New Yo

Say You're Sorry

"Fans of Lisa Gardner and J. D. Robb will enjoy this outing and be on pins and needles waiting for the next installments."   —*Publishers Weekly*

"Complex, thrilling, and impossible to put down.... An engrossing and exciting start to a new series, and one that busts genre stereotypes along the way."
                                                            —*BookPage*

"Chilling and remarkably complex, this is a thriller that, for all its length, will keep minds sharp and night-lights burning. An excellent series start."   —*Library Journal*

"Rose's *Say You're Sorry* delivers on the promise of a pedal-to-the-metal thriller with plenty of developed characters and converging mysteries.... To call this book a page-turner is an understatement."   —*USA Today*

"Jam-packed with wall-to-wall action and heart-stopping, page-turning suspense."   —*Harlequin Junkie*

"Karen Rose never fails to give a fantastic, well-written thriller that is intense, always on the edge, with fantastic characters, evil villains, and a wonderful couple you care for."   —The Reading Cafe

Monster in the Closet

"An emotionally charged thrill ride. With deep characters, an intriguing plot, and breathless action, Karen Rose's latest book is a real page-turner!"
    —#1 *New York Times* bestselling author Lisa Jackson

KAREN ROSE

INTO THE DARK

BERKLEY
New York

BERKLEY

An imprint of Penguin Random House LLC

penguinrandomhouse.com

Copyright © 2019 by Karen Rose Books, Inc.
Excerpt from *Closer Than You Think* by Karen Rose copyright © 2019
by Karen Rose Books, Inc.
Penguin Random House supports copyright. Copyright fuels creativity, encourages
diverse voices, promotes free speech, and creates a vibrant culture. Thank you for buying
an authorized edition of this book and for complying with copyright laws by not
reproducing, scanning, or distributing any part of it in any form without permission.
You are supporting writers and allowing Penguin Random House to continue to
publish books for every reader.

BERKLEY and the BERKLEY & B colophon
are registered trademarks of Penguin Random House LLC.

ISBN: 9781984805287

Headline UK hardcover edition / November 2019
Berkley hardcover edition / November 2019
Berkley mass-market edition / November 2019

Printed in the United States of America
1   3   5   7   9   10   8   6   4   2

Cover art: woman © JNemchinova/Getty Images
Cover design by Adam Auerbach

To Christine. I'm so glad I have you in my life.

As always, to Martin. I love you.

ACKNOWLEDGMENTS

Erica and Penny Singleton for telling me your story. Penny, I'm so happy that your beautiful heart continues to beat. Erica, we're all blessed because you kept a clear head and knew just what to do. Wishing you both happiness and health. You already have love.

Geoff Symon for all the forensic know-how. (Even though I sometimes have to rewrite scenes and replot clues because forensic TV shows have lied to me all these years.)

Marc Conterato for the medical assistance in *all* things. Thank you for never being too busy to talk to me.

My lovely Starfish for all the plotting.

Sarah Hafer for your editing expertise.

Caitlin Ellis for all the things you do to keep the biz (and me) running.

Claire Zion, Jen Doyle, and Robin Rue for all your support.

As always, all mistakes are my own.

Prologue

Cincinnati, Ohio
Saturday, March 9, 1:30 a.m.

Run. Don't look back. Just run.

Michael Rowland clutched Joshua tighter and gritted his teeth against the sharp rocks and twigs digging into his feet. And he ran as fast as he could.

Blinking away tears, he focused on reaching the end of the driveway, at the bottom of the big hill.

Get to the road.

And then? He didn't know. He'd figure it out when he got there.

He'd figure it all out when he got there.

Where is "there"?

Shut up. Shut up and run.

He fought the urge to look behind him. He wasn't sure if he'd knocked Brewer out or not. Even if he had, the asshole could come to, and the minute he did, he'd be coming after them. Checking to see wouldn't make a bit of difference. It would only slow them down and make it easier for Brewer to catch them.

He'll kill me, Michael thought. Of that he had no doubt. But he'd do worse to Joshua. Joshua, who was only five. So Michael kept running.

He was approaching the cluster of trees that Joshua called the "forest." At one time it had been an orchard. Now it was totally overgrown. Branches grew every which way and bramble bushes had nearly taken over.

Damn bramble bushes. Michael's feet were bleeding now. *It doesn't matter.* He ignored the pain, welcoming the cover of the trees. *Move. Move.*

He found another burst of speed, ducking under branches, grateful for the agility drills that his coach had made them do. Michael was fast—the fastest on the JV soccer team, even though he'd been the youngest. But he needed to run faster. *Please let me be faster.*

The flickering light that marked the end of the driveway was closer now, barely visible through the trees. He'd run about halfway. Another quarter mile to go.

He felt the yank on his foot a millisecond before he was pitching forward into the darkness. Airborne.

Joshua.

Michael tilted his body at the last moment, hitting the ground on his shoulder. A burst of pain had him swallowing a grunt, the last-minute tilt giving him enough momentum to continue rolling to his back, then around to rest his elbows on the ground, his arms still clutching Joshua tightly.

He dragged in a breath, blinking as he got his bearings. He hunched over Joshua, in case Brewer had been on their tail. But there were no kicks. No hits.

Nothing.

Michael lifted his head and looked around. No one was behind him. It hadn't been Brewer grabbing his foot. *Must have been a tree root.*

Maybe he had knocked Brewer out. The thought filled him with dark satisfaction.

He glanced down at Joshua. Still asleep. Not dead. Just drugged. He wondered what had been in the syringe the bastard had been injecting him with. Michael said a small prayer of thanks for the extra soda he'd had before bed. If he hadn't needed to pee, he wouldn't have been awake to see Brewer plunging a needle into his brother's arm.

He frowned at Joshua's peaceful little face. *Should I take him to the hospital?* He wasn't even sure how to do that. He'd have to figure that out, too, once he'd gotten them away from Brewer's house.

He took another moment to watch his brother's chest rise and fall. *At least he's not dead.*

When he'd staggered down the stairs—his own sight blurry from the punch Brewer had thrown to the side of his head when he'd tried to grab the syringe—he'd seen Brewer carrying Joshua toward the front door. For a terrible minute, he'd thought Joshua was dead. He hadn't been moving.

Michael hadn't hesitated to find out. Whatever Brewer had planned, it wasn't good. Leaping from the third step onto Brewer's back, he'd knocked the man down.

Brewer had released Joshua long enough to punch Michael a second time, this time in the gut. Stumbling backward, Michael had grabbed the iron shovel from the fireplace and swung it with all his might. Brewer had been leaning down to pick up Joshua from the floor when Michael had hit him in the head with the shovel. Brewer had gone down on his knees and Michael had pushed him away from his little brother.

Who *had* been breathing. *Thank God.*

Then Michael had picked Joshua up and run.

Wincing at the pain in his shoulder, Michael pushed to his knees, gently settling Joshua on the ground so that he could do a three-sixty search.

So many times in his life he'd wished he could hear. Never so much as this moment. If Brewer was following, Michael wouldn't be able to hear a twig breaking or the sound of labored breathing.

Brewer could be hiding anywhere. Michael didn't trust the bastard as far as he could throw him.

Stop wasting time. Get to the road.

Drawing a deep breath, he picked Joshua up and cradled him against his good shoulder. He took a step and had to bite back a scream.

It hurts. God, it hurts. The pain was shooting from his shoulder, up his neck, to the back of his head now. He hoped he hadn't whimpered.

Taking another look around, he started walking again, slowly. Yeah, it hurt. But he'd suck it up. He'd had worse, after all. Lots of times. Thanks to Brewer.

For a moment he wished the man was dead, then he shook his head hard. *No.* Not dead. Just in jail. *Where other bad guys—bigger, meaner bad guys— will hurt him every day of every year for the rest of his miserable life.*

That would be . . . What had his teacher called it? *Oh, right. Poetic justice.*

He came to the edge of the old orchard and peered into the night. He could see the flickering light at the end of the driveway again. He was glad he knew it had always flickered. Otherwise he might be worried that he had a concussion.

He took a step out of the trees, then froze. *Shit. Oh shit.*

He scrambled back under cover and lay down out of sight, the pain in his shoulder making his eyes tear up. He blinked the wetness away and stared at the car making its way down the driveway toward the main road. It was too dark to see the make, model, or color, but that didn't matter, because Michael already knew it was a 2018 BMW 530i. Alpine-white exterior with a tan leather interior. Brewer was very proud of his car.

The car was moving super-slowly. Maybe five miles per hour, if that. It stopped, then crawled another few feet forward.

He's looking for us. Oh God. What do I do? Pulse rocketing, Michael tightened his hold on his brother.

He'll kill me. And then he'll take Joshua. To where, he had no idea. But it would be bad.

And then . . . another set of headlights pulled into the driveway from the main road. The vehicle was barely visible in the flickering light, but Michael could make out a dark SUV. Maybe black.

The SUV stopped and a man got out. A big man. A big bald man. The flickering light reflected off his head as he strode from the SUV to Brewer's BMW, now at a complete stop.

Because the SUV had blocked its exit.

The man crossed around to Brewer's door and yanked it open. A second later he was pulling Brewer from his car by the shirt collar and dragging him to the SUV. Once they were on the driver's side, Michael could see that Brewer was oddly limp.

If Michael hadn't been so scared, he would have cheered. Finally someone was bigger than Brewer and giving him a taste of his own medicine.

Michael frowned when Brewer twisted in the man's grip, because he looked like he was moving in slo-mo. Brewer reached into his pocket, but the man threw him to the ground and grabbed something from his hand.

Oh my God. It was a gun. Brewer had brought one of his guns. *He would have killed me with it.*

But now Brewer's gun was in the big man's hand. Michael held his breath, waiting for the man to shoot the monster who'd made their lives a living hell for nearly five years—ever since the day he'd married their mother, Stella.

Who was as useless as spit.

But the man didn't shoot Brewer. He pocketed the gun, then yanked Brewer to his feet and pinned him against the SUV. Then he put his big hands around Brewer's throat.

Brewer struggled.

Until he didn't anymore.

Michael's mouth fell open as Brewer's body went

limp once again, falling to the ground in a crumpled heap. The big man took a step back, fists on his hips as he stared down, shaking his head.

Oh my God. He'd killed him. The big bald man had killed him.

Abruptly aware that he was breathing hard, Michael clenched his jaw closed so that the man wouldn't hear him.

Luckily the man was focused on Brewer. He opened the hatch of the SUV and tossed Brewer in, as if he weighed no more than one of Joshua's action figures.

Slamming the hatch closed, he walked to the BMW's driver's side and leaned in. When he straightened, he tossed something in the air and caught it one-handed.

The keys. He'd taken Brewer's car keys.

The man then opened all four of the BMW's doors and the trunk, searching for something. When he didn't find it, he closed the doors, pocketed Brewer's keys, backed the SUV to the main road, and drove away.

Michael let out a quiet breath. *No keys.* He didn't know how to drive yet, but he could have figured it out. Now the car was no longer an escape option.

But now I don't need to escape. Brewer is gone.

And Michael was so tired. His mother wasn't home tonight. She was out partying with her friends, getting stoned again. Which was probably the reason Brewer had been so bold. He usually snuck around to do his dirty work.

But now there would be no one in the house to hurt them.

Besides, Michael knew where Brewer kept the rest of his guns, and he knew how to use them to keep his little brother safe. *I'll take Joshua home. Get some sleep. And in the morning I'll figure out what to do next.*

He'd made it back through the orchard when Joshua's eyes blinked open. His mouth curved when he saw Michael's face.

"Hi," Joshua said.

Or at least that was what it looked like he'd said, and Michael was pretty good at guessing people's speech. Especially Joshua's. Michael had been watching his brother speak since he'd uttered his first words.

Michael smiled down at him, despite the pain in his shoulder. "You okay?" he voiced, because his arms were full and he couldn't sign.

Joshua nodded sleepily, his eyes closing once again.

Michael shuddered with relief. They'd dodged a bullet tonight and Joshua seemed none the wiser.

And Brewer? *Good riddance. I'm glad he's dead.*

Cincinnati, Ohio
Saturday, March 9, 2:15 a.m.

The river was high tonight, Cade thought as he watched the churning water flow past his vantage point above the bank. Nowhere near flood stage, but the current was still fast and deadly. Perfect for his needs.

Turning from the river, he stared down at the body in the back of his SUV, glad the miserable SOB was dead. *Good riddance.*

It had been close tonight. Too close. He'd assumed the asshole had been incapacitated by the Taser that he'd fired into the back of his neck, but somehow John Brewer had managed to move his arm enough to draw a weapon.

That hadn't happened before, not in the four years that he'd been performing this service for the community.

He drew the Taser from his coat pocket and held it up to the rear hatch light, studying it. It looked okay. Maybe it hadn't been fully charged? Or maybe it was broken. That did happen from time to time. He'd read the news stories of police being forced to shoot a suspect with their gun after the Taser didn't work, but he'd always figured it was the cops making excuses.

He pressed it to Brewer's chest and squeezed the trigger, causing the body to twitch.

"Well, fuck." The Taser *did* function. At least some of the time. Maybe Brewer had been on something. That might account for it. However he sliced it, the man's response had thrown him off his game.

He hadn't planned to kill the bastard in his own driveway. He'd planned to wait. To do it here, on the riverbank, miles from the nearest neighbor, where no one would hear his screams.

He scowled at John Brewer's handsome face. *Son-ofabitch got off too damn easy.* Too many people had been taken in by his fake charm.

My boss included. Normally Richard was a shrewd judge of character. *Me excluded, of course.* Cade was pretty sure Richard wouldn't condone his extracurricular "service" to the community, were he to find out. Although, who knew? Stranger things had happened.

He'd never considered that Richard would engage in human trafficking, but that was exactly what his boss had done earlier that evening. Brewer had been trying to win back the property title he'd lost before and Richard had allowed the slimy bastard to add his five-year-old stepson to his stake when the small stash of heroin he'd brought to the game didn't meet the minimum table requirements.

The super-secret game that Richard hosted allowed no actual currency to be wagered. Instead, a constant flow of unique and valuable items—some legal, but most black-market—changed hands from week to week. Cade had often wondered what the winners did with some of the stuff, which had included land, luxury vehicles, stolen masterpieces, and exotic animals—live and parts.

He'd concluded that the participants often had their eye on a specific prize, and that they probably sold off the rest of what they won as quickly as possible. Usually through Richard.

In addition to running a successful gambling operation on the Ohio River, his boss was also a "procurer" for the wealthy in the Midwest and beyond. Richard knew what some people wanted and what others had. He brought them together, enabling them to trade in a civilized fashion.

Up until tonight, people had never been included among the prizes to be won. A few times there had been offers of human organs brought to the table, which had shocked Cade enough. But never people. *At least not to my knowledge.*

That was a troubling thought. Cade wondered how many times items had been traded under the table while he'd stood guard outside the door. He wondered if Richard had allowed Brewer to participate tonight because he'd known one of the others at the table would want the boy.

He wondered if he'd have to kill Richard, too.

It was with disgust that Cade realized Brewer had wanted his house back enough to sacrifice his own stepson. It hadn't even been Brewer's own house. Up until a week before the game, the property had belonged to his wife. Richard nearly hadn't allowed it, but then Brewer had wagered something else that technically belonged to his wife—her little boy.

Richard always said that desperate men played lousy poker, and Brewer proved that true. He'd lost big and left the game shaking and pale.

The winner of tonight's game had gleefully arranged to meet Brewer to take possession of the boy, but the exchange wasn't going to happen, because that man was currently . . . indisposed.

Cade yanked away the blanket covering the figure lying in the back of his car. Staring back at him were eyes that were wide and full of horror. And perhaps a little defiance? *If that's what it is, I'll get rid of it with my first slice.*

He was always glad to rid the world of a pedo. Seeing the pure fear in their eyes, hearing their screams? It made his chosen crusade all the sweeter.

He smiled down at Blake Emerson, the pedophile who'd been bold enough to buy a little boy at a poker game. "Hi," he said to the appropriately terrified man, then pointed to Brewer's dead body lying beside his captive. "You two have already met, so I won't bother introducing you. Not that he'll say much, because, y'know, he's dead. It's true that Brewer had a less painful death than you'll have, but that isn't my fault." He shrugged. "That's sometimes how it goes. But please know that if he'd lived, I would have given you both equal torture. It doesn't really matter at the end of the day, though. You'll both be equally dead."

And Brewer's five-year-old stepson would be safe, as would other kids who might have been future victims of this particular pedophile.

On the other hand, the boy hadn't been in Brewer's car, so maybe the asshole hadn't been planning to make the transfer after all. Maybe Brewer had just been intending to escape. Which didn't matter, because he'd made the offer in the first place.

Cade frowned. Or maybe Brewer had already taken the child. Maybe he'd hidden him somewhere he could easily retrieve him. Maybe he had been on his way to retrieve the boy so that he could give him over to his new "owner."

Bile burned his throat.

"Shit," he muttered. He needed to make sure the kid was okay, but he couldn't drive back to Brewer's house with a live prisoner and a dead body in the back. It was too risky. He pulled the Sawzall from its box in the back of the SUV and waved it in front of the pedophile.

"You want me to saw off a piece of you first? No?" he answered for the man, who couldn't speak through his gag. "Good choice. Now you can see exactly what's going to happen to you. And you'll still be alive to feel every slice."

He dragged Brewer's body from the back of the SUV to the ground and fired up the saw, making sure the bound pedophile had a clear view.

"First his fingers," he explained to his terrified audience, "then his dick, because he was willing to sell his kid to you. I'll *start* with your dick, though. Because you would have taken that little boy and destroyed his life. From there on, it's pretty standard. Arms and legs. Then, his head. That's where it gets nasty, especially if you're still alive, like you will be. Really a shame that Brewer's dead. I would have liked watching him struggle and squirm. You'll give me that, though."

And when they were through, Cade would check on the boy. Just to make sure he was okay.

Cincinnati, Ohio
Saturday, March 9, 5:40 a.m.

Michael shifted in the chair in the corner of Joshua's bedroom, trying to get comfortable as he kept watch over his little brother, who slept peacefully, unaware that anything had happened tonight. At least there was that. Joshua wouldn't have the memory of being drugged by their stepfather. Of their escape through the old orchard.

Michael had tried to sleep in his own bed. He truly had. God only knew, he was exhausted enough. But every time he closed his eyes, he saw Brewer jabbing Joshua with a syringe and carrying him away. He'd tried to force his brain to see Brewer going limp under the big bald man's hands, but his brain kept seeing the bastard getting up and walking away. That wasn't what had happened, but until Michael knew for sure that Brewer really was dead, he'd be on pins and needles, waiting for his mother's husband to come home.

And watching over Joshua. It wasn't like anyone else was going to. Their mother had never been what anyone would call maternal, but she'd gotten much worse since Brewer had entered their lives.

He shifted again, then froze as a familiar rumble beneath his feet sent an even more familiar bolt of fear through his body.

The garage door. Someone had opened it.

Someone is here.

Michael shot to his feet, fumbling for the gun he'd taken from Brewer's safe. Tucking it into the waist of his jeans at his back, he looked around the room wildly, nearly scooping Joshua up into his arms.

But again he froze. There was no time. Someone was coming.

Someone is here.

Brewer? Or . . . He remembered the big bald man tossing Brewer's keys into the air. Had the man come back? Had he killed Brewer and come back? *For us?*

Oh God. He saw me. Knows I saw him kill Brewer. He thinks I'll tell. He'll kill me, too.

Michael's brain told him to *run*, until his gaze fell to his little brother, still asleep. *I'll keep you safe. I won't let him touch you. I promise.*

Stepping back, Michael hid behind the chair and drew the gun. He'd kill whoever walked through that door. Unless it was his mother. Her, he'd let live. Although she didn't deserve to.

He'd gone to her, terrified and bleeding. Scared. He'd told her what her husband had done, the first time it had happened more than two years ago. And the second. And the third. But she hadn't believed him. Or she'd claimed as much.

You're lying, she'd told him. Michael could still feel the sting of her slap across his face. It was a wonder she hadn't broken any of his teeth. But he hadn't been lying about all the things her husband had done to him.

He'd threatened to go to the police, hoping they'd believe him, but his mother told him that they'd take him away—and maybe her, too. He and Joshua would go to foster care, but not together. They'd be separated, she'd told him, and everyone knew what happened to kids in those homes. Joshua would be hurt and it would be Michael's fault. Unless he stayed quiet. So he had, enduring his stepfather's "visits" in the night, hoping that Brewer would just go away.

Now he had. *Because he's dead.*

He shuddered, pushing those thoughts from his mind. *Not now.* He couldn't lose it now. Later, he'd fall apart. Later, when Joshua was safe.

Joshua, the only reason he'd stayed in this house. *This hell.*

Michael clutched the gun in both hands, willing them not to shake. Willing his eyes to stay open, even though he wanted to clench them shut and pretend none of this was happening. Because the door was opening. Slowly.

He held his breath, his heart hammering in his chest. *No, no, no.* It couldn't be Brewer. Brewer was dead. *Please let him be dead. Please let this be Mom. Please.*

A shadow appeared in the doorway. Big. Hulking.

It was the man. The bald man. The man who'd killed Brewer with his bare hands. He was here. He stepped into the room, the moonlight from the window reflecting off his head as he stopped at the foot of Joshua's bed.

Michael could see his face clearly. Memorized his features. Every detail, so that he could tell the police.

No, no, you won't. You can't tell the police. Because they wouldn't believe him. His mother would tell them he was a liar. Just like she'd done when he'd told her that her new husband came to his bed at night.

She'll find a way to blame me. That's the way it's always been.

He glanced at the gun he held in his shaking hands. *I won't need to tell the police, because I'm going to kill him.*

Except the man didn't touch his brother. He simply stood there, his gaze fixed on Joshua. There was no anger on the man's face. None of the lustful leering that Michael had seen so often in Brewer's eyes. Actually, the man looked . . . relieved. And that didn't make sense.

The man's gaze jerked up and Michael wondered if he'd made a sound. But the man didn't come closer. He just turned on his heel and left the room.

Michael sagged back against the bedroom wall, letting out the breath he'd been holding. A few minutes later he felt the rumble of the garage door going back down.

He crept to the window and peeked out into the night. And sucked in a breath when he saw the big man running down the driveway, toward the flickering light at the road, a suitcase in his hand.

He was gone.

Michael and Joshua were alone again.

Michael's entire body began to shake. He stumbled to the chair just as his legs gave out. He didn't have to wonder what would have happened if the man had discovered him there. He'd have put his hands on Michael's throat and choked him until he'd gone limp, just as he'd done to Brewer.

Oh God. Oh God. I would have been dead. And Joshua would be all alone, unprotected. He glared at the gun in his hand. He'd frozen. He should have shot the man as he'd stood next to Joshua's bed, but he'd frozen.

I won't freeze next time. If he comes back, I'll be ready.

Chapter One

Cincinnati, Ohio
Saturday, March 16, 11:30 a.m.

Diesel Kennedy blew his whistle and gestured for the kids to join him on the sideline. "That's good for today, guys. Come on over."

He smiled at the ten kindergartners ambling off the field. They were all too cute in their shin guards and little cleats. Only two of the boys had any soccer competence at all. The others missed the ball, fell down, ran into one another, and generally looked like they were doing a Three Stooges routine. But they tried so hard and seemed to be having fun, which was the real win Diesel was looking for when he coached their team.

He'd been coaching for the past five years, determined that no child under his care would experience what he had growing up. He'd had no male role models and the one man in his young life, the one who should have protected him, had left him forever scarred. Diesel strove to teach good values to every child he coached, how to win and lose, how to work together. But he also taught them how to speak up for themselves. How to ask for help.

He knew the signs of abuse and, as a state mandated reporter, informed Children's Services when he suspected a child was being harmed. Over the last five years of coaching, he'd been involved in rescuing four children from abusive situations.

He wasn't saving the whole world through coaching, but he could take comfort in knowing that four little boys were safe today who might not have been. He'd continue to save one child at a time. In the meantime, he'd continue teaching sportsmanship and teamwork—beneficial to any child.

He held up a hand for them to high-five as the team gathered around him, many having to jump up to reach his palm. At six-six, he towered over the five-year-olds, making them crane their necks to meet his gaze.

"You guys did so well today. You made me very proud." Ten little faces beamed up at him. "Now, let's talk about next week. We have our first game! Are we excited?"

"Yes, Coach Diesel!" they replied.

"What happens if we win?" he asked.

"Ice cream!" they shouted.

"That's right." He lifted his brows. "What happens if we lose?"

They looked at one another, then one of the boys frowned, likely searching his memory, because Diesel had delivered this spiel before and after every practice for the past two weeks. "Ice cream?" he asked timidly.

Diesel gave him a grin, extending his fist for the boy to bump. He searched his own memory for the name of the boy with the dark hair and dark eyes, and the dent in his little chin. . . . *Right. Joshua Rowland.* "That's right, Joshua! Whether we win or not, we get ice cream. Winning is fun, but not the most important thing. The three most important things are what?" He held up three fingers, waiting expectantly.

"Have fun!" they shouted.

He nodded. "That's one. And two?"

"Do our best!"

"Very good. And the third?"

They looked at one another again quizzically, then back up at him for the answer.

Joshua raised his hand once more. "Be nice?"

The other boys repeated the answer, nodding fiercely, expressions abashed at not remembering.

Diesel hid his smile. They really were too cute. "Exactly. Be good sports, which means we'll be nice. If we lose, we smile. We congratulate the winners. And then after the game, we go out for ice cream. If we win, we accept their congratulations and go out for ice cream. Either way, we get ice cream. Except . . . what one thing might keep us from getting ice cream?"

"Being bad sports," they said.

"You got it." He looked over his shoulder at the parents who'd gathered to pick up their children. "Moms and dads are here. Line up, shoulder to shoulder, and wait until I call your name. Mrs. Moody will pass out your snacks. What do you say to Mrs. Moody?"

"Thank you, Mrs. Moody!" they chorused as his assistant coach got them lined up and handed out the snacks and juice boxes. Shauna Moody was a nice, motherly woman whose son had played soccer with their league all through school and was now in college and doing well. She credited the league with keeping him engaged and out of trouble, and now that he'd graduated, she wanted to give back. She showed up every week to hand out snacks and bandage boo-boos.

Diesel turned to the waiting parents with his clipboard. He made it a point to greet each adult doing pickup before allowing them to leave with a child. Over the years, he'd coached kids stuck in the middle of custody disputes, and he always wanted to be sure he recognized the person doing the picking up. The last thing he wanted was to allow a child to be taken by the wrong person. Terrible things could happen when the wrong person had access to a child.

This Diesel knew from experience.

The parent of the ninth child on his list hesitated before smiling timidly. "You're really good with them," she said, sounding surprised.

He steeled himself for what he thought might be coming, because he'd seen the censure and suspicion in this mother's eyes from the first practice. "I do my best."

And he did. No one had given him any kind of good attention when he was five years old. He wanted these kids to have a better role model than he'd had. Which, honestly, wasn't too hard to achieve. Most of the adults in his life hadn't given him very much at all.

If this mother wanted to remove her son from his team, he'd be polite. And then he'd call the first child on his waiting list, which right now was at about twenty-five names.

The parent—Mrs. Jacobsen—tilted her head as she studied him. "I owe you an apology, Mr. Kennedy. The first time we showed up with Liam for practice, I saw your tattoos and . . . well, I thought you would be . . ."

Diesel's lips curved, because it appeared the conversation wasn't going to go as he'd feared. "Mean? A thug?"

She laughed nervously. "Something like that. We try to teach our son not to judge a person by their appearance, but I'm afraid I did that with you. But you came highly recommended by my friends, so I allowed Liam to join the team. I'm so glad I did. I was wrong, and I'm sorry."

"Thank you," he said graciously. "I hope Liam enjoys himself." He looked down at the boy and gave him a wink. "He's a neat kid."

Liam beamed. "'Bye, Coach Diesel."

Diesel waved as they left, then looked down at his list with a silent sigh. One name left unchecked. One child unclaimed. He turned to find Joshua Rowland sitting on one of the folding chairs with Mrs. Moody, his little face pinched as he searched the parking lot for his mother's car.

Mrs. Brewer had been late picking up her son from every practice. Diesel had needed to call her cell phone to remind her. She always gushed that she'd been so busy and was so sorry, but Diesel got the feeling that the woman was more concerned with attracting attention to herself than with caring for her son.

He dialed her cell, got her voice mail, and left a polite message. Then he gave Joshua a bright smile. "Your mom's running a little late. Maybe you could help me put away the soccer balls while we're waiting for her."

Joshua jumped up, eager to help. So eager to please.

Diesel's heart hurt. The boy reminded him of himself. Children this eager to please were prime prey for predators.

They put the equipment in the bed of Diesel's truck, and he let Joshua shove the tailgate closed, unable to keep from smiling at the way the child dusted his hands together and gave him a satisfied nod.

But the boy's satisfaction was a facade, because he was searching the parking lot from the corner of his eye. The pinched look returned when there was still no sign of his mother.

He looked up at Diesel, tears filling his eyes. "What do I do? I don't know the way home."

Mrs. Moody, who'd been silently watching them from the sideline, came over and gave the boy a hug. "We won't make you go home by yourself, sweetheart," she said. "We can take you."

Joshua glanced at her, then back up at Diesel. "Okay. I'm sorry."

Diesel crouched down so that he was on Joshua's level. "No need to be sorry, my man. Things happen."

Joshua swallowed hard. "She's been really sad lately. She . . ." He bit his lip. "She sleeps a lot."

Diesel's jaw tightened. These were dicey situations. A parent suffering from depression wasn't necessarily unfit. He needed to tread carefully here. Joshua's mother had appeared normal when she'd dropped him off and he didn't seem to be neglected. His clothes were dirty now, but they'd been clean when he'd arrived. He looked to be well fed, and Diesel had never seen suspicious bruises on him.

"Who watches you when she sleeps, Joshua?" he asked.

Joshua brightened. "Michael does. He takes care of me."

Diesel made his lips curve, even though his trouble-meter was pinging loudly. Michael was Joshua's older brother, but the boy was only fourteen. Diesel had seen enough of these situations while investigating story leads at the *Ledger*, the newspaper he'd worked at for the past seven years. Too many older siblings were left to care for the younger ones. Sometimes this was necessary, like when a single parent had to work multiple jobs to keep the family fed, but Joshua Rowland's mother wasn't a single parent. She was married to a man named John Brewer, whom Diesel had never met. He assumed that Brewer hadn't adopted the boys, as they had a different last name, but that could be for any number of reasons and didn't indicate an issue in and of itself.

Brewer appeared to be financially successful. The family lived in a well-to-do part of town, where homes were huge and called "estates." Mrs. Brewer wore designer clothes and drove an expensive car. According to her parent info sheet, she didn't work one job, much less multiple.

She should have had time to take care of her children, or money to hire a nanny. If she was leaving child care to her older son, that meant something else was going on.

He forced his voice to be as gentle as he could make it, which wasn't easy. It was normally gravelly and rough, so he made sure he was smiling benignly. "What does Michael do for you?"

"Washes my clothes. Plays with me. Reads me stories at night and fixes my breakfast when I wake up. Eggs and bacon," Joshua added proudly. "Because he says I'm growing and cereal's not good enough."

"He's right," Diesel said. "I can see you growing right now."

Joshua giggled, as Diesel had hoped he would. "No, you can't."

Diesel's lips twitched. "Well, maybe not *right* now, but I did before. Who picks you up from school?"

"Michael does. He walks me home." Joshua's smile dimmed and he bit his lip again. "But Michael's sad, too. And I can't make him be happy."

Diesel glanced at a sympathetic Mrs. Moody before returning his attention to the forlorn little boy. "Why is Michael sad?" he asked softly.

Joshua shrugged, looking down at his feet. "Mama yells at him a lot. Especially since Uncle John left."

Oh shit. Diesel's trouble-meter started pinging again. "Uncle John?"

"Her husband." Joshua frowned. "But not my daddy. My daddy's gone. To heaven."

"Okay." Calling his stepfather "uncle" also wasn't an issue in and of itself. But all together . . . "And why did Uncle John leave?"

Another shrug. "Mama says it's Michael's fault. But Michael's good."

"I'm sure he is, honey," Diesel murmured. "Does . . ." He drew a breath. "Joshua, does your mom ever . . . hit your brother? Or you?"

The misery in Joshua's eyes was his answer.

Fuck. Diesel's heart sank even as his resolve grew. No one would hurt this child. No one had saved Diesel, but by God, he'd make sure no child that crossed his path would endure what he had.

His heart hurt for these kids, the neglected ones. The abused ones. He felt a physical pressure on his

chest and realized he'd pushed the heel of his hand to
his heart, reminding him that he'd been living on borrowed time for years. There were whole blocks of time
when he nearly forgot that he carried a bullet in his
chest, courtesy of an Al-Qaeda insurgent. A bullet
hovering too close to his heart to be removed. One day
it would move, piercing his heart and ending his life.

But he was used to it now, the notion that his personal clock was running down. He was going to make
the most of however many years—or days—he had
left. Taking care of other people's kids was his life's
mission.

Joshua Rowland had just become priority one.

Cincinnati, Ohio
Saturday, March 16, 11:30 a.m.

"Mom!" Glancing at the clock on the wall, Michael
shook his mother's shoulder, roughly voicing her
name even though she hated to hear him speak.

It hadn't always been that way. She'd never encouraged him, but she hadn't hated him. But that was before Brewer had come into their lives. It hadn't been
perfect before the bastard, but once he'd moved in with
them? That was when everything had gone to hell.

She'd been erratic before meeting the man, had
even been a drug user. All that had changed. And in
the last year it had gotten much, much worse. She'd
never hit him before Brewer, either. Now . . .

She sometimes used her fists, but usually she'd
hurl whatever happened to be in her hand at the time.
This morning it had been a bowl. He'd been busy
cooking Joshua's breakfast and hadn't seen her coming at him.

He touched the side of his head gingerly, grimacing at the blood on his fingers. He'd cleaned it as best
he could. It would stop bleeding eventually. His head
would stop pounding. Eventually.

Right now, Joshua was more important.

"Mom." She should have been at the soccer field, picking up Joshua. She should have stayed there, waiting for him. But she hadn't. She'd come home, staggering inside with that glassy-eyed look that never boded well.

She'd been high, probably popping pills while in the car. And now she was passed out, a syringe on the end table. But she was breathing, so at least she wasn't dying. He had half a mind to contact the cops and have her sorry ass carted off to jail for heroin possession and child neglect, but for now his main concern was Joshua.

He was supposed to be picked up by now. What if the coach left him there? What if Joshua tried to walk home? The practice field was six miles away. What if some pervert stole him? What if the big bald guy was waiting for him?

Oh God. Oh God.

Michael grabbed his phone and house keys. He stole a quick look at his mother's car keys, then shook his head, immediately regretting the action. His head hurt and he was dizzy. He couldn't have driven a car even if he knew how. His bicycle would have been just as dicey, but that wasn't an option anymore.

John had sold his bike a few months back. Said he'd needed a little cash. Which would have been bad enough, but John hadn't paid for the bike to begin with. Michael had bought it with the money he'd made mowing lawns.

But none of that was important now. He had to get to Joshua. He was going to have to run.

He was glad he was fast.

Cincinnati, Ohio
Saturday, March 16, 12:05 p.m.

Fuck. Diesel shoved back the rage. Kept his voice calm. "Does your mother hit both of you?" he pressed, and felt a small frisson of relief when Joshua shook his head.

"Just Michael," he whispered. He blinked, sending tears streaking down his face. "She throws stuff at him. Says he ruined her life. Why is she so mean to him?"

Diesel drew another steadying breath. "I don't know," he said, then shifted his gaze behind him when Joshua's eyes abruptly lit up with relieved joy.

"It's him. Michael's here!" He ran for his brother, who was crossing the parking lot at a sprint. When he got to Joshua, he dropped to one knee and opened his arms, breathing hard.

Until Diesel stood up and turned to face him. Then Michael Rowland's face drained of all color and he fell backward, landing on his ass. His arms came around Joshua and he held him so tightly that the little boy squirmed. All while Michael stared at Diesel like he'd seen a ghost. He was no longer breathing hard. Diesel wasn't sure if the kid was breathing at all.

"Michael, lemme go!" Joshua pushed on Michael's chest, trying to free himself. "You're squishing my hands."

The teenager didn't let go, continuing to stare at Diesel. Diesel had seen that expression before. Stark terror.

But why? To his knowledge, he'd never seen Michael Rowland before. He shot Mrs. Moody a quick look, seeing that she was as bewildered as he was.

Carefully, Diesel approached the brothers, his hands lifted, palms out. "Michael?"

"He can't hear you!" Joshua panted, still trying to get free of his brother's viselike grip. "He talks with his hands."

Oh. Okay. Diesel knew a few signs. Well, more than a few, actually. He'd been studying for a year and a half. Ever since he'd first laid eyes on Dr. Danika Novak, whose younger brother, Greg, was deaf.

Greg had approached him more than two years ago for help doing a little "computer sleuthing," as

Diesel liked to call it, because "hacking" sounded clumsy, lacking in finesse, and he took pride in his art. Diesel had hoped that spending more time with Greg meant that he'd be spending even more time with Greg's sister, but so far that hadn't happened. Not yet.

Diesel hadn't lost hope. Not yet.

He wished that Dani were here right now. She'd know what to say. What to do to calm this terrified kid. But she wasn't here. *I'm on my own.*

Slowly, he dropped to his knees, trying to make himself smaller. Less threatening. He signed haltingly, hoping the kid understood him.

"Don't be scared. I won't hurt you. Promise."

Michael blinked, his gaze focusing on Diesel's hands, so Diesel repeated the signs, then added, "I'm Coach Diesel." He spelled the letters of *coach* and his name because he didn't know the signs for those words. "It's nice to meet you, Michael."

Michael stared another moment longer, then lifted his eyes to study Diesel's face. He seemed . . . *there* now. Coherent. Back from wherever his mind had gone when he'd first seen Diesel.

"Are you okay?" Diesel signed.

Very slowly, Michael nodded, his shoulders visibly relaxing. He loosened his hold on Joshua, who wiggled out of his grasp, his little hands flying like the wind as he signed to his brother.

Blinking, Michael turned his attention to Joshua and signed back.

Diesel caught enough of the signs to know that Joshua had demanded to know what was wrong with Michael—and to ask where their mother was. Michael's reply was less frenetic, telling Joshua that he was sorry. That he'd thought . . .

Diesel frowned, unable to understand what the teenager was saying. He wasn't sure what Michael had thought. But he did see the boy tell Joshua that their mother was asleep.

The slight hesitation as Michael signed "asleep" told Diesel that the woman was either stoned or drunk. How Mrs. Brewer could have gotten wasted so quickly was puzzling. She'd dropped off her son less than two hours ago. She hadn't seemed impaired at the time, but he'd known enough functional addicts to realize that she could have become adept at hiding a buzz.

"He says he's sorry," Joshua supplied. "He thought you were someone else. You look like someone else."

Someone else who'd had the power to terrify this young man. Another uncle, maybe? Diesel couldn't be sure, but he *was* sure that he didn't want to take these kids back to that home. Not until he was sure they'd be safe.

"He says that my mom is asleep," Joshua continued. "He tried to wake her up to come get me, but he couldn't, so he came instead."

"Okay," Diesel said aloud, then signed, "Does your mother need a doctor?"

Joshua's eyes grew wide. "You can sign?" His back had been to Diesel when he'd signed the first time.

"A little," Diesel answered, both speaking and signing, but his attention was back on Michael. "How did you get here?"

The boy shrugged, wincing as he did so. "Ran."

It was Diesel's turn to stare. He knew where the family lived from the address Mrs. Brewer had listed on the registration form. "That's . . ." He held up his fingers, trying to remember the sign, and finally spelled it. "That's five miles."

"Six." Michael shrugged again, this time with only one shoulder. "I'm fast."

"He's a soccer star at his school," Joshua said proudly.

Michael rolled his eyes and shook his head.

Diesel was still stunned. "How long did it take you?"

"Thirty minutes."

Which meant he'd probably set off when his mother should have been leaving to drive here. It also meant this kid wasn't just fast. He was record-setting fast.

Which wasn't important right now. "Does your mother need a doctor?" he repeated.

Michael stiffened again. "No," he replied, the sign terse and final. "She is *sleeping*." He put emphasis on the final sign, letting Diesel know that the teenager understood what he was really asking.

Diesel rubbed his head, the slightest stubble tickling his palm. He needed to shave again soon. "Okay, Joshua, I don't sign well enough to say the next stuff, so you're going to need to interpret, okay?"

Michael poked Joshua with a scowl, and Joshua signed what Diesel had said. Both brothers nodded.

"I can't let Michael take you home. He's not on my approved list." Michael started to protest, but Diesel held up his hand and continued. "I can drive you both home. Mrs. Moody will come with us."

He considered Michael's wince when he'd shrugged. Something wasn't right and Diesel was going to find out what. "But before we leave, I noticed your shoulder seems to be hurting. Are you okay?"

Michael nodded, his eyes narrowing. "Yes," he signed, just as tersely as he'd signed the "no."

"No, he's not," Joshua protested and Michael turned to him with a glare. "You're not," Joshua insisted, his signs as curt as Michael's had been. "His shoulder hurts. His head, too. It was bleeding this morning."

Jaw taut, Michael signed, "I'm *fine*," with enough force to hurt himself.

Once again, Diesel held up his hands, palms out. "If you're bleeding, you should let Mrs. Moody check you out. She's a retired nurse."

"She's real nice, Michael," Joshua added after he'd relayed Diesel's words.

Mrs. Moody came forward slowly, as if approaching a wounded animal. She smiled that motherly smile that Diesel had loved at first glance. "How do I sign 'please,' Joshua?" she asked.

He showed her and she followed his instructions, circling her flat palm over her heart. "Please?"

Michael took a mutinous step back, arms crossed over his chest.

Diesel sighed and started to sign again. "If it gets infected"—he had to spell that word out—"you'll get sick, and then who will take care of Joshua?"

Michael met and held his gaze for a long, long moment. Then he finally nodded and bowed his head, so that Mrs. Moody could take a look.

Mrs. Moody was gentle and quick, her expression telling Diesel that what she saw wasn't good. "It's a bad cut," she murmured. "It needs a thorough cleaning and stitches. At least two or three. It's still oozing blood." She took a step back. "Joshua, can you ask him when this happened?"

Joshua apparently didn't need to ask. "At breakfast," he said, signing as he spoke. "Mama hit him with a bowl." He then relayed to his brother what Mrs. Moody had said about stitches.

"No." Michael voiced the word, his tone flat and unyielding.

"It's still bleeding," Mrs. Moody said softly. "You could get very sick."

Fear flashed in Michael's eyes as Joshua interpreted. "No doctors," Michael signed. "Mom . . . will be mad. She won't pay."

Diesel had to swallow back his rage once again. "What if I could take you to a doctor who would fix you up for free?" he signed. "She signs, too. Her name is Dr. Novak. She's very nice." And never far from his thoughts. His pulse skittered at the chance of seeing her today.

She'd made it very clear that her rejection of his

clumsy advances had had "nothing to do with him."
He hadn't believed her, of course, but had foolishly
held out hope, just the same. Today, he'd be content
with just seeing her.

Her presence calmed him like no one else's could.
He'd even conquered his idiotic phobia of white lab
coats, just to be near her without a panic attack. And
in the end, he hoped his patience would be rewarded.

He hoped he could be hers, for just a little while.

It was pathetic. He knew that. But he was okay
with it.

Michael stared at him for a long moment, clearly
considering a visit to Dani's clinic. "She's Greg's
sister?"

Diesel was surprised. "You know Greg Novak?"

A nod. "He goes to my school. He's a senior."

That made sense. Greg lived with his older brother,
Deacon, not far from Joshua and Michael's house.
"Yes. Dr. Novak is Greg's sister. Can we take you
to her?"

He held his breath until Michael reluctantly
nodded.

Relieved, Diesel smiled. "Good. Mrs. Moody, can
you get up into my truck?"

She chuckled. "I might need a boost." She held out
her hand. "Joshua?"

Joshua trustingly put his hand in hers and walked
to Diesel's truck. Diesel turned to Michael. "Ready?"
he signed.

Michael's nod was sullen, but at this point Diesel
didn't care. He'd get the kid stitched up, then he'd get
Dani to find out why Michael had been so terrified.

Diesel had seen terror like that before, and it
was never caused by something small. A man who
looked like him had hurt that boy. Or threatened to
hurt him.

He was going to find out who that man was. And
he'd make sure that Michael and Joshua were safe.

Indian Hill, Ohio
Saturday, March 16, 12:25 p.m.

Finally, for fuck's sake. Cade rolled his eyes. If his leg wasn't cramping, he might be impressed with his boss's stamina. But his leg *was* cramping and he needed to piss something fierce because he'd been hiding in Richard Fischer's bedroom closet for the past *four fucking hours*, listening to his boss grunt and moan as he'd pounded into whichever one-night stand he'd brought home from the casino the night before. Every time he thought they were finished—or unconscious— they'd start back up again.

Cade didn't know the woman's name. He didn't care. He just wanted her to leave. Luckily Richard wasn't one to cuddle. His boss was already trying to get rid of the woman.

"But I thought we could have lunch," the woman whined.

"Nope." Richard's flat refusal was followed by a slap.

The woman yelped. "That hurt!"

"You know you love it," Richard said with a lewd chuckle.

"I'd love it more with lunch," she grumbled. Her tone went sly. "Come on, baby. We can go out to eat, then come back and fuck some more."

"I said no." Richard's voice had grown abruptly cold. "My guests never stay over. You're lucky I didn't throw you out after the first round."

Cade could hear shuffling sounds outside the closet door. She was gathering her clothes, which— thankfully—she'd left on the floor. The clothes had been his first warning that Richard's date was still in the house when he'd slipped into his boss's bedroom *four fucking hours ago*, thinking the man would be sleeping alone. Because Richard never allowed his dates to sleep over.

Cade had heard the toilet flush and jumped into

the closet seconds before a nude woman had sauntered out of the en suite bathroom and back into Richard's bed, where she'd woken him up for "round two." Cade had been lucky to duck out of sight in time. He didn't want to have to kill the woman, too. He would have, of course, but then he'd have to deal with her body and he didn't know who might look for her afterward.

Plus, it sounded like she'd suffered enough by simply enduring sex with Richard.

The woman huffed. "Like you could have thrown me out. I had to roll you off me. You fell asleep as soon as you came. Which I didn't, by the way," she added viciously. "Not once. I faked it. Every single time."

The closet door abruptly shook as Richard shoved the woman against it, and Cade pulled his Sig from his pocket. If Richard opened the door now, Cade would have to shoot them both. This wasn't what he'd planned. Richard was supposed to have been alone and his death was supposed to look like an accident.

He held his breath, eyeing the door as it shook and rattled, but it didn't open.

"You're a fucking liar," Richard snarled and the woman cried out.

"You're *hurting* me. Take your hands *off* me. I'll tell everyone that you're a lousy lay. That you can only get it up with Viagra."

Well, Cade thought, that made sense. Richard was a diabetic on insulin. But still. *I'm not sure I could keep it up for four hours even with Viagra.* Richard had done the woman at least three times since Cade had arrived. There was no telling how many times they'd gone at it before he'd fallen asleep on her.

"You're lucky I don't snap your neck," Richard growled. "If I hear one whisper of your lies in my club, I will."

Cade rolled his eyes again. *Like Richard can snap anything more than his fingers.* Although he might rethink that. A certain level of fitness was required to go for four hours. According to the Viagra ads, Richard should probably be consulting his doctor.

The door shook once more and the woman whimpered as her head thudded against the thin wood. "Now get out," Richard snarled.

"Let *go* of me," she protested. "I'm going. I'm going!"

"Yes, you are. And I'm going to escort you out, to make sure you don't steal anything on your way."

Their footsteps faded, along with their arguing voices, and Cade let out a sigh of relief. Opening the door enough to confirm he was alone, he slipped out of the closet and into the bathroom, where he emptied his bladder, pulled on a pair of surgical gloves, then waited for Richard to return.

He heard the front door slam and Richard's muttering as he stomped back into his bedroom. Cade peeked around the bathroom door in time to watch Richard slump onto his bed, loosening the tie on his robe. "Motherfucking bitch."

Cade stepped out of the bathroom. "Yes, she was."

Richard sat bolt upright. "What the hell? What are you doing here, King?"

Scott King was the name Cade had given Richard when he'd applied for the casino's head of security position. King, because its original owner wasn't using it. Because the original owner was long dead, at Cade's hand. King, because the irony always made him smile.

If good old Dad could only see me now. Cade's smile seemed to relax Richard a bit. "I'm going to kill you," Cade said cheerfully.

Richard gave him a sour look and pulled his robe tighter. "That's not funny. How did you get in here?"

"You gave me a key, remember?"

"So that you could feed the damn cat!"

"And water the plants. And bring in the mail. Et cetera." Cade pulled a velvet tie from his pocket and had Richard's wrists bound before the man could react. It had taken years to perfect that move, especially while wearing gloves, but the practice had been well worth it. "Looks like you shouldn't have trusted me."

Richard stared at him. "What the fuck?" He yanked at his bond. "Untie me. Now."

"Sorry," Cade said, then paused, considering the word. "No, I'm not. I'm not sorry at all. But *you* will be." He forced Richard's hands over his head and secured the bindings to the wrought-iron headboard.

Richard seemed to finally realize that Cade meant business. He jerked, but Cade was already restraining his ankles the same way as he had Richard's hands.

"Stop this," Richard demanded. "What is this? What the *fuck* are you doing?"

"I told you. I'm killing you."

Richard stopped his thrashing, the color draining from his face. "What? Why?" When Cade didn't answer, Richard sucked in a huge breath, preparing to scream. Ready for this, Cade stuffed a gag in his boss's mouth.

"I'd planned to do this while you were asleep, but your lady friend was still here," Cade said conversationally. "Have to admit, that startled me. I'd figured she'd be long gone. I had to hide in the closet. But no worries. I'll dose you up and be on my way."

The vial and needle he pulled from his pocket had Richard's eyes widening comically. Cade chuckled. "You really should have been more careful with your insulin dosage." He stuck the needle into the vial and pulled the plunger until the syringe was full.

Terror had filled Richard's eyes and he tried to thrash some more, panic making him strong. His muffled pleas were like music to Cade's ears.

Cade pulled Richard's robe away from his abdomen, pushed the needle into his skin, and emptied the syringe, despite the man's desperate movements. When he was finished, he set the bottle and syringe on the bedside table, arranging them as if Richard had dropped them there. He then pulled his stethoscope from his pocket. He'd wait until he was positive that Richard was completely dead.

He sat down on the edge of the bed, Richard's eyes following his every move. Cade knew it was time to get serious.

"I was hoping last week's transaction during the poker game was a one-time thing," he said coldly. "That maybe you hadn't known that John Brewer was using his five-year-old stepson as his stake so that he could stay in the game. That maybe you hadn't known that Blake Emerson was a pedophile and had bought Brewer's stepson. But you did." Richard shook his head hard, but Cade ignored him. "Brewer's dead, by the way. So is Emerson. I killed them."

Richard's muffled "no" was to be expected. Cade was unmoved.

"I might have believed you, but I listened carefully last night. You know, through the door where you were having your super-secret poker game. I heard Brian Carlyle say that he had 'seasoned merchandise' that hadn't yet been 'branded.' You know what his merchandise was? Of course you do. You vetted Carlyle and his stake, just like you vetted all the others. I found your database, Richard. I'm not sure why you kept such detailed records. That was asking for trouble." Cade never recorded his kills. He didn't need to. He remembered each one.

"Carlyle's merchandise was his fifteen-year-old niece." Cade leaned in, furious. "You knew," he hissed. "Just like you knew Paul Engel liked young girls. You knew and you allowed it. You profited from it. You're disgusting."

He leaned back, noting the cold sweat on Richard's forehead, the way his breathing had slowed. *Excellent.* "You might have noted that I said that Paul Engel *liked* young girls. Past tense. He's dead. He died very painfully. So did Brian Carlyle. Unfortunately, I want your death to appear to be an accident, otherwise the cops will start looking at me for it. If I had my way, I'd be cutting off your fingers and then your toes. Then all the other parts you hold dear. Just like I did to them. While you were sleeping with Miss Motherfucking Bitch, I was busy cutting up your clients and throwing them in the river. I'm sure you'll be quite relieved to know that Carlyle's niece is safe and her creepy uncle won't ever touch her again."

Richard's eyes slid closed.

Cade nodded, satisfied. "I'll take that as a yes. Now, hurry up and die. I have places I need to be."

Chapter Two

Cincinnati, Ohio
Saturday, March 16, 12:45 p.m.

Dani Novak closed her eyes wearily. Conversations with her aunt and uncle never ended well these days. *Who am I kidding?* There was no "these days" about it. Conversations with Jim and Tammy Kimble had never ended well. They had ended less well since Jim had lost his insurance benefits along with his police pension. Which Jim had a way of blaming on everyone except himself, of course.

"You said this was an emergency, Uncle Jim." She gritted her teeth, trying to keep her voice low because she wasn't alone in the little exam room. "Aunt Tammy needing a refill on her anxiety medication is not an emergency and I'm not her doctor. Call her actual doctor. I'm with a patient."

She knew she would be ignored. Trying to reason with her uncle was like spitting into the wind. Her words were always flung back at her, somehow worse on the return trip.

"Oh, yeah," Jim said sarcastically. "All those patients at that *clinic*." He said *clinic* like it was a dirty word. To him, it probably was. The Meadow Free Clinic served the lowest economic bracket of the city, the people Jim had always looked down on. "You'd rather sew up gangbangers than take care of your actual flesh and blood. Well, I guess your patients get what they pay for. It's not like you're going to get anyone else to come to you, seeing as you're . . . y'know."

Dani drew a breath, trying not to show that the arrows had found their mark, because they had. *Your patients get what they pay for.* Which was nothing, in Jim's mind.

Seeing as you're . . . y'know. Yes, she knew. Jim hadn't spared the descriptors since learning that she was HIV positive, and today would be no exception. *Whore. Stupid. Dirty.*

Believing her ex-fiancé when he'd said he was clean might have been stupid, but she was no whore. Nor was she dirty or even ashamed of her HIV status. She fervently wished that the whole world didn't know about it, but she'd been outed against her will by one of her brother's former classmates. How the kid had found out, she didn't know. She didn't really want to know. She could only push forward and make the best of the hand she'd been dealt, which included refusing to cower to bigots.

Even when they were her own family. Especially then.

Seeing as you're . . . y'know. Yes, she did know. She lifted her chin. "A good doctor."

"Diseased," Jim spat out. "God, I can't believe how stupid you were. And that you touched people without them knowing. Your aunt can barely hold her head up in church. I thought I raised you better, but I can see—"

She wanted to remind him that she could not transmit the virus to anyone as long as her viral levels were undetectable, which hers had been for years. She wanted to remind him that even if she were detectable, HIV wasn't transmitted through touch, and that she'd followed every rule and policy put in place by County General Hospital while she'd been an attending physician in the emergency department. But she'd been down that road before and knew it was useless. Her uncle didn't want to believe facts.

He's an asshole and abusive. Let it go. "Good-bye," she interrupted. "Call Tammy's doctor." She ended the call and took a few seconds to regroup and force her lips to curve in a smile before turning back to the others in the room.

Tommy and Edna watched her, pity in their old eyes. Dani's friend Scarlett Bishop was visibly angry, but Scarlett knew the family well. Scarlett had worked with Dani's cousin Adam on the homicide squad for years, and he had gotten it from Jim and Tammy worse than Dani had. God only knew how he had survived growing up in the Kimble house.

Dani's older brother, Deacon, barely had survived. And her younger brother, Greg? *I should have gotten him out. I should never have let Jim raise him.*

But she'd been too young to fight Jim back then. Young and confused and grieving the loss of her parents. At least Greg didn't have to live with Jim and Tammy anymore, having moved in with Deacon and his wife, Faith.

And none of that belonged in her mind right now. She needed to focus on the elderly man on her exam table. "So where were we?" she asked Tommy. "Oh, right. Pneumonia with a side of gout."

"I'm fine." Tommy negated his claim with a racking cough. He fell back against the exam table, exhausted. "I'm fine, Dr. Dani," he wheezed. "Just fine."

Dani lifted her brows. "Really, Tommy? That's what you're going with?" The older man had already survived two bouts of pneumonia. This was his third.

Edna, his street companion, shook her head. "He's a stubborn fool, Dr. D."

Tommy set his mouth as stubbornly as described. "Shut up, Edna. I'm fine."

"You're not fine." Scarlett Bishop pushed away from the wall in impatience. She had a soft spot for Tommy and Edna, who'd lived on the street for years.

But every time she or Dani tried to get them into housing, the pair would return to the street. "You promised me that you'd listen to what the doctor said. Tommy, you *promised*."

Tommy looked away. "Not goin' to a shelter."

"No," Dani said softly. "You're going to the hospital, Tommy. You're really sick. You have pneumonia. Again."

Edna's sigh was heavy. "The winter was too hard on him. You'll go to the hospital, Tommy, and that's that."

"Tommy." Dani met his eyes, hoping like hell that he saw the truth in hers. "If you want to see the summer, you will go to the hospital. Detective Bishop will take you. Won't you, Detective?"

Scarlett nodded. "Absolutely. Please, Tommy. I've gotten used to seeing that face of yours. I want to see it—and you—on your stoop this summer." She gave the man a sweet smile. "Please? For me?"

He sighed. "What about Edna? Where will she go tonight? She can't be alone on the street, and somebody could hurt her if she goes to the shelter."

"She can go to the hospital with you," Dani said. "Tell them she's your wife."

Edna snorted. "I ain't his wife. I'd'a killed him years ago if I'd married him."

Dani chuckled. "Just say it, Edna. They'll probably bring in a comfortable chair for you to sleep in and give you a breakfast tray in the morning."

Edna rolled her eyes. "Okay. Just this once." She glared at Tommy. "Don't you be gettin' any ideas, old man."

"Wouldn't think of it." Struggling to sit up, Tommy accepted Dani's gloved hand, grunting his thanks. "Fine. I'll go." He wagged a finger at Scarlett. "But only for you."

Scarlett's smile was relieved. "Thank you. Come on. I'll take you and Edna to County right now." She helped Tommy down from the exam table and into the wheelchair he'd been put into the moment he'd walked into the clinic.

Dani gave Edna her cane, then opened the office door. "Nurse Jenny? Can you call County and let them know Mr. Jenkins is coming in?" She squeezed Tommy's hand. "Be nice to the hospital nurses, okay? They can make or break you."

Scarlett took hold of the wheelchair handles and pushed Tommy into the waiting room. And stopped short.

"Diesel?" Scarlett asked. "What brings you here?"

Dani sucked in a startled breath. *Diesel. He's here. Oh God. He's here.*

She closed her eyes for the briefest of moments, calming her racing heart and schooling her features into the mask she always wore around him. The one that said she didn't notice him. That she didn't care. That she didn't want him.

Because she *did* care, and she *did* want him. She really did. But she didn't want him to know. Didn't want to give him hope.

Because he did hope. Still. It was common knowledge among their circle of friends that Diesel Kennedy had been head over heels for her for a long, long time. They thought she didn't see it. But she saw. She'd seen from the very beginning.

From that first moment when he'd walked into her clinic eighteen months ago—six feet, six inches and two hundred seventy-five pounds of solid muscle—she'd known. He'd stopped short, dark brown eyes going wide, skin abruptly paling so that his magnificent tattoos had stood out in stark contrast. He'd staggered backward out of the door that day, never saying a word. But there'd been want in his eyes, want that she'd understood, because she'd wanted him, too, just as suddenly. And so very much.

He was everything she'd ever desired. Big. Built. Bald. Tats covering his skin. She'd wanted to touch them that day. And every day thereafter.

But that was an impossibility.

She'd tried to let him down easy, with as much of the truth as she was able—or willing—to tell. She'd tried the "it's not you, it's me" speech, except she'd let him believe that she meant her positive status and not that she'd poisoned the only other relationship she'd had. The memory of her final moments with Adrian intruded, leaving her shaken and bitter. She wasn't going to hurt Diesel the way she'd hurt Adrian. She couldn't.

So she'd told him a partial truth, cited her status, tried to convince him that any kind of relationship was hopeless. He hadn't cursed or whined or stomped off. He'd just looked her in the eye and nodded with that quiet reserve he wore so well.

He hadn't gone on to someone else.

She wished he would. And was perversely glad he hadn't.

He'd simply gone on doing the same things he always did. He worked for Marcus O'Bannion at the Cincinnati *Ledger*, the newspaper Marcus had inherited from his grandfather. Diesel was their IT guy, using his online skills partly to support investigations for their reporting, and partly to dig up extortable dirt on lowlifes who preyed on defenseless women and children. He and Marcus continued to build houses for those in need through the organization Marcus had founded, modeled on Habitat for Humanity. He continued to coach kids' sports. He continued being a good friend to them all, their entire circle of friends.

All except me. Because they both knew that he wanted to be more than friends. *And so do I. God help me, so do I.*

And because she wanted him so damn badly, because he was such a good person, she'd stepped back, intent on letting him live his life. *Without* me.

It was for the best.

Lifting her head, she pasted a professional smile on her face and followed Scarlett into the waiting room, turning to her nurse as she passed. "Jenny, can you get the room ready for the next patient?"

"Sure, Dani." Jenny's eyes flicked to the doorway, where Diesel stood with an older woman and two boys, brothers from the look of them. The little one looked warily hopeful. The older one appeared sullen and ready to bolt. "Mr. Kennedy called about ten minutes ago. Asked if you were on duty today. The older boy is deaf."

"Ah. Makes sense." Dani nodded, hoping like hell her mask held up. Because Diesel was looking at her longingly, hiding nothing. Everything he felt—and wanted—was right there in his gaze. He was an open book. *Hard*cover. Each page clean and white.

And I'm a tattered comic book, she thought derisively. With every page encrypted so completely that even the NSA couldn't make a lick of sense out of a single word.

Shoving all thoughts aside, she focused on the sullen teenager at Diesel's side. "Hi," she signed. "I'm Dr. Dani."

The teenager nodded stiffly. "Michael Rowland," he spelled.

"Your name sign?" she asked, and signed hers—her right hand in the letter "D," following the sweep of the white streak in the front of her otherwise black hair. There since birth, it was her most distinctive feature.

Michael signed his—left hand in an "M," right hand "kicking" up into it.

She smiled at him. "So you love soccer."

"He does," the little boy said, signing simultaneously. "Me, too. I'm on Coach Diesel's team."

She lifted her eyes to Diesel, steeling herself for the now-familiar look in his eyes. "Coach Diesel. It's always a pleasure to see you."

He nodded once. "And you, Dr. Dani. This is my assistant coach, Mrs. Moody. She's a retired nurse."

"Mrs. Moody," Dani said with a nod, then leaned

down, not needing a fake smile for the little boy. He was a darling. "And who are you?"

"Joshua," he said, showing her his name sign. "My brother's head is hurt. It's bleeding. His shoulder, too."

"We'll get him all fixed up," Dani promised, still signing so that Michael could follow the conversation. "Just give me a few minutes to talk to your coach, okay?"

Joshua's expression was sober. "He said you'd take care of everything."

Dani's eyes shot up to Diesel's in question. "Well, I'll do my best. Why don't you sit over there with Mrs. Moody and your brother? I'll be back in a sec."

Diesel leaned in to Scarlett and murmured something that Dani didn't catch. She reached behind her ear to hike the volume on her processor, wincing when the sounds flooded in. She'd been born deaf in her right ear and wore a hearing device that diverted all the sound into her left ear. Usually having it at a low setting was fine for one-on-one, but if someone was whispering, she needed to turn it up.

"—need CPS," Diesel was saying and Dani's heart sank while Scarlett nodded her understanding.

"I'll call Adam to come in," Scarlett said. "He signs, too. We'll get a statement."

"I'll call him," Dani said, her smile tight because she was annoyed, actually. *Had I known parental abuse was an issue, I would have called Adam myself.*

Scarlett gave her a nod. "Thanks, Dani."

Joshua's curious stare had locked on Tommy in the wheelchair. "What happened to you?" he asked the old man, his small hands unmoving at his sides.

Michael nudged his brother and gave his head a hard shake. "Not polite," he signed. "Apologize."

So Michael can speech-read, Dani thought. *Just a little, perhaps, but that's enough for me to be on guard. Good to know.*

Joshua obediently apologized and Tommy patted

his head, telling him it was good that he was willing to admit when he was wrong. Tommy glanced ruefully at Dani as he said the words, and she knew that was all the apology she'd get from the old charmer.

"See you soon, Tommy, Edna. Coach Diesel? Let's talk."

Cleveland, Ohio
Saturday, March 16, 12:55 p.m.

Grant Masterson cursed under his breath as he searched the stack of paperwork for a copy of his client's 1099. He'd just had it in his hands. *Dammit.*

He paused to close his eyes and take a deep breath to calm his racing heart. He was exhausted. The last time he'd slept? He opened his eyes to glance over at the cot he brought into his office every year at the beginning of tax season. Whenever it was, it was too long ago.

Maybe he'd take a quick—

"Grant?"

His gaze swung to his open door, where his assistant stood, looking nervous. Grant swallowed what would have been a nasty reply. "Yes, MaryBeth?" he asked, as civilly as he could. MaryBeth had been working the same hours he had and the dark circles under her eyes confirmed it.

I need to hire more people.

"There's a woman who says she needs to see you." She held up her hand when he started to repeat his instructions that he not be disturbed. "Her name is Tracy Simon. She says it's urgent."

Grant felt the blood drain from his face. *No. Please, no.* Tracy was his brother's partner on the force. No good came of visits from police officers to the next of kin.

Let him be alive. Please.

He stood, his legs like rubber. "Send her in, please."

MaryBeth gave him a concerned look, but knew

better than to ask him if he was all right. Or maybe she was simply tired of his reply of "fine" whenever she did.

She didn't ask much anymore, he thought numbly. Not since January, more than a year ago.

My God. Had it been that long since— He shook his head hard. He still couldn't think his sister's name without a sharp stab of pain. He sent up a silent prayer. *Please don't let me lose Wesley, too.*

Except those prayers hadn't been answered with his sister, so why would God start listening now?

Tracy Simon entered his office and quietly closed the door. She was normally a cheerful woman, but today she looked grim.

Grant choked out his question before she could begin. "Is he alive?"

She swallowed hard. "I don't know."

Grant sank into his chair. "What does that mean?" he whispered.

She sat in the client chair. "Wesley's been taking a lot of weekends off lately. For some of them he's used his vacation time, others he's taken sick leave. A lot of sick leave, Grant."

Grant shook his head, confused. "Is he sick? He hasn't said a word."

She shrugged. "I don't know. All I know is that he took vacation days this time. When I saw him last Friday morning, he said he'd be back Thursday morning. He never showed up for our shift. For the last three days I've called his cell and his home phone and got no answer. He's going to be put on suspension, although I'm surprised it hasn't happened before now. I'd hoped you'd know what was going on, but it doesn't look like you do."

"No," Grant murmured. "I don't. Do you know where he's been going?"

"No. Again, I hoped you'd know." She hesitated. "I think he might be drinking. I mean, like, a *lot.*" She shrugged again. "Something's wrong. I stopped by his place and knocked, but he didn't answer. I'm afraid he's somewhere hurt or sick."

Grant scrubbed his hands down his face. *Not again,* he wanted to groan, but kept it silent. Wesley's partner didn't need to know that he'd likely thrown away a whole year of sobriety. Or maybe not a whole year, if he'd been disappearing for a long time.

Goddammit, Wes. You would pick the busiest fucking time of the year to go AWOL. You'd better be sick or hurt, or you will be when I find your drunk ass in whatever gutter you've passed out in.

He took another deep breath, then another. Yes, his brother had suffered a loss. *But we all did. I miss her, too, but you don't see me crawling into a fucking bottle.*

Because Grant had responsibilities.

He lifted his gaze to meet Tracy's sympathetic one. "I'll ask my wife to stop by his apartment. We have a key for emergencies." Not to feed a pet or water plants, because Wesley had nothing alive in his apartment. *If you don't count the mold growing on the old food in his fridge.*

Tracy rose, a faint smile on her face. "Thank you. Let me know what you find, okay? I like him. He's been a good mentor to me. I've covered for him a time or two, but I can't do that anymore."

"Of course you can't," Grant said gently when he really wanted to scream. "I'll let you know whatever I find."

"Take care," Tracy said. "And try to get some rest."

"After April fifteenth," he said wearily. When the door had closed behind her, he called his wife with a sigh. Then winced when he heard screaming children in the background. "Hey, Cora," he said, hoping she wouldn't sound too frazzled.

"Grant," she breathed hopefully and his heart squeezed. She was hoping he was calling to say he was coming home to give her a break.

He was going to disappoint her again.

"I need a favor."

There was a beat of harsh silence on the other end, followed by a tense "What?"

"It's Wes. He's disappeared. His partner just left my office. He's gone AWOL."

Cora sighed. "Oh no. You don't think he's . . . you know."

Yes, Grant knew. "I don't know if he's drinking again or not. I was hoping you could get a sitter and go check on him."

She sighed again, exasperated. "Like I'll be able to find a sitter at this short notice. It's Saturday afternoon, Grant. Besides, if I could get a sitter, I'd go to the spa or the mall or the gym or anywhere but your brother's apartment."

"Cora—" he started, but she cut him off, her tone shrill and exhausted.

"I have an idea. Why don't you come home and watch your children and then I can go?"

Their three children—fourteen-month-old twins and a month-old singlet—were enough to exhaust an Olympic athlete. It was no wonder Cora was tired. She had no help, because he'd been working ridiculous hours. Guilt pierced him. Sometimes he hated his job. Especially in March and April.

He gentled his voice. "Tell you what, honey. I'll get you a sitter *and* I'll go to Wes's to check on him. You can take the afternoon to do anything you want to do."

"I want to have a few hours with you," she whispered. "I miss you."

"I miss you, too, baby," he said regretfully, understanding why a third of his peers were divorced. He hoped he could make it up to her after April fifteenth. "Soon we'll have a lot of time. I'm sorry."

She sighed again, this one sounding defeated. "I know. I'm sorry to be demanding. I know you're upset about Wesley. I'm just so tired."

"I know, baby. I'll find you a sitter."

"That's okay, Grant. I'll get some sleep when I put

them all down for a nap. Go check on your brother.
We're fine here."

"I love you. I don't deserve you."

She chuckled, and he felt better. "I love you, too.
And no, you don't. Call me when you find Wes."

"I will." Grant disconnected, then grabbed his keys
and wallet. "MaryBeth?" She met him in the hallway,
clearly curious about his visitor, but too polite to ask.
"Does your niece still do nanny work?"

"Au pair," she corrected primly. "And yes. She's
just returned from a year in Germany. Would you like
me to send her to your house?"

He smiled. "Yes, please. And call my wife to let
her know that she's coming. I'll be back soon." He
hoped.

He gave a last look at his desk, its surface barely
visible under all the stacks of tax returns. *Goddammit, Wes. Couldn't you have fallen off the wagon on
April sixteenth?*

Cincinnati, Ohio
Saturday, March 16, 1:05 p.m.

Keenly aware of the big man behind her, Dani walked
to her office and sat behind her desk, waiting until
Diesel came in and closed the door. There were so
many things she wanted to say to him. *Do* to him. But
she knew any relationship with Diesel Kennedy would
only end in heartbreak for both of them.

So she kept her thoughts focused on the most important thing—the two boys in her waiting room.
"You asked Scarlett to call CPS?"

"Yes," he said, and she winced, his booming voice
sending a shard of pain through her ear and into her
head.

"Sorry," she said, and turned the volume down. "I
turned it up to hear what you were whispering to
Scarlett. In here, I don't need it at all. Have a seat,
Coach."

He met her gaze unflinchingly, clearly understanding what she'd done by putting the desk between them. Distance was key to her sanity.

He was close enough, though, that she could detect his scent, and it was as it always was—delicious. Like verbena soap and light sweat. Common enough, but on him? Really, really good.

She concentrated on not sniffing the air like a puppy. *That would be humiliating.*

He was close enough that she could read his lips. Which were firm and full and . . . *No, no, no. Do not look at his lips. He'll know.*

He was too damn close. That was all.

So find out what's going on so that you can open the door and air the room out. You don't want to be leaping over the desk and into his lap.

She cleared her throat. "I'm wearing my lab coat."

Which was *so* not what she'd planned to say.

He nodded. "I've been working on that phobia. Desensitizing."

When he'd first met her, he'd experienced panic attacks whenever he saw her in a white lab coat. But not today.

"Why?" she asked and clenched her jaw. She hadn't meant to ask that, either.

He tilted his head, the light from the window highlighting his jaw, which was square and strong.

Like all of him.

"I didn't want to be triggered by doctors anymore," he said. His gaze dropped to her mouth briefly before rising to her eyes.

She nearly fanned herself. "That's good. I mean . . . good." She closed her eyes and drew a breath, aware that her nostrils were flaring but unable to change the fact. "So . . . Michael Rowland."

"Yes," he said quietly. "I need your help. *He* needs your help."

She opened her eyes, locked onto his. "Why CPS, Diesel? What's going on at his home?"

He settled his big body into the chair. There wasn't an ounce of fat on that man. Anywhere. "I don't know exactly," he finally answered. "Joshua said their mother hits Michael. She threw a bowl at him this morning. That's what needs to be stitched. I also saw him wincing when he shrugged, then later he only used one shoulder to shrug." The side of his mouth lifted sadly. "I guess teenagers have to shrug to communicate, so he couldn't stop altogether."

She couldn't help it. She smiled at him. Really smiled. "Yeah, I know that from experience. My brother Greg has the shrug down to an art form."

He swallowed hard, his chest rising as he drew a breath of his own. He was staring at her mouth again. Then he blinked, jerking his chin up.

"Michael says he knows your brother. From school. That you're Greg's sister was the one thing that convinced him it was okay to come in."

"I'll use that, then. I've got contacts in CPS." She lifted a brow. "As do you."

Scarlett had told her long ago that some of Diesel and Marcus's best tips for *Ledger* investigations had come from social workers who'd been frustrated at being unable to remove children from abusive parents who knew how to work the system in their favor. Or rich parents who knew how to buy their way out.

His only reaction to her statement was a slow blink. "Yours are more appropriate for today's problem, though."

"True. I'll call Maddie Shafer. She's quick and sensitive to kids with special needs like Michael. I take it you don't want to take the boys back to their home."

"No. Joshua is mine to keep safe."

Her heart squeezed so hard that it hurt. This big, scary-looking man was as protective as the day was long. She should know. He'd once saved her life.

She had the scar to remind her of the day she'd been dragged away by a killer who'd plunged a knife into her gut and left her for dead. She'd been caring for Decker Davenport, an FBI agent who worked with her brother Deacon, after Decker was shot by a local gang to stop him from sharing what he'd learned while undercover. Dani's attacker had been a supplier of drugs to the gang and had feared Decker's information could bring him down as well. Knowing that Dani was Decker's private physician, he'd tried to use her to obtain Decker's location. It had been Diesel who'd been watching over her, who'd stopped her abduction, and who'd gotten her to the hospital after her attacker's knife sliced her open. She still remembered the feel of his big hands as he'd carried her into the closest ER.

He hadn't known that he was risking his own life that day. But he'd found out in a hurry. They'd taken the clothes he'd been wearing and tossed them into a biohazard bag because they'd been covered in her blood. Her HIV-positive blood.

She'd expected the knowledge to drive him away, but it hadn't. Not in all this time.

Diesel Kennedy was a protector. She'd do her best to help him because the world needed men like him. Children needed to know that there were still people to protect them, especially kids whose parents had abdicated that responsibility.

"Do you have any kind of parental permission to have Michael treated?" she asked.

He shook his head. "He's not on my team. Only Joshua is."

She sighed. "I can't treat him, then, not until CPS tells me to."

"His head's bleeding, Dani," Diesel said quietly. "Can you at least bandage him up even if you can't do stitches?"

"Of course. I'll ready a room for him," she said, standing. "And as soon as CPS arrives, I can stitch him up."

Diesel stood as well. "He ran six miles in thirty

minutes with a head wound," he offered. "I don't know if that has worsened his injury or not."

Dani's eyes grew wide. "Wow. The kid is fast. Let's make sure he doesn't run from us."

His lips quirked again. "From us. Sounds like a plan."

She needed to correct him. Needed to tell him that nothing had changed for her. That there was no "us." It wouldn't be a lie. She wanted him as much as she always had. But that there could never be a "them" remained equally true.

She needed to say the words, but they would not come. "Right," she murmured, then waited for him to leave first. But he remained where he stood, silently challenging her to move past him. She should have told him to go, but those words wouldn't come, either.

She squeezed by him, unable to keep from drawing one last breath to fill her head with his scent.

And watched him do the same.

God. She opened the door, let the cooler, non-Diesel-scented air of the waiting room fill her lungs. "Jenny, can you prep a room for Michael, please? I'll need a suture kit." She moved closer to her nurse and murmured, "I need to call Maddie Shafer at CPS and my cousin Adam. We need them here for the exam."

Jenny nodded. "Will do."

Dani turned to Michael to tell him what would happen next, but froze once again, her mouth dropping open in shock. Diesel was signing to Michael. *Diesel.* And he was doing pretty well, too.

She didn't know he could sign. Where had he learned? When had he learned?

Why had he learned?

"You can sign?" she blurted.

He turned to her, his eyes more compelling than they'd ever been before. He nodded, holding her gaze for a moment that seemed to stretch on and on.

"I thought I might need it in the future," he said

quietly. "To talk to Greg." He didn't even blink, his message coming across loud and clear.

Game on.

Dani swallowed hard, her control faltering. He'd learned to sign to talk to Greg? He didn't interact with Greg except at holiday parties.

He'd only interact one-on-one with Greg if . . . *If we become "us."*

She took a giant step back, bumping into the counter. Unable to say a word, she turned and fled to her office to make her calls. She needed a few minutes to shore up her defenses. And then she'd tell Diesel Kennedy—once and for all—to back off.

And then?

I'll be lonely. But he'll be safe.

Indian Hill, Ohio
Saturday, March 16, 1:45 p.m.

Cade pulled the stethoscope away from Richard's chest. *Finally.* It had taken hours longer than he'd expected. But his boss was finally and definitely dead.

An insulin overdose would do that to a man. Unfortunately, Richard hadn't died as painfully as he'd deserved. He'd died in his own bed, in his own house. He'd probably been unconscious for most of the fun. He should have been awake, meeting the same fate as the others.

Richard had known. He'd done it *twice*—trafficked human beings *twice*. Actually, he'd done it more than twice, but Cade hadn't been aware of that until he'd broken into Richard's very private database. Twice, however, would have been enough.

Cade would have preferred to kill him with the Sawzall, dumping him in the river, too, but Richard would be missed and possibly connected to his missing guests. That would connect to Cade, and that would be bad.

Plus, he needed Richard's death to appear natural, if premature, so that he could get another job. It was easier to say you'd left your old job because your boss had had a heart attack. Far more difficult if the guy had mysteriously gone missing.

So he'd used Richard's body against him. The man had suffered from type 1 diabetes and had been insulin dependent for years. Cade had seen him injecting himself a number of times.

He'd given him an extra dose. Or ten. The timing was convenient. Richard wouldn't be expected back at the riverboat casino until Wednesday night, and by then all the insulin would be out of his system.

There were no super-secret poker games during that time, and Richard often left the normal casino operation to his manager. There would be no suspicion of any foul play.

Cade would show up on time for his shifts, behaving as if nothing was wrong. And then when Richard's body was finally found, he'd be so damn sad.

He turned to Richard's mirror and practiced his sad face. Then laughed because his sad face needed some work. That was okay. He had a few days to perfect it.

Stowing his stethoscope in his gym bag, Cade slipped out of Richard's house via the basement door, setting the alarm and locking it behind him with the key Richard had given him months ago. He had a minute to get past the cameras before the security system engaged.

The basement door opened to the backyard, which had an eight-foot-high privacy fence. Tall enough that Cade didn't have to slouch to keep his head from being seen as he jogged to the back gate. His SUV was parked on the next street. He needed to hurry. He had an appointment with his father in the nursing home.

He visited his dad every Saturday, rain or shine. The old man couldn't say anything to him, but he listened. Cade never held back.

Major Konrad Kaiser—US Army JAG Corps, Retired—had controlled Cade's life when he was younger. He'd been a firm believer in "spare the rod, spoil the child." No one could ever say that Cade had been spoiled. Or that his mother had.

But Konrad was smart enough to know where to hit. And when. There were never visible marks for a teacher to see and report. Not that it would have stuck.

Major Konrad Kaiser—US Army JAG Corps, Retired—knew the law. Knew how to get around the law.

And knew powerful people who'd gotten him out of trouble the two times he'd "gone too far." That was what he'd called it both times he'd hit Cade's mother too hard. The first time, she'd landed in the hospital. Cade had been ten.

The second time, she'd landed at the bottom of the basement stairs after Konrad had snapped her neck with his bare hands. Cade had been almost twenty-one and he still had nightmares about what he'd seen that night.

God, he hated the SOB. His father had never let Cade have the last word. Until he'd had a "stroke" four years before. He was supposed to have died, but he'd been found too soon. That had taught Cade the value of proper planning. And making sure that his victim was actually dead before he walked away. He'd bought the stethoscope the very next day.

That particular outcome, however, hadn't been a bad one. Cade liked this version of his father—a pathetic old man who was dependent on strangers to feed him, wash him, and change his diapers.

Cade got the last word every single week now.

Chapter Three

Coach Diesel hadn't said anything since he and Michael had entered the small exam room. Michael wasn't exactly sure what had happened in the waiting room, but there was tension between the doctor and Coach. It had started the moment he and Joshua had walked through the clinic's front door with Coach and had gotten worse when Coach had returned from talking with the doctor in her office.

Even Joshua had noticed it. He'd kept looking from Coach to the doctor to Mrs. Moody, who'd stayed quiet. Mrs. Moody was sitting with Joshua in the waiting room right now. She'd had crayons and a coloring book in her big purse, and Joshua was happily coloring when Michael had been led back to the exam room.

It seemed that Mrs. Moody didn't actually say a whole lot. Michael hadn't seen her lips move more than once or twice since he'd run up to Joshua at the practice fields. But she smiled sweetly and her touch had been gentle as she'd checked the wound on his head.

Which hurt like crazy. His head was pounding, but it was bearable. He'd had a lot worse. He stiffened as a new thought struck. Would the doctor ask to see more than his head? Would she ask him to take off his pants?

He swallowed hard. He'd say no. He'd fight them. He didn't need the doctor seeing *that*. Hell, he didn't need to see it, either. It had been over a week since the last time, and he was still seeing red streaks in his briefs.

Goddamn Brewer. Michael forced himself to breathe. To calm down. Because thinking about Brewer made him remember the night the man had been killed. Which made him think about the huge bald man who'd killed him.

Who'd returned to the house to look at Joshua. Why? Why had he done that? He'd returned Brewer's car to the garage and left the man's keys on a peg near the front door before coming up to look at Joshua. Why?

Why hadn't he simply stolen the car and sold it?

The man had also taken a suitcase and some of Brewer's clothes with him that night—a few suits, shirts, jeans, underwear—like he'd been packing for a trip.

No way Brewer's clothes would have fit him. Brewer was five-ten with a beer belly. The man who'd killed him was closer to the size of Joshua's coach.

And now the coach was suspicious. He was being nice and all, but Michael wasn't stupid. He knew the big man was biding his time before pressing him for why he'd been so terrified when he had first seen him at the soccer field. He certainly didn't want to tell the coach about the guy who'd killed Brewer. Coach already knew that his mother had thrown the bowl at his head that morning. Joshua had a big mouth.

Michael couldn't blame his brother, though. He was only five and the coach was a nice man. *I hope. Please let him be a nice man. Please don't let him be like Brewer.*

The door opened and four women entered, crowding the already cramped space. One was the doctor, two were women Michael had never seen before, and the fourth—

Michael blinked. The fourth woman was taller than the others and she wore a uniform. *A cop.*

They'd called the cops. Michael jerked his gaze to Coach Diesel. "I didn't do anything," he signed, his heart beating like crazy once again.

Diesel nodded calmly. "We know."

Dr. Dani stepped close to him, leaning in to sign in very small movements that the other three women couldn't see. It was as close to privacy as they would get. "She's not here because you did anything. She's here because your mother hurt you. She'll take your statement. That's all. She's a friend of mine. She won't hurt you, Michael."

Michael's chest suddenly hurt and it was hard to breathe, because everything was starting to fall into place. His mother's words bounced around his mind— if the cops took Joshua and him away from her, they'd separate them and Michael wouldn't be able to watch over his brother. Terrible things would happen. Joshua would get hurt. *Like Brewer hurt me.*

That couldn't happen. Michael could not allow that to happen. Ever.

Don't panic. Not now. Please. "One of them's a social worker," he signed, pointing a trembling finger at one of the women.

Dr. Dani nodded. "And the other is your interpreter."

Michael didn't care about the interpreter. "The social worker will take Joshua. She'll put him in foster care. She'll separate us."

Dr. Dani held up both hands to calm him before resuming her signing. "I'll do my best to see that that doesn't happen, okay?"

Michael swallowed hard. The doctor's best wasn't nearly good enough. "I need to go." He tried to push past her, but Coach Diesel stood and blocked his path.

"Michael, please. Wait," he said. "Don't jump to . . ." He grimaced before spelling out *conclusions*, his hand clumsy. "Not yet. Let Dr. Dani help you and then we'll figure this out. But you guys can't go home. What if your mother throws something and hits Joshua next time?"

Michael shuddered, his eyes filling with helpless, frustrated tears. "She only throws stuff at me."

"And if she misses?" Coach asked. "For now, trust us. We want to help you. Okay?"

Michael clenched his jaw. "I got no choice, do I?"

Both the doctor and Coach sighed. "Yes, you do," Dr. Dani signed. "You have choices. But none of them are good ones. Sorry."

And she *was* sorry. Michael could see that. Coach was sorry, too.

And his mother *had* nearly hit Joshua recently. In the last week, since Brewer had "disappeared," she'd been especially out of control.

She thought that her husband had left on a trip without telling her. She thought he was having an affair. That he'd divorce her. That her kids had cost her a good life. She thought Brewer was leaving her.

Which was why the big bald killer had taken Brewer's clothes. So everyone would think that he'd just left. And because the bald guy had left the car there in the garage, that Brewer was coming back. Someday.

Only Michael and the big bald killer knew different.

No one else could ever know. Because that man would come back for Michael. And maybe for Joshua.

Michael couldn't let them be separated. He'd let the doctor stitch him up, then he'd take Joshua and run. He wasn't sure where, but he'd find a place for them to hide.

And then? Where will you hide? How will you take care of him?

Damn, my head hurts. Wearily, Michael dropped into his chair, rubbing his forehead. "Fine," he signed sullenly.

Coach sat back down and the doctor pulled up a stool and sat in front of him. She was very pretty, but in a way that made him frown. It wasn't the white streak that framed her face, because her brother Greg had one, too, and Michael was used to seeing it. It was something else . . .

Oh. "Your eyes are two different colors," he signed before he realized he was going to. He winced. "I'm sorry. I was rude."

But it was true. One of her eyes was a deep brown and the other a bright, bright blue. Just like Greg's.

She just smiled at him. "They are. I was born with them. Takes folks a little while to get used to, but you should see my older brother. His are downright spooky."

Michael wanted to ask questions, but she was pointing to the women. "This is Maria Catalano. She's your interpreter."

Catalano was older than his mother and had gray hair. "You've worked with an interpreter before?"

Michael nodded. "I have one in school." So he knew the rules. She'd interpret everything anyone said so there'd be no secret conversations behind his back.

She'd also voice whatever he signed for the social worker and the cop, so he needed to keep any mutterings in his head and his hands still. He'd gotten in trouble with his teacher a few times when he'd signed his displeasure at a grade or protested an assignment. Of course, he *had* called the teacher a bitch, an opinion he continued to stand by. He just wished he hadn't signed it for the interpreter to see. He made a note to keep his opinion of the adults in this room unsigned.

"This," Dr. Dani continued, "is Maddie Shafer. She's a social worker. She's here to support you and Joshua."

He gave the social worker a brusque nod and figured he might as well tell the truth at this point. Some
of the truth, anyway. Enough to keep Joshua safe. If
they separated them . . . He'd have to deal with that
later.

"My mom did this," he told her, pointing at his
head. "She's always taken drugs, but it's gotten worse
in the last week. She's passed out at home. But she
was breathing when I left."

The social worker nodded, her face serious. She
was young. Really young.

Michael narrowed his eyes at her. "How old are
you?" he asked, not caring that he was being rude again.

"Twenty-seven," she said. "I know I look young,
but I've been doing this job for five years. I've already
got an emergency foster home that will take both of
you. This is until I investigate your mother, okay?"

Michael slumped in relief. *Both of us.* Then his
mind jumped to the next sentence. They were going
to investigate his mother.

"She won't like that," he signed. "She might not
answer the door, even if she isn't still passed out. If
she's awake, she won't be nice to you. She'll lie to you.
She'll tell you that *I'm* lying."

Maddie Shafer gave him a smile that reminded
him of a shark. "Let me worry about your mother.
My priority is making sure you and Joshua are safe.
Officer Cullen will accompany me."

The lady cop signaled the interpreter, who began
signing for her. "Does your mother have access to any
weapons?"

Michael hesitated. Then nodded as he carefully
considered his answer. "My stepfather's gun safe is
full of guns." One of which was under his own pillow
at home. If the cops found it, they'd ask questions.
They might charge him with possession of a weapon.
If they pressed, he'd ask the doctor to check his other
wounds. Once she saw that his ass was still bleeding,
she'd be able to tell them that he had been . . .

He fought not to cringe, swallowing back the bile that burned his throat at the memory of Brewer's rough hands. Of the pain that could still steal his breath.

Of the word that he still couldn't say. Even in his mind.

When she saw all that, she'd tell them that he'd had a right to keep a gun under his pillow. And she wouldn't know that he hadn't put it there until after Brewer was dead.

Because he was still afraid that the big bald guy would come back. Which sounded completely crazy. So he wasn't going to talk about *that* unless he had to.

The cop was talking again. "How often does she hit you?"

Again he hesitated. He wanted to make his mother sound bad enough that they'd take him and Joshua out of the house, but not so bad that they thought he was lying.

"She doesn't hit that much," he said, opting for as much of the truth as he dared. "She just throws things. Usually I'm fast enough to duck."

The lady cop's smile was sweet and sad, her eyes filled with what might have been understanding. "Until today, huh?"

He shrugged. "She's got me a few times. Once with a vase. Once with a knife." He pulled up his shirt enough to show the scar on his left side. "It bled a lot, but then it was okay."

The lady cop studied the scar silently before her eyes rose to meet his. "Did she take you to the hospital?"

"Not that time."

The cop tilted her head. "Other times?"

He nodded once. "When my stepfather hit too hard. Three times that I remember. Two broken arms and a break here." He pointed to the bone over his right eye. That one had terrified him. He'd been afraid he'd lose his eye and he didn't even want to think about having to understand ASL with only one good eye.

"Where did she take you?" the cop asked. "Which hospital, I mean?"

"Not around here," he said. "We drove a long time." He glanced at Dr. Dani. "Free clinics like this one."

Dr. Dani grimaced. "She didn't give your real name, did she?"

He shook his head. "Never."

Dr. Dani looked at the lady cop, signing and speaking at the same time. Michael wondered if Greg knew how lucky he was. Stella Rowland Brewer had never learned sign language. No more than the basics, anyway. *Yes, no. Come, go. Bad.*

Always *bad.* Michael had come to expect it. And accept it.

"We can x-ray Michael's bones and show the evidence of older, healed breaks," Dr. Dani said.

"Thank you." The lady cop never broke eye contact with Michael, and he appreciated it. At the same time, it freaked him out. "I'm not saying that what she did was okay *ever,* but did she say why she was angry this morning?"

Michael wanted to close his eyes, because his head hurt. But the lady cop was watching him so steadily that it freaked him out even more.

"The milk was bad," he said. Because Brewer wasn't home to buy more.

Because he's dead.

The cop's lips thinned. "Okay. Miss Shafer and I will go to your house." She pointed to the social worker. "While we're gone, you'll stay here with Dr. Dani."

Dr. Dani was smiling kindly. "I'll stitch you up while they're gone. Any questions before they leave?"

Just one. "Yeah. Who is our emergency foster placement?" Because Joshua's safety was the most important thing. Just like always.

Dr. Dani pointed to herself. "Me. Is that okay?"

"You?" the interpreter signed, widening her eyes to show surprise, her head tilted toward Coach Diesel to show Michael who had spoken.

Dr. Dani's smile faltered, just a little, her eyes growing cool as her gaze shifted over Michael's shoulder to where Coach Diesel sat. "Yes, Coach. I'm a licensed provider of emergency foster care. I'm normally called in when deaf kids are involved." She returned her gaze to Michael, her eyes warming. "Okay?"

Michael nodded, relieved. He knew she wouldn't try to hurt either of them. *Maybe I can get some sleep.* Because he'd stayed up all night, every night, watching over Joshua since the big bald man had come into his brother's room.

Her eyes went cool again. "I hope that's okay with you, too, Coach."

Ouch. Michael didn't need to hear to know that was sarcasm.

"Of course," the interpreter signed, ducking her head a little to indicate shame. Coach Diesel had been schooled. "Officer Cullen," she continued on Diesel's behalf, again tilting her head toward the coach. "I thought Scarlett was going to call Adam."

Michael knew Scarlett was the detective who'd taken the old man to the ER. *Who is Adam?* But he didn't ask. He just kept his eyes on the interpreter, because the doctor's hands were busy taking care of him and the interpeter was speaking for her.

"I spoke to him," Dr. Dani said. "He got called to a scene, so Officer Cullen came instead." She pulled her phone from her pocket, brushed Michael's hair aside, and took some photos of the cut on his head.

"For our records and for the police report," she told him, angling the phone so that Michael could see the screen, too.

Wow. Michael grimaced. That was a bad cut.

The interpreter was waving her hand to get his attention. The cop was talking again, handing him a white card. "My numbers," she said. "You have a phone?"

He nodded warily. If she wanted to take his phone, he'd fight her.

"Use it to text me," she said, "if you have any concerns or if you feel unsafe. Text 911 first if it's an emergency."

He took the card, then the one offered by the social worker, who smiled kindly. "Stay with Dr. Dani until I come back. Have you and your brother eaten today?"

"Joshua had breakfast," Michael said, evading the question, but the social worker's eyes narrowed, like she'd seen right into his brain.

"Dr. Dani will get you *both* some food, then." She patted his hand. "I'll be back as soon as I can with information."

"Thank you," he voiced. Once the cop, the social worker, and the interpreter had left, he slumped in the chair. He was exhausted.

"I'll do your stitches first," Dr. Dani told him. "Then food." She set a tray holding a curved needle with thick thread, gauze, scissors, and a syringe on the counter. "This won't take long. I'm going to numb the area first. You'll just feel a pinch."

Michael gritted his teeth against the sting of the anesthetic she injected, closing his eyes when his empty stomach began to pitch. *Don't throw up. Do not throw up.*

He counted backward from one hundred, then did it again until Dr. Dani touched his cheek. "All done," she signed when he opened his eyes. Then she frowned. "You're very pale. Are you feeling sick?"

Michael shook his head, instantly regretting the movement. "No," he lied. "I think I need to eat," he added, which was totally true. He hadn't eaten a real meal in days. His stomach growled even as it gurgled. *Do not throw up.*

Coach Diesel appeared in front of him, giving his

good shoulder a light squeeze. "You did good," he signed. "Where would you like us to take you for lunch?"

Dr. Dani's brows shot up. "Us?"

Coach Diesel smiled, and anyone could see the challenge in it. "Yes, us. Me, you, Michael, and Joshua. Joshua is my responsibility." He spelled the word out awkwardly.

"Responsibility," Dr. Dani said, showing him the sign. "And no, Joshua is now *my* responsibility."

"I promised him ice cream," Coach said.

The doctor narrowed her eyes at the big tattooed man. "You did not."

Coach glanced at Michael, blinking innocently. "Didn't I?"

Michael knew that the team got ice cream after games. He had no clue if Coach Diesel had or hadn't offered it after today's practice, but the coach had been kind to Joshua. *And to me.* Guys had to stick together. So he nodded to help the man out. "He did. Joshua is excited about it."

Dr. Dani rolled her eyes. "Of course he is. Well, I haven't taken my lunch hour yet and I don't have another appointment till later this afternoon, so we'll go. I can examine your shoulder when we get back."

Michael's gaze shot to the coach accusingly. "You told her about my shoulder, too?"

"I want you to be okay," the coach signed, his expression sober.

It was hard to be mad at the guy. Plus Michael was hungry. Hopefully the coach would make sure that wherever they went to eat had burgers and fries.

Cleveland, Ohio
Saturday, March 16, 2:50 p.m.

Grant Masterson stood in his brother's apartment, not understanding what he was looking at. He'd emptied the contents of the safe, laying each piece out on the dining room table.

Wesley wasn't here, and hadn't been in some time, if the expired milk in the fridge was any indication. It wasn't until Grant had seen that all his brother's suits were gone from his closet, along with his suitcases, that he'd opened the safe.

The combination hadn't been difficult—09-29-96. Their sister's birthday. It was almost as if Wes had set it up so that Grant could easily unlock it.

No almost about it, Grant thought grimly as he stared at the stacks of cash and piles of paper. He'd counted the cash twice, not believing the total the first time.

Five hundred thousand dollars, all in crisp one-hundred-dollar bills.

There was *five hundred thousand dollars* in his brother's safe. Grant closed his eyes briefly. "What have you done, Wes?" he murmured. Because his brother had not earned this money. Not as a cop. And not from his investments, either, because Grant did his damn taxes.

Grant's first clue that something super-illegal was going on had been the box of latex gloves that Wes had left in the very front of the safe. Hands trembling, Grant had pulled on a pair and begun sifting through his brother's private life.

He had found a partial answer to where Wes had gotten the money in a sack that had been in a small lockbox, tucked inside the safe. That combo had also been easy—the date they'd discovered that their sister had run away.

The day Grant had lost Wes, too. First to the bottle, then to the obsession of finding their sister, and now to . . . whatever all of *this* was. Because the sack held a brick of something white. Heroin, he guessed.

My God, Wes. How could *you? Drugs?* Wes was a vice detective, for God's sake. "What have you done?" Grant murmured again.

He needed to find out. And fast.

He pulled out a chair and sat in it heavily. Then be-

gan skimming each page in the stack. They looked like
receipts, printed from a computer. Rent, utilities . . . All
in the name of Blake Emerson. And all for an address
in Cincinnati.

Which did not make any sense. At all. They'd both
been to Cincinnati, multiple times. It was where their
sister had run away from. But they'd stayed in hotels.

Who the hell was Blake Emerson? But then he saw
the signature on one of the pages. It was Wes's handwriting. *What the hell?*

He Googled the address on the receipts and gaped
at the result. It was a luxury apartment in Cincinnati's downtown. Stunned, he continued scanning the
receipts—food from very expensive restaurants, a
new car.

A Bentley, for God's sake. A two-hundred-thousand-
dollar Bentley.

Grant put the paper down on the table, his head
spinning. *Breathe. Just breathe.* Was his brother ex-
periencing some kind of mental breakdown? How
long had he been stealing drugs and selling them?
Had he always lived a double life?

"Who *are* you?" he whispered, hearing his own
desperation. Quickly, he went through the rest of
the documents. More receipts, but they seemed to go
back only six months. So perhaps this double life was
new.

Under the earliest rent receipt, he found a small
envelope containing a key. A label hung from the
thin key ring, bearing the same address as the luxury
apartment.

Grant put it aside and kept going. His hands stilled
when he neared the bottom of the stack. "Oh fuck."

It was an obituary, printed in the Cincinnati *Ledger.* Detective Bert Stuart of the Cincinnati PD had
been killed in his own home by an intruder who was
never identified.

Grant swallowed hard. Detective Bert Stuart had
been the cop who'd refused to investigate their sis-

ter's disappearance, insisting that she'd run away voluntarily.

He set the obituary aside and his blood ran cold when he saw what was under it. It was a copy of the police report they'd filed on their sister's disappearance. In the margin, in Wes's handwriting, was scrawled: *Never filed*.

Grant shook his head. That made no sense. Of course it was filed. The detective had come to them in their sister's dorm room and—

Grant covered his mouth with his gloved hand. The detective who was now dead. Murdered. "My God, Wes, *what have you done*?"

This was not the brother he knew. The brother he loved. Wes was a good man. A good cop. Except . . .

Grant forced himself to look at the brick of heroin. Except Wes *wasn't* a good cop. He couldn't be. Could he?

Dreading what else he'd find, Grant flipped to the last page in the stack. It was another police report, also written by Detective Stuart, but this one had a red stamp that said FILED. The number on the report was exactly the same as on the report filed on their sister's disappearance, but it was for a petty theft incident that occurred a few days after their sister disappeared.

Wes was right. Her missing person report had apparently not been filed at all.

There was a sticky note in one corner, with the letters *L O T R*.

LOTR? *Like . . . Lord of the Rings?* That didn't make sense, either. Grant loved the books and the films, but Wes absolutely *hated* them.

Only one thing in this whole mess was clear. He grabbed his cell phone. "Hey, Siri. Call Cora at home." When his home phone began to ring, he hit the speaker icon with one gloved knuckle. "Hey, honey."

"Grant!" Cora exclaimed. "MaryBeth's niece just got here. Is this for real? Can I keep her?"

Grant frowned, trying to figure out what she was talking about, then remembered his assistant's au pair niece and almost smiled. Cora sounded like a kid asking for a puppy. "You certainly can. She comes highly recommended."

"I know! I'm so . . ." Her voice broke a little. "Thank you," she whispered.

"You're welcome." He cleared his throat, dreading this. "Look, honey, I'm at Wes's apartment and he's not here. But I think he might need me."

Cora's end of the phone went silent. "Where is he?"

"Cincinnati." It was all he could tell her. All he could force himself to say. Telling her about the drugs, the cash, the ritzy apartment would only worry her fruitlessly.

"He's gone to look for her again," she murmured.

Because Wes hadn't given up looking for their sister, convinced that she hadn't run away. Grant just didn't know what to think. "Maybe. I need to find him."

She blew out a breath. "What's he done now, Grant?"

Grant stared at the table. At the money. The heroin. The receipts. "I don't know. But he needs help. Can you get along without me for a few days?"

"I guess I'll have to," she answered, a little bitterly. "You'll take off at tax time to help your brother, but not to come home and see your own wife and kids."

Grant chafed at that. "That's not fair, Cora."

"No, it's not." She drew a deep breath and let it out. "Go find your brother. Then—" She broke off in a huff.

"Then?" Grant prompted warily.

"Then tell him that you're done. Your children need you at home. I want you here. With me."

Grant rubbed his head, his loyalties torn. "All right," he murmured. "I will."

She sighed wearily. "Do you need me to pack you a bag?"

"If you wouldn't mind."

"All right. Come home. I'll have it waiting along with some food for you to take on the drive."

He felt a little piece of his heart settle. If Cora was making him travel food, it meant she wasn't too angry with him. He could only pray that he found Wes quickly.

Villa Hills, Kentucky
Saturday, March 16, 3:00 p.m.

"Hi, Mr. Kaiser." The receptionist at his father's nursing home shot Cade a flirtatious smile. "I was hoping I'd see you today. You're later than usual."

Because I was stuck babysitting my boss, who took way too long to die.

"I got hung up at home," he lied smoothly. "How are you, Millicent?"

"You know how it is." She actually batted her lashes. The woman was always throwing herself at him. It made him wonder if she was so aggressive with everyone. "Same old, same old." She resettled herself, propping her generous cleavage atop the arms she'd folded on her desk. "Hey, I've got a pair of Cyclones tickets for tonight. Interested?"

It was abundantly clear that it wasn't minor league hockey she was interested in. Cade had to admit he was tempted. He liked hockey and he loved cleavage. And after listening to Richard bump and grind for four fucking hours, he'd earned a little fun of his own. "Maybe." He returned her flirtatious smile with one of his own. "Do you come with them?"

More eyelash batting. "I do."

"Give me your number. I'll call you if I can move some things around."

Rising fluidly, she leaned forward, giving him an even better view of her very impressive rack, and wrote her number on the back of one of the nursing home's business cards. "My cell."

Cade slipped the card into his shirt pocket. "I'll

call you," he promised with a wink, then set off for his father's room. The nursing home was a lot nicer than the place Cade would have picked out for the man who'd given him nothing but bad memories. Unfortunately Konrad Kaiser had known how much his son hated him and had prepared for this eventuality by securing his spot at the home himself. He'd placed all of his money into a trust, going so far as to specify his nursing home, hospice, and funeral arrangements, too. After his death any remaining funds, including the sale of the Kaiser family home, were to go to his church.

And, having been an attorney, he had made sure the trust was unbreakable. Cade could not touch one penny. He'd tried. Several times.

Which was why he'd opted to leave his father here in this nursing home, in his semivegetative state, where strangers changed his diapers, rather than finishing the job. *I'd be a suspect for sure.*

A nurse was exiting his father's room as Cade approached. She was new, young, and hot. Far hotter than the receptionist. "Can I help you?" she asked cautiously.

"I'm Cade Kaiser. Konrad's son." This was the only place that knew his real name. He hated that, but it was unavoidable.

The nurse smiled at him. "I'm Nurse Jillian. I'll be working with your father. The other nurses mentioned that you visit on Saturdays. It's nice to meet you."

"Likewise. I know I'm a little late today," Cade said, feigning apology. "How's he doing?"

"The same. But I'm sure he'll be happy to see you. Have a good visit."

Bullshit. His dad hated it when he visited. That was why Cade never missed a Saturday.

"Hey, Dad," he said cheerfully as he entered the room. He grabbed a chair and pushed it close to his father's bed. "It's Saturday again. Which means that it's time for your favorite son to visit."

He chuckled to himself because he was his father's only child. "I see you got a new nurse on the floor. She's a hottie, or didn't you notice?"

His father's gaze held his for a long moment before flicking away to focus on the television mounted over his bed. It was Konrad's way of getting the last word without uttering a sound.

"I don't think so," Cade said, and got up to find the remote so that he could turn off the TV. Instead he stopped in his tracks when he saw what was on-screen.

"Oh . . . fuck," he whispered. Divers in dry suits were standing on the Ohio side of the river. It appeared the camera was positioned on the Kentucky side, but it had a hell of a telescopic lens. Flanking the divers were two men in suits.

One had dark hair, the other bright white.

Cade recognized the guy with white hair. He'd gotten a lot of press coverage in the last few years, all of it good. FBI Special Agent Deacon Novak was a media darling. And a damn good cop.

The chyron at the bottom of the screen read: *Divers Search Ohio River for Body Parts.*

He swallowed hard. *Fucking hell.*

Relax. No way they can trace those parts to you. You were careful.

Yes, he had been, but he'd also thought he'd been careful enough that the parts would never be found in the first place. *Fucking hell.*

He gave himself a little shake and turned up the TV volume. And listened.

The first body part found had been a head, dragged up by a fisherman early that morning. The guy must have come along shortly after Cade dumped Brian Carlyle and Paul Engel, the most recent perverts.

What had the fisherman seen? *Did he see me?*

Cade needed the man's name. He needed to make sure that the fisherman didn't remember anything that might lead the police to him.

They'd been diving all morning, according to the newscaster, pulling up the remains of at least three individuals. On the case were Agent Novak and Detective Kimble, members of the Major Case Enforcement Squad, an FBI/CinciPD joint task force.

Cade would have to make sure they didn't cause him any trouble. He'd never had to kill a cop, but if it came down to them or him?

I'll choose me every damn time.

But first things first. He switched off the TV. He needed to find that fisherman.

Cincinnati, Ohio
Saturday, March 16, 3:15 p.m.

"Did you two get enough to eat?" Dani asked the Rowland brothers.

They'd gone to the diner around the corner from the clinic where Dani and her staff ate all their meals. Some people were still nervous about walking around in the Over-the-Rhine neighborhood, but Dani had never had a problem, even after midnight.

If she'd had any qualms before, she felt as safe as a vault walking around with Diesel Kennedy. The big man had held Joshua's small hand in his enormous one as they'd walked. It made her heart hurt.

But it still changed nothing. Their lunch had been cozy, and Dani would be lying to herself if she didn't admit that she'd pretended it was real, that she and Diesel and the boys were a family. But it was a fantasy, and a dangerous one at that.

She couldn't get too comfortable with the man. She would not lead him on. She'd been accused of being thoughtless and cruel by the last man in her life. She wouldn't be cruel to Diesel Kennedy.

Joshua sat back in the booth across from her, patting his stomach as he leaned into Diesel's huge arm. "I'm gonna bust," he said, his signing considerably slower than it had been before he'd eaten. His eyes were drooping sleepily. "I ate all my burger and my vegetables."

Michael shook his head. "Fries are not vegetables."

"Potatoes," Joshua insisted. "Right, Coach?"

Diesel's lips twitched. "Well, technically potatoes are vegetables, but they generally don't count as nutritious. Especially when they're fried. But it's okay to treat ourselves every now and then. You'll need to eat some legit veggies later."

It was a good answer, Dani had to admit. "Can you fit ice cream?"

Michael shook his head. "No. I'm stuffed. Joshua needs to wait, too."

Joshua frowned. "Do not."

Michael gave him a look. "Remember what happened the last time you ate too much?"

Joshua grimaced. "Okay, you're right." He looked up at Diesel. "Can we have some ice cream later?"

"We can," Diesel promised.

"Should we bring food for Mrs. Moody?" Joshua asked, clearly stalling.

"No," Diesel told him. "She had to go home, remember? She can get her own lunch. But that was thoughtful of you to ask."

Dani was about to agree when her phone buzzed and she checked her messages. "Maddie Shafer and Officer Cullen are back," she told the boys. "They want us to meet them." She lifted her eyes to Diesel. "I texted them before we left that we'd be taking the kids out for food."

Joshua seemed to deflate before their eyes. "Did the police lady arrest Mom?"

"I don't know," Dani answered honestly. "I guess we'll find out when we talk to them."

Joshua drew a deep breath and glanced at his

brother. "I don't want to go back. But Michael can't go back." His lip trembled. "She hurts him."

"If you go back, I go back," Michael signed fiercely. "You're not going to be alone."

The four of them sat in silence for several seconds. Then Diesel slid out of the booth and held out his hand to Joshua. "The bill's paid. Are you ready?"

Joshua gripped Diesel's hand like his life depended on it. "No," he whispered.

Michael had put on a stoically brave face during the meal, but any pretense was gone. He appeared more miserable and terrified than any kid should ever be.

"We need to go," Dani signed softly. "Let's see what we're dealing with before we get upset, okay?"

He nodded once and slid out of the booth, waiting until Dani had done the same before replying. "Okay. And even if it goes wrong, thank you for trying."

Dani's throat closed. She was glad she could sign, because there was no way she'd be able to speak at that moment. "You're welcome. You can call me anytime. I mean that. Now, let's go."

The mood walking back to the clinic was considerably more grim than it had been on the way to the diner.

Dani had a bad feeling about this. If everything had gone well, Kendra Cullen would have just told her so. Instead, her text telling Dani to bring the kids back had been curt and to the point. Too curt, and that wasn't like Kenny at all. They'd known each other for years. That message had read like they were strangers.

And maybe I'm just imagining things.

She glanced up at Diesel, only to find his eyes on her. They shared a long look that spoke volumes.

He was worried, too. And if there was one thing she knew about Diesel Kennedy, it was that his instincts were top-notch. She'd be dead if they weren't. He'd had a feeling she was in danger all those months ago and had been waiting behind the clinic, watching over her. He'd been right, because she'd been stabbed that day.

"Thank you," she murmured.

He smiled down at her, making her heart stutter. "For what?"

"Saving my life a year and a half ago. I don't remember if I ever thanked you."

"You did." His expression became wryly self-deprecating. "The day I visited you after your surgery. The day you told me to find someone else. Very politely, of course."

"The day I told you that it wasn't you, it was me," she said quietly, but firmly.

He shrugged his shoulder and she bit back a sigh. She'd lost count of the number of times she'd wished she could lean against that shoulder. Diesel was kindness and strength.

And he did need to find someone else.

"We'll finish this conversation later," he said as they reached the clinic door and pulled it open. "After you."

Dani entered, Michael right behind her. Diesel brought up the rear, Joshua still clutching his hand.

Taking in the scene before her, Dani came to an abrupt stop. Kendra Cullen and Maddie Shafer, the social worker, were back. So was Maria, the interpreter. But they weren't alone.

Adam and Deacon were there, too, looking grim. That wasn't good at all.

None of them looked happy. This was *so* not good.

"Michael, the man on the left with dark hair is my cousin, Detective Adam Kimble," Dani said calmly, signing as she spoke. "The man on the right is my brother, Special Agent Deacon Novak. Gentlemen, this is Michael Rowland and his brother, Joshua."

Adam stepped forward, his brows knit in a scowl. He started to speak, but before he could, Michael broke the silence.

"Coach Kimble?" he voiced thickly.

Adam opened his mouth and closed it again, looking even unhappier than he had before.

"You know each other?" Dani asked, surprised.

Michael nodded and went back to signing. "He coached my baseball team a few years ago. I joined up because he could sign. That doesn't happen often." He sucked in a breath, his spine stiffening, sudden panic filling his eyes. He took a step back, his wild gaze swinging to Adam. "You're a cop. Why are you here?"

"That's a very good question," Diesel said calmly. He gripped Michael's uninjured shoulder with a steady hand. "Please answer, Detective Kimble."

Adam seemed to brace himself as he met Michael's gaze squarely. It was a small gesture, but Dani noticed it because they'd grown up together, for much of their childhood sharing the same house. It was why Adam signed so well. Greg had been more like a little brother to him than a cousin. He still was.

"We saw Officer Cullen and Miss Shafer at your house, Michael," Adam signed. "They were talking to your mother about her throwing the bowl at your head. We were there to talk to her about something else. Your stepfather's remains were pulled from the river this morning."

Dani gasped, her eyes on Michael.

Who didn't look as surprised as he should have.

Oh no. Oh God.

Joshua, on the other hand, was frowning up at Diesel. "What's 'remains,' Coach Diesel?"

Diesel swung the little boy up into his arms and held him against his hip. "It means they found your stepfather's body," he answered quietly. "It means your stepfather is dead."

"What?" Joshua shook his head hard. "No. He went away. Mom said so. Like, on a trip. Not to heaven, like our real dad."

"Maybe you can take the boy into one of the offices, Coach Diesel," Adam said.

"No!" Both Michael and Joshua cried out at once. Michael clutched Joshua's hand.

"I'm not leaving Michael," Joshua added mutinously.

Diesel leaned his forehead against Joshua's. "Then you need to listen, okay?"

"Okay," Joshua whispered, but his eyes filled with confused tears. "Okay."

Adam was regarding Michael levelly while Deacon stood silent in the background, watching everyone. Deacon was good at that.

"You don't look surprised," Adam signed.

Michael clenched his jaw. Then looked away and shook his head.

Adam came closer, hunching down a little so that he was at Michael's eye level. "Why aren't you surprised, Michael?" he signed, so very gently.

"I didn't do it," Michael declared, his desperation clear.

And Dani believed him. She met Diesel's worried eyes. He did, too.

"We found the gun," Adam said. "Under your pillow."

Gun? Shit. This was getting worse by the moment. Michael swallowed hard. "I didn't do it."

Diesel held Michael's shoulder again, turning him around to face him, then letting him go so that the hand not supporting Joshua was free. "Say nothing," he signed tersely. "Do not say another word. We'll get you a lawyer. Do you understand?"

Michael's eyes widened. Then he nodded, trembling.

Joshua was sobbing, his face buried in Diesel's shirt.

Maddie Shafer stepped in to join the small circle, the interpreter trailing behind her to sign her words.

"He is a minor, Detective Kimble. If you're going to question him, we'll do this right. Downtown, recorded, with his lawyer and me." She looked at Dani. "And his emergency foster parent." She pulled a folder from her bag. "Sign this, quick."

Dani scanned the paper in the folder and signed on the dotted line. It was the standard form she'd signed many times before when fostering in an emergency.

"Done." She handed the folder back to Maddie, then turned to Michael. "I won't leave you. I promise."

Chapter Four

The room had gone still, Adam having stepped back to stand with Deacon, leaving Dani to talk to Michael with as much privacy as they could allow.

Dani knew Adam and Deacon as well as she knew herself. Both her cousin and her brother were good cops. More than that, they were good men with integrity. They wouldn't have come for Michael if there wasn't a very good reason.

A dead stepfather and a gun under his pillow were pretty good reasons, but Dani's gut was telling her to believe Michael's claims of innocence. She wasn't sure why, exactly, because her gut had failed her stupendously in the past, and believing the wrong man had done her life-changing harm. Believing her ex-fiancé had left her alone and HIV positive.

But this wasn't like that. Not at all. Michael was not Adrian. Adrian had been a grown man who'd lied to her about his HIV status. Michael was a scared kid who'd been abused.

Dani held his eyes, hoping he could see her promise and that he believed her. "I won't leave you," she repeated, her signs forceful. "Do you understand me, Michael?"

For a long moment, he just stared at her with hopeless fear. Then he nodded once. "What about Joshua?"

Diesel tapped Michael's shoulder, waiting until the boy slowly lifted his gaze. "I'll watch over him," Diesel told him. "If that's okay with you."

"It'll be okay," Joshua promised, but he hadn't stopped crying. Still in Diesel's arms, the child held out a hand to his brother. "It'll be okay," he whispered.

Visibly trembling now, Michael took Joshua's hand and held it against his cheek. He turned to the social worker. "You won't let him go home?"

"No," she promised. "Dr. Dani is his emergency foster parent, too."

Michael swallowed hard. The teenager was trying to be brave and it was breaking Dani's heart to watch. He let his brother's hand go. "Our mother will clean up her act," he signed, as the interpreter voiced for him in a low murmur. "She'll say all the right things. She'll make you think she's not on drugs anymore. But when you go away, she'll go back to her old ways." He blinked back tears. "Don't let her take him. Please."

Maddie glanced at Kendra Cullen from the corner of her eye. Kendra gave the social worker a slight nod. Drawing a deep breath, Maddie said, "Officer Cullen arrested your mother for possession of heroin. She was obviously impaired when we arrived. She'll be tested for drugs."

Michael seemed to digest this. "So Joshua is safe for now."

Maddie nodded. "Yes."

"But I'm not," Michael signed, dropping his eyes to the floor.

No one was able to refute that, and the room was silent for a long moment. Dani gripped Michael's good shoulder gently. She hadn't finished examining him, but she'd do so before he was taken into custody. On that she wasn't budging.

She waited until Michael looked up at her. "We're going to get you a lawyer."

Michael swallowed again. "I don't have money to pay a lawyer."

"You let us worry about that, okay?" Dani looked up at Diesel. "Do you have the name of a good lawyer?"

"I do. I'll call him right now." Diesel lifted Michael's chin. "Not one word, okay?"

Michael nodded shakily and said nothing.

"Use my office," Dani told Diesel. "Joshua, can you stay with Coach for a little while?"

Diesel took a sniffling Joshua into the office to make the call, and Dani turned to Adam and Deacon. "Are you *sure* the body you found was that of Michael's stepfather?"

Both men nodded, and she blew out a sigh. "All right, then." She signed as she spoke. "Michael came to me for medical attention. Now that I'm his emergency foster parent, I can authorize this. I've already sutured the cut on his head and documented the injury. His shoulder is also hurt, and he may need to wear a sling to protect it. I'll examine him now, before you take him downtown." She met Adam's gaze, then Deacon's, daring them to cross her. Neither man did, for which she was grateful. "Nurse Jenny will assist me. I assume we'll need police presence during the exam?"

Both men nodded again. "We need to do this cleanly," Deacon said, also signing. He'd been rusty when he'd returned to Cincinnati two and a half years ago, but daily interaction with their younger brother, Greg, had quickly honed his ASL skills. "It's also to protect you, Michael. Hopefully we can clear this up easily. If not, and if the prosecutor ends up pressing charges, we'll want everything done according to procedure. That way no one can accuse you of having your story fed to you by your doctor."

Michael's eyes shot to Dani's, filled with a mix of

shock and . . . anger. "He thinks you'd do that? Your own brother?"

"No." Dani offered him a smile. "But he thinks an overzealous lawyer might try to make a jury think so. He's protecting you. Would you be all right with him staying in the room with us?"

Michael's eyes shifted again, but not before she saw the flash of panic. He closed his eyes and when he opened them, they were expressionless. "Can Officer Cullen do it instead?" he asked.

God. Dani kept her own smile gentle even as his panic and his words made a terrible kind of sense. She'd seen that reaction before. Too many times.

Someone had hurt him. Someone male.

"It's fine," Deacon said softly. He'd caught the nuance, too.

So had Adam, even though her cousin said nothing. Only because she'd known him her whole life did she know that the twitch of his eye signaled guilt. He'd been Michael's coach, she recalled. He would feel guilty that he hadn't known—and hadn't helped this boy. The guilt was unwarranted, but Adam felt things so much more deeply than most people knew.

"Should I call Meredith?" he asked quietly when Dani walked past him on her way back to the examination room. His wife was a child psychologist who specialized in treating traumatized kids. "I can ask her to meet us at the precinct."

"That's a good idea," Dani murmured. "Thanks."

Cincinnati, Ohio
Saturday, March 16, 3:45 p.m.

"That's fu—"

"Children," Diesel growled into the phone, cutting off his best friend before he could drop the f-bomb. Yes, it was fucked up. This whole situation was fucked up, but he didn't want Joshua hearing that. It had been bad enough that Joshua had heard him recount the story to Marcus O'Bannion.

Marcus was technically Diesel's boss at the Cincinnati *Ledger*. When he'd inherited the newspaper from his grandfather, it had been failing, but he, Diesel, and the rest of the *Ledger*'s investigative team had brought it well into the black. They'd broken a lot of high-profile stories. To do so sometimes they needed an inside edge during an investigation, a peek at their target's computer.

Computer sleuthing sometimes happened. That was where Diesel fit in.

"Sorry." Marcus's wince was clear in his tone. "I'm not on speaker, am I?"

"No, but Joshua is sitting with me." Diesel had tried to put the child on one of the kid-sized chairs at the table in Dani's office that was stocked with crayons and paper, but Joshua had clung, wrapping his little arms around his neck so tightly that Diesel had found it hard to breathe. So he'd relented, and Joshua now sat on his lap, cheek pressed to Diesel's chest, small hand clutching his shirt. "Close enough to hear you."

"Sorry," Marcus said again. "Poor kid. What do you need me to do?"

"Michael needs a lawyer. Can you call Rex Clausing and ask him to meet Dani at the precinct? She's Michael's emergency foster parent and will be present during any questioning. This kid really needs Rex's help."

"I just texted him," Marcus replied. A little ding chimed at Marcus's end. "And he just replied. He'll be there. The kid's last name?"

"Rowland. Michael Rowland."

"Got it. What else?"

"I need my laptop. Can you go by my house, get it, and bring it to me?" Marcus was one of the few who had a spare key to Diesel's house. They'd met in

Ranger school seventeen years ago and had been
friends from the get-go. There was no one Diesel
trusted more to have his back, unless it was Marcus's
brother Stone. The entire O'Bannion family had made
him one of theirs, and he was damn grateful.

"I'm at Dani's clinic right now, but I'll take Joshua
to the *Ledger* once Dani and Michael leave with Deacon and Adam."

"Which laptop?" Marcus asked, because Diesel had
three. One was for games, one was for e-mail and bills,
and the third was the machine he used for his less-than-
always-legal searches. It was souped-up and powerful,
its browsing history undetectable on the Web.

"The turbo." He glanced down at Joshua, who was
staring up at him with wide eyes. But he didn't say a
word, because Diesel had asked him to be quiet while
he was on the phone. *What a sweet kid.* His mother
should have been on her knees thanking God for her
sons, not getting high and throwing bowls at their
heads. "Michael didn't do this, which means someone else did. I'm going to do what I always do."

"Follow the money," Marcus said grimly.

"Yep." Because it always came down to that in one
way or another. "Also, does Gayle still keep a stash of
candy in her desk?"

Joshua's eyes lit up at that and Diesel smiled down
at him, giving him a wink.

"If she doesn't, I'll stop by the store and pick some
up," Marcus said. "You want some crayons and
stuff, too?"

"Wouldn't hurt. Thanks, Marcus. See you soon."

Cincinnati, Ohio
Saturday, March 16, 4:00 p.m.

Michael winced at the ball of fear lodged in his gut.
It actually hurt. What was the doctor going to do?
What was she going to ask?

He'd seen the understanding in her eyes when he'd

asked if the lady cop could be the witness instead of one of the two men. Dr. Dani knew.

Dammit.

He'd followed her into the same exam room he'd been in before. Sitting on the paper-covered table, he watched as the lady cop took position in the corner, her expression kind.

Shit. She knew, too. His face flushed hotter than fire. Now they'd all know. They'd tell the two men outside. They'd tell Coach Diesel. *Everyone will know.*

His stomach churned in misery as the nurse came in. She looked businesslike, at least. The interpreter came in last and met his eyes.

"I'm here for you," she signed without voicing for the others. "I'm bound to confidentiality. You get that, right? I'll never share what you say with anyone outside this room."

He nodded. "I get it." It didn't really help. She'd still know. And he wasn't worried about her telling anyone anyway. It was the others who'd tell. Especially the cop. She *had* to report abuse. So did the doctor and nurse. They were required to by law. Just like teachers. Which was why he'd never told any of his teachers.

He fought the tears stinging his eyes. He would not cry, dammit. This was humiliating enough without him crying.

The interpreter closed the door and suddenly the room was very crowded. More crowded than it had been before, even though Coach Diesel had also been here, taking up more space than two of the women put together.

At least the social worker had stayed outside to talk to the two detectives, but this room was too crowded. Too many people. Michael's chest began to hurt, his breath coming faster and faster, and he clamped a hand over his mouth, afraid he'd be sick. *Fan-fucking-tastic.*

Dr. Dani had been preparing to check his shoulder, but from the corner of his eye he saw her pause, her gloved hand slowly rising to touch his face, like she was afraid he'd bolt.

His gaze shot up to meet hers. Gentleness. That was what he saw and felt. *All* that he saw and felt. She was stroking his face gently, her oddly colored eyes so patient.

No blame. No mockery. No questions. Just . . . gentleness.

"Breathe with me," she signed with her free hand, then placed it on her chest. He watched as she breathed in and out, realizing that he was matching her pace without even trying. The nausea slowly went away, leaving him . . . tired.

"So tired," he signed and she smiled sadly.

"I know. You can rest later. I'm not going to leave you."

He swallowed hard. "They'll put me in jail. You can't stay with me then."

Her jaw tightened, not in anger, but in determination. "I'll fight for you, but try not to worry just yet. I want to check your shoulder, okay?"

He thought about his bruises, the deep scratches from the night he'd fallen in the woods, Joshua in his arms. The bruises had faded, but some of the scratches were still there. *They'll think I fought him. They'll think I did it. That I killed him.*

His anxiety rose once again and his head spun.

Dr. Dani's hand cupped his face again, squeezing lightly so that he looked at her. "Breathe, honey. Breathe with me."

He tried. He really did. But he was so damn tired. He felt the sob surging from his gut, clogging his throat. He tried to fight it, but he couldn't. It broke free and he dropped his head, unable to keep his cries silent.

He hated to cry out loud. Hated the sounds he made. His mother used to tell him that he sounded like an animal when he cried. So he'd learned to cry with no sound at all.

But not today. He could feel the sobs coming out of his throat and the tears coming out of his eyes and he couldn't stop them.

Dr. Dani's arms came around him and held him tight, rocking him gently, stroking his hair.

Like he wished his mother had done, every time he'd cried. But she never had. Not once.

Tentatively he reached around the doctor's back and gripped handfuls of her white coat. She nodded against his cheek and he held on until he exhausted himself with weeping and was able to choke back the stupid sobs. They'd seen. All the women in the room had seen him cry.

Heard him, too.

God.

New humiliation washed over him. But he was too tired to panic anymore. Someone tucked some tissues into his hand and he pulled back from the doctor's warm hug to mop his face and blow his nose, his eyes now fixed downward. He couldn't face her. Couldn't face any of them.

He drew a deep breath through his nose, hoping he wasn't snorting too rudely. Then froze. He drew another deep sniff, realizing he could smell chocolate.

He looked up then, but all he saw was Dr. Dani, dabbing at her own eyes.

She cried, too. For me. It was . . . a lot more than he'd expected.

His hands were moving before he realized it. "You smell like chocolate."

She smiled, blinking away more tears. "My shampoo," she answered, then drew a breath of her own. "I'm not going to tell you that everything will be okay, because I don't know what's going to happen. Except that I won't abandon you."

"Or Joshua?"

She nodded firmly. "Or Joshua."

He chanced a look around, saw that the other women were waiting patiently. His interpreter's eyes were wet, as were the nurse's. And the cop's. That surprised him. No one looked angry. No one looked disgusted.

They just looked sad.

He turned back to the doctor. He trusted her word, that she wouldn't abandon his brother. Still, Joshua was not her responsibility. *He's mine.* He'd do what he needed to do to get him back. Starting with this exam. Nervously he ran his fingers through his hair, wincing when he brushed over the stitches he'd all but forgotten with the arrival of the detectives. "Okay, I'm ready. You can check my shoulder."

He just prayed she wouldn't need to see anything more. That she knew that he'd been hurt by a man was humiliating enough. Her seeing it? All the women seeing it?

That was too much.

Cincinnati, Ohio
Saturday, March 16, 4:00 p.m.

Diesel looked up from the page he was coloring when someone knocked on Dani's office door. Joshua's gaze flew to his, frightened, the crayon he held breaking in two in his tight grip.

"Don't worry," Diesel said. "No one will hurt you here."

Joshua nodded, but he bit his lower lip with his tiny little baby teeth. He looked at the broken crayon in his hand, his scared eyes filling with new tears. "I broke it."

"Dr. Dani won't be mad," Diesel reassured him, cupping his cheek, his own hand looking like a bear's paw next to the small boy's face. "Let me see who it is," he said when whoever it was knocked again.

He'd expected it to be Dani or her nurse, but Adam and Deacon stood outside the door. The much shorter social worker stood in front of them, her fist raised to knock again.

Diesel threw a look over his shoulder when he heard a thump behind him. Joshua had backed away, knocking his chair over. He was trembling, his face pale.

"I won't go with her," the boy said defiantly, but his voice broke. "Or them. They lied. They said Michael was bad. They *lied*."

Diesel cast a glance at Adam and Deacon before turning fully to face Joshua. "Hey," Diesel said as soothingly as he knew how. "They never said Michael was bad. They said they wanted to talk to him. That's not the same thing."

"But you called a lawyer." Joshua pointed a finger at Diesel accusingly. "You said he didn't do it." He lifted his little chin, even as it quavered. "Did you lie, too?"

Shit. Why did this kid have to be so smart?

Diesel fought back a wince, forcing himself to smile. Convincingly, he hoped. "No, Joshua, I didn't lie. I don't think Michael did this, but the police have to talk to everyone when they find a body. Anyone who is asked to talk to the police needs a lawyer. That's just common sense."

"Gee, thanks," Adam muttered, but Diesel ignored him.

Joshua swallowed. "Even me?"

Diesel wasn't sure if he wanted to smile or cry. "If they talk to you, Miss Maddie here will be like your lawyer, okay? Dr. Dani and I are going to keep you safe. I know you don't know us very well, but you can trust us, Joshua. I promise. Now, give me a minute to talk to the detectives."

He turned back to Adam and Deacon. "What's up?" he asked calmly.

"We need to ask you a few questions," Adam said. "In private."

"No!" Joshua shouted. "You said you wouldn't leave me."

The social worker entered the room. "He won't, Joshua. Coach Diesel's going to be just outside this door. I'll wait with you, but he'll be right back."

Joshua blinked, sending tears down his face. He said nothing, and Diesel felt like dirt. He made himself smile. "If you get scared, yell for me and I'll come back, lickety-split. That's fast, Joshua."

"Okay." The mutinous look on Joshua's face said that he wasn't buying any of this, but he still righted the chair in which he'd been sitting and dropped onto it, his thin arms crossed over his chest.

Diesel cleared his throat, feeling helpless. He wanted to assure the child that it would all be fine. That Michael would be all right. But he didn't know that for sure.

"Fine. I'll be outside this door." He moved back as Maddie stepped forward to sit at the table with a scowling Joshua.

Closing the door behind him, he blew out a breath. "Shit."

Adam clasped his shoulder and gave it a hard squeeze. "You did good, Diesel. It's hard for all of us when kids are involved. We'll try to make this quick."

"Thanks. What do you need to know?"

"Everything you know about these two kids," Deacon said.

Diesel frowned. "I don't think Michael killed anyone, for starters."

Adam and Deacon shared a glance. "Neither do we," Adam murmured softly.

Something in Diesel settled. "Why not?"

Seeming to hesitate, Deacon ran a hand through his spiky white hair. "Off the record? I don't want to see this on the front page of the *Ledger*."

"Off the record," Diesel promised and was filled with a kind of pride when Deacon took him at his word.

"Okay," Deacon said. "A fisherman pulled a head out of the river this morning. That started the investigation."

Diesel recoiled. "God. You said a body."

"Actually, we said *remains*," Deacon corrected. "We found John Brewer's remains."

Adam grimaced. "We think we have all *that* body's parts."

Diesel swallowed against the images in his mind. He'd seen headless bodies. He'd seen disembodied heads. He'd seen bodies in all kinds of pieces. Because war fucking sucked and his brain never forgot anything he'd seen. "There were more?" he forced himself to ask.

Adam nodded. "The divers pulled out two heads, but a number of arms and legs—enough for more than two men. So definitely more than one victim. They're still searching. So far, none of the parts have gunshot wounds, so Michael having a gun under his pillow isn't a definitive connection. We'll do DNA testing to match up the parts, to make sure we have all of Brewer's remains. The ME will issue cause of death at that point."

Diesel swallowed hard, bile rising in his throat. "Jesus. Poor fisherman."

"Yeah." Adam shook his head. "Not anything that he's likely to forget."

No, it wasn't. For the fisherman or the divers or the cops forced to watch. "How do you know it was Brewer?" Diesel asked.

Deacon lowered his voice even further. "His is the only body part we've ID'd so far. He had a plate in his head, we're assuming from an earlier injury. It was . . . visible." He made a face. "Fish."

Diesel choked back his need to gag at the image of the fish consuming the man's flesh. "Fuck."

Adam nodded. "That's what we said. But the plate had a visible serial number, so we took a photo and made some phone calls."

"Anything implanted into a person's body has a serial number," Diesel said quietly. This he knew from experience. "For traceability in case of a recall or other problem."

Both men gave him measuring looks. "You know this how?" Deacon asked.

"Because I've got my share of metal plates and pins." Diesel shrugged when their eyes widened. "Shrapnel. Anyway, that's what they told me at the VA hospital. That every piece they put in me has a serial number. They keep my contact info, just in case, although I wouldn't be surprised if there was a recall and I was never notified." He didn't place much trust in the VA hospital. His experience hadn't been so good.

He felt the pressure on his chest before realizing he was rubbing the worst of his scars with the heel of his hand. He dropped his hand to his side, both men following the movement with curious eyes.

No, his experience hadn't been good at all. The surgeons had done their best, he supposed, but in his case their best hadn't been nearly good enough. Some days he almost forgot about the bullet they hadn't been able to remove.

Almost.

It would kill him someday. He needed that day not to be today. He had work to do. Kids to help. And maybe a doctor to woo.

She'd said no again today, but her beautiful mismatched eyes had said yes. So he wouldn't push. He'd wait patiently, just as he had for a year and a half. And if she never actually said yes, he'd still come whenever she needed his help.

Until the bullet moved. It wasn't something he could change, so he tried not to worry about it. *Yeah, right.* Every day was a ticking clock.

"So," he said, and Adam and Deacon returned their attention to his face, questions still in their eyes. "The kids. I know that the mother never stays to watch Josh practice. I know she's late every week. I know she's tried to come on to me in very inappropriate ways, despite being married." He looked over his shoulder at the exam room. "Joshua said she threw a bowl at Michael's head this morning. Michael said he ran six miles to pick his brother up."

Both men lifted their eyebrows at that. "With a head injury?" Deacon asked.

Diesel nodded grimly. "And I know that when he saw me, he nearly passed out from fear." And that when he sat down for lunch, the boy had winced. And when he rose from the table he had given the seat a quick swipe with his fingers, surreptitiously checking his fingertips as if he worried he might have left something behind. *Like blood.* "I think that he's been hurt by a man, in addition to his mother's throwing things at him."

Deacon blew out a harsh breath. "He didn't want either of us in the exam room. He specifically asked for Kendra. Did he tell you who the man was?"

Diesel shook his head. "No. He never actually said there *was* a man. That's my opinion." *Based on my own experience.* But there was no way he was revealing that to these men. Only one other person in their circle of friends knew his secret—Decker Davenport, an FBI agent who'd been investigating a child pornography ring.

Diesel had given Decker some evidence that he'd gathered from a related *Ledger* investigation, evidence that had hit way too close to home. And for some reason that he still couldn't fathom, he'd unloaded his sick baggage onto the agent, who'd promised not to tell anyone. And Diesel knew he hadn't, because he hadn't detected a change in the way the rest of their friends looked at him.

There would have been a difference, had they known. They wouldn't have been able to help themselves. Decker had earned his trust, not something

Diesel gave easily. He sensed Michael didn't give it easily, either.

"I hope I can get Michael to trust me enough to tell me," he murmured, then froze at the sound that suddenly exploded from behind the closed exam door.

His eyes slid closed, his chest suddenly tight. He knew that sound.

Sobbing. Desperate, uncontrollable sobbing for a pain so deep that nothing could help it. Nothing could heal it. It just went on and on and on until it clawed out of a person's throat. Michael's throat. *My throat.*

Because he'd made that same sound right after he'd spilled his secret to Decker Davenport. The man had simply grabbed his shoulders and let him cry until he'd cried it all out.

But he hadn't cried it all out, because new tears burned his eyes. Tears for Michael. Tears for himself.

Tears that he couldn't blink back. They rolled down his face and he wiped them away with the heel of his hand, just as the tortured sobbing quieted. His mind cleared enough to realize he'd just cried in front of two cops.

Fantastic.

No, he told himself. Deacon and Adam were far more than cops. They'd become his friends over the last year and a half. He let out a shaky breath and forced himself to open his eyes, not exactly sure what he'd see in their expressions. He knew it wouldn't be scorn. Pity, maybe? Embarrassment on his behalf?

But that wasn't what he saw. Not at all. Deacon's jaw was clenched as he stared at the door, and Adam was swiping his hand across his own eyes.

Adam gave Diesel a sad glance. "It's hard when it's kids," he whispered. He squeezed Deacon's arm. "You okay?"

Deacon nodded, finally tearing his eyes from the door. "That might account for the gun under his pillow," he murmured. He drew a breath and straightened his spine. "Regardless of what happens, we need to get that kid into therapy."

"What are you going to do with him?" Diesel set his jaw. "Please say you're not going to drag him downtown now."

"We have to," Deacon said quietly. "I don't want to, but we need to do this by the book. When we do catch the person who did this, we need to show that we didn't play fast and loose with the investigation. Michael is, for now, my sister's foster child."

"And my cousin's," Adam added. "We'll be lucky if we aren't asked to recuse ourselves. We can't let any defense attorney say we looked the other way with Michael because of his age, his disability, or his foster home."

"We're just going to question him about his stepfather," Deacon said. "At this point we don't have any evidence linking him to Brewer's murder other than his mother's claim that he's responsible."

Diesel swallowed back new rage. "She blamed Michael?"

Deacon shrugged. "But she's in custody for possession. Michael's story is more believable than hers. We'll likely release him into Dani's care."

And mine. But something still nagged at him. "What did his stepfather look like?"

Deacon frowned at him. "Why?" he asked suspiciously.

Diesel's temper flared, but he held his tongue. "I'm curious," he said mildly.

Deacon's expression said that he wasn't fooled. "Brewer was about five-ten, a hundred eighty pounds, dark hair."

So . . . nothing like me.

"Why?" Adam repeated, equally suspicious.

Diesel shrugged. "I told you that Michael nearly fainted when he saw me. I got the impression that he thought I was someone else."

"Ah." Adam's eyes sharpened with understanding. "Someone who wasn't five-ten with dark hair."

Diesel nodded. "Exactly."

"We'll keep our eyes open for someone big and bald, then," Deacon promised. He frowned again, glancing up at the clock on the wall. "Dani's taking an awful long time with that exam."

"She probably gave him time to chill a little after the crying jag," Diesel said, although he feared there was more to it than that.

"I hope you're right," Deacon murmured.

Ohio River, Cincinnati, Ohio
Saturday, March 16, 4:15 p.m.

Cade got out of his car, giving his padded gut a surreptitious pat. He was armed to the teeth. Just in case. He pushed his sunglasses up his nose, then tugged on his knitted cap, making sure it was snug. His bald head would stick out like a sore thumb here. It was cold enough for a cap, so he wasn't obvious.

He needed to remain that way. He'd parked at the end of a very long row of police and crime scene investigation vehicles, all pulled into an orderly line at the edge of the gravel road that was little more than a trail. Seemed all these investigators had hiked from here to where he'd parked his SUV when he'd dumped his newest bodies, twelve hours before.

Shit. There were three cops standing guard along the crime scene tape and five CSU techs wearing coveralls, their shoes protected with booties.

They're looking for evidence. Of me. Shit. He fought the urge to swipe his hand over his bald head. That would be obvious. He knew he'd left no body hair behind, because he had none, but who knew what else they might find?

Like tire treads. *Shit.* Some guy was squatting next to where he'd parked while dumping Brian Carlyle and Paul Engel early that morning. The guy, who wore an FBI jacket over his coveralls, was making a plaster mold.

Cade glanced at the tires of his SUV. *Shit, shit, shit.*

Terror caught hold of his lungs and for a moment he couldn't breathe. *Get out. Get out of here. Now.*

But that would also look suspicious. Drawing deep breaths, he calmed himself. *What was I thinking, coming here?*

He hadn't been thinking at all. He'd panicked. He'd searched online for the fisherman's name and found it nowhere. *Nowhere.* That meant it was being withheld by the cops. Which meant the man had seen something.

Which means he saw me.

Shit.

No. Do not panic. That's what got you here. Don't run, it'll get you noticed. Just breathe. And wait. And listen.

He got his best information by simply listening.

And sure enough, a young man approached with stumbling steps, stopping at the crime scene van. He reached inside the front passenger door and pulled out a pack of cigarettes. His hands shaking, he took out a cigarette and tried to light it, but his finger kept missing the lighter's wheel. He was clearly distressed.

Cade took another deep breath, gathered his composure, and approached. "Can I help you with that?"

The man glanced up, his eyes a little wild, his face alarmingly pale. "Thanks."

Cade took the lighter and lit the end of the cigarette, watching as the man sucked in a shaky breath and blew out a cloud of smoke.

"Shit," he muttered, then took another drag, holding it in this time. When he blew it out, he seemed calmer. "I quit smoking a year ago," he said, disgusted.

"Tough day?" Cade asked quietly, already knowing the answer. If this guy had been at the crime scene, he'd observed what the divers had brought up.

I'd be smoking something a helluva lot stronger than that. Fresh, the body parts weren't repellent at all. But after sitting in the water . . . some of them for weeks?

Yeah. The guy had a right to be shaken up.

The man laughed bitterly. "You could say that." His eyes narrowed. "Who are you, anyway?"

"Dennis Kagan," Cade answered. Kagan was one of his aliases, and happened to be the name on the driver's license in his wallet at the moment. "I'm with the *Ledger.*" Which was a total lie, of course, but this guy wouldn't know it. "And you are . . . ?"

"Not happy," the man said curtly. "Go away. I don't talk to reporters."

Cade clenched his jaw, then forced himself to relax. "We pay for information."

It was the guy's turn to clench his jaw. But he hesitated. "Not interested."

Cade was about to press him further when an annoyed voice called from behind the crime scene tape.

"Akers! Break time's over!" The guy who'd been taking a plaster cast of the tire treads ducked under the crime scene tape and stalked halfway to where they stood, his expression intense. "We've only got two hours of daylight left. Let's move." He started to turn, then reversed to stare at Cade. "Who the hell are you?"

"Oh fuck," Akers muttered.

Cade's gut rolled over. *Fuck.* "Reporter," he managed.

Intense Guy grew angry. "Really, Akers? You're talking to a reporter after I expressly forbade it?"

Akers's jaw tightened. "I didn't!" he fired back. Then muttered under his breath, "Asshole." He flicked the ash from his cigarette, ground it out on the van's tire, then put the butt in his pocket.

Intense Guy glared. "I heard that."

Akers smiled too sweetly. "Sorry, Agent Taylor. I meant, I didn't, *sir.*"

"I'm sure you did," Agent Taylor said levelly. "You. Reporter. You need to leave now." He waved at a cop.

"Officer, please show this man out. Akers, come with me."

Akers pushed away from the van and followed Agent Taylor back to the crime scene. Cade put both palms up in a gesture of surrender. "I'm going," he said.

Making a mental note of their names, he got back into his SUV before the cop reached him, grateful that he'd at least thought to change his license plates before he'd driven over here. He'd change them back once he got back to the city.

He glanced in the rearview mirror as he did a quick three-point turn in the gravel, skidding off the road a little before regaining control. The cop wasn't following him. He blew out a relieved breath. *Good.*

"That was stupid," he said aloud. And it was. Rushing over here had been idiotic. But he'd come away with a few pieces of information.

First, he hadn't had to shoot his way out of there, so they didn't suspect him. Or at least the CSU team didn't suspect him.

Second, Akers was bribable. He hadn't appreciated being dressed down by Agent Taylor. Cade would find him and get the name of the damn fisherman.

So although coming here had been stupid as hell, it might have been worth it.

Chapter Five

Dani willed her hands to be steady as she checked Michael's stitches to make sure they were intact after he'd raked his fingers through his hair. On the outside, she was confident and calm, just as a good doctor needed to be. Inside she was still trembling.

Michael's sobs had rattled her, but it was the blood on the exam table that had left her shaken. She'd seen it as soon as she'd taken the boy into her arms as he'd cried his poor heart out. She'd felt helpless and angry at his mother and whoever else had hurt him. And then she'd seen the blood spreading on the white paper and she'd wanted to kill his stepfather.

She'd wanted to strangle the bastard with her bare hands.

She swallowed hard, focusing on his stitches, on her own breathing. *In and out. Stay calm. Stay steady.* But it was difficult. He'd hurt Michael. He'd put that hunted look in the boy's eyes. And if Michael *had* killed the man while defending himself, she'd fight for him like a mother bear protecting her cub.

And now she had to ask him about it. In front of a nurse, an interpreter, and a cop. Both her nurse and the interpreter were bound to confidentiality, but

Kendra would have to report it. Michael had been through enough hell already, and now she'd have to ask him about it in front of witnesses.

The presence of the interpreter was a necessary burden that was one of the many difficulties that came with deafness. There was no privacy when dealing with the hearing, nonsigning world. There was almost always an interpreter involved. Very few doctors signed. Even fewer therapists. So even when Michael was physically recovered, he'd probably still have to deal with an interpreter when he got therapy.

And this boy will get therapy. I'll make sure of it.

Of course, the presence of a cop was all on the heads of his mother and stepfather—the two people who should have taken care of him. Who had instead thrown a bowl at his head and assaulted him, causing rectal bleeding.

She glanced over at the interpreter. Maria was a nice person, evidenced through many previous encounters. She had interpreted for Greg more than once over the years and Dani was happy that she was the one assigned to Michael today.

Maria was watching Michael carefully, waiting for the smallest twitch of the boy's hands that signaled communication.

"Your stitches are still intact," Dani said. "Keep your hands out of your hair, okay? I'll bandage you up and then I'll check your shoulder."

Maria interpreted exactly what Dani had said, then voiced, "Then I'll go with the cops?" when Michael replied.

"*We'll* go with the cops," Dani corrected. She covered the wound with a bandage, placing the tape carefully. "I had to shave a little of your hair, but when you comb it, nobody will know."

"So not bald like Coach Diesel?" Michael signed with a nervous roll of his eyes.

Dani forced herself to smile, even though she wanted to cry. Michael was trying so hard not to fall apart. "Certainly not." She handed the suture tray to Jenny, removing the gloves she'd worn and putting on the new ones Jenny handed her. "I can take it from here," she told her nurse. "Dr. Kristoff should be here soon to take the rest of my shift. Can you make sure he's up to speed?"

"Of course. We've got a patient scheduled for a well-baby in five minutes. I'll get them settled." Jenny moved to the back corner to throw the gloves and bloody gauze in the biohazard bag, but then she stopped, her gaze fixed on the bloody paper covering the exam table. She looked at Dani, her eyes sad. "I'll take care of everything else," she added, touching her pants, indicating that she'd find a clean set of scrubs for Michael.

"Thanks." Jenny was an amazing nurse. She knew exactly what people needed before they asked. But her departure from the room meant one less person to bear witness to Michael's pain. Dani wished she could get rid of the interpreter and Kendra, too, but that wasn't possible. She returned her attention to Michael. "Let me take a look at your shoulder now. Can you take off your shirt?"

He nodded, grimacing as he did so. Dani's heart clenched. He was so thin. She'd felt his sharp edges when she'd held him, but she hadn't realized how bad it was until she saw his ribs so very clearly.

And there were bruises on his chest. Faded, but still visible. She sighed. "I'm going to need to document the bruises, Michael."

He narrowed his eyes. "I fell down."

Right. If she had a nickel for every abuse victim to say those words . . . Especially because two of the darkest bruises had the distinct shape of the toe of a boot. She'd seen that before, too.

She met his eyes for a long moment. Finally he looked away. "Whatever."

She snapped a few photos. "What happened here?" She pointed at healing cuts on his upper arm.

"Was running. Fell down."

"Running without a shirt? In this weather?" she asked and he shrugged again. She sighed and probed his shoulder, listening for his sharp intake of breath. "Probably just a strained muscle. We can ice it when I take you and Joshua home with me. You're a little underweight." A lot underweight. "Have you been feeling okay otherwise?"

A one-shouldered shrug. "I'm fine. I just haven't felt like eating."

Oh, honey. "Okay. You can put your shirt back on." It wasn't bloody, at least.

He quickly pulled his shirt on. "Are we done?"

"No." She drew a breath and looked him in the eye. "I need to get you some pants to wear," she signed without voicing.

Behind her, Maria voiced her words quietly for Kendra's benefit.

All the remaining color drained from Michael's face. "No. Please."

Dani's heart shattered a little more. She knew he wasn't refusing to change his clothes. He was begging for her words not to be true. "You've bled through these."

Michael's gaze flew to Kendra before returning to meet Dani's. His eyes were wild and afraid. "No more doctors. Please."

"I can't promise that, Michael. Not without knowing a little bit more. How long have you been bleeding?"

He dropped his gaze to his hands. "Two weeks." When he looked up, it was only enough to see Dani's hands.

"Steady or off and on?"

"Off and on."

"Is it worse after you have a bowel movement or is it random?"

Even with his head bowed, Dani could see his pale face flush with humiliation. "When I use the bathroom."

"Okay, then." Dani exhaled quietly. "Who did this to you, Michael?"

Michael's chin jerked up, his gaze flying once again to Kendra. He shook his head hard. No communication was necessary. He wasn't telling.

"All right," Dani said, voicing as she signed. "I'm going to need to clean the area and pack it with gauze."

Michael turned his face away, new tears sliding down his cheeks.

Goddammit. She hated causing the boy more pain and humiliation. She relented. If he bled primarily after a bowel movement—or a six-mile run followed by the extreme stress of being accused of murder, not to mention the body-racking sobs—this was probably a minor fissure that would repair itself.

She tapped his arm gently, waiting until he looked at her miserably. "I understand. I'll find you something to wear and leave you some gauze. We'll give you privacy to clean yourself up. When we get to my house, I'll give you some fiber supplements. It'll help you not to strain, which will help you heal. But if you don't heal, we'll need to see a specialist."

He nodded, looking away again. "Okay," he signed, his fingers barely moving. "Thank you."

Dani patted his knee. "Let me get you the scrubs."

"You're going to report this?" he asked, glancing at her.

She sighed. "I have to. I'm sorry."

He nodded once. "I know."

Dani turned to Kendra. "Is this sufficient?"

Kendra's nod was grim. "Oh, yeah." She reached for the doorknob. "If he lets you document the rectal tearing, we can add it to the report." She looked like she wanted to say more, but pursed her lips and left the room.

The interpreter hesitated, then walked into Michael's line of sight. She quickly relayed Kendra's closing comments, then gave Michael her card. "Text me or video-call me if you need help. I'll come."

Michael took the card and closed his eyes. He looked so damn tired.

Dani motioned for the interpreter to leave first, then she followed, closing the door behind her. There was a heavy silence in the reception area. Deacon, Adam, and Diesel waited, seeming to realize that the women needed a moment to center themselves.

Kendra sat on the edge of the intake desk, arms crossed tightly over her chest. The interpreter sank into the chair, her skin appearing gray under the harsh lights.

Stripping the gloves from her hands, Dani rested her weight against the exam room door, closing her eyes, feeling as weary as Michael had looked. Normally she went to her office to cry in private after a stressful exam such as this one, but today she had an audience. "Where is Maddie?" she asked, realizing the social worker was not with them. "And Joshua?"

"In your office," Diesel said quietly, his voice suddenly much closer than it should have been.

Dani's eyes flew open to find him standing in front of her, his expression concerned. And his eyes . . . They were red. He'd been crying. He must have heard Michael's sobs and been moved to tears.

Dani lost another piece of her heart to the gentle giant. *Dammit.* She didn't want to want him. But she did. At that moment, she wanted nothing more than to lay her head on that solid chest and feel those muscled arms wrap around her.

That wasn't going to happen, but for the life of her she couldn't remember why. She stared up at him helplessly. "He needs some pants," she whispered.

Diesel's throat worked, his gulp audible. His red-rimmed eyes filled with the pain of understanding. "I have an extra pair of sweats in my truck, but they'll swallow him whole," he whispered back. "He'll know that I know."

God, he *did* understand. Dani found herself leaning into him, resting her forehead on his chest. Their bodies touched nowhere else. Until he brought a trembling hand to her hair and stroked it. It felt so good. Too good. So good that she should make him stop. But she didn't.

She couldn't.

"He'll be okay," Diesel murmured into her ear. "We'll make sure of it."

Tell him there is no "we." Tell him. But she didn't. Instead she nodded unsteadily before straightening her back. His hand fell to his side and she had to force herself not to grab it and put it back on her hair.

She moistened her lips, nervous now, because his eyes were drinking her in. "Can you take Joshua somewhere for a little while? We need to go to the police station and I don't think Michael will want him to know about this. Or for you to know, either," she added, one side of her mouth lifting. "I think he's got a case of hero worship where you're concerned."

Diesel nodded. "I'll take Joshua to the *Ledger*. Marcus is out buying crayons. He might be buying candy, too."

She smiled. "I think a little candy sounds like a good plan. I'll let you know when we're done at the police station. I *will* be taking Michael home with me. He will *not* be kept at the police station." She threw a stern glance at her brother and cousin, who hadn't said a word—not with their mouths, anyway. Both sets of eyes were full of questions as they looked from her to Diesel and back again.

Gossips, all of them.

Diesel chuckled, bringing her attention back to him. "I pity anyone who even tries to keep him from you. You have my cell phone number?"

"Yes," she said simply, unwilling to admit that she'd memorized it long ago.

"Then I'll get out of here for a little while." He went into her office and closed the door.

Dani rubbed her temples. "Jenny?" she called.

Jenny came out of the storeroom, a set of scrubs in her hand. "They'll be a little short on him. They're mine."

Deacon drew in a breath when he saw the clothing in Jenny's hands. "Give me a minute. I've got a pair of Greg's sweats in my trunk. He and Michael are about the same size. And they're actually clean. His baseball practice got canceled yesterday and he left his gym bag in my car. Does Michael need anything else?"

"Thanks," Dani told him. "Just the sweats will be fine. And if Michael asks, I had them in my car, okay?"

Deacon saluted as he headed out the door. "Yes, ma'am."

Her office door opened and Diesel appeared, a sniffling Joshua riding on his hip, the little boy's arms tight around Diesel's neck. "He heard Michael crying," Diesel murmured.

Dani rubbed Joshua's back. "I'm taking care of him, okay?"

Joshua nodded, his face pressed to Diesel's strong chest.

"I'll see you and Coach Diesel in a little while."

Joshua lifted his head, his face tearstained. "You won't let him go to jail?"

"I'm going to fight my hardest," Dani promised.

"That's what Coach Diesel said." Joshua studied her hair solemnly. "Are you an X-Man?"

Dani laughed. "I wish I were." She touched the white streak in her hair. "But I wouldn't be Rogue, because she hurts people with her touch. I'd hate to do that."

"Yeah," Joshua agreed. "That would suck. She has to wear gloves." He pointedly glanced at the purple exam gloves she still clutched in one hand. "Like you do."

Dani sighed. She did have to wear gloves when she administered exams. That was standard practice. But she sometimes wore them while simply talking to patients as well, usually at their request.

She knew the facts about HIV. She was a doctor, for God's sake. She knew exactly how the disease was transmitted. She also knew that her levels were undetectable, that she was as unlikely to infect anyone as any other member of the population. But some of her patients weren't so certain about her.

It wasn't a secret that she was HIV positive. Patients at the free clinic couldn't afford to boycott her services, but many still recoiled from her touch.

So I guess Rogue and I have something in common after all.

She chanced a glance up to see Diesel studying her through narrowed eyes, like he was trying to figure her out. *Good luck with that, buddy.*

She patted Joshua's back. "You go with Coach Diesel, sweetheart. He'll take care of you, and I'll take care of Michael. I promise."

Cincinnati, Ohio
Saturday, March 16, 5:00 p.m.

Michael clenched his teeth to keep them from chattering. He was so cold, even though the inside of the detectives' car was warm. They had the heater on high, at Dr. Dani's request. Still, he shivered uncontrollably.

He stared out the window as the buildings went by. They were taking him to the police station. To question him. About Brewer's murder.

Tell them the truth.

God, he wanted to. But his hands were shaking, too. He shoved them into the pockets of his jacket and closed his eyes, misery overwhelming him.

Misery and humiliation. And fear. They knew. The doctor had to have told them that his ass was bleeding. She was obligated. By law.

He hunched into himself, wishing he could just . . .

die. It would be easier. So much easier. They were going to say he'd killed that bastard Brewer and they'd put Joshua in foster care somewhere. The doctor couldn't keep him forever. She was only an emergency foster parent.

He jumped when Dr. Dani touched him, a brief graze of her fingertips over his cheek. He turned to look at her, focusing on her mismatched eyes. "What?" he voiced. He knew he sounded snarky and ungrateful.

She smiled at him. Sweetly. Not meanly. Not like his mother did. Dr. Dani's smile made him want to believe her. He slowly drew his right hand from his pocket.

"Sorry," he signed.

"It's okay," she signed back. Her mouth wasn't moving at all. "I don't want you to sign anything or say anything when we get there. There will be reporters outside the police station. Probably cameras. They're not waiting for you specifically. They're waiting for a statement from the cops on the body that was found this morning, but they may take pictures and video of you. You're a minor, so they most likely won't use the photos or your name, but you never can tell about the media these days. They'll want to provoke us into saying something, especially when they see Deacon and Adam. Do not respond to them. Do not make eye contact. Don't even sign to me. Nothing will be private until we get to an interview room. Got it?"

He nodded, huffing out a choked breath. *Most likely?* He could end up on TV and then everyone would know he'd been accused of murdering his piece-of-shit stepfather. But he'd worry about that later. For now, he was too terrified about being dragged off in handcuffs. "Are they going to put me in jail?"

"No. They don't have any evidence. Right now they have your stepfather's body, your mother's accusation, and the gun you hid under your pillow."

"How do you know?"

She tilted her head. "Did you do it?"

"No." He snapped the sign.

"Did you ever fire that gun?"

"No."

She looked like she wanted to ask more questions, but the car was slowing down. And stopping. In front of the police department.

Michael stared at the neat lettering at the front of the building. CINCINNATI POLICE. They were going to put him in jail. He was going to jail. With real criminals. Who'd . . . He choked out a sob as his gut roiled.

He hunched tighter into himself. *God.* "I'm going to throw up."

Dr. Dani wrapped her fingers around his wrist, pressing his pulse point gently with her thumb until he turned his head to look up at her. "No, you're not going to throw up," she signed with her free hand. "You're going to breathe with me. Just like we did before. Okay?"

He nodded, too scared to refuse. She put her hand on her chest, lifting and lowering it as she breathed deeply. Within a few breaths he was matching her rate and she let go of his wrist.

"Better?" she asked.

He blinked at her. He was still terrified, but he no longer felt like he'd hurl. *At least there's that.* "A little."

"Okay. I saw about twenty reporters waiting outside the police department. They're going to be yelling at you and you might see flashes of light from their cameras. You're not going to look at them. You're going to keep your hands in your pockets until we get inside. You'll go through a metal detector inside the door, and they'll tell you to take your hands out of your pockets. Detective Kimble told them you were coming and that you'd have an interpreter, so nobody's going to get in your face inside."

"Will it be the same woman as before?"

"No, she had to go to another appointment. But I

know this interpreter and he's nice, too. He's interpreted for my brother a few times. He's one of the only interpreters in the city certified to interpret in legal situations. He's good."

Not the same woman. *That's good.* But a man? *Shit.* At least this guy didn't know. Not yet, anyway. "Okay."

"When you've gone through the metal detectors, you put your hands back in your pockets. You have no privacy until we get to the interview room. Got it?"

He nodded. "Yeah. No privacy." He was used to that.

She stuck her hand into her big purse and pulled out two baseball caps—one had the Bengals logo, the other the Cincinnati Reds. She handed him one. "Put this on. Keep your head down. Lobby security will make us take our caps off, but let's not make it easy for these reporters to take pictures of you, okay?" She twisted her long hair into a knot and put her cap on over it, hiding the white streaks in her hair. "I'm recognizable. I don't want anyone tracking you to my house afterward, because that's where we'll be going. Got it?"

He nodded and put his own cap on. He hoped she was right, that they'd be going to her house. *Please don't let them put me in jail. Please.*

One of the men in the front must have said something to her, because she nodded. "We're ready."

It was just like Dr. Dani had said, from the moment they got out of the car until they were through the metal detector. Reporters and flashing lights. He kept his head down and put one foot in front of the other.

Don't throw up. Don't throw up.

A guy about thirty years old was waiting just inside the door and quickly introduced himself as Andrew, the interpreter. He smoothed the way, going through the metal detector first, then standing where

Michael could see him as he interpreted the officer's instructions.

It was . . . calm. The reporters outside had been yelling. He hadn't heard them, but he could see their mouths and their faces. He'd seen enough yelling people in his life to know. They had taken video and film, but Dr. Dani never left his side, her hand on his back the whole way. Detective Kimble had walked on Michael's left, Agent Novak on the doctor's right. Protecting him. All of them had protected him.

At least no one had gotten in his face. Nothing freaked him out faster than people getting in his face.

Unless it was seeing his stepfather being murdered.

Tell them. The words chanted in his mind with every step he took through the hallways that seemed endless, walking past cops who turned to watch as he was escorted toward what he hoped was the interview room.

No. He looked around him frantically. He needed a restroom. Because he was feeling like he was going to throw up again. But Dr. Dani put her hand on his good shoulder, squeezing until he glanced up at her.

They'd stopped outside a doorway that looked like all the other doorways they'd passed. "Breathe," she mouthed, her hand on her chest.

Once more he breathed with her until he felt better. He started to take his hand from his pocket to tell her that he was okay, but remembered what she'd said and shoved it back in. She gave him a nod of approval.

Detective Kimble pointed to a door at the far end of the hallway. "That's where we're going."

It was another hundred feet. It felt like a thousand, even with Dr. Dani's hand on his back. *Don't let them put me in jail. Please.*

He'd heard stories of what happened to deaf kids in lockup. No one could communicate with them, no one would protect them. They couldn't hear who was coming and got beaten up. Or worse.

By the time Detective Kimble opened the door to the interview room, Michael was shaking so hard he could barely walk. Dr. Dani helped him to a chair and knelt in front of him so that she was directly in his line of sight. He dragged his trembling hands from his pockets, shoved them through his hair. The tug on the bandaged stitches made him wince as he held his head in his hands. He was rocking himself and he hadn't even planned to. He couldn't make himself stop.

"You're scared," she signed. "I get it. But you're making yourself sick." She squeezed his knees lightly. "Can you trust me?"

He blinked away tears. "I'm so scared," he voiced, his fingers clutching his hair.

Gently she took his hands from his hair and put them in his lap. "You have pretty hair, Michael. Don't yank it out or you'll look like Coach Diesel after all."

He snorted a shocked laugh, which was probably what she'd been going for, because she smirked before looking over her shoulder. Sitting at the table were Miss Maddie the social worker, Andrew the interpreter, and a man he'd never seen before. About Coach Diesel's age, he thought, but dressed in a suit that had an actual vest. With a pocket watch chain.

"Who is that?" he asked Dr. Dani.

"Your lawyer. His name is Rex Clausing." She spelled out the name carefully. "He's a friend of Coach Diesel's. Diesel says you can trust him."

"Do you know him?"

"No. I've never seen him before."

Michael frowned. "Then how do you know who he is?"

"Because he said his name when we came in."

When she'd looked over her shoulder at him. *Okay.* That made sense. But the man did not look like a friend Coach Diesel would have. Coach was big and rough and looked like he should be in a motorcycle gang or lifting weights in a sweaty gym. The lawyer—Rex Clausing—looked like a professor.

He was too neat. Too smart-looking. Too . . . something that Michael didn't trust.

Dr. Dani squeezed his knees again to get his attention. "What?" she asked. "Your face went pale again."

"What do I have to tell him?"

Dr. Dani's expression softened. "You tell him everything that you can."

Michael swallowed, glancing over at the lawyer again before returning his focus to the doctor. "I can't." He leaned forward and she shifted so that no one could see what he signed. Giving him privacy. "He'll think I did it. He'll think I hated Brewer because . . ." He swallowed again. "You know."

"I know. But he can't protect you if he doesn't know. I'll stay with you."

"What about the cops? Don't I get to talk to the lawyer without them first?"

Dani's lips curved. "You watch TV cop shows, too, huh? They're going to leave so that you can talk to Mr. Clausing. In private."

He glanced again at the lawyer, who sat patiently. He looked calm.

But I still don't like it. I don't trust him. I can't trust him.

"He's too fancy to be Coach Diesel's friend."

Dr. Dani's eyes widened. "What? No, honey. Coach has all kinds of fancy friends. Some of his best friends are super-rich."

"Can you ask him again? Please? Make sure this guy is who he says he is."

Dr. Dani hesitated. "Do you want Coach here with you when you talk to the lawyer? Would that make you feel better?"

Michael wanted to say no. He didn't want Coach to know. He didn't want anyone to know. He was surrounded by people that he'd never met before this afternoon and they were expecting him to trust them. Just like that.

He wanted to trust them. He really wanted to. But

if they put him in jail, Joshua would be alone. Coach had helped them. He'd taken care of Joshua.

He made Michael feel safe.

He jerked a nod, blinking back new tears. Dammit, he hated to cry. Especially in front of all these cops. "But he's with Joshua. I don't want Joshua here. Not in the police station."

"I agree. Let me see what I can do."

Michael dropped his chin. "They'll be mad if they have to wait. The lawyer might leave."

"I think they can all wait a little while longer. I'm more worried about you. You need to be able to think and communicate. And you can't do that if you're afraid."

Michael nodded slowly. "Okay. Call him. Please?"

She stroked his cheek and he leaned into her touch. "I will. Right now."

Chapter Six

Marcus O'Bannion leaned against Diesel's desk in his office at the *Ledger*. "He's a cute kid."

Diesel looked up from his computer screen to check on Joshua, who sat at the worktable between their office manager, Gayle, and Marcus's wife, Detective Scarlett Bishop, who worked with Adam and Deacon. The worktable was normally cluttered with printouts, maps, competitors' newspapers, and coffee cups, but today it was covered with puzzles and pages from the coloring books Marcus and Scarlett had bought for Joshua.

Diesel smiled when Joshua grinned at something Scarlett said. The boy had cried all the way from the free clinic to the *Ledger* office, but Gayle's grandmotherly hugs—and the candy she'd given him—had distracted him just enough. Then Marcus and Scarlett had arrived with enough toys and candy for six children. That Joshua had met Scarlett earlier that afternoon put him further at ease.

"You're spoiling him," Diesel said, but he could hear the warmth in his own voice. "Thanks, man."

Marcus clapped him on the shoulder. "You're welcome. I had to put back half the stuff Scar put in the cart. She's practicing."

Diesel frowned. "Practicing what?"

Marcus was staring at his wife, a sappy expression on his face. "Mothering."

It took Diesel a full second and then he pushed to his feet and grabbed Marcus into a bear hug, lifting him until only his toes touched the floor. "Oh my God. That's . . ." He let his friend go, gripping his arms so that he could make eye contact. "Wonderful. Absolutely wonderful."

Marcus smiled and Diesel's heart squeezed. His friend's smiles had been a rare occurrence before meeting Scarlett Bishop. Now they were a daily given. A daily gift. He and Marcus had been through a lot together since they'd met in boot camp. War had made them brothers, but the years after had made them the best of friends.

Unfortunately, there were things even best friends didn't tell each other. He didn't think Marcus would think any differently of him if he knew about his childhood. About the abuse he'd endured. But Marcus had a past of his own and there was no way Diesel was adding to his friend's load.

And now? Even more of a reason. Marcus was going to be a dad. Time to put all the dark years behind them and start fresh. Children were one of the best reasons to live in the light.

"When?" Diesel asked.

"In six months. We haven't told many people yet. Just our immediate families." Marcus grinned. "My dad and Keith are beside themselves. They've already started on a nursery."

Jeremy O'Bannion had been like a father to Diesel in the years since his move to Cincinnati. At first the man had welcomed him out of sheer gratitude, because Diesel had pulled Marcus out of a Baghdad firefight one night. But then he'd been welcomed for himself. Jeremy and his husband, Keith, included him as one of their kids. They never forgot his birthday, and he'd had a place at their table on every major holiday for years. They were his home.

The thought of the two men as grandparents made him grin. "I'll just bet they are. Keith's probably bought a baseball bat and glove already, and your dad's picked out wallpaper with all the best organs. Hearts, spleens. Bladders." Jeremy had been a surgeon before suffering permanent damage to his hands in a fire.

Marcus laughed. "Yes to the baseball, no to the bladders. Scar's folks aren't far behind. Her mother's knitting already. At least this isn't their first grandchild, so the pressure's a little less from them. I've been so close to telling you, but Scarlett threatened to make me cook dinner for a month if I told before now. She hasn't even let Deacon and Adam know yet. She doesn't want CPD to know. She's afraid they'll be weird about it."

Diesel crossed his arms over his chest. "She *is* going to take a desk job when she starts to show, though. Right?"

Marcus rolled his eyes. "It's 'under discussion.'" He used air quotes. "But enough about me. What are you finding about the boy's stepfather?"

"Enough to know the guy had severe money troubles." Diesel sat behind his desk and Marcus pulled up a chair. "And a taste for young boys," he added in a murmur.

Marcus grimaced. "Oh God. Not Joshua."

"I don't think so. But maybe his brother."

"The one you asked Rex to meet downtown?" Marcus's eyes widened as the significance sank in. "Oh shit. That's not going to look good for Michael. It goes to motive."

"Yeah. Deacon and Adam told me that they don't think Michael did it. But I hate the thought of him getting dragged downtown. He's had a shit day."

Marcus frowned. "They couldn't have questioned him at the clinic?"

"No." Diesel told him what Deacon and Adam had explained. "I mean, I get it. I do. They don't want anyone coming back later and pointing a finger at Michael, citing preferential treatment. But . . . God, Marcus."

"Yeah," Marcus murmured. "You'll be good for him, though. Sounds like he could use a good male role model."

Warmth at Marcus's words spread through Diesel's chest, softening the edges of the sadness, the helplessness, the absolute *rage* that had all but suffocated him since he'd heard Michael's sobs in the clinic. "Thanks. That means a lot."

"It's true." Marcus scooted closer, so that he could see the screen. "Follow the money?"

"It's an adage for a reason." Diesel pointed at the spreadsheet he'd been studying. "I downloaded his most recent bank statements. Guy had his online bank account bookmarked and the password saved by his browser."

"He deserved to get hacked, then," Marcus said airily.

Diesel snorted. "Well, he certainly didn't make it hard for me to do. I was surprised the cops hadn't locked his accounts down, but I guess they're a little slow on the draw. He was spending money at three times the rate he was making it. And . . ." He clicked to another tab. "He sold his house."

Marcus blinked. "To whom?"

"I don't know yet. I haven't had time to drill into the transaction. The buyer is buried in shell corporations." He cracked a knuckle, then wiggled his fingers. "I was about to start in on that."

"What makes you think he has a thing for boys?" Marcus whispered.

Diesel clenched his jaw until it hurt. "Found some links to kiddie porn in his browser history. And photos. Not as hard-core as some of the shit I've seen on this job, but still . . . well, the photos aren't going to look good for Michael, either."

Marcus winced. "He had photos of Michael?"

"Yeah. And a few of Joshua." Diesel swallowed hard. "Bath time." The rage was back and he fought it down so that he could breathe. It was a good thing that the fucker was already dead, otherwise he'd kill him himself. "I didn't make copies of any of his porn. The cops will find it when they search his computer. He tried to hide it in a partition on his hard drive, but a five-year-old could have found it."

"So Michael had motive."

Diesel felt sick, imagining the cops questioning the kid. "Yeah. But he didn't do it. I just . . . don't believe he did."

"You've always had a good gut," Marcus said softly. "He's not you, though."

Diesel's gaze flew to his friend's face, his mouth falling open, panic freezing his heart so that it skipped a beat. He could feel the color draining from his face. "What?"

Marcus dropped his gaze to his hands. "I know nothing, Diesel. I promise. But I've watched you take on sex offenders for years. It's personal for you, just like it is for me. But different, too. My brothers were hurt, not me. My rage is once removed. Yours . . . isn't." He glanced up. "I don't need to know what happened to you. Not unless you ever want to tell me. I've never told a soul what I think, and I never will. But I don't want to see you get hurt. You've gotten attached to this kid so fast . . . You don't really know him. I don't want you to be blinded by your need to help him. Just be careful, okay?"

Diesel forced himself to let go of the breath he'd been holding. *Exhale. Nice and easy. Marcus cares. I know he does. He only wants to protect me. Like I protect him.* "Do the others know?"

That the team at the *Ledger* could tell his vendetta

was personal hadn't really occurred to him. It should have, of course. They were all reporters. Keen eyes. Keen minds with the ability to see connections others could not.

"No," Marcus murmured. "At least I don't think so. Nobody talks about you, D. I promise."

"Okay." Closing his eyes, he tried to calm his now-racing heart. "Okay."

Marcus gripped his forearm. "I'm sorry. I shouldn't have said anything."

"It's . . . it's okay. I'll be okay. I hope Michael will be, too." Diesel opened his eyes to see that Marcus's had become too bright. Too shiny. "It's okay, Marcus."

Marcus pursed his lips and nodded. "Let me know if you need me to run any interference for you. I'll do whatever you need." His throat worked. "You know I've got your back, D. Me and Scar and everyone here."

"I know." Diesel dug deep and found a smile—and a subject change. "So, you're going to name the baby after me, right?"

Marcus's laugh held the echo of a sob, but he flicked the back of Diesel's head as he stood up. "I don't think so. Elvis O'Bannion? I think Scarlett would kill me in my sleep, and she'd have every right."

Diesel rubbed his head with an exaggerated scowl. "Ow. But it's fair. I wish to God I knew what my mother was thinking when she named me."

"I think there were heavy-duty delivery drugs involved."

Diesel was about to agree when his cell phone buzzed. He frowned at the call. Most people texted. Then he saw the ID. "It's Dani." He hit ACCEPT as Marcus sat back down, waiting. "Hey," he said, "are you done at the station already?"

"No," Dani said. "Can you figure out a way to come down here? I think Michael needs you. He had a panic attack on the way in and he's about to have another."

Diesel was already packing up his laptop. "Didn't Rex get there?"

"Yes, but, um . . . Michael doesn't believe he's your friend," she said with a trace of wry humor. "He's too fancy."

Diesel snorted. "Did you tell him I don't just consort with WWE types?"

"I did. I even told him you had super-rich friends." She sighed, abruptly sober. "I think you make him feel safe. I don't know what to do about Joshua, though. There's a crowd of reporters outside the station. I don't want his photo in the news. It's bad enough they took pictures of Michael when we walked him in."

Diesel's temper simmered. "They can't them. He's only fourteen."

"They're not supposed to, but you know as well as I do that some of those guys with cameras would sell their mothers for a buck. I don't think they were aiming for Michael. They were shouting questions at Deacon and Adam."

It didn't matter. "Dammit. Adam and Deacon should have taken him in through the back."

"I said as much, but they said there were more reporters there. All the networks and major news outlets."

"Hold on." Diesel looked at Marcus. "Can you and Scarlett watch Joshua for a little while?"

"Of course, as long as he's okay with it. Whatever you need."

On the other end of the phone, Dani sighed her relief. "Tell them thank you for me. When you get here, text me. I'll ask Deacon to come up and escort you."

"Will do. Thanks, Dani."

"No, thank *you*. See you soon."

Diesel hung up, staring at his phone for a few heartbeats. She'd never called him before. Hearing her voice had him both calm and tense at once. He wanted to take a moment to remember how he'd felt when she'd leaned into him. How soft and silky her hair had been.

But he had places to be. Kids to help. And maybe a doctor to woo face-to-face, rather than just dream about.

Marcus's lips had curved. "Finally?"

Diesel's cheeks heated. "Finally what?"

"Dani?"

Diesel didn't try to play dumb. But he also couldn't let Marcus get the wrong idea. "It's just for the kids. Don't get your hopes up. I'm not."

Marcus stood up and leaned in close. "Liar. If you need me, I'm here."

Marcus knew him well. *My hopes already are up.* But Marcus also understood that Dani had kept him at arm's length for eighteen long months.

Diesel shrugged. "I have to accept that she might not ever let her walls down." Somehow that hurt more than having Marcus know that he had been abused as a kid.

"Is it her status?"

Diesel nodded. "That's what she said when she told me to find someone else."

Marcus frowned. "Did you tell her that you were okay with the risk?"

"I did. It didn't change her mind." He zipped his laptop case, unwilling to discuss it any longer. Shouldering the bag, he went to where Joshua was happily coloring. He bent down on one knee. "Hey, buddy. Everything's okay, but Michael asked me to be with him at the police station. He's a little scared and I'm going to keep him company. Are you okay staying here with Miss Scarlett, Mr. Marcus, and Miss Gayle?"

Joshua glanced at the adults around him, then nodded, pointing at Scarlett. "Yeah. She's a police lady. My teacher says it's the police's job to help us."

Diesel ruffled the boy's hair. "That's right. Miss Scarlett is good at helping people."

Joshua stared up at him guilelessly. "Like the old man in the wheelchair today."

"Just like him." Diesel booped Joshua's nose. "I'll be back before you miss me." Rising, he murmured to Marcus, "I'll text you when I know something." His gaze flicked to Joshua. "Keep him safe, okay?"

"You know it," Marcus vowed.

Diesel did. Which was the only reason he was able to get into his truck and drive away.

Cincinnati, Ohio
Saturday, March 16, 6:00 p.m.

Deacon walked Diesel to the interview room and stopped outside the door. "I'll wait out here until Michael's talked to his attorney," Deacon said. "Adam's checking in with CSU. The two of us will come in when Clausing calls us, okay?"

Diesel nodded. "And nobody's in the observation room?" Because simply turning down the speaker didn't constitute privacy when dealing with sign language.

"No one. I'll turn on the light on the observation side, so you'll be able to see if anyone enters. But I'll stand guard. You have my word, Diesel. No one will spy on Michael."

"Thank you." Because Deacon's word was as good as gold.

Deacon hesitated. "See if you can get him to tell us who the bald man is, the one he thought you might have been. The one who scared him."

"I will. Do you or Dani know the interpreter?"

"Yeah. Andrew's a good guy. He's interpreted for Greg more than once, and a few times it was because Greg had gotten into legal trouble. The guy knows the courts. And he is bound to confidentiality."

"Yeah, well, there are a shit-ton of reporters out there who'd pay a pretty penny for an inside story on this case. Especially one including an abused kid with a disability who's been accused of murder."

Deacon sighed. "I can't guarantee that Andrew is untouchable, but in my experience, he's been discreet. That's all I can give you."

"It'll have to be enough for now, I guess. Thanks, Deacon."

Deacon clapped him on the shoulder. "Good luck."

I hope we don't need it, but I'm pretty sure we will, Diesel thought as he entered the interview room. Michael was sitting in a chair, hugging himself, so pale that Diesel was surprised the kid hadn't passed out. Dani sat beside him, a tenseness beneath her exterior of calm. Rex sat quietly, hands folded in front of him, the picture of the proper lawyer, and Diesel could see how Michael might doubt their friendship.

Hell, half the time Diesel wondered why *any* of them were his friends, but he was grateful that they were. The team at the *Ledger* was more like a family.

My family.

His gaze moved past Maddie, the social worker, to a man he'd never seen. Andrew, the interpreter.

Diesel would be doing a thorough search of his background and finances. Just in case the guy got greedy.

"Diesel. Thank you for coming." Dani gave him a smile that made his pulse skitter. It was mostly relieved, her smile, but there was also something else there. Trust. That she trusted him with this was enough to make him hope.

If nothing else, it was a damn good place to start.

"Always." He'd always come when she needed him. The woman had no clue just how much power she held over him. But this was about the boy looking at Diesel like he was his salvation. He sat next to Michael, bumping shoulders with the kid. "You okay?" he signed.

Michael shook his head. "Scared," he signed back.

"I understand. But Rex is a very good attorney. I've known him for years. I'd trust him with my life."

Michael nodded, seeming to relax a little. "I don't want to tell anyone anything. This is . . ." He clenched his eyes shut for a few seconds before starting again. "What happened to me . . . it's so embarrassing."

"I get it," Diesel signed, hoping the kid could see the seriousness in his eyes. "But if you were mugged, would you be embarrassed to tell?"

"No, but this is different."

"Of course it is. But for now, for the next hour or however long it takes us to get through what you have to say, pretend in your mind that you were mugged. Tell Rex everything just like you would then, okay?"

"Okay." Michael turned to Rex, squaring his thin shoulders. "I'm ready."

Diesel glanced at Dani, his pulse stumbling again. She was looking at him with gratitude and respect and a bit of awe. *Add those to trust, and I can work with that.*

Rex smiled kindly. "I know this is difficult, Michael. Please know that I'll do everything I can to get you through this. Plus you have Dani and Diesel. Let's start at the beginning. Your stepfather, John Brewer, is dead. Your mother accuses you of doing it."

"But I didn't!" Michael interrupted. The interpreter's voice clearly communicated the boy's dismay.

Rex nodded. "I hear you."

"Do you believe me?"

"I can't know that until you tell me everything. I want to believe you, Michael. I know Diesel and Dani already do, and that's powerful. Okay, so you had a gun hidden under your pillow. Those are basically the facts we have right now. That your mother accuses you doesn't mean that I think you did it. But it's a fact that she's accused you. Do you see the difference?" When Michael nodded, he went on. "I want to note all the facts we have. To do that, I'll be asking you for your opinions, too. Okay?"

Michael nodded again, suspicion in his eyes. "Okay."

"Why did your mother accuse you of killing your stepfather?"

Michael swallowed hard. "She knew I hated him."

"Did you hate him?" Rex pressed.

Michael nodded again, his jaw setting with fury. "I did."

Rex held the boy's gaze. "Why?"

"Because he beat me. And . . . did other things. He'd come to my bed and—" Michael pressed a fist to his mouth.

Diesel placed his hand between Michael's shoulder blades, anchoring him. "Think of it as a mugging," he signed one-handed. "You didn't do anything wrong."

"She said I did." Michael's hands shook as he signed. "She said I seduced him."

Diesel bit back a roar of rage. "I don't believe you did that. You shouldn't believe it, either."

Michael nodded shakily and turned back to Rex. He took a deep breath and signed, "He raped me. And when I told my mother, she said I was lying—at first. But then she found bloodstains on my sheets and got so mad at me. She said I seduced him. That I was the reason he didn't want her anymore."

Rex jotted notes on the legal pad in front of him. "What did you say to your mother?"

"That she was wrong." Michael lifted his chin. "That I'd go to the cops."

Rex's smile was gentle. "That was very brave. What did she say then?"

"She said she'd throw me out. That I'd have to go to the homeless shelter." Michael gritted his teeth, but a tear leaked out of his eye. Angrily, he dashed it away. "I'm fourteen. I'd end up in the system. And I've heard the stories about kids in the system. Plus, that would leave Joshua alone. I don't think the bastard hurt him, but if I left, he might. I wasn't going to let that happen. So I shut up and stayed."

"For your brother," Rex clarified.

"Yes."

Rex took a moment, and it was only because Diesel had known him so long that he knew the man was shaken. Rex had a good heart under his Armani suits. Diesel hadn't been lying when he'd said that he'd trust him with his life.

"Okay," Rex finally said. "Where did you get the gun?"

"From Brewer's safe."

Rex's brows went up. "You knew the combination?"

"I watched him open it once. He didn't know I was there."

"Weren't you afraid he'd miss it?"

Michael shrugged. "He had five more. I got the one at the back."

Diesel wondered what else was in the bastard's safe. The contents would fall into the hands of the cops soon enough, if they hadn't already been entered into evidence. He wished he could get a look at that haul.

Brewer's finances were hinky as hell.

"Do you know how to fire a gun?" Rex asked, jotting more notes.

Michael nodded. "I found a YouTube video with captions. I didn't fire it, but I practiced loading, aiming, and flipping the safety."

"The police will be able to verify that the gun hasn't been fired recently," Rex said. "So I don't want you to worry too much about having it. They have the gun now. When did you take the gun from your stepfather's safe?"

Michael drew a deep breath, let it out. Glanced at Diesel, looking for encouragement.

Diesel nodded. "You can trust him."

Michael squared his shoulders. "Last Friday night. Or maybe it was Saturday morning by then. A week ago. I don't remember what time, but it was still dark outside."

"Why then?" Rex asked. "If he'd been abusing you all that time, why did you get the gun just last week?"

Another deep breath, another shuddering exhale. "You won't believe me," he said, his face the picture of misery.

"We believe you, Michael," Diesel signed.

"It's stupid. It sounds stupid to me, and I saw it."

Rex put his pen down. "What did you see, Michael?"

Michael gave Diesel another quick glance before returning his full attention to the lawyer. "I saw a man kill my stepfather."

Diesel's eyes widened and he looked at Dani, who'd turned to him, her expression equally stunned.

Rex blinked once. "Who was it?"

"I don't know. But I think he broke Brewer's neck." Michael had grown pale again, dangerously so.

Dani tapped the boy's shoulder. "Breathe," she told him, and together the two took long, deep breaths. "Maybe you should start with the beginning of this part," she said once Michael no longer appeared to be on the brink of fainting.

"I woke up to pee that night, and I saw Brewer going into Joshua's room. So I followed him and . . . I saw him sticking a needle into Josh's arm. A big syringe. I grabbed Brewer and we fought. He threw me on the floor and I was dizzy. By the time I got up, he was down the stairs, carrying Joshua to the front door. Joshua was sound asleep. I think he didn't wake up because of the drug."

"So you followed?" Rex asked.

Michael nodded. "I got Joshua away from him before he reached the front door and we fought some more. He kicked me in the ribs a few times. That really hurt. So I . . . I grabbed a shovel from the fireplace and hit him with it. After he fell down, I grabbed Joshua and ran."

"Where were you going?" Rex asked.

"I didn't know, but I needed to get Joshua away from him, so I ran. I was going to the road. I guess I was going to try to stop a car so I could take Joshua to the ER. He was out cold. I didn't know how much Brewer had given him, or what he had given him, but Josh is so little. He could have died. Anyway, I got to the old orchard and tripped on a branch or something. I went down, but I didn't drop Josh."

Dani had stiffened where she sat, her cheeks flushed with anger, and Diesel wondered which part of the exam she'd done corroborated this part of Michael's story.

Rex shot a questioning look at her, before turning to Michael. "Did your stepfather follow you?"

"Yeah. At first I thought maybe I'd knocked him out with the fire shovel, but he came after us in his car, down the driveway. I hid in the orchard. That's when another car came up the driveway—an SUV—and blocked Brewer's car. A man got out, dragged Brewer from his car, and . . . he put his hands on Brewer's neck and he went limp. But that was after Brewer pulled a gun on him."

Rex looked up from his notepad. "What did the man do with your stepfather?"

"Put him in the back of his SUV. Then he drove away."

"And left Brewer's car in the driveway?" Rex asked.

"Yes. For then."

Rex's brows went up. "He came back?"

"Later that night. I was standing guard in Joshua's room with the gun."

"That's why you got the gun," Rex said. "Because of the man who killed your stepfather?"

"Or Brewer. I didn't know he was dead then. I thought he might come to, then come back. I wasn't going to let him try to take Joshua again."

Again Rex smiled gently. "How many nights have you guarded Josh, Michael?"

"Every night since then."

Dani's expression softened with sympathy. "You must be so tired."

Michael nodded wearily. "I really want to just go somewhere and sleep."

"You can do that when we're finished," Rex promised. "Where was your mother Friday night and Saturday morning?"

"She has rich friends in Louisville. She was partying with them."

"Does she do that often?" Rex asked.

"Once or twice a month. Sometimes more."

Rex noted it. "And your stepfather was always home then?"

Michael swallowed. Nodded.

"That's when the abuse happened?" Dani asked him.

Another nod. Two tears ran down Michael's face and Diesel's eyes stung. Michael's mother had basically sold her sons for a good time.

At least my mother didn't know, Diesel thought. It would have killed her if she had.

Diesel squeezed Michael's good shoulder very lightly, just to remind him that he was there. "You said the man who killed Brewer came back. Have you seen him since he left in the SUV?" he asked the boy.

Michael sagged in his chair. "Yes," he voiced in a ragged whisper. He was growing too weary to even sign.

"When?" Rex asked.

"A few hours after he took Brewer away in his SUV. I was in Joshua's room and felt the shaking of the garage door opening. I thought Brewer was coming back."

"You didn't think it could be your mom?" Rex asked.

Michael shook his head. "She'd be too stoned to walk, much less drive home. She didn't get home until Monday morning."

"Did the man come into your house?" Dani asked.

Michael's expression became haunted. "He came into Joshua's room. He was so . . . big. I had the gun in my hands, but they were shaking." He shook his hands to demonstrate. "I was hiding behind the chair."

"So he didn't see you?" Rex asked carefully.

"No. I don't think so. He just came in and stood at the foot of Joshua's bed." Michael frowned. "Like he was . . . checking on him or something. I just hid there, frozen, until he left," he added, his mouth bending in disgust. "Lot of good I was."

"You were amazing," Dani said. "You saved Josh from your stepfather that night. He's here because of you, Michael."

"I guess so."

Rex tapped the table, getting Michael's attention. "Can you describe the man?"

Michael's gaze darted up to Diesel, half-guilty and half-apologetic, confirming Diesel's suspicion that he'd been afraid of a man who resembled him.

"He was bald," Michael told Rex. "Really big. Like Coach. But not Coach," he insisted. "I saw the guy's face. It wasn't Coach Diesel. The man had no tattoos." He sighed. "Sorry, Coach."

Diesel took his hand off the boy's back so that he could sign. "It's okay. I thought as much." He looked at Rex, continuing to sign as he spoke. "When Michael arrived at the soccer practice field this morning, he was so shocked when he saw me that he fell backward. He was having a panic attack, I think. But then he realized I wasn't the person he was afraid of and we were fine." He locked gazes with Michael. "We are fine, right?"

Michael's nod was immediate and firm. "Hell, yeah."

Rex's lips twitched as he wrote it all down. "Got it. The police will probably want you to sit with a sketch artist and describe the man, since you saw his face. Will you do that, Michael?"

"Yes. But they won't believe me."

Rex put his pen down. "*We* believe you. Besides, they don't have enough evidence to keep you. I want you to tell them everything you told me. If they don't believe you, we'll begin investigating on our own, so that we can back up your story with facts."

Michael's eyes grew wide. "You can investigate? Like the cops?"

"Sometimes better than the cops," Rex said with a smile. His eyes flicked knowingly to Diesel. Like he knew Diesel had already begun. "I have a private investigator on my staff at the law firm."

Michael frowned. "I can't pay you."

Rex leaned across the table, his hand extended. "Some work I do for free. If you'll let me, I'll represent you."

Michael shook his hand, then dropped it to sign. "For free? Seriously?"

"Seriously. It's called pro bono and it's legit. You won't owe me anything. Plus Diesel is one of my best friends. I'm happy to do this for him and for you. Although I think we'll be okay. I think the detectives will believe you. At least enough to search for the facts themselves. Kimble and Novak are good men."

"They're my family," Dani said. "My cousin and my brother. They won't rest until you're safe and they know the truth."

Michael finally relaxed—so much so that he swayed in his seat. Diesel put an arm around his shoulders. "Just a little longer, kid," he signed one-handed. "Then you'll go to Dr. Dani's house to sleep."

"Will you stay?" Michael asked.

Diesel risked a glance at Dani, relieved when she nodded once. "I will. I'll keep you safe. You and Joshua."

Michael tilted until his head rested on Diesel's

shoulder. "Thank you. I don't know why you're being so nice to us, but thank you."

Rex stood. "I'll go get the detectives. Hopefully we'll be out of here soon."

Cincinnati, Ohio
Saturday, March 16, 8:30 p.m.

Cade blinked hard, trying to stay awake. He was fucking exhausted. He hadn't slept in over twenty-four hours and he wouldn't be able to sleep until he'd taken care of the fisherman. Which was why he was sitting in a darkened SUV outside a darkened house, waiting for CSU tech Charlie Akers to get home.

He'd been able to find everything he'd needed on Mr. Akers's social media, including his most recent photo, which confirmed he was the same man Cade had met at the crime scene, and that Akers complained a lot about money.

That explained the man's minute hesitation before declaring he wasn't interested in what Cade would pay for information. Akers had left himself open to convincing. Cade could be very convincing.

Sitting up straighter, Cade slapped both his cheeks to wake himself up. "Come on, Akers. Get your ass home."

As if obeying his command, a car pulled up in front of the small house, stopping long enough for Akers to stagger out and wave to the driver. Cade rolled down the window.

"I'm good," Akers said loudly, with a slur to his words. "You can go."

The man was totally drunk. While that might make him more pliable, Cade hoped he wasn't so drunk that he'd forget what he'd heard at the crime scene.

"You sure, man?" the driver asked. "I can walk you to the door."

"Yep. I'm just fine." Akers waved him on. "I'm gonna go to sleep."

"You do that," the driver agreed. "Maybe things won't be so shitty tomorrow."

"Yeah, they will be," Akers said sadly. "'Cause Quincy fuckin' Taylor is still my fuckin' boss and I'll still be on fuckin' suspension."

Suspension? That was good news. Akers's anger might make him more inclined to spill the beans.

The car drove away and, pulling on a pair of surgical gloves, Cade got out of his SUV, reaching Akers just as the man stumbled, nearly falling to his knees.

"Whoa, there," Cade said. "Let me help you."

Akers looked up at him, frowning. "I know you. You're that fucking reporter that got me fucking suspended."

"You got suspended? You didn't even tell me anything."

"I know!" Akers said vehemently. "Fucking Agent Taylor. He didn't believe me."

"He's a prick." Cade led Akers up the front steps, giving him support when his knees started to buckle again. "Seems like you should at least get paid for information if you're being suspended. I mean, you're doing the time without doing the crime."

"S'true. All of the above." Akers fished his keys from his pocket, closing one eye and squinting at the lock. Cade took the keys and opened the front door. Akers stumbled in and spun, pointing one finger at him. "You need to go."

"I will. Let me help you first." He put his arm around the man and led him to his bedroom. "You sure you won't take my money? Seems like you earned it."

Akers nodded. "I did." He squinted. "How much?"

"Five grand." Like hell, but Akers was too drunk to know better.

"That's a lot," Akers said. He dropped backward

onto the bed, resting on his elbows. "Depends on what you want to know."

"The name of the fisherman."

"Why?"

"Because nobody else has it. I'll get a scoop and my boss won't fire me."

"Somebody should keep their job," Akers muttered. "Sorry, though. Can't tell."

Cade had to focus on not clenching his fist and punching Akers's lights out. He smiled instead, backtracking and coming in from a different angle. "Why didn't Agent Taylor believe you?"

Akers's head fell backward, like he was too tired to hold it up. "'Cause I might have talked to a reporter in the past."

Cade's lips twitched. "Might have?"

Akers harrumphed. "Fine. Did. It was just a little thing."

"Did you get paid for that?"

"No," Akers said sullenly.

"Then let me pay you, since you're already kind of convicted, dude."

Akers raised his head slowly, blinking owlishly. "I am, aren't I?"

Cade said nothing, just let Akers ruminate on this truth for a few seconds. *If I have to, I'll get the fisherman's name with a threat.* He still had his gun, after all. But he'd have more confidence in the information if it were freely given.

"Garrett," Akers said abruptly.

Cade managed to conceal his excitement. "That's his name?"

"Yep. George Garrett. He was a fucking mess, I gotta say."

I guess so. Cade felt a tiny bit of pity for the man who'd wanted to catch some crappie, but had pulled up a human head instead. "Do you know where he lives?"

"That'll cost you extra, *dude*." Akers began to laugh as only the truly drunk could do. "Double."

"Fine. I'll pay it," Cade lied.

"Fine. Somewhere in Oakley. Don't remember the street."

"That's okay. That'll be sufficient." He pulled Akers to his feet. "Come on, you need to take a little trip."

Akers frowned and struggled. "No. Wanna go to sleep."

"Don't worry. You will." Cade hoisted the man over his shoulder and carried him to the entrance of the basement stairs, right off the kitchen. Akers was fighting him now, the surprise of being lifted like a sack of potatoes having sobered him up enough to know something was not right.

Duh. Having a stranger follow you into your house shoulda been your first clue, Einstein.

Setting the man on his feet, Cade gripped his head and twisted, satisfied at the cracking sound. He then gave Akers a little shove, watching as he tumbled down the stairs, landing in a heap. Gingerly, he walked down himself, careful to touch nothing until he got to Akers's body. He wouldn't leave prints, but he might leave a mark in the dust that coated the railing and the walls. Pulling his trusty stethoscope from his coat pocket, he listened to be sure Akers's heart beat no more. It did not.

He knew it would look like an accident. After all, he'd watched his father kill his mother in the exact same way.

Now to George Garrett's house. And then I can sleep.

Chapter Seven

Dr. Dani's house looked nice, Michael thought as he got out of Coach Diesel's truck. Opening the back passenger door, he unbuckled the safety belt on Joshua's booster seat and started to scoop him into his arms, because Joshua had fallen asleep within minutes of leaving the newspaper office.

His little brother had chattered nonstop as they'd walked to Coach's truck, telling Michael about the coloring and the treats and the toys and his trip into the basement to see the old-fashioned printing press. Coach Diesel's friends had taken good care of him, the one named Marcus even buying the booster seat for Joshua because he was too young to sit in a car without one.

Michael was more than grateful. Joshua would never need to know any of what Michael had shared with the lawyer, then the cops. At least the cops were pleased with the sketch the police artist had done based on his description.

They'd seemed to believe him. It was a weight off his shoulders. But the bald man was still out there, still a threat to both Michael and Joshua. More so now if he found out that Michael had seen him so clearly.

A light tap on his good shoulder had him straightening his spine in a rush. His gaze jerked up, then higher still because Coach Diesel stood next to him, hands moving. He'd driven them from the police station to the *Ledger* office and then here, since Dr. Dani had left her own car at the clinic.

"Let me get Joshua," Coach signed. "You go inside with Dr. Dani." He looked up and down the street with narrowed eyes and Michael realized he was looking for someone.

The bald man? Reporters? Either way, Michael wasn't going to argue. He pulled his hoodie up and hurried to Dr. Dani's front steps. She'd opened the door ahead of him, but before letting him in, she abruptly turned to face him.

"Do you like dogs?" she asked. "Joshua, too?"

Michael nodded. "Yeah. Why?"

She gave an exaggerated sigh of relief. "I forgot to ask before we started for home. I have a dog. He's extremely . . . enthusiastic."

Michael eagerly stepped around her, then laughed when a golden retriever crawled across the floor on its belly, commando-style, its tail wagging triple time.

She shook her head, smiling at the dog. "I told him 'down' and he knows hand signs." She showed Michael the correct sign, then shrugged. "Technically, he's still down, but he's very excited to meet new people, so he crawls like that."

Michael dropped to his knees, patting his thighs, laughing again when the dog bounded to him. A second later his face was getting bathed by the dog's tongue. He buried his face in its soft coat and hugged its neck.

"He smells good."

"He should. He had an appointment with the groomer today. She has one of those vans that comes to your house. We're friends, so I gave her the key. She takes Hawkeye into her salon and makes him beautiful."

Him. The dog was male. And named Hawkeye. "You named him after the Avenger?" he asked. The hard-of-hearing Avenger who wore hearing aids. It was the name he'd have chosen for a dog if he ever got one of his own.

"I did. I've been deaf in one ear since I was born. I thought Hawkeye was a great name for my dog, even though he has amazing hearing." She leaned down to scratch behind the dog's ears. "Right, boy?" She looked over her shoulder and signed the dog back to the down position. The dog instantly obeyed, but its tail never stopped wagging.

Coach Diesel was coming through the door, Joshua tucked into his big arms, the little boy still asleep. Dr. Dani quietly closed the front door after him, looking at the dog with her finger pressed to her lips. She pointed Coach toward the stairs, then gestured for Michael to follow her. He did, Hawkeye scrambling to walk at his side.

Dr. Dani had a room for each of them. Nice rooms with soft beds. Posters on the walls. Everything looked new. And safe. She pulled the blanket on the bed back and Coach put Joshua in it so gently that Michael's throat hurt. No one was gentle with Joshua. *No one but me.*

He lifted his eyes toward the ceiling. *Thank you,* he thought. If there was a God, he should be thanked, because this day could have ended up so much worse. Yes, the cops had talked to him about Brewer's murder, but he'd had a fancy lawyer and Coach and Dr. Dani hadn't left his side. The cops seemed to believe him. He wasn't in juvie, so he called that a win.

This foster situation was turning out to be okay. A nice house, a safe neighborhood, a foster parent who was kind *and* who signed, a cool dog, Coach Diesel to keep them safe . . . And he and Joshua got to stay together. That was the most important thing.

Dr. Dani covered Joshua up, then opened the closet door, revealing boxes labeled PANTS, SHIRTS,

PJ'S, SOCKS, and UNDERWEAR. She rummaged in the PJ's box and pulled out a pair of Spider-Man pajamas. She put them on the foot of the bed, then pointed at the stuffed animals on the closet shelf below the boxes.

"Pick something you think he'd like," she signed to Michael without voicing, so they didn't wake Joshua.

Michael went straight for a soft dog plushie. "He has one kind of like this at home," he signed, then carefully placed it next to his sleeping brother.

Dr. Dani gave Michael's shoulder a pat. "This room is safe. Nothing that can hurt a small child in here. The windows are locked." She tugged on one to demonstrate and it didn't budge. "They're also alarmed." She pointed up at the ceiling, where there was a strobe light, dark at the moment. "If the house alarm or smoke alarm goes off, the lights strobe. Your room has the same. It's set up to be secure and safe for deaf and hearing kids."

Wow. He had not expected any of this.

She showed Michael a baby monitor on Joshua's nightstand. "I carry the receiver in my pocket. It vibrates when there's sound. If Joshua wakes up and is afraid, I'll know and can get to him quickly. Your room has the same setup, plus I have a panic button for older kids. Press it if you need anything, okay?"

He nodded, overwhelmed. "Thank you. So much."

She smiled at him, then the two of them turned to find Coach Diesel filling the doorway. He'd been staring at them. Or at Dr. Dani. Michael wondered what their deal was, but knew better than to ask.

He wasn't sure *they* knew what their deal was, but he'd caught each of them looking at the other when they thought no one noticed. Kind of like high school, he thought with an eye-roll. Dr. Dani was even blushing. He didn't know older ladies like her still blushed. She had to be at least thirty. Maybe older. But he knew better than to ask that as well.

Coach moved out of the way and Dr. Dani showed Michael to his room. It was . . . super-nice. Posters of sports stars—hockey, baseball, football, even soccer—covered one wall. A second wall had photos of dancers, ice skaters, and musicians. The third wall was floor-to-ceiling shelves. Covered with books.

Michael's pulse gave a little start. He loved books. There were none at his house. It wasn't a question of affording them. They had money. Their real dad had left them money in his will. It was supposed to be enough for them to live comfortably, which, for Michael, included books. His mother just never saw the point.

He glanced at Dr. Dani to see her smiling at him. "You like books?" she asked.

He nodded. "I love the library at school. I go whenever I can. I take Joshua to the public library, too. We take the bus. Can I . . . can I read any of them?"

She grinned at him. "Take your pick."

He reached for Brian K. Vaughan's *Runaways*, but yanked his hand back at the last minute. "What if I have to leave before I'm done reading it?"

Dr. Dani's smile faded a little. "Then you can take it with you. I can get another." She took the book from the shelf and placed it in his hands. "It's yours."

Holding the book to his chest, Michael stepped back as she made her way to the closet and started rummaging in the boxes she kept there. Coach Diesel had followed them into the room and now stood staring at the shelves of books. Kind of like he'd never seen them before. Michael wondered if this was the first time Coach had been here.

That was interesting. Watching the two of them might be more fun than TV.

Diesel pulled a sci-fi novel from a top shelf and showed the cover to Michael. "I like this one. Have you read it?"

Michael shook his head, unable to hide his surprise. "No. *You* like sci-fi?"

Coach's lips twitched. "I do. I'm a gamer. I love sci-fi and fantasy stories. Books or movies or games, doesn't matter to me."

Michael perked up. "You're a gamer? Me, too."

"Tomorrow I'll go home and get my system, if Dr. Dani says it's okay."

She looked over her shoulder at them with a nod. "Fine with me." When she turned, she held pajamas, sweats, and an unopened package of briefs. She put them on the end of the bed.

"Coach, would you mind letting Hawkeye out? He can run in the backyard for a few minutes."

Coach Diesel gave her a slow nod, some kind of unspoken, unsigned communication passing between the two of them.

When Coach and the dog were gone, Dr. Dani led Michael to the closet at the end of the hall. "Bathroom is first door on your left. Towels are in here. Hang them up if they're still clean. If they need to be washed, take them downstairs to the laundry room in the basement. I'll show you how to run the machine. You can wash your own clothes."

He nodded, relieved. He didn't want anyone seeing his bloody pants or briefs. It was humiliating enough as it was. "I will. Thank you."

She gave him a knowing look, then opened the closet door and reached for a first aid kit on the top shelf. "Gauze and salve for your injury," she said, all business.

His cheeks flamed, but he nodded. *Think of it as a mugging.* Coach's suggestion had worked with the lawyer and it worked here, too. He relaxed and took the first aid kit from her. "Thank you," he said again.

"If you need anything, text me. My cell phone number is on the card next to the bed. If you start bleeding, you need to let me know. You can text me or write a note and leave it on my desk if you aren't comfortable telling me in person, but you need to tell me. I won't embarrass you, but if you continue bleeding, I need to get you to another doctor."

He drew a breath and nodded. "I promise."

"Okay." She pulled a few bright red plastic bags from the top shelf. "Biohazard bags. It's just good practice to put your bloody gauze in one of these and seal it up. If you leave the bag in the cabinet under the bathroom sink, I'll check there and collect it."

He took the red bags gingerly. "Okay."

"What about allergies? Food? Medication? For either you or Joshua?"

He shook his head. "Nothing that I know of."

"Who's your doctor?"

"I don't have one. I guess Joshua did, because he got his shots when he was a baby. I went with my mother when she took him to his doctor visits. She was kind of messed up then. My dad had just died. In Iraq. She drank a lot before then, but the drugs started after my dad died. She was pretty stoned the whole first year. She got a little better, but then it got a lot worse."

Dr. Dani's expression softened. "So you've always taken care of Joshua?"

He nodded once, grateful that she understood. "Yeah." He'd been the one to hold Joshua while the doctor stuck him with needles. He'd given his little brother his baths, changed his diapers, rocked him to sleep, fed him during the night. His mother had simply checked out.

"I took care of my little brother when he was an infant, too," Dr. Dani said. "My mom and stepdad died when I was sixteen. Teething and midnight feedings were *so* much fun, am I right?"

He huffed a chuckle. "So much fun."

She looked to one side, head tilted like she was thinking, then nodded. "Do you get services in school? Speech therapy, anything like that?"

"No, but I do have an interpreter, just like Greg."

"No hearing aids or cochlear implant?"

He shook his head again, sadly this time. "My dad—my *real* dad—once told me that my mom was afraid to let them cut my head open. He wanted me to have the surgery, but she insisted it wasn't safe. But it is. And now it's too late." He was fourteen, long past the time doctors did the implant surgery. Usually they operated on kids under two.

She lifted her brows. "Of course it's safe, and it might not be too late. You're a little old now, but if you're interested, we can still look into it. For now, relax. I'm going to make dinner and maybe watch some TV. If you want to eat with Coach and me now, that's fine. If you want time to yourself, that's fine, too. If you get hungry, there's food in the fridge. Help yourself to anything you find, just don't eat in your room, okay? I hate mice."

Michael grimaced. "Mice?"

"I've never had them, and I don't want to start." She looked around the corner, but they remained alone. "The basement is a rec room with video games and a TV." She smirked. "I'm a gamer, too, but don't tell Coach. I don't think he knows."

"You planning to hustle him?" he asked.

"Maybe. I haven't decided yet. Take a shower, get comfortable. We'll talk about all the serious stuff later, okay?"

"Okay."

"Any questions?"

"Yes." *Why are you doing this for us? What are you going to want from us? And why do you have biohazard bags in your closet?* But that wasn't the question that rolled off his hands. "Are you rich?" He immediately winced. It was rude, but he'd asked and now he couldn't take the question back.

She blinked her mismatched eyes in surprise. "No. Barely middle-class. Why?"

He gestured around him. "All this. The nice furniture, the books, the strobe lights. It all costs money.

We had money and my mom never put in emergency strobe lights." He'd always wondered what might have happened had there been a fire. He wondered if his mother would have bothered to wake him up.

He was sure Brewer would have left him to die.

"Well, I'm nowhere near rich. I'm house poor, actually. I used to be an ER doctor, and that paid well, but the clinic can't afford those kinds of salaries. I pay my mortgage and bills, but that stretches every penny."

He frowned. "So you take in foster kids for the money?"

Something flashed in her eyes. It looked like hurt. "I'm sorry," he signed.

"It's okay. It's a reasonable question. No, I do this because I had a deaf teenager come through my clinic last year. They'd been hurt."

Michael swallowed. "Like me?"

She nodded once. "I wasn't certified for emergency placement then, so they went into the foster system."

"They?"

"The teen was trans. Their pronoun is 'they.'"

Michael sucked in a breath that burned. He'd heard horror stories about what bullies in the foster system did to both deaf kids and trans kids. A deaf trans kid? *Shit.* "What happened to them?"

"Kids snuck up on them. Hurt them. They didn't die, but it was close. They're forever traumatized."

"So you became an emergency foster parent."

She nodded. "Yes. As for all the nice furniture and gadgets? You remember me telling you that Coach has rich friends?"

"Yeah," Michael answered cautiously. "The rich guys just gave you money?"

"Pretty much." She smiled. "See—and you might have to make a chart later to remember all this—my brother Deacon who you met today? His wife is named Faith. Faith's uncle is the rich guy. His name is Dr. O'Bannion. You remember Marcus, Coach's friend from the newspaper office?"

"The one who took care of Joshua. Yeah. And?"

"Dr. O'Bannion is also Marcus's dad. He is very nice and very generous. When I was getting this place ready for kids, Dr. O'Bannion showed up on my doorstep with his checkbook. All the books, the games, the clothes in the closets, the jungle gym out back—it's all because of him."

Michael frowned. "Why did *he* do it?"

Her smile was gentle. "Sometimes people are just nice, Michael. It's okay to trust. We're good people. We *will* take care of you." She closed the closet door. "Take your time. Dinner won't be ready for an hour or so. We can watch a movie after if you want to."

Michael's eyes burned. "Thank you."

She cupped his cheek. "You're welcome. You're worth it."

He watched her go down the hall toward the front of the house. When she was out of sight, he blinked and the tears streaked down his cheeks.

No, I'm not worth it. But Joshua is.

Cincinnati, Ohio
Saturday, March 16, 8:50 p.m.

Dani stopped outside of her kitchen doorway for just a moment, just long enough to brace herself. She was about to be alone with Diesel Kennedy. And it scared her to death, because she wasn't sure what she wanted anymore.

She swallowed hard as she peeked around the doorframe to where he sat at the table, staring at his laptop, the expression on his handsome face one of intense concentration. He rubbed the back of his neck with one of his huge hands.

Hands that had held her so damn gently. Hands that had held Joshua so gently. Hands that had encouraged Michael when the boy had been so scared.

Think of it as a mugging, Diesel had told Michael. And it had helped the boy get through the telling of his abuse.

It had been a . . . specific thing to say, the expression on his handsome face oddly personal. She wondered about it now, watching him glare at his computer screen. Wondered if the advice had come from his own experience. But that was not a conversation she felt comfortable initiating. If he felt like sharing someday, she'd listen.

As if sensing her presence, he abruptly shifted his gaze from his computer to where she stood, one of his dark brows lifting in question. But he said nothing. Just watched her watching him.

Busted. Dammit.

Cheeks heating, she entered the kitchen, going straight to the freezer, grateful for the frigid air cooling her face. And for the freezer door that hid her from his intense scrutiny. "I got Michael settled," she said, simply for something to say.

"Good," he replied, the single word sending a shiver down her back.

She leaned farther into the freezer, clutching the door handle for support. She loved his voice, the gruff growl of it like a firm stroke over her skin.

"Are you okay?" he asked cautiously.

She closed her eyes, her face reheating despite the cold air surrounding her. "Of course," she lied. "Why wouldn't I be?"

"Because you've been staring into the freezer for over a minute and haven't touched anything." He drew a breath and let it out in a loud whoosh. "If you want me to leave, I can watch the house from outside."

Dani jerked her head out of the freezer and looked around the door in surprise. "No. I don't want you to leave."

His massive shoulders relaxed. "Okay. I thought I was . . . y'know, making you uncomfortable."

Well, yeah, she thought. But not the way he thought. She closed the freezer door and went to the sink to fill the kettle. "Of course not," she said, then clenched her jaw. This was ridiculous. They were acting like they were Michael's age.

She put the kettle on and turned to face him, leaning against the counter. "Meredith says you like tea. I have some chocolate mint. Would you like that?"

He relaxed further, and she had to fight to keep her eyes on his and not drop to his lips, which were curving in a smile. He had the nicest mouth.

He had the nicest everything. She could admit it, even if only to herself.

"I would," he said. "I'm kind of a chocolate addict."

"Me, too, but I try to limit my chocolate intake." She made a face. "I'm careful with my nutrition. Helps keep my immune system healthy."

He nodded, his eyes never leaving hers. "That's important. You've got a physically demanding job, especially considering so many of the people you see on a daily basis are communicably sick. And now, fostering two boys? Two boys who come with a helluva lot of stress? You need to stay well."

She narrowed her eyes, studying his face, searching for any indication that he was setting her up. Waiting for the inevitable "but." But no "but" followed. He was serious. Absolutely sincere.

His eyes narrowed back at her when she remained silent. "Why are you looking at me that way?" he asked.

"Because my family says that, but then they suggest that I should stop working so much or that I should give up medicine entirely or that I shouldn't foster kids who might be 'dangerous.'" She used air quotes.

He tilted his head to one side, appearing distressed. "Who says that to you? Deacon?"

She chuckled a little darkly. "No, he knows better. I have kicked his ass in the past and I can do it again."

His lips twitched. "I'd pay money to have seen that. How old were you?"

"Thirty-three." She grinned at him, suddenly at ease. "It was last month. He was testing my self-defense moves. Snuck up on me. Ended up staring at the ceiling."

He returned her grin, making her heart flutter again. "Then he deserved what he got," he said decisively. "Does Adam say you should quit?"

"Never. And if he thinks it, he's smart enough to keep it to himself. He's seen me kick Deacon's ass."

"Then who wants you to quit?"

Sighing, she got mugs from the cabinet and filled the teapot infuser with loose tea, just as she did every evening, finding comfort in the routine. "My aunt Tammy, mostly. She and my uncle Jim took us in after my mom and stepfather died, and we'd lived with them off and on before that." She winced, remembering. "Not the happiest environment for kids. Adam got it worse than we did. Uncle Jim was a drunk. Still is."

The kettle boiled and she filled the teapot. Taking it and the mugs to the table, she sat directly across from Diesel with a sigh. "He'd hit Adam sometimes. Mostly he was emotionally abusive. Adam's still struggling with it."

Diesel nodded. "I know. He's talked to me about it a time or two, when I'm over at their house visiting Meredith. She's good for him."

Dani smiled. Adam had never been happier since he and Meredith Fallon had finally gotten together after a year of dancing around each other. *Kind of like Diesel and me,* she thought, her smile fading.

She couldn't offer Diesel what he really wanted—the happily-ever-after that all their friends had found. She wanted that, too. But she'd also wanted it with Adrian, had even accepted his marriage proposal, only to later break him. Literally.

Roughly she pushed aside the mental picture of

Adrian's body lying on the rocks, his final words ringing in her ears. *Are you happy now? I hope you're a better doctor than you were a lover.*

She was. She was a damn good doctor and that would have to be enough. Maybe someday she could be a better lover, a better person, but that wasn't today.

She wasn't ready. Not yet. Maybe not ever. And Diesel Kennedy was too nice a man to have to settle for anything less than a woman who could love him completely. And not "maybe someday," but now.

"Meredith's very good for him," Dani agreed quietly. "She's exactly what he needs." *And I'm not what you need, even though you think I am.*

Diesel's eyes narrowed, but he said nothing as he reached for the teapot and filled their mugs. He just watched her, his gaze steady and unyielding.

Kind of like the man himself.

"So your uncle and aunt want you to quit?" he finally asked.

"Yes." She nodded, grateful that he'd pulled back to the topic at hand. "They've never gotten over my diagnosis. You know, my status."

He didn't blink. "That you're HIV positive," he said, putting it right there on the table between them.

She fought the urge to flinch, although just barely. After nearly four years of living with HIV, she still hated to hear the words spoken so baldly. Some days she almost managed to forget she had it.

Almost.

She nodded briskly. "Right. Tammy and Jim are convinced that I'm hiding information about my condition, that I'm sicker than I claim." She rolled her eyes. "Or that I'll give it to a patient or to one of them. That's mostly Jim. It doesn't matter that my levels are undetectable and have been for years. It doesn't matter that I'm diligent about protective wear. They're constantly reminding me that my clock is ticking and that life is too short to slave in a free clinic for people who 'don't deserve it.' Every so often they ask me if I've got AIDS yet. Aunt Tammy's even found long-term care for me, you know, for when I 'succumb.'"

Diesel grimaced. "God."

"Yeah," Dani agreed bitterly. "They treat me like spun glass. Like my life is already over. I've gone as far as showing them my latest lab results. Always undetectable. But they don't believe me."

His brows drew together. "Why would they mistrust you?"

She sighed. "Because I didn't tell them about my status. They had to hear about it on the news when I was outed." When a kid at Greg's school had somehow found out and spread the word, two and a half years ago.

Diesel's mouth tightened. "I read about that."

She chuckled bitterly. "In the *Ledger*?"

He nodded once. "Not at the time it happened. Marcus and Stone were in the hospital and we were all busy keeping the paper running."

"I remember," she said, pushing her bitterness aside, because so many other things had been happening at the time her status was revealed to the whole city. A serial killer had been on the loose, Deacon on his trail. The man had been after Faith, and after discovering that Faith and Deacon were lovers, had abducted Dani and Greg to lure her to him. "That was a busy week."

His gaze darkened. "That bastard hurt you."

"Not really. He busted my lip, but it healed. He hurt Deacon a lot worse." Her older brother had nearly died when he'd been stabbed while taking the killer down. She sighed, remembering her younger brother's terror. "Greg still has nightmares about it. He was abducted along with me."

"I know." Diesel's eyes were still dark, anger glittering in the chocolate depths. He looked . . . *dangerous*. It gave her an unwelcome thrill. "The bastard tried to use the two of you to force Faith into surrendering herself to him."

And it might have worked, but for Faith's quick thinking. Dani owed a lot to her sister-in-law.

She forced herself to smile. "We're all okay, though. Greg saw a therapist for a long time, and the nightmares seem to be more infrequent."

"And you?" he asked, so seriously that it made her heart hurt. "Did you have nightmares?"

Dani's smile faded. "Sometimes I dream that I'm trying to stop Deacon's bleeding but he dies anyway. I thought I'd lose him for sure that night." But most nights she dreamed of Adrian, his body lying broken on the rocks.

"But you're a damn good doctor," Diesel said gruffly. "Which is why I can't believe your family would want you to quit. Don't they understand how HIV is transmitted?"

She studied him carefully, remembering the night she had been stabbed outside the clinic. Diesel had been there, watching over her. He'd been the one to carry her into the ER, her blood all over him.

"Do *you*?" she asked. "Because you never freaked out when I bled all over you. You never even asked me if my levels were detectable."

He blinked, his anger abruptly gone. In his eyes she saw a sweetness that hurt her heart even more than his caring about her nightmares.

She had to look away. *I don't deserve that sweetness. I'm going to hurt him.*

"I know how it's transmitted," he said quietly. "I was a little rattled when the doctors put me in a decontamination room, checking me for open wounds. I didn't know about your status until then. But I figured that you wouldn't have been endangering your patients if your levels were detectable."

Swinging her gaze back to his face, Dani sucked in a breath. "Really?"

"Really." He sipped at his tea and made an appreciative sound. "This is good."

He was trying to change the subject and she wasn't sure why. "Diesel," she said, leaning across the table urgently, gripping his forearm. "You got tested, right? I told you to that day you visited me in the hospital." When she'd told him that she wasn't looking for a relationship and that he should move on and find someone else. "I know the doctors told you to. I made sure they did."

He froze, his eyes dropping to where she was touching him. When he looked up, the sweetness was gone, replaced by a hunger that made her suck in another breath, shivers racing all over her skin. She let him go, breathing hard, wanting to look away again, but unable to.

"Did you get tested?" she whispered. "Please tell me you did."

He leaned forward in his chair until their faces were only inches apart. "Every six months for the last eighteen," he whispered back. "But I knew I'd be negative. You were working in the emergency room at the time. I knew you wouldn't knowingly place anyone in danger, so you had to be undetectable. Undetectable means untransmittable, right? That's what the experts say."

"Right," she murmured, but his closeness had shivers running down her spine. Her gaze slid to his lips, wishing she could feel them on her own. *Just once.* But once would never be enough. So she eased back into her chair and closed her eyes, flattening her hands on the table, willing her heart to slow to a normal rhythm.

Which would be so much easier if he weren't looking at her. Even with her eyes closed she could feel his gaze, heavy and wanting.

And she wanted, too. So much.

She swallowed hard. "Every six months?"

"Yes," he said quietly. "I'm fine, Dani."

"I should have asked you directly long before to-day. I'm sorry."

She flinched when his hand covered hers, large and warm. "Given how your uncle and aunt have been treating you, I guess I understand why you didn't want to bring it up," he said calmly. *Soothing me.*

The seconds ticked by as neither of them moved. He sat patiently, his thumb caressing her skin, as shame washed through her.

Look at him. He deserves that much. She opened her eyes and found him staring at her, just as she'd known he would be. There was no recrimination in his gaze. "I'm glad you're okay," she managed to choke out. "I still should have asked you. Thank you again . . . for saving my life."

"You don't need to thank me. I wouldn't have been able to watch you die, even if I'd known your status before you were stabbed." He held her gaze for several more hard beats of her heart, then pulled his hand away.

She almost grabbed it back. Almost.

"Returning to my original question," he said, "don't your aunt and uncle understand how HIV is transmitted?"

She blew out the breath she'd been holding, grateful once again that he'd pulled them back on topic. "I really don't know. I've explained it to them. It's really just Jim who's the ass about it. Tammy doesn't fight him on anything, though. Which is why I'm so glad that Greg lives with Deacon and Faith now. Living with Tammy and Jim wasn't good for him. Jim has very strong beliefs, most of them ones I don't agree with. He pretty much hates anyone who isn't like him."

"Which is why you didn't tell them about your status," Diesel said, then shrugged one massive shoulder. "Makes sense to me."

Do not look at his shoulders. Focus. "My brothers knew and so did Adam. But none of us had told Tammy and Jim. I asked the boys not to. When the news broke . . ." She stared down into her tea, feeling her cheeks heat as she relived the humiliation of the entire community learning of her medical status. "Tammy and Jim were very angry with me. They had a right to be, I guess."

Diesel's chair creaked a second before his hand entered her field of vision, one thick finger tipping her chin up. Once again, his face was a breath away from hers.

Expression fierce, he held her gaze. "Why were they angry with you?"

She swallowed hard, unable to look away. His eyes were dark and held a touch of wildness that made her heart beat faster. "Because I was stupid enough to get HIV. Because I was selfish enough to keep on working. Because I was cruel enough not to tell them before."

"So they could already be telling you to quit?" he gritted out, clearly angry himself. But on her behalf. "That your 'clock is ticking'? That the people you serve at the clinic don't deserve care? *They* were selfish and cruel. Not you."

"I can be selfish," she whispered, her eyes stinging. *I've been selfish with you, secretly basking in your attention, knowing I can never be what you need.*

His head tilted as he studied her so intently she wanted to look away. But still she couldn't.

"I would hope so," he said softly. "I hope you can be selfish, at least sometimes. You're always doing things for other people. You deserve to do something for yourself."

She blinked once, sending hot tears streaking down her cheeks. Wishing she could have him. Wishing she could at least try. "You're too nice, Diesel. You're going to get hurt."

His eyes flickered with . . . what? Apprehension? Regret? "Who's going to hurt me, Dani?"

She drew a breath. "Me."

Chapter Eight

Leaning across the table, her chin still resting on his fingertip, Diesel held his breath as he asked her, "How will you hurt me?" His whisper was harsh. "And why?"

Her beautiful eyes, one dark brown, the other royal blue, shimmered with new tears that broke his heart. Misery was written all over her face.

When all he ever wanted was for her to smile at him.

The moment stretched on as she continued to stare up at him. He wanted to push her again. To make her tell him why she believed she'd hurt him. Because she did believe that. But he could see her trembling and knew that if he pushed, she'd flee.

So he waited, not moving a muscle. Still holding his breath.

"You want me." Her barely audible words were like a sledgehammer to the chest because she sounded so sad. So hopeless.

"Yes." It was pointless to deny it, so he didn't even try. He'd wanted her from the first moment he'd laid eyes on her, eighteen months before. If it made him pathetic, then so be it. He regretted nothing.

She blinked again and more tears fell. "You shouldn't want me. I'm not good for you."

He'd expected something like this, but it still hurt. "For me? Or for anyone?"

"For anyone."

Okay. He could work with this. He hoped. He brushed his thumb over her chin, then her lower lip. "I have one question and I want an honest answer." When she opened her mouth to speak, he pressed his thumb over her lips, silencing her. "Please."

If he sounded desperate, he didn't care. He *was* desperate.

Her nod was nearly imperceptible, but the power of it made him weak in the knees. "Do you want me?"

Once more he held his breath, waiting for her answer. Seconds ticked by as they remained frozen, him bent across the table, her looking up at him like she'd just lost her best friend.

Then, just when he was about to straighten his spine and concede defeat, her eyes slid closed.

And she nodded, her sorrow palpable.

He hadn't realized he could be full of joy and dread at the same time. "Why does this hurt you?" he asked as gently as he could. His voice was a perpetual growl, but he didn't want to growl at Dani. Never at Dani.

She blinked her eyes open in surprise. "Me? Hurt me? I . . ." She trailed off as her mismatched eyes flickered in sudden confusion. Then she licked her lips nervously as the confusion became regret. "I lost someone."

Diesel frowned, not having expected that explanation at all. He'd been sure she was going to cite her HIV status, and he was ready for that argument. He'd been ready ever since the doctors had told him to get tested after being exposed to her blood. "Who?"

"His name was Adrian."

Was. Slowly he let out the breath he'd been holding. Past tense. "He died?"

She flinched. "Yes." Then gave her head a small shake. "We were . . ." She hesitated, licked her lips again. "Happy."

But she looked even more miserable than she had before. And he had even more questions than he'd had before. Who the hell was Adrian? When had they been together? How had they been together? Lovers? Married? He swallowed back a growl at the thought of anyone touching Dani like that.

Then he forced himself to calm down and think. He wouldn't do himself any favors grunting like a possessive caveman.

Think, Kennedy. Who the fuck is Adrian? But he couldn't recall any of their mutual friends mentioning an old boyfriend, much less a husband.

How had Adrian died? And exactly how *happy* had they really been? Because she looked like she was about to cry, and he didn't want that.

Steadying himself, he cupped her cheek in his palm, his heart perking up when her eyes closed again and she leaned into his touch. Hope flared in his chest, bright and hot and . . . painful, because if she didn't mean it, it was going to hurt like hell.

It would hurt worse if he never tried.

"So," he murmured, latching on to her—albeit reluctant—admission. "You want me. You just don't want to want me."

She hiccuped a stunned little laugh, her cheeks going all rosy. "Yes."

"Not a bad starting place," he said lightly.

She shook her head, her cheek brushing against his palm because she hadn't pulled away. Nor had she opened her eyes. "You're incorrigible."

"Like that's the first time I've heard that." He caressed her skin with his thumb, relaxing an iota when her lips curved. He leaned in a little closer until he could smell the light scent of chocolate in her hair. His courage was bolstered by the rapid flutter of the pulse at the hollow of her throat. Her mouth was *right there*. So damn tempting. But he'd never take anything from her without permission. "Dani?" he whispered.

Her eyes slowly rose to meet his and he sucked in a breath. He still saw sorrow, but there was also heat. Hunger. And a yearning that was every bit as strong as his own.

He could hear the seconds ticking by, loud drumbeats in his head. Or maybe that was his pulse, because his heart was pounding like it would break free from his chest.

Finally she spoke, the single word not a question, but an answer. "Yes."

He reached for her, cupping her face in both hands. His trembling hands, he realized. He was shaking like a leaf. And then, after what had seemed like an eternity of waiting, he kissed her.

It was sweet. *She* was sweet. She smelled like chocolate and tasted like the chocolate mint tea they'd been drinking. *God.* He shuddered hard. He wanted her in his arms, but he didn't dare let her go even to move around to her side of the table. He didn't want to scare her away. He didn't want to do anything to jeopardize this moment.

Because he was *kissing* her and she . . . He couldn't suppress the growl that rose in his throat. She was kissing him back. He heard the scrape of a chair across the floor and then she was standing, leaning into the kiss, her hands gripping his wrists, running up his arms, over his shoulders, cradling his face.

She hummed a quiet moan, then pulled back way too soon, resting her forehead against his. Panting.

He'd made her pant. She might not want to want him, but she did, and he'd take it for now. But then she spoke and his confidence began to crumble at the edges.

"Oh God," she whispered, and his heart skipped an apprehensive beat.

He was afraid to ask, but he needed to know. "Oh-God-good or oh-God-bad?"

Her chuckle was shaky. "Both?" She lifted an equally shaky hand to caress his skull, her hand fanning back and forth in a rhythm that calmed his fears. But then she dropped her hands to his wrists, holding him in place as she pulled farther away, creating an unwelcome distance. "I don't want to hurt you."

He straightened, sliding back until he held her hands over the table. He wouldn't tell her that she wouldn't hurt him, because she had the power to destroy him, and that scared him to death. "Let's just see, okay?"

She bit her lower lip, still plump and wet from his kiss. "I can't promise you anything."

He met her eyes directly. "I didn't ask you to. Let's take it a day at a time."

She opened her mouth to say something, but was interrupted by a throat being cleared. As one they shifted to look at the doorway, where an uncomfortable Michael stood. Dani yanked her hands away like she'd been caught shoplifting.

Diesel wanted to snap at Michael for interrupting them, but pushed his annoyance down. It wasn't the kid's fault. In fact, he might have done them a favor, because Diesel was pretty certain he didn't want to hear what Dani had been about to say.

Dani gave Michael an awkward wave. "Hey."

Michael's gaze flicked from Dani's face to Diesel's. "I'm sorry," he signed. "I'm hungry."

Diesel didn't miss the sheer relief that passed over Dani's face. "I'll work on dinner," she said brightly, then turned to the fridge, where she stuck her face in the freezer a second time in less than an hour.

It's okay, Diesel thought. She could back off if she needed to. Because he'd seen the longing in her eyes, the need. She might not want to want him, but she did.

He smiled at Michael. "You settling in okay?"

Michael's smile was shy. He held up a copy of *The Hobbit.* "I started this one."

"A classic. I liked that one." Diesel sat down and

patted the seat next to him. "Why don't you read while I work?" He opened his laptop and briskly typed in his password. Which was Dani's birthday—the numbers and letters scrambled for security purposes, of course. Not that he was admitting that to anyone.

Michael sat. "Why is Dr. Dani staring into the freezer?" he signed without any sound. "Is she okay?"

Noting the white-knuckled grip Dani had on the freezer door handle, Diesel bit back a frown, his lips still tingling from their first kiss. Their first, because there *would* be a second. *Please, God, let there be a second.* "Don't worry," he signed, also without sound, certain that Dani wouldn't appreciate them discussing her. "She'll be fine." *I'll make sure of it.*

Cincinnati, Ohio
Saturday, March 16, 9:30 p.m.

Just once, Dani mocked herself. She'd known one kiss would never be enough. Not with a man like Diesel Kennedy.

Diesel.

There hadn't been anyone else since Adrian. Not a single man who'd caught her eye, who'd made her look once, much less twice. Not until Diesel Kennedy had entered her clinic eighteen months ago.

She'd known then. Known he'd be a problem, with his chocolate-brown eyes, his tall, broad frame. His ink. She shivered. *God, his ink.*

He pressed every button she possessed. That day and today.

I can't promise you anything.

I didn't ask you to.

And he hadn't. That was the problem. If he asked, she could say no. Resolutely, emphatically no. But the man never asked for anything.

He should. He should demand it. He should demand to know for sure. He should demand to know if she'd ever be ready.

She'd thought he would ask, all through these months, but he hadn't. He'd stayed cautiously on the periphery of their circle of friends. Watching her. Wanting her.

At least he wasn't watching her now. She'd felt his eyes on her as she'd hung out in the freezer for so long that even Michael had looked worried when she'd finally emerged, a frozen macaroni and cheese casserole in her hands.

Michael had been reassured with a smile and busied himself with the book he'd chosen. But Diesel had silently watched as she'd prepped dinner, preheating the oven and making a salad. But he'd finally returned his attention to his laptop.

Which he was currently frowning at, a deep groove etched in the center of his forehead. She clutched a dish towel, fighting the urge to press her lips to that groove, to see it smooth. To watch his shoulders relax.

And then to kiss him again.

Abruptly his gaze flicked right, to where Michael sat, the boy's lips moving soundlessly as he read. Diesel opened his mouth as if to ask Michael a question, then snapped it shut, shaking his head before looking up to meet Dani's eyes.

His were worried, and she wondered what he'd seen on his screen. It involved Michael, she was certain.

She clucked her tongue for Hawkeye, who sat next to Michael, leaning on the boy's leg. Michael was absently stroking his head and Hawkeye was in heaven. The dog always seemed to know when the kids needed him. Michael wasn't the first foster kid Hawkeye had glommed on to.

The dog immediately began to trot over, but Dani stopped him with a hand signal. "Bring your brush," she told the dog, pleased when he ran from the room.

Michael's eyes widened when Hawkeye reappeared with the brush carefully held between his teeth.

"Nice trick," Diesel murmured, then added the signs for Michael.

"No bite marks in the wood, either," Dani signed. "Good dog," she praised, scratching Hawkeye's back in the place that made his eyes close and his leg kick.

"Did you teach him?" Michael asked her, a grin lighting up his face.

"Yes," she said, "but not by myself. One of our friends has a shelter. I got Hawkeye there when he was just a puppy. My friend helped train him. Delores is amazing. Maybe you can meet her."

"I love dogs," Michael said wistfully.

"Then you should definitely meet Delores." Dani held out the brush. "Can you brush him? He loves it. But in the basement, if you don't mind. If you do it up here, his hair goes everywhere, and I hate pulling it out of my dinner. There's a TV down there. And an Xbox," she added.

Again, his eyes widened. "I can play it?"

"Of course! Have fun."

Michael took the brush and gestured for Hawkeye to follow him. When his footsteps quieted, Dani shut the door to the basement. "I don't want him to see what we're saying if he comes up more quietly than he went down." She took the seat next to Diesel. "What have you found?"

"Stuff that doesn't make any sense." He pointed to his screen. "I started checking Michael's stepfather's finances when I was at the *Ledger* this afternoon."

"I figured you had. Are you the private investigator that Rex Clausing mentioned? The one working for his law firm?"

"One of them." Diesel hesitated. "I hacked into Brewer's home network."

Dani blinked, unsure why this was something he felt the need to admit. "I know. You're a hacker. One of the best, according to Deacon and Adam. You've helped on a lot of their cases. Kate and Decker's, too." Kate and Decker were FBI agents who sometimes worked with Deacon, and who had been firmly enfolded in their circle. "Did you think I didn't know?"

He shrugged uneasily. "I wasn't sure how you'd feel about it. It is illegal, y'know."

Her lips twitched. He was . . . cute. Not a word she'd ever thought she'd associate with the man. But he was. And sweet, too. "I'm not the goody-goody everyone thinks I am."

His brows shot up, his cheeks growing flushed. "You're not?"

"No. I've even recorded Major League Baseball without permission. It's a slippery slope," she insisted when he snickered. "I could go all *Ocean's 8* any day now." She'd loved the heist comedy with the all-woman cast. She and her friends had watched it together one night and laughed till they'd cried.

"I can see it now," he said. "You, Scarlett, Faith, Meredith, and Kate, sneaking into Jeremy O'Bannion's wine cellar to steal his Château Lafite Rothschild, all wearing black masks that Kate knitted for you, armed with Mer's pink tactical pens with the engraved hearts that she buys on Amazon."

Dani laughed, unexpectedly charmed. And momentarily breathless at the smug smile of pride that curved his lips. It made her want to kiss him again.

She swallowed and shook her head, giving herself time to gather her composure. "Nah, the girls and I don't need any thousand-dollar wine. We're good with the stuff in the box. Now, fine chocolate? *That* we might risk prison for." She pointed to his laptop. "Seriously, if you hacked the Pentagon, I wouldn't tell. You've saved my life and the lives of my friends so many times . . . We owe you discretion."

The twinkle in his eyes dimmed and she wondered what she'd said.

"You don't owe me anything, Dani," he said quietly. "Everything I've done has been freely given."

Oh. Way to go, Novak. Make him feel like you're obligated by gratitude. She was filled by the sudden need to make him feel wanted. For himself.

Because he was. *And at some point I might even admit that to myself.*

She sighed. "That was ham-handed of me. What I *meant* is that you are part of our circle, the family we've made, because of *you*. Not because we owe you. Even though we do. I would never reveal your secrets." She thought of him encouraging Michael in that dreary room at CPD. *Think of it as a mugging.* "*Any* of your secrets," she added. "I promise." She let her words hang between them for a few seconds, then pointed to his laptop. "So what have you found?"

He continued to stare at her for a few heartbeats more, then, closing his eyes, he cleared his throat. And shifted uncomfortably in his chair.

Heat flooded her face as his reason for the movement registered. She glanced down, unable to stop herself. And then closed her own eyes.

Holy hell. He was . . . very proportional. *Everywhere.* Sexual arousal washed over her in a mighty wave and she clenched her thighs together.

There'd been no one in so long. No one since Adrian. Her hand moved, her fingers outstretched and aching to touch him, but she yanked back, closing her fingers into a fist.

Stop it. This isn't going to happen. Nothing is going to happen.

A loud scraping sound had her opening her eyes—in time to see him shoving his chair away from the table. He stalked to the freezer, opened the door, and stuck his head inside. Laughter bubbled up from somewhere deep inside her and she let it out, conscious that it was the second time in minutes that she'd sounded so happy.

He leaned back, glaring at her around the freezer door. "I'm glad you think this is funny."

"Not funny," she said quickly, anxious not to offend him again. "Not funny at all."

He simply raised his dark brows in clear disbelief.

"Okay," she amended. "It's funny. The freezer, I mean. You gotta admit it."

His lips twitched. "Okay, I admit it." He closed the freezer and retook his seat with a heavy sigh, his small smile gone. "What are we doing here, Dani?"

Nothing. But that wasn't true. Denying that there was something between them was disrespectful. Whatever the something was, it wasn't going to go anywhere, but she didn't say that.

Because she didn't want it to be true.

She drew a breath and let it out. "For now, we're helping two little boys who may be in danger from a big bald guy who killed their stepfather."

He nodded. "Right." He scrubbed his hands over his face, then focused on his laptop screen. "Like I said, I started searching through Brewer's financials this afternoon."

"Follow the money," Dani said. "I've heard Deacon and Adam say it often enough. Where did it lead you?"

"Brewer was spending a lot, but wasn't bringing much in. He sold their house two weeks ago, but the transaction didn't result in any kind of bank deposits, cash or otherwise."

"He didn't deposit anything in his or his wife's accounts? Did he use the money to buy something else?"

Diesel shook his head. "I don't see any record of a purchase. And his wife had no accounts in her own name. His name is on all of her accounts, and it appears he's slowly been bleeding her dry for at least a year. She had her own account, one with a sizable balance, but that was more than a year ago. She added him to her account and now the balance is close to zero."

Dani frowned. "If he didn't deposit it or buy something, then he must have found *somewhere* to cash the check for the house sale. Maybe he got a cashier's check at another bank." She had the sinking feeling that she knew what had happened to the money. She'd seen it before, just not on this scale. "Maybe he used the money to pay someone off. Someone who doesn't take checks."

"That's what I was thinking."

She pursed her lips. "Either drugs or gambling."

He nodded. "What do you know about that?"

"My father—my biological father—gambled and drank. Couldn't keep a job. That was why my mom had to move us in with Tammy and Jim. My father gambled away all of our money and then got himself killed in a bar fight. There was nothing left for us. No insurance, no nothing."

At least Adrian had left her a little money to pay off his debts. He'd also left her HIV positive.

Diesel's dark eyes softened in compassion. "I'm sorry," he murmured, then turned to his computer screen. "I think you're right about Brewer using the proceeds to pay off debts. The rate of his spending sure looks like he had some kind of addiction. The problem is, there's no record of the house sale. Nothing saying how much he sold it for. If I knew that, I could look for notations on a debt of that size."

"If there's no record, then how do you know he sold it?"

"Because he transferred the deed to a shell corporation. I still haven't dug through all the layers to see who bought it, and I've been at it for a while."

She glanced at the clock on the wall. "You were sitting here for less than thirty minutes while I started dinner."

"I started this afternoon in my office at the *Ledger*." He frowned in clear irritation. "I can usually dig to the bottom of a shell much faster than this."

"So whoever bought Brewer's house is very smart,

or has employed someone who is. That tells you something."

"Yeah," he muttered, sounding disgruntled. "What I do know, though, is that the house was the boys' mother's. It had belonged to her first husband, their father. He died before Joshua was born. He was army. Died in Iraq. She transferred the title to Brewer only two weeks ago."

"Not at the time that they got married?"

"Nope."

"What did Brewer do for a living?" she asked.

"He was an attorney, but it doesn't appear that he'd practiced for quite some time—a few years at least. There may be another explanation for what happened to the money he got for the house, other than gambling or drugs." Hesitating, Diesel glanced over his shoulder at the closed basement door. "Blackmail."

A shiver ran down Dani's spine. Mindful that Joshua was upstairs, could come down at any moment and hear them, she leaned toward Diesel and whispered, "Someone knew about Brewer molesting Michael?"

Diesel's jaw clenched and her feeling of trepidation grew.

"What?" she demanded in a harsh whisper. "Tell me."

He leaned in to whisper in her ear. "Brewer had photos on his hard drive."

"Oh my God." Dani mouthed the words, her voice having fled from her throat. "Of the boys?"

Diesel nodded grimly.

She covered her mouth, tears stinging her eyes. "No."

"I'm not telling the cops unless I have to. If they find them, then they find them, but I don't want anyone to have any more reasons to suspect Michael."

Dani nodded, swiping her eyes with the heels of her hands. "Dammit. I hate this. I hate to know this. I hate that it's true."

Diesel looked away. "I thought you should know. But maybe I shouldn't have told you."

Instinctively she reached for his face, cupping his cheeks and pulling him so that he looked at her again. "Yes, you should have. You did the right thing. Doesn't mean it's not hard to know." *Think of it as a mugging.* If she'd been unsure that Diesel had been speaking from experience, the shame in his eyes drove all uncertainty away. "The boys did nothing wrong. I hate that they were hurt, but they did nothing wrong." *And neither did you,* she wanted to add, but of course she did not. "I needed to know so that we can get them the right help, but this changes nothing. I will care for them—and *about* them—regardless."

Gratitude flickered in Diesel's dark eyes and Dani wanted to cry again.

"I don't think Michael knows about the photos," he murmured, gesturing to the basement door. "In them, he appears to be either asleep or in the shower."

Bile clawed at her throat at the thought of Michael being photographed when he thought he was alone and safe. "Let's not tell him unless we have to."

Diesel shook his head. "I think whether or not we tell him depends on whether any of the photos were uploaded. If they were, he needs to know how to protect himself should he ever be recognized. Either way, those kids are gonna need therapy. Lots of therapy. Both of them."

He suddenly looked exhausted, chin dipping, shoulders slumping, and Dani wanted—no, *needed*—to comfort him. Before she could overthink it, she laid a hand on his forearm and felt his muscles twitch at the contact.

When he lifted his chin to look at her, she gave him an encouraging smile. "Meredith is a good place to start." Adam's wife had helped a lot of kids, victims of all kinds of trauma. But she specialized in providing therapy to children and adolescents who'd been victims of sexual assault.

"I know." Diesel dropped his gaze to where Dani was touching him, staring for a long, long moment before covering her hand with his, making her shiver at the unexpected warmth. "I'm going to ask her to take Michael on as a client. Unless you know of a therapist who signs."

"Faith does, but she's not fluent. I can ask around. Until then, Mer can hire an interpreter." Dani knew that she should probably pull her hand away, but it felt too good sandwiched between his palm and his arm. "Can you find out if anyone else has hacked into the stepfather's hard drive?"

"I'm going to try after dinner. But first I'm going to identify who owns the shell corporation that bought their house." He attempted a smile. "Whatever you're making smells really good."

"Macaroni and cheese casserole. Comfort food for Michael and Joshua. My stepfather, Bruce, used to make it for us if we'd had a bad day."

"So your mom remarried?"

"After my father died, yes, but not for several years. And we didn't have Bruce that long. He and Mom died in a car accident when Greg was a baby. We ended up back with Tammy and Jim. But for a while, when we lived with Mom and Bruce, we were really happy."

Diesel's smile was sweet. "I'm glad you had that for even a little while."

He hadn't had any happiness. She didn't know how she knew that, but she could tell. She also strongly suspected he wouldn't want to talk about it. Rising, she pressed a quick kiss to his forehead, clearly surprising him as much as she surprised herself. "You'll figure out the shell corporation," she said confidently. "Maybe you just need to feed your brain. Bruce's mac-a-chee is a most excellent source of carbs."

She started to back away, but her hand was still trapped between his arm and palm. He scooped it into his and brought it to his lips, pressing a kiss to her knuckles before letting her go.

He stared her squarely in the eye, his earlier weariness nowhere to be seen. He was all challenge now. "Then bring it on."

For a moment she couldn't draw a breath. Then his mouth quirked up and she laughed. How was it that this man could make her laugh when she should be telling him "no" in no uncertain terms?

She opened her mouth to say exactly that, but instead heard herself say, "All right."

Chapter Nine

Grant Masterson stood in the enormous walk-in closet of his brother's Cincinnati apartment, mouth agape once again. He'd never seen so many suits outside of a clothing store. And they were expensive suits. He recognized a few of the designers, and those were ones he'd overheard on the television when Cora was watching some fancy awards show.

And shoes. *My God.* How many shoes could one man wear? He blinked, doing another dazed three-sixty. And then his gaze fell on a mirror.

That was slightly ajar. Because it was a door.

He'd pulled on the latex gloves he'd found in Wes's Cleveland safe before he'd touched anything in this building—even the elevator button. He'd been in luck, because the doorman's post was empty, a sign saying he'd be back in five minutes, so there had been no one to ask him questions about Wes that he couldn't answer.

Wes's Cincinnati apartment was astonishing. A wall of windows allowed a view of the river that Grant expected was a main factor in the price.

But the contents of this closet alone had to be worth

more than fifty grand. Grant thought of the brick of heroin that he'd carefully replaced in the safe, and wondered how many other bricks there had been.

A quick Google search had revealed that the street price for the single brick was close to six hundred grand. When he'd added up all the receipts he'd found and added the five hundred grand still in the safe . . . Wes had to have started out with at least three of the bricks. That was nearly two million dollars' worth of heroin.

It had left him dizzy and nauseated.

His cop brother had *sold heroin*. Those drugs were on the streets of Cleveland, being shot into the arms of addicts of all ages. And why?

For this apartment. These suits. Those shoes. And whatever was hidden behind the mirror.

He opened the mirror enough to peer in and frowned. There were more clothes hanging on a rack. He activated the flashlight on his cell phone and walked into the hidden room, about the size of a normal person's closet.

His frown deepened. Uniforms. He grabbed the sleeve of one and pulled it out enough to see that it was a repairman's coveralls. A Velcro patch on the left breast pocket was empty, but a strip of Velcro attached to the hanger held at least a dozen name tags, each with the name of a different local business—the cable company, power company, gas company, phone company, plumbers, electricians, and a pest control firm. Next to the coveralls were a priest's cassock and doctor's scrubs.

Grant backed out of the closet, drawing a deep breath as he positioned the mirror as he'd found it. Wes had done undercover work during his years in the vice department. Those uniforms might be for that.

Or Wes had been using them to buy and sell the drugs he'd hidden in his home safe.

His safe, which had the simplest of all combinations, one that Wes knew Grant would immediately try.

Had Wes *wanted* his brother to find his stash? To find all that cash? If so, then *why*?

"Undercover," Grant whispered. "Please let it be that."

Drawing another breath, he detected the smell of cigarette smoke. Wes didn't smoke.

Wes doesn't sell drugs, either. Except that he does.

Grant turned to the suits, sniffing them, then stopping when he got to one that had a stronger scent of smoke than the others. Figuring that this would be the suit his brother had worn most recently, he hesitantly put his gloved hand in the pocket. Finding it empty, he checked the other and pulled out a matchbook and a half-empty pack of Lucky Strikes.

I guess he does smoke. And then Grant saw the matchbook cover.

Oh. The background was black, both the lettering and the logo white. The lettering used an Old West font. *LOTR.* Below the letters was a simple drawing of an old-fashioned paddleboat on a winding river.

He held his phone to his mouth. "Siri, search Ohio River paddleboats and L-O-T-R." He waited impatiently for the results screen, then gave a single nod. "Not *Lord of the Rings*," he murmured to himself. *"Lady of the River."*

It was a riverboat casino, just over the state line in Indiana.

Of course it was. He added gambling to Wes's growing list of sins. Then he thought of the detective's obituary. Murder? Had his brother gone that far?

Where was Wesley? Grant knew where he had to start. Most of the casinos on the Indiana portion of the Ohio River were permanently docked, but the *Lady of the River* was not. According to their website, this was one of their selling points. The boat went out onto the river three times a week—Monday and Wednesday afternoons for business parties, and

Friday evenings, where it was first come, first served until the boat sailed at seven p.m. It remained docked during the rest of the week.

It offered a full range of games and slots, elegant bars, live entertainment, and a handful of well-appointed hotel rooms, which carried an ungodly price tag.

"*Lady of the River*, here I come." He started to drop the matchbook back into the suit coat pocket, but paused, turning it over instead. Nothing was printed on the back, which surprised him. Usually a business would add an address, a phone number, or at least a website somewhere. Not sure what he was expecting, he flipped the front of the matchbook up.

Bingo. A very small playing card—the Joker—was printed in gold, which made it pop from the black background. Below the card was the word *Walden* and what appeared to be a date, *03/08*, also printed in gold. March eighth was two Fridays ago.

But what was Walden? "Hey, Siri, search for Walden."

The first items in the results referred to Walden College, but the next was a Wikipedia link to a book by Henry David Thoreau. The bio for Thoreau answered the question.

Henry David Thoreau's best friend was Ralph Waldo Emerson.

"Blake Emerson," he muttered. The name on the rental agreement for this apartment. It could be a coincidence, but Grant didn't think it was.

Pocketing the matchbook, he headed into the bedroom. He'd searched the living room for a safe, but found none.

He glanced around, noticing a throw rug that didn't exactly match the decor. He was a little impressed with himself, he had to admit. *I suppose all those HGTV shows that Cora watches are coming in handy.*

He nudged at the rug with his toe, satisfied when

he revealed the corner of an in-floor safe. It, too, opened with their sister's birth date. The dread that had become his constant companion intensified as he lifted the safe's door.

Reaching inside, he pulled out two wallets. One held Wes's detective shield and police ID card. The other held his driver's license and credit cards. *He hid them because he's undercover,* he thought hopefully. *Please let him be undercover.* He opened the wallet with the detective shield and studied the photo of his older brother. They were three years apart, but looked enough alike that many people mistook them for twins, especially from a distance.

He hesitated, then put the shield in his own pocket. "In case he's in trouble," he muttered to himself. If Wes was in trouble, he might need someone to vouch for him.

Reaching into the safe again, he pulled out a gun he recognized as Wes's service weapon. He checked the chamber and the magazine. It was unloaded, so he set it aside. His breath caught in his throat, because the next gun he pulled out was not one he recognized. It had no serial number, the plate having been filed off.

Shoulders bowing with dread, he checked the chamber. One bullet, ready to go. He studied it until he figured out the release mechanism to empty the magazine.

It was a nine-bullet clip, but he counted only five bullets. Plus the one in the chamber . . . Three were missing.

Once again he thought of the dead detective and swallowed audibly.

Hands shaking, he replaced the clip and released the slide, covering the chamber. Setting the weapon aside, he reached into the safe once again and pulled out a cell phone.

A single tap to the screen had his eyes filling with tears. It was Wes's phone. No question. The wallpaper was a photo of . . .

Grant blinked, sending the tears down his cheeks. "Baby girl," he whispered hoarsely. It was their sister in her cap and gown and Wes in his dress uniform, arms around each other, smiling. A huge sign behind them read CONGRATULATIONS, GRADUATES!

Grant remembered the day. He'd taken the photo. They'd been so damn happy.

And then she was gone.

Please don't be gone, Wes. I can't lose you, too.

Grant swiped upward, certain he'd need a password. But he didn't. He frowned, wondering why Wes would be so careless. He started to touch the apps on the screen, then hesitated. What if this was a trap and the phone was set to auto-wipe itself if anyone tried to look at its contents?

He shook his head. "Don't be ridiculous," he told himself. Now he was getting paranoid.

He checked the screen, but he'd waited too long and it had gone dark. He swiped up again, but the angle was now different and the words *Face ID* popped up on the screen.

Grant had a similar phone, so he held it to his face. But it wouldn't wor—

"Well, shit." Apparently, facial recognition wasn't completely precise in its discrimination, because Grant could open his brother's phone.

Encouraged, he touched Wes's calendar and swiped back day after day until a single entry popped onto the screen. *LOTR Poker.* The date was two Fridays before, at nine p.m. The same date he'd found on the matchbook.

Relief soothed him. At least he had a lead. He found another calendar entry on Wes's phone, on March first, the Friday before the matchbook date. *LOTR. Richard.*

Grant continued to swipe, but found nothing more than a few shopping lists.

He checked the contacts for a Richard but found nothing. There were only Wes's known friends, family, and coworkers. Other than the wallpaper photo, the only photos on the phone were of Grant's kids.

Grant returned everything to the floor safe, hesitating when he handled the loaded gun. Should he take it? Would he need it?

Maybe, but he decided it was safer to put it back. If he were caught with an unregistered gun, he'd be in a hell of a lot of trouble.

He walked back to the living room and took another look at the amazing view. "I hope whatever you're doing is worth it, Wes."

Then he found the riverboat on Google Maps and plotted a route.

Cincinnati, Ohio
Saturday, March 16, 10:45 p.m.

Michael sat back in his chair with a sigh. His plate was scraped clean, his stomach truly full for the first time in weeks. He glanced up to see Dr. Dani smiling.

"It was good?" she asked.

"Really good," Joshua said enthusiastically, shoving another bite into his mouth. He'd padded down the stairs midway through dinner, rubbing his eyes sleepily and claiming the smells had woken him up. He pointed to the creamy noodles in his bowl. "This is my favorite."

"It's really good," Michael echoed. He liked macaroni and cheese out of the blue box—it was better than the crap they served at the school cafeteria—but Dr. Dani's was the best he'd ever had. He wondered if she'd show him how to make it, so that he could make it for Joshua when they left this house.

It was only temporary foster care, after all.

She tilted her head, studying him with those weird, mismatched eyes that seemed to see a lot more than he wanted to show. "How long since you've eaten a good meal, Michael?"

Joshua's spoon froze midway to his mouth, his smile fading as he waited for his brother to answer. Michael tried to laugh it off. "Well, I usually make dinner, but I wouldn't call it good."

Joshua's eyes narrowed. "He doesn't eat when he cooks at home. Only I do."

Coach Diesel turned in his chair so that he could see both Joshua and Michael. "Why, Joshua?"

"Because there isn't enough." Joshua gave him what Michael thought of as his "old-man" look. It hurt that Joshua knew that look. *He's just a kid.* He shouldn't have to worry about stuff like that.

Michael sighed. "I eat at school."

Diesel frowned. "Your mother doesn't buy you food?"

Michael lifted one shoulder in a half shrug. "She doesn't eat much."

"Because she's high?" Dr. Dani asked, compassion in her eyes.

Michael's gaze darted to Joshua. He would give anything to keep this conversation from his little brother. But Joshua knew the truth about their mother's drug use. They'd both seen her high. *Damn it all.*

"Yes," Michael acknowledged. "Brewer never ate at home. He went out a lot. Business meetings, he said. There wasn't a lot in the pantry. So . . ." He trailed off, looking at his hands, shame heating his face. He hated that they pitied him.

After a few seconds, he looked up through his lashes to see Dr. Dani and Coach Diesel silently communicating across the table with their eyes. Both of them cut to look at Michael when they realized he was watching them.

Coach Diesel looked serious. "How long has it been since you went to school?"

Michael glanced at Joshua. "A week." Since Brewer was killed and that big bald man came into Joshua's room. He guessed he'd be able to go back, now that Joshua had Coach and Dr. Dani to watch over him.

Coach's lips pressed in a tight line. "So . . . no real meals all last week?"

Joshua's eyes grew big. "Michael!"

Michael was about to look away again when Dr. Dani turned to him with a smile. "Well, you'll eat well from now on. Send me a text with your favorite meals. I'm going to the grocery store tomorrow."

Joshua tugged her sleeve. "And me? My favorites, too?"

"Of course." She ruffled Joshua's curls. "I already know you like mac-a-chee. And I'm betting you'll like what I have for you next." She waggled her brows. "Chocolate brownies."

Joshua bounced in his chair. "Can I help make them?"

"Of course," she said. "Michael, do you want to help?"

Michael shook his head. "I just like to lick the bowl."

"Same," Coach said, his expression relaxing again. "So . . . are you going to school on Monday?"

Michael looked at Dr. Dani. "Am I?"

She bit at her lip. "I don't want you to fall further behind, but I also don't want to risk reporters bothering you."

Or the big bald man, Michael thought, grateful they hadn't mentioned him in front of Joshua. "I can stay out a little longer. I won't be any trouble. I promise."

Dr. Dani's eyes were kind. "I know you won't. I have to go into the clinic on Monday for at least a few hours, but maybe Coach Diesel can stay here? Just in case anyone pesters you."

"I sure will." Coach shot him a challenging look. "Did I hear Dr. Dani mention Xbox?"

Michael grinned in spite of himself. "You did. She's got *Cuphead*."

Dr. Dani tilted her head. "That's the cute one with cartoon cups? It looks fun."

Michael wanted to laugh, but held it back. When he'd logged on, he'd found that she'd been playing the game last and was up to the final level, "Inkwell Hell." She was good. But she didn't want Coach to know.

Coach was smiling at her the way guys did when they were going to tell girls how things worked. "I'll show you how to play."

"I'd like that," she said, her mismatched eyes twinkling. "Now, let's clean up the dinner dishes so we can make brownies, because Joshua needs a bath and it's *way* past both your bedtimes. Luckily we can sleep in tomorrow. Normally we eat at six thirty and bedtime would be eight for Joshua and nine thirty for you, Michael, but this whole day has been a little peculiar."

You can say that again, Michael thought.

Joshua snuggled into her side. "I saw the Spider-Man pj's. Can I wear them?"

She kissed the top of his head. "You may *have* them."

Joshua hugged her neck, his smile bright and free of worry. "Thank you!"

Michael closed his eyes and wished they could stay here forever.

Cincinnati, Ohio
Saturday, March 16, 11:50 p.m.

Slouching in the driver's seat, Cade watched the taillights of the cruiser pause at George Garrett's house before continuing down the street.

Cade checked the time. The police drive-bys were spaced approximately an hour apart. The two closest had been forty-five minutes apart, so he had at least that much time before the next cruiser came by.

Finding the right George Garrett hadn't been terribly difficult. There had been several listed in the white pages, but only one had a vanity plate containing the letters DRFISH. Dr. Garrett was a pediatrician, lived alone, and had no dog, his Lab having died of old age during the holidays.

Facebook was *such* an asset. Garrett's page confirmed that he spent all his free time in the boat currently parked in his driveway, and that he'd planned to fish the Ohio this morning. He was supposed to have been joined by a friend, but the man had begged off at the last minute, citing a spring cold.

Lucky bastard, the friend. He'd missed out on the gore and . . . what was to come.

Cade didn't think Dr. Garrett would come to the door if he knocked. It was too late for legitimate visitors. But the doctor was still awake. Cade could see his shadow passing back and forth behind the thin shade covering what was probably a bedroom window. The man was pacing.

He couldn't blame him. Not an easy sight to unsee, a disembodied head being pulled from the water. *And if the good doctor was unfortunate enough to see my face as well?* He might have. Cade had been dumping the bodies of the two men he'd killed after last night's poker game after dawn. The fishermen had usually started out by then.

Cade would find out soon enough. He patted the pockets of his jacket, making doubly sure he had his gun in one pocket and his lockpick set in the other. Starting his SUV, he drove around the block and parked on the street behind Garrett's house, just in case he needed a quick getaway. The fences were four-footers, and he could jump those with no problem.

Pulling a ski mask over his face, he got out of his SUV and, keeping to the dark side of Garrett's house, headed to the back door. Even if the man had the place alarmed, Cade would have at least thirty seconds to make the shot and get out. He'd done it far faster in the past.

The dead bolt was tricky, but the lock on the door handle was no problem. Glancing at his watch, he noted the time and pushed the door open. Sure enough, there was a red light on an alarm panel just inside the door, so he needed to hurry.

Heading straight for the room where Garrett was pacing, he opened the door—and blinked at the barrel of the gun in Garrett's shaking hand. *That* was unexpected.

"You don't have a license for that," Cade said. He'd checked.

Garrett's laugh held a note of hysteria. "Really?" He showed his cell phone's screen, where a call to 911 was active, then pointed at the wall behind Cade. "I was afraid you'd come. I have an alarm panel in here. I saw it flash red. The cops are on their way."

Fuck. Then I suppose I have nothing to lose. Betting that the doctor couldn't make a shot with his hand shaking like that, Cade pulled out his own gun and shot him in the head in a fluid motion that left Garrett only enough time to gape in shock. He fired again, aiming at the fallen doctor's head to be sure it was a kill shot, then turned and ran like hell. He exited the way he'd entered just as the alarm began to shriek.

He'd jumped the fences and gotten his SUV down the street, about to turn at the stop sign, when the cops sped past, headed toward Garrett's house. Cade carefully turned the opposite direction, making sure he broke no laws.

Shit. That had been close. *Too close.*

But worth it. *I was afraid you'd come.* Garrett *had* seen him. *So now I've tied off all the loose ends.* All he needed to do was get home without attracting any attention. And sleep. God, he needed to sleep.

It might be time to pull up roots and move to another location. He didn't even have to get a new ID. It was a natural thing, right? His boss would be found dead sooner or later—of natural causes, thank you very much. Who knew what would become of the casino? Of course employees would search for other opportunities.

That was what he'd do. He'd get some sleep and then he'd figure out where to start over.

Cincinnati, Ohio
Sunday, March 17, 1:00 a.m.

Diesel looked up from his laptop when Dani came down the stairs and flopped onto the other end of the sofa. She'd changed into a pair of soft sweats that hugged every one of her curves. With an effort, he lifted his gaze from her curves to her face. And smiled. He was here, in her house. He'd kissed her and she'd kissed him back. He couldn't wait to see if she'd kiss him back again. "You okay?"

She blew a hank of white hair off her face. "I had to mop the floor and change my clothes after I gave Joshua a bath. He's quite enthusiastic. I was soaked."

Diesel was happy his laptop covered him sufficiently, because most of the blood in his brain had rushed south at the thought of her wet. And changing her clothes. He cleared his throat. "It was the sugar from all those brownies."

She laughed softly. "Probably. But he was so happy, I couldn't say no. And Michael is so . . . content when Joshua is happy."

"They're both asleep?"

"Joshua is. Michael asked that he be allowed to leave his light on to read. But I think he just doesn't like the dark. I showed him that his lamp has a nightlight setting. He was grateful." Her eyes, so strikingly different, filled with tears. "I hate that these kids are so damn grateful. I hate that Michael hadn't had food in a week because he was caring for Joshua."

"But we can respect that, right?" Diesel asked softly, because he did. "Michael did the best he could."

She sighed. "Of course. I know you're right." She

shifted so that her legs stretched out in the space between them. "Is this okay? My feet are killing me."

Her feet were mere inches from his thigh and his hand moved of its own volition, cupping one foot and tugging her closer until he could reach both feet. She made a startled sound that turned into a quiet moan as he began rubbing her soles.

"That feels too good," she murmured, her eyes sliding closed.

I can make you feel even better, he wanted to say, but held the words back. Not yet. "How long were you on shift before we got there today?"

"I got there at seven, clinic opened at eight. Busy morning. Mmm." She shivered when his thumb dug deep into her heel. "Right there. Don't stop."

Diesel closed his eyes and drew a deep breath, knowing he'd hear those words in his dreams tonight, but in a different context. "You have to go in tomorrow?" he asked, his voice going gruff.

"I'm scheduled for a few hours, but I'm going to call in a few favors. Hopefully I can get coverage through the first part of the week."

"I can stay with the boys," he countered, feeling a little defensive.

Her eyes, one blue, one brown, opened and locked on his. "I know you can. I trust you to do so. But I want to be here, too, just for the first few days. They all break my heart, all the kids who come through here as fosters, but these two . . ."

"Yeah," Diesel agreed. "They need you."

"They need you, too. Both as a male role model and for the investigation that I interrupted." Gently, she tapped her toe against his laptop. "What did you find while I was becoming a mermaid up there?"

He shifted again, even more grateful that his laptop covered him so well. "I found the parent shell corporation."

She beamed at him. "I knew you would." Sliding

back to sit up straighter, she pulled her feet from his grasp. "Tell me."

Feeling brave, he patted the cushion closest to him. "Come and see."

She studied him for a long moment, then scooted over until their hips almost touched. "Show me, then."

He filled his head with her scent, then focused on his screen, which displayed the end of his search. "I had to dig." Which was a gross understatement. "Whoever put this setup together did not want to be found out. I still don't know who or where the true owner is. There are too many layers and proxies." He glanced over at her, to find her staring at his screen. "You know what a proxy is?"

"I do. They're servers that connect other servers, usually to keep the users' identity hidden. My brother Greg was doing a little extracurricular work on his computer a few years back. Managed to hack into the school's e-mail system."

Diesel knew about this. He also knew that Greg was a much better hacker than he'd been a few years ago. Because Diesel had taught the kid himself, at Greg's request. Greg had heard about Diesel's hacking from his older brother, Deacon, and had approached Diesel independently. It was why Diesel had learned sign language. Not that Dani needed to know that right now. He had the feeling that she wouldn't be too happy to know her brother had such mad skills.

Diesel knew that Greg had managed to hack into his school's e-mail system and sent a message, supposedly from the school nurse, that a student in their classes was HIV positive. The kid in question was not, but that kid had been the one to expose Dani's status. By spreading the word that the other boy was also positive, Greg had hoped to discredit any information the boy spread about his sister.

Greg had come to Diesel, asking for his help in figuring out how the kid had learned Dani's secret to begin with. It hadn't taken much effort to get into the kid's e-mail, where they found he'd been in the ER one day for a sports injury and had seen Dani taking her pills. Recognizing her because of the identical white streaks she and Greg shared, the kid had become curious enough to take a photo of the pill bottle in her hand, and a short Google session later, he'd figured out her status. He'd e-mailed a friend to discuss blackmailing her, but word had spread before they could do so, and Dani's career at County's ER had been ruined.

Unfortunately, that kid was now dead. In the wrong place at the wrong time, he'd crossed paths with a killer. Which meant both Diesel and Greg had been forced to swallow their rage at the discovery and move on.

But the memory still made Diesel want to hit something.

"Greg was trying to protect me," Dani continued. "Got him a five-day suspension. Deacon's relationship with the principal was the only thing that kept Greg from getting expelled. I made him promise that he wouldn't hack anymore."

"I bet Deacon was a Goody Two-shoes in school," Diesel said, trying to change the subject, because he hadn't known Greg had made that promise. *Although I would have still helped him.* Because Diesel had also needed to know who'd ruined Dani's career. He'd have to get Greg to come clean with his sister, or he himself would have to at some point. Diesel couldn't lie to Dani, not about something so important as this, even if she never changed her mind about wanting him.

Dani laughed at his assumption about Deacon's good behavior. "Not so much. That's why he had a good relationship with the principal."

Diesel was genuinely surprised. "He was in her office a lot?"

"Oh yeah. Adam even more. But Deacon was charming, even then. Made things easier for me when I started high school, because I *was* a Goody Two-shoes."

"But not anymore," Diesel said slyly. "All that recording of Major League Baseball without permission . . . You badass, you."

She grinned at him, startling him into a smile of his own. "Tell me about the shells and proxies."

Right. He tore his eyes away from her grinning face. "Lots of proxies."

"You said that already."

She was laughing at him, but he couldn't be offended. It was a knowing laugh, like she was aware of what she did to him—and liked it. It was a nice change. And a good start toward her wanting to want him.

"So I did. Anyway, I found this operation at the core." He turned his laptop.

She leaned in to see, then leaned in farther, squinting. "What am I looking at? It's just . . . boxes with arrows connecting to more boxes with arrows."

"That was the problem. There are over eighty businesses interconnected with LJM Industries, the company that bought the Brewers' house. Some of them are connected to two, some three, and some even four other businesses, which are, in turn, connected to other businesses."

She glanced up at him. "It's like a snarled ball of string."

Diesel nodded. "That someone snarled on purpose, which is why it took me so long to figure it out. And now that I've untangled it, I still don't understand it. It's like a maze, but all the threads lead to this one company." He highlighted a separated thread connecting LJM Industries to a single entity.

"Raguel Management Services?" she asked. "What does it do?"

"Nothing, from what I can see. It's the name that's interesting. Have you heard of Raguel?"

She looked up at him. "Should I?"

"Not unless you've studied religion."

She looked surprised. "You have, I take it?"

"I've dabbled." He'd more than dabbled, minoring in religious studies in college. "According to the book of Enoch, Raguel was an archangel. A watcher."

Her eyes widened. "Oh." Then she frowned. "Book of what?"

"Enoch. In the Bible he gets one line—Enoch walked with God and then he 'was not,' because he was taken straight to heaven. But there's a whole book of Enoch—two of them, actually—that aren't considered canon. What you really need to know is that Raguel was tasked with delivering justice and vengeance."

Her wide eyes flicked up to his. "Oh. Wow. That *is* an interesting name, then." She leaned in closer, studying the various business entities on his laptop screen, all of which somehow also linked to LJM Industries. After about a minute of silence, she murmured, "I wonder who LJM is. Or maybe was?"

"Who?" That LJM was a person's initials wasn't an unreasonable assumption, as many small businesses were named with their owners' initials, or those of a founding group. But he didn't want them to run with their first assumption. "Why do you think LJM is a person? It could represent a group, like 'P&G' stands for the last names of its founders. Or it could stand for something totally different than a person."

"That could be true, except for the business names here." Still leaning over him, she pointed to the list he'd compiled as he'd untangled the mess, then turned her head.

His breath caught in his chest because her mouth

was only inches from his. She froze for a few pounding heartbeats, then ran her tongue over her lower lip. It wasn't a display; she wasn't being coy. That made the little movement that much harder to resist.

But resist he did. She was starting to trust him. He'd be content with that. For now. Hopefully she'd do more than just cuddle next to him in the very near future.

"What businesses, Dani?" he asked gruffly and her nostrils flared before she jerked her gorgeously mismatched gaze back to his laptop.

"Well," she started, but had to clear her throat when her voice cracked, which cheered him immensely. "*Well.* A few of these business names are also ways to describe a girl—or at least her hobbies. When I look at this list, I see a scrapbook of snapshots showing a girl's life." She pointed to the list. "You've got 'Skating Princess' and 'LG Varsity Dancing Divas' right here."

He shrugged. "'Skating Princess' doesn't have to be a person. It could be a company that makes clothes for skaters. Same with the 'Dancing Divas' business."

"True, but midway down the list is 'BittyBaby Mama.' That's what first made me think that LJM is—or was—an actual girl."

"What the hell is a Bitty Baby?" Diesel asked warily.

She smirked, amused. "A doll. Have you heard of American Girl dolls?"

"No. Should I?" he asked, parroting her words from earlier.

Her lips twitched. "Not unless you've either been a little girl or bought presents for one."

"I can truthfully say no to both."

She smiled at him. "They're dolls based on historical characters, aimed at the eight-and-up crowd. They introduced Bitty Babies later. They were targeted to younger girls, maybe three to five years old. They were also less expensive." Her expression became wistful. "My mom bought me a Bitty Baby when I was nine."

Tenderness warmed his chest. "So you were a Bitty Baby Mama, too?"

"I was. I'd wanted the Felicity doll, because she was a 'big girl.' I'd even asked Santa for her, on the off chance he was really real. I was so excited when I unwrapped the box, but almost cried when I opened it and saw a Bitty Baby instead of Felicity. Then Mom told me that she'd been saving for a year for Felicity, but only saved enough for the Bitty." She glanced up at him. "I remember making myself look excited because she'd been so happy giving it to me but then so sad when I was disappointed. She was happy again, and that's my best Christmas memory."

Diesel found himself smiling down at her. "That's a nice memory."

"It really is. See, my mom worked hard to feed us because my father was a drunk. I didn't realize until I was older what a sacrifice she'd made, spending over fifty dollars on a single doll. When I finally understood, I was glad I'd hidden my disappointment."

"You were only nine," Diesel murmured. He remembered being nine. Remembered how hard his mother had worked to feed him, which was why he'd never told her about . . . He swallowed back the flinch that had become instinctive whenever he thought about the man who'd hurt him like Brewer had hurt Michael. He'd only been six when it started, but even then he'd known that telling his mother would hurt her, so he'd kept his mouth shut. He now knew that he should have told her anyway, that he'd been manipulated into silence. His mother would have protected him, whatever it took.

"True. But I knew it wasn't right to hurt her feelings." Dani's mouth quirked up. "Turns out that my mom knew I was pretending. She told me later that she'd been pretending to be happy, too, after seeing my disappointment. That was the first Christmas we

had at Bruce's house, after Mom married him. Bruce
made a good living and we could afford things we
couldn't before, living with Jim and Tammy. Four
years after the Bitty Baby, she was finally able to give
me the Felicity doll." Her smile softened. "I cried,
then she cried." She chuckled. "Poor Bruce and Deacon had no idea what was going on."

Diesel found that he had to clear his throat. How
he wished his mother had known he'd only been pretending to be happy. "Do you still have the dolls?"

"Oh, yeah. I was tempted to sell them on eBay
when I was a poor med school student, but I could
never bring myself to do it. Felicity was my memory
of happy times with Bruce and Mom. And selling
Bitty Baby would almost have been like selling a real
child. I'd been that baby's mama." She tapped his laptop screen. "Just like LJM was."

Diesel highlighted "BittyBaby Mama" and focused on the list of companies, shoving his roiling
emotions down deep. None of this was about him. It
was about learning as much as he could about Michael's dead stepfather and the bald man who'd killed
him. Right now, LJM and the transfer of ownership
of Brewer's house was their best lead.

Now that he knew what to look for, he saw more
company names that fit Dani's theory. "Here's 'Jonas-
Bro Fan' and 'Bieber Girl.'" He grimaced. "Can't say
I'm a fan of LJM's taste in music."

Dani laughed softly. "So you agree that LJM is
probably a person?"

He nodded absently, still staring at the long list.
Her theory was based purely on supposition, not
much more than a guess. Still, as guesses went, it was
a good one. He could float with it for a little while.
"Almost all of the other business names could represent elements in a girl's life as she grows up, so yes.
I'll leave my mind open to other possibilities, but for
now let's assume that LJM is a person and all these
company names describe her in some way. We'll run

with it for a little while. If we don't get anywhere, we'll start back at the beginning."

"Okay." Then she frowned. "But *why* would they name all these companies after LJM, whoever she is? You said that the shell companies were hard to untangle, which suggests that they have something to hide. But if they've named all these companies after a person, that's not very stealthy."

"No, it's not." He shifted to study her confused expression, wanting to understand her thought process. He had the feeling that her brain was as beautiful as the outside of her. "So why do it?"

"I'm guessing that they're either clever or stupid. Assuming that they're clever, they've decided to hide in plain sight." She glanced at him. "Right?"

"Makes sense. Somehow LJM links to Brewer, because they bought his house. But if LJM is a person and not actually a company, then that narrows our search for a connection."

Her pleased smile was quick, then gone as she returned her attention to his laptop. "'BittyBaby Mama' and 'Skating Princess' have me thinking of little girls, but 'varsity' in 'LG Varsity Dancing Divas' indicates she was in high school. Or maybe both? Maybe LJM grew up?"

"With you so far. What does the 'LG' stand for?" Scanning the list, he thought he knew, but he wanted to see if she'd come to the same conclusion.

Dani ran her finger down the list, stopping at the name he'd noticed. "Here's a company called 'La-Grange Lacrosse Laurels.' So maybe the 'LG' in 'LG Varsity Dancing Divas' means LaGrange. High school girls also play lacrosse, so it doesn't contradict 'varsity.' Maybe LJM was a lacrosse player at LaGrange High School? Is LaGrange a place?"

Adrenaline had Diesel's skin tingling as he opened a new browser tab and did the search. "It is, up in Lorain County, near Cleveland."

"Makes sense." She snapped her fingers and pointed

again. "This business is called 'Geneva OTL Getaway.' Geneva-on-the-Lake is a resort town near Cleveland."

"I've been there. It's nice. And I agree with everything you've said so far. But why did you say that LJM is or *was*?"

Dani shrugged. "Because you said that all the companies link from LJM to Raguel the vengeance dude."

His lips twitched. "The vengeance dude. Absolutely." He winced when she poked him in the side. "Ow. That hurt."

She scoffed. "No, it didn't. It hurt me worse. You're like poking a brick wall. I think I broke my finger."

He lifted the finger to his lips and kissed it. "There. Better."

She huffed, flustered, a blush making her cheeks rosy. "It's fine, thank you. Focus, Diesel." She pointed the finger that he'd kissed at his laptop. "You've got this entity here, LJM, that bought the Brewers' house, but no money actually changes hands."

"That I've been able to find."

She waved his words away. "Either way, a week later Brewer gets killed by a mysterious bald guy who just breezed back by to check on a kid that Brewer had sedated and had been trying to remove from the house. Which isn't threatening at all." Sarcasm poured off her.

She was intoxicating like this, her mismatched eyes alive and sparkling. He had to force himself to listen to what she was saying.

"I'm thinking it's safe to say that Brewer is—was— a bad man," she said dryly. "He tried to do *some*thing to Joshua. Thankfully Michael saved Joshua from whatever that was. He *raped* Michael. He took photos of both of the boys and neglected them while their addict mother didn't feed them enough food and threw bowls at their heads. Maybe Brewer also hurt this LJM person, and the Raguel vengeance dude"— she glared up at him, daring him to laugh—"was out to ruin Brewer."

Hearing the word *raped* effectively eliminated any desire he might have had to even smile. "That makes sense."

She sighed, sounding frustrated. "But why all the companies? What purpose do they serve? If LJM is about revenge, why not connect it straight to Raguel? Why tangle it up with all these shell companies?"

"Because whoever bought Brewer's house does have something to hide. It took me forever to unwind all these companies."

She rolled her eyes. "It took you a few hours."

"For a task like this, a few hours seems like forever."

"Well, the company names have significance. Someone took a lot of time setting them up and then tangling them together. Once we figure out what they have to hide, the companies should make more sense."

We. She'd said *we,* making his heart flutter hopefully. "Like I said, your theory makes sense. Very smart." He stole a quick glance at her, wishing he had the words to tell her just how much she impressed him. "But I already knew you were smart."

Her brows lifted pointedly. "Thanks?"

Shit. Apparently those weren't the right words. Flustered, he squared his shoulders. "You know, you've got the whole doctor thing going on." When her brows lifted even higher, he looked around the room exaggeratedly. "Do you have a ladder? I seem to be in desperate need of one."

Her lips twitched. "To climb out of the hole you keep digging deeper?"

He nodded, wincing. "You *are* smart. It's just one of the things I like about you." He blew out a breath. "It was a compliment. Just a poorly delivered one."

She chuckled. "Then I'll say thank you." Backing away so that she no longer leaned over his arm, she regarded him thoughtfully. "So this whole hacker thing. Where did you learn it?"

He nearly sighed with relief at her topic change. She was asking him questions about himself now. Which hopefully meant that she wanted to know him better. That was a good sign. "Taught myself, mostly. They didn't teach hacking in the comp-sci program at Carnegie Mellon," he added with a smirk.

"I guess not. So . . . Carnegie Mellon. That's in Pittsburgh, isn't it?"

He nodded. "Steelers fan, through and through. Sorry about that."

"I won't hold it against you," she said. "When did you graduate?"

"Seven years ago, after I got a medical discharge from the army."

"You served with Marcus," she said quietly.

He wasn't surprised that she knew that. Their circle of friends was pretty tight and nearly as tangled as the entities he'd just unwound. Her sister-in-law, Faith, was Marcus's cousin, so it made sense that Dani and Marcus had crossed paths. "Yes. In Iraq."

"That's what Marcus said. He also said you saved his life."

"He would have done the same for me."

"I know he would have. But he also said you saved the lives of four other people and got hurt in the process. You spent a long time in the hospital, recovering. Which was why you used to have PTSD triggered by white coats."

Not exactly true. His fear of white coats had started years before he'd been old enough to escape to the army. "The key words are 'used to have,'" he said evasively. "I don't anymore." He'd overcome it. For her.

She held his gaze for a long moment. "I'm glad." Then her eyes abruptly widened and she nearly dove at his computer screen. "White coats," she said, scanning the list of entities strung out in an untangled line.

He leaned in to see where she was looking. "What about white coats?"

"That was the name of one of the businesses. APG White Coat Distribution."

"Okay?" He frowned. "And?"

"I went to medical school at UC."

"I knew that. Undergrad at Xavier, med school at the University of Cincinnati, residency in St. Louis." She flinched visibly when he mentioned St. Louis, and he felt immediate regret when her eyes shuttered. What had happened to her there?

But then he knew. It was the same look she'd had when mentioning Adrian, her dead lover. "Sorry," he murmured. "I didn't mean to bring up bad memories."

She swallowed hard. "It's okay. It's just that St. Louis is where I met Adrian."

Knew it. He wanted to growl, but instead simply nodded. "I figured that."

"You would." She forced a smile. "You're smart, with that comp-sci thing."

This time he pointed at the screen because he couldn't bear to see the pain tightening her face. "White coats and UC Med School?"

She nodded hard once. "Right. Look at this business—APG White Coat Distribution. I think LJM went to med school at UC. There's a ceremony all entering med students participate in—the White Coat Ceremony where they get—"

"Their white coats," Diesel finished. "So it's a distribution."

"Yes." She was nodding emphatically again and he was relieved to see the spark return to her eyes. "Exactly. The 'APG' stands for the Arnold P. Gold Foundation, which sponsors the ceremony."

"And why UC?" But Diesel saw the entry she was pointing at and answered his own question. "Bearcat Medical Services." The mascot for the university was a bearcat. "Okay. Got it."

"LJM may have gone to UC undergrad, too," she said. "Scioto Associates. Scioto Hall's a dorm, and med students don't generally live in the dorms." A triumphant smile tipped her lips. "We may be able to get her name."

He'd already figured on searching—or hacking, if he needed to—the med school's rosters to find students with the initials LJM, but he wanted to know how Dani would approach it. "How?"

"We know when she was an undergraduate, because Scioto Hall was closed for years. It got renovated and didn't reopen until . . ." Her brows furrowed. "I'm not sure of the exact date, but I can look it up."

Diesel quickly typed out the search. "Reopened in 2016. Renovation started in 2014, but it hadn't been used for a residence hall since 2008."

"All right. If she got her white coat, then she'd at least finished her first year of med school. Let's start with last year's ceremony. She would have had to have graduated from undergrad in 2017. Still in time to live in Scioto, but just barely, because the 2016–17 term was the first time that students lived there in a decade."

Diesel liked the odds better now. "We have a one-year window of her possible attendance at UC's medical school."

Dani frowned. "Unless she was an undergrad student in 2008, when Scioto Hall last housed students."

"Unlikely. All of these businesses were established within the last year. A few within the last nine months."

"I wonder why they added more companies later. They're not real companies, are they?"

Diesel shook his head. "No. They might hold money for a little while, until it can be transferred to one of the other companies, which is what was happening here. Money moved all around these businesses, feeding LJM Industries. Other than that, they're empty. Shells."

She made a face. "Makes sense, given that they're

shell companies, right? Which ones are the most recent?"

Diesel highlighted a few lines in his spreadsheet. "'Laurels Lilies, Rosemary & Poppies,' 'Seahaven 42N x 82W,' and 'Brothers Grim Consulting.' No, wait. That's Sea*heaven* 42N x 82W, not Sea*haven*."

Dani sighed. "She died. LJM died."

Again, he agreed but wanted to hear her thoughts. "How? Why?"

"If you mean how and why did she die, I don't know. If you mean why do I think she died, then 'heaven' and 'lilies' were enough for me. Poppies are for remembrance, and in some cultures represent death or eternal sleep." She took out her phone and did a Google search. "Rosemary is also for remembrance. And, y'know, there's Raguel, the vengeance dude."

He smiled at her. "The vengeance dude clinched it."

She smiled back, then sobered. "What is '42N x 82W'?"

"Coordinates." Diesel looked it up on the map. "*In* Lake Erie, a few miles offshore."

She looked over his shoulder. "Near Cleveland. That's her heaven, in the lake. I bet they dumped her ashes there. And 'Brothers Grim Consulting'? Could this be her family, looking for revenge?"

He returned to the window with the list of companies. "It's certainly possible. Like I said, we can run with the theory for a while."

She frowned at his screen. "It's . . . all here, for anyone to figure out."

"Anyone who can untangle the business entities and who knows about white coat ceremonies and Scioto Hall," Diesel countered.

"True. But why would they do this? I could make a few phone calls tomorrow and get her name. Why would the vengeance dude be so careless?"

"Maybe he isn't being careless. Maybe he—or they—wanted someone to know. Maybe they wanted someone to be afraid—if whoever they're aiming for took the time to figure it out. I'm betting the 'Brothers Grim' didn't believe anyone would. They're operating under the radar. Way under."

"It still doesn't make sense. Why go to all the trouble of tangling the companies if they wanted someone to figure it out? Why name them the way they did in the first place? Why give away the clues?"

"Good questions. I don't know. It's still possible that LJM isn't a person at all."

She speared him with an intense look. "Do you believe that?"

"No," he admitted. "I think LJM is a person and someone's out to avenge her. But it's not simple. None of this is simple."

Dani rubbed at her temples. "I still don't see how this connects to Brewer. Except that he was murdered shortly after LJM bought his house. That could be a coincidence."

He tilted his head. "Do you believe that?"

The slight eye-roll was the only indication that she'd recognized that he'd once again used her exact words. "Deacon always says that there are no coincidences."

"That's been my experience as well. Also, I can't find any record of money changing hands for the house, which was what raised my initial suspicions," Diesel reminded her. "LJM is cash rich. Why park money in the company if they had no intention of spending it?"

"Cash rich? How much money are we talking about?"

"A million, give or take."

Her eyes widened. "A million *dollars*? How do you even know that?"

"I shouldn't, actually. Ohio small businesses don't have to file annual reports, so there's no formal record of LJM's net worth." He minimized the list of companies and opened another document. "I found this on Brewer's computer. It's a copy of LJM's bank statement, dated March first. There's no letterhead and no signature on the attached note, which is hand-written and dated Saturday, March second. The name of the bank and all account and routing info were redacted. Both the note and the statement were scanned and saved to Brewer's hard drive."

"'Dear Mr. Brewer,'" Dani read softly. "'As you can see, all is in order. You will transfer the title to your house as agreed and then we will forward the payment.'" She looked up at him, eyes narrowing. "This bank statement clearly says LJM. So the company and Brewer *are* connected somehow. You could have led with that, you know," she added grumpily.

"I'm sorry." He truly was. "I didn't mean to keep it from you. We got wrapped up in the business names and I got distracted." By more than the business names. It was becoming harder to focus every moment she sat beside him, her scent filling his head.

"It's okay." She bit her lip, distracting him even more. He stared at her mouth, wanting to be the one doing the biting.

Easy. Back off. Give her time, however much she needs. She was talking again and he needed to listen. He jerked his gaze back to her eyes. "What?"

She shot him a knowing look, her cheeks flushing prettily. "I *said*, LJM clearly planned to send the money once they got the deed. But after Brewer transferred the deed, he went missing and they couldn't find him to pay him. Maybe they were waiting for him to show up and accept payment for his house. Brewer's only been dead for a week or so."

"Killed by a mysterious big bald guy," Diesel reminded her.

She frowned. "So are we saying that the mysterious big bald guy who killed Brewer is actually Raguel? *He's* the avenging angel? That sounds like an even bigger leap than I made by assuming LJM was a person."

"It is a leap, but it's a possibility we should consider. The bald guy could have nothing to do with LJM. Brewer was a piece of work. It makes sense that he had enemies. It could be completely unrelated. All we know is that LJM got his house."

Her frown deepened. "But *why* does LJM want the Brewer house? And won't they have to ID themselves if they want to take possession of it?"

"Not necessarily. They could use a third party to close the deal and throw Brewer's wife and the boys out."

"If they were still *in* the house," Dani said fiercely. "Which they are not and, if I have anything to say about it, never will be again."

Diesel stared at her for a long, long moment, his heart beating double time. What might his life have been like if he'd had a Dani Novak in his corner when he'd been a terrified little boy?

"Thank you," he whispered, his throat gone rough. "Thank you for protecting these kids and all the others who come through your home."

She swallowed hard, her eyes becoming bright with tears. "You, too," she whispered back. "You *are* protecting these kids. You brought Michael and Joshua to me. You've protected children every time the *Ledger* runs a story on a pedophile who's been caught or exposed. You don't think I know who's responsible for those investigations? Who's hacked into computer systems to get evidence or to find these bastards' other crimes that put them in jail and away from innocents? I'm not stupid, nor unaware." Her hand slid over his forearm in almost a caress before gripping him tight. "*You* do this. *You* protect the children, too. So thank you."

Diesel closed his laptop, his own eyes stinging. "I . . ." He cleared his throat and started again. "I can't look at this screen anymore tonight. I need to sleep."

Immediately releasing him, she moved to stand,

but he gently grabbed her hand. "I'll do a walk-around first. I won't be able to sleep until I know you're secure."

"All right. I'll get you a blanket and a pillow. Can you sleep on this sofa? Deacon has before, but you're . . ." She trailed off, eyeing him up and down in a way that could only be called appreciative. In a way that heated his blood yet again. "You're taller than he is."

That hadn't been what she'd been about to say, but he didn't challenge her. "I'll be fine. I've slept on a lot worse."

"But I don't want you to be uncomfortable here," she murmured. "I don't have any spare beds now, or I'd—"

He pressed a fast, soft kiss to her mouth because he thought he'd explode if he didn't. "I'll be fine. I promise." Then he stood, careful to keep his laptop positioned over his groin, because his cock wanted to be in *her* bed. With her.

In her. He shuddered, barely able to bite back a groan when she looked up at him, her eyes gone dark with desire. *She wants me. Thank God.*

But he didn't make a move. *Not yet. Not like this.* Not with two kids upstairs who might come down at any moment. *Not until she completely trusts me. Not until she tells me that she wants me. Out loud.*

Patience, he told himself. He'd been patient for eighteen months. He could last a little while longer.

He took a step back, putting necessary distance between them, feeling a spear of satisfaction when her face fell in obvious disappointment. "Get Hawkeye," he said. "I'll walk him while I do my perimeter check."

Chapter Ten

Grant Masterson's feet hit the dock and he drew a strangled breath of frustration. An hour and a half sitting in that damn riverboat casino and he hadn't heard or seen anything resembling the poker game he'd been looking for, even after "getting lost" in the upper level. But he knew that the matchbook was the invitation. He'd picked up another matchbook from the bar and, while the front was the same, the back had been different, printed with the full name of the riverboat and its address. There had been no fancy gold writing on the inside.

He had to figure out how to get an invite to the game. He needed to find Wesley's contact. Richard.

He leaned against the small fence surrounding the dock, listening as guests straggled off the riverboat. Some complained about the rigged games. A few crowed over their winnings, but they were definitely in the minority.

But the games that people were complaining about were the vanilla variety. Slots, blackjack. Nobody mentioned a high-stakes game. But if they weren't invited to it, they wouldn't know about it.

He had a gut feeling that the game he wanted was exclusive and, if the cash Wes had been throwing around was any indication, only for the very rich.

He ducked into the shadows and waited another hour for the riverboat's employees to begin filing out as the shift changed. One of the last out was the woman who'd been called over to settle a dispute between a dealer and a guest. She'd identified herself as the manager. Hopefully she knew Richard.

Grant followed her to her car, stepping into the light from the streetlamp as the woman was pulling her keys from her purse. "Excuse me," he said quietly.

She gasped and spun around, a small spray can in her hand. "I have no money!"

Shit. Pepper spray. *That's all I need tonight.* Grant froze, his hands where she could see them. "I'm not trying to rob you. I swear."

Her eyes darted back and forth frantically, but they were alone in the parking lot. She tilted her body to bring the pepper spray closer to his face, her eyes narrowing. "I saw you tonight. In the casino. Not drinking and not gambling. Why are you following me?"

"I'm looking for Richard."

She didn't move, her finger still on the spray tab. "He wasn't working tonight."

"Not working on a Saturday night? That doesn't make sense."

She gave him a haughty look. "He's the owner. He can work when he likes."

The owner? he thought, irritated. *Could have mentioned that, Wesley.* But at least this was helpful information. "When will he be working again?"

"Not until Wednesday. Why?"

"I want to talk to him." Grant drew a breath, wishing he had his brother's talent for effortlessly spinning tales. "I'm in town for the week for a convention and I heard he has an exclusive poker game going. I wanted to get an invite."

She shook her head. "All of our games are played

in the open, right on the floor. Nothing special, nothing exclusive."

But her eyes had flickered, just a little. She knew, all right.

"I have several friends who've played," he tried again, but he could hear his own desperation. "They say it's a high-stakes game. Just what I'm looking for. They all said to ask for Richard."

"Sorry, can't help you. Can you go away now? I'd like to go home and I'm not putting this pepper spray down until you're a block away."

Grant's jaw tightened. "I suppose I have no choice. You say Richard will be back on Wednesday?"

"That's right. Now leave or I'll scream for the cops."

He wanted to tell her to go ahead, but because he wasn't sure what Wes was doing, he backed away, his hands still up. "I'm leaving. Relax, lady."

She glared at him until he was out of her visual range and he watched as she unlocked her car with shaking hands.

At least he knew which Richard he was looking for. He'd go back to Wes's penthouse apartment, get online, then figure out the last name of the man who owned the *Lady of the River* casino. And where that man lived.

Hang on, Wesley. I'm here, looking for you. Just . . . be all right, okay?

But he had a sinking feeling that he was already too late.

Cincinnati, Ohio
Sunday, March 17, 9:30 a.m.

It was a beautiful day. Blue, cloudless sky, fresh ocean air on her face, the rumble of the powerful Harley between her thighs as they rounded curve after curve, the waves crashing against the rocks below. Her arms were wrapped tightly around a solid waist, her cheek pressed against a broad, muscular back.

She was happy. Again.

And then she wasn't, because the motorcycle engine revved. She was standing off to the side, watching helplessly as it careened over the cliff, hanging suspended in midair for long, long seconds while the face she'd loved stared at her with hatred.

You did this, *he said.* I hope you're happy now. You killed me. *Then Adrian dropped out of the sky to the rocks below and she screamed and screamed.*

Dani woke up with a jerk, her heart racing, her mouth open, her breath coming in jagged pants. Caught in that moment when she wasn't sure what was real and what was the dream. Was she awake? Had she actually screamed out loud this time? She lay motionless, getting her bearings. Thinking it through.

Her throat was dry, but it didn't hurt, so she probably hadn't screamed out loud. She didn't do that every time she had the dream. And she smelled bacon and coffee, so she was awake.

Someone was making breakfast.

Diesel. *Oh God.* Diesel Kennedy was in her kitchen, making breakfast for the boys. Michael and Joshua. *Who need me.*

So pull yourself together, Danika. Put Adrian out of your mind and focus on those two kids. Who need you.

Easier said than done. The dream always left her shaken and filled with self-loathing. Not the face she wanted to show the boys. *Who need me.*

It was a mantra that worked. Had worked ever since she'd been sixteen years old and suddenly responsible for her infant brother. *Greg needs me.* It had gotten her out of bed every morning as she'd raised him, even though she'd completely botched that job. It worked every day that she woke up now, wishing she could just . . .

She wasn't sure what. Be somewhere else? Be

some*one* else? But the clinic needed her. The patients who had no other health-care choices needed her.

Michael and Joshua need you. So move your ass and be who they need. Do not let them down.

Like she'd let Adrian down. He'd needed her, but she'd been selfish. *So damn selfish.* Adrian was dead, gone out in a blaze of glory. *And, like it or not, it's my fault.*

She drew another breath, relieved that her heart no longer threatened to beat free of her chest. She had regained enough control that she was able to force a smile when her bedroom door opened slowly and a little face cautiously peeked in.

"Good morning, Joshua. You can come in, but next time knock first, okay?"

His face pinched. "I'm sorry. Coach told me to, but I forgot."

"It's okay." And it was. She always slept in sweats when she had foster kids in the house, so that she'd be decent if one of them needed her during the night.

She swung her legs over the side of the bed and found her fuzzy slippers, wriggling her toes as she slid her feet inside. The comfort took the remaining edge off the unsteady feeling left by the nightmare.

Joshua giggled. "I like your slippers."

She shoved the remnants of remembered horror from her mind as she lifted her foot. "So do I. Big Bird always makes me happy. Did you sleep okay last night?"

Joshua nodded, but his smile dimmed. He ducked his head back into the hall for a moment before returning to meet Dani's eyes. "Michael slept on my floor."

"I know." Dani gently tousled the boy's hair. "I got up to check on you in the middle of the night and he was there." And it had broken her heart. Children needed to feel safe, but it was clear that Michael didn't trust her. Yet. That was okay, though. "He probably wanted to be there in case you woke up in the night and didn't know where you were."

Joshua gave her one of those old-soul looks that said he knew so much more than he should. "He's scared."

"Well, he's allowed to be, but he'll get used to me and then he'll know that you're safe here."

"I know already." Joshua punctuated his words with a hard nod. "You gave him a blanket."

"I didn't want him to be cold while he was taking care of you."

"He's always taking care of me, but I can't take care of him," Joshua said sadly. "I'm too little. Everyone says I'm too little to do anything."

Dani knelt in front of him. "But you did take care of him, Joshua. Yesterday you got him to talk to Coach Diesel, who brought you guys to me." She poked him playfully. "You did that."

Joshua sucked in a breath, his belly going round. "I did!"

"Yes, you did. Now, I'm thinking Coach told you to wake me up because he made breakfast. Is that right?"

His eyes widened comically. "I forgot again! He made chocolate chip pancakes."

Dani frowned. "I don't have chocolate chips in the pantry."

Joshua shrugged and turned to the door. "I know. His friends brought some over. They're downstairs eating. You should come before they're all gone." He started to race away, but she called him back in mild alarm.

"Joshua? Which friends?"

"Miss Merry and . . ." He frowned a little. "That policeman from yesterday. Not the one with white hair. The other one. He *says* he's your cousin," Joshua added suspiciously.

Dani chuckled. "Well, he *is* my cousin. His name is Mr. Adam. Go eat. Tell Coach I'll be down in a few minutes."

She closed the door, relieved. Adam and Meredith were here. Maybe Meredith could talk to Michael about therapy. Diesel had probably invited her over for that reason, asking her to bring chocolate chips to make her visit less formal.

Quickly she got ready, changing out of her sweats into a pair of jeans and a sweater the exact color of her blue eye. She added a dash of makeup that she normally would not have worn. Because Diesel was in her kitchen, she could admit.

And he'd kissed her last night. Several times. Then left her wanting more.

Which was smart on his part, she could also admit. He always left her wanting more. Glancing at her door to make sure it was still closed, she opened her sock drawer and pushed the socks aside, revealing a beautiful hand-knitted lace shawl.

It was black with a jagged white stripe that stretched across its length. She caught sight of herself in the mirror. *Like my hair.* She'd found the shawl on her chair at the clinic one morning about a year ago, wrapped in shiny foil paper. There'd been no name attached indicating the sender.

She hadn't realized that it was from Diesel until later, when Meredith had pointedly told her that Diesel had learned to knit. Dani hadn't confirmed to Meredith that she knew Diesel had made the delicate shawl, but she had a feeling Meredith was aware that she knew.

Dani hadn't thanked him. But she wore the shawl whenever she went out, and she knew he'd seen it around her shoulders. It allowed her to pretend that it was Diesel's arm around her, instead of the lace he'd created with those big hands of his. *I need to thank him. I need to acknowledge this beautiful gift.* She met her own eyes in the mirror. *I need to acknowledge the beautiful gift of his affection, too.*

Even if she would never accept it. No matter how much she wanted to. Her dream had been the stark reminder she'd needed to shut down her fruitless desire to belong to him. Because, God help her, she still wanted to.

She closed the drawer and opened another, staring at the neatly folded, frothy lingerie. She didn't touch the letter that she'd hidden under her best underwear. She didn't have to. She knew its contents word for word. Short and bitter, they were Adrian's last words and she'd forever hear them in his voice.

I said I was sorry, but you didn't care. Are you happy now? I hope you're a better doctor than you were a lover. Have a great life. Would have loved to spend it with you.

"Dr. Dani!" Joshua's shout from the bottom of the stairs ripped her from her memories. "Breakfast!"

Yes. Breakfast. And then she'd have the discussion with Diesel that he wouldn't like, but needed to hear. *Find someone else.* And she'd mean it this time.

She found everyone gathered around her table when she got downstairs. Adam and Meredith, Joshua—who was sneaking bites of bacon to a very grateful Hawkeye—and Michael. And Diesel, of course.

Diesel was dressed in jeans and a tight black Henley that showed off every one of his muscles. Unfortunately the long sleeves also covered most of his ink.

Which was good, she told herself. The ink was too much of a distraction. Too much of a turn-on.

She deliberately looked away from Diesel to her cousin, whose eyes were . . . worried. That was not a good sign.

"Good morning," she said brightly, hoping the boys hadn't seen Adam's concern. "I see we have our own chocolate chip delivery service."

Meredith laughed. "Only because Diesel promised to make pancakes," she said, while Adam signed her words for Michael. She turned to speak directly to Michael, even though Adam was still interpreting, and Michael clearly noticed. Most people spoke to the interpreter, not the deaf individual. But Meredith had learned proper etiquette through her conversations with Greg. "I got hurt a little while back and Coach Diesel came to take care of me. He would always make me chocolate chip pancakes. His are the best."

"How did you get hurt?" Michael signed and Adam voiced.

"I got stabbed by a very bad man," Meredith told him.

Beside her, Adam winced. It had been a terrifying experience for both of them. It had also been when Diesel and Meredith had bonded, each becoming the sibling the other had never had. Dani had been a little envious of the time Diesel had spent at Meredith's side, which had been foolish and selfish. He and Meredith were platonic friends, nothing more. Besides, she'd told Diesel to find someone else.

It didn't seem like he'd listened to her. *And you're grateful. Say it.*

Fine. I'm grateful. Even though she'd be repeating the directive as soon as they were alone.

"Well, yeah," Joshua said, stuffing his mouth full with a last bite of pancake. "If he stabbed you, he was very bad."

Michael frowned. "Close your mouth when you chew, Joshua." He looked at Meredith with concern. "But you're better?"

Meredith smiled at him. "I am. Michael, there's a box by the front door. Can you take it to the basement? I brought some fun stuff for Joshua, a model airplane kit for you, and a few books, since I hear you like to read."

Michael looked first to Diesel, then Dani for confirmation when Diesel just pointed to her.

I should probably be annoyed by that, but I'm not. Diesel had earned Michael's trust. "It's fine," Dani assured him. "You can trust Meredith."

Once the boys and Meredith were in the basement, Dani turned to Adam. "What happened?"

Adam scrubbed his palms down his face. "The fisherman is dead."

It took Dani a moment, but when it hit her, she sank into the chair next to Diesel's. "The guy who found the body parts?" She noted that Diesel looked grimly unsurprised. "They told you already?" she asked him.

Diesel nodded. "When I called to ask them to come over. You were still asleep, but I didn't think you'd mind if I invited them."

"Of course I don't mind," Dani said, then turned to Adam. "Who was he?"

"His name was George Garrett," Adam said. "He called 911 last night because there was an intruder in his house. Garrett had a gun, but he didn't use it. His killer had a gun with a silencer. The entire altercation was caught on the 911 tape. Garrett told the guy, 'I was afraid that you'd come.'"

Dani blinked in surprise. "So he saw who dumped the body parts?"

Adam shook his head. "No, or at least he told us he hadn't seen him. But he was worried that the killer would come after him, even though we took pains not to leak his name to the press. I think he was speaking more generically when he said 'you.'"

"Weren't you protecting him?" Dani asked.

Adam sighed. "We had cruisers doing drive-bys, but it appears the killer was watching and timed his attack just after a cruiser had driven away. Garrett's house had a security system, so he saw the alarm light go off when the killer broke in through his kitchen door. From the moment Garrett called 911 until the shot was fired was less than thirty seconds. The guy was in and out. A real pro."

"So having an alarm system won't help," Dani murmured, suddenly chilled.

Diesel placed his big hand in the center of her back. "But having me here *will*. Garrett didn't use his weapon. I will."

She glanced at him wryly. "That shouldn't make me feel better, but it does."

"It should," Diesel said seriously. "Adam, how many people know that Michael witnessed Brewer's murder?"

New fear skittered down Dani's spine. "Oh God. All those reporters outside the police station yesterday. They have Michael's photo."

Adam patted her arm. "The press thinks he was brought in on suspicion of Brewer's murder. Not that many people know he saw the killer. Only the people who were in the room with you, plus Deacon, our boss Lynda Isenberg, the sketch artist, and me."

"That's too many," Diesel growled. "That sketch Michael gave to your artist was online last night and on the TV news this morning. Brewer's killer knows that someone saw him. Or he will as soon as he opens his computer or turns on the TV. What are you going to do to keep the kids safe? To keep Dani safe?"

Dani's heart melted a little more. She and her foster sons were not Diesel's responsibility. At least they shouldn't have been. But Diesel had made them so.

Adam lifted a shoulder in fake nonchalance. "When a reporter assumed that George Garrett had given us the sketch, we might or might not have corrected him. When they asked us if we'd taken Michael into custody for the murder, we might have said, 'No comment.' Now all the reporters assume it was Garrett who saw the killer. The press still thinks Michael is a suspect in Brewer's murder—a fact that was helped by his mother's fifteen minutes of fame. Unfortunately, because of the mother, the press also knows that the kids went to foster care, so *then* we had to let them think we'd put him in protective custody in a safe house. Which is why you don't have reporters camped on your front lawn, so you're welcome for that."

Dani looked at Diesel, saw that he was once again unsurprised. "What did their mother tell the press?"

Diesel's jaw was so tight it was a wonder he didn't break his teeth. "She got out on bail this morning. First thing she did was sell an interview to a gossip rag about how her son had killed her husband and abused her as well. She identified Michael by name, so now the various news outlets are replaying her words. Some claim that they can divulge the name of the minor because he's already been exposed."

Rage boiled from Dani's gut to her throat. "Bitch. I hope I don't meet her."

Diesel wasn't finished. "She also said that she was going to fight for her son."

Dani scoffed. "By accusing him of lying when he reports abuse, starving him, and throwing bowls at his head?"

Diesel shook his head. "She meant she was going to fight for Joshua. To get him back."

Dani felt a sudden calm. "Over my dead body."

Adam frowned. "Don't say things like that."

Dani turned on him. "She will *not* take that baby back. I might not be able to keep them long term, but she will not get either of them back."

"Ditto," Diesel said grimly.

"Hey, I'm on your side," Adam said. "I'm just preparing you. Right or wrong, judges will sometimes give the kids back to the biological parent."

Dani nodded, still trembling with anger. "I know that, but thank you. Forewarned is forearmed."

"Are the boys and Dani safe here, Adam?" Diesel asked.

Adam gave him a kind smile. "If you're here? Absolutely. If you need to go anywhere, call me and we'll get someone else to stand guard." He pushed away from the table. "Meredith has her own car, so she can leave when she's ready. I need to get back to work. Deacon and I have victims' families to inform."

Dani shuddered on his behalf. She knew the toll that speaking to victims' families took on her cousin and brother. "How many?"

Adam suddenly looked older. "They've identified seven people from the parts divers brought up. I don't know if there will be more. They haven't identified all the parts yet."

The thought of the bodies didn't make her sick, but the thought of that man just walking into Joshua's room? She had to steel herself so that she didn't throw up.

"God," she whispered. If the bald man who'd killed Brewer really was the same one who'd bought his house without paying for it . . . That man had killed six others? Why? Thoughts of all they'd learned the night before flooded her brain.

What did this have to do with LJM, the UC med student?

She stole a glance at Diesel and saw he was giving her a "say nothing" look. So he hadn't told Adam what they'd uncovered. She wondered why.

She'd find out before she blew the whistle and told her cousin herself.

Walking Adam to the door, she reached up to give him a hug. "Take care of yourself, okay?"

"You, too," he murmured in her ear. "And I don't know what is or is not happening between you and Diesel and it's not my business. But he's a good guy, okay? Let him stay. I'll feel better if he's here to keep you safe."

She felt her cheeks heat as she rocked back on her heels. "No, it isn't your business, but I agree and I will let him stay."

"Good enough." Adam dropped a kiss on her forehead, then paused, his hand on the doorknob. "Oh, I almost forgot. Faith is bringing Greg over later. He thought he could cheer Michael up. He also said he'd gather his schoolwork from his teachers and bring it by tomorrow."

Dani smiled, pleased. "Excellent. It'll be good for Greg, too. Maybe they can do homework together and I won't have to nag Greg so hard to do his."

Adam laughed. "Good luck with that. 'Bye, Diesel!" he called over his shoulder.

Dani shut and locked the door behind him.

"Arm the alarm," Diesel said.

She jumped a little because he was right behind her. "I didn't hear you come over here," she said, doing as he'd instructed. Now that they knew this killer could move faster than an alarm would sound, it was prudent to take extra precautions.

"Sorry. I didn't mean to startle you." He reached a tentative hand toward her hair. When she didn't stop him, he pushed it aside. "No processor?"

"I don't wear it in the house normally," she said. Which was why she hadn't heard him. Without her processor, she was completely deaf on her right side.

"Do me a favor. Put it on. I want you aware of every sound possible."

Right, she thought. *Completely deaf on one side, I'm more vulnerable.* She took her processor from her pocket and slipped it onto the back of her head, where it fixed to her skull with a small snap, all while Diesel continued to hold her hair.

"It's a snap," he said, curiosity in his tone. "Not held by a magnet?"

She fought a wince. She hated the snap, but it was a feature of the processor. "Cochlear implant processors are magnetized, but they're only for people who are profoundly deaf. This is a Baha processor, because I have hearing on one side." She turned it on. "I'm not hearing everything you can, but more than I would have."

"Good."

"Um . . . You can let go of my hair now."

He grinned down at her. "Do I have to?"

She laughed and swatted his hand away. "Yes." Then she sobered. "You didn't tell Adam about LJM and all the other businesses and that someone bought Brewer's house a week before he was killed."

"No, not yet. First, he didn't ask me. But mostly

because we don't know anything for sure yet. If I showed him what I had, it would taint his investigation because it's information I got without a warrant." He shrugged. "Y'know, illegally."

She ignored his last statement. "Will you tell him?"

"If he asks me directly, yes. And when we get a name to go with whoever LJM is, or was."

"And her Brothers Grim," Dani added.

"Especially them. Especially if one of them turns out to be big and bald." He tugged her hand. "Come on, you need to eat breakfast."

She let herself be pulled back to the kitchen. "Are you going to make me a chocolate chip pancake, Coach?"

He was headed for the stove, but turned to face her, his expression earnest. His voice dropped an octave, like crushed velvet stroking her skin. "I would make you anything you wanted."

Her mouth opened on a silent "Oh." *Tell him. Tell him that this will never work. Tell him to find someone else.* But her mouth wouldn't form the words.

He grinned again. "But for this morning pancakes will have to do."

She couldn't help it. She laughed again. "While you're cooking, I'm going to call Jeremy O'Bannion. He teaches a class at the med school." Marcus O'Bannion's father had been a skilled surgeon before burns from a car accident had scarred his hands. Now he taught others. "He might remember an LJM."

Diesel hesitated. "I might have already asked him."

Her brows shot up. "Oh, really? Might have?"

He looked sheepish. "You slept really late, Dani."

She hadn't slept all that late. "Did you sleep at all?"

"As much as I normally do. Jeremy is checking and said he'd call if he found the name we're looking for."

As much as I normally do was not a real answer, but she let it go when another thought occurred to her, one that really should have occurred to them both the night before. "We should check missing-person reports and newspaper articles for the death of a med school student. It wasn't that long ago." She frowned. "We should have heard about it in the news, actually."

She was reaching for her phone to check when Diesel put a cup of tea on the table in front of her. "I looked," he said. "There was nothing in the news. No mention of any missing med students with the initials LJM. No missing med students period."

Well, shoot. She'd been so sure last night. It had made so much sense.

"Is . . . Is it okay?" Diesel asked from where he stood at the stove, pointing his spatula at the tea.

She took a sip of the tea. It was the same blend she'd made for him the night before. "Oh, yes," she said sourly. "It's made perfectly, too."

Of course it was.

He looked confused and she realized that she was glaring at him. "I'm sorry. I'm not irritated with you. Exactly."

"Sounds like it," he muttered, but because he'd insisted she wear her processor, she heard him.

"It's not you," she repeated. "It's just that you've been so damn productive while I've been lazy and sleeping."

He flipped a pancake. "Is this a competition?" he asked mildly.

She blew out a breath, sending her hair flying back from her face. "Of course it isn't. Except when it is, but that's just me and not your fault," she said firmly.

He plated two pancakes and set them in front of her. "Except when it is my fault," he said. "I haven't been in a relationship before, but I know how this thing works. When in doubt, it's always the guy's fault."

She should have been distressed that he'd called this odd thing between them a relationship, but she found herself chuckling. "Adages exist for a reason."

She tasted the pancakes and couldn't stop the low moan that hummed from her throat. "You're a good cook, too?"

He shrugged, his muscles flexing. "I like to eat, so I took lessons."

"In your vast amounts of spare time," she said dryly, noting with interest that his cheeks darkened, his blush charming her. Diesel Kennedy was a dangerous man. *I want him. I don't want to, but I do.*

God, please don't let me hurt him.

Straightening her spine, she shifted her train of thought back on track. "Maybe she isn't dead, then. LJM, I mean."

"Oh, I think you were right. I'm pretty sure she's dead."

When he said no more she gestured with her fork, as if she was conducting an orchestra. "Because?"

His big hands clutched one of her stoneware mugs. "Remember I said that those last three companies had been established later than the others?"

"Yeah. Seaheaven with the Lake Erie coordinates and the other with the remembrance flowers. Lilies, rosemary, and poppies. Plus the Brothers Grim."

"Exactly. They were established at the same time as Raguel Management Services, last June."

"Nine months ago. Okay. And?"

"More like *but*. Do you know what I mean by parent and child companies?"

She made a face. "I'm a doctor, Jim, not a business manager," she said, pleased when his warm chuckle told her that he'd caught her *Star Trek* reference. "But it sounds like the parent is first and the child is connected, like a franchise."

"That's exactly what it means, Bones," he said, smiling when she smirked. "LJM is the main parent company in this mess. Raguel was formed by LJM, so Raguel is a 'child' of LJM. All of the other companies are ultimately connected to either LJM or Raguel, but most list one of the other companies as the parent. Some of the companies are parents of the other children. That's how it got so tangled up. You have eighty companies all tied to each other in different ways."

"Got it. Tangled. But who formed LJM?"

He nodded in approval. "Good question. LJM was formed by Raguel, two months *before* Raguel was formed."

She narrowed her eyes. "How is that possible?"

"It shouldn't be. I checked the documents attached to Raguel and found that it had a name change in June. Raguel's previous name was LJM S&R, which was established in *January*, so before all the others. When Raguel was formed in May, LJM changed the name of its parent company from LJM S&R to Raguel. I'm not sure why it wasn't caught by the small business office in Columbus, but it wasn't."

"LJM S&R. Search and rescue," Dani murmured. "Was it a search and rescue business?"

He shook his head. "I don't think so. I can't find any mention of it online." And he'd searched all night for one. "Plus, it was only active from January to June."

"When the name was changed to the angel of vengeance." She rubbed her temples. This was like a circular puzzle made of only one color. "If we take the business name as another clue, we can assume that LJM went missing, probably in January last year. Why would someone need a company to search for a missing person? I guess they might if they hired a private detective or something and wanted to keep their spending separated from their day-to-day accounts for tax reasons. Is that possible?"

"Yes. But I wouldn't know for sure without seeing their financial records, and I haven't figured out where to start with that. This is a tangled-up mess."

"You'll figure it out," she said, confident that he would. "But the name change itself is the most significant thing. Whoever was searching for LJM stopped searching. They established Raguel, Seaheaven, and the Rosemary & Poppies businesses because they knew she was dead."

He nodded. "Then their mission became vengeance."

"You couldn't find any record of a missing med school student? No police reports or newspaper articles or anything?"

"Nothing. Of course, this might be because there was no med school student who went missing, then died. This tangled-up mess of companies could be completely unrelated to Brewer and the bald man and Michael."

"But you don't think so."

"No, I don't. We know that LJM and Brewer are linked, both through Brewer's house and through the copy of LJM's bank statement on Brewer's hard drive. What we don't know is if or how any of this mess"—he waved at his computer screen—"connects to Brewer. That LJM was a real person feels . . . right, though." Another shrug of his shoulders, this one sad. "I want to believe that someone's been actively looking for her. That someone missed her."

She leaned close, her hand covering his before she could stop herself. "Then let's find out who that someone is."

Chapter Eleven

Cade opened one eye, groaning when bright sunshine hit like a sledgehammer. He'd forgotten to pull the shades in his bedroom when he'd tumbled into bed the night before. Who put a bedroom window facing east, anyway?

Evidently the guy who'd built this house, an old pedo who'd gotten what he'd deserved after luring a kid into his van with the tired old story about a missing puppy. Weren't parents supposed to be teaching their kids not to fall for that shit?

And weren't parents supposed to be watching their kids?

Luckily for the child in question, Cade had been there to save him, because the child's parents had failed on both counts. The pedo had made all the usual excuses, of course. Cade hadn't listened. The man had already drugged the little boy.

Cade had left the child on a park bench, then waited out of sight until a beat cop had come by and taken him to the hospital. Then Cade had taken the old man to the woods at the river's edge, cut him up while he'd still been alive to feel every slice, and fed him to the fishes.

Now he wondered if the man's bones would be among those the divers pulled out of the Ohio River. Probably not. It had been four years since Cade had dumped him into the river. Silt would have covered any remains by now.

And even if the cops did find the old man, Cade wasn't sorry. The piece of shit had needed to die. *I'm just happy I was there to do it.*

The old pedo had been the first, but there had been others since. The home health nurse in Indianapolis who'd stolen the life savings of her patients. Several other pedos—male and female.

There was also the man who'd beaten his wife nearly to death in front of their son, but who'd been out on bail the very next day, returning home to finish the job a few months later. That one hit far too close to home and he'd taken particular satisfaction in hearing the murdering bastard's screams.

The cops hadn't protected any of those victims. *So I did.*

Not all of the doers had ended up in the river. Some, like Richard, were staged as accidents, especially if they were people Cade knew. Some, like his father, had lived in spite of Cade's best efforts. Some, like the good doctor last night, were simply unfortunate collateral damage. *Gotta break a few eggs to make an omelet.*

Speaking of which, he was starving. He'd skipped too many meals yesterday. He swung his legs over the side of the bed with a grunt. He'd pulled a muscle as he'd run to his SUV after killing Dr. Garrett.

"I'm getting too old to be jumping fences like that," he grumbled aloud. But some ibuprofen would take care of his aches and pains. Thirty wasn't *that* old.

He fried a few eggs on the ancient stove that had come with the house. All the appliances were tottering on the edge of life, but now that he was leaving town, he was happy that he hadn't cared enough to replace any of them.

Clearly the old pedo who'd built the place hadn't cared, either. The man had had money. Cade had found piles of cash in a lockbox in the basement, which was fitting because the basement was where all the pedo's money had been spent.

Cade had been in heaven when he'd discovered the secret room filled with weapons behind a fake wall. So many handguns. Rifles—new AK-47s and AR-15s, and vintage submachine guns dating from World War II and Vietnam. Then there were the grenades. So many grenades. And they still worked, too. Cade had checked. He hadn't checked the potency of the Claymore land mines, though. The old pedo's house was a mile from its nearest neighbor, but a Claymore explosion might be heard or felt from that far away. He wasn't sure, so he didn't risk it.

He loved the weapons room. Unfortunately, to get to it, he had to walk by the other special rooms the pedo had built behind the fake wall. One was a small jail-like cell, with a bed, desk, sink, and toilet. No windows. One door.

The other room had been the stuff of Cade's nightmares. The size of a small closet. Airtight. Soundproofed. Cade had unlocked the door with the keys he'd removed from the pedo's pocket after he'd killed him, and found the body of a teenage boy.

He shuddered now, standing in the old man's kitchen, remembering the horror he'd felt at the sight. Then soothed himself with the knowledge that the boy's parents had closure. He'd put the body in the old man's van and left it where the cops could find it. The kid was identified pretty quickly. He hadn't been dead long. He'd been fourteen when he was killed, eleven when he was taken.

The old man had kept that kid a prisoner for three years. Then left him to die in that airtight room when he was finished with him, which, Cade guessed, was why the old man had been in the park—to get a new kid. The ME had confirmed that the boy had died of cerebral hypoxia as a result of suffocation.

But the parents got closure, he reminded himself. *I did that. I also took the filthy pedophile out of the breathing population, like I did last week and last night.*

He'd saved Brewer's little stepson. Hell, he'd saved countless kids.

Cade wasn't sorry for any of the things he'd done. He was, however, sorry that he hadn't been more careful this time.

Flipping the fried eggs onto a plate, he sat at the table, his tablet in hand. He forced himself to click on the *Ledger*'s front page, wondering—with not a little dread—what the paper had to say about George Garrett's death.

He'd been sloppy last night. And lucky.

But still skillful. He'd made it in and out of the doctor's house in thirty seconds. He hadn't heard the alarm blare until he'd cleared the back door. That hadn't been sloppy or lucky. That had been talent.

Even so, seeing Garrett's gun pointed at him had left him rattled. And that he had raced out to the crime scene yesterday without a disguise?

The hell of it was, he probably hadn't needed to. Once his panic and adrenaline had faded, Cade had considered the layout of the forested area near the river dump site. There was no way Garrett could have seen his face. He'd done all that nonsense last night for nothing.

Disgusted with himself, he pushed his plate away, no longer hungry as he read the *Ledger*'s headline: KEY WITNESS MURDERED. He let out the breath he'd been holding as he scanned the article. Nobody had seen him enter or exit the house.

It had been a clean kill. The article did mention the 911 call and quoted Garrett as saying, "I was afraid you'd come," speculating that the man had recognized his killer. That was okay, though. Nobody knew who the intruder was. Garrett's security cameras had captured him, but the picture quality was poor and his face had been covered with the ski mask anyway.

Cade clicked to the TV news website to see if they provided any more detail. When the home page loaded, his breath froze in his chest.

"Oh my God," he whispered. Because there he was. *My face.* It was there. *For everyone to see.*

For a long moment, he could only stare. It was a sketch, but a damn decent one. Anyone who knew him would recognize him. Anyone who saw this sketch would know he was a person of interest.

He gritted his teeth, breathing through his nose to calm his suddenly racing pulse. *No one can find me here.* This place still belonged to the old pedophile, who, as far as the government knew, was still alive and collecting his social security. Cade kept the taxes and the utilities paid. There was no one to tie him to this house. His check from the casino went to a PO box. The address the nursing home kept on him was his childhood home—not that he would ever set foot in that place again, unless it was to burn it down.

Which he'd considered doing, many times. But the equity in the house was keeping his father in the nursing home. Without it, Cade would be expected to care for the old bastard. Which was not gonna happen, because—

Dammit. Pay attention. He jerked his focus back to the very real and present danger—that his *face* was on the *news*.

Garrett *had* seen him. But how? And was that even important anymore? He'd killed the man. Garrett couldn't testify against him. But that wouldn't stop the cops from putting Cade in a cage.

"I need to get out of here." Merely starting a new job somewhere else was no longer an option. *Run.* He needed to leave the country. He needed a new life.

He'd tossed his tablet to the table and pushed out

of his chair when he froze again. The next story had popped up. This one with video.

AREA TEEN QUESTIONED IN DEATH OF RIVER VICTIM.

He slowly sat down and turned up the volume. A reporter's voice-over accompanied the video of a young man being walked toward CPD headquarters, escorted by the two cops he'd seen on the news story in his father's nursing home room. The white-haired Fed, Deacon Novak, and his CPD partner, Adam Kimble. There was a third person with them, a woman who had her hand on the kid's back. Both she and the kid wore ball caps that hid their faces, but every so often the woman would look up and glare at a reporter who came too close.

"Michael Rowland, stepson of river victim John Brewer, was brought in to CPD for questioning this afternoon regarding the apparent murder of his stepfather."

Cade frowned. "That's not Brewer's stepson." Brewer's stepson was a little kid. Five years old, tops. The kid on the screen was a teenager.

Shit. Did Brewer have *two* kids?

"Police have withheld the teen's name due to his minor status," the reporter continued, "but his mother has come forward, claiming that her son both killed her husband and assaulted her, beating her on numerous occasions."

The video of Michael walking into the police station switched to a clip of a woman wearing wrinkled but expensive clothes. Her skin was sallow and her hair was snarled and dirty.

"He killed my John," she said tearfully. "I tried to control him, but Michael was just too angry, all the time. He was always a difficult boy, but in the last year he's become violent. He kept threatening to kill John and now he has." Big tears gathered in her eyes and spilled down her face. "And now I'm afraid for me and my little boy, Joshua. I've lost my husband. Are they going to take my little boy, too?"

They cut to the reporter, who stood in front of a large school building. "Michael Rowland is a freshman at Albert Sabin High School. We were here earlier during the annual Spring Fling dance talking to faculty and students, who were stunned at the news. Many expressed disbelief that Michael could be involved. School administrators declined to comment, and we were told by his fellow classmates that Michael keeps to himself. But the students believed that this was due to the teen's disability. Michael is deaf and uses an interpreter during his school day."

The video cut again, showing the reporter standing in front of the courthouse, looking concerned. "We should note that the victim's wife, Stella Rowland Brewer, was released on bail for drug possession charges this morning and Michael and one other child were removed from her custody into emergency foster care." She made a pained face. "So this story is far from straightforward. We'll continue to investigate. I'm Kelly Henry and this is *Action News.*"

Cade stared at the screen long after the segment had ended. He hadn't known about another kid when he went to Brewer's house to check that the five-year-old was safe. He'd looked in the other bedrooms. One was the master, where he'd packed Brewer's clothes into a suitcase so it would look like he'd gone on a trip.

The other was a stark guest room, bed made with military precision, the furniture and walls devoid of anything personal.

The third was Joshua's room, where the boy had been sound asleep. But he hadn't looked for any other kids. *I should have. Why didn't I?*

Because he'd considered his job done that evening. He'd killed John Brewer and Blake Emerson, the guy who'd tried to buy Brewer's stepson. He'd cut them up and dumped their parts in the river. He'd gone back to check on the kid, for God's sake, because it was the fucking right thing to do. He'd been exhausted, dammit, so he'd come back here to sleep.

He clenched his eyes shut, trying to focus. "Okay," he said aloud, the sound of his own voice anchoring him in the empty kitchen. "Either way I have to get out." Because his *face* was on the damn *news*. "At least they don't know my name." They didn't know any of the names he'd been using, real or fake. "Yet."

He could run right now. He could be in Canada in five or six hours. But if they caught him? They had an only-decent sketch at this point. They'd need an eyewitness to make any charges stick. If Garrett had been the one who'd seen him, that loose end was snipped. But if Garrett *hadn't* been the witness?

He pushed to his feet and began to pace the small kitchen, feeling caged and angry. *Why am I even worrying about this? I killed scum that should be dead. I killed kiddie rapists and wife beaters. I killed traffickers and thieves.*

Why should he be worried that they'd catch him and send him to prison? But he knew it was because of the collateral damage, like George Garrett.

In his heart, Cade knew that Garrett hadn't seen him at the river. But Michael Rowland lived in Brewer's house. "He could have seen me."

New panic rose to choke him, because unlike George Garrett, the teenager was still breathing. He ran his palms over his head, digging his fingers into his skull. The sharp pain short-circuited the panic and he could think again.

He dropped into the chair and pulled his tablet close. It was time to be smart. Yesterday he'd run crazy, worried that the fisherman had seen him. He'd taken care of the threat, but had made some mistakes. Now he was going to go slowly. He'd determine whether the kid was a threat.

If so, he'd eliminate him, just like he'd eliminated George Garrett, though he'd do it a lot more carefully. Then he'd leave. Change his face. *Do something.*

He'd *definitely* quit doing the cops' job for them. He'd leave the kiddie rapists and traffickers and wife killers and thieves to prey on anybody they pleased.

Not my circus, not my monkeys. It was time he took care of himself. The question was, how exactly would he determine if Michael Rowland had been the one to give the cops his description?

If Michael had seen him, perhaps he'd told someone. Someone other than the cops. A friend, maybe. Or a teacher.

Where did that news report say he went to school?

Cade found the news report and watched it again. Albert Sabin High School. He located it on the map, then realized it was Sunday. They'd be closed today.

Besides, he couldn't just waltz in and ask for Michael Rowland. First, he'd be recognized in five seconds, because his *face* was on the fucking *news.* Second, he doubted Michael would be at school tomorrow.

Nor would he find the teenager in Brewer's house. Both children had been removed from the home into emergency foster care. He needed to locate the foster home into which they'd been placed.

He considered the boys' mother. Her expensive clothes couldn't hide that she was an addict. He highly doubted she'd been told where her sons were. Hell, she thought her teenager had killed that prick Brewer.

He stilled. *Wait. Why?* Why would she think that? Was there evidence that pointed to the kid?

Would it be possible to frame the kid for the murders?

Then he remembered George Garrett. "Shit." Garrett's security cameras had caught him, and even though Cade's face had been covered, Michael Rowland was barely five-foot-eight and so damn skinny.

There was no way the kid could be mistaken for Garrett's killer.

George Garrett is gonna come back to bite me in the ass, he thought grimly.

So he was back to finding where Michael Rowland was being kept. He rewound to the start of the news story and slowed the speed of the video, advancing it frame by frame as he studied the teenager. The cops walking him into the police department didn't look like they believed he was guilty. They looked protective. But the cops weren't going to tell him anything, either.

He wasn't even going to chance asking.

He paused the video, freezing a frame that showed the woman walking beside the boy. She looked more than protective. She was snarling at the reporters.

For the first time since he'd seen his own face on the news, Cade smiled. "I'll start with her." She'd guarded Michael like he was her own kid. She'd know where he was hiding.

Cincinnati, Ohio
Sunday, March 17, 10:40 a.m.

"That would be great, Miles," Dani said into the phone, breathing a sigh of relief. Dr. Miles Kristoff had agreed to take her shifts at the clinic for the next four days. "I'll owe you one."

"No, you won't," Miles said kindly. "You worked Christmas and Thanksgiving for me for the past two years so that I could spend the time with my kids. You deserve the vacation. Where are you going to go?"

"Nowhere. I've got two new foster kids and they need me."

"Oh." He was quiet for a moment. "The boy on the news?"

Dani sighed. "Yeah. But let's not spread that around, if you don't mind. We haven't had any reporters skulking about and I'd like to keep it that way."

Miles made a rude sound. "Vultures, you mean. I get it. They won't get a word from me. Let me know if you need anything else."

Diesel looked up from his laptop when she ended the call. He'd been scowling at his screen for the past hour, while she'd cleaned the remnants of his chocolate chip pancakes from the kitchen and the boys played downstairs with Meredith. "Everything okay at the clinic?" he asked.

She nodded. "I'm off for a few days. That will at least give me time to get them settled and resolve their school situation." She bit at her lip, glancing toward the front window. They'd kept the drapes shut in case a reporter came by, but she actually had a larger concern. "I'm worried about their mother," she confessed.

Diesel closed his laptop and gave her his undivided attention, which didn't really help matters. When he looked at her like that, she felt powerful and important. And she realized once again how much she was going to hurt him.

He'd been worshipping her for eighteen months. There was no way any woman could live up to that. *Much less me. No matter how much I want his fantasy to be true.*

She busied her hands making tea so that he wouldn't see them tremble. "The courts favor the biological parent," she went on. "If Stella Brewer makes a fuss, a judge might give her another chance."

"So what will you do?" he asked simply, as if there was no question in his mind that she had a plan.

She liked that about him. A lot. He hadn't once questioned her competency, when so many men had.

Even Adrian had, and even though she knew he'd been striking out at the time, emotionally devastated and in pain, his words had hurt. *Are you happy now? I hope you're a better doctor than you were a lover.*

She pushed the words away, focusing on the ones that mattered. *The kids need me. Michael needs me.*

"I want to get Michael x-rayed, to document previous abuse. He said that his mother took him to different clinics, always giving false names. If I can pull one or two of those records into the open and match them with a scar or a healed break, we can show gross negligence on her part and endangerment of a child. She might not have caused that particular injury, but she left him in an environment where she knew he was being abused. That way, if she tries to say she threw a bowl at his head because of the stress of her missing husband, we can show this has been a pattern all along."

"What can I do to help you?"

Which was exactly what she'd expected him to ask, even as she'd dreaded it. He offered his support so sweetly. No strings. *He should want strings. He should demand them.*

"For now, nothing. I may need you to do some creative searching later, though, if I can't find what I'm looking for on my own."

"You only need to ask."

She swallowed hard, because that statement was rife with nuance and double meaning. "I know." The kettle boiled and she poured water into the teapot and carried it to the table. "I'll start by asking Michael what he remembers about the clinics he was taken to. I hate to upset him, but he's going to find out sooner or later that his mother is making noises about getting Joshua back. I'd rather he hear it from us."

Us. The word had flowed from her mouth before she'd realized it was coming. She hadn't intended to say it, even though it was truly one of the nicest words. And right now, one of the scariest.

He hadn't missed her slip and his dark eyes flashed with something hopeful.

Which made her feel even worse. So she powered through. "But for now, I'd like to look at that list of businesses, so we can figure out who LJM was. Have you heard from Jeremy O'Bannion?"

"I got a text." Diesel's tone had gone wary, as if he sensed her panic. "He didn't have any records of her in his home office, so he's going in to his office at the university to check, but he's got some fundraiser or other to attend first. He'll get to us as soon as he can."

"All right, then. Can I look at the list?"

Diesel rummaged in his laptop case and brought out a stack of papers, neatly stapled in the corner. "I used your printer last night to make a hard copy. Hope you don't mind."

"No, of course not." She scanned the list of businesses compiled into a tabular format from the state government's database. Eighty business entities took up four pages and were more words than her brain could process at the moment.

Falling back on what worked for her, she drew a spiral notebook and a pen from one of the kitchen drawers.

"What are you doing?" Diesel asked in confusion.

"I'm going to write them all out."

"Longhand? With *paper*? And a *pen*?"

She had to laugh at his horrified tone. "Yes. The act of writing helps one's brain dissect and retain information. I started doing this in med school. It was the only way I got through HGA with an A."

He continued to watch as she started copying out each business name, still apparently disbelieving that she'd actually write with a pen. "What's HGA?"

"Human Gross Anatomy. *Oh.*" Something clicked in her brain and she ran her finger down the printed table until she found the entry she was looking for. "Aminus HGA." She pronounced it *AH-minnus*, just as she'd heard in her mind every time she'd read through the list. "But it's not *AH-minnus*. It's *A-minus*. Like, the grade. If all of these business names refer to one person—LJM—then she got an A-minus in Human Gross Anatomy during her first year of med school at UC."

He blinked. "You're right. Does Jeremy teach HGA?"

"No, but he'll know the prof who does. He doesn't have to check all med students in the files. He can narrow it down to who got an A-minus in Human Gross Anatomy in the years that LJM went to UC. Based on . . ." She ran her finger down the list of companies. "Here. 'Scioto Associates.' I took that to mean that she lived at Scioto Hall when it reopened, while she was an undergrad. That had to have been 2016 or later because the dorm was closed for renovations before that."

Diesel nodded thoughtfully. "When do med students take HGA?"

"We took it the first semester of our first year— that was the fall semester."

"Okay." He picked up her pen and began to make notes in the margin of the list he'd printed out. "If she started med school directly after graduation, that means she was a first-year student two and a half years ago. LJM S&R was established in January of last year, so if we assume that's when she went missing, she took HGA this past fall, fall a year ago, or fall two years ago."

"Not this past fall," she corrected, taking the pen and circling one of the businesses. "'APG White Coat Distribution.' She would have received her white coat for finishing her first year. So we've narrowed down when she took HGA to either one or two years ago."

"I'd forgotten about the white coat thing," he murmured.

"I didn't. The white coat ceremony was a huge milestone. It would have been for her, too." She shook her head, staring at the list, which made so much sense in one respect and so little in others. "But I still don't understand why whoever set up these compa-

nies left all these clues—especially the 'Brothers
Grim.' If we're able to track LJM down, we can figure
out whoever it was who built this tangled mess."

Diesel shrugged. "Like I said before, maybe they're
hiding in plain sight. And maybe they don't think anyone will go to the trouble of dissecting all this." He
grinned abruptly. "Are you sure that you really want
to be a doctor? You're looking like you're enjoying
this detective gig."

She'd stiffened at the first part of his question, but
relaxed when she realized he was teasing. And once
again, not criticizing. "I like puzzles, but the thought
of the physical danger is enough to send me running
back to sick patients and insurance paperwork."

Just then, the basement door flew open and Michael strode through, determination on his tear-
streaked face and Hawkeye on his heels. In his cupped
hands, he held tiny pieces of paper, ripped into what
looked like confetti.

Before Dani or Diesel could say a word, Meredith
appeared, her face serene. It was a mask she wore
when her emotions threatened to tear her apart.
Which was usually the case after she'd talked to children who were hurting.

Meredith silently followed Michael, reaching into
the cupboard for a glass mixing bowl, into which he
dumped the paper. She put the bowl into the sink,
then looked over her shoulder.

"Matches?" she asked Dani.

"Second drawer on your right," Dani said, reading
between the lines. Michael and Meredith had talked,
and the scraps of paper were the remnant of that conversation. Meredith knew a few signs, but she was far
from fluent, so they'd communicated via paper and pen.

A glance at Diesel told her that he'd also arrived
at that conclusion. There was pain in his eyes and his
jaw clenched reflexively. But he said nothing, just
watched.

Meredith handed Michael a match. The teenager

gave Dani a questioning look and Dani nodded. "Do it," she signed.

With hands that shook, Michael lit the match and dropped it into the bowl. Fire whooshed up, but quickly burned itself out. After a minute, Meredith ran tap water over the smoldering mess, dumped it down the sink, then turned on the disposal.

"Finished," Meredith signed with a flick of her hands.

Michael's expression was grim, but still determined as he turned to Dani. "Can I meet with her?" he asked, pointing to Meredith.

Dani maintained her own serene face, not showing her relief. Therapy was exactly what Michael needed. Therapy with Meredith was even better. "Of course."

"And next time I'll hire an interpreter for you," Meredith said and Dani signed her words. "No more writing it out."

Which was the law, but Meredith would have done it regardless because it was the right thing to do. So many providers tried to refuse to pay the cost of interpreters. Dani was grateful that securing the service for Michael's therapy would be one fight she wouldn't have to take on at the moment.

"I just got the next few days off," Dani told him. "We'll make an appointment and I'll take you."

"*We'll* take you," Diesel corrected. "Nobody goes anywhere alone for a while."

Michael drew a breath, then closed his eyes and exhaled on a sob. And in that moment he was a fourteen-year-old boy who was terrified and hurting.

With an audible swallow, Diesel came to his feet, hooked one big hand around Michael's neck, and pulled the boy in for a hug. Michael froze for a split second, then wound his arms around Diesel's solid strength and cried into his chest, his sobs tortured and desperate.

Diesel's hand shook as he stroked Michael's hair gently, the giant man giving comfort to a scared little boy. And hopefully taking some comfort for himself.

Think of it as a mugging.

Yeah. Diesel's experience is personal, all right. One had only to look at his face to see the agony there. Yet he was here. Helping.

Dammit, Diesel. Why didn't you find somebody better than me?

Dani didn't realize she was crying until Meredith put a tissue in her hand.

"He's gonna be okay," Meredith murmured. "We're going to make sure of it."

Which one of them? Dani wanted to ask, but of course she didn't. Instead she cleared her throat. "Does he know about his mother?"

"That she wants Joshua back?" Meredith shook her head. "No, not yet."

Great. That would be yet another blow. "All right. I'll tell him. And Joshua?"

"He fell asleep on the sofa downstairs. He didn't see any of our conversation."

"Good. I'll bring him up and put him to bed."

Meredith brushed Dani's hair away from her face, tucking it behind her ear. "And you? Will you be all right?"

Dani scoffed quietly. "I'm always all right."

Lie, lie, lie. She wasn't all right. Not at all.

Meredith's sober look said that she knew Dani was lying. "My door is always open to you. You know that."

Dani looked away. "I know. Thank you."

"I'm going home now. Call me if you need me. Call me if Diesel needs me."

Dani sucked in a breath and met her friend's clear green eyes. And saw perfect understanding there. Understanding and truth and sorrow as Meredith's serene mask slipped away for the briefest of moments.

"He's a good, good man," Meredith whispered, then leaned in close. "Don't hurt him. Please."

Pain radiated through Dani's chest. Her friend

hadn't bought her clueless act. Meredith knew that
Dani had been aware of Diesel's feelings all this time.
And Meredith expected her to do . . . what? The right
thing? The wrong thing?

Clearly, the thing that would hurt him. Because
Meredith knew people. *She knows me.*

Dani came to her feet. "I'm going to see to Joshua.
I'll catch you later."

Chapter Twelve

Indian Hill, Ohio
Sunday, March 17, 11:05 a.m.

Grant slunk down behind the steering wheel as a bright blue Mini Cooper pulled into the driveway of Richard Fischer's gated Indian Hill home. He was glad it was too early for the trees to have leaves, because he could just see the huge, sprawling house from where he sat. The garage alone must have held six cars.

A tall, curvy blonde hopped out of the Mini Cooper and tapped a code into the security panel mounted on the big iron gates. Getting back into her car, she drove through the gates, but they didn't close behind her.

Not giving himself time to second-guess, he followed her through the gate, but stopped just inside while she continued up to the house. The driveway curved, so she couldn't see that he'd driven in after her.

He inched his car up the drive until she was once again in view. She'd gotten out of the car and was stalking up to the front door. She rang the bell, then waited, arms crossed over her chest, foot tapping.

Grant got out of his car and, after hesitating a moment, slowly approached the woman, who was now banging on the front door with both fists and screaming for Richard to "Open up, you fucking asshole!"

Either Richard wasn't home or he was deliberately not answering the door. Given the woman's wrath, Grant wasn't sure he'd have answered the door, either.

"Excuse me, ma'am," Grant said and the woman spun around, a gasp on her lips and her hand pressed to her heart.

"Fucking hell," she hissed. "You scared the shit out of me."

Grant tried to smile. "I'm sorry. I didn't mean to frighten you. I take it that you're trying to talk to Mr. Fischer?"

She snorted in a very unladylike way. "Give the man a gold star," she said sarcastically, then narrowed her eyes. "Who are you?"

He nearly gave her his real name. Then he thought of all the pains Wes had taken to hide his identity. If this woman was a cohort of Richard's and if Richard was somehow involved in Wes's disappearance, Grant would follow his brother's example. "Lin Jackson." It was his father-in-law's name, but it was the best he could do with a split second's warning.

I'm an accountant, for God's sake. Wes is the creative one. So sue me.

"Sergeant Lin Jackson," he added when the woman gave him a "so what" look.

"Oh." She nodded, appearing satisfied. "You're just the person I need to talk to. That bastard has my diamond earrings."

"Oh, dear. And you are . . . ?" He took out his phone and prepared to note the name.

"Dawn Daley." She leaned in to watch him type it in. "D-a-l-e-y. Make sure you spell it right. I want those earrings. They were my mother's."

"He stole them?" Grant asked carefully.

"Yes!" Dawn grimaced. "Well, not exactly. I left them on the nightstand in his bedroom yesterday. When he kicked me out."

"You live here, then." Which was how she'd known the security code.

She grimaced again. "Well, no. I would have liked to, of course, because the house is a fucking mansion, but Richard Fischer is a fucking asshole."

"I got the asshole part," Grant said dryly. "So you were his houseguest." This woman had been inside the house. She'd been with Richard. She could give him information. "How well do you know Mr. Fischer?" he asked.

She looked embarrassed. "Not well. I kind of met him Friday night."

Friday night. The night of the poker game. Excellent. "On his boat?"

She nodded. "Paid a mint for that ticket, too. The Friday night cruise tickets are expensive, but I was hoping to meet him. I . . . work for the casino." Another grimace. "I wait tables."

So she'd wanted a leg up the corporate ladder and instead she'd gotten kicked down a few rungs. The lady had a bone to pick. Wes had often told him that this made otherwise hostile witnesses more cooperative.

"Why are Friday nights expensive?" he asked.

"Because the boat leaves the dock on Fridays. It can only carry a certain number of people. I guess they charge admission to make up for the losses."

"Do you ever work on Fridays?"

"No. Only a few servers work Fridays—the most senior people. I've only been there a year. I always wanted to know what made Fridays so special. So I saved up and bought a ticket." She shrugged, trying for nonchalance, but Grant saw the disappointment in her eyes. "Richard saw me at the bar and decided he'd take me home."

"Was it worth it? The ticket price, I mean," he added when her penciled brows shot up her forehead.

"Oh." She laughed. "Not really. The clientele is richer. I saw a lot of fur coats, which I didn't know was even still a thing." She wrinkled her nose in distaste. "The bar jacked up the booze prices, I can tell you that. I nursed a twenty-five-dollar martini until Richard came downstairs and spotted me, then he bought the drinks."

Downstairs? "What's upstairs?" Grant asked, tilting his head and trying to look mildly curious. Hopefully secret poker games requiring a special invitation.

"The suites. There are only, like, ten of them and they're hella expensive, but the boat is really old, so people like to spend the money to stay there."

"Was he alone when he came down?" Grant asked with a sly wink, implying that there might have been another woman, but hoping that there would have been several poker players.

"Yes," Dawn said. "I mean, it wouldn't have stopped me if he had been with someone, but he hadn't. He smelled like smoke." She wrinkled her nose again.

Grant remembered seeing the No Smoking signs everywhere when he'd been on the boat the night before. "The casino allows smoking?"

"No, and that makes for a lot of angry people, I'll tell you. They take it out on the servers. Filthy-mouthed fuckers who don't tip for shit."

"Maybe the upstairs guests can smoke."

She shrugged. "I asked him that, because the smell of smoke was heavy in his jacket. He kind of laughed and said those clients were rich enough that they could do anything they wanted. Wish I'd bagged one of them. None of 'em could be a bigger asshole than Richard."

Grant made himself chuckle, even though he wanted to be sick. Wes was posing as a rich man. He'd sold heroin for the cash to play a role. Had Wes really come to Cincinnati looking for their sister or had he succumbed to the temptation that taunted the vice detectives? Had he become one of those men who believed he could do anything? Like shoot a detective with an unregistered gun?

He forced his mind back to his search. Dawn didn't sound like she'd know about the poker game he was seeking, but he needed to find a way to ask. "That sounds like it's over my pay grade. Are the upstairs rooms for sleeping or for gaming?"

She gave him a narrow-eyed stare. "Why?"

"I'm curious. I'll never be able to afford that kind of game, but I've played in Vegas a few times."

"Well, I don't know," she said brusquely. She started for her car, but he shifted so that he stood in her way.

"One more question, Miss Daley. Please. Who does work on Friday nights?"

Her eyes narrowed further. "Why do you want to know?"

"I'm searching for someone," he said honestly. "They might have been on the riverboat at some point. But no one I've talked to during the normal hours has seen her." He wasn't sure why he'd substituted *her* for *him* at the last moment, but he was glad he had because Dawn's eyes softened.

"This is personal, isn't it?" she asked.

You have no idea. "Yes, ma'am." He drew a breath and steeled himself. "My baby sister."

"Let me look at her photo. Maybe I've seen her."

His hand genuinely trembling, he found the photo of his sister on his phone. "This is her."

Dawn studied the photo intently, but ended up shaking her head sadly. "I'm sorry, I haven't seen her, either. You should ask Scott King. He works most days, but always on Fridays. He's the security manager."

Grant hadn't realized how tightly he was holding his shoulders until they relaxed a little. Talking to the security manager might be a better idea than trying to talk to the riverboat owner. "Thank you," he said sincerely. "I appreciate it."

He began to turn back to his car, but had one more question. "If you don't live here, how did you know the security code?"

She rolled her eyes. "I watched Richard type it in. He was so high by the time we got here that he didn't notice I was watching him."

"You drove with him when he was high?"

Her smirk was matter-of-fact. "It was the only way to get into the house. Are you going to report my earrings?"

He nodded. "Of course. Daley—D-a-l-e-y."

She smiled. "Yes. They're dangly earrings with diamonds. Diamond chips, actually. Clip-ons. They aren't worth much, but they were my mom's."

Grant's eyes unexpectedly stung. He'd make sure Wes reported them when he found him. "I hope you get them back," he murmured, then got into his car and drove back to Wes's apartment.

Harrison, Ohio
Sunday, March 17, 1:15 p.m.

"Thanks for fucking nothing." Ending the call, Cade tossed the burner phone to his kitchen table in disgust. "Un-fucking-believable," he snarled. Not a single reporter knew who the woman was. Or if they did, they wouldn't tell him.

The fuckers kept telling him to "read about it on my blog page," or "watch the video on our website." He had and none of those had anything about the kid other than what he'd gotten from that first report. *Assholes.*

He rubbed his head, sighing. Part of it might have been that he'd scared them. Not the few at the beginning, because he'd been nice to them—so damn nice—but they hadn't told him squat. He might have gotten a little hostile with the others.

Still. He gritted his teeth. "So much for freedom of goddamn information."

He was becoming more confident that the kid knew something. If the press was to be believed, the cops were being very tight-lipped.

He saw me. Cade knew it. But this was a fourteen-year-old kid. He needed to be sure before he pulled the trigger.

He pressed his thumbs into his skull, forcing himself to think. What did he know? "Not fucking much," he grumbled. Just that the kid's name was Michael Rowland, he was Brewer's stepson, and his mother was a haggard bitch who was either lying through her teeth or stupid, because her teenage son had not killed her child-selling bastard of a husband. *I did.*

He knew that Michael had probably been hiding that night, because Cade hadn't seen him. He replayed the video report in his mind. He knew that the kid was a freshman at Albert Sabin High School. And that he was deaf.

Oh. Wait. If he'd talked to the cops, he'd have needed a translator or whatever those people were called. He pulled his tablet close and did a search on sign language translating services. There were only two that were local.

He scanned the page, looking for what, he didn't know. He'd know it when he saw it. He hoped.

Okay, they were called "interpreters." Both companies provided them for all kinds of different things—schools, hospitals, doctor and other medical professional visits, and legal proceedings.

Legal proceedings. He'd known that he'd know it when he saw it, and there it was. Only one person in each interpreting service was certified to interpret in court. So he was down to two people. He'd try one, then the other.

He frowned at his screen. How should he go about hiring an interpreter? Clearly he couldn't just call and say he was the client. Could deaf people even use the phone? How did that even work?

Luckily there was an FAQ section that covered what he needed to know. Michael wouldn't have hired his own interpreter, even if he had been an adult. The responsibility for hiring and payment of interpreters was that of the provider.

In this case, the court or the cops. Cade thought about it. If he were an attorney, he could call on behalf of his client. He could be Dennis Kagan again, the ID he'd been carrying yesterday. He'd told only the CSU tech his name, and that guy was dead, so he wouldn't be repeating it.

As for his "client"? He grabbed the old phone book that had come with the old pedo's house and opened it at random. He closed his eyes, poked at the page, then opened his eyes. "David Peele it is."

The FAQ also covered the confidentiality the client could expect from the interpreter, and Cade realized they might refuse to tell him anything.

But that wouldn't be a huge deal. Cade knew how to get information out of people.

Now, which service to call first? He flipped a coin, then dialed.

"How can I help you?" a cheery female asked.

"Hi, my name is Dennis Kagan. I'm an attorney and need to hire an interpreter for my deaf client. He's being held at the police department off Ezzard Charles Drive. I've never done this before. How do I go about hiring someone?"

"Oh, dear," the woman said. "Our court-certified interpreter is out of town this weekend. We've been referring clients to the other interpreting service. If you have a pen, I can give you their number."

"Not necessary. I can see them here on my computer. I did a search. Thank you." He ended the call, feeling suddenly cheery himself. He dialed the other number and repeated his spiel. This time he was rewarded.

"Our interpreter will meet you at the police department in one hour," a more reserved voice told him.

Cade nearly asked them who to expect, but then

spotted the only certified legal interpreter's photo on the company's website. His name was Andrew McNab and he appeared to be early thirties and slender.

This shouldn't be too hard at all.

Cincinnati, Ohio
Sunday, March 17, 3:10 p.m.

John Brewer had been *such* a sonofabitch, Diesel thought, barely managing to suppress a growl. An abusive, conniving, manipulating sonofabitch. He was glad the man was dead, because he wanted to rip Brewer's head from his neck.

But he needed to keep his cool, for Michael's sake. The boy had cried his eyes out while holding on to Diesel like he'd never let go, but eventually his sobs had quieted. Dani had given him a cup of tea and assured him that Joshua was napping comfortably in his bed upstairs.

Diesel hadn't even been aware of Dani carrying Joshua up from the basement. His sole focus had been the boy crying for the innocence that had been so cruelly ripped away from him. And from fear that his world was about to come to an end.

"Temporary," Michael had whispered in a voice that was a little slurred, but understandable. The whispered word had been his response when Diesel had assured him that everything would be okay, that he was safe in Dani's house.

Temporary. In that moment, Diesel had known exactly how the boy felt.

But now Michael was napping on the sofa, Hawkeye sprawled at his side, half in his lap. And Diesel had returned to work.

Only to find that John Brewer had been an even bigger sonofabitch than he had already known.

"Her name was Laurel," Dani said abruptly, jerking his attention from the numbers he'd been scowling at for the past hour. "LJM. The 'L' is for Laurel."

Diesel looked up from his laptop. Face cupped in her hands, Dani sat with her elbows propped on the kitchen table, staring at the list of more than eighty LJM companies she'd written out longhand.

They'd worked in silent harmony after Meredith had taken her leave, with breaks for hot tea or for Dani to stir a pot of chili she had cooking on the stove. Or for her to check on Joshua as he napped, or to drape a blanket over Michael when he'd fallen asleep, clutching Hawkeye as desperately as he'd clutched Diesel.

It was so domestic, it almost hurt. Because Diesel wanted this so much. Wanted the homey kitchen, the dog, the kids, the quiet Sunday afternoon with Dani Novak. He wanted *her*. He wanted it all.

"Okay," he said simply, unsurprised that she'd figured out the med student's name. "How do you know?" Because they were still waiting on Jeremy O'Bannion to give them a lead on medical students with those initials.

"Laurel is the only name that appears multiple times. 'Laurels Awards & Trophies,' 'LaGrange Lacrosse Laurels,' and 'Laurels Lilies, Rosemary & Poppies.'" She leaned back in her chair. "The first few times I read over these names I took 'laurel' to mean either an award or a plant."

"So did I."

"Well, one of the businesses does refer to awards— the 'LaGrange Lacrosse Laurels.' They must have won some kind of championship. I guess my brain put in commas instead of apostrophes for the other two businesses. These two actually refer to 'Laurel's,' as in the possessive."

His chest warmed with pride. "Nicely done, Doctor." He leaned forward to kiss her cheek, but she pulled away, her back going stiff.

Her head dipped once, but she didn't smile. Her eyes had become colder, her expression remote. Something had changed since that morning and he didn't like it. They were back to the way they'd been all those months after she'd told him to find someone else.

"Thank you," she murmured politely. "If Jeremy can't find her, I figure we can dig into the records from her high school to get her last name. If she graduated from college two or three years ago, she must have attended high school four years before that. And if she did play lacrosse we can get her name. She may have been on the dance squad, so we can cross-check."

Diesel did a quick Internet search. "LaGrange High School has a dance team and they're called the 'Dancing Divas,' so 'LG Varsity Dancing Divas' makes sense." He bristled with the excitement that always accompanied a hunt. It was better than feeling ragey at Brewer's malice. Or numb at Dani's obvious rejection. "That could work."

"Once we get her last name, either through Jeremy or the high school, we'll be able to trace to the Brothers Grim."

"That assumes they are her actual family. 'Brothers' could mean a lot of things, although it's a place to start."

Her eyes narrowed. "Whoever they are, they can lead us to the vengeance dude."

"Possibly. Although I'm sure whatever his real name is," he said lightly, "it won't roll off the tongue in nearly the same way as 'vengeance dude.'"

She rolled her eyes at his teasing, which he'd managed pretty convincingly, if he did say so himself. Because he was really feeling desperation clawing at his heart. She was sitting here with him physically, but had pulled away emotionally.

"What did you find?" she asked.

Diesel frowned at the numbers on his screen. "The boys *had* trust funds."

Dani stilled. "Had?"

Diesel nodded grimly. "Brewer had regular direct

deposits coming in from another bank. At first I thought they were his income, but that's deposited into another account that matches with his reported income on his tax forms."

Her dark brows lifted. "You can see his tax forms?"

"Only because he kept copies on his hard drive."

"How do you know the money came from the boys' trust funds?"

"Because he kept the e-mails detailing the transfers."

She pressed her lips tightly together. "How much did he take?"

"All totaled, more than a million dollars."

She gasped. "Oh my God."

"Half of it was an inheritance that Michael Rowland Senior left to the kids when he was killed in Iraq. That money and the house itself were passed down through the boys' biological father's family. The other half was probably Rowland Senior's death benefits. If he had maximum coverage, his family would have received four hundred grand. There's also the death gratuity."

Dani winced. "Death gratuity? That sounds awful. Like it's a tip for dying."

Diesel agreed with her. "I know, but that's what the military calls it. There's also the surviving family benefits. It's not much—maybe a grand a month—but the boys will be entitled to that until they're eighteen."

"That's something, I guess."

"Not much," Diesel said with disgust. "The life insurance and the paternal inheritance were invested and the dividends plus the GI benefits should have been enough to pay the children's expenses until they turned eighteen. But it's all gone."

Dani's eyes were narrowed and angry. "I'm surprised that the mother hadn't taken it all already."

"I'm not sure that *she* took any of it. Brewer was the trust funds' trustee."

Her mouth fell open, surprised. "How did he manage that?"

"He was Rowland Senior's attorney. Brewer used to be part of a firm downtown and another attorney from the firm set up the trust before the boys' father was deployed. For whatever reason, Rowland appointed Brewer as the executor. Brewer's been steadily draining money from the fund for the past four years, a little at a time. It sped up in the past year."

"Doesn't someone keep an eye on the trustees?"

"Supposed to. The trustee submits a report detailing the money spent and for what purpose. Brewer did this and kept copies on his hard drive. But I think he faked some of the reports. One says they spent money on cochlear implant surgery for Michael. We'll have to ask him if he has an implant, but he wasn't wearing a processor."

Dani's jaw tightened. "He doesn't have a cochlear implant. I asked him yesterday. That surgery runs about fifty grand, and it went right into Brewer's pocket. How did he claim a surgery that never happened?"

Diesel shrugged. "He has a doctor's letter and copies of bills, but he could have forged those. It looks like he mostly stayed just under the minimum he was allowed to withdraw until the past year. That's when most of the money was taken. He would have needed to submit his report soon."

"And he wouldn't have good reasons for spending the money. He needed to replace what he'd taken or he'd be charged with stealing. So he sells his house." Dani swallowed hard. "And maybe his stepson?"

Diesel had to swallow back his own anger. "Possibly." He'd assumed the same thing. "Whatever he was doing with Joshua the night Michael fought him, it wasn't anything legit. Nothing about this whole mess is legit. Looks like Brewer withdrew the money in cash every month after it was deposited."

"Are we back to him needing money for gambling and/or drugs?"

He nodded. "Looks like. The good news is that, because Brewer kept all of his e-mails, there are several references to casinos and bookies."

"So you're back to following the money."

"Or the lack thereof. Hopefully the court required Brewer to be bonded with an insurance company when they appointed him trustee. Maybe some of the money can be reimbursed."

"I hope so." Folding her hands on the table, she leaned back, putting distance between them. Her whole demeanor became reserved. Not angry, just remote enough to send a shiver of dread down his spine. "What will you do next?"

What will you do next? You, not we. The question hit him hard because she asked it in the same tone that she'd take with a banker or a lawyer or . . .

A stranger. A wave of loneliness washed over him and his chest felt tight. He drew in a slow breath, holding it, trying to calm his now rapidly pounding heart.

He managed to keep his expression impassive, but it was hard. That she'd firmly put them back in the friend zone was a bitter pill to swallow. Hell, it wasn't even the friend zone. They were in the colleague zone. She was making it perfectly clear.

"*I'll* keep searching." *Because there is no more "we." No more "us."* Not that there ever had been anything real between them. Just his stupid hopes and dreams. It was high time he accepted it. But it hurt. So much that the need to punch something was almost more than he could control. *I need to get out of here. Away from her. From this.*

She opened her mouth on what was sure to be a protest, but he stopped her with an upheld hand that visibly trembled. "I need to go out for a little while. Check the casinos. But I don't want to leave you alone." Because even though she'd pushed him away, he still cared. He was still responsible for her and the boys. He would stick with this until the boys were safe, until their immediate future was resolved. But he needed to get away for a little while. Needed to be able to breathe.

"We'll be okay," she said levelly. "Maybe I'll ask Kendra to come over and watch a movie with us later."

Officer Kendra Cullen was a good choice. She was an even better choice if her Fed boyfriend accompanied her. Not that Diesel didn't have confidence in Kendra's abilities, but Special Agent Jefferson Triplett was as big as Diesel and could protect Dani and the kids as well as he could.

He smiled tightly. "That sounds good."

She gave him a knowing look. "I'll ask her to bring Trip with her."

"Am I that obvious?"

She nodded. "Yeah, you are, but that's okay. If it makes you feel better, I'll even ask Scarlett and Marcus."

And that was it, the straw that broke his back. The thought of Scarlett and Marcus, married and happy, Scarlett expecting their first baby. Diesel was so damn happy for them, but it was one more reminder that his friends were paired off, living their forevers.

While I . . . sit here. In this house, with kids who weren't his, the homey kitchen where he was just a visitor. *And with the woman who isn't mine.* And as much as he wished it, she might never be. He could feel her impending rejection.

He'd welcomed the interruption when Michael had thrown open the basement door because it meant he could go a little bit longer without her saying the words he dreaded. *Find someone else. This isn't going to work.*

Go away.

Dani squared her shoulders, straightened her spine, and schooled her features, turning to him with an expression that was prim but firm. She was getting ready to say it again. Getting ready to tell him to find someone else. And he couldn't stand to hear it.

Abruptly he pushed to his feet, overwhelmed by the panic clawing at his gut. Because this wasn't enough. *I'm not enough.* This wasn't *real.* None of this was real and he'd been a fool to pretend that it was.

Dani stared up at him, brows crunching together in consternation, and he knew he needed to say something, because the words he dreaded most were about to fall from her lips.

So he said the first thing that came to mind. "Thank you."

She tilted her head warily. "For what?"

For letting me pretend for a little while. "Not giving me a hard time about protecting you. I know this is temporary for you." He drew a deep breath that sliced at the inside of his chest. *Temporary.* Michael had been right. They were all just temporary. Hell, Michael had a better chance of permanence here than Diesel did. "I know you asked me to stay because of the kids. And that's okay." *No, it's* not *okay. Not at all. I'm not okay.* "But thank you for taking my need to protect all of you seriously."

Her mouth had fallen open, and he waited, hoping she'd tell him that he was wrong, that this wasn't *temporary*, that she wanted him there as much as he wanted to be there. But she didn't. She sat staring up at him, a host of emotions warring in those beautiful mismatched eyes.

She wanted him. He knew that. But she still didn't *want* to want him.

Hurriedly he packed his laptop in its case. "If you can call Kendra and Trip, I'll call Scarlett and Marcus." Then he'd get out of this sweet, cozy house and do what he did best—catching sonsofbitches who hurt people.

Harrison, Ohio
Sunday, March 17, 4:30 p.m.

Cade stared down at the man lying in the fetal position on his basement floor. Andrew McNab was a lot tougher than he looked. And a lot more honorable.

Cade was reluctantly impressed. The guy had not given the kid up. Hadn't said a word other than that he wasn't going to divulge any client's business. For the first half hour, anyway.

That had changed when Cade had broken one of McNab's ribs. Then the man began to chant that he didn't know, over and over.

Grabbing McNab had been the easy part. Cade had been waiting for him in the parking lot of the police station. All he'd needed to do was shove a gun against the man's back and McNab had gotten back into his car and, with Cade in the backseat still pointing the gun, had driven them to where Cade had directed he go.

They'd ditched the guy's car and switched to Cade's SUV, making the trip back to the old pedo's house in silence. Because Cade had tied and gagged McNab.

He'd figured the man would sing like a fucking canary once he saw Cade's face and realized he was the one from the news, but McNab hadn't. He'd been terrified, but he hadn't given Michael up.

Cade was regretting showing McNab his face. A guy like Andrew McNab didn't deserve to die, but now he'd have to kill him.

"I'm going to ask you one last time," Cade said, because even though he admired the guy, McNab was trying his patience. "Did Michael Rowland provide the police with my description?"

McNab groaned. His face was pretty messed up. *I might have been more impatient than I thought I was.*

Cade's knuckles were beginning to swell, so he pulled his gun from its holster and aimed it at the interpreter's head. "Last chance," he said with true regret.

McNab rolled to his back so that he looked up, meeting Cade's gaze squarely. "You're going to kill me either way. So why would I tell you anything?"

It was a fair question. "So it doesn't hurt anymore?"

"So it's not my last chance," McNab said.

Annoyed, Cade kicked him hard. McNab coughed, but looked at him defiantly. "Why are you asking me? Why not just kill Michael and be done with it?"

Cade blinked. "Because he's just a kid. I have to be sure."

"Well, you'll need to get your guarantee from somebody else." McNab spat, his spittle tinged with blood. "I'm not going to help you kill that kid." He cradled his broken rib with one arm. "He's been through enough."

"So you did interpret for him?" Cade was pleased. The man hadn't even admitted that much until now.

Something flickered in McNab's slitted eyes, nearly swollen shut. But Cade saw it. Dismay. McNab hadn't meant to say that.

"Thank you," Cade said. "Close your eyes. It'll be easier."

The defiance was back in the interpreter's eyes. "How will you talk to him?"

Cade blinked again. "What?"

"Are you going to just shoot him in the head or are you going to bring him here and beat him to death?"

Cade flinched. "I . . . I'm not sure." He hadn't thought that far. "Probably just shoot him."

"Just like that? You aren't going to tell him why?"

"He'll know why." But Cade considered the interpreter's words. If he did need to talk to Michael for any reason, it'd be smarter to keep McNab alive. At least until he'd taken care of the boy.

He grabbed McNab's collar and dragged him into the cell where the pedo had kept his prisoners. Cade had already checked the man for weapons, and he was clean, which made sense, as he'd been planning to go into the police station. He slammed the cell door shut and checked that he had the key.

Then he went into the weapons room and stocked up, arming himself. He selected three more handguns, an automatic rifle that he'd converted from semiauto himself. And two of the old pedo's vintage grenades.

He'd never had to use one, but if he was surrounded and needed to make a quick getaway, he could use them as a distraction.

Because he'd had time to think about this while questioning the interpreter. He still didn't know where Michael was. Consensus among the reporters online was that he was in custody in a safe house somewhere. Probably well guarded.

Cade wasn't going to be able to get into a safe house. But if he could find out where it was, he could smoke Michael out. And then he'd shoot him.

Or bring him back here and drug him. That might be easier. *On both of us.* He wasn't relishing the cold-blooded murder of a fourteen-year-old, especially now that McNab had so bluntly asked him his plans.

He scanned the shelves to figure out what he had that could be used to smoke the kid out. A smoke grenade wouldn't do it. He needed real smoke, from a real fire. He could go old-school with matches and gasoline, but if it was a safe house, the cops would have cameras set up. Whatever he did, he'd need to do it from far enough away that the cops couldn't see him coming and stop him.

His gaze fell on the glass bottles on one of the shelves. They were covered with years' worth of dust. But the can sitting next to the bottles was new. No newer than four years, though, which was when Cade had chucked the old pedo into the river.

It was tar. Next to the tar was a neatly wound coil of fuses. And a small gasoline can. Cade shook it. It still had some gas in it.

He knew exactly what those bottles were for. Sometimes low-tech was best, and a Molotov cocktail was about as low tech as it got. Only thing lower would be a rock.

He busied himself making up the concoction and gently pouring it into the bottles. He'd smoke out the kid and snatch him in the confusion of a fire.

But first he had to find the safe house. He had been unsuccessful in discovering who the protective woman in the news video was, the one who'd guarded Michael as they'd walked into the police station.

But Michael's mother might know her identity. And even if Stella Brewer truly didn't know, she could still be useful. She'd said that she wanted to get her little boy back, that she'd fight for custody. That would take a while, but a sympathetic judge might grant supervised visitation in a neutral location. If that happened, all he'd need to do was follow her to that location, then follow the five-year-old back to the safe house.

It was a plan. One way or another, he'd find Michael Rowland.

Chapter Thirteen

Dani was hiding in the kitchen because the troops had, apparently, arrived. Neither Kendra nor her burly boyfriend, Trip, could come, because they were working tonight, but Scarlett and Marcus had come right away, bringing their three-legged bulldog, Zat, and their old sheltie, Baby Bop.

Kendra and Trip had apparently asked Kate and Decker to come in their stead, because the two federal agents had just arrived along with Kate's dog, Cap. Dani knew Kate had brought Cap for the boys, Michael especially, because the aging dog was a therapy animal. Which was nice and all, but Hawkeye had Michael covered. Dani's dog hadn't left the teenager's side all day.

That left all the other dogs for Joshua to pet. The little boy was in heaven, all smiles and giggles.

Yet Dani was hiding in her kitchen, washing pots and pans. Normally she loved socializing with their circle of friends, although they rarely came here. Usually they hung out at Meredith and Adam's place or with Marcus and Scarlett in their big yard on top of the hill with its barbecue grill, gazebo, and horseshoe pit, plus a magnificent view of the city.

But today they were here, and her little house was full to bursting with people.

All except the one who was supposed to be here.

Diesel was gone. Abruptly. And, she feared, maybe finally.

She had no idea if he'd come back. He'd left to go to the casino to investigate Michael's stepfather. Without a good-bye. Or a wave. Or a smile or a hug.

Certainly without a kiss. Which wasn't a surprise. She'd been psyching herself up to tell him to find someone else, once and for all, but she hadn't been able to speak the words. She'd tried, several times, as they'd sat at her table sorting through Brewer's financials and the tangle of LJM, but the words got caught in her throat every single time. Her body language must have been sufficient, however, because he was gone.

She scowled at the pot she was scrubbing in the kitchen sink, replaying the final few minutes of their conversation. He hadn't said good-bye. What he had said was . . .

Temporary. That he knew she considered this *temporary*, that he was only there to protect her and the boys.

Which was true.

But she didn't want it to be true. She didn't want it to be temporary.

But that was how it would have to be.

The doorbell set the dogs to barking. She considered answering it, but there were plenty of people in her living room to do that, so she kept scrubbing the pot. The barking got louder, interspersed with cries of, "Zeus! Goliath! Down!" and "Zeus! Goliath! Settle!"

Oh, great. Now Faith was here, too. Dani loved Deacon's wife, but her arrival made Dani wonder who had invited her. She blew out a breath and scrubbed the pot harder as the answer unrolled itself in her mind. Earlier that morning, Adam had mentioned that Faith would be bringing Greg over to spend time with Michael.

Dani wouldn't be surprised if Faith already knew about the conversation that she and Meredith had had earlier in the afternoon. *He's a good, good man. Don't hurt him. Please.*

Meredith and Faith were joined at the hip because they worked together, both therapists in the child counseling practice Meredith had built. That they'd already compared notes and agreed that Dani would probably hurt Diesel was fairly inevitable. *Great. Just great.* Because of course they'd been right.

I hurt him.

"What's wrong?" Faith asked.

Dani didn't spare a glance at her sister-in-law, who'd leaned one hip against the counter. She'd known Faith was standing there, had felt her sharp scrutiny.

"Did you bring Greg with you?" Dani's younger brother lived with Deacon and Faith, the three of them getting along like champions.

Not like it had been when Dani had been solely responsible for Greg's welfare—and behavior. That had never ended well. Greg loved her, but she'd never been able to give her little brother what he'd needed when he'd needed it.

Just one more relationship I fucked up.

"Yes. He's talking to Michael, signing so fast that I can't follow."

"That's good." And it was. Michael deserved all the friends he could get.

"And you?" Faith asked gently. "Are you good?"

No. Not at all. I'm not good. I'm shitty. A shitty person. The kind who hurts generous men like Diesel Kennedy.

And Adrian. Because she'd hurt him, too. Yes, he'd also been at fault, but she'd purposely hurled words intended to hurt him. She'd denied him forgiveness when he'd begged. And now he was dead. "I'm fine," she said dully.

"Yeah, no," Faith drawled. "Try again."

"Don't ask questions you already know answers to, then," Dani snapped.

"Okay," Faith said, sounding unruffled. "Meredith suggested that Michael could use a friend. Greg had already planned to come over, though. He brought a bag in case you wanted him to stay for a few days."

Dani tensed. "So you and Meredith talked." Of course they had.

"We did," Faith said levelly.

Tears stung Dani's eyes and she swallowed hard. "What else did she tell you?"

Like she couldn't figure that out on her own. *Don't hurt him. Please.*

"That Michael could use a friend, like I said," Faith said. "And that maybe you could, too."

"Great," Dani muttered, the tears stinging harder. "Pity, too. Just fantastic."

"Knock it off, Dani," Faith said sharply, then softened her tone at Dani's involuntary gasp. "You know I love you. And, for the record, neither of us pities you. We might want to smack you upside the head, but we don't pity you."

Dani choked on a surprised laugh. "Well, okay." She blinked, sending the tears falling, but she didn't look away from the pot that trembled in her blurred vision.

Faith's hands came into view, tugging the pot away. "You're going to scrub off the copper plating and expose the metal, which'll probably poison and kill you."

Dani looked at her then, shaking her head. "Not one part of that makes sense, Faith. That's not . . ." Then she saw the gentle compassion in Faith's eyes and sighed. "You were kidding. Right."

"Well, not about smacking you upside the head," Faith said wryly. She handed Dani another pot, knowing she needed to keep her hands busy. Faith knew her well.

And loves me, Dani reminded herself.

Faith slid her arm around Dani's shoulders, giving her a hard hug. "Talk to me, Dani. We're all worried about you."

Dani's throat grew tight. "He left."

There was a momentary pause. "Diesel?" Faith asked carefully.

"Yeah." It came out a whisper, harsh and broken. "Why?"

"I'm . . . I'm not sure." *Liar.* The word he'd used bounced around her brain. *Temporary. He thinks he's temporary.*

Because that's what you told him. In words and deeds.

"Really? You really don't know?" Faith's reply was gentle, but firmly knowing.

"No." Dani drew a breath when Faith's hug tightened. "I . . . fucked it up. And I didn't even mean to." *Liar.* "Well, yeah, I guess I did."

"How did you . . . fuck it up?"

Hearing Faith's delicate repetition of the curse word almost made Dani smile. Almost. Then she remembered the look on Diesel's face when he'd said he was temporary. *I hate that word. I hate that I made him feel that way.*

Right now, she hated herself, too. But that was nothing new.

Dani drew a careful breath because her chest was too tight inside. "He's so nice. Too nice."

"I don't know him well," Faith murmured. "Only through Mer. But she thinks the sun rises and sets with him."

He's a good, good man. "I know." Dani wasn't sure which thing she was referring to—that Mer liked him or that Diesel was a good, good man. *Both.*

"How did you fuck it up, Dani?"

"I pushed him away. Too many times. I guess he finally believed me."

Another pregnant pause. "Did *you* believe you?"

That was a damn good question. "I don't know. I wanted to believe me. I wanted to believe that I wanted the best for him."

Faith's next pause held confusion. So did her voice. "That's not you?"

Dani laughed bitterly. "That is *so* not me."

"Okay, then. I think this is a bit more complicated than I thought. Tell me why you think you're not good for him. And if it's just him or anyone."

Dani glanced at Faith from the corner of her eye, appreciation momentarily overriding her misery. "You're really good."

Faith's lips twitched. "I have a little experience on the workings of the Novak mind. You didn't answer my question."

Dani forced herself to consider it, because she didn't want to answer. "Anyone. Especially him."

"Honest, at least," Faith murmured. "The 'anyone' will take some time. Why especially Diesel? What makes you not the best person for him?"

"Because he's so nice," Dani snapped, suddenly angry. Who with, she had no idea. *Liar. It's you. You're mad at yourself.* The sudden burst of fury seeped away like a rapidly leaking balloon. "He's patient and kind and he helps people."

"So do you. Why aren't you the best person for him?"

"He's worshipped me for a year and a half. Put me on a pedestal."

"That's hard to live up to. But *why are you not the best person for him*?"

"He . . ." Dani swallowed hard, remembering his expression as he'd held a sobbing Michael, just hours before. "He opens his heart. For anyone to hurt."

"You think you'll hurt him."

"I already have," Dani whispered, then cleared her throat. "I've gotten too used to being alone the last few years. I wouldn't be good company."

"Oh, Dani." Faith's words were sweet and full of

caring and made Dani want to cry again. "You haven't been alone for a few years. You've been alone since you were sixteen years old."

Dani blinked, sending new tears down her face. "What?"

"You've been alone since your mother and Bruce died. Since Deacon went away to college, leaving you alone with Greg."

"Deacon didn't leave me alone," Dani declared, shocked out of her tears. "I was with Jim and Tammy."

Faith's gaze was pointed. "Like I said—alone. Did you cry back then, Dani? After your mom and Bruce died and Deacon left for school?"

Dani had a sudden image of herself at sixteen, sitting in a rocking chair holding Greg, who'd only been a year old. She'd curled around the baby in her arms, rocking him and sobbing, but quietly. Because Jim had come home from his shift with the police force "cranky," and Tammy had urged her not to let him hear her cry.

Tammy had told her that she'd had to do the same when she cried over losing her only sister, or risk Jim's anger. She had cautioned Dani not to make Jim mad. Or he'd make them leave and then she and Greg would have no one. So Dani had cried as silently as she could.

"Yes," she whispered, shaken by the memory.

"Who did you cry on? Or with?"

"There was no one." No one to comfort a grieving girl who missed her mom and stepfather so damn much. Whose life had been uprooted yet again.

"The definition of 'alone,' wouldn't you agree? You learned not to lean on anyone because there was no one to lean on. There's power in that, actually." Faith's tone continued to be soft. Soothing. Comforting, even. "There's power in not needing anyone. Makes you *feel* strong." She let the *feel* hang between them.

"*Feel* strong," Dani murmured. "Not *be* strong."

Faith pulled her close again. "Yeah. It's like a statue made of thin plaster. It might look like marble from afar, but let someone close enough to touch and . . ."

"Its true self becomes clear." My *true self becomes clear.*

"That can be very bad if the plaster person doesn't like her true self."

Dani dropped her gaze to the pot in the sink and began scrubbing it. "I know. I don't like my true self." She said the words matter-of-factly, because they were accurate. She'd known it for some time. "So I don't let anyone close enough to see me."

"That's kind of the easy answer," Faith said.

Dani jerked her gaze up to glare at her sister-in-law. "What? I said what you wanted me to say, didn't I?"

Faith smirked. "Yeah, you did. If you told a patient they smoked or drank too much, or ate too much sugar, and they said, 'Sure, Doc, I smoke, drink, and eat too much,' what would you say to them?"

Dani rolled her eyes, getting the point. "I'd tell them that talk is cheap. Actions speak louder. To make the lifestyle changes required to fix the problem."

Faith dropped her arm from Dani's shoulders and retuned to leaning her hip against the counter, her smirk gone. "Easier said than done."

Dani sighed heavily. "Yeah. I know."

"So what are you going to do about Diesel?"

Dani's hands paused on the pot and she blinked at Faith in surprise. "Don't you mean what am I going to do to do like myself?"

"That'll take more time. You've been *you* for your whole life. I don't have a magic wand. You're going to have to put the time into therapy to fix that."

Annoyed, Dani pressed her lips together. Of course Faith would recommend therapy. She was a damn therapist. "Did *you* get therapy?"

Faith surprised her again by nodding. "I did. I still do. So I'm not being cute or condescending. If you want to make those fundamental changes, you'll seek therapy, but it's not an overnight cure. In the meantime, you could find happiness with Diesel. Do you want that?"

Dani looked away. "Yes." *More than anything.*

"Then what are you going to do?"

"You mean right now?"

"Not this second, but soon. If you've hurt him, you need to fix it. If you want him, you should tell him."

"I did tell him," Dani admitted. "Last night. But I told him that I didn't want to want him."

Faith winced. "Ouch."

Dani forced herself to say the word that had been echoing in her mind. "He said I considered him *temporary*. That I only wanted him here because of the boys."

Faith's wince deepened. "And you said . . . ?"

"Nothing. I just . . . watched him go." Dani wanted to smack *herself* upside the head. "I just kind of froze."

"Is he coming back?"

"I don't know. I *think* he will, if only to guard the kids. He made a promise and I don't think he'll break it."

"And if he does come back?" Faith asked.

The doorbell rang, saving Dani from having to answer. Which was good, because she had no idea what she'd do. And because the issue still existed.

Right or wrong, she was not good for Diesel Kennedy.

Cincinnati, Ohio
Sunday, March 17, 8:20 p.m.

Cade stood at the back of Brewer's property, staring up at the house. There was a single light on upstairs. Stella Rowland Brewer was home, it seemed.

He'd parked his SUV a half mile away and hiked, just in case there was police presence. Which there was. A single cruiser sat in the driveway, close to the house. There were two cops inside the car. There were no other police cars out front or anywhere along the perimeter. He'd made sure of that.

The cops were taking turns doing perimeter checks. Every thirty minutes or so, one would jog around the house, checking doors and windows.

Cade could handle the two cops if he had to. He'd prefer not to have to kill them, but he would if it came to it. But in an effort to avoid doing so, he would get in and out of the house and interrogate Mrs. Brewer in the fastest possible time.

He wondered if the woman knew what her husband had been up to, gambling away their home, then gambling away her five-year-old son. When he'd first overheard Brewer at Richard's poker game, he'd assumed that the man's wife had not known. Brewer had mentioned that delivery needed to occur that very night, because his wife was out of town. But now, after seeing her interviewed by the TV news, anything seemed possible. With heroin addicts, all bets were off. They'd do anything to feed their habit, including selling their own souls.

Patting his coat pockets, he confirmed that he had his weapons and the gift for Mrs. Brewer. He'd found the heroin in the pocket of Blake Emerson, the guy who'd tried to buy Joshua Rowland. Cade hoped she'd be enticed enough to tell him what he wanted to know. If not, he'd have to resort to more violent means.

Which was fine, especially if she'd known or even suspected what her husband was doing. If she'd willingly put her son in danger, she deserved everything she got.

He carefully approached the house from the rear, staying in the shadows. The place hadn't had an alarm system when he had been here the week before. If one had been installed in the meantime, he'd be very surprised.

A light came on in the kitchen as he lurked near the back door that led to the garage. A woman paced nervously back and forth by the window, a glass of wine in her hand. This was even better. He could discuss things with her in the kitchen and be closer to his escape route. He'd been antsy about having to go to her bedroom, especially after having George Garrett pull a gun on him the night before.

He pulled out the key ring he'd taken from Brewer's pocket the night he'd killed him. He lucked out when the first key fit the lock. He slipped into the garage and pulled the door closed, locking it. If the cop outside did his perimeter check before Cade was finished, there would be nothing to raise suspicion.

An inner door in the garage led to a laundry room. Cade pulled his gun from his pocket and racked the slide. *There. Ready for any surprises.*

He cracked the laundry room door, knowing from his last trip to the house that it opened into the kitchen. Brewer's wife was still pacing, the bracelets on her right arm jangling. She was muttering to herself.

"Goddamn cops. Goddamn Michael. Goddamn John. Goddamn them all," she chanted, her hands shaking so hard that the wine sloshed from the glass she carried. "Need a little. Just a little. Just a little."

Excellent. Stella Rowland Brewer was stuck in her house, cut off from her dealer and her supply. Cade withdrew the bag of powder from his other pocket, palming it in one hand as he opened the door.

"Mrs. Brewer?"

She wheeled around, wine going everywhere, though she didn't notice. Her eyes fixed on his gun before lifting to his face. "It's you. The guy my son claims killed my husband."

"Yes. So he *claims.*"

"Did you do it?"

"No," he lied smoothly. "I need your help to clear my name."

Her eyes narrowed. "Why the gun, then?"

"I wanted to ensure that you didn't scream."

She tilted her head. "Have you killed the cops outside?"

"No," he answered, amused.

"Dammit. They won't let me go. I'm a prisoner here in my own home, even though I made bail."

"They're keeping you from leaving? Did you tell your lawyer?"

Her jaw clenched. "They'll let me leave. They just follow me. I can't go anywhere and no one wants to help me," she added in a whine.

"I want to help you." He held up the bag of white powder and watched her eyes lock on to it like tractor beams. "I have a proposition for you."

She licked her lips nervously. "What?"

"Like I said, I want your help to clear my name. Your son has made life difficult for me. My face is all over the news. I can't go anywhere for fear of capture."

She swallowed hard, her gaze not faltering from the bag he held. "Yet you came to a house guarded by cops."

"I'm not guilty, but I am careful. I hiked through the back of the property and they didn't see me. Will you help me or not?"

More lip licking. "What do you want me to do? They're not allowing me any visitation or communication. I can't make Michael tell the truth. Not that he ever listened to me anyway. He's a bad kid."

"I want to talk to him, but I can't get close, either. Does he have any friends at school? Anyone he's mentioned? Somebody who could tell me where he's being kept?"

"We don't really talk. Can I have that?" She pointed to the bag in his hand.

"When we're finished," he said, annoyed with her already. "Do you know where he's staying right now?"

"He's in foster care." Her eyes went sly. "Give me a little and I'll tell you where."

He wondered if she knew. "Tell me where and I'll give you the whole bag."

"How do I know you're not lying?"

"How do I know *you're* not lying?" he countered.

She blew out an angry breath. "CPS told my lawyer that his foster home is run by a woman who signs. You know, in ASL, because he's deaf."

That made sense. "And the woman's name?"

She took a step forward, then stopped when he gestured with his gun. "My lawyer says the only emergency foster care with someone who signs is with a woman named Novak. Dani Novak. Her brother is some kind of hotshot cop."

Well, shit. If the woman was Deacon Novak's sister, the most recent news reports he'd seen online also made sense. Reporters were speculating that the kids were in a safe house. Special Agent Novak would never allow his sister to be an accessible target.

He held the bag of heroin behind him when she took another step forward. "I think you're lying. Your son is in a safe house."

"I know that," she said, licking her lips desperately. "I told you that I don't know where. But the Novak woman is with him, wherever he is."

"Okay." Cade could work with that. "Does your son have a girlfriend?" Because a teenage boy might tell his girlfriend where he was, just so she wouldn't worry.

Stella barked out a nasty laugh. "You're kidding, right? What girl wants to take on a boy who can't even talk? I kept trying to get him to talk, but he never would. Wouldn't even try. His teachers keep saying I should learn sign language or whatever." She waved with the hand holding the wineglass, which was now almost empty. "I don't have time for that shit. Someone else can take him. I'll take Joshua back but not Michael. He's too much trouble."

"Joshua is your five-year-old." He was unimpressed with Stella Rowland Brewer. She was not nurturing.

"Yeah, he's cute. People like him. He gets them to give me things. I'll keep him."

She talked about her son like he was a dog or an inanimate object. Cade had a feeling he wasn't getting any additional information from this paragon of maternal virtue. Time for the true test.

"I actually knew your husband. Were you aware that John was gambling?"

She inched forward, her eyes on the prize he held. "Sure, but not a lot."

"He gambled away your house."

Her face paled. "What? That's impossible."

"I was there. I heard him. And when he ran out of money, he tried to win it back by offering up a five-year-old boy."

Her eyes flickered, then hardened. "Because of Michael," she said, her voice a vicious hiss. "He turned John bad."

Cade didn't think he'd like what came next. "Exactly how did Michael do that?"

"Seduced him," she spat. She took a few more steps, her shaking hand outstretched. "I told you what you wanted to know. Now give me the stuff."

Cade dropped the bag into her hand, knowing she wouldn't call for the cops. She was too afraid they'd take her "stuff."

She took a taste, her eyes sliding closed. "Oh God. I need this."

"So you knew that your husband was molesting your son?" he asked smoothly as she dropped to her knees by the kitchen sink.

Grabbing bottles of various cleaners and tossing them aside, she crowed when she pulled out a laundry soap bottle with a wide cap. She dumped the contents on the floor—her drug paraphernalia. Rubber tubing for the tourniquet, a syringe, and a number of used needles.

Cade grimaced, deciding he'd shoot her from a few feet away so he wouldn't get splashed with her blood. Who knew who else had been using those needles?

She didn't look up at his question. "I knew John and Michael were doing it, yeah. But Michael asked for it. Michael wasn't John's type. My husband liked women."

In that moment Cade wished like hell that Michael hadn't been the one to give the cops that sketch. The interpreter had been right. Michael *had* been through enough. He hated having to kill him. *I'll make it painless,* he decided.

"You can bring me more tomorrow," Stella declared, mixing the heroin with water.

He laughed softly. This woman was truly insane. "Or?"

"Or I'll tell everyone that you did it, even if it was Michael who really did."

She didn't see the bullet coming. She was too busy drawing the concoction she'd mixed into a syringe. The silencer emitted a small pop and Stella's prepared syringe fell to the floor. The woman's body followed.

Crouching down to stay out of sight of the window, Cade shot her in the head again, just to be sure. Then he put a final shot in her chest. Where her heart should have been, if she'd had one. At least she wouldn't be able to get her hands on the five-year-old ever again.

He checked his watch. He'd been here less than ten minutes. Still another twenty before the cop outside came round again. He'd be able to exit the house and hike back to his car with no trouble at all.

Next stop, Dani Novak's house.

Chapter Fourteen

Cincinnati, Ohio
Sunday, March 17, 8:25 p.m.

A cacophony of barking, the sound of Joshua's happy laughter—and the need to escape Faith's knowing gaze—had Dani drying her hands and joining the others in her living room. Marcus's younger brother Stone had arrived with his girlfriend, Delores, and the Russian wolfhound mix that Delores never went anywhere without.

The front door was open, and through the storm door glass Dani could see Marcus and Stone engaged in an intense conversation, but it was Joshua who grabbed her attention. He stood face-to-face with the enormous dog, completely fearless as Angel sniffed at his neck and licked his face.

Joshua loved dogs. He'd been wholly unafraid of Hawkeye as well, but it was clear that Dani's dog had attached himself to Michael.

Delores had her hand on Angel's collar, wordlessly restraining the well-trained animal, whose tail wagged. She was telling Joshua that Angel helped her take care of all the dogs at her shelter until they found their forever homes.

Joshua turned to smile at Dani. "She has dogs and

they need forever homes. Can we get another dog for me?"

Dani opened her mouth, unsure of how to respond, but Michael answered for her, signing brusquely to his brother.

"No, Joshua. This place is only temporary. We don't live here. We'll have to leave soon."

Temporary. Oh God. Dani reeled for a moment, feeling like all the breath had been knocked out of her as Joshua's little face crumpled.

"Oh," he whispered, his hands pulled tight to his body as he signed back to Michael. "I forgot."

The room went silent as everyone turned to look at Dani, waiting for her to say something. To do something.

This had happened before, she told herself, even as a sense of panic swamped her. Previous foster children had fallen in love with Hawkeye. Had wanted to stay. Dani had always been gentle as she'd told them that she was only a . . .

A temporary stop. *God. I hate that word.*

This felt different, this situation with Joshua and Michael. And she realized that she wanted it to *be* different. She wanted it to be . . . un-temporary.

But life rarely worked the way she wanted.

Joshua stepped back from Angel the wolfhound, his eyes downcast. "Sorry," he said to Delores. "I can't have a dog. Maybe when I grow up I'll be able to help one."

Dani sank to her knees in front of Joshua, pulling him in for a hug, patting his thin little back as he sagged against her, sad when he'd been so happy only moments before. She glanced at Michael, whose eyes were flinty, full of warning. But there was also entreaty there, a sad awareness that he was too young to know.

"Don't get his hopes up," Michael signed. "Please."

Dani gave him a nod, then pulled away from Joshua to use her hands so that Michael could understand her, too. "I am usually an emergency foster provider," she said. "That means I'm a quick stop when kids are in danger at home."

"Like Michael," Joshua said. "Because Mom threw a bowl at his head."

"Yes," Dani said, grateful that Joshua didn't know about the abuse John Brewer had inflicted on Michael. "Usually kids stay with me for just a few days."

Joshua's mouth pinched, but he nodded stoically. "So we have to go."

"I don't know," Dani said honestly. She felt like she was saying that a lot today. "I have had a few kids stay longer, so I don't know. What I can promise is that I won't let you go anywhere that's not safe."

"But we're still temporary," Joshua said in a small voice.

Dani wanted to promise him the world. But she didn't want to hurt him any more than he'd already been hurt, so she just gathered him close and held him again, whispering behind his ear while signing behind his back so that Michael could see. "I know it's hard right now. I want to promise you that it'll get better, that you can stay here, but the truth is, I don't know what's going to happen. I *can* promise that I won't lie to you. Ever."

"Okay," Joshua whispered into her neck, then pulled back enough to sign. "Can I still have the Spider-Man pj's?"

Dani's heart hurt. He'd gone from asking for a dog to asking to keep a pair of pajamas. "Yes, sweetheart."

"Can . . . can I go to my room?"

She let him go. "Sure," she said unsteadily. "I'll be up in a little while to give you a bath."

He turned away, the picture of dejection walking up the stairs. Still on her knees, her eyes burning, she watched Michael follow him.

The silence in the room was oppressive. Then Kate sighed. "You can't save everyone, Dani. Sometimes shit happens. You can only do what you can humanly do. And like it or not, you're human, not Wonder Woman. I see this every day on the job. I want to help all of the people I meet, especially the kids. But I can only do my job and do it well."

Murmurs of agreement rippled from the others.

"I see it, too," Scarlett said. "And the small things are important. You and I helped Tommy and Edna yesterday, and they're safe and warm tonight. Tomorrow they'll go back to the street. We can't stop that. But we can be there the next time they need help."

But Michael and Joshua weren't two elderly homeless people who'd been living on the street for years and knew how to keep themselves safe. Michael and Joshua were children. *I need to do more.*

A hand on her elbow had her looking into her brother Greg's concerned eyes, mismatched like her own. "Not your fault," he signed and tugged her to her feet. "You're keeping them safe. That's a lot. Michael knows that. He told me so. He's grateful for all you've done—this house, the lawyer, all of it. He just can't let himself get used to it."

Because it's temporary. Just like Diesel, she realized with a start. He'd said that she thought him temporary. And she did, but not like he thought.

She knew he'd leave, because she couldn't let him stay. She couldn't let him stay because he'd leave. It was a vicious cycle.

One that needed to stop. She just wished she knew how.

"I want to do more," she told Greg, not voicing her words because she was afraid she'd cry if she tried. Do more for the boys, more for Diesel. *More for me.*

Greg tucked her hair behind her ear, the gesture so grown-up that she blinked. "I know," he signed. "But while they're here, they'll be happy. And when they leave they'll remember you as the lady who kept them safe."

"You grew up when I wasn't looking." She forced a smile. "Deacon's done a good job raising you."

Greg frowned, then a sad understanding crept into his expression. "Dani, *you* raised me. Not Deacon. He was off having a career. *You* kept me safe all those years with Jim and Tammy. You're the one who missed your senior prom because I had an ear infection. You're the one who came home every night you were in college instead of partying like the other kids. You read me stories and made sure I learned to read, too. You're the one who checked my homework and made sure my hearing aids worked. You're the one who went to bat for me every time I messed up. That was *you*." He swallowed hard. "If I turn out good, it's because of *you*."

The sob rose in Dani's throat and she couldn't fight it back. There, in front of everyone, she broke down, leaning into Greg's shoulder and crying like a child. Slowly, his arms rose to close around her and awkwardly he patted her back.

Another loud sob broke behind her. "What did he say?" Scarlett demanded tearfully from the sofa. "What did he say to make her cry like that?"

"I don't know," Faith said, sounding bewildered. "They were going too fast for me to follow."

"Uh, Scar?" Kate asked carefully. "Why are you crying if you don't know what they said?"

"I don't know!" Scarlett wailed, sniffling loudly. "Damn pregnancy hormones."

"Pregnancy hormones?" Faith echoed. "Oh my God. Scarlett!"

Pregnancy hormones? Grateful for the distraction, Dani pulled from Greg's arms and patted his cheek. "Sorry," she signed, then pointed over her shoulder where Scarlett was getting hugs, which started all the dogs barking again. "Seems like Scarlett just told everyone she's pregnant."

A slow grin spread over Greg's face. "Cool." Then he sobered. "Are you okay?"

"Yeah. I think I am." *I hope I am.*

And she hoped she could make Diesel understand why she kept him at arm's length. Her fear of being left alone being only one reason. Because there were a lot of other issues. Her status being the most obvious one.

Adrian being the other. Adrian and her status were wound together like a hopelessly snarled ball of Kate's yarn. She'd need to figure out how to tell Diesel the truth so that he'd know . . . what? *That it's not him, it's me?* That sounded lame, even to her own mind.

As to the issue of the boys . . . She didn't want to stop being an emergency provider, because there were deaf and hard-of-hearing kids who needed her, but for Michael and Joshua? *Maybe I can make it permanent for them.*

The storm door opened abruptly and Marcus strode in, his expression forbidding. "Why are you crying?" he asked his wife. Then he realized what she'd shared and he shook his head, his mouth tipped up in an indulgent smile. "You spilled the beans? You're the one who's been insisting that we keep it a secret, and you told everyone?"

Scarlett sniffled. "I couldn't help it. Dani made me cry."

Marcus raised a questioning brow as he closed and locked the front door.

Dani just shook her head. She didn't have the energy to go through that again. "Where is Stone? Isn't he coming in?"

"No. He's gone to the casino to back Diesel up."

The casino where Brewer had gambled away first his house, then his stepson. Where he might have crossed paths with his killer. A sense of relief rolled through Dani, because Stone would keep Diesel safe. "Good." She didn't want Diesel to be alone.

Even though I will be.

Cincinnati, Ohio
Sunday, March 17, 8:35 p.m.

Cade checked that the ski mask was properly positioned before driving past Dani Novak's house. For now it covered only the top of his head, but he could yank it down in half a second to cover his face if he needed to. Only when he needed to, though. It wasn't cold enough to warrant the mask and its presence might make an overly observant homeowner suspicious enough to call the cops. Novak's quiet little neighborhood seemed the type to have a host of overly observant homeowners, with its tree-lined streets and minivans in every driveway.

Except for Dani Novak's driveway. Hers looked like an SUV dealership. He counted four in total: a Subaru, an Escalade, and two Jeeps.

Two men stood on the front porch, deep in conversation. Both were tall. One of them was at least Cade's size. Good to know what he'd be up against.

He wished he'd thought to put his headphones on, because his long-range mike would have picked up their conversation. But it also picked up his engine's noise, so he'd wait until he'd found a place to park before using the listening device.

The front door was open and he could see a small slice of a living room through the storm door glass. Even with his windows up, he could hear barking.

There were dogs in the house. *Dammit.* Lots of big dogs from the sound of them. He hated it when people he needed to kill owned dogs. Invariably the animals tried to protect their owners. Sometimes the worst monsters had really nice dogs.

He'd have to get a sedative to knock them out. He never killed the dogs, just helped them take superlong naps. *I'm not a monster, for God's sake.*

There were enough people in that house that *someone* would know where the safe house was. He needed to wait until that someone came out. Then he'd follow.

And how will you know who the right someone is?

That was when he saw her.

Oh, hello, Doctor. She was entering the living room from what was probably the kitchen. It was definitely Dani Novak. He'd Googled her name and found her photo. He could see the streaks of white in the front of her hair, stark against the rest, which was very black.

His pulse kicked up when one of the men on the porch turned to look at his vehicle. He kept driving, grateful that the windows of his SUV were tinted darkly enough to hide his face and that he'd muddied up the license plates. He was so close to his goal, he couldn't allow himself to be noticed now. If Dani was here, either the kids were, too, or she'd leave to go to them soon.

He'd find a place where he wouldn't be noticed and then wait until either she came out or all the visitors left. Then he'd listen and watch.

Lawrenceburg, Indiana
Sunday, March 17, 9:40 p.m.

Diesel didn't glance up when two beers were placed in front of him, keeping his eyes on the crowded riverboat casino. He wasn't sure what he was looking for, but John Brewer had kept receipts from drinks at the bar on the *Lady of the River*, on more than one occasion. So he'd wait and watch.

"I didn't order those," he stated flatly, pointing to the new drinks. He'd been nursing the same beer since he'd arrived an hour ago.

A solid form dropped into the booth beside him with a resounding thunk, the voice as familiar as his own. "If you're going undercover at a bar, you need to at least look like you're consuming alcohol in some form," Stone O'Bannion said dryly.

Diesel blew out an impatient breath. "What are you doing here, Stone?"

Marcus's younger brother was another of Diesel's oldest and most trusted friends. But he didn't want the man here at the moment.

"Keeping your investigation from going tits-up." Stone sipped at his beer. "You look like you're loaded for bear and maybe even carrying a badge. Nobody's going to do anything suspicious with you sitting there looking all pissed off and righteous."

Diesel finally looked away from the crowd of people. He glanced at Stone, who appeared to be studying the blackjack table, but whose eyes were constantly roving. Looking. Watching. The man was a skilled journalist, having gone undercover for several dangerous assignments even before being embedded with troops in the Gulf. If it happened in a room, Stone O'Bannion saw it.

"You're right," Diesel murmured. He was too tense. Too angry. Too grim. If Brewer had been up to something, no one would tell him. "Hope I didn't blow it."

"Maybe, maybe not." Stone wriggled, sliding down in the seat, making himself comfortable. Seemed that he planned to stay awhile. "But never fear," he added with overly bright sarcasm. "I'm here to help you. First thing, loosen that grip your jaws have on your teeth before they crumble into dust."

Diesel glared, wanting to tell Stone to leave him alone. But Stone's staying was probably not a bad idea, because Diesel hadn't been aware that he was broadcasting rage. "I'm not good company," he admitted, realizing now that he'd been in a state of furious agitation ever since leaving Dani's house. Working his jaw back and forth to loosen it, he sighed. "Sorry in advance for anything I say or do that's shitty."

Stone shrugged shoulders nearly as wide as Diesel's. "You sat with me when I was detoxing. I think you've seen me worse."

That had been bad, Diesel had to agree. Stone had

been trying to kick the heroin habit he'd developed once he'd returned from serving in the Gulf.

They all had their demons, he supposed, wondering if Stone, like Marcus, knew that Diesel's zeal in catching pedophiles was personal. "Did Marcus tell you to come?"

"Yep. Said you made him promise to stay with Scarlett at Dani's house, to help her keep them safe." Stone snorted. "Like Scarlett needs any help with that. That lady cop is the baddest badass of us all, even preg—" Biting off the word, he gave Diesel a cautious side-eye. "Did Marcus mention anything special today?"

"That Scarlett is pregnant? Yeah. And she *is* the baddest of us all, even pregnant. But . . ." Diesel sighed. "What did Marcus tell you?"

"What you told him when he got to Dani's house." Stone glanced around them meaningfully. "And based on the dead pediatrician and all those bodies they've pulled from the river, I'd say you have a right to want all hands on deck over there."

Diesel raised a brow. "How many hands were on deck?"

Stone shuddered. "Too many cops. Too many people, period. Kate and Decker, Scar and Marcus— that's a cop and two Feds. Poor Marcus."

Diesel knew that Stone's protests about all the cops who'd become part of their lives over the past few years were purely for show. Scarlett and Stone had become very close, but Stone had to maintain his prickly shell.

"Marcus can take care of himself," Diesel said, shaking his head.

"I sure hope so. Anyway, Delores loves all the ruckus, so I dropped her and Angel off at your doctor's house and split."

Diesel pressed the heel of his hand to his heart to blunt the pain that lanced his chest. "Not my doctor," he said, his voice a breath away from breaking. *Just because I wish it were so, doesn't make it so.*

Stone drew in a slow breath and let it out as he

studied Diesel's profile. "Marcus didn't tell me that part, just the business part."

Because Diesel hadn't told Marcus. He'd looked so happy in his little family bubble with Scarlett and the baby she carried. Diesel hadn't had the heart to burst it.

Stone's expression softened. "What happened? Should I talk to Dani?"

Diesel shook his head hard. "No. *God, no.* She's . . . allowed to want who she wants. And she's allowed not to want me." He held up his hand when, frowning, Stone started to say more. "I'm glad you took Delores over there." Stone's petite girlfriend was the sweetest of their circle, and her animal shelter had sourced nearly all of their pets. Angel, her wolfhound, was nearly as big as she was, but just as sweet. Unless someone tried to hurt Delores or Stone. Then the dog was a fierce protector. *Just what Dani and the boys need.* "Michael and Joshua will love Angel. They've already fallen for Hawkeye."

Stone's nod was both thoughtful and sad. "Okay. Well, then, what do you need from me? I'm here to watch your back."

"I don't know. I think there's . . . *business* happening here." Diesel looked around, wondering if they could be overheard. It might be paranoid on his part, but this situation had already bypassed weird. "Special business."

It was how they referred to their special *Ledger* investigations, those in which powerful people, usually men, had gotten away with terrible crimes. Those investigations usually resulted in the powerful men being punished, either by the judicial system or via very strong suggestions that they back away from their families and allow the *Ledger* team to relocate the wives and children somewhere safer.

Stone gave him a nod of understanding. "Then we watch." He lifted his brows, indicating a skirmish in its early stages. "At least we'll be entertained."

Two very drunk men were arguing with each other while a woman tried to separate them. One of the men roughly pushed the woman aside, making her stumble on her high heels and fall flat on her butt.

Diesel tensed. "This is getting really ugly. Is she all right?" he asked, while the second man, apparently avenging the woman's honor, let out a huge roar and lunged for the man who'd shoved her.

Shouting for security, two of the dealers stepped in and restrained both men. The room seemed to draw a relieved breath—until someone helped the woman to her feet and she reentered the fray, her fists swinging. Bystanders began to yell for security, too, just as the woman delivered a stunning left hook to the first man.

"I'd say she's all right," Stone said.

"King!" A woman rushed at the table where Diesel and Stone sat, her face flushed, her expression irate. "Why are you just sitting there? Get off your ass and do your damn job—" She stopped abruptly when she reached them, blinking at Diesel, her irate expression gone blankly confused. "Um . . . I'm sorry, sir. I'm *so* very sorry. I thought you were someone else. Please excuse me."

She backed away, bobbing her head, continuing to apologize. When she was gone, Stone turned to Diesel with a perplexed frown.

"What the hell, D?" Stone asked.

Diesel was staring after the woman, who'd run into the back, where presumably the offices were. A minute later, a guy in a double-breasted suit rushed out with two uniformed security guards in tow. The skirmish was broken up and the crowd returned to the gaming tables.

"That's the second time in two days that I've been mistaken for someone else," Diesel murmured. "That woman—I think she was the manager—called me King."

"I'd say you're more of a baron," Stone joked, then

sobered when Diesel didn't laugh along. "Who was the other person?"

"Michael Rowland." Diesel grabbed his phone from his pocket and opened up the *Ledger*'s home page. Front and center was the sketch of the bald man Michael had seen kill John Brewer.

Stone was looking over his shoulder. "I can see the resemblance. You think it means something?"

"It could. Michael sees this guy . . . y'know." Diesel folded his fingers to look like a gun and tapped the photo, unwilling to say the words in case there were eyes and ears spying on them.

"I get it," Stone said. "And the victim frequented this casino."

"He did. It's not a coincidence. Stepdad and this King guy—the one that the manager thought was me—their paths could have crossed here. Maybe something happened between them that led to the killing."

Just then the woman came back carrying a tray with two beers. "Gentlemen, please accept my apologies. I feel terrible having talked to you that way."

Diesel gave her a smile. "Not a problem. I have to say I'm curious, though. I'm not usually mistaken for someone else. Who is my doppelgänger?"

The woman chuckled as she set the beers in front of them. "Our security manager, Scott King. I remembered after I yelled that he's off for a few days."

Scott King. Now Diesel had a name to go with the face of the man who'd probably murdered at least Brewer, and maybe the others who'd been pulled from the river. For a moment he considered keeping the information to himself, but he knew he needed to tell Deacon and Adam ASAP. The man was a killer. He might have found at least one of his victims here, in the casino. And this was information Diesel had found in a mostly legal way, one that could be backed up in court if need be.

He held his phone out to the woman. "Is this King?"

She looked at the photo and . . . froze. "Oh my God. That's him." She grabbed Diesel's phone and scrolled to the story, turning pale as she read. "*He's* the one who killed that fisherman? I didn't . . ." She pressed her lips together and handed back the phone. "I shouldn't talk to any cops without my boss and our legal counsel."

"Well, we're not cops," Diesel said.

Her eyes narrowed. "I don't believe you. You look like cops. Both of you."

Stone winced. "Ouch."

Diesel elbowed him. "We're with the *Ledger*."

She took a step back, her face growing even paler. "That's worse. I'm sorry. I can't talk to you anymore." She practically ran back to the office.

"And I think that's our cue to exit stage right," Stone murmured. "If I can still breathe with this knife in my heart. Saying we look like cops. She knows how to hurt a guy."

Diesel rolled his eyes. "Come on, drama queen."

"Drama *king* to you, *Elvis*," Stone said lightly, but he got up from the booth and headed straight for the exit. "If you can be a King, so can I."

Ignoring Stone's taunting use of his first name, Diesel was calling Adam as they headed for the door. The detective answered on the first ring.

"Diesel? What's up?"

"I found the man in the sketch, or at least I know where to find him. His name is Scott King and he's the security manager on *Lady of the River*."

"The gambling riverboat?" Adam asked.

"One and the same," Diesel said. "The general manager mistook me for him, and now that she's realized we've made the connection she's busy circling the wagons, calling in the owner and their lawyer. I know it's not your jurisdiction, but I'd recommend you get someone over here fast, before they start destroying any evidence you might find useful."

"Thanks, man. Should I ask why you're at the casino, since you don't gamble?"

"Probably not. Catch you later." Diesel motioned to Stone. "Let's go."

Stone led the way, creating a path for them, like Moses parting the Red Sea. "Shit," he said as they made it through the exit and onto the riverboat's main deck.

Diesel glanced around him, looking for threats. "What?"

"We left two perfectly good beers on the table back there."

Diesel snorted a surprised laugh. "You asshole. I'll buy you another beer."

"You'd better," Stone said, then grunted. "Sorry, man," he said to a customer coming in.

The man looked them over, his expression oddly wary. "You work here?"

"Nope," Stone said, without breaking a smile. "We're cops."

Diesel had his hand out, ready to slap Stone upside the head, when the man, who looked to be about thirty-five, stepped aside. "By all means, Officers. Is everything okay in there?"

"I might not pick tonight to gamble," Stone said. "Especially if you have any unpaid parking tickets." Without blinking, he passed by, leaving the stranger looking confused and alarmed.

Diesel sighed. "My friend is not well. He's not a cop." That he himself also wasn't a cop he left unsaid. And he wasn't sure why. "But he is right about choosing a different night to gamble. Sorry," he added, shaking his head at Stone's back in exasperation. "Like I said, he's not well."

"I hope . . . your friend gets help?" the man said uncertainly.

"Me, too. Have a nice evening." Diesel jogged after Stone, still shaking his head as he got into the passenger seat of Stone's Escalade. "You are going to get us in so much trouble one of these days."

Stone just grinned and started the engine. "Where to?"

Home, Diesel wanted to say. But he bit it back, because the home he'd been visualizing had a cozy kitchen where the woman he craved was sipping her tea and smiling across the table at him as a dog snored at their feet.

"My house," he said, hearing the terseness in his own voice. "I left my truck there." And his computer. He hadn't wanted to risk the sensitive information held on his hard drive, so he'd left his laptop locked up. "I took a cab over here."

Stone pulled out of the parking lot just as two black-and-white cruisers raced in. "Your house it is."

Lawrenceburg, Indiana
Sunday, March 17, 10:15 p.m.

Grant Masterson watched the two men walk away, feeling like he should know the guy who'd claimed to be a cop. He had one of those faces that was familiar in a déjà vu kind of way. The other guy—the actual cop—was massive, bald, and tattooed. Yet even though he spoke in a low growl, he was curiously soft-spoken.

Still not someone I'd want to meet in the dark, he thought, then gave the ramp onto the riverboat a cautious look. He wasn't sure whether he should go into the casino or not. He was hoping he'd find Scott King on duty tonight, because he'd been unsuccessful in finding the casino's security manager's home address. He hadn't been able to find anything at all on Scott King, actually. Which he supposed was understandable for a guy in the security industry. They were paranoid bastards. Grant did the taxes for a security firm, and getting them to reveal anything was like pulling teeth.

But even if he didn't get to talk to either Scott King or Richard Fischer, he might meet someone who'd seen Wesley. Still, he hesitated. If those guys were to be believed, something was about to go down.

Grant wondered what they knew. Following his gut with Dawn Daley had yielded information, so he followed his gut again, pivoting to follow the men to their vehicle.

He got close enough to see them get into a dark SUV and begin driving away.

He turned back to the riverboat, but froze at the sound of sirens. *Yeah, those guys know something, and that something's going down right now.*

Slowly he backtracked to his own car, not wanting to attract the attention of the police. If Wes was okay, he was involved in something very wrong. Something that required him to sell heroin and keep an unregistered gun in his home safe. Alerting the police could, at best, land Wes in prison. At worst, it could blow his Blake Emerson cover, putting him squarely in the sights of those he'd gone to such lengths to infiltrate.

And if the cops haul Wes out of the casino in handcuffs?

Grant guessed he'd be looking for a good attorney. He hoped like hell he'd be looking for a good attorney. And not an undertaker.

He watched, heart in his throat, as uniformed officers stormed the casino's entrance. They were carrying assault rifles. *What happened to you, Wesley?*

Bridgetown, Ohio
Sunday, March 17, 10:45 p.m.

Diesel strode into his house, conscious of Stone closing the door behind them. They hadn't spoken after Diesel had asked Stone to drive him here. They'd been friends long enough for Stone to know when to back off and just be there.

Stone slumped in the chair opposite Diesel's desk,

watching silently as Diesel pulled his laptop from the safe and started it up. "Scott King and Cincinnati," Diesel muttered as he typed the name into the search engine he always started with when doing a background check.

He frowned as he scanned the results, which included the individuals' most recent DMV photos. "Nobody matches."

"Could he be disguised?" Stone asked. "It'd be easy enough to wear a wig to cover his bald head."

Diesel shrugged. "Maybe," he said, and ran a hand over his own scalp, where stubble had begun to grow. He needed to shave it soon. "But nobody fits his body type. It's more likely that Scott King is a fake name."

"But surely he'd have to undergo a background check to be a security guard in a casino," Stone said, frowning. "What with all that money lying around."

Diesel gave him a sharp look. "I know how to do my job, *Montgomery*."

Stone's cheeks flushed. "Don't call me that."

Diesel rolled his eyes, because Montgomery was Stone's real first name. "You can call me Elvis in public and you get mad when I call you Montgomery? At least I have the courtesy to do it when we're alone."

Stone tried to glare, but had to laugh. "You caught that, huh?"

"I'm not deaf." But he stumbled over the word as soon as it left his mouth, because Dani *was* deaf, half-deaf, anyway. And Greg and Michael were completely deaf, yet they managed to pick up what was being said or done around them. Using the word as he had seemed . . . wrong. "I heard you," he corrected himself.

Stone's brows lifted. "Somebody is becoming politically correct."

"It's not being PC. It's being respectful," Diesel insisted, ignoring Stone's knowing smirk. "You're probably right about the background check, though. If he got the job in security and the job is legit, there should be something on him—a DMV photo, an apartment rental contract, or something. I'm expanding the search region to the tri-state area and I'll go national if I have to, but that takes more time." He typed in *Kentucky*, *Ohio*, *Indiana*, and *security*. And frowned again.

Stone leaned forward in the chair. "What?"

"This." He enlarged the screen and turned it so that Stone could see. "A guy named Scott King, age thirty-two, went missing from his job as a security guard in a nursing home."

Stone's eyes lit up. He lived for the hunt. "In Indianapolis. He went missing a year ago. How long has this King guy been with the casino?"

Diesel did another search. "Here's a forum that rates casinos." He scanned the entries until he came to one that mentioned King. "One casino guest had an altercation with a 'big bald guy' named King who had him thrown out for 'winning too much.'"

Stone huffed. "Counting cards, he means. Which shouldn't be against the rules. If you can count 'em, then more power to you."

Diesel rolled his eyes. "You only say that because you can count cards."

"Not anymore." Stone gave his best choirboy face. "I've reformed."

Meaning that Delores had asked him to stop. The woman had Stone wrapped around her finger without ever raising her voice.

Vicious jealousy ripped through Diesel's gut, startling him. *No. This isn't me. I'm happy for them.* He just wanted the same thing.

"Maybe it's time for you to move on, D," Stone murmured.

Diesel's gaze shot up to Stone's, found it filled with compassion and hurt on his behalf. "What? Move on to what?" he demanded, feigning cluelessness. Better to pretend than to take the pity. *I hate pity.*

Stone sighed. "Fine. It's just that the look on your

face just now . . ." He shook his head. "Never mind. When was that complaint filed by the card counter?"

Diesel returned his focus to the laptop screen, grateful for the reprieve. Because Stone was right. Maybe it was time to move on. "A year ago, which fits the time frame of the real security guard's disappearance. There are similar complaints on here, but all are newer."

"Will you go to Indy to check out the missing nursing home guard, to see if the riverboat's big bald security guy stole his identity?" Stone asked.

Diesel opened his mouth to say yes, but remembered Michael and Joshua. He'd promised to keep them safe, and he couldn't do that from Indianapolis. He couldn't do that from his house, for that matter.

"No. I'll go back to Dani's until the kids are safe. I promised them."

Stone nodded, understanding. "I figured as much. If you send me the info, I'll go. Delores might like a little road trip."

"Thanks," Diesel said, his throat suddenly thick. "I'm grateful."

Stone's smile was sad. "You know I'd do anything for you, Elvis."

Diesel swallowed hard, because the name hadn't been a taunt that time. "Thanks, Montgomery." He cleared his throat. "While you're doing that, I'll be trying to break into the casino's server. I want a home address for big bald 'Scott King.'"

"Will you do that here?"

Diesel hesitated. "Who's still at Dani's house?"

Stone did a quick text. Then smiled before he looked up. It was an expression that none of them had ever seen on his face before he met Delores. She made him truly happy.

Diesel waited for the jealousy, but it didn't come. Instead, there was a loneliness so intense that he had to fight not to press his hand to his heart. Because it hurt more than it had when he'd taken the bullet aimed at Marcus in Iraq all those years ago. And that bullet had nearly killed him.

Some days he'd wished it had. Today . . . He closed his eyes when they stung. *Today is not one of those days,* he told himself fiercely. *It's not.*

"Diesel?" Stone asked softly.

Diesel forced his eyes to open, silently cursing when the tears that stung his eyes trickled down his face. "I'm okay."

Stone pursed his lips. "No, you're not, but you will be. Delores says that everyone is still there—Kate, Decker, Marcus, Scarlett, and Faith. They're watching *The Avengers*. Kate's pick."

Diesel had to smile at that. "Of course it was." Kate was the ultimate Avengers fan. Then he frowned. "Wait. That's not appropriate for a five-year-old."

Stone typed out another text and smiled again at the response. "Delores says that Joshua was tucked into bed before they started the movie. They watched *Tangled* with him before supper. Take a look." He slid his phone across the desk.

Diesel sucked in a sharp breath at the photo that Delores had texted. Dani's living room was full of people, on sofas and the floor. Dani sat next to Greg, his arm around her shoulders and her head on his. Michael sat at her feet, his back against the sofa, Hawkeye in his lap. Unable to stop himself, Diesel zoomed in on her face and released the breath he held in a slow shudder.

"She's been crying," he whispered. Her eyes were red-rimmed and swollen.

"Yeah." Stone sighed. "That happened as I was leaving."

Diesel jerked his gaze up. "What?"

"She was upset. I could hear it through the storm door when Marcus was updating me on the casino situation. I texted Delores before I drove away to make sure everything was okay. She said that Joshua asked if they could get a dog for him, because Hawkeye was Michael's dog. Michael told him no, that they were only temporary. The kid looked like a kicked puppy and it ripped Dani up."

Temporary. God. Diesel rubbed his mouth with the back of his hand. New tears threatened, but he'd be damned before he let any more fall in front of Stone. He did *not* want his friend's pity. "But she must have dealt with it."

Stone shrugged. "I don't know. I left when the water-works started. Dani's tears triggered Scarlett's and she blamed her hormones." He faked a full-body shudder. "I took my cue to exit stage right." Then he met Diesel's eyes directly. "You'll have to ask Dani if she dealt with it."

"Right." Diesel busied himself, using his mouse to cut, paste, and send Stone all the information he'd found on the "real" Scott King. "You've got all you need to go to Indy. Thanks again."

Stone stood, grabbing his phone, which Diesel hadn't been aware he was still holding in his clenched fist. Diesel almost asked him to send him the photo of Dani, but he managed to tamp down the urge.

"I'll let you know what I find," Stone promised. "How much longer will you be here?"

"I'm going to try to get into the casino's server from here. My Internet connection is better than hers."

"Of course," Stone said wryly. "So . . . how much longer will you be here?"

"I'll give it three hours. If I haven't been success-ful, I'll come back."

"All right. We'll make sure she's covered until you get back." Stone looked like he wanted to say more, but turned for the door. "Talk to you soon."

The front door closed and the house was silent. Stifling. Oppressive.

Diesel wanted the barking of a dog, the happy squealing of a little boy, the victorious cry of a teen-ager when he beat Diesel on the Xbox. He wanted the cozy house with its warm kitchen where chili bubbled on the stove and the kettle whistled.

He wanted Dani's house. He wanted Dani.

His phone dinged with a text from Stone. The photo of Dani's living room.

Talk to her was the texted message.

Diesel had to close his eyes. "I did," he said to the empty room. *She doesn't want to want me.* He'd meant what he'd told Stone earlier—it was Dani's right not to want him. He wasn't going to push. Not anymore. If she changed her mind, the ball would be in her court.

With a harsh sigh, he turned to his computer and began organizing his cyberattack on *Lady of the River*'s network.

"Scott King," he muttered aloud. "I'm coming for you. You have a lot of explaining to do."

Chapter Fifteen

Cincinnati, Ohio
Sunday, March 17, 11:30 p.m.

"Okay, lights out," Dani told Michael when *The Avengers'* final credits rolled. "You have to get back on a schedule. You won't be out of school forever."

Michael stood up from where he'd been lounging on the floor. "Is Coach back?"

Dani shook her head. "Not yet." She still hoped Diesel would come back, but that hope was starting to falter.

You could call him and ask him.

I could. I could also remove my own appendix. It would be equally painful. The look on Diesel's face as he'd left still haunted her.

Temporary.

She forced a smile for Michael. "But don't worry. We'll be safe. One of these guys will stay until Coach gets back."

"And I'm staying over for a few days," Greg signed, offering Michael his fist, which Michael bumped. "I'll take the couch in the basement. I have to go to school tomorrow, but I'll get your homework and help you get caught up."

"Thanks." Michael gave the waiting group a melancholy wave, then signed, "Thank you to you all, too. Nice meeting you."

Dani voiced his words for the others, then followed Michael and Hawkeye upstairs. "Let me check your stitches," she signed without voicing.

Michael inclined his head obligingly. The sutures were dry, the wound healing nicely. She tapped his shoulder, indicating he should look up.

"You're looking good," she told him, still not voicing because his injuries were private. "How is the other thing?"

Michael looked away before dragging his gaze back, his face aflame. "Better. No more blood."

"Good. Don't forget to take the laxative pills. They'll help."

Michael's quick eye-roll spoke volumes. "Okay. Fine."

She gave him a smile. "Don't stay up reading too long, okay?"

He smiled back, shyly. "I won't. Thank you," he added in a burst of sign.

She tilted her head. "For what?"

He gestured around him. "All this. Getting your friends to watch over us. Not hating me because of what I said to Joshua."

She sighed. "Well, you told him the truth. I am temporary emergency housing. But you guys are in a unique position. I'm hoping you can stay the max time, which is thirty days." And then? *We'll see.* But she wasn't promising anything until she had hard facts. There was no way she'd further disappoint these kids.

His smile was wobbly. "Better than nothing. Good night."

Dani watched him go, then descended the stairs with a sigh, only to be met by the sudden barking of seven dogs at a knock on the front door. The dogs were quickly hushed by their owners, and Marcus gently pushed her aside when she started for the door.

She glared at him. "I would have checked who it was first."

"He promised Diesel he'd keep you safe," Scarlett murmured as she made her way back into the living room. She'd raced for the half bath as soon as the movie had finished, bemoaning her constant need to pee. "Marcus won't break a promise to anyone, especially to Diesel."

Marcus, Stone, and Diesel were a tightly knit group, Dani thought, grateful that Diesel had a strong support system. He was likely going to need it. She still hadn't figured out what she'd say to him when he came back.

If he came back.

It wasn't the security she was worried about. She had no doubt that any one of her gun-toting friends or family would stay with her until everything was safe.

Or maybe she should request a safe house for the boys. Part of her rebelled at the notion. This house was set up for Michael. And it was Dani's home. It had taken her a long time to fix it the way she wanted it. She'd have to wait and see what happened. Her friends wouldn't be able to stay with her forever.

Of course, if the boys' mother came after Joshua, Dani wouldn't need assistance from anyone. She'd knock the woman on her skinny ass before she got close to the little boy. She looked down, unsurprised to see that she'd clenched her fist.

"Dad? Keith?" Marcus's curious voice cut through her thoughts. "Come on in."

Dani looked up to see Marcus opening the front door wide for Jeremy O'Bannion and his husband. For a moment she was startled that they'd dropped by so late, but then she remembered.

Oh, right. Laurel. LJM Industries, the company that had bought the Brewers' house. Jeremy was supposed to have asked his colleagues about her today.

Both Jeremy and Keith kissed her cheek and Keith

held out a casserole dish. "We made a lasagna for you guys. I figured you're not used to cooking for so many."

Dani took the dish, touched. "Thank you, Keith." She'd gotten to know the two men through Deacon and Faith, as Jeremy was Faith's uncle. The couple hosted their circle of friends often, and Keith was a fabulous cook. "I'm sure Michael and Joshua will love it. Especially Michael. He's missed a few meals." Because that mother of his hadn't bought enough food for both boys. If her hands hadn't been full of lasagna, they would have clenched into fists again.

"It's Diesel's favorite," Keith explained.

Of course it is. Diesel was part of Jeremy and Keith's family through Marcus. The family Diesel had made. It made sense that they'd know all his favorite foods.

She realized that he hadn't talked about his family. And she hadn't asked, even after he'd asked about hers. *I'm selfish. God, he deserves better.*

Faith leaned over and sniffed at the dish. "Keith's lasagna is the best." She hugged Jeremy. "Hey, Uncle Jeremy. You missed the movie. *The Avengers.*"

He kissed her cheek as well, but didn't return her smile. "Don't close the door, Marcus. Troy's right behind us."

"Okay," Marcus said, sounding surprised. A few seconds later, Special Agent Luther Troy entered, a big Tupperware bowl under one arm like a football. Kate's partner at the FBI, Troy was closer to Jeremy's age, and laughingly referred to himself as "Uncle Luther" to the rest of them.

"Dani," he said, giving her a one-armed hug. "The lasagna was part of my cooking lesson today. I hope it's good." He tapped the lid of the bowl. "I made cookies for the boys. I know you don't keep a lot of sugar in the house."

Dani had gotten to know Troy, since they were both frequent visitors to the O'Bannion house. Troy had an ulcer and had eaten a lot of bland foods until Keith started teaching him to cook flavorful meals that met his dietary requirements. Dani's antiretroviral meds sometimes irritated her stomach, so she was thankful for the cooking tips as well.

"I'm sure Michael will love it," she assured him. And given Michael's rectal bleeding, Keith's recipes might be easier for him to digest as well.

Faith had been joined by Kate, and both were giving Troy and Jeremy worried looks. "What's going on here?" Faith asked.

"We asked Jeremy to do some research for us, Diesel and I," Dani said. She had no idea why Troy had joined them, but his presence made her worry escalate. "Have a seat. I'll put this away, and—"

"I'll do it," Faith interrupted, grabbing the dish. "Just don't start until I get back. I don't want to miss anything important."

Dani winced. She wasn't sure that Diesel would want everyone to know what he'd discovered, because they'd know that he—She stopped herself short. They all knew that he hacked. Every single person in the room had been the recipient of information that Diesel had gained through hacking.

"That's fine." She took a seat next to Greg, who was watching impatiently.

"What's happening?" he signed. "Why are they here?"

"Hi, Greg," Keith signed awkwardly as he sat next to her brother. "How's everything?"

Greg smiled at him. "Fine. And you?"

Greg lived with Faith and Deacon, and often visited the O'Bannion house. Unfortunately, although Jeremy and Keith were learning to sign, neither was very proficient. Keith tried hard, but claimed that his big hands were too clumsy.

Which made Dani think of Diesel's big hands, which signed fluidly. And had held her so tenderly. Mentally she gave herself a hard shake. She was *not* going down that road to nowhere.

Jeremy had trouble signing because of the severe burns to his hands he had suffered in the car accident that had ended his career as a surgeon. After the accident, he'd become a professor in the medical school.

Which was why he was standing in her living room. Diesel had asked him to use his med school contacts to find out who Laurel of LJM Industries was. From the sober expression on his face, he'd found something, and it didn't appear to be good.

Dani briefly considered telling Greg to go downstairs, but her brother had grown up so much in the past few years. Michael was going to need a friend, and that friend would need to be careful until the big bald killer was caught. Greg might not agree to the precautions if he didn't know why. He was a lot like Deacon that way. Rules needed to make sense.

"I'll tell you when Faith gets back," she told Greg. "It's a long story and I only want to tell it once."

Jeremy gestured to Marcus to move so that he could sit next to Scarlett. Once he had, he gave her a frank appraisal. "Are you eating okay?"

"Like a horse," Scarlett muttered.

"Good," Jeremy said, patting her hand with his gloved one. "I want my grandchild to be healthy."

Scarlett beamed at him, and Dani felt a pang of envy. She knew that it was medically possible—and safe—for her to have children, even with her positive status, which was a miracle on its own. But she'd decided that she didn't want to be a mother to an infant again. As Greg had reminded her earlier, she'd raised him.

And of course, there was the issue of needing a father for a baby. *Diesel would be a good dad,* she thought, stifling a sigh. Just another reason he needed to find someone else.

Faith returned and sank to the floor, sitting crosslegged. Instantly she was flanked by her two dogs. "I'm here," she signed with a flourish. "Please begin."

Greg rolled his eyes. "Is this about Michael? Shouldn't he be here?"

Dani shook her head. "Not yet. I have other things to tell him, too, but he's had a rough few days. I wanted him to have at least one low-stress day." But then she thought of the way he'd sobbed in Diesel's arms. The kid wasn't going to have any low-stress days for a long while.

She explained to the others what she and Diesel had found, careful not to say that Diesel had hacked into Brewer's computer to begin with. "Based on some of the business names, I think her first name was Laurel," she finished and looked to Jeremy expectantly, ready to interpret his reply for Greg.

Jeremy nodded. "You're right. Laurel Jo Masterson. She graduated with her undergrad degree almost three years ago. She'd completed her first year of med school and had started the second. I didn't know her, as she wasn't in any of my classes." He gave Dani a respectful nod. "She did take Human Gross Anatomy and she did get an A-minus. Having that information helped her HGA professor remember her."

Delores looked confused. "Why didn't you just ask the registrar for students with the initials LJM?"

"They didn't have enough for a warrant," Troy said, "and the university would require one. One of the reasons I came along. I might have flashed my badge a time or two to smooth the way."

Scarlett was biting her lip. "I assume you haven't told Deacon and Adam anything about this."

Dani shook her head. "Not yet. We don't actually know anything yet. Will you tell them?"

Scarlett frowned, then sighed. "I have to. But not until we know something solid that connects to an existing part of the investigation so that we can legally start probing. Otherwise anything we learn will be inadmissible in court. Jeremy, what did you find out?"

"Laurel Jo Masterson dropped out of med school a month into her second year," Jeremy said. "She submitted the proper paperwork, but not in person. She mailed it to the office. When I finally got her name from her HGA professor, I called one of my old friends in the office and asked if she remembered her. She did, because Laurel's brother came looking for her in January, at the beginning of the spring semester, when she didn't return home for Thanksgiving or Christmas. The family had been receiving e-mails from her, but no one had actually talked to her, and the brother was worried. My friend confirmed to the brother that the office had received Laurel's withdrawal documents at the end of September. It was the first the brother had heard of it."

"Brothers Grim," Dani murmured. "Why didn't her disappearance make the news?"

"That's what took me so long to find out," Jeremy said. "And why I asked Troy to come with Keith and me as we asked our questions."

"I went because I wanted Jeremy to have a witness," Keith explained, "because he was talking to young female medical students in their apartments. It might have looked unprofessional."

"I was also nervous about Jeremy going alone," Troy added, "because, even though you didn't tell him why the young woman was important, we figured something was up because Diesel was involved. And the kid you took in was accused of murder yesterday. I didn't want whoever actually committed the murders getting to Jeremy and Keith because they were asking questions."

Dani grimaced. "I'm sorry. I never intended to put you in danger."

Jeremy shook his head. "Don't be ridiculous. You've put yourself in danger by bringing the boy into your home. We didn't end up having any trouble at all. At least, not of the violent variety. I'm glad Troy came with us, because he was able to locate Laurel's old roommate, who'd moved several times, moving up to a more expensive apartment each time."

"That's not suspicious," Kate said dryly.

"That's what we thought," Troy agreed. "When we finally found the roommate, she told us that Laurel said she was leaving school to run away with her boyfriend, an older man she met at a party. She claimed Laurel had e-mailed her that she was spending the holidays with this guy. The roommate said she told this to the brother, who was very upset and didn't believe her. But CPD did believe that Laurel had simply run away and therefore did not open an investigation, even though the insistent brother was a Cleveland cop."

Dani blinked in surprise. "A cop?"

Jeremy nodded. "The roommate said that the cop visited her several times, until she threatened to get a restraining order. He accused her of making up the story that his sister had run away, but she insisted she'd never have done that."

"Do you have the name of the roommate?" Dani asked.

Jeremy handed her a piece of paper. "I made notes of everything we found. You think that Laurel Masterson is dead?"

"Yes," Dani said sadly. "And her brothers are out to get revenge against whoever killed her."

"One of her brothers is Grant Masterson," Marcus said, looking at his phone's screen. "I just ran the search. A Cleveland accountant. Married with three kids."

"And the cop brother?" Scarlett asked.

"He introduced himself to my friend in the office as Wesley Masterson," Jeremy said. "It's on that paper."

Marcus was already typing the cop's name into his phone. "Wesley Masterson is a detective with the narcotics department. He was written up in one of the Cleveland papers when he got a commendation after going undercover for three years."

"Is either Grant or Wesley big and bald?" Dani asked.

Marcus shook his head. "Nope. Neither are bulky. Both about five-ten."

Dani frowned, putting the pieces together in her

mind. "He was undercover for three years? When did he come out from under?"

Marcus checked the article. "January before last."

Dani sighed. "So he would have been undercover when she initially went missing. He didn't know she hadn't come home for the holidays until it was too late. Of course he was frantic."

"And feeling guilty that he wasn't there for her," Keith added quietly. "I would."

Jeremy patted his hand. "I would, too."

"Ditto," Scarlett agreed.

Greg's forehead was furrowed. "So if this LJM Industries bought Michael's house, does it mean they killed his stepfather? That a Cleveland cop killed his stepfather?"

Dani shrugged. "Good questions. Maybe? We don't know. But they connect somehow." She glanced at Scarlett. "Is that enough to tell Deacon and Adam?"

Scarlett nodded slowly. "The sale of the house will come out when they start searching Brewer's financials, if they haven't done so already. This case, what with the way Brewer's body was dumped and Michael's testimony about watching Brewer getting murdered, smacks of a hit. Running financials on the victims will be among the first things Deacon and Adam do. LJM will be on their radar soon, so yeah, tell them."

A quiet rapping on the front door had the dogs barking again. Once again they were shushed. Dani looked anxiously at the stairs while Marcus opened the door.

"Joshua can hear us if he wakes up," Dani murmured, still signing for Greg's benefit. "Can you run up and check on him, Greg?"

Greg gave her a sideways look. "You're trying to get rid of me." But he got up to do as she'd asked.

Marcus was letting Stone into the house, and Stone had been with Diesel. Dani craned her head to see if Diesel would follow him in, but he didn't.

"He's at his house," Stone told her without her having to ask.

Disappointment swamped her, leaving her stammering for words. "Is he . . ." She cleared her throat, viscerally conscious of the quake in her voice, because everyone was watching her. "Is he coming back?"

Stone nodded. "Later, yes." He turned to Delores. "I told him we'd stay here until he came back."

Delores just smiled, and leaned up to kiss his cheek. "I figured we would. Are you hungry? I'll fix you a plate of lasagna," she went on without waiting for his answer. "Scarlett, Kate, and Faith, wanna help me out?"

The three women looked from Dani to Stone and back to Delores. "I guess we do," Kate said.

"I could eat," Scarlett added with a shrug.

Greg came back downstairs, looking troubled. "Joshua's sound asleep, but Michael's sleeping on the floor next to him."

"He did that last night, too," Dani said. "He will until he feels safe." *And then he'll be shipped off to someone else.*

Temporary. Dammit. She was becoming more determined to change that every time that damned word entered her mind.

Delores waved at Greg to get his attention. "Can you walk all the dogs, Greg? And, Marcus, can you go with him to keep watch? Decker, can you do a perimeter check?"

"I did one," Troy said. "When we got here."

Delores merely smiled. "Then Decker can go with Marcus, Greg, and the dogs." She merely lifted her brows at Jeremy, Keith, and Troy, who wordlessly stood and followed her into the kitchen.

A minute later, Dani was looking around at the empty living room, bewildered. "They're all gone."

Stone chuckled. "People underestimate Delores because she's little and sweet, but she's a dynamo."

His whole demeanor softened when he talked

about Delores, and Dani's heart squeezed. *Diesel looks at me that way.*

So why was she fighting this so hard? *Oh, right. Because I'll break his heart.* She thought about the look on Diesel's face when he'd walked away. *I already did.*

"How is he?" she asked quietly.

Stone sighed, the softness in his face transforming into worried sadness. "Not great. I don't know what happened between you and I don't need to know, but he thinks you don't want him."

She closed her eyes and swallowed hard, not sure of what to say.

"Is it true?" Stone murmured.

She shook her head. "No," she whispered, unable to lie any longer.

"Then I assume you have a very good reason for making him think so." He hesitated so long that she opened her eyes to find him looking at his hands. "When I met Delores, I . . ." He trailed off, his cheeks growing ruddy. "I'm a recovering addict. You know that, right?"

Dani knew it. It was common knowledge in their circle of friends. "Yes."

"Did you know it was Diesel who stuck with me when I went through detox?"

"No, but I'm not surprised to hear it." Diesel had sat with Meredith as she'd recovered from her injuries the year before. He possessed a gentleness that made Dani's heart hurt. "He's loyal."

Stone's nod was fierce. "He found me delirious and seizing with withdrawal. Got me into rehab. And never told a soul. I'd be dead if it wasn't for him. So would Marcus. Diesel took a bullet for him in Iraq. Still carries it. Right here." He thumped his chest with a meaty fist. "VA docs said they couldn't remove it. Said that someday it would . . . slide. Just a smidge. And pierce his heart. He's been a dead man walking for years."

Dani's breath froze in her lungs as her blood ran cold. "What?" The word was a soundless gasp.

"He doesn't talk about it. But he won't go to any more doctors about it."

"Because he hates white coats and hospitals," she whispered.

"Exactly. You know that song 'Live Like You Were Dying'? That's what he does. He builds houses with Marcus for women and their kids after they've run from domestic violence. He coaches the Pee Wee leagues. He volunteers all over the city, trying to make the lives of kids better. He works overtime at the *Ledger*, finding dirt on lowlifes who've slipped through the justice system. He never sleeps, Dani."

She covered her mouth with her hand, horrified. Yet . . . it made sense. It all made sense. He was a man living on borrowed time.

Which was the first thing she'd address. "How long has he been carrying the bullet in his chest?"

"Ten years."

She squared her jaw. "That will change. I'll find a doctor to take it out."

"He won't go. And that isn't why I told you about it. He doesn't want you to *fix* him, Dani. He just wants you to *want* him. That's all he's ever wanted— to be wanted. We do—our family, I mean. We want him. We love him. He's one of us. We're all a little broken. You're not the only one who travels with baggage."

"I know," she managed.

"*Do you? Do you really*? I'm an addict. Heroin. I am a fucked-up man. And not always a nice person. When I met Delores, I told her that I was fucked up, a real SOB. I told her that she'd be better off picking someone else."

Oh. Stone's true message finally broke through. "What did she say? Clearly, she didn't listen."

He smiled again. "Like I said, everyone underestimates Delores. She's sweet, but the woman has a spine of steel. She told me that it was her choice. Got

right in my face and informed me that I didn't have
the right to tell her what to think or who to love. That
if my addiction was a problem, she'd tell me so, but it
wasn't." He shrugged self-consciously. "I still have
bad days, but she stays. She loves me. I don't deserve
it, but it doesn't make it any less true."

Dani swallowed hard. "How did you know?" she
asked hoarsely.

His smile became sad. "That you feel like you
don't deserve him?"

She nodded, unable to speak for fear of losing it
for the second time that evening.

"I didn't," he said. "Not until this minute. But I suspected. I've watched him watching you for months.
I've watched you watching him when you thought no
one was looking. You want him, but you tell him no.
You're not stupid and you're not mean. I can only assume there are other issues in play. Your HIV status?"

"That's one," she allowed. He was wrong on the
mean, though. *I am not a nice person, either.*

"Well, I'm not a doctor or a shrink or even a nice
guy, but I am a good judge of people and I think you
should talk to him. Tell him what's standing in your
way. And then take a page out of Delores's book and
let him make his own choices. He's a big boy, Dani.
He can deal, one way or the other."

She drew a deep breath. "Okay. I will. When he
comes back." Because he would come back, if only
for the boys.

Stone tilted his head, studying her. "Good. Oh,
and by the way, we got the name of the big bald guy
and gave it to Adam."

Dani's jaw dropped. "What the . . ." She narrowed
her eyes. "What happened?"

"We were in the casino on the *Lady of the River*
and a fight broke out. The manager mistook Diesel
for the security manager, whose name is Scott King.
Diesel's tracking him now."

Dani ground her teeth. "And when Diesel finds him?"

"I don't know, and that's the truth."

She shook her head, exasperated. "You couldn't have led with that?"

"You didn't ask what we found," he pointed out. "You asked how he was. I simply answered your question."

She scowled. "Is he planning to do something stupid, like go after this King guy all by himself?"

Another shrug. "Diesel's gonna do what he's gonna do."

She exhaled carefully, working to keep her cool. Diesel might *think* he was going after Brewer's killer by himself, but that was *not* going to happen. "You say he's at his house? Where is that?"

"I'll take you to him," Stone said. "Not a suggestion," he added when she opened her mouth to protest. "Big bald guy is out there and I'm not getting on Diesel's shit list because I let you drive alone."

Let me? Really? She was tempted to argue, but decided to leave it for later. Mainly because he was right. "Let me grab my coat." She turned for the closet, but stopped. "I can't leave the boys."

Stone rolled his eyes. "They'll be safe. Scarlett's a cop, Marcus was a US Army Ranger, and Keith was a Marine. Kate, Decker, and Troy are Feds. Kate's a goddamn sniper."

"Okay. You're right."

He gave her one of those soft smiles that he normally reserved for Delores. "I'll ask Marcus to stand guard outside the boys' bedroom door. Nobody will touch them. I promise."

She looked up into his face, seeing nothing but sincerity. "I know I'm overprotective, but . . . well, thank you."

He patted her shoulder. "Get your coat. I'll tell Delores where we're going."

Cincinnati, Ohio
Sunday, March 17, 11:30 p.m.

"I don't like any of this, Grant," Cora said after he'd described the scene at the riverboat casino that evening.

Grant sank into the buttery leather of Wesley's living room sofa, so soft that he thought he'd fall asleep right away. "Me, either," he said with a jaw-cracking yawn.

"If he's gotten involved with something this bad, maybe you should get a hotel. What if those guys come looking for him?"

Grant tried to shake the sense of dread brought on by her words. *What if they already have come looking? What if they've found him?* "I'll be fine. I'm so tired, hon, I don't think I can move to find a hotel. If I don't get any answers by tomorrow, I'll consider it. How's that?"

She blew out an aggravated sigh. "Probably the best I'm going to get, so I guess I have to take it. How much longer do you think you'll be gone?"

"I don't know. How's MaryBeth's niece working out? Is she the au pair extraordinaire that MaryBeth claimed?"

"Better. I got to sleep last night for the first time in weeks."

Grant smiled. "You sound better. Maybe we can keep her for a while."

"Can we afford a live-in au pair?"

Not really was the actual answer, but Cora sounded so happy that he wasn't going to say that out loud. For a tiny moment, Grant thought about the stacks of cash in his brother's safe. And he'd be lying if he said he wasn't tempted.

But that was dirty money and would lead to absolutely no good. Wesley's current predicament was testament to that. "Yes," he said.

Cora chuckled. "No, we can't, but I love you for trying. I'll enjoy this little reprieve and then maybe we can find a part-time helper." She made a kissing sound. "Come home to me, Grant. I don't need a full-time nanny. I just need you."

Grant's chest tightened. This was what he'd wanted for his brother and sister—a simple life with someone who loved them. "I love you. Kiss the kids for me."

He ended the call and shoved himself off the couch. As soft as it was, it was no substitute for a bed. He'd fallen asleep on it last night and woken with a stiff back. He went to Wesley's guest room and pulled back the cover on the bed.

And frowned.

There were no sheets on the bed. He checked the other guest room and found the same thing. The beds had been made up to look guest-ready, but they weren't. He began picking up items in the second guest room—lamps, knickknacks. Every one of them still bore the price tag. He picked up a framed photo and realized it was the photo that had come with the frame.

This room was a model. It wasn't real. The first guest room was the same.

This whole apartment was a fake. But intended to fool whom?

Grant found sheets on Wesley's bed in the master bedroom and kicked off his shoes. He stripped off his clothes and went to bed in his boxers, half expecting masked men with guns to come in and shoot him, thinking he was his brother.

Cora had made him paranoid. But what if she was right?

With a sigh, Grant got up and opened the floor safe. He retrieved Wesley's service weapon and set it on the nightstand. In the nightstand drawer was a full clip. He inserted it into the magazine and racked the gun to fill the chamber.

If Cora's "bad guys" came, he'd at least have a fighting chance.

He turned off the light and stared up at the ceiling, hearing every bump and creak in the night. *Tomorrow I'm getting a hotel.*

Cincinnati, Ohio
Sunday, March 17, 11:50 p.m.

Dani checked on the boys when she went upstairs to get her coat. Joshua was curled up in the bed, his arms tightly clutching the stuffed dog she'd given him. And Michael was on the floor, just as Greg had said.

At least he had a blanket tonight. She made a mental note to give him the inflatable mattress tomorrow night. If he was going to keep sleeping on Joshua's floor, he should be comfortable.

She found Stone in the kitchen, eating a plate of lasagna while Delores quietly beamed at his side. All conversation stopped as soon as Dani entered.

"I'm ready to go," she said and suddenly everyone's eyes were on her and she was fighting not to drop her gaze to the floor.

Great. Just great. They all knew she was going to Diesel. There was not a single shred of privacy in their circle. But then Jeremy gave her a small nod of approval and her heart settled. Faith's uncle—and Marcus's dad—had become a surrogate father to them all, especially sweet as most of their circle of friends didn't have the best parental relationships.

They'd made this family together, and it was every bit as strong as a family connected by blood.

The silence in the room was about to become awkward when the doorbell rang. Dani started to quiet the dogs when she realized they weren't barking. Because Delores had sent Marcus, Decker, and Greg out to walk them.

Troy went to open the door. Dani didn't miss the way his hand rested on the weapon on his belt, and a cold shiver ran down her back as she was once again reminded of the dangerous predator who wanted the young man asleep on the floor upstairs.

Over my dead body. She looked at the faces around her kitchen, taking comfort in the confidence that any one of these people would protect those boys with their lives. It was only that knowledge that was allowing her to leave them.

The front door closed and Troy reappeared, his expression an odd mixture of annoyance, fierce determination, and . . . something else Dani couldn't identify. But her attention was captured by the man pushing the jacket hood off his head as he followed Troy.

"Agent Taylor?" she asked, eyes widening at the disheveled state of the man who ran the crime scene lab for the local FBI field office. She only knew him slightly, but he was a friend to both Deacon and Adam, so he was okay in her book.

"Quincy?" Kate asked, her surprise clear. "What are you doing here? And what the hell happened? Are you okay?"

Because the man was clearly upset. He had dark circles under his eyes, and his hair looked like he'd repeatedly run his fingers through it.

"Yeah," he said to Kate, then turned to Dani. "I'm so sorry to intrude at this hour, but I saw the lights on and all the cars out front and knew you were awake. I was hoping to talk to Diesel. Is he here?"

"Not right now," Dani answered warily. "Can I help you?"

He sighed. "I'd kind of hoped to pass this on privately, but that's not really possible with your group, is it?"

"Not really," Dani said sympathetically. "What's wrong, Agent Taylor?"

"Quincy," he corrected. "Look, I'm not here. Got it?"

Troy rolled his eyes. "Just get on with it, Quince," he snapped, drawing curious stares from all over the room. Troy flicked his hand at them all. "I'm tired and it's late. What is so important that it couldn't wait until tomorrow?"

Something briefly flickered in Quincy Taylor's eyes and then it was gone. *Amusement?* Dani wondered. But Quincy was regarding her seriously again. "You read about George Garrett, the fisherman that was murdered, I assume."

"No," Dani said, "but Adam told us about it."

"Well, we wondered how the killer had gotten Garrett's name," Quincy said. "We kept his name out of the press. But when I saw the sketch CPD made based on Michael Rowland's description, I realized that I'd seen him." He glanced over at Troy. "He came to the crime scene yesterday. Was talking to one of my techs."

Troy stiffened. "Shit."

Dani sucked in a breath at the same time. "What? One of your techs told a stranger this man's name?"

"Probably not at the crime scene," Quincy said. "We're thinking that Scott King went to my tech's house last night. Akers was found at the bottom of his basement stairs with a broken neck."

Dani sank into a chair. "It wasn't an accident, was it?"

Quincy shook his head. "No. We were supposed to think it was. I've just come from Akers's house. Dani, this killer went to considerable trouble to get George Garrett's name."

Dani made herself breathe. "Then he killed Akers and Garrett."

"Yes. We believe that Garrett was killed because Scott King believed he'd seen him. King risked coming to the crime scene. He risked being seen by cops. By Feds. By *me. I* saw him there. I walked up to him and he didn't run. My coveralls have 'FBI' in giant letters across the back. King was that desperate to eliminate anyone who'd seen him."

Dani's blood ran cold. "Michael saw him."

Quincy's nod was grim. "I know. I also know that no fewer than three reporters had received calls by the time I left the Garrett crime scene this afternoon. All said that a man claiming to be one of Michael's teachers had called asking if they knew where his foster home was located. All of them told him that they'd heard he was in a safe house and the location was restricted information."

"Because Deacon and Adam spread that rumor after Garrett was murdered," Dani murmured. She swallowed back the fear that was clawing up her throat. "He's looking for Michael. He knows that Michael saw him. How?"

Troy exhaled quietly. "Probably because of all the articles about Michael online today. His mother talked to any news service that'd listen. The *Ledger* didn't run her story, but all the other news sites did. The interview she gave where she accused Michael of killing Brewer and assaulting her went viral. If King didn't know Michael was hiding in Joshua's bedroom before, he's figured it out by now."

Dani had to close her eyes against the wave of pure rage that washed over her. "I wish Scott King had killed their mother, too," she hissed and wasn't one bit sorry that she'd said it aloud, even in front of cops and Feds. She opened her eyes to see them all nodding. "Do Deacon and Adam know about Akers?"

"They do now. I told them," Quincy said, "but they're at another scene."

"The riverboat," Dani said. "Stone told me that he and Diesel had learned Scott King's name. Did they find King there?"

"No," Quincy said. "I'm on my way over there now, but I . . . wanted you to know that you need to be even more careful than you have been."

"Thank you." She squeezed his hand. "I'm sorry about Akers."

"Me, too. I'd suspended him because I thought

he'd talked to a reporter." He sighed. "I hope that didn't make him vulnerable to King."

"I think King had targeted Akers before you suspended him, Quincy," Troy said with compassion, then turned to Kate. "I texted Deacon when I saw the report of the riverboat raid. Asked if they needed help questioning the riverboat patrons. He just texted back and said they did. They're trying to get the staff processed."

Deacon and Adam were on an FBI/CPD joint task force and the two organizations sometimes lent each other personnel as needed. It wasn't common for Dani's CPD friends to be working with her FBI friends and vice versa, but it did happen when the case was high profile enough or when multiple crime scenes were involved, which was certainly true for this case.

Kate glanced at Dani. "I'm off duty tonight. I'm going to stay here."

"I figured you would. I told him I'd help." Troy shook his head. "I can't believe you all hadn't heard about it. It was all over the news."

"We were watching *The Avengers*," Kate said, lifting her chin.

Troy chuckled. "That explains everything. I'll take this one, but I don't have a car. I came with Jeremy and Keith."

"I can give you a ride there," Quincy said. He pulled the hood of his jacket back over his head. "But I'll be there for a while. You'll need to find your own ride home."

"Thanks," Troy told him, then leaned in to kiss Dani's cheek. "Be careful. Don't go doing anything stupid like going after this King guy or the boys' mother, okay? I don't care how justifiably furious you are."

"Okay," she said. "Thanks, Troy. And thanks for the cookies. The boys will love them. So will Diesel. Thank you for stopping by, Quincy. I'll make sure Diesel knows about Akers, too."

Quincy nodded and Troy gave her shoulder a final squeeze before following Quincy out the door.

Dani sat for a moment, letting the new facts percolate through her mind. "This really changes nothing," she said after a moment. "We knew the killer was, y'know, a killer. We knew he might come after Michael. We've been keeping the boys safe. We'll continue to do so. The only thing that's new is that now we know all the protection really *is* necessary. Right?"

"Right," Stone said. "So do you still want to go to Diesel?"

"Oh yeah," Dani said darkly. "It's even more important now that he not go after King on his own." She stood up. "Let's go."

Stone put his hand on her back as he walked her to his Escalade, watching the street as cautiously as Deacon or Adam would.

"Thank you, Detective Stone," she said sweetly, knowing it would get his goat. At the moment, she needed a little levity.

Sure enough, he gave her a dark look that was as fake as a three-dollar bill. "You want to go back inside, Dr. Novak?"

She sighed. "No, I'll be good, I promise. Just take me to him, okay?"

"Okay," he conceded grumpily. He opened the car door and helped her in. "Buckle up. Click it or ticket and all that shit." He slammed the door hard, then climbed in his side and slammed his own door. "You're mean." But his eyes twinkled and Dani had needed to see that.

"I'm *so* mean," she agreed, then sighed again, because she was only partly joking now. "We should hurry. No telling what the man's gotten himself into in the time he's been alone."

Chapter Sixteen

Cade breathed a sigh of relief as the black Escalade pulled away from Dani Novak's house. The place was fucking Grand Central Station. He'd parked far enough away that he wouldn't be seen by the people constantly coming and going from the house, but close enough that he could still hear outdoor conversations with his long-range mike. He settled in, then waited and waited for her to come out.

The Escalade had left earlier, driven by the burly guy who'd been talking on the front stoop when Cade had first arrived. He'd run a search on the plates, but came up with nothing useful. The vehicle was registered to a nonprofit called Patrick's Place, which was a dog shelter.

A Hummer had arrived a few hours after the Escalade left, carrying three men. That vehicle was registered to a cooking school, run by a Keith O'Bannion. It made sense because it looked like two of the three men had brought food.

Which was likely needed because the house was filled with people.

The Escalade had returned shortly after the Hummer's arrival. The bulky man went into the house and a few minutes later a teenager had come through the door. Cade had been momentarily elated, but it hadn't been Brewer's stepson.

The kid had been followed by two men—different from the three who'd arrived in the Hummer. One of the men was the other guy who'd been talking on the front stoop when he'd arrived. The kid was walking seven fucking dogs. *Seven.* The two men each took a couple of the leashes and that seemed to calm things down.

Cade had no idea who any of them were, but at least the dogs were no longer in the house. However, there were still *way* too many people in there for him to make a move. So he'd waited some more.

The final visitor drove a Toyota Tundra and had slowed once, passing the house entirely before turning around to park across the driveway. The driver was a man, but that was all Cade could see, because he wore a jacket with a hood. He'd emerged a short time later with one of the guys from the Hummer. They'd been quiet, not saying a word as they'd walked stiffly to the truck.

This was the quietest group of people Cade had ever trailed. Nobody said anything as they walked to and from the house.

Until Dani Novak had *finally* emerged. With the bulky Escalade driver, who was a cop. Detective Stone, she'd called him. Then she'd promised to "be good" so that the detective would take her "to him."

To him. The cop was taking the doctor to the safe house. Cade was so glad he'd been patient. Taking off his headphones, he started his SUV and slowly followed them, keeping them in view. He'd have the kid in his sights soon enough.

Bridgetown, Ohio
Monday, March 18, 12:55 a.m.

Diesel stared at the monitor on his right, willing Ritz to hurry. He'd run the password-cracking program dozens of times since developing it years ago. Ritz had never met a password it couldn't crack. Normally he used it to gain access to the accounts of the targets of the *Ledger*'s "special investigations," those individuals who'd abused their families, but who'd slipped through the justice system. Tonight he was sifting through the passwords in the casino's administrative database.

His network entrée had been through Jodie Spaeth, the general manager who'd mistaken him for Scott King. Unfortunately, her personal e-mail had been the target of a data breach two years ago, when a department store's network had been hacked. Fortunately for Diesel, those usernames and passwords were publicly available. Miss Spaeth had made his work very easy indeed by using the same password on her work e-mail.

Which, according to her social media, was the name of the dog she'd lost to cancer the summer before. Her username and password had provided him access to nearly everything on the riverboat's network. Including the database of all employees along with their encrypted passwords—a nonsensical hash of letters and numbers at the moment. Diesel could see Scott King's name, but the hashed password that followed wouldn't be useful until it was decrypted, and that was Ritz's job.

Once Ritz had cracked the encryption, Diesel would have access to all of King's personnel data—including his address, phone number, and the phone number of his emergency contact, which would be a good place to start searching if he'd gone into hiding.

And then? What will you do?

Give the information to Deacon and Adam if they hadn't already found it, of course, he told himself. He didn't need to see King go down with his own eyes. In Diesel's mind, the man had done a public service, ridding the world of John Brewer. The cops would ensure that King was punished for the other murders—and that the bastard was never able to hurt Michael.

He turned back to the monitor on his left. He'd been running background checks on all of the casino's staff—those he'd been able to find in places other than the server.

The general manager, Jodie Spaeth, seemed to be doing well. She lived in a very nice home in Mount Adams and drove a new Audi. He'd have to dig into her financials to determine if she was in debt. She'd seemed genuinely surprised that the security man she knew was wanted for murder, but people in debt could often be persuaded to look the other way by lawbreakers.

The riverboat was owned by Richard Fischer, forty-six. His photo showed a hometown-looking man with a warm smile. His image exuded warmth and vitality.

Diesel didn't trust him as far as he could throw him.

Fischer's net worth was staggering, if the news reports could be believed. He'd certainly need to be filthy rich to sustain his lifestyle. The man owned a gated home in Indian Hill, not too far from Jeremy's mansion. That whole neighborhood was filled with mansions. According to DMV records, Fischer owned a Ferrari, a Bentley, and a classic Corvette.

The *Lady of the River* was the smallest of all the riverboat casinos along the Ohio River, and Diesel was surprised—and suspicious—that Richard Fischer was making enough of a profit to finance his lifestyle.

He'd started to dig into Fischer's background when his cell phone buzzed with an incoming text. He glanced at the right-hand monitor, hoping for a miracle, but the program was still churning.

The text was from Stone and read **TALK TO HER,** in all caps. Diesel typed **WTF?**, and hit SEND when there was a knock on his door.

No, not a knock. Someone was banging on his front door.

What the hell? He shoved away from his desk and

ran to the door, his pulse jumping from normal to stratospheric as panic set in. Thoughts of Dani and the boys tumbled through his brain as the banging on the door got louder.

I should have stayed. Goddammit. What if—

He threw open the door and gaped. Dani stood on his welcome mat, her fist raised as if poised to bang some more.

She glared up at him, then released her fist, pressing her palm flat to his chest and shoving him backward. Stunned, he stumbled, regaining his balance in time to see a black Escalade driving away.

Stone. And then the text made sense.

His phone buzzed in his hand and he glanced at the screen as Dani slammed his door shut behind them. It was another text from Stone.

You're welcome. Don't fuck this up.

Diesel tore his gaze away from his phone to Dani's face. She was furious, her mismatched eyes narrowed and shooting sparks.

God, she was gorgeous like this.

"Don't even," she snapped when he opened his mouth—to say what, he had no idea. So he closed his mouth and followed her as she strode into the kitchen and pointed at one of the chairs at the table he'd built himself.

"Sit," she said curtly.

He sat obediently and watched as she took the chair closest to his. Folding his hands in front of him, he waited for what would come next.

She assumed a similar pose, then drew a breath and slowly released it. Lifted her chin. Held his gaze, hers boldly challenging. "I'll cut to the chase. You will *not* go after this bastard Scott King all by yourself."

He blinked. "Okay," he said simply.

She frowned, obviously not expecting that answer. "Okay? Just . . . okay?"

He fought a smile because he valued his life. "Of

course. I never planned to. What made you think . . ." The thought trailed off as the truth became crystal clear.

"Stone," they said together.

She crossed her arms over her chest. "He said you were going after him by yourself." Then her lips flattened, her shoulders sagging. "No, he didn't. I asked him if you were and he said, 'Diesel's gonna do what he's gonna do.'"

Diesel licked his lower lip to hide its twitch. "Classic Stone. A nonanswer to best fit his agenda."

"Which was to get me here so that I'd talk to you." She blew out a breath. Closed her eyes. "I'm sorry, Diesel. I shouldn't have barged in here like I did."

All the texts made sense now. "It's okay," he murmured. "Where are the boys? Are they all right?"

"The boys are fine. They're at home with an entire platoon watching over them."

That thought made him smile. "Good. Can I get you something? Tea? Water?"

Her hand gripped his arm when he started to rise. "No. Nothing. Just . . . give me a minute to regroup."

He retook his seat, resumed his pose, and waited.

Bridgetown, Ohio
Monday, March 18, 12:57 a.m.

Pulling the ski mask down to cover his face, Cade parked his SUV out of sight of the small safe house surrounded by trees and watched the Escalade until its taillights disappeared. He'd followed that goddamn Escalade out to the middle of nowhere, worried all the while that Detective Stone would stop any minute to find out why he was being trailed, but he hadn't. *Hell of a detective he is.*

Stone had dropped Dani Novak off at the house, waiting only until she was inside before driving away. Cade figured there had to be at least one more cop in there guarding the kid.

Grabbing his listening device, he ran to the house, keeping his head down so that he couldn't be seen from the windows. He stopped at the far corner, which appeared to be the garage. He didn't want to be seen and he was closest to his SUV here—critical in case he needed to get away fast.

He didn't dare look in the windows, but he could hear voices just fine from where he crouched at the corner closest to his SUV. The house wasn't that big and his listening device was delivering their voices to his headphones as clear as a bell. Once he established that the kid was here, he'd crawl around the perimeter, listening for an indication of which room was Michael's. Hopefully the kid would be asleep. At this point, he was done fooling around. There'd be no bringing the boy back to his house.

He'd do a fast double tap through the window and be on his way.

He held his breath, focusing on the voices. Two people were talking, one male and one female. The woman's voice belonged to Dani Novak, but he didn't recognize the man's. It was deep and gravelly, like he'd been asleep for five years.

"Classic Stone," the man said. "A nonanswer to best fit his agenda."

"Which was to get me here so that I'd talk to you," Novak said quietly. "I'm sorry, Diesel. I shouldn't have barged in here like I did."

Cade frowned. *What kind of name is Diesel?*

"It's okay," Diesel murmured. "Where are the boys? Are they all right?"

Cade froze. *Fuck, fuck, fuck. Where are the boys? Fuck.*

"The boys are fine," Novak said, a smile in her voice. "They're at home with an entire platoon watching over them."

Cade ripped the headphones off, so furious that he wanted to scream. This was *not* a safe house. Michael Rowland was *not here*. He was back at Novak's house, with seven dogs, an entire fleet of SUVs, and a fucking *platoon* of people.

Motherfucking sonofabitch.

Well, at least Cade knew for sure now. He'd go back to her house and wait for the platoon to disperse. Surely all those people hadn't planned to stay there all night. It shouldn't be so hard to get to one teenage kid.

He'd pivoted in his crouch, pointing his body toward his SUV, when he heard the crack of a twig. He froze again.

The Escalade-driving Detective Stone was fifteen feet away, staring at him. A heartbeat later the man began to run, headed right for him.

Cade didn't think. He just reacted, simultaneously twisting out of the detective's path and lifting his gun to fire at the man's broad chest, pumping a second bullet into his leg. Stone dropped like . . . well, a stone, going down to his knees.

"Sonofa*bitch*," the detective hissed. He tried to rise, but Cade grabbed him by the coat collar and smacked his head with the butt of his gun. Hard.

With a groan, the big man closed his eyes, unconscious. Cade tried to drag him back to his own SUV, but the fucker was way too heavy. He got him halfway, which was about fifty yards from the house. No one inside could hear if he called for help.

And speaking of help, Cade patted the man's pockets, taking his cell phone and his car keys. He shoved the big man to his side and pulled his wallet from his back pocket. As he opened it, his mouth fell open. Stone had to be carrying a thousand dollars in cash. Cade grabbed the cash, tossed the wallet, and ran to his SUV.

He passed Stone's Escalade as he drove down the driveway. The fucker had doubled back. *Well, he got what he deserved.* He'd bleed out before anyone realized he was out there.

Cade pulled over when he got to the main road.

His hands were shaking. That had been too damn close. He was tempted to leave the kid alone and just run.

But juries loved eyewitnesses. Especially orphaned eyewitnesses with inspirational disabilities. Michael Rowland had to go.

Bridgetown, Ohio
Monday, March 18, 1:00 a.m.

Diesel held his breath, waiting for Dani to compose herself, both dreading and anticipating what she'd have to say. But she was touching him and that had to mean something. *Right?*

Her grip loosened and her fingers began a caress that made his heart beat even faster, if that was possible. *She's here. In my house. At my table. Touching me.*

She was quiet so long that he worried she wouldn't say anything, but then she opened her eyes and met his squarely. He saw honesty, determination, and something else that he didn't think he liked. It looked like shame.

"I am not the person you think I am," she said quietly.

It was not what he'd expected her to say. "Who do I think you are?"

"Nice. Kind. A good person." Her jaw tightened. "A worthy person."

His first reflex was to deny her words, to insist that she *was* that person. But this was important. And maybe the reason she'd rejected him all these months.

He gentled his voice as much as he could. "Why aren't you that person, Dani?"

"Did you know that Deacon was married once before? Before Faith?"

Diesel frowned at the non sequitur. "No, I didn't."

"Only for a few months. Her name was Brandi. She was an addict, but she lied and told him that she was clean. He was a lot more trusting back then. I knew that she was using, but I knew that Deacon wouldn't believe me if he didn't see it with his own eyes."

"So you set it up so that he would? See with his own eyes, I mean."

She looked away. "I knew her dealer. We all went to the same high school."

"Wait. Deacon got married in high school? Was Brandi pregnant?"

Her gaze shot up, horrified. "No. I never would have tempted her with drugs if she'd been pregnant." She shook her head. "No. It wasn't like that. Deacon was a senior. I was a sophomore. Bruce and Mom had just died, and they left us the house. But Uncle Jim said we needed to sell it. Deacon didn't want to. He wanted to get a job after graduation and support us— Greg and me. Greg was just a baby. And . . ." She let out a breath. "Jim didn't want him. Greg, I mean. Greg doesn't know this, and Deacon and I promised we'd never tell him."

"He'll never hear it from me," Diesel said. "Why didn't Jim want him?" But he thought he knew and the very notion made him angry.

"You know we carry a syndrome, right?" she asked.

He nodded. "Waardenburg. A genetic syndrome that causes deafness and loss of pigment in hair, skin, and eyes. I looked it up right after I met you."

"To explain our family freak show," she muttered.

"No!" His explosive answer had her looking up at him warily, but he didn't care because there was nothing further from the truth. "I wanted to know what made you *unique*. You intrigued me, Dani. I couldn't get you out of my mind."

Something flickered in her eyes, an emotion he couldn't identify. He hoped it was a positive one.

"Thank you. You're in the minority. A lot of people were intrigued, but not in a good way. Jim was one of those people. He thought Mom never should have had kids, because the syndrome is hereditary. He said she got off lucky with me and Deacon because we could at least hear, even though we were 'freaks.'"

Diesel couldn't control the growl that escaped his throat. "He said that? In front of you?"

"All the time. Especially when we went to live with him after our biological dad died. Both Deacon and I had dark hair and a white streak in the front. And, of course, the eyes."

Diesel couldn't help it. He reached out and skimmed his thumb across her cheeks, under her eyes. "Beautiful," he whispered fiercely.

One side of her mouth lifted. "Where were you when I was a kid getting made fun of every day?" She shook her head. "Anyway, Mom married Bruce and we moved out of Jim and Tammy's house. Jim told Bruce to make sure he didn't make any more freaks with my mom, that statistically she was due for the 'mother lode of deformity.'"

Diesel closed his eyes, needing a moment to control the absolute rage that flamed through him. "Your uncle is a fucking SOB."

"Yeah, he is. He was worse when Greg was born, because he had all the same issues Deacon and I did, but he was a hundred percent deaf. And then Mom and Bruce died. Jim was so angry. He said he was going to have to clean up Mom's mistakes again."

Diesel realized he'd balled his hands into fists, visualizing slamming them into Jim Kimble's face. "Greg is not a mistake. He's bright and funny and he loves you."

That made her eyes well up. "I know. But thanks." She blinked and scrubbed the tears from her face with her sleeves. "Deacon was determined that Jim wouldn't take custody of Greg. He figured if he got married, we could live in Bruce's house and the state couldn't take Greg away. Or the house, for that matter."

Diesel's brows lifted. "I'm thinking that didn't work."

Her laugh was bitter. "No. He was only seventeen. He just wanted to protect us. But he'd gotten a full ride to Miami of Ohio and I didn't want him giving up an amazing scholarship to work a nowhere job just so we could keep the house. I tried to tell him that Brandi was bad news, that she hadn't changed, but Deacon thought he loved her."

She said the last words with a sad wag of her head that made Diesel very afraid. "You know that love exists, though. He's found it with Faith."

She met his gaze. "Oh, I know. That's not why I hate what came next."

And herself, he'd wager. The shame he'd glimpsed earlier was now front and center. "What happened?"

"Like I said, I knew the dealer. I cozied up to him, told him to meet me at my house after school. I figured he would and Brandi wouldn't be able to resist. Deacon was working an after-school job, but I planned to call him home with an emergency and he'd catch her in the act."

"But that's not what happened."

"No. I got delayed by one of my teachers, who was concerned that I hadn't been doing my homework. I mean, my mother had just died. Homework wasn't a priority. The dealer showed up at my house and he and Brandi did lines of coke before I got home. But Brandi had been using all along, and Greg got into her purse."

"Oh my God," Diesel breathed, horrified.

"It could have been so much worse, but yeah. There was just coke dust in her purse, but it was enough to nearly kill Greg. I got home just as he was seizing and called 911. The dealer ran. I'd been the one to ask him to the house, so I wasn't in any hurry to tell the cops he'd been there. Brandi hid, and at that moment, all I cared about was Greg. Of course Jim blamed Deacon. Said that Brandi had to go. Deacon agreed, but Brandi cried and he let her stay one more day so she could pack her things.

"Deacon and I sat with Greg in the hospital all night, but I made him go home the next day to make Brandi leave. He . . ." She rubbed her forehead. "He caught Brandi and her dealer in Mom and Bruce's bed, doing lines of coke. He called the cops and Jim was on duty. Jim gave him so much shit that day. Said that Deacon wasn't capable of taking care of Greg. That he was a danger to Greg." She swallowed hard. "I got what I wanted. Deacon gave up fighting for custody and agreed to sell the house. He went off to college and Greg and I moved in with Jim."

"And you took care of Greg. How old were you, Dani?"

"Sixteen."

"Greg getting hurt wasn't your fault. It wasn't Deacon's, either. It was Brandi's fault. She was unconscionably careless. She could have put the baby in his crib, but she didn't, did she? She left him to crawl around and get into her purse."

"I didn't feel guilty about Greg," she said, but he couldn't believe her. He wondered if she even believed herself. "But I never told Deacon the truth. I've let him think he was at fault all this time."

The shame was all he could see now, and it hurt his heart. "Dani, honey." He knew he shouldn't touch her, but he couldn't stop himself. He covered her hand with one of his and with the other he cupped her cheek. "Brandi would have been using whether or not you brought the dealer to your house. Granted, that was not a wise thing to do, but you were sixteen. We all did foolish things at that age."

He himself had been busy starting fights and vandalizing the belongings of innocent people when he'd been sixteen. There had been . . . extenuating circumstances, true, but he'd done it, all the while knowing he was doing wrong.

"I *know* that," she hissed, but she didn't pull away.

"But I let Deacon carry the blame for that for all these years. That is not nice. That is not what nice people do, Diesel. And it's not the only bad thing I've done."

Ah. This was merely exhibit one in her campaign to make him believe that she wasn't worthy of him. He was a little afraid to hear exhibit two. And if there was an exhibit three, he was going to need a drink.

"Did you try to tell Deacon?" he asked.

She frowned. "Yes, of course, but . . ."

His brows lifted. "But?"

"He was busy blaming himself," Dani admitted. "So I let him."

"Do you really think he would have blamed himself less if you'd told him?"

She dropped her gaze to his hand. Then leaned into the hand that cupped her face. "No. Probably not."

"And maybe you should have tried harder." He stroked her cheek with his thumb, catching a tear that fell. "But you were grieving, too. And then you were busy taking care of Greg and going to school. *And* you were stuck with Jim, while Deacon got away. I think you more than paid your debt to the family in general."

More tears fell. He wiped them away tenderly, and that made her cry harder.

"You shouldn't be nice to me, dammit. Why are you so damn nice?"

He sighed. "Because I like you too much to be mean. Trust me, I can be a real SOB when I want to."

"When?" she demanded. "When you're volunteering all over town? When you're coaching children in Pee Wee so that they can have a good male role model? When you're putting yourself in legal jeopardy hacking into assholes' computers so that you can keep them from hurting their families by ruining them on the front page of the *Ledger*? When are you an SOB, Diesel? *When?*"

He exhaled. "Well, I curse at telemarketers. Especially the ones who tell me that they work for Microsoft and that my computer needs fixing."

She stared at him for a long moment. Then snorted. "No fair making me laugh."

He grinned. "It worked, didn't it?"

Her smile disappeared, and she pulled free. "No. It just delayed the inevitable."

Diesel sighed. "All right. Hit me with exhibit two."

She narrowed her eyes. "I'm being serious."

He met her eyes soberly. "So am I. Tell me, Dani. Tell me why I shouldn't care about you. Tell me why I shouldn't fall in love with you."

She sucked in a startled breath. "Diesel."

He shrugged. "I'm tired of pining away like a lovesick teenager. I'm putting it on the table."

"You can't love me."

"Not right now, because—as you've so succinctly established—I don't know you. But I believe I could." He gestured with his hand. "Bring it on, Dr. Novak."

She huffed angrily. "You are a frustrating man."

"I know," he said dryly. But she was still here, so he hadn't fucked it up yet.

She cocked her jaw. "Adrian."

He swallowed. "Your lover. Who died." He managed a calm nod even though everything inside of him wanted to lash out at the man she still . . . what? Loved?

"He was my fiancé."

Diesel blinked. That was unexpected. "So, more than a lover."

"Yes. Another thing I never told Deacon."

He tilted his head at that. "Why didn't you?"

"Because he wouldn't have approved, and then Adrian was dead." She pursed her lips. "And I was HIV positive, so telling him that my *fiancé* had given it to me made me look even stupider than if I'd gotten it doing drugs or making a mistake with a casual boyfriend, which is what I did tell them. Deacon, Greg, and Adam, I mean."

Diesel shook his head. "Wait. I missed something. Maybe several things." He ran his palm over his head, felt the stubble scratch his skin. "First, saying you were stupid is victim-shaming. Would you do that to a patient?"

"No, but—"

He held up his hand. "No buts. You were not stupid. Especially since contracting HIV from someone you should have been able to trust wasn't stupidity. It was a betrayal."

A muscle in her jaw twitched. "You don't know the details."

He'd hit a nerve, he could see. "Maybe not, but you *were* engaged, right?"

"Yes." Her chin lifted. "I told you that already."

"Just establishing the logic. If you were engaged, you trusted him, yes?"

"Yes, but—"

He pressed his finger to her lips. "Stop. Yes, you trusted him. Did you ask him his status? Yes or no, Dani."

She nodded silently.

"Okay, good. Did he tell you he was negative?"

"Yes," she said against his finger, then pulled his hand away. "But I never asked to see proof."

"Why should you have?" he asked, exasperated. "You trusted him. You loved him enough to agree to marry him." And for that alone, he hated the bastard. "You shouldn't have needed proof. What's really wrong, Dani? Because none of this makes sense. You're too smart to blame yourself for contracting HIV."

Her eyes narrowed again. "I'm not smart enough to have avoided contracting it to begin with."

"That sounds like your uncle talking," he snapped. He'd guessed, but he knew he was right when she flinched. "He said that to you, didn't he?"

She visibly sagged. "Yeah, he did. Many, many times."

"And we've already established that he is a fucking SOB." *Who I want to tear limb from limb.* But he didn't say it, because she thought he was nice. *On second thought . . .* "I want to kill your uncle with my bare hands. Does that make me nice?"

"It makes you protective," she said calmly. "So, yes. Nice."

He threw up his hands. "For God's sake, Dani. What is really bothering you? Because so far you're just blowing smoke up my ass."

Anger flared in her eyes. "It's my fault Adrian died, okay?"

Chapter Seventeen

Cincinnati, Ohio
Monday, March 18, 1:05 a.m.

Michael jerked awake, knowing instantly that something wasn't right. He'd felt the floor move—just a small movement, but enough to wake him. This was why he'd slept next to Joshua's bed. If someone came after his little brother in the night, he'd know.

He didn't really expect anyone to come after Joshua. At least, he hadn't last night when Coach had been downstairs, asleep on the sofa. He trusted the big man whose skin was covered with tattoos. But tonight there were others in the house, and Michael didn't know them. He didn't completely trust them.

Although he knew Coach did. So he didn't leap from where he lay on the floor. But he did open his eyes a slit. And stiffened. A man stood in the doorway, his face and body in shadow.

It wasn't Greg. Michael had been aware that Greg had checked on them earlier in the evening. So had Dr. Dani. He'd smelled the chocolate of her shampoo. But the man standing there was taller than Greg and a lot more muscular.

The man didn't move for the longest time. Just stood there, looking at them.

Michael grew tenser with each second that passed. Carefully, he slid his hand along the floor, reaching for the knife he'd hidden under Joshua's bed. It was a simple steak knife from the silverware drawer in Dani's kitchen, but it was sharp enough to do some damage. Especially if the man wasn't expecting it.

After a few more seconds that felt like years, the man sat on the floor just outside the door to Joshua's room, leaning his back against the doorjamb. His face was visible for a split second as he moved. It was Marcus, the guy who owned the newspaper. The guy who'd gotten Michael a lawyer with a fancy suit who worked for free. The guy who was Coach's best friend.

According to Greg, Coach and Marcus had served in the war together. The two were shot at by the enemy and Coach took the bullet intended for Marcus.

Michael hoped it was true. He wanted to believe that Coach was a legit hero. He wanted to believe that the two men were best friends—and that they were both good. He let out the breath he'd been holding, hoping Marcus couldn't hear the frantic beating of his heart.

He watched as Marcus sat patiently, quietly. And then Scarlett came to sit beside him. Marcus put his arm around her shoulders and together they . . .

They guarded them. That was what they were doing. *They're watching over us.* Because the man who'd killed Brewer was still out there.

Michael didn't think anyone was getting by Marcus. Or especially not by his wife, Scarlett. She was a cop. A homicide detective, even. A real badass, again according to Greg, who was a fountain of information.

Slowly, Michael's heart resumed a normal rhythm. Sliding the knife back into its hiding place, he let himself go back to sleep.

Bridgetown, Ohio
Monday, March 18, 1:20 a.m.

Diesel drew in a slow breath. Slowly, he flattened his hands on the table. "How was Adrian's death your fault?"

Pain mixed with the anger in Dani's gut. "He was a big guy. Covered in tats."

Diesel was quiet for a beat. "Like me."

She nodded, her lips twisting into a smile that was both rueful and bitter at once. "Apparently I have a type. Big, bad, bald guys with tats. I wanted you from the first moment you walked into my clinic." When he'd stared at her face, then panicked at her white coat and stumbled backward through the door to the street.

"I looked like a crazy man."

"No." She smiled sadly. "You'd bent down to talk to a little boy with such gentleness. I knew you were nice."

"Too nice for you?" Maybe he was finally getting it.

"Yeah. But you have the whole bad-boy thing going on." She waved her hand, indicating his body. And tats. And bald head.

He attempted a smile. "I can grow my hair back."

She huffed a chuckle, shaking her head. "Diesel."

"Dani," he replied, levity gone. "Tell me about him so we can put it behind us."

Her eyes shot to his. "Put it behind us? I told you that it's my fault he's dead and you say that we'll put it behind us?"

"Yes," he said firmly. "Talk. Where did you meet him?"

She glared at him. "In the ER. I was a resident. He'd ripped up his knee when he fell off his Harley. He was accompanied by a cop."

"Because?"

"He was under arrest," she snapped. "For forging a prescription."

He didn't react at all. "Why?"

She blinked at him. "Why what?"

"You wouldn't have fallen in love with someone who was hurting people. Why did Adrian forge a prescription?"

Her shoulders slumped. "You're not going to see me as anything other than nice, are you?"

"Probably not. Tell me, Dani. If this has kept us apart for eighteen months when we've both wanted each other, then I deserve to know."

"You're right." He was. So she'd make herself tell this story that she'd never told another soul. "He was a recovering addict. Like Stone. Only he didn't have a lot of money like the O'Bannions. He'd gotten help from a church-run rehab program in St. Louis. He volunteered there for years afterward. Up until he died."

"So he was a nice guy, too?" Diesel asked wryly.

She shot him a pointed stare. "Yes. He was. He was always helping at the church, building things. He made blocks for the kids to play with, because the church didn't have the money for toys. One of the kids in the shelter run by the church got sick. Really sick. She needed medicine, but her mom didn't have insurance or the money to pay for the drugs. The pharmacist had turned her away. Adrian did have insurance. So he forged a prescription for the medicine, with his name as the patient. It wasn't a narcotic, which let him plead down to a misdemeanor. He took the deal and served six months."

Diesel studied her face. "You took the kid her medicine, didn't you?"

Stunned, she nodded. "I did. How did you know?"

"Because I've watched you for months. I know you better than you think I do. You could have lost your residency had you been caught," he observed.

"It was worth it."

He smiled. "See? Nice."

She rolled her eyes. "Adrian came by after he got

out of jail. The nuns had told him what I did and he
came to thank me. One thing led to another and . . ."
She shrugged. "I was a goner."

"Why didn't you tell your family about him?"

She scoffed. "After Brandi, I was bringing home
an *addict*? With a *record*? No way. I knew what Jim
would do. I wasn't going to let that happen. Not to
Adrian."

"So how was it your fault, Dani? Because I don't
believe it was."

She huffed. "We'd been together for two years
when he had another motorcycle accident. Put him in
the hospital this time, not just a trip to the ER. He
had a concussion and a broken arm. They tested him
for HIV because he needed surgery for the arm."

"And he came back positive."

"Not just positive. He had AIDS."

His eyes widened. "He'd had it for a while, then."

She nodded. "And because we were engaged, and
I was on the pill, we'd stopped using protection. The
doctor told me to get tested."

"And you were positive, too."

She nodded wearily. "I was . . . shocked. I mean,
Adrian had told me he was negative and he believed
that. But I asked if he'd been tested and he said
he had."

Diesel frowned. "Didn't they test him when he
came to the ER?"

"No. I wondered the same thing once I found out
our status, so I went back into the system and checked
his records. He'd refused to consent to the test."

Diesel clenched his teeth. "He lied to you."

She looked up at him. "Yes. I was really angry. I
wanted to hurt him. I felt so powerless. I should have
waited until I'd calmed down to see him. I had no
business visiting him when I was so angry, but I did.
And I said some horrible, hurtful things. Called him
terrible names. Accused him of infecting me on purpose. Then I slapped his face and called him a killer.

All while he lay in a hospital bed, recovering from surgery. I slapped an AIDS patient."

"You slapped the man who lied to you. I think your anger was justified."

"Ugh." She wanted to throttle him. "Of *course* my anger was justified, but not what I did when I was under its influence." She closed her eyes. "I was like Jim."

Diesel made a strangled sound. "You are nothing like him. Were you sorry?"

"Afterward, yes. Of course I was. I tried to apologize, but Adrian wouldn't see me. I'd hurt him too much."

Understanding finally dawned in his eyes. *Finally.* "And you think you'll lash out and hurt me like you hurt him."

"Yes," she said, relieved. "You get it now?"

"I get that you were upset and said things you didn't mean. I get that you tried to apologize and he sulked."

Dani clenched her hands into fists. "God*dammit*, Diesel."

He shrugged. "How did you kill him?"

"I never said I killed him. I said it was my fault that he was dead." She drew a breath, the memory of that day playing in her mind. "He committed suicide."

"How did he do it?" he asked calmly. "Gun to his head so that you'd be the one to find him?"

It was close enough to the truth to stun her into speechlessness. "No," she finally whispered. "He drove his motorcycle off a cliff in California. Into the ocean."

Diesel's face maintained an outward calm but his dark eyes were snapping with fury. "Did he make a video and send it to you?"

She shook her head slowly, stunned even more that he'd guessed almost exactly right. "No video. He bought me a plane ticket and asked me to come out to be with him. Said he'd always wanted to see the Pacific coast, so he was driving the length of it before he died. He said that he wanted to share it with me. Said he forgave me."

Diesel tilted his head back so that he stared at the ceiling. "*He* forgave *you*."

It sounded wrong when he said it that way. "Yes. So I went. We talked it over. Rode up the coast and marveled at the views. I rode with him and it was like old times. Just the two of us. And then he pulled off to a scenic overlook, we got off the bike, and he kissed me. It was the first time he'd touched me like that since I'd arrived. I'd hugged him around the waist while we'd been on the bike, but that was all. He gave me a letter and told me not to open it until 'after.' I asked him what he meant, but he didn't answer. He got back on his bike and drove away. I thought he'd abandoned me at first. I opened the letter, but it was only one sentence: *Tell the search and recovery team to wear gloves.* Then he came thundering back. He'd picked up a lot of speed."

A muscle twitched in Diesel's jaw. "He drove off the cliff in front of you."

Dani nodded numbly, remembering it all in vivid, Technicolor detail. "He never even tried to stop. The drop was eighty-five feet."

Diesel drew in a breath. "*This* is what you call your fault?"

He's angry. Good. "He left another letter at the hotel where I'd left my luggage. He said that he might have tried to fight for us if I hadn't betrayed him when he was in the hospital. That I'd killed him as sure as if I'd shot him with a gun."

He ground his teeth audibly. "You did not betray him. You sure as hell didn't kill him. He could have fought for his life. He could have taken the cocktail. He could have found out that he was positive long before he developed full-blown AIDS and *not given it to you*. And if he didn't want to fight, he could have OD'd on sedatives. He could have arranged to be found by someone who didn't know him. There were lots of things he *could* have and *should* have done."

Dani retreated behind the mask she wore when people around her became angry. "All those things are true, Diesel. But my point is, when he needed me most, I became like Jim. I was not nice. Under stress, I am not nice."

Diesel shoved to his feet, his chair flying backward to clatter on the floor, making her jump. "You did *not* become like Jim," he snarled. "And wipe that look from your face. Right now. Don't pretend you don't know what I mean. That's the face you wear when things get heavy. When you have to deal with confrontations. I've seen it too many times, Dani. I will *not* be the cause of it. You wanted to talk? Let's talk now, shall we?"

"Not if you're going to yell at me," she managed in her frostiest voice.

"I will damn well yell!" he shouted. "And so will you. Do you know how to yell? Have you ever done it? When was the last time you really yelled at someone?"

Her mouth opened, but no words would come. She licked her lips and tried again. "When I yelled at Adrian in the hospital," she whispered.

Diesel's fury seemed to disappear. He leaned against the kitchen island, his hands gripping its edge so tightly that his knuckles were white. But his big body sagged. "And before that? Had you ever just yelled because you were mad, Dani?"

She tried to remember. But came up blank. "No. That was the first time."

"And it ended very badly," Diesel ground out. "I'm betting that you didn't yell when you lived with Jim, before your mom married Bruce. Or Jim would have thrown you all out." He turned his head to stare at her, still leaning against the island like he was mid-pushup. "Did you?"

She thought about her younger self. And realized he was right. "No."

"And when your mom married Bruce. Did you yell then? Or were you afraid that Bruce would stop loving you and your mother if you misbehaved?"

He was right again. "No. I mean yes. No, I didn't yell. Yes, I guess I was afraid he'd leave."

"And then he left anyway," Diesel murmured.

She flinched. "Bruce didn't *leave*. He *died*."

"Same outcome, wasn't it? You were alone and living with Jim again. Right?"

Her throat had suddenly become thick. "Yes. It was the same."

"And then Adrian left you, too. Left you with a huge burden."

Her eyes burned. He had. She nodded because words were impossible.

He turned to lean his hip against the island, his handsome face sad but determined. "You leave before you can get left," he said. "You leave before it's even possible to get left."

"I'm comfortable being alone," she whispered, but she didn't believe it. Not anymore. Faith had said the same thing. And she'd been right. So was Diesel.

"Bullshit," he snapped. "That really means you're scared. Maybe subconsciously you want me to prove to you that I won't leave. I can't do that. You either trust me or you don't. But I can't force you to do either." He rubbed both palms over his head before dragging them down his face. "I could make you really happy, Dani. I know I could. But you have to want it, too. If not with me, then with someone else." He smiled so sadly. "Otherwise you're going to spend your life alone. I don't want that for you. Even if it's not me sharing it with you."

He held her gaze for another moment before turning away and digging into his pocket for the keys to his truck. "Come on," he said gently. "I'll take you home."

Home. Where two "temporary" boys waited. And when they were gone, she'd be alone again. Her future suddenly stretched before her, silent and gray.

One place setting at her table, a single indented pillow. No laughter.

He makes me laugh. He makes me . . . happy. And Dani desperately wanted that. Wanted to laugh. Wanted to be happy. Wanted the kisses and the shared meals. The shared bed.

She was on her feet before she knew she was going to move. *"Wait."* She hesitated, then crossed the kitchen to stand before him, gripping one hand with the other so hard that it hurt. His eyes were wary, his body held rigid as if he was bracing himself against a blow, and that hurt more.

"I don't know how to do this," she admitted.

He drew a breath that filled his chest. "Do what?"

"Be with you. I don't know how to not mess it up. I don't know how to make you stay. But I want to try. I do want this." She swallowed. "I want you."

His big hand trembled as he pushed her hair behind her ear, then cupped her cheek again. She leaned into the contact, her eyes closing as she felt her heart settle. *Yes. This is right. This is where I'm supposed to be.*

"You need to be sure, Dani," he croaked, his voice breaking. "If you change your mind, I—"

He what? If she changed her mind, what would he do? Her nightmare abruptly changed, Adrian's broken body on the rocks becoming Diesel's. Her gaze jerked up to meet his, and she suspected that the instant fear that had filled her was now apparent on her face, because he rushed to soothe.

"No, Dani, not that. If you change your mind, I'll survive. I won't take my life." His eyes filled with pain and then tears. "Is that what you're afraid of? That if you hurt me, if you make me angry, I'll kill myself?"

She did. She hadn't even realized it until that moment. "Yes," she whispered.

"Well, I won't," he said fiercely. "I won't ever even threaten it. I promise you that. But it will hurt me."

Relief made her hand shake as she lifted it to trace her fingertips over his lips, so soft and warm. "I don't want to hurt you. Ever."

He caught her wrist in his big hand, holding it like it was fine china as he kissed her fingers. "Then don't," he said simply. Sweetly. "Just be with me. That's all I want."

"You should want more," she whispered. "You deserve more."

He shook his head. "I want you. I deserve you."

She opened her mouth to challenge him, then remembered Stone's words. *Take a page out of Delores's book and let him make his own choices.* She'd do that. But first he needed all the information. "I come with baggage, Diesel."

"We all do."

"My baggage is . . . extra. You said you needed me to be sure. I need the same thing. I need you to know what you're giving up."

Once again, he seemed to brace himself, but this time it seemed like it was for an argument rather than a physical blow. "Okay. Shoot."

"You love children. I . . ." She lifted her chin. "I don't plan to have any babies."

He shrugged. "There are too many kids who need homes. Who need families to love them. Kids like Michael and Joshua. A child doesn't need my DNA for me to love him. Or her." He hesitated. "Although I'd like to know why. Is it your status? Or the syndrome? Or your career? Any are reasonable, but I'd like to understand."

It was a fair question. "All of the above? I mean, I know that women who are positive can safely carry and birth an HIV-negative baby, but there are risks."

"And if one of your positive patients wanted to have a baby?"

"I'd tell her the risks and recommend counseling, just in case her baby is born positive. I know positive women who choose to give birth and I'm happy for them, I really am, but I don't think *I* could handle passing the virus to a baby. And if that baby was deaf *and* HIV positive?" She shook her head. "If it happened, I'd be there for my child, don't get me wrong. But I'm happy fostering kids that need me. I also love my career, and a baby changes everything." She looked down to stare at their shoes, not wanting to see his disappointment at her next confession. "And I know it's selfish, but I raised Greg. I was basically a single mom at sixteen. I've done the midnight feedings. I've been through teething and colic and chicken pox. I'm okay with not doing that again."

He hooked a finger under her chin and lifted it so that she looked at him. There was no trace of disappointment. No censure. Only tenderness and hope.

The hope nearly broke her. *Please don't let me hurt him.* But this time her prayer was because she was keeping him, not sending him away.

"Not selfish," he murmured. "Honest. And I understand your reasons. I can live with them, as long as adoption remains on the table."

"It does," she said.

His smile stole her breath. "Good. Next?"

"My levels are undetectable, but that could change. I could get . . . sick."

His gaze didn't falter. "I know. You're asking again for me to prove I won't leave. I can only give you my word, Dani. I'm not afraid of sickness."

One corner of her mouth lifted. "Or doctors. Not anymore."

He brushed a kiss over her lips, sending shivers rippling across her skin. "It was a phobia worth conquering."

She closed her eyes, wanting to preserve the moment, the feeling of his mouth on hers, but she needed to finish this. "I could die, Diesel," she whispered against his lips.

"So could I. I could get hit by a bus tomorrow."

Stone's words returned, chilling her. *Or that damn*

bullet could pierce your heart, you stubborn man. That issue she planned to address ASAP, but she let it go for now.

She leaned in, resting her forehead against his solid chest, unable to meet his eyes for this next part. "You'll need to wear . . . you know. Protection. Always. When we have sex."

Because we will. She wanted it. She wanted him. She always had.

"God. Dani." She felt his big body shudder. "I know," he growled, and her knees actually buckled. Clutching his shirt with both hands, she held on as his arms tightened around her. Holding her close.

Where I belong. It was crystal clear. She belonged here. With him. In his arms. *Why did I deny this for so long?*

He smelled so good. She inhaled, filling her senses with him until her knees were solid again, then leaned back to look up at him.

"I . . ." The thought trailed away because . . . *Oh my God.* His face was flushed, his jaw taut, a muscle twitching in his cheek. And his eyes . . . She stared, mesmerized. They were dark and intense. And hungry. He was so hungry.

So am I.

Tightening her hold on his shirt, she yanked him down and kissed him hard. He froze for a split second before exploding into movement. Another growl rumbled in his chest as he took control of the kiss. One big hand slid down her back to palm her ass, the other slid up to tangle in her hair. She felt herself being lifted off her feet as if she weighed nothing and her control was severed. Her arms went around his corded neck, her legs around his powerful thighs, and she clung to him like a vine.

"So damn hot," she mumbled into his mouth. "You are so damn hot."

He swung her around so that her ass pressed

against the kitchen island and he pressed against her. All of him.

Oh God. He was hard. And huge. She wriggled, trying to get closer. "I want you," she whispered. "All of you."

His groan was guttural. Broken. Molten. He tugged on her hair, roughly tilting her head for his next kiss. He simply . . . took her. Took her mouth. Took her breath away. He ripped his mouth away and buried his face in her neck. He was panting.

And so, so hard.

"I've waited so long," he said hoarsely. "Be sure, Dani. Please."

She kissed his ear, taking a second to catch her breath. "I'm sure. But only with condoms. Always. Forever, Diesel. I won't have you exposed. *Promise me.*"

Abruptly he lifted her to sit on the island and released her hair before taking a step back. His eyes were wild, his pupils blown. But before she could even form a question, he was digging in the pocket of his jeans.

He took her hand and pressed something into her palm. A brown plastic prescription bottle, she realized. Lifting it, she examined the label and the last of her resistance crumbled to dust. The name on the prescription label read *Elvis Kennedy*. The prescribing doctor was Dr. Jeremy O'Bannion.

The bottle had originally held thirty pills. There were two left.

"Truvada," she whispered, her throat too thick to speak. Tears filled her eyes, blurring the label. She blinked, wiping at her eyes with her free hand so that she could see his face. "You're taking Truvada?"

He nodded wordlessly, his gaze never leaving her face.

Truvada. Pre-exposure prophylaxis. Medication to reduce the risk of contracting HIV. This was . . .

"For how long?" she asked hoarsely.

"For the past six months," he answered, just as hoarsely. "Jeremy wouldn't prescribe it until I'd tested negative for a solid year."

Because she'd exposed him the day he'd saved her life.

He took a step closer when she continued to stare at him. "You told me to find someone else that day in the hospital, but I wanted to be prepared. In case you changed your mind." He stood between her legs, hands on the island on either side of her hips. Caging her in. He leaned in to whisper in her ear. "Was I wrong?"

Slowly she shook her head. "No. You weren't wrong." Still gripping the bottle, she wrapped her arms around his neck. "We still need condoms."

His lips curved in a grin that was wolfish and wicked. "I have a whole box."

"Where?"

"Next to my bed. I was optimistic."

She shivered hard. "Show me," she demanded.

He stiffened in surprise, his eyes widening. "Now?"

"Yes, now. We've waited long enough." She kissed him until he growled again, making her smile against his mouth. "Take me to bed, Diesel."

Chapter Eighteen

Diesel took the prescription bottle from her hand and set it blindly on the counter. *Take me to bed, Diesel.*

This was happening. It was finally happening.

He slid his hands to her ass and lifted her from the counter, but then hesitated. "Be sure," he whispered, letting her see all the emotions coursing through him. Hope, fear, arousal. All roiled around the one emotion he couldn't yet say aloud.

Love. He felt it with every fiber of his being, but he was afraid to say it, afraid that she'd bolt.

"I'm sure I want this. I'm still not sure that I'm good for you, but Stone told me tonight that we can't make those decisions for other people. You said I need to trust that you won't leave. I say you need to trust that I'm sure." She kissed him softly. "I'm sure that I don't want a life without you, so I'm doing what I never do. I'm taking a leap of faith."

Stone's text made even more sense now. *You're welcome.* Diesel was more than grateful. He'd owe his friend for life.

"Tighten your arms around my neck," he ordered

softly, closing his eyes when she obeyed. He shuddered, arousal beating back the other emotions until it was all he knew. He lifted her easily, his ego basking in her pleased sigh.

"I knew you'd be able to carry me," she whispered into his ear, then kissed down one side of his neck and back up the other.

The caresses shot straight to his cock and it was all he could do not to break into a run. "You don't weigh anything," he said roughly, quickening his pace, which made her laugh softly. Expectantly.

Breathlessly.

She raked her teeth over his throat. "Hurry, Diesel."

He was never more grateful that he had a small house. He shoved the bedroom door open and kicked it closed with his foot before slowly lowering her to the mattress with the care she deserved.

For a moment, he stood and stared down at her. *She's in my bed. Her hair spread on my pillow. Finally.*

She held his gaze for a few hard beats of his heart before rising to her knees, the movement fluid and graceful. But then she grabbed handfuls of his shirt and yanked him forward. He stumbled, his knees hitting the edge of the bed.

"I like your T-shirts," she said. Letting go of the fabric, she began unbuttoning the shirt, starting at the top. "This hides too much. Your T-shirts show off every one of your muscles." She made quick work of the buttons, making another pleased sound when she revealed his chest, but when he said nothing, she glanced up at him uncertainly through her lashes, her teeth biting her lower lip as her hands flattened on his pecs. "Is this all right?"

He could only nod. *She's touching me.* He'd fantasized about this moment so many times. But reality was . . . To say it was better was the understatement of the fucking century. He covered her hands with his, moving them back and forth over his chest, sucking in a breath when her fingertips grazed his nipples.

Her uncertainty fled. "You like that," she murmured and again he could only nod. Her lips quirked up. "Good to know. How about this?" She licked one nipple delicately before latching on to the other and abruptly sucking hard.

A groan filled the air and he realized it had come from him. His fingers threaded through her hair and he tugged gently, tilting her face up so that he could take her mouth.

Mine. She's mine. God. This time the groan was hers as he ate at her mouth, licking and nipping until she opened for him. "Finally mine," he muttered.

"Yes." She pushed his shirt off his shoulders then pulled away from the kiss, breathing hard, her eyes on his tats. She touched him again, skimming her fingertips over each curve and angle of the designs he'd had inked onto his skin, pulling another groan from his throat. "These are magnificent." She looked up. Her eyes were mismatched in color, but were filled with the same aroused determination. "Next time I want to run my tongue over them."

Next time. His cock pulsed in his pants and his hips thrust forward, all on their own. *"Dani."* It was the only word he could summon, but it must have been enough, because she smiled at him.

"Diesel." Her fingers trailed over the tats that ran down his sides, over his obliques, then dipped lower, toying with the button on his trousers. "How far down does the ink go?"

"Find out," he growled, and she smiled again.

"Oh, I plan to." Eyes on his, she popped the button and deliberately slid his zipper down. "Still good?"

He swallowed hard, wondering at what point she'd gotten the upper hand. Then realized she'd always had it, and he was totally okay with that. "Yes," he hissed because her hand had slid under his briefs, her fingers closing around him.

Her gaze dropped to her hand, then shot back up to his face, stunned desire apparent. "Oh my God. Diesel. I . . ." Her words trailed away as she returned her focus to her hand, sliding it up and down while her other hand tugged at his trousers and briefs, yanking them down.

His head fell back as she worked him, his grunts and moans the only sounds in the room. They weren't the prettiest sounds, but he'd lost the power of speech.

Until something warm and a little rough stroked over him and his head snapped forward. She was bowed over him, her tongue licking daintily. But her eyes were on his again. She stuck her tongue out for him to see.

"No cuts. But no more than this without protection."

He wanted to protest because he wanted to feel her mouth surround him, hot and wet, her lips forming a tight seal as she sucked, because he was almost there. He wanted to remind her of the science—that her levels were undetectable and that he was on Truvada, the combination reducing any risk to nearly none.

But *nearly* wasn't going to be enough for her. Not right now, at least.

He took a step back, hands fisted at his sides, needing a moment to breathe. To steel himself against begging for more of her mouth on his dick. To control himself because he was one tiny stroke from coming and he wanted this to last longer.

After a few deep breaths, he realized that he was completely naked while she still wore all her clothes. That he could change.

He gripped her hands in one of his, gently moving them behind her back. "Hands off for a minute or two," he said gruffly. "You make me lose my mind."

A slow smile spread from her lips to her eyes. "Thank you."

He had to chuckle at her expression of sheer satisfaction. "You're welcome." He took the hem of her sweater and gave it a caress. It was almost as soft as she was. And the color matched her blue eye perfectly. "I like this."

Her smile turned shy. "I picked it out this morning hoping you would."

"I'll like it better off." Gently he pulled the sweater over her head, intending to place it on his dresser, but then he saw the bra she wore and was speechless once again. The sweater ended up on the floor, somewhere near his shirt.

She was beautiful. He'd known she'd be, but . . . God. The bra was a frothy scrap of lace that cupped her breasts lovingly, while actually managing to cover very little. One good yank and he could tear it to shreds. And suddenly that was exactly what he wanted to do.

"Was that expensive?" he found himself asking.

"Not really, wh—"

He didn't let her finish her question. He took the lace in his hand and pulled it apart, growling at the sound of ripping lace. The bra lay in tatters at her sides, held onto her shoulders by the straps.

Leaving her perfect breasts bare. He stared, only vaguely aware of her shocked gasp. Her skin was the same dusky bronze all over, answering a question he'd wondered about since first laying eyes on her.

"That shouldn't have been so hot," she murmured. "But it was."

"You're beautiful."

Her hands remained behind her back, but her gaze raked him up and down, muddying his brain as much as a physical touch. "Hurry, Diesel."

The words spurred him into motion. Pushing her to her back, he fumbled with the snap on her jeans. She'd settled her hands at her sides, but now took over the snaps and zipper.

"If you tear my jeans, I won't have anything to wear home."

"That's okay with me," he said, then pulled the denim down her legs, leaving her in only her panties. They matched the bra that he'd ruined. Lacy and covering almost nothing. He drew a breath before slowly tugging the lace down her legs, exposing pubic hair, neatly trimmed. The panties ended up on the floor.

Leaving her naked. Bronze skin and beautiful curves. *This is it. She's here. Naked in my bed. And watching me.* With eyes that promised more than her words had. He wondered if she knew.

And then he didn't care because she let one knee fall to the side, opening herself to him. She was already wet. So wet he could see her glistening.

He wasn't sure what to touch first. "I want to taste you."

Her eyes flickered, doubt replacing some of her gorgeous arousal. Because HIV could be transmitted through vaginal secretion. *Dammit. Damn me.*

Needing to get them back to where they'd been, he backtracked. "But I won't. Not now. Maybe in the future. But know that I want to. You smell . . ." Kneeling between her legs, he leaned down and drew a deep breath, filling his head with her intoxicating scent. "So damn sweet."

He placed a chaste kiss on her abdomen, then set his fists on either side of her shoulders, lowering himself slowly until he could kiss her softly. "You're more beautiful than I dreamed. And I dreamed, Dani. A lot." He kissed her again, deepening the kiss until she was moving beneath him, her hips lifting in a rhythm that beckoned him to hurry.

Blindly he reached into his nightstand drawer and pulled out a condom. Pushing himself to his knees, he rolled it over his cock while she silently watched, her mouth fallen open, her breaths coming in short pants.

"Now?" he asked.

"Please." She licked her lips. "Please, Diesel."

He hesitated. He was not a small man. "I don't want to hurt you."

She narrowed her eyes. "Do I need to draw you a diagram? Send you an engraved invitation? I want you, dammit." She grabbed his shoulders and pulled him down onto her, their faces a hairbreadth apart. "I want this. And I like it rough, so do not treat me like spun glass or I swear to God I will take over."

She was completely serious. And it was sexy as hell.

He drew back enough to see between them, wanting to remember the moment when he filled her for the first time.

He pushed into her slowly. Wanting this closeness— this feeling—to last forever. Her whimper had his gaze jerking up to hers.

But it wasn't pain he saw. It was impatience. She wound her legs around his hips and thrust up, forcing him in the rest of the way. He let out a sharp bark of surprise before groaning because she was so tight, gripping him so hard that he nearly came then and there.

She gasped, her eyes closing, a satisfied cat-in-cream smile curving her lips. "You feel so good," she whispered. "So good."

He'd lost his words again, so he began to move, slowly. Methodically. Committing every moment to memory. She met him thrust for thrust, her eyes opening to lock with his.

This was more than sex. He knew it as clearly as he knew his own name. It was just . . . more.

But too soon the slow pace was no longer enough. He sped up, increasing the strength of his thrusts. Her eyes were wide now. Wide and wild.

"Oh my God," she whispered. "Don't stop. Don't ever stop."

"I won't," he promised, although he knew he couldn't hold out much longer. His thrusts became frantic, determined that she'd come with him. "Now, Dani. Let me see you. Come for me now."

Her back arched, exposing the long line of her

throat. He kissed it, then found his mouth opening over the curve of her shoulder. He wanted to bite, but he backed away with a groan, his orgasm hitting him like a high-speed train. His vision grew dark and his body gave a few last frantic thrusts as he came harder and longer than he ever had before.

She stroked him through it, her hands on his back, her body clenching around him. Her voice whispering sweet things that didn't penetrate the fog in his brain.

He fell forward, catching himself on his forearms so that he didn't crush her.

"Mmm," she hummed. "You are a beautiful man, Diesel Kennedy. And when you come, you're . . . magnificent. Yeah, that's a good word. Magnificent."

She was, too, he thought, but his mouth wasn't working.

Her hands slid up his back, cupping his head, her fingers working magic on the base of his skull, which was pounding almost painfully.

"Breathe, Diesel," she whispered and he realized he hadn't been.

He sucked in a lungful of air and let it out. "Are you all right?" he asked, his face buried against her neck.

"I am so much better than all right," she said with a smile he could hear. "I wondered how it would be with you. I wasn't nearly creative enough."

He laughed quietly. "Same." He lifted his head. "I need you," he confessed.

To his relief, her smile didn't falter. "I need you, too."

He hung there, watching every blink of her eyes, every flicker in their mismatched depths. But he saw truth. She was beautifully sated. *I did that. And she needs me.* She didn't yet feel the same love that he felt. Not yet. But it could be. That was enough.

"I need to move," he finally said. "Need to deal with the condom."

"I know. I wish you didn't. I wish you could stay inside me forever."

"Well, I can visit again," he said playfully.

She grinned. "I know. It's the only reason I'm letting you go."

"The others will know," he said, abruptly worried that this would bother her. "I'm not going to be able to hide my smile."

She shrugged. "Let them know. I'm proud that you're mine, Diesel Kennedy. Proud that I finally got over myself and let you love me."

His eyes widened. "I never said—"

She smirked. "You didn't need to." Her smirk softened to a smile. "It's in everything you do. Every word you say. Every way you look at me." She stroked her fingers over his cheek. "Give me time. I'll get there, too. I promise."

He swallowed hard. *More than good enough.* He pulled out of her reluctantly, watching her wince. "You're not okay."

"You're . . . proportionately sized." She winked at him. She seemed lighter. Freer. Younger. At peace. "Have I thanked you for that yet?"

Diesel felt his cheeks heat. "I didn't want to hurt you."

She rolled her eyes, her own cheeks growing rosy. "I'm fine. I loved it, okay?"

He could see that she meant what she'd said. "Okay. I'll be right back."

She smiled at him serenely. "I'm not going anywhere."

Cincinnati, Ohio
Monday, March 18, 1:50 a.m.

I should have made sure that Detective Stone was dead. Cade drummed his fingers on his steering wheel as he sat a few houses away from Dani Novak's, which still seemed to be bustling with activity. All the SUVs that had been there when he'd left to follow the Escalade were still there, plus *another* SUV had arrived in the fifteen minutes that he'd been sitting here, watching. He had no problem identifying the man who'd used his own key to open the front door without even running his plates. The bright white hair and leather trench coat were Special Agent Deacon Novak's trademarks, according to the press. Dani's brother had stopped by to visit. How sweet. *Not.*

How utterly *fucking* annoying, because the house was still lit up like a goddamn Christmas tree. The lower floor, anyway. Every light was on, including the floodlights, which wouldn't go off for another minute or two. He'd been timing them as people had come and gone, measuring how close he could get to the house before the lights were triggered.

But the upstairs was dark. Michael Rowland was asleep in one of those rooms.

Just waiting to identify me in a lineup.

I should just drive away. But he couldn't. He couldn't leave the eyewitness alive. He'd never left an eyewitness alive. Except his old man, and who was he gonna tell? And even if the bastard found a way to accuse him, who'd believe him?

Cade had been the model son, visiting every damn week. Every nurse in that place would vouch for him, no question.

Even the detective tonight hadn't seen his face, and he'd left no evidence behind except for the slugs in the guy's body, and Cade had tossed the gun into a creek just before he'd gotten back on the main road. He'd stopped a few blocks later to get some food, changing the plates on his SUV, just in case he'd been captured on a camera. He currently sported plates he'd found in the old pedo's garage when he'd first taken possession of his house.

Cade had looked the plates up online and found they belonged to a man who'd been reported missing ten years before but had never been found. Cade wondered if the old pedo had killed the guy, too, but he'd never found any evidence in the house. Even in the cell in the basement. Or the airtight room.

For all Cade knew, the man could be buried in the backyard, which had kind of creeped him out, if he was being honest. But that didn't matter anymore. Once he'd eliminated Michael Rowland, Cade was leaving town and driving north.

There had to be ways into Canada that avoided border control. He'd figure that out once he got away. He could even use his real name. No one was looking for Cade Kaiser, only Scott King.

With a grunt of discomfort, Cade settled behind the wheel of his car, hoping all the people in Dani Novak's house would just leave.

And if they never did?

He scowled to himself. He'd still have to force Michael out into the open, so his plan to set the house on fire was still the best option. But with so many people pouring out of the house, it might be harder to get Michael in his sights without shooting anyone near him. More people than just Michael would die.

He wasn't going to worry about that. If they'd fucking leave, they'd all be fine. *It's their own fault they're in danger.* Plus, taking out a few more people would cause enough of a distraction that he could get away without being noticed. And if Deacon Novak was one of the casualties, all the better.

Novak was investigating him. The man was a living legend in this town. If Cade could take him out of the equation . . . Yeah, the cops would redouble the efforts to find him—or Scott King, anyway. But Special Agent Novak's death would throw them into disarray for just enough time for him to get over the border.

It was something to consider. But first, he had to start the fire. He thought about the Molotov cocktails in the box on the passenger-side floorboard. He'd need to get close enough to the house to break the window and throw them in. Easier if the house was quiet and dark.

He idly wondered if Amazon delivered flame-throwers, then snorted to himself.

I really need to sleep. Maybe that would be best. Maybe he'd think more clearly after a few hours' rest. *And maybe in that time they'll move Michael to a real safe house and I won't be able to find him.*

No, he needed to stay awake, alert, and wait for the "platoon" inside to go the fuck home. Then, as if in answer to his command, the door opened.

Cade sat up straighter. Were the assholes finally leaving? He didn't expect everyone to go, just enough people that he'd be able to slip in and out unseen.

But . . . no. *Fucking hell.* He slumped, cursing his frustration. It was the other teenager, the one who'd been walking the dogs. He was accompanied by the same two men as before, each of them taking a couple of leashes, but this time they walked in a tight formation, as if they expected to see something.

Or someone. *Fuck.*

Cade sank down in his seat, out of sight. They didn't know he was here. If they did, he'd be surrounded by police cruisers so fast he wouldn't be able to blink.

Who was the kid? *I should have asked that question a long time ago.* Kids meant vulnerabilities. Especially a kid who was important to Dani Novak.

Still slouched in his seat, he put on his earphones and pointed his mike at the group. But they were quiet. Strangely quiet.

Yeah, it was the middle of the night, but Cade had expected to hear some murmured conversation. Something. Yet there was nothing. Only the panting of seven fucking dogs.

Then one of them murmured, "Far enough. They've all peed. Let's go back."

Cade scrunched his body, making sure he was not visible at all. He heard the door slam closed, but he didn't relax. He half expected to see a face staring at him through one of the SUV's windows, that the slammed door was a ruse to make him think he was alone again in the darkness.

But that didn't happen. Nothing happened. He strained to hear the conversations inside the house, but he was too far away, dammit.

Pulling himself upright in the seat, he did a quick Google search on Dani Novak. Her picture popped up—her white streaks stark against the black of her hair. He expanded the search to include her family and blinked at the results.

Of course there were articles on her brother Deacon, but she had a second brother. Greg. Who'd been kidnapped along with Dani a few years ago.

Cade enlarged the photo so that he could study the young man's face. Yeah, that was the kid he'd seen walking the dogs. He'd been wearing a ball cap, so Cade hadn't noticed that the boy had white hair, too. And he was deaf.

Like Michael.

Stella Brewer had said that Dani Novak was the only emergency foster provider who knew ASL. That made sense now, knowing that Greg Novak was deaf. The lack of spoken conversation between Greg and the two men as they'd walked the dogs also made sense.

He wasn't sure how he'd use the information, but it was certainly worth considering. Especially if Greg and Michael were friends.

If the "platoon" never went home, he'd need a way to draw Michael out of the house, and invitations from friends were a good way to do that.

Definitely something to consider.

Bridgetown, Ohio
Monday, March 18, 2:30 a.m.

Diesel's arms tight around her, Dani rested her head on his chest, luxuriating in the feeling of being held by this man who . . . *Loves me.* Diesel *loved* her. She had seen it in his eyes as he'd worshipped her with his body.

She'd always thought that "worshipping" with bodies was a silly, trite phrase in old-fashioned wedding vows. But not anymore. She'd seen it with her own eyes. Diesel loved her. She'd wanted it to be true for her, too. It would be true, someday. She was already a little of the way there.

But one step at a time. She was here. In his bed. Her body was deliciously sore in all the right places and she could hear the steady thumping of his heart against her good ear. She brushed her fingertips over the tattoo that started at his heart, covered his right pectoral, then wandered over his shoulder and down his arm.

At first glance it looked like a beautiful, swirling design that existed simply for its artistic merit alone. But now that she studied it up close, she could see that it was a combination of a number of designs, each one flowing into the next.

She lifted her head to kiss the Star of David over his heart. "Tell me about this."

His chest rose, then fell as he took a deep breath. "It's for my mother."

Oh. "Is she . . ." Dani hesitated. "Is she still alive?"

"No. She died when I was fourteen. Car accident."

She kissed the tattoo again. "I'm sorry."

"Thank you. She was . . . nice." He said *nice* with more than his usual gruffness.

Nice. There was so much left unsaid in that one little word. She'd come back to it later. They had time. She traced her finger from the memorial to his mother to the interconnecting designs on his pectoral. They were blocks from the periodic table, she realized with delight. Five of them—Dy, S, O, and N—surrounded by test tubes, beakers, an atom, and a molecule. "Who is Dyson?"

His lips curved and she relaxed. Clearly this was a better memory. "My high school chemistry teacher."

"Is he still alive?"

"Yes. He's one of the best men I know. I didn't know men could be kind until I met Walt."

Think of it as a mugging. Oh God, Diesel. Who hurt you? Her heart ached, but he was smiling now, so she smiled, too.

"Do you still see him?"

"Yep. At least once a year. Every New Year's Day, I head back to Pennsylvania to visit him. The next day, I drop my backup drive into my safe deposit box. I've been doing that for a while now."

"Your backup drives. Do they have evidence of your . . . investigations?"

He lifted one brow, raising his head to look her in the eye. "I keep forgetting how smart you are."

She gave him a wry look. "Flattery will get you everywhere, but I'm smart enough to know when you're changing the subject. I'll consider your answer a yes." She slid across his chest so that she could see the tats on his right shoulder.

He groaned softly as she pressed her breasts against him, grinding a little for maximum impact. "You're mean, you know that?"

"I thought I was smart," she replied tartly, and he laughed.

"Touché, Dr. Novak."

The design on his shoulder was another blending of symbols. "A Celtic knot. For the Kennedys?"

"For the O'Bannions. They're more my family than my father ever was." His jaw tightened. "He walked out on my mom before I was born. Never knew him."

She kissed his shoulder. "Then I'm glad you have the O'Bannions." She traced her finger along the lines of script that ran around his biceps, like a barber pole. She peered closer. "Are these tiny little numbers?"

"My first hacker code," he said, amused.

She smiled at him, watched his expression soften.

Just like Stone's did when he talked about Delores. "What did you hack?" she asked.

He mimed zipping his lips shut, but she poked him in the side.

"Seriously," she insisted. "I want to know."

He drew a deep breath, as if bracing himself. "A government agency located in a special building with five sides."

Her eyes widened. "You hacked into the Pentagon?"

He pressed a finger to her lips. "Shh. You can't ever tell."

She narrowed her eyes. "Are you bullshitting me?"

He threw back his head and laughed. "God, I'm *so* glad you're finally mine. No, I'm not bullshitting you. But I could get into so much trouble, so you can't ever tell."

Finally mine. He'd said the words in the throes of passion and it had been hot. But hearing him say them now, when they were simply enjoying each other's company? *Priceless.* "How old were you?"

"Seventeen going on fifty," he replied, growing serious. "I shouldn't have done it. I was a punk with more book smarts than brains. I was headed for a life behind bars until Walt Dyson turned me around."

Her throat tightened. "I'd like to meet him and thank him."

Diesel looked a little nervous at that. "He wants to meet you, too."

"You told him about me?"

He nodded, still so serious. "I did. He could see that I was different. Sad. He wouldn't let me leave until I'd told him why."

She swallowed hard. "I'm sorry."

Once again he pressed his finger to her lips. "Don't be. This here—us—happened when it was right for you. You're here now."

She nodded, still feeling sorrow for the sadness she'd caused him, but he was right. She wouldn't have

been ready before. "I am most definitely here now."
She continued her perusal of the tat covering his arm.
"This looks like an army patch."

"Rangers."

She blinked at him. "You were a Ranger?"

"For a few years. Then I got shot up and sent
home."

When he'd taken the bullet meant for Marcus. The
bullet that was still hanging around in his thoracic
cavity. She slid back to lie against his side. He was
covered in scars, some long and jagged and some
short and neat. She'd seen similar scars on military
vets she'd treated in the ER and in the clinic. "You
were hit by shrapnel."

"Yeah. IED on the side of the road. Same story as
so many others. We were thrown out of the Humvee
and one of the guys in my platoon broke his neck."
He swallowed hard. "He was conscious when they
gutted him. I tried to get to him, but they were shooting at us. I had to lay down cover for the others."

She traced the perimeter of the scar a few millime-
ters from the Star of David over his heart. It was
round and puckered. A gunshot wound. "They got
you."

"Yeah," he said gruffly. "I took another couple in
my hip and thigh."

Those bullets didn't still reside in his body, though.
"This was the one meant for Marcus."

"Yes. He was working on one of the other injured
guys. I saw the gun pointed at him and . . ." He blew
out a breath. "We'd met in basic training. I was prepared to be alone for my tour. I trusted Walt Dyson,
but nobody else. And then I met Marcus and he
just . . . bullied me into liking him. I didn't meet Stone
till later, but he did the same. Just steamrolled right
over me."

"You couldn't let Marcus get hurt. I understand
that."

He met her eyes once again. "I know you do." He

let his head fall back to the pillow. "I woke up in the hospital and freaked."

"All the white coats," she murmured. "They became associated with your trauma." That explained so many things.

Except for the flicker of hesitation in his dark eyes. She opened her mouth to ask about it, but a phone alarm sounded from somewhere on the floor, and he stiffened.

"That's mine," he said as he extricated himself from her arms. He bent to retrieve his cell phone from his pants pocket and Dani hung over the side of the bed, enjoying the view.

"*Yes,*" he hissed gleefully when he'd checked his phone screen. He stepped into his boxer briefs and wiggled his butt as he pulled them up his body.

"Oh, yes," she murmured, smiling when he turned to grin at her.

"You were checking me out."

"I was, and no woman alive would ever blame me." She pointed to the phone. "Yes what?"

"Ritz is finished. Sorry, but I need to check on the program I was running."

Dani swung her legs off of the bed, reluctant to leave their haven but knowing their respite was never going to last all night. They needed to get back to the boys because all their friends needed to get home.

Shit. She'd forgotten to tell Diesel about Quincy's visit. They really needed to get home. Scott King was out there, hunting Michael.

She pulled on her clothes, shaking her head over the ruined bra. But she couldn't be sorry. That had been the hottest thing ever.

Well, except for the whole orgasm part. That had been . . . exceptional. She tucked the tattered white lace into her purse as she walked through the kitchen.

She found him in his home office, bare-chested and typing madly on a keyboard. She started to admire his muscled chest, but found herself distracted by the hardware that filled the room.

"I thought computers had gotten smaller," she said as she took in the stacks of . . . she wasn't quite sure what. It wasn't actually one big computer, just a lot of smaller computers stacked upon each other. There was a shelf of what looked like stacks of DVD players. They sat next to four computer tower units, stacked in a two-by-two group. There were windows in the room, but they were covered with blackout shades. A whiteboard on the far wall was filled with what looked like gibberish. She wondered if it was code.

She hoped he wasn't still hacking into the Pentagon, although it looked like he might have more computing power than the "special building with five sides."

Diesel's desk held three large monitors and three keyboards. He moved from one to another like a concert pianist, his fingers flying over the keys. One look at those big hands had her shivering.

He could do amazing things with those big hands. And she had the feeling she hadn't experienced a fraction of what he was capable of doing.

He looked up and saw her studying his setup. "Those are my servers. The four towers are mostly old units I don't want to part with. I'm kind of a hoarder," he said with a shrug, then turned back to his monitor.

She squeezed behind his desk, leaning over his shoulder to see what he was doing. His screen was filled with columns of more gibberish. Combinations of letters and numbers that made absolutely no sense at all.

"What is that?"

"Hash," he said succinctly. "Encrypted passwords."

"Whose?" she asked cautiously.

"*Lady of the River*'s. That's where Scott King works. These are the passwords of every casino employee. Including Scott King."

"How did you get their passwords?"

He looked over his shoulder at her. "I hacked in. That's what I do."

Her lips twitched because he was so damn cute. "Okay. Did you find the password you were looking for?"

"Yep," he said with satisfaction. "Ritz cracked the password hashes."

It took her a second, then she snorted. "Your program is called Ritz and it's a password *cracker*?"

He grinned. "Yeah. I thought it was hilarious when I programmed it, but I think there was beer involved."

She laughed and kissed his shoulder. "I see. So what is Scott King's password?"

He looked back at her, rolling his eyes. "GoodTo-BeKing666."

She sighed. "Of course it is. What will you do now?"

"I'm going to get his address, phone number, and every other piece of information the casino's admin stores." His hand shot out to clasp her neck, pulling her face close. "But first I want to kiss you again."

"Please do," she murmured, then startled when his phone played a few bars of a song she couldn't place.

He stiffened. "It's Scarlett."

Dani sucked in a breath. "The boys."

"Don't worry yet," he said, then hit ACCEPT and pushed the speaker icon. "Scar? What's up?"

"You need to go outside right now," Scarlett said, her voice tense. "Stone's out there somewhere in your yard. Scott King shot him."

Diesel shot to his feet. "What the fuck?" He shoved the phone at Dani. "Get the details. I'll get dressed." He set off for his bedroom at a run.

Dani headed for the front door. "What happened, Scarlett?"

"You'd just gone into Diesel's house. Stone pretended to drive away, but he doubled back. He'd seen a vehicle tailing you all the way to Diesel's and figured he'd investigate on his own."

"Stupid man," Dani muttered. "I'm on my way outside."

"You are not," Diesel declared. He'd put on jeans and a faded Bengals jersey and was shoving his feet into his boots. "King might be out there still."

"No, he's not," Scarlett said. "He's here."

Both Dani and Diesel froze. "He's where?" Dani demanded.

"King's here, but don't worry. He's waiting outside. He thinks we don't know he's there. But we have it covered." She drew a breath. "Deacon's here and he's explaining everything to Michael. Just take care of Stone. He told Marcus that he already called 911, so help is on the way. Tell us how bad it is as soon as you know. Poor Delores is about to lose her mind." Scarlett hesitated. "He told Marcus to tell her that he loves her."

Shit. Everyone knew that Stone loved Delores, but saying it that way made it sound dire. Diesel met her eyes and she could see that he'd assumed the same.

"Okay. We'll call you back." Diesel ended the call. "If I tell you to run, you run."

"I will. I promise." Diesel had already saved her life once. She wouldn't ask him to do it again.

Chapter Nineteen

Cincinnati, Ohio
Monday, March 18, 2:45 a.m.

Michael jerked awake. There were hands on him. His heart went into overdrive and he rolled away, his fingers finding the kitchen knife he'd hidden under the bed. He popped up into a crouch, ready to fight, his pulse thrumming hard in his head.

Nobody touches Joshua. Nobody. Breathing hard, the hilt of the knife firmly in his clenched fist, he stared at his attacker.

Who stared back out of the weirdest eyes Michael had ever seen. Each one was half-brown and half-blue. Mesmerized, Michael froze.

Then jumped when a hand shot out to grip his wrist, and that fast the knife was gone, taken from his hand. But it had been done gently, he realized.

And the man was signing to him. Fluently. "Easy. Just breathe. I'm sorry. I didn't mean to scare you. I'm Deacon Novak." His fingers spelled the name with quick dexterity. "We met yesterday."

Deacon Novak. Michael fell onto his ass, trembling, his brain waking up in a rush. Deacon was Dr. Dani's brother. But yesterday he'd worn sunglasses. Now his eyes were uncovered. *Whoa.* She'd told him that her brother's eyes were stranger than hers. Damn, was she right.

Deacon was still signing. "Are you all right?"

Michael realized that he'd pressed his palm to his still-racing heart. He nodded. "What's wrong? Where's Dani? And Coach?" He whipped around, his heart nearly stopping when he saw the bed was empty. "Joshua!" he shouted, not caring how stupid he sounded when he voiced.

Deacon's hand was on his shoulder. Still gentle. "He's okay," the man said calmly. "He's with my wife. Faith. She's the redhead."

"Zeus and Goliath," Michael signed, his hands shaking. "Her dogs."

"Yes." Deacon's mouth quirked up. "Goliath chews shoes, so be careful."

Michael smiled slightly, his body coming down from the adrenaline rush. But only a little, because something was still wrong. He could see the worry in the man's weird eyes. "Where are Dani and Coach?"

"They're helping one of our friends. Delores's boyfriend, Stone."

"Wolfhound. Angel," Michael signed, his tension rising again. "What happened to her boyfriend?"

"He was shot by the man who killed your stepfather."

Michael sagged against the side of the bed. "He's here? Looking for me? You have to get Joshua away from here. Keep him safe."

"We're going to keep *both* of you safe," Deacon signed firmly. "Now I need you to pay attention. I need you to be calm. Can you do that for me?"

Michael closed his eyes for a brief moment and nodded. When he opened them, he saw that Deacon had extended his hand to help him up. "Come with me. I'll explain as much as I can. But we need to hurry."

Michael followed the man into the hallway, and Deacon shut the door. "I wanted you away from windows. You're safe here."

"Where is Joshua?" Michael demanded.

"In the basement, eating cookies with my wife. He thinks they're camping. He has no idea that anything's wrong and we don't want to scare him, okay? Can you fake not being scared?"

"I don't know," Michael said honestly, and Deacon smiled.

"Fair enough. This is the situation. I'm telling you so that you'll be prepared, and so you trust us. Okay? We just got a call from Stone. He's at Coach's. In his side yard, to be exact. He was shot about an hour and a half ago and hit on the head. When he came to, his phone was gone and he was too weak to move, but Stone's a tough guy and I'm sure he'll be fine. Dani's taking care of him right now."

"Okay," Michael said, his heart slowing. Not a normal rate, but he no longer felt faint. Something about Deacon's manner calmed him. He was like Coach that way. "How did Stone call you guys if he didn't have a phone?"

Deacon smiled approvingly. "Good question. You're thinking now. Stone is a suspicious sort. He's also a reporter, so he has sources who like to stay anonymous. Because of that, he always carries a burner phone. You know what that is?"

Michael nodded. "A throwaway phone. I watch TV."

That made Deacon grin. "Okay. Well, he had a burner phone, but it was hidden in his damn boot, so he had to get to it and that took a while. He called his brother Marcus before he even called 911. He knew that this guy was looking for you. That he'd probably been following Dr. Dani, thinking she'd lead him to you. He wanted to warn Marcus that the man was coming."

Michael's shoulders lowered as some of the tension seeped out of him. These people really did care. Marcus and his wife had guarded him and Joshua, sitting by the door. All Dani's friends had gathered to protect them. And Delores's boyfriend, Stone, had put Michael's safety over his own. "Oh."

Deacon's smile was warm. "Yeah. Stone likes to pretend he's a gruff badass, but he's really a marshmallow inside."

"Like Coach."

"Exactly. There's a good reason those two are friends. Anyway, Greg just told us that he'd noticed an SUV that shouldn't have been parked in front of one of the neighbors' houses. He'd been walking the dogs." Deacon rolled his eyes. "All seven of them. God. How did we get so many dogs?"

"Greg said it was because of Delores and her shelter."

"It's because we're all saps," Deacon said, but he smiled and Michael suspected the white-haired man was probably as big a marshmallow as the others. "Anyway, we believe he's out there."

"Did you call the police?" Michael asked.

"Well, yes," Deacon said. "But we *are* the police. Scarlett's a detective and Kate, Decker, and I are FBI agents. We will protect you."

"Why don't you just go out and arrest the guy, then?"

"Another good question. See, we had no evidence that you'd killed your stepfather when we brought you in for questioning on Saturday, but we don't have any evidence that he did, either, except for your eyewitness account. Now, we believe you, but we can't prove this guy has actually done anything. Nobody else has seen his face, and it's not a crime to sit outside on a street."

Michael stared at the man. "You're going to let him go free?"

Deacon looked offended. "Of course not. But right now he'd be stupid to break into this house. There are too many of us here. So we're sending a few of the people away. Stone will be going to the hospital, so Delores, Jeremy, and Keith have gone to be with him."

"Who are Jeremy and Keith?"

"Oh, they may have arrived after you went to

sleep. Jeremy is Marcus and Stone's dad. Keith is his husband." Deacon's brow lifted, almost like he was challenging Michael to say something bad about that. But Michael wouldn't. He was cool with it. One of his favorite male teachers at school had a husband.

"Okay," Michael said. "That leaves the cops. And Marcus, Faith, and Greg."

Deacon nodded. "Marcus is Stone's brother. He needs to be at the hospital, too. Scarlett will go with him. I'm telling her it's because Marcus needs her, but it turns out that she's pregnant and Marcus won't leave if she stays."

That made sense. Michael had seen the protective way Marcus had hovered over his wife. "What about Faith and Greg?"

"Greg's going with Marcus and Scarlett. Faith will stay here so that she can communicate with you if I'm busy. Outside of me, Dani, and Adam, Faith is the best signer of our group."

"Busy," Michael repeated. "That doesn't mean 'shot,' does it?"

Deacon laughed. "No. Been there, done that, got the T-shirt. And the scars. Plus, I've been out working on a case. I'm wearing a Kevlar vest."

Working my case, Michael thought, but didn't ask. Mentally he counted all the people who'd been in the house. "What about Kate and Decker?"

"Ah. This is where our plan comes in. We want him to *think* I'm the only one here with you guys, so Kate and Decker are going to pretend to leave. They're going to drive away and park on the next street, then come back here. We want to catch him trying to come in."

Fuck no. No way in hell. Michael lifted his chin. "And if he manages to?"

"We'll take him down. But he won't get in. Dani's house is as secure as my own. I designed the security system myself."

"And if he continues to just sit out there and be a creeper?"

"Then we'll have one of our undercover agents follow him when he finally decides to leave. We've got the neighborhood surrounded."

Michael thought about it. "Why don't you just move Joshua and me, too?"

"We're going to. We're securing a safe house for you both as we speak. If we can get you out without compromising your safety, we will. Otherwise, we're going to sit tight until we can."

"You could drive one of the cars into the garage and smuggle us out that way."

Deacon grimaced ruefully. "Have you *been* in Dani's garage?"

Michael shook his head. "No. What's in it?"

"'What's not?' is a better question. So many boxes. She gets donations for the clinic and the shelter downtown and keeps them in there. Clothing, toys, you name it. So unless we want to move it all out—which would basically be a neon sign that we're moving *you* out—we need to do it a different way. You ready to pretend you're camping?"

Michael took a deep breath. "Yeah. Thanks, Deacon."

Deacon gave him a hard nod. "You're welcome."

Cincinnati, Ohio
Monday, March 18, 2:45 a.m.

Oh my God. Finally. Cade rolled his eyes as the SUVs began to pull away from Dani's house. The Hummer was the first to leave, with two of the men who'd arrived in it. The third man had left earlier. This time it also carried a small blond woman leaning heavily on the arm of the more slender of the two men. The man kissed her cheek, then helped her up into the backseat of the Hummer before getting into the front passenger seat. The heavier man already had the Hummer started and they drove away.

They'd been just as quiet as the dog walkers had been. Were they *all* deaf?

The red Subaru was the next to leave. One of the adult dog walkers, along with a woman and Greg Novak, Dani's brother. The Subaru's license plate had been hidden by all the vehicles parked behind it but Cade would be able to see it once they'd driven past him. Hunkered low enough that they couldn't see him, he waited until they passed, then lifted his phone to snap a photo of the plate, hoping he'd get a decent picture.

He checked his phone and nodded. It was blurry and off center, but he could make out the numbers and guess at the letters. It wouldn't take him long to do a lookup. Greg being Dani's brother, she might be open to a trade.

One of the Jeeps was the next to go. This was a big blond guy and a redhead. The man kissed her lightly before helping her into the car. Cade rolled his eyes.

He got a photo of their plate as well. One never knew what might be helpful information later. Hopefully there would be no later. Hopefully Michael would be taken care of before the sun rose. But it was wise to have contingencies, especially since nothing had gone to plan since he'd killed that motherfucker Brewer.

There were only three vehicles left—the Chevy Suburban that Deacon Novak had shown up in, a smaller-model Jeep than the one that had just left, and a sedan he hadn't been able to see earlier because it had been surrounded by behemoth SUVs. He noted all the license plates.

A quick search showed that the sedan belonged to Dani and the smaller Jeep belonged to Faith Novak, who was the Fed's wife, according to the article Cade had read. Her presence didn't matter to him. He could disable a woman if he needed to. He hoped he wouldn't need to. All he really needed to do was sit and wait for Deacon and his wife to go to sleep. Then the house would be quiet. *And I can take care of Michael.*

Bridgetown, Ohio
Monday, March 18, 2:45 a.m.

"I'll go to Stone," Dani said, stopping Diesel at his front door. "You go get some clean towels and a pair of scissors or a sharp knife." She was digging in her purse and brought out a sealed plastic bag filled with disposable gloves. "I'll also need a flashlight, unless you have outdoor floodlights." She gave him a slight shove when he stood there, staring at her. *"Go."*

Diesel stared. "You're crazy if you think I'm letting you go out there alone."

"Scott King is not out there. Stone is, and he's been there for over an hour, dammit. He's been unconscious and he's got to have lost a lot of blood. Bring a blanket, too." She opened the door and glared at him. *"Go!"*

Diesel cursed under his breath, but turned to do as he'd been told. It took him a full minute and a half to gather all the items she'd demanded. A minute and a half during which he cursed Scott King to hell.

"Dani!" he shouted as he left the house at a run, his arms full.

"Over here," she called back. "To your left."

Diesel found her kneeling at Stone's side, stethoscope in her ears and holding a small penlight between her teeth. One of her gloved hands put pressure on his leg, the other held the bell of the stethoscope to his chest.

Dropping to Stone's other side, he spread out one of the towels and dumped all the supplies on it. Then his breath caught. Even in the small light provided by the penlight, he could see that Stone looked bad. He was pale, sweaty, and trembling, teeth gritted against the pain. But conscious. *Thank God.*

"What do you need first?" Diesel choked out.

Dani glanced up at him. "Are you going to be okay?" she asked.

"Yeah." He gripped Stone's hand in his and grunted when Stone squeezed hard.

"Then I need you to shine the flashlight on the leg wound. It's worse than the wound in his chest. That bullet hit closer to his side and it's a through-and-through. He's lost more blood from his leg, and he's still bleeding." She glanced up again. "Keep holding his hand, because this is going to hurt like a bitch."

"Thanks, Doc," Stone gasped. "Such optimism."

"Would you rather be surprised when it hurts like a bitch?" she asked, not sparing him a glance as she searched the stuff she'd emptied from her purse onto the ground. Coming up with a foil packet, she tore it open and Diesel caught a whiff of alcohol. Leaning over Stone, she found the knife Diesel had brought out and cut Stone's pants up the inside of his leg, slicing at the fabric at his upper thigh.

"Guess not," Stone gasped. "What else you got in that bag, Doc Poppins?"

Dani snorted. "Only my emergency stash of M&M's, but there's no way I'm giving them to you, Detective Stone."

Stone's laugh turned into a moan as she swabbed the area around the wound with the alcohol wipe. "Mean. You're so mean."

Diesel looked between them, missing the joke. "Why did you call him that?"

"Private joke," Stone said, then moaned again when Dani pressed a clean towel against the wound. He was squeezing Diesel's hand so hard that Diesel swore he felt his bones pop.

"I need your belt, Diesel," Dani said.

Without a word, he set down the light, pulled off his belt, and handed it to her. He repositioned the light and took Stone's hand again.

"Stone, Scarlett said you called 911. When was

that?" Dani slid the belt around Stone's thigh above the wound and tugged it, then tested to be sure the towel soaking up the blood was still in place.

God. Stone was still bleeding. And he wasn't squeezing Diesel's hand as hard. *He's getting tired.* That couldn't be good.

"Few minutes before you came out," Stone ground out as Dani balled up the blanket, using it to elevate his legs. "Shitty signal out here, Diesel. You need to live closer to town."

"Sorry," Diesel said because he didn't know what else to say. "Where's your phone?"

Stone pointed vaguely to the ground. It took Diesel a moment to find the phone because it was black and turned on its back. It was a flip phone. Glancing at Stone's foot, Diesel saw that his boot was gone. Somehow Stone had managed to kick his boot off and contort his body so that he could get his hands on the burner he always kept hidden there.

"Did King take your phone?" Diesel asked, and Stone nodded wordlessly. Diesel let go of his hand to pick up the phone and immediately heard a tinny voice urgently calling for someone to respond. "Hello?"

"This is the operator. I asked Stone to stay on the phone. Who are you and what is his condition?"

"I'm Elvis Kennedy and this is my property." Diesel glared at Stone, who was snorting and mouthing, "Elvis." "The patient is Montgomery O'Bannion. Stone's a nickname. He's conscious. A doctor's with me and she's providing first aid."

"Put it on speaker," Dani commanded, so Diesel did, holding it out so that Dani could talk to the operator. "This is Dr. Novak. I'm a trauma doctor. The patient has two gunshot wounds, one to the right side of his chest and one to the upper thigh. He's lost a significant amount of blood." She looked at Stone. "What's your blood type?"

"B," Stone told her, then managed a grim grin at Diesel. "You two talked?"

Diesel nodded as Dani continued to speak to the 911 operator, telling her the extent of Stone's injuries and that his pulse was thready. "Yeah," he mouthed back. "Thank you, brother."

Stone closed his eyes, lips curving in a soft smile. "Good."

His grip abruptly slackened and Diesel panicked. Stone looked suddenly way too peaceful. *"Stone?"*

Dani immediately gripped Stone's wrist, then dropped it to put the stethoscope's eartips in her ears and listen to his heart. She pulled the eartips out. "Operator, how far out is EMS?"

"Less than five minutes."

"Tell them to pick up the speed," Dani said urgently, but somehow still calmly. "The patient has gone into cardiac arrest. Starting chest compressions."

Diesel froze. *Cardiac arrest? Chest compressions?* "What?"

Dani placed her hands in the middle of Stone's chest, one atop the other. She started pumping, her mouth moving as she silently counted. "Diesel, it's better for Stone if one of us breathes for him. I can, but I'd prefer you do it." She looked up, meeting his eyes directly. "Do you know how?"

He nodded, focusing on her mismatched eyes because he felt like he was going to throw up. "CPR certification was required to coach." He propped the flashlight on Stone's hip, aiming the light at Dani's hands, then moved to Stone's head and shoved the fear from his mind. He could do this. He *had* to do this.

He tilted Stone's head back gently, closed his nose, and began breathing into his mouth, conscious of Dani watching him.

"That's good, Diesel. Keep it up. Every fifteen compressions, you breathe for him once. I'll count." She began to count quietly and Diesel held on to the sound, letting it ground him.

Don't die, Stone. Don't you dare die.

Together they worked on his friend, Diesel breathing into Stone's mouth and Dani continuing chest compressions, her voice maintaining its calm, soothing tone as she counted. *She must have been so damn good in the ER,* Diesel thought, realizing for the first time what she'd lost when she was forced to quit her job at County Hospital.

It felt like they did CPR for an hour, but it couldn't have been more than a few minutes before Diesel heard the sound of sirens in the distance. He'd breathed for Stone eight more times before the ambulance turned onto his property.

"Diesel. Diesel, honey, you have to back away now."

Diesel shook his head when someone tried to pull him away from Stone, then realized that Dani had stopped counting. She was gently pulling his arm.

"Help's here," she whispered in his ear. "Come on, honey. Come with me."

Numbly he rose to his feet and let her guide him away from the two paramedics who had already placed the paddles on Stone's chest. He flinched when Stone's body arched at the first jolt of electricity.

He could only watch as the medics repeated the process twice more, horror finally setting in.

"Got a pulse," one of them declared. "Ready for transport."

"Where are you taking him?" Dani asked.

"Mercy West," the medic called over his shoulder as they lifted the stretcher into the ambulance.

"Diesel." He blinked down at Dani when she put her hands on his cheeks and tugged his face down to look at her. She leaned up to whisper in his ear. "The police are here. They may ask to go inside. You should shut Ritz down."

He blinked again, comprehension returning in a rush. Hands shaking, he took out his phone and opened the app he'd designed for just such an emergency. One tap of his screen, and all of his computers shut down. Now the cops couldn't search them without a warrant.

"Done," he murmured.

She looked impressed. "Wow." She smiled up at him. "You did good tonight, Diesel. Kept your head. Kept Stone alive. I'm proud of you."

He felt his face heating. "Your voice calmed me."

"I'm glad." She ran her thumbs across his cheeks, wiping at moisture there, and he realized he'd been crying at some point. "Call Marcus. Tell him what's happening. Tell him that Mercy is a good hospital. One of the attendings is one of the finest cardiac surgeons in the area."

"Thank you," he whispered. She'd known just how to make him feel better.

She leaned up to place a soft kiss on his lips. "Make sure the boys are okay. I'll talk to the cops."

Cincinnati, Ohio
Monday, March 18, 3:30 a.m.

Cade had waited long enough. The house was dark and quiet, and if he waited much longer, the sun would come up. Detective Stone's body would be found and they'd know that someone had followed him and Dani Novak out to the house in Bridgetown.

Then they'd move Michael and he'd have lost his chance.

It had to be now or never.

But he was prepared. He double-checked his inventory. Two Molotov cocktails. A lighter. A spare lighter. One rock.

In the event of a necessary contingency, he wore two handguns in shoulder holsters, an AR-15, backup guns at each ankle, and three switchblades—all from the old pedo's weapons room. And, if things went truly south, he had the grenades in his jacket pockets.

He hoped they still functioned. They were at least

fifty years old, relics from the Vietnam War. He'd never had to use them, but he'd never tried to smoke out a house where a Fed was watching over children, either.

Hell. He was planning to smoke out a house where a *Fed* was watching over *children*.

So that I can kill a fourteen-year-old kid.

Just leave. Turn your SUV around and drive to fucking Canada.

He closed his eyes. He really wanted to. Michael Rowland had already been through hell. But if Cade got caught on his way to the border, he'd fry for sure. Even if he did manage to cross the border, he could still get caught and, best case, spend the rest of his life behind bars. And wouldn't his father find that hilarious?

Michael's eyewitness testimony could send him to prison. Avoiding prison was worth both the risk and whatever guilty conscience he experienced later.

Pulling the ski mask down to cover his face, Cade started his SUV and slowly approached, hugging the wrong side of the road so that he was closer to Dani's house. He rolled to a quiet stop at the end of her driveway. This was it.

Go! He got out of his car, crouch-walking alongside Deacon Novak's Suburban, so that he couldn't be seen. The street was deserted now. No cars. No people walking umpty-million dogs. When he was inches outside the range of motion sensors, he put down the rock and lit the fuse on the Molotov, holding the bottle in his left hand. He had about ten seconds before it blew.

He dropped the lighter into his pocket and picked up the rock, then stood and hurled it at the window before passing the Molotov to his right hand. He leaned backward, ready to launch it through the broken glass.

But the window wasn't broken. It wasn't even nicked. The rock had simply bounced off it.

Shit. Impact-resistant glass. He'd have to be content with a fire on the outside of the house. It would still force them out. He'd started to pitch the bottle toward the house when a woman's voice barked out of the darkness.

"Stop! FBI. Toss the bottle into the street. *Now.*"

Cade spun toward the voice, immediately recognizing half of the last couple to have left Dani Novak's house. The redhead who'd kissed the blond man now held a rifle like it was a lover.

FBI. It was a trap. Not taking time to think, he hurled the bottle toward her, pleased when she turned and leaped out of the way, sliding on her belly. The bottle shattered, spreading fire all over the lawn.

The woman had tricked him, doubling back. The man was likely here, too.

FBI. *Fuckers.*

Sure enough, a male voice growled from behind him. "Hands in the air. Or I will shoot you, make no mistake."

Fuck, fuck, *fuck*. Heart racing, Cade slowly turned, leading with his left shoulder. He lifted his left hand while his right reached into his pocket and withdrew the grenade, keeping it palmed and out of sight.

Shit, damn, fuck. The big blond man was standing next to the open door of Cade's Sequoia. Any grenade explosion would destroy his own transportation.

I'll have to shoot him instead. He reached for his gun, but was stopped when the Fed fired a warning shot at the ground in front of him.

"I said, hands up," the man snarled.

Asshole. Cade pulled the pin and tossed the grenade at the man's feet. He had only a split second to enjoy the shocked look on the man's face before the Fed turned and sprang forward, better than any long jumper Cade had ever seen. Sailing over the grenade, the Fed landed on his stomach with his arms outstretched, reaching for Cade.

But Cade was already running and the Fed grasped at air. He'd sped between Novak's house and her neighbor's by the time the grenade exploded behind him. He ducked as hunks and shards of metal— remnants of his own vehicle—rained down. Grabbing the pistols from their holsters, he ran, fueled on adrenaline, rage, and fear.

But it was his leg that was hit, not his head. Searing pain tore through his thigh and he looked sideways to see the redhead holding her rifle, aiming it at him again. She'd rounded the burning lawn, coming at him from the back of the house.

He whipped his arm to the side and fired repeatedly, not caring where it hit as long as it slowed her down, then felt rather than heard the gun clicking on empty. He couldn't hear anything right now. Between the woman's rifle fire, his own gunfire, and the grenade, his ears were seriously ringing. *Shit.* He half hobbled, half ran forward, grateful that Novak lived in a no-fence neighborhood.

Damn HOAs were good for something, after all.

His knees nearly buckled when another hot shard of pain pierced his leg—the same damn leg. He'd been hit again.

Fucking Feds.

Cade didn't slow down as he swung the rifle from his back, one-handed, and pulled the trigger, spraying bullets behind him. With his other hand, he found the second grenade and pulled the pin, then tossed it over his shoulder. A few seconds later, the ground shook and dirt rained down around him, leaving him in a smoky haze.

And then he saw his escape.

A woman had opened the door at the back of her house and was peering out. Cade made a run for the door and shoved his way inside before she could draw the breath to scream.

He pointed the rifle at her. "Don't scream and I won't kill you."

Cincinnati, Ohio
Monday, March 18, 3:33 a.m.

Michael gasped when the second explosion rocked the house. He'd felt them, which meant they had to be close. Hawkeye crowded his leg, the poor dog trembling. The dog didn't leave him, nor did he bark. But he was growling. Michael had his hand on Hawkeye's neck and could feel the sound vibrating in his throat.

The other dogs were barking, though. They stood, their attention focused on the stairs, bodies jerking with every bark.

They were in the basement of Dani's house, he and Faith sitting on the sofa while Joshua lay on the floor, curled up in a sleeping bag. "Camping," Faith had called it. Joshua had already been asleep by the time Michael had come down the stairs with Deacon Novak.

Joshua wasn't asleep anymore. If the explosions hadn't woken him, the dogs' barking did. But Joshua didn't look scared. Mostly confused.

Michael was grateful that Faith had kept Joshua from being afraid. But those explosions changed everything. He saw her fear before she quickly hid it away, because Joshua was sitting up and rubbing his eyes.

"What was that? Why are the dogs barking?" Joshua asked, signing clumsily with his small hands, like he always did when he first woke up. Then his eyes suddenly filled with excitement. "Fireworks? Can we go see?"

No, not fireworks, Michael thought dully. The explosions felt like bombs. *Because of me. Because some asshole is trying to get to me. To kill me.*

He lurched to his feet, unable to sit any longer. Unable to pretend to be calm and unafraid. He waved at his little brother, signing that he was going to the bathroom.

I just need a minute. Just a minute, that's all. He closed himself in the small bathroom and stared at his reflection in the mirror. His eyes were wide. Wild. He'd scare Joshua if he went back out looking like this.

Run. Every nerve in his body was telling him to run. To lead this monster as far from Joshua as he could. But that was what the man wanted. Michael understood that. His stepfather's killer supposedly couldn't get into this house with its security system designed by Deacon himself. *So he's trying to lure me out.*

Michael also understood that as soon as he stepped out of the house he'd be dead. And then no one would watch over Joshua.

Actually, that wasn't true, he thought. Coach would. Dani would. Her friends would. Still, Michael had no desire to be dead. *So I'll stay put.*

He splashed cold water on his face, then drew several deep breaths, just like Dani had shown him the day he'd gone to the police station.

When was that? Less than two days ago. *This is insane. My life is insane.*

Drying his face, he returned to the cozy basement room, where Faith was now sitting on the floor with Joshua, rubbing his back comfortingly.

"See?" she signed. "I told you he'd only be a minute." She gave Michael an approving nod. "I think we should have more cookies."

That made Joshua grin, and Michael forced himself to smile. He sat on the sofa and forced himself to wait. Forced himself to breathe. Forced himself to eat a cookie. And to wait some more.

Deacon finally returned to them, expression grim and clothes smelling like smoke. But he, too, forced a smile for Joshua. "Did you save me any cookies?"

Joshua laughed. "Yes. One," he teased, because there were at least a dozen more in the plastic container. He held one up to Deacon. "They're good. Try it."

Deacon nibbled at the cookie. "They are good. Joshua, I saw a box of Legos in the toy box in the corner. Can you get them for me?"

Michael came to his feet, positioning himself so that he could see both Deacon and the toy box. He did trust these people, but he still found he couldn't breathe when Joshua was out of his sight.

Joshua ran to obey and Deacon turned to Michael and Faith, signing rapidly without speaking. "King set a fire in the front yard. We extinguished it. He also threw a grenade at Decker and another at me when I tried to follow him."

Faith slapped her hand over her mouth. She hadn't made a sound, because Joshua never looked up.

"Is Decker okay?" Michael asked.

Deacon nodded, still not voicing. "He knew how to escape it. He took cover under my SUV, but he caught some shrapnel before he was able to roll under it. He's bleeding, but it doesn't look too bad. Kate's with him and we had two ambulances on standby."

Faith looked over her shoulder to check on Joshua and, seeing him still searching the toy box, asked, "How did he start a fire?"

Deacon glanced at Michael and sighed. "He threw a Molotov cocktail at the house. Do you know what that is, Michael?"

Michael nodded. "I told you. I watch TV."

One side of Deacon's mouth twitched up. "So you did." He sobered. "He tried to break the front window first by throwing a rock at it."

Faith's smile was dark. "I hope it bounced back and hit him in the head."

"I wish." Deacon scowled. "He was standing far enough back that he didn't trigger the floodlights."

"So he'd been watching the house for a while." Faith's signing was less fluid than Deacon's, but she was understandable, and that was all that was important right now. She looked at Michael. "The windows are made with hurricane glass. They're all impact resistant. You can't break them with a rock or even a hammer."

Michael understood Deacon's confidence now. "That's why you knew he couldn't get in."

Deacon nodded. "Exactly. The doors are set in three inches of steel and I installed cameras and an alarm system. Just like at our house. Nobody's coming through that door. But if you stay here, he'll wait us out. We're moving you ASAP."

"Where?"

"To a nice place," Faith told him. "You'll like it there. Go ahead and pack up the Xbox and your clothes and I'll help Joshua gather some toys and his clothes."

"What about Coach and Dani?" Michael asked, feeling new panic rise.

"They're going to meet you there," Deacon promised.

"How is Stone?" Faith asked.

Deacon's face went grim again. "He's going to be okay."

But Michael didn't need to be able to hear to know that Deacon wasn't so sure.

Faith exhaled slowly. "Okay. I'll go to the hospital as soon as we have the boys settled."

"I think Jeremy and Marcus would appreciate it." Deacon leaned in to press a kiss to her forehead. "Dani had to do chest compressions and Diesel breathed for him."

Faith closed her eyes. "God."

Michael sank to the sofa. Chest compressions meant that the guy's heart had stopped. *He'd died. Because of me.*

"He's a tough bastard," Deacon said. "EMS brought him back with the paddles."

Faith nodded unsteadily, then opened her eyes to focus on Michael. She sat next to him and made him look at her. "Your face says you think this is your fault. It's not. It's the fault of the asshole who shot him and who tried to kill you. Not your fault. You did nothing wrong and everything right. Do you understand me?"

Michael nodded, too. They were nice words, but . . . "Is he going to die?"

Faith shook her head. "He didn't the last two times he was shot, so odds are good that he'll be his own grouchy self by lunchtime."

"Two times before?" Michael gaped. "This is his *third* time getting shot?"

She nodded again, firmly this time. "And that doesn't count the time he was shot in Iraq. My cousin really is a tough bastard. All of us are. So you need to be tough, too. It's kind of a club requirement."

It was silly enough to make Michael smile, which was just in time, because Joshua returned with a concerned frown.

"I couldn't find the Legos in the toy box," he said.

"No?" Deacon tilted his head. "Maybe I was wrong. I know another place they could be. Let's go check." He held out his hand and Joshua took it trustingly.

When Michael and Faith were alone, she squeezed his knee. "Dani and Deacon are two of the best people I know. They'll make sure you're okay."

Michael let himself believe it because he was too scared not to. "I'll pack up the Xbox so that Dani can beat Coach at *Cuphead*."

Faith grinned wickedly. "Video it with your phone, please. I want to see the look on Diesel's face when Dani kicks his . . . cup."

Michael laughed. Maybe it would be okay after all.

Chapter Twenty

The cops were doing door-to-door searches. Cade leaned against the wall of the house he'd entered and made himself think. Which was hard because his leg *hurt*. The wounds weren't fatal, not like those he'd given Detective Stone. The first bullet had hit a few inches above his knee, the second a few inches below, both far enough away from the femoral artery that he wasn't going to bleed out.

He didn't think he'd dripped any blood as he'd run, and they hadn't seen his face, so they couldn't identify him if they did manage to catch him. Plus he'd bought his escape with the grenade, his timing perfect. The smoke and dust thrown up by the exploding dirt had kept them from seeing where he'd gone, but they knew he couldn't have run that far.

The cops were driving along the street, announcing the danger via loudspeaker. *"A dangerous criminal is on foot in your neighborhood. Keep your doors and windows locked. We will be conducting door-to-door searches."*

They'd be here soon. *So think, dammit. Be prepared.*

"You," he said to the woman who stood trembling

before him wearing Minnie Mouse pajamas and a
robe. "What's your name?"

"Evelyn," she whispered. "Please don't hurt me."

"I said I wouldn't, as long as you don't scream.
Are you here alone?"

She nodded, but her eyes flicked to the left. Cade
followed her line of vision and smiled. *Perfect.* He
limped through the kitchen to the living room, where a
baby lay in a playpen, gurgling happily at the toys dan-
gling over its head.

Shouldering the strap to his rifle, Cade scooped
the baby up. The kid was cute. Maybe a year old. He
didn't know much about babies. "Where's your husband?"

"I don't have one," Evelyn rasped.

Her ring finger was bare, so she might have been
telling the truth. "Come with me."

She was wringing her hands as tears rolled down
her face. "Don't hurt my baby. Please."

He wheeled on her, giving her a glare that made
her whimper. "I will not hurt your baby unless you
scream or say or do anything that pisses me off. Give
me your phone. Now." Supporting the baby with one
hand, he held out his other. *"Now."*

Evelyn dug into the pocket of her robe and handed
it to him, her hand shaking like a leaf in a hurricane.
He pocketed the phone and motioned her to the
stairs. "You first. And do not try anything."

She obeyed, whimpering all the while. But she
obeyed.

Her bedroom was nicely furnished, as were the
two spare rooms—one as a bedroom and one as a
study. No sign of a husband. He checked the closets
for suits and wingtip shoes and found nothing but
women's clothes. And aprons. Lots of aprons that
were made from heavy plastic, decorated with a dog
driving a big van.

"What do you do for a living, Evelyn?"

"I'm . . . I'm a groomer. Dogs and cats."

"When do you leave for work?" He could respect the fear causing her hesitation. But he had places to go. *Like anywhere but here.* "When, Evelyn?" he repeated, lifting the rifle just enough to press his point.

She exhaled, squaring her shoulders. "At six thirty. My first appointment is at eight, but I have to drop Jimmy at day care first."

Six thirty could work. Assuming he could hide from the door-to-door searches until then. "We'll figure that out. What do you drive?"

She frowned again. "A-a-a car?"

He fought for patience and lost. "What *kind* of car?" he snarled, and she flinched. *Good. I want her to be afraid of me.*

"A Civic."

That wasn't going to work. There was no place he could hide in a vehicle that small. Then something clicked. He pulled one of the aprons from the closet and pointed to the printed logo. "Zoom 'N Groom? You have a pet grooming van?"

She swallowed hard. "Yes."

"Is it here?"

"In my driveway."

"I didn't see a dog grooming van in your driveway last night." He'd passed by this house on his way to Dani Novak's.

"It's just a white van. I have a magnetic sign. I take it off at night."

"Why?"

"Homeowners association rules."

"Ah. No commercial vehicles in the driveways." He smiled at her and was gratified to see her flinch. "You're a rule-breaker, Evelyn. I like that."

She took a step back. "What do you want from me?"

"Just a ride. And for you to get rid of the cops when they knock on your door. Tell them whatever you want, as long as you don't mention me and you make them leave." He paused, giving her a long, hard look. "You will help me, because once you drive me out of here, I'll leave you and your baby alone. Do you understand?"

She swallowed hard again, her gaze dropping to the baby in Cade's arms. "Yes."

"Good. Now bring me whatever first aid supplies you have."

Bridgetown, Ohio
Monday, March 18, 3:45 a.m.

Diesel could feel his body vibrating with the need to get away from the police and get to Stone. His friend's heart had stopped beating. Just . . . stopped. Diesel had been through a lot in his life, but he wasn't sure he'd ever been so terrified as he was when he'd heard Dani say *cardiac arrest* and *chest compressions*. Stone would be at the hospital by now and Diesel was a breath away from ditching the questioning cops and getting himself and Dani to the ER as fast as his truck could carry them.

The sight of the Chevy Tahoe coming up the drive had his gut relaxing a fraction. When Adam got out, Diesel didn't think he'd ever been as glad to see a cop.

Adam strode over to them, noting Diesel's arm around Dani with a raised brow. "I'm glad at least one thing went right tonight."

Diesel pulled her closer, letting the chocolate scent of her hair fill his head. Yes. That had gone more than right. He needed to hold on to that. "How is Stone?"

"In surgery," Adam said quickly, then hesitated. "The boys are fine."

Dani stiffened. "What happened?"

Adam tried to smile, but it looked forced. "There was a commotion at your house. Your front lawn will need to be resodded," he said lightly, then sighed when neither Dani nor Diesel relaxed an iota. "King attacked the house. Tried to set it on fire with a Molotov cocktail, and it could have been bad. He threw a rock first so that his bottle would land farther into the living room. It was filled with a tar mixture, so it would have stuck to the carpet and walls and everything else it touched."

"But that didn't work," Dani said flatly. She looked up at Diesel. "Impact-resistant windows, all through the house."

"Smart," Diesel said. "So the Molotov just bounced off the window?"

Adam shook his head. "No, the *rock* bounced off the window. King threw the Molotov at Kate when she confronted him. She's a damn good leaper, luckily. Her hands have some burns, but she's mostly unhurt. Decker was up next and King threw a grenade at him."

Dani gasped, her hand flying up to cover her mouth. "God."

Diesel frowned. "Did you say a grenade? An honest-to-God *hand grenade*?"

"I know, right?" Adam shook his head again. "But yes, that's exactly what I said. Decker saw it and his army training kicked in. He threw himself under Deacon's Suburban, but got a piece of metal in his thigh—from King's own vehicle, which King blew up instead of Decker. Satisfyingly enough, Kate shot King in almost the same place that Decker got hit. Deacon got him, too. So King's wounded."

"And in custody?" Dani asked darkly and Adam scowled his frustration.

"No. Fucker came armed to the teeth with handguns and a converted AR-15."

"Converted to full auto?" Diesel asked.

"Yep. Sprayed bullets at anyone who approached him. Then tossed a second grenade that blew a crater in one of your neighbors' backyards. When the dust cleared, he was gone. He has to have ducked into one of the houses nearby. We have the neighborhood surrounded and roadblocks at every exit. We're doing door-to-door searches now."

"The boys must be so afraid," Dani murmured.

"Deacon says that Joshua thought the grenades were fireworks," Adam said. "Michael knows the score, but he's holding it together. He keeps asking for you two, though."

"We have to go to them," Diesel said quietly.

Dani's gaze shot up to his. "You wanted to go to Stone."

"Stone's got a lot of people at the hospital right now," Diesel said. "And as much as I want to be one of them, those kids need us."

Adam frowned. "Faith and Deacon won't leave them. You know that, right?"

"I know." Diesel knew that Deacon and Faith would have protected those kids with their lives. "But Faith is Stone's family. She needs to be at the hospital, for Jeremy if nobody else. If it was you in the hospital, Adam, Dani would want the same." He knew that Faith was as close to her cousins, Stone and Marcus, as Dani and Deacon were to their cousin Adam. Cousins were more like siblings in their circle of friends. "Those boys are legally Dani's responsibility. They're morally my responsibility. And Dani is just mine, so I go where she goes."

"The big ones always fall the hardest, y'know?" But Adam grinned, clearly happy with the change.

Dani ignored him, her focus on Diesel as a smile curved her lips. "Thank you."

Diesel felt his own mouth curve of its own volition. "Anytime."

Adam cleared his throat, reclaiming their attention. "Pack a bag, Diesel. I'm your chauffeur tonight."

"Where are we going?" Dani asked.

"Where we always go," Adam told her with a grin. "You're movin' on up, Dani."

That told Diesel exactly where they were going—a condo belonging to one of Adam's friends. The guy was always out of the country, so he let Adam use the place whenever he needed it. It was the penthouse floor of an exclusive tower in Mount Adams. The condo was luxurious, the view of the river phenomenal.

"I'll need my laptop," Diesel said cautiously.

Adam nodded once. "The network's secure. And private."

Translation: *Do what you need to do.* Diesel felt pride knowing he'd earned the detective's trust.

"I'll be right back." He released his hold on Dani, placing his trust in Adam to keep her safe until he'd returned.

Cincinnati, Ohio
Monday, March 18, 4:15 a.m.

It wasn't a great plan, Cade conceded, but he was running out of time. He'd cut two boxes that had once held toilet paper, taping them together to form one large hollow box that still looked like two boxes sitting next to each other. On top of the hollow box, he'd stacked others holding what the labels claimed.

"It'll be snug, but I think Junior and I will fit." It was unlikely that the police would come into the house, but he wanted to be prepared in case they did. If the cops searched the garage, all they'd find would be a tiny Honda Civic and a bunch of boxes. Luckily, Evelyn bought everything in bulk.

"What if Jimmy cries?" Evelyn asked, her voice shaking.

Cade gave her his best extra-cruel smile, the one he practiced on his father when the nursing home staff wasn't looking. "Let's hope he doesn't."

Evelyn closed her eyes, swaying on her feet. Cade hoped the kid would stay quiet. For the most part, he simply watched Cade with wide, interested eyes. As long as he had a bottle or pacifier, he was golden, and his mama was very attentive. In fact, she hadn't let the baby out of her sight, except for the time she'd run to get his bottle warmed up.

Must be nice to have someone bring you bottles. A bottle of booze would make an amazing pacifier, because Cade's leg *hurt*. Not like he would die, but it was sore as hell. He hoped the FBI agent who'd taken the grenade was hurting a lot worse.

And of course, Detective Stone wasn't complaining anymore. He'd be long dead by now.

Cade stilled. Unless he wasn't. "Fuck," he muttered aloud.

"What?" Evelyn asked.

"Nothing," Cade grunted. But it wasn't nothing. It was a big something. Deacon Novak and those two Feds had evacuated the house. That was why everyone had left. And that was why they'd been so quiet, not speaking to one another.

They'd known he was out there, watching them.

And then there were the dogs. *Dammit.* Those fucking dogs. He hadn't thought about it at the time, but not one of them had brought out a dog when they left Dani's house. All seven of those fucking dogs were still in the damn house.

They hadn't seen him inside his SUV and he'd switched the plates so that the vehicle itself was untraceable. The only way they could have known he was there was if Stella Brewer had told them—and she hadn't because she really *was* dead—or if Detective Stone had.

The man had known all along that Cade had been following him to the house in Bridgetown, because he'd doubled back to confront him. He must have realized that Cade was looking for Michael and told the others. That was only possible if the detective had somehow survived and called them. How had he done either? Cade had shot him twice *and* had taken his phone.

Right now he didn't care how they'd found out. He only cared that they'd tricked him.

Motherfuckers.

He realized his fists were clenched when Junior

started to fret. He drew a deep breath and forced himself to calm down. To breathe and to think.

It didn't matter what the Feds had known. It only mattered that he get away.

The doorbell rang, its sound muted here in the garage. It was showtime. Cade turned to Evelyn. "You're going to go to the door and you're going to tell the cops what?"

She licked her lips, terror flickering in her eyes. "That nobody's here. That I need to get to work. To please let me pass through the roadblock."

"And if they ask where Junior is?"

"I'll say that he's with my mother."

"And where will I be?"

"In the box."

"Now tell me what will happen if you say a word that makes the cops suspicious."

"My . . . baby . . ." She faltered.

"Say it."

She closed her eyes. "Dies."

"Very good, Evelyn. Now go."

He waved her toward the door to the house and climbed behind the hollow box, taking care not to topple the stack he'd so artfully arranged. Grimacing, he lowered himself to the floor and slid into the hollow box from its open back. For his part, Junior remained quiet, and Cade held his breath that the baby would continue to cooperate.

He didn't like this. He didn't like having no way out. But it could work. He really hoped it did work. He really hoped Evelyn was a good actress, because he *really* didn't want to kill the baby.

Cincinnati, Ohio
Monday, March 18, 6:20 a.m.

Dani paced the length of the safe house's living room with its tall windows that would provide the most amazing views of the river when the sun came up.

Which was going to be soon. She'd visited this luxurious penthouse condo several times in the past when she'd cared for her friends who'd hidden here. With one entrance and a dedicated elevator that now had a twenty-four-hour Cincinnati PD guard, its security was top-notch. As amenities went, it offered everything anyone could want.

If one had to hide, it didn't hurt to have to do it here.

But the boys weren't here yet and she became more worried with every minute that ticked by.

"Dani, honey, relax," Diesel rumbled from behind her.

His big hands lifted to rest on her shoulders and it felt like the only thing keeping her contained within her own skin. "I can't. What's taking Deacon so long getting them here?"

"He's being careful. They have standard operating procedures for transporting witnesses so that they're not followed. You told me this yourself."

"That was before he was more than two hours late without calling us."

He leaned in to kiss the side of her neck. "You were so calm when you were saving Stone's life. What's all this about?"

She turned into his arms, exhaling when they wrapped around her, holding her tight. "I think it's all finally hitting me. Scott King tried to burn down my house. Stone's in ICU, Decker needed thirty-two stitches for shrapnel wounds because King blew up his own SUV . . . And the boys are out there somewhere and I don't know where."

He stroked her hair. "You want me to say something to make you feel better or just listen to you decompress?"

The chuckle that bubbled from her throat shouldn't have surprised her. This man was adept at making her laugh when everything looked bleak. "You did just make me feel better, so thank you."

"Anytime. It may make you feel even more better to know that Stone's awake. Marcus texted me. Delores is with him and he's being cranky with the nurses."

"Good. Not that he's tormenting the nurses, of course. He really ought not to do that. Nurses can make his life either comfortable or really uncomfortable."

"Apparently Delores keeps trying to tell him that." Diesel swayed them back and forth, rocking her where they stood. "And Decker says to tell you that his ass cheek hurts because that's where he took the biggest piece of shrapnel, but he's 'had a lot worse.' His words, not mine." His fingers began moving, massaging the tight muscles of her back. "I'd tell you to go to sleep, but you wouldn't listen."

"Not until they get here."

"They're here," Adam said from his post by the front door. "They just pulled into the parking garage. They'll be up in less than a minute."

It was still a long, long minute before the door opened and Joshua bounded in, still wearing his Spider-Man pj's, his new stuffed dog under one arm. He made a beeline for Dani, throwing his arms around her and holding on tight.

"We did an adventure," he told her solemnly when he finally let go. "We went in a van with no windows after another van pretended to drive away with us."

"A decoy," Diesel said.

Joshua nodded. "That's what Mr. Deacon called it. Then another van left *after* us, so it was like a trick. The third van had the dogs. They went to Delores's house because she has places for them to sleep. Then we changed vans. The first one was white and the second one was . . . white." His forehead crinkled. "So was the third one." His sunny smile returned. "And Miss Faith gave us cookies."

"So many cookies," Deacon groaned, signing the conversation for Michael, who walked sedately at his side. Hawkeye trailed behind them, never more than a snout's length from Michael. "I kept telling Faith that the sugar would keep him up all night, but she said that would be your problem, Dani."

Dani's eyes met Michael's and she saw true exhaustion. And fear. And maybe some guilt. Faith had texted her that Michael blamed himself for Stone's and Decker's injuries. They'd have to work on the guilt later. The fear she understood because she felt it, too. The exhaustion, however, she could fix right now.

"You look tired, Michael," she signed. "I fixed a room for you. I'll show you where it is. Even though I know you'll sleep on the floor in Joshua's room."

Michael just nodded.

Diesel picked Joshua up and swung him around, making the little boy laugh. "I think you need to brush those cookies off your teeth, then off to sleep for you, too."

"Do I get a story?"

Diesel looked at Deacon. "Did we bring any books?"

"I did." Michael dug in his backpack and pulled out five children's books.

Joshua leaned over, still in Diesel's arms, to take the books. "This one!"

Diesel laughed when he saw the title. "*No, David!* I like this book."

Dani stared at him. "You've read *No, David!*?"

"Of course." Diesel righted Joshua on his hip. "Sometimes when the weather is bad or if a parent is late picking up a kid, we read. Right, Joshua?"

Joshua grinned. "Right, Coach."

Dani guessed that Diesel would be tucking Joshua in tonight, and that sent a nice shiver down her spine. *Like a family.* She patted the little boy's back as he and Diesel passed by. "Good night, sweetheart."

"Good night," Joshua said. "Even though it's almost morning."

Dani motioned Michael into the room that would be

his and showed him the adjoining bathroom. "You and Joshua will share this bathroom. Both bedrooms have doors that lead into it. There are no strobe lights for the smoke detector, but I'll ask Coach Diesel if he can install them tomorrow. He's good with stuff like that."

Michael nodded numbly and let his backpack slide off his shoulder and onto the bed. "I'm tired." He spared a weary stroke for Hawkeye, who was practically sitting on Michael's feet, leaning his body into the teenager's leg.

"You should be. It's been a long night." She sat in the chair next to the bed. "Did Deacon tell you what happened?"

Michael's eyes were haunted. "Those men got hurt because of me. Stone and Decker. They're in the hospital because of me."

"No, honey. They got hurt because a killer wants to get away with murder."

"And I can identify him."

"Yes. I won't lie to you. You are a thorn in this killer's side. But Decker was doing his job. And Stone was . . ." She shook her head. "Well, he should have called for help before he went after the guy on his own. He should have called for help as soon as he realized he was being followed. I'm sure his father, his brother, Delores, and everyone else is telling him that, now that he's awake."

"Joshua still doesn't know what happened. He thinks there was just a fire, but not the shooter. We tried to make it fun for him. Deacon and Faith were really nice."

Dani smiled. "They are nice. And you must have been successful because he doesn't look scared at all. Just hyped up on sugar."

Michael's laugh was weak, but there. "Yeah, well, I think Faith was running out of ideas to keep him busy after we kept driving around and switching vans. The last switch, she went to the hospital, and we came here."

"You all did well. You especially. You've held up better than anyone has any right to expect, Michael. I'm proud of you."

Michael's gaze dropped, but his cheeks pinked up. Dani rose and cupped his face in her palm, lifting his chin so that she could sign to him. "Try to sleep. We have guards outside and no one has ever broken into this place. It's like a fortress and too tall for anyone to throw Molotov cocktails. You're safe here. We'll figure everything out after we wake up and have some eggs and bacon."

This got her the grin she was hoping for. "Bacon makes everything better."

"It really does." She brushed her hand over his hair. "Good night, hon. You'll find toothbrushes in the bathroom. And if you get hungry, the pantry has food. The milk in the fridge is new and there's cereal. Eat whatever you like."

She wanted to say more. She wanted to tell him that he wasn't temporary, that she'd fight to keep him. But she wasn't going to make promises she couldn't keep, so she flicked on the bedside light to its dimmest setting and left him to go to bed, making a mental note to get him a night-light ASAP.

She found Deacon sitting at the kitchen table with Adam, both men looking as exhausted as she felt. But she could hear Diesel's rumbling growl and Joshua's giggly rendition of the final lines of *No, David!* and that made her smile.

Deacon's mouth curved a little, too, but quickly flattened, putting Dani on instant alert. "What's wrong?" she demanded.

"Let's wait until Diesel is finished with the story. I don't want to go through it twice." He pointed to a duffel bag on the floor beside him. "Faith packed a few things. Toys for the kids, some changes of clothes. She packed you some clothes, too, and all your medications."

"Thank you," Dani said, relieved. "I always keep

enough for two days in my purse, but I appreciate knowing I don't have to worry."

Deacon patted her hand. "And Michael packed a Ziploc bag full of kibble for Hawkeye. He wouldn't leave until he'd done it. The kid loves that dog."

"I'd say it's mutual," Adam commented, because Hawkeye had ignored the adults, plastering himself to Michael's side. He cast a sidelong glance at Dani, letting her see his concern. "It's gonna hurt him when he has to give that dog up."

"I know" was all she could reply, but inside she was strengthening her resolve to keep these boys as long as was humanly possible.

They sat in silence a few minutes longer until Diesel joined them. He sat beside her, instantly noting the tension at the table. "What's wrong? Is it Stone?"

"No." Deacon motioned them to keep their voices down. "Stone's the same."

"Did you catch King?" Diesel whispered warily.

"No," Deacon murmured again. "They're still doing door-to-door searches and checking every vehicle that leaves the neighborhood. It's Stella Brewer. She's dead."

Dani's heart missed a beat. "What? When?"

"Sometime last night," Adam said.

She huffed out a harsh breath, finding it hard to draw another. Diesel's big hand was on her back, rubbing circles and helping her get the words out. "Am I . . . Are we—Diesel and I—are we suspects?"

"No," Deacon said. "You were with cops and federal agents all evening. Diesel, you were likely with Stone. We'll get him to confirm that later. Someone came into her house, we think with a key, or she let them in. No sign of forced entry. She was found with a bag of heroin, two bullet holes in her head, and another in her heart."

"We're trying to trace the heroin now," Adam offered. "It's a very pure grade."

Diesel rubbed his face with his free hand. "Scott

King." He looked at the two detectives. "Michael said the guy returned Brewer's car to their garage the night Brewer was killed. He must have kept Brewer's keys."

Deacon nodded. "Makes sense. The two cops who were watching her house found her an hour ago when they tried to get in to use the bathroom. They were supposed to have eyes on the front and the back, but they were sitting in their squad car and doing perimeter checks every half hour."

Dani suddenly remembered Quincy Taylor's visit. "One of the CSU techs is also dead. Quincy believed that the tech was responsible for identifying the fisherman that King thought was an eyewitness. Quincy saw King at the crime scene."

Diesel drew in a sharp breath. "King was desperate enough to go to the crime scene to get information? No wonder he's after Michael. He's snipping his loose ends. Did you get anything from the riverboat?"

Both Adam and Deacon shook their heads. "We're getting warrants for their employee records," Adam said, "but their attorney is fighting it. I did hear from Scarlett, though, that you two have a suggestion for where we should start looking. Something about a med student?"

Diesel stiffened beside her and Dani squeezed his hand. "Jeremy found her," she said. "Her name is Laurel Jo Masterson."

"LJM Industries," Diesel murmured. "You should check Brewer's financials. Specifically the transfer of the title to his house. It was bought by LJM Industries two weeks ago."

"Laurel's got two brothers," Dani told him. "One is an accountant and one is a Cleveland cop." She told them about how Laurel went missing and her brother insisted that she hadn't run away, but that Laurel's roommate claimed she'd gone off with her older boyfriend.

"How does this connect to Scott King?" Deacon asked.

"We don't know yet," Diesel admitted.

Dani noted that he wasn't sharing the fact that he'd discovered Scott King's e-mail password on the casino's network. Probably because he didn't yet have anything concrete to share.

"Do you need us?" she asked. "Because I need to sleep." She'd forgotten to take one of her pills in the commotion last night and had finally taken it several hours too late. It shouldn't make a difference to her antiviral levels, but missing sleep was an excellent way to open herself up to illness.

She couldn't get sick now. She had two kids that needed her.

"No," Deacon told her. "Go to sleep. I'm going back to the hospital to sit with Faith and Jeremy."

"And I'm going home," Adam announced. "Meredith has been texting me every hour wondering if I'm okay. I'm going to sleep for a few hours before I tackle all these crime scenes again. Both CPD and the FBI have ponied up people to stand guard, here and at the hospital, in case King tries again. You're covered."

Dani stood up and tugged on Diesel's hand. "Come on. I'm about to fall asleep on my feet. And you need to sleep, too," she added before he could say that he needed to work some more.

Diesel followed her to the master bedroom, both of them ignoring the pointed looks from her brother and cousin. Dani closed the door. "You can search Scott King's e-mail after you've slept." He opened his mouth as if to argue, so she added, "Besides, I'll sleep better if you're with me." She sat on the bed and kicked off her shoes. "Please?"

"Okay," he said. "But just for a few hours. As long as King is out there, none of you are safe."

Without another word, they found toothbrushes and took care of their nightly routines. Dani opened the bag that Faith had packed for her and reluctantly chose a loose T-shirt and flannel pants to sleep in, because she really wanted to feel Diesel's bare skin against hers. But as long as there were kids who might need them in the night, they'd need to be more circumspect.

She came out of the bathroom, pausing for a moment to appreciate the sight of Diesel shirtless in the bed. She'd long wondered what he looked like under his tight T-shirts. He'd more than surpassed her imaginings. The man was seriously cut, with a six-pack that would make any breathing woman drool.

He gave her a knowing smirk and lifted the blanket. "You wanted to sleep, Doc. So come and sleep."

"Just . . . appreciating." Dani slid under the covers and sighed happily when he wrapped his muscular arms around her. She rested her head on his solid chest, her good ear pressed to his steadily beating heart.

After a minute, she lifted her head to kiss his chin. "I like this," she whispered.

Lips curving, he drew a deep, contented breath. "So do I."

But as tired as she was, her brain wouldn't stop racing. She ran her palm over his skull, his stubble tickling her skin. "Why do you shave your head?"

He opened one eye. "My hair started to fall out after I got hurt, back in the army. Not all of it, just . . . in patches. So I shaved it. Why?"

"Just curious." She rubbed all over his skull. "You have no bald spots now."

Both of his eyes were open now. "You want me to grow it out?"

"Only if you want." She lifted her brows. "Bald is a sexy, badass look on you, but I bet your hair is pretty."

He snorted. "No. It's just brown. Not like yours." He tucked her white streak behind her ear. "Yours is unique. But I have wondered why Deacon's went completely white and yours didn't."

It was her turn to snort. "It did. But you'll be very

discreet and not notice when I go to the hairdresser every few weeks to get the black part . . . re-blacked. My white streaks are the only authentic part of my hair."

He laughed quietly. "Still, I like it. I'll be very discreet." He trailed his fingertips over her lips. "What's really wrong, Dani? I'm thinking that it's really not our hair that's keeping you awake."

She rested her forehead on his chin for a moment before lifting her head to meet his eyes squarely. "I never told Michael that his mother was threatening to fight for custody of Joshua. Now I'll have to tell him she's dead."

He threaded his fingers through her hair, pulling her down to kiss him. "We'll tell him together. Now sleep."

She lay in the dark for a long time, listening to the steady thumping of his heart. Until his breathing evened out and his light snores were a quiet rumble in her ear.

She pressed a kiss to his heart. Now she could sleep.

Chapter Twenty-One

Cincinnati, Ohio
Monday, March 18, 7:45 a.m.

"I understand that you're searching everyone," Evelyn said, her tone to the cop patient, but holding a thread of desperation that Cade figured the cop would attribute to her being late for her first appointment. So far she'd been a pro. "But the police searched my house and van already. You can call and ask them."

"I understand." The cop was condescending. "I'm sure your first appointment will also understand. We have a manhunt ongoing. That's a little more important."

Yes. Cade was aware. He'd hid in the garage with Junior while the police had searched Evelyn's home thoroughly. They'd actually searched the boxes that Cade had stacked atop the box in which he and Junior were hiding.

Just when Cade had been certain he'd be found, the cop had left, thanking Evelyn for her cooperation.

Now they were sitting in a long line of vehicles waiting to be searched at the roadblock, going out of Dani Novak's neighborhood. As getaway vehicles went, the pet grooming van was, in some ways, ideal. The windows in the back were small and close to the ceiling, more for ventilation than viewing, and there was a decent place to hide—for a petite woman. For Cade, not so much.

Nevertheless, he had stuffed himself and Junior into the dog bathing tub. Luckily Evelyn had clients with very large dogs and had bought the largest model. It had an inset "base," like a false bottom, that enabled the tub to be used for smaller dogs. Cade was hiding under the inset base.

Luckily, Evelyn kept her equipment clean. There was a strong odor of dog shampoo and disinfectant, but it wasn't exactly unpleasant. And if it got him out of this dragnet, he'd have sat in dog shit.

But he was glad he hadn't had to, because his leg was on fire. The Feds' bullets hadn't done a lot of damage, but Cade was afraid the wounds were getting infected. He had antibiotics back at the old pedo's house. He just had to make it until then.

"Of course," Evelyn was saying to the cop. "I'll open the back door for you."

Well, fuck. Cade tightened his hold on the rifle. If that inset base was lifted, he'd start firing. God help anyone who got in his way.

The back door creaked as Evelyn opened it.

"This is a pretty nice setup," the cop said. "Very clean."

"Thank you," Evelyn said, sounding like she was speaking through clenched teeth.

Heavy footsteps sounded just outside his hiding place and Cade could hear the van's cabinet doors being opened and closed. He held his breath, freezing when Junior made a disgruntled sound. Not a cry. But he wasn't being quiet. *Just a little longer, Junior.*

Everything went silent outside the tub, and then Cade heard the thump of a fist on the inset top. Junior opened his mouth. Cade clamped his fingers over it. *Do not cry, Junior. Do. Not. Cry.*

"Okay, ma'am," the cop said. "Everything seems in order here. We're sorry for the inconvenience."

"That's okay," Evelyn said, her voice trembling. "I hope you catch him."

The doors closed and Cade finally released the breath he'd been holding. They were free. He waited until the van began to move at a decent speed before cautiously pushing the inset base out of the way.

He let out another breath. He was alone in the back. No cops.

Yes.

He opened one of the bigger drawers, finding stacks of towels. He set Junior on the towels, giving his head a pat. He was so glad that the kid hadn't cried and he hadn't had to smother him. That would have sucked.

Carefully he slid the small window in the side of the van open, recognizing the area at a glance. He'd told Evelyn to drive to a secluded area near the Mount Airy Forest once they were through the roadblock. She'd drop him off and he'd let her go.

Except that wasn't exactly the way it was going to happen. He laid out a few of the nylon dog leads and cut up some towels in preparation, then waited, watching the scenery pass by for another thirty minutes, until the van slowed and Evelyn pulled over. She'd followed his instructions well.

She opened the back doors and scanned the interior for Junior.

"He's right here," Cade said. "Not a problem. He's a good kid."

He waited until she leaped into the back and raced for the baby before grabbing her and shoving one of the cut-up towels in her mouth. Quickly he tied her hands and feet with the dog leads and lowered her to the floor of the truck. He put Junior beside her.

"We need to go a little farther and I need for you not to know where I'm getting out," he said. "Don't want you to call the cops on me the moment you drive away."

The flash of impotent fury in Evelyn's eyes told

him that she'd planned to do exactly that. Then he could see nothing of Evelyn's eyes because he tied one of the towel remnants over them.

"Sit tight. You'll be free soon." He got out of the van and slammed the doors closed. "And *I'm* free now." He needed to figure out how to stay that way. First, though, he had to find a safe place to regroup because his leg was throbbing. He needed to clean it properly, without having to hold a damn baby. Once it healed, he'd be able to make his escape. When he ran, he needed to be able to actually *run*.

He'd have to figure out a way to change his appearance, because there was no way he was escaping a conviction if he was caught.

One thing was certain—he was not getting to Michael Rowland. They had to have that kid in a safe house six miles underground by now.

Cincinnati, Ohio
Monday, March 18, 8:30 a.m.

Grant Masterson toasted a bagel and made a cup of coffee with Wesley's space-age machine. The bagel was the only food in the fridge that hadn't passed its ex-date. He'd eaten takeout the day before. If he stayed any longer he'd have to buy food.

Munching on the dry bagel, he opened a browser window on his laptop to the local news. He wanted to see what had happened the night before with the casino raid. Whether there was any mention of Richard Fischer or Scott King. Or Wesley's alter ego, Blake Emerson.

As soon as the news page loaded, he nearly choked on the bagel.

"Holy shit," he panted when he could breathe again. There on the front page was a photo of the *Lady of the River* with the headline: SEARCH FOR RIVER KILLER COMES UP EMPTY.

"River killer? What the actual fuck?" Grant

scanned the article and was glad he hadn't taken another bite, because the suspect was none other than
Scott King, the security manager he'd gone to the casino to find.

"Casino owner Richard Fischer did not respond to
requests for comments," he read aloud. *Because he's
not there,* Grant thought. *He's left town. Or he's hiding in that mausoleum he calls a mansion.*

He clicked on the link to the River Killer story
and sagged in his chair. Seven dismembered bodies
had been brought out of the river on Saturday. He
skimmed until he got to the part he was looking for.

"A fourteen-year-old boy was questioned in the
death of the first body to be identified, Mr. John
Brewer. But later eyewitness testimony pointed local
law enforcement to search for this man—Scott King.
Riverboat patrons told us that John Brewer was a frequent visitor to the casino at the *Lady of the River,*
where Scott King manages security."

Grant studied the sketch of King and fought a
shudder. He was very glad he hadn't met the man last
night. He had a mean look to him.

Returning to the article, he read on, then frowned.
The first of the identified victims, John Brewer, had
last been seen Friday a week ago.

That was the same day that Wesley's Cleveland PD
partner, Tracy Simon, had seen Wes, with no word
from him since. His brother had been to that same
casino, participating in some kind of secret game.
Dread prickled down Grant's spine and a shudder
broke free, his stomach churning. He pushed the
half-eaten bagel away, his appetite suddenly gone.

Seven dismembered bodies, he thought numbly.
He had his phone in his hand, ready to call the police,
before he realized his intent. Did one of those bodies
belong to his brother?

Wait. He put the phone down, pushing it away as
he'd done the bagel. If Wes was alive, Grant would be
flagging him to the cops.

"And if he's dead?" Grant whispered to himself. Then shook his head hard.

He was jumping to conclusions. There was no evidence that his brother was dead. There was no indication that Wesley had even known John Brewer. It could be a giant coincidence.

But if you find a connection? If Wesley did know John Brewer?

Then I'll go to the cops. I'll ask them if any of the bodies they found is Wes.

Hoping to find something in the news to alleviate the dread that slowly choked him, Grant clicked back to the home page. And stared, openmouthed. *The hits keep coming.* Because staring back at him was a photo of the man he'd seen leaving the casino the night before—the one who'd claimed to be a cop, but who wasn't. The one who'd seemed vaguely familiar.

Now Grant knew why.

AWARD-WINNING PHOTOJOURNALIST CRITICALLY WOUNDED. Grant slowly scrolled, his dread increasing as he read. "Stone O'Bannion was the victim of multiple gunshot wounds last night while on the property of his friend and coworker Elvis Kennedy. Doctors at Mercy West say that Mr. O'Bannion is in critical but stable condition. His family has asked for privacy during this time.

"Both Mr. Kennedy and Mr. O'Bannion are employed by the Cincinnati *Ledger*. Neither was available to comment on this developing story, but an individual with knowledge of the case said that the shooter was Scott King, the man suspected of the river killings and of the murders of pediatrician George Garrett, the fisherman who discovered the bodies on the Ohio side of the river early on Saturday morning, and Charlie Akers, a member of the crime scene investigation team.

"After shooting Mr. O'Bannion, Scott King is believed to have continued on to the home of Dr. Danika Novak, who manages the Meadow Free Clinic.

Witnesses say there was a major firefight between the
suspect and law enforcement. An FBI agent was injured, but is now in stable condition. Those involved
in the investigation believe that the target of the
home attack may have been Michael Rowland, the
young man seen with Dr. Novak on Saturday afternoon. Michael was originally suspected of killing his
stepfather, John Brewer, but police now believe
Brewer's killer was Scott King."

Grant frowned. All of this was troubling, but none
of it directly connected to Wesley. Except that Wesley and Scott King were connected through Richard
Fischer and the *Lady of the River.*

He looked around the apartment, trying to orga-
nize his thoughts. Everything he'd learned so far was
via items Wesley had left behind, and he couldn't
help believing that his brother had *wanted* him to find
them. Why else would he choose a safe combination
that Grant would easily guess?

Maybe there was something else here. A file. A
book. *Something.* He finished his coffee. He had
searching to do.

Cincinnati, Ohio
Monday, March 18, 12:10 p.m.

Michael woke with a start. He was alone. Well, not
completely alone. Hawkeye lay beside him, using Michael's butt as a pillow. He reached back to scratch
behind the dog's ears, sliding to sit up, feeling momentary panic when Joshua's bed was empty again.

But then he smelled food. It took him a few seconds to realize that he wasn't in Dr. Dani's house.

Safe house. They'd moved them to some fancy
condo at the top of a building and Michael had no
idea where they were. He'd been forced to give up his
phone, too. Deacon had explained that it could be
used to track them and promised to get him a burner
the next day.

We'll see. So far everyone in Coach and Dr. Dani's group had been pretty straight with them. Michael hoped they continued to be. For Joshua's sake.

I can take care of myself.

Hawkeye at his heels, he made his way to the kitchen, where a man in a black suit stood at the stove, flipping grilled cheese sandwiches in a pan. Joshua was already sitting at the table, a sandwich on his plate, cut into squares the way he liked it.

"Good morning," Joshua signed. "It's really afternoon. We slept a long time."

Michael nodded, his head still foggy. He pointed to the man at the stove. "Who's that?" he signed.

Joshua frowned in concentration as he tried to spell the man's name. "Troy." He nodded once, pleased with himself, and that made Michael smile. "He's an FBI man, like Mr. Deacon and Mr. Decker. He makes a good cheese sandwich."

Troy turned then, the pan in one hand. He pointed to Michael, then to the pan, with a raised brow.

Michael nodded. "Please," he voiced, and sat down.

Troy brought him the sandwich on a plate. He'd cut it into squares, just like Joshua's. It had been a long time since anyone had cut his sandwich into squares.

"Thank you," he signed, and Joshua voiced it.

Troy smiled and signed, "You're welcome."

"I taught him that," Joshua said, grinning so that cheese squished in his teeth.

"Close your mouth," Michael signed gently, then booped Joshua's nose. "Silly."

Troy got a pad and pen and wrote: *Sorry I can't sign well. Coach and Dr. Dani are still asleep.*

Michael nodded and took the pen. *How are Stone and Decker?*

Troy smiled and wrote *Doing well* next to Decker's name and *Awake and cranky as usual* next to Stone's.

Good. Some of the load lifted from Michael's shoulders.

Troy wrote something else on the notepad and passed it to Michael. *Not your fault.*

Shaking his head in denial, Michael was still grateful that the agent would try to make him feel better. *Thank you.*

Joshua looked over Michael's shoulder. "Coach!"

Michael looked to see Coach's big body filling the doorway. *I want to be that big someday.* Then no one could hurt him. Ever again.

"I smell food." Coach rubbed Joshua's head affectionately. "Is it good?"

Joshua nodded. "Mr. Troy is a good cook."

Troy winced. "Not really, but I'm learning."

"You made the cookies," Michael remembered. "Faith told us. They were good."

Troy's eyes widened when Joshua voiced his words. "*Were?* They're all gone?"

Michael shrugged. "Not all. Most."

"But I made three dozen cookies."

"It was a rough night," Coach said, signing for himself.

Troy's nod was understanding. "Yeah, I guess it was."

"What are we gonna do today?" Joshua asked.

"Not much," Coach told him. "You guys are kind of stuck here for a little while."

"Because Dr. Dani's house caught on fire," Michael said.

Joshua's nose wrinkled. "From the firecrackers. I remember. I smelled it. But Mr. Deacon put it out. He's like a superhero."

Coach laughed. "Don't tell him. His ego will get big."

Troy pointed to his plate. "Eat," he signed clumsily, then shivered dramatically.

"He means it'll get cold," Joshua signed.

Michael chuckled. "I got that." As he started to eat, Coach's face changed, getting that soft look that he got every time Dr. Dani came around. Sure enough, Michael smelled chocolate seconds before Dani took the seat next to him.

She and Coach shared a look, but it wasn't a happy one. Michael pushed his plate away. Had they had a fight? Were they breaking up? Were they even together?

But Coach put out his hand and Dr. Dani took it, squeezing hard. Troy seemed to know what was going on, because he excused himself and left the room.

Coach held out his arm to Joshua, who'd also felt the change in mood. Joshua's sunny smile was gone as he climbed into Coach's lap.

Dr. Dani straightened in her seat and gave Coach's hand another squeeze before signing to Michael. "I have news for you both. It's about your mother."

Michael recoiled, pressing back in his chair. "Did she get out of jail? Is she . . ." He had to fight to breathe. "Is she coming for Joshua?"

Dr. Dani shook her head. "I . . ." She looked at Coach helplessly, then back at Michael. "She's dead."

Michael frowned. "What?" He didn't understand. Except that he did.

Joshua's face had grown pale and he was trembling in Coach's arms. Joshua did understand, Michael thought, and he wished to God that he didn't.

"Was it the drugs?" Michael asked, feeling suddenly very calm. And cold.

Dani shook her head again. "No, honey. She was killed. Someone broke into her house and killed her."

Michael's mouth fell open. *Oh God.* "Him. Scott King."

Dani nodded. "They think so." She turned to focus on Joshua. "I'm so sorry, baby," she signed, her hands shaking and her mouth barely moving.

I'm not. Michael pulled his plate close and picked up a square of grilled cheese. He bit into it, barely tasting the cheese. But he was hungry, and people other than the school cafeteria ladies were feeding him for the first time in . . . forever.

He was going to eat what he could, whenever he could, because who knew how long Dani would keep them?

Joshua began to cry. "What's gonna happen to us, Michael?"

Michael put down the sandwich, his stomach churning again, but for a different reason now. Hawkeye put his head on Michael's knee and he petted the dog a few times before answering. "I'll figure it out. I've always taken care of you, haven't I?"

Joshua nodded uncertainly. "But where will we live? Dr. Dani is temporary. You said that."

Dani closed her eyes. Pressed her lips together. A tear trickled down her face. She looked at Coach and murmured something that Michael couldn't catch.

Coach wiped the tear from her face. "Whatever you need," he voiced back without signing, but Michael could read his lips well enough to understand. Joshua was no longer signing, having turned his face into Coach's chest, crying like his heart would break.

He's only five years old, dammit. Stella was an awful mother, but Joshua still loved her.

Dani turned her body so that Michael could see her hands, but Joshua couldn't, even if he had been looking at them. Coach had both arms around him now, rocking him and whispering in his ear. Michael couldn't understand what he was saying, but Joshua must have, because his skinny little arms came up to wrap around Coach's neck. Coach held him like the child he was, meeting Michael's eyes with such sadness that Michael almost cried himself.

But he wasn't going to cry. He'd cried enough for Stella and John Brewer. Because they'd hurt him. But now they were both dead and he wasn't sorry. He was scared, though. Because as big as he might have talked about taking care of Joshua, he'd heard the stories about foster care. He knew they'd be separated.

He'd run away with Joshua before he let that happen.

Michael jumped when Dani laid her hand on his arm. "Hey," she signed without using her voice. "I'm not going to tell Joshua because he's so young. You're old enough to understand the system, though. You get what may and may not happen, and what I am and am not allowed to do. I'm going to do my damnedest to become a permanent foster parent for you two. I don't want you sent somewhere else."

Michael stared at her, his heart beating like a wild thing. "Possible?" he asked.

"Possible." She tilted her head. "Probable. But not definite. I won't ever lie to you. I'm going to try. I'm making the calls today. So don't worry for now. I'm going to take care of you for as long as I can."

Michael swallowed hard, overwhelmed. "Thank you."

She smiled sadly. "You're worth it."

No, he wasn't, but Joshua was. "I'm not sorry she's dead," he signed, glancing at Joshua to make sure that he still couldn't see him.

Dani nodded. "Me, either."

"Same." Coach let go of Joshua long enough to do the sign one-handed, then resumed his rocking.

"You're not a bad person for not being sorry," Dani told him. "But this is something that Meredith can help you with."

Meredith. The counselor lady. He wondered if she had a dog, too. "I liked her."

"I'm glad."

He hesitated. "Last night . . . when we were in the FBI van leaving your house, I talked to Faith. She signs pretty well. Because of Greg."

Dani nodded, saying nothing, so he gathered his thoughts and went on.

"I asked her why she wasn't going to be my therapist and she said . . ." He swallowed hard, still unable to believe it.

"What did she say, sweetie?" Dani asked, her signs soft.

"That I was your family and she was your family. So I'm *her* family. And she thought it would be better for her to not be my therapist."

One side of Dani's mouth quirked up. "My brother married a very smart woman with a very big heart."

"Did she know you were going to try to make us permanent?"

Both sides of Dani's mouth smiled now. "I think she did. I hadn't told her, but she knew I was upset that you felt temporary. That you *were* temporary. I think she knows me better than I know myself sometimes. Are you okay with Meredith being your therapist? She'll make sure she always has an interpreter for you."

Michael nodded. "I don't have family. Other than Joshua." Dani's eyes grew shiny with tears, and he knew she understood what he was trying to say. *If it means I can have a family, then yes, I'll do anything.* "And I understand if you can't make it happen," he added quickly. "The permanent thing. But I appreciate you trying."

Dani reached out slowly, giving him time to move, but Michael didn't. He wanted her to touch him. Wanted to feel her stroke his hair. Sighed when she did. This was the way moms were supposed to be.

"You are worth it, Michael."

Michael's eyes burned and he could only nod.

"Eat if you can. Let me and Coach do the worrying for now, okay?"

"Okay," he whispered.

Please, God. I won't ask for anything else for the rest of my life if you let us stay with Dani and Coach forever.

Cincinnati, Ohio
Monday, March 18, 1:30 p.m.

"I'll put the permanent conservatorship paperwork through ASAP," Maddie promised. Maddie was one of the better social workers Dani had worked with. If she said she'd take care of the paperwork, she would.

"Thank you. These kids have been through hell. Especially Michael."

"I know," Maddie said quietly. "I could see it when I met them. More so, now."

Which was only two days ago. *My life has turned upside down in two days.* And it was mostly good. Crazed killers and getting her house nearly set afire, not so good. But the rest of it? *Diesel and the boys? All good.*

"Do you think you'll pursue adoption?" Maddie asked.

"I think I will. But for now, I just know I don't want these kids going to anyone else. I don't want them separated, and Michael needs a signing foster parent."

Maddie laughed softly. "I'm already on your side, Dani. You don't have to convince me. I saw your house on the news. You guys are safe, right?"

Dani looked around at the opulent condo with its impact-resistant windows, its single point of entry, Special Agent Troy standing guard inside, and at least three more guards between the dedicated elevator and the parking garage.

Not to mention Diesel, who was sitting on the sofa, staring at his computer screen like he was trying to hypnotize it to do his will. That man would protect them. Dani had no doubt. He still held Joshua, who'd cried himself to sleep in the big man's arms. Diesel showed no sign of letting the little boy go.

He'd make a great dad. She'd always thought that, even when she'd been desperately trying to convince herself that she didn't want to want him. Once they were more settled, they could talk about joint parenting. For now, the children would be Dani's legal responsibility. Still, Diesel's words to Adam last night replayed in her mind and warmed her heart.

Those boys are morally my responsibility. Dani is just mine.

"Yes," she answered Maddie. "We're in a safe house." And Agent Troy had assured her that this phone line was secure or she wouldn't be using it. "Deacon and Adam know where we are, but we can't tell Children's Services."

"I get it, Dani. That's the definition of 'safe house,'" Maddie teased. "I'll send you the paperwork by e-mail. Do you have access to a printer?"

"Yes. I'll fill it out and have one of the guards deliver it to you. Thank you."

"This really is my pleasure. 'Bye, Dani."

Dani ended the call and was about to tell Diesel about it, but he was readjusting Joshua on his shoulder so that he could bang away on his laptop. He was digging deeper into the casino's network. He'd told her that much.

Which leaves LJM Industries and the Mastersons for me. Marcus's search the night before had revealed that Wesley was a cop with Cleveland PD and Grant was an accountant. She'd start with the cop. He was unlikely to be at his desk—Deacon, Adam, and Scarlett rarely were—but she hoped the switchboard would be able to connect her to Wesley Masterson's cell.

Taking herself into the room she shared with Diesel, she sat on the bed and fired up her own laptop, Googling the number for the Cleveland PD switchboard. She expected that her request to be connected with Detective Wesley Masterson would net her either the guy's cell or his voice mail, so she was surprised when a woman answered.

"This is Detective Tracy Simon. How can I help you?"

"I'm not sure," Dani said. "I'd like to speak with Detective Masterson."

"He's out of the office. Can I take a message?"

Dani blinked at her curt reply. "When do you expect him to return?"

A beat of hesitation. "This is his partner. Can I ask who's calling?"

"My name is Dr. Dani Novak. I'm calling from Cincinnati on a personal matter. Can you have him call me when he gets back?" She gave the woman her cell phone number, knowing that Adam had her phone in his possession and would let her know if she had any missed calls.

"Of course," Detective Simon said. "Thank you for calling."

Dani ended the call and frowned. "That was weird," she muttered.

"What was?" Diesel asked from the doorway. He wasn't carrying Joshua anymore.

"Where's Joshua?"

"I just put him to bed."

"Did your arms finally get tired?" she asked.

Diesel looked offended. "My arms did not get tired." Offense gave way to sheepishness. "I needed to swear at my computer. I didn't want him to hear."

She smiled at him. "Good call, then, putting him to bed."

He came over to sit on the bed next to her. "You got the ball rolling at CPS?"

"I did. Maddie's going to pull strings to fast-track my paperwork."

"Good." He leaned in to kiss her mouth and she hummed against his lips.

"I like this."

"Told you," he said smugly.

"No," she replied primly. "You said you could make me happy. Which you are."

"Good." He kissed her again until they were both breathless. He pulled away, adjusting himself, which made her even more absurdly happy. "So what was weird?" he asked.

"I called Cleveland PD to talk to Wesley Masterson. He's one of the Brothers Grim," she added, because Diesel hadn't been with her when Jeremy had visited the night before. She told him about the partner's response. "It's like she wasn't expecting him to come back."

He considered it. "Didn't you say the other brother was an accountant? Call him."

"His name is Grant." She looked up his firm and placed the call, putting it on speaker.

"Hello, Masterson Accounting. This is MaryBeth. How can I help you?"

"May I speak to Grant Masterson, please?" Dani asked.

"He's not in the office at the moment."

"All right." *Lunchtime,* she signed to Diesel. "Can I leave my number and ask him to call me back? It's urgent."

MaryBeth sniffed. "It's always urgent this time of year. He'll get to your tax return as soon as he can."

"This isn't about my taxes," Dani said, irritated with the woman, but maintaining her calm. "It's personal. When do you expect him back in the office?"

Another beat of hesitation, almost identical to the one when she'd spoken to Wesley Masterson's partner. "Who is this?" MaryBeth demanded.

"My name is Dr. Dani Novak. I'm calling from Cincinnati."

The woman's intake of breath was audible. "Give me your number. I'll let him know when he returns."

Dani gave MaryBeth her cell, then pressed, "When do you expect him back?"

"Mr. Masterson has taken some vacation time. I'll pass on your message."

The line clicked as MaryBeth ended the call.

Diesel's brows had lifted. "An accountant doesn't just 'take vacation' a month before April fifteenth. They're pedal to the metal, practically living in their offices."

"I know. I wonder if he took his wife on 'vacation' with him."

Diesel reached for her laptop. "I can find his home number."

Dani didn't doubt that for a moment. "Go for it."

Less than a minute later she was placing the call. She again put it on speaker.

"Hello?" a woman answered.

"Hi. I'm trying to reach Grant Masterson. Is he home?"

"No, he's not," the woman said. "This is his *wife*." Dani didn't miss the emphasis on *wife*. "Can I help you?"

"I hope so. My name is Dr. Dani Novak. I'm calling from Cincinnati."

The woman sucked in a panicked breath. "Oh my God. Is he okay? What happened? I told him to get a hotel."

Dani looked at Diesel, her eyes wide. "I'm sorry, Mrs. Masterson, I didn't mean to frighten you. I'm not your husband's doctor. I've never met him. This is a personal call. I'd like to ask him about Laurel."

Dead silence. "What?" the woman finally asked.

"Laurel," Dani said gently. "Your husband's sister."

"I know who Laurel is," the woman snapped. "Do you have her? Is she alive?"

Dani stared at Diesel, who shrugged. "No, I don't have her," Dani said. "And I'm sorry, but I don't know if she's alive or not. I take it you haven't seen her, either."

The woman sighed. "No. She went missing from Cincinnati a year and a half ago. Her roommate told us that she'd run off with her boyfriend."

"She was a med student."

"She was," the woman agreed sadly. "Threw it all away."

"You believe the roommate, then?" Dani asked cautiously.

"I don't know," Mrs. Masterson admitted. "I know my brother-in-law is convinced that she didn't leave of her own free will. Why? How are you connected to Laurel, Dr. Novak?"

Dani hesitated. "I'm not," she admitted. "Not directly. But I am connected to something that might belong to her." *The boys' house,* she signed to Diesel, who shook his head at her, but fondly. "Can you have your husband call me? It's very important."

"Of course." A baby started crying in the background. "I need to go."

Dani sighed when the call ended. "I did bad?"

He smiled at her. "The boys' *house*? Really?"

"Well . . . LJM owns the house that should belong to the boys. It was their father's house first. And I'm connected to the boys. So I'm connected to the house and LJM. LJM is Laurel. So yes. Really."

His smile became indulgent. "Is that the story you're sticking to?"

She pretended to pout. "Fine. I panicked."

"Then I take back my comment about you giving up medicine to be a PI. You should keep your day job."

She laughed. "So noted."

He traced his fingertip across her smiling cheeks. "You are so pretty when you laugh."

"I've done it a lot more often the past few days."

"Good. Who are you calling next?"

Dani pulled his hand from her face. "I can't think when you touch me like that."

His dark eyes lit up with unfettered joy. "Outstanding." He waggled his brows. "Do you want to take a break from thinking?"

She kissed his fingers, chuckling. "Yes, but now is probably not the best time. We'll take a break from thinking later, once Michael's gone to sleep."

Diesel sobered. "Yeah. I know." He lay on his side, propping himself on his elbow. "So who will you call next?"

"I thought maybe the university or her old high school. Maybe Wesley Masterson is wrong and she did leave of her own free will. Maybe Laurel's communicated with some of her friends."

"Lots of maybes," Diesel said, "but all good questions. You need help?"

"No, I think I've got this, and I need something to do or I'll go stir-crazy. I'm not used to sitting still."

"Me, either. Especially when sitting still doesn't give me what I'm looking for."

"What were you looking for? You were staring at your laptop like you were trying to hypnotize it."

He snorted. "I wish. I had to do it the old-fashioned way. I was looking for other databases on the casino's server and found several, which is normal. One is for e-mail. There's also an HR file with all the employee records, including salaries, overtime, payroll, et cetera, plus there's an inventory database and one for their VIP clients. We'll come back to that one later. All those databases are normal for a company doing business."

"What's not normal?"

"The super-secret database that only two people have access to—Scott King and Richard Fischer. Richard's the owner of the riverboat."

"Oh. Is it a security thing? King was the security manager, right?"

"Yes, he was the security manager, but I don't know if this is for security. Maybe, but in my experience the general manager would also have access, as would the IT manager. They don't. I'm doing the same kind of password search I did last night."

Her lips twitched. "The Ritz Cracker."

He grinned and her heart did a little stutter-hop in her chest. He was the handsomest man when he grinned like that. Well, he was handsome all the time, but he got that light in his eyes when he grinned. "Exactly," he said.

She leaned in close to him and whispered in his ear. "I seem to recall passing the time quite pleasurably while Ritz did its cracking last night."

He drew in a deep breath. "You're evil."

She kissed his ear. "I know. I'm sorry."

"No, you're not," he growled and she very nearly went back on her resolution to wait until Michael was asleep.

"You're right. I'm not sorry at all." She nuzzled his neck. "For what it's worth, you're testing my resolve. A lot."

He laughed and rolled off the bed, coming to his feet like a graceful dancer. "Good. Serves you right."

"It really does. What are you going to do now?"

"What I've done for the past year to work off my sexual frustration. Knit."

Her mouth fell open. "*That's* why you knit?"

He nodded, amused. "Well, it's a general stress reliever, but mostly sexual stress, yes. I've made you *so* many pairs of mittens this year."

She clapped her hands, delighted. "I can't wait to wear them." She put her laptop down and caught him at the door, pulling his head down for another kiss. "Thank you for the shawl you made me last year. It's beautiful."

"I want you to wear it," he murmured.

"I have. I wore it to Meredith's Christmas party."

He chuckled darkly. "That's not how I visualized you when I was making it."

She slid her hands up his chest, letting herself enjoy the flex of his pecs under her palms. "No?"

"No. I saw you wearing the shawl and nothing else."

A sensual shiver danced over her skin, and her hips thrust forward of their own volition. "God, Diesel." She clasped her hands at the back of his neck and pulled his head down, bringing their mouths together hard. The kiss was hot and raw and she wanted nothing more than to lock the door and rip his clothes off.

"You tempt me," he whispered against her lips when they came up for air. Then he took a firm step back. "Get to work. Call Laurel's friends. I'll see you later."

Chapter Twenty-Two

Cincinnati, Ohio
Monday, March 18, 2:30 p.m.

Grant didn't check the caller ID as he answered his cell. "Yeah?" he mumbled, staring at the book he'd found, the page covered with Wesley's handwriting.

"What's wrong?" Cora asked, the panic in her voice jolting him back to reality.

"I'm okay." *No, I'm not okay.* "I just . . . I'll tell you when I see you."

"Grant, come home. *Now.*"

That got his attention. "Why? What's wrong with the kids?"

"Nothing, they're fine. But this lady called. Her name was Dani Novak. She said she was a doctor. In Cincinnati. At first I thought something had happened to you, but she said it was about Laurel."

Dani Novak. Grant let out a slow breath. She was the woman whose house had been attacked last night by Scott King. And now she was calling him . . . "About Laurel?"

"Yes. I looked her up, Dr. Novak, I mean. She went to UC's med school, too. Maybe she knew Laurel from there. Maybe she knows where Laurel is."

"What did she say?"

"That she was connected to something that belonged to Laurel. She left her cell number. I told her that you weren't home. Grant, what the hell is happening?"

Grant stared at the book, then at the world globe that he'd found on the desk in Wesley's office, the sphere now split into halves. He'd known as soon as he found the globe that that was where Wesley had hidden something important. A battered world globe was where they'd hidden their treasures when they were kids.

He hadn't expected a call from Dani Novak, though. "Wesley came here looking for Laurel." He still hoped, even though everything he'd found said otherwise.

"I know that. We figured that on Saturday. Grant, I'm scared. What's going on?"

"I think Wes stopped looking for Laurel," Grant whispered, his throat thick.

"Oh God." Cora was quiet for a long moment. "She's dead?"

"I don't know, but I think so. And I think he found the man who killed her."

Cora's swallow was audible. "Is that man dead?"

Grant looked at the three names on the page. Detective Bert Stuart, Anatoly Markov, and Clinton Stern. Anatoly Markov's name had a line drawn through his name. As did Stuart's and Stern's. All with dates. The date next to Detective Stuart's name matched up to the obituary's account of the day he'd died. "I'm pretty sure he is."

Cora stifled a sob. "Oh my God, Grant. Who was it?"

"You remember Detective Stuart, the one who said he'd filed the missing person report for Laurel? He didn't."

"What do you mean? You mean that he lied? Why would he?"

"I don't know. Maybe he was bribed. Maybe he was in on it."

"And Wesley killed him?"

With the unregistered gun in his safe, missing three bullets. Three names with lines through them. Three bullets. "Yeah."

"Grant." Cora was sobbing openly now. And so was Grant.

"I know, baby," he whispered. "I know. I need to give this information to the . . ." He almost said *police*, but he wasn't sure who was trustworthy. That detective who'd managed Laurel's missing person report hadn't been. "To the right people," he decided, wiping his eyes with the back of his hand. "But I'm going to take photos of the documents I found and upload them to a cloud account. Username is where we had our first date. Password is the date you first told me you loved me."

"I love you now." Desperation filled her tone. "Don't tell me things like usernames and passwords like you're not coming home. *Come home now!"*

"I will come home. But I have to get this information to the right people. Cora . . ." He faltered and cleared his throat, his voice hoarse and shaken. "Laurel was my little sister." *And Wes* was *my big brother.* Because now, Grant was pretty sure that Wesley was dead, too.

Cora's sobs were breaking his heart. "Your children need you alive. *I* need you alive."

"I'll be okay." It was an empty promise. He knew that. So did she. "Send me Dr. Novak's phone number. I'll call her."

"Okay," Cora said through her tears. "Please come home, Grant."

"I will. I promise. I love you. Kiss the kids for me."

He ended the call and turned to the next page in the book he'd found in the globe. It was actually a diary, bound in green leather and decorated with purple flowers. Grant knew instantly why Wesley had chosen it—the purple flowers were Texas mountain laurel. Their sister's favorite.

The next page was filled with another list of names.

This one longer. All of the names were recorded in Wesley's chicken-scratch scrawl. There were columns of names, dates, and . . . items. All kinds of items. One name stood out over the others.

John Brewer. He appeared twice. The first time was the week before Brewer had disappeared. The second time was the day he'd last been seen. The same day that Wesley last made contact with his Cleveland PD partner.

Grant now had proof that John Brewer had somehow, somewhere crossed paths with Wes. It had to have been on the riverboat. It and its security manager, Scott King, were the only common denominators. Where he'd only dreaded the possibility before, he was now certain that Wes was one of the bodies the police had pulled from the river on Saturday morning.

His gut roiled and he had to swallow back the bile that burned his throat. One of the seven dismembered bodies.

Wes. My God. Then his jaw tightened, resolve giving him strength. *Whoever did this to you needs to pay.*

But who could make that happen? The police were the obvious first answer, but Grant didn't trust the Cincinnati cops. Not after Detective Stuart had swept Laurel's disappearance under the rug.

He considered his options. The other group that exposed wrongdoing was journalists. And thanks to his aborted visit to the riverboat last night, he happened to know of a few journalists.

Making a quick decision, he opened a new browser window and searched for Stone O'Bannion and the Cincinnati *Ledger*. If O'Bannion had been targeted by King, it was possible that the reporter had gotten in the killer's way. If that was the case, he might prove to be an ally.

The man had a number of bylines in the local paper. Many of them were exposés of criminals, mostly pedophiles or those guilty of domestic violence.

Stone O'Bannion seemed to be a man dedicated to finding justice.

Grant then searched the other man mentioned in the article about Stone's recent shooting. Elvis Kennedy. Grant was unsurprised to see a photo of the soft-spoken bald man from the casino staring back at him from his laptop screen. Known as Diesel, according to one article. He was listed as the *Ledger*'s IT person. But he was also a decorated veteran of the Gulf War. Earned a fucking Purple Heart. And he coached Pee Wee soccer and baseball, and had been given civic awards for building low-income housing.

Both men seemed like upstanding citizens. Both had faced pressure from the police for their journalism, but hadn't given up their sources. Stone had even spent time in jail for refusing to name the source on an exposé he'd done of a high-profile corporate president who'd been accused of domestic violence.

Grant needed to meet these men again. Needed to talk to them. Needed to be sure he was choosing the right people to handle the information he'd found in Wesley's globe.

I'm going to pay a visit to Mr. O'Bannion and Mr. Kennedy. He wasn't sure where to find Kennedy, but he knew exactly where Mr. O'Bannion was—Mercy West, recovering from being shot last night.

Grant flipped the book to the first page and began taking photos. If he was comfortable with Stone and Diesel, he'd hand over the documentation.

He just needed to figure out how to get close enough to Stone O'Bannion to have a private conversation. His gaze drifted to his brother's secret closet. And Grant thought he just might have an idea.

Cincinnati, Ohio
Monday, March 18, 3:45 p.m.

Diesel glanced out of the corner of his eye when the sofa cushion next to him depressed—too gently, actually. Michael could use a good fifteen or twenty pounds to get to a healthy weight.

He'd felt the boy's eyes on him for the last few minutes, but had waited for Michael to come to him. The kid had had a shock that morning and had tried valiantly to hide it, eating his cheese sandwich like he hadn't just been told his mother had been murdered.

He hadn't been successful, of course. Diesel was an expert on valiantly hiding his hurts and he'd seen right through the boy's attempted nonchalance.

Of course, Marcus saw right through mine, too. So maybe Diesel wasn't as good at hiding as he'd thought.

He finally looked up and gave Michael a smile. "Hey."

Michael was frowning at Diesel's hands. "Are you . . . knitting?"

Diesel looked at the knitting needles he held. He put his project in his lap, glanced at his laptop to confirm that Ritz was still cracking passwords, then gave Michael his full attention.

"Yes. You wanna learn?"

Michael blinked at him. "But . . . girls knit."

Diesel gave himself an exaggerated once-over. "I'm knitting," he signed, "so that's obviously not true. It wouldn't be true anyway. Some of the most famous designers are men. And some of the most dangerous women I know are knitters. You met Kate last night, right?"

"Yeah," Michael answered cautiously. "Married to Decker, owns Cap, the therapy dog. Captain America decals on her nails."

Diesel grinned. "That's her. She taught me how to knit. It's a stress reliever for me. Plus, it helps me focus when my brain's going all Sonic the Hedgehog."

Michael's lips twitched at the reference. "Kate said the same thing when she was knitting last night. Said she was making a sweater for Cap. He's getting old and his bones get cold. What are you making?"

"Socks." He really had made far too many pairs of mittens while pining for Dani and figured it was time for a change. "Yarn's soft." He held the ball of yarn out to Michael, who tentatively touched it with one finger, then smiled.

"It is." He hesitated, studying the partially knitted sock. "That's not going to fit you. It's too small."

Diesel extended his leg, turning his size fifteen boot one way, then the other. "Nope. Which is fine, because they're not for me."

Michael hesitated again. "If that's the leg, it looks too big for Dr. Dani, too."

"Because they're not for her, either." He'd intended them to be for Dani, but once he'd put a room's distance between himself and her intoxicating scent, he'd been able to think more clearly. He'd made her a ton of scarves, shawls, and mittens. He had enough holiday and "just because" gifts for her to last for a long time. She didn't need any more. But Michael did. And once he'd felt the boy watching him so timidly, he'd known he'd made the right call. "Hold up your leg."

Michael complied, something like hope creeping into his eyes.

Diesel dug into his bag and found his knitting kit, pulling out a measuring tape. "Measure your leg, about two inches below your knee."

Drawing a visible breath, Michael again complied and told him the measurement.

Diesel eyed the sock-in-progress. "Perfect." He rolled up the measuring tape and stowed his kit. "You wear a size eight shoe?"

"Eight and a half."

"I guessed pretty close."

Michael swallowed hard. "They're for me?"

Diesel met the boy's eyes and nodded. "They're for you."

Tears filled Michael's eyes and he lurched to his feet, abruptly interested in the vase of flowers on the coffee table. He dashed at the tears, took a few seconds to regroup, then turned to face Diesel. "Nobody's ever made me anything before."

Diesel's heart cracked. "I'd say you're due, wouldn't you?"

Michael looked at the floor, then back at Diesel, the raw hope in his eyes painful to witness. "Did she mean it?"

Diesel didn't have to ask what the boy meant. "Yes. She meant it. She's already called Children's Services and started the process."

Michael seemed to wilt, one hand rising to cover his mouth, the other reaching out to steady himself as he lowered to sit on the coffee table. As soon as his butt hit the glass, he lurched back to his feet. "Sorry. I didn't mean to sit there."

"I think it's strong enough to hold you," Diesel said. He patted the sofa. "But cushion is more comfortable than glass."

Michael sank onto the sofa, dropping his face into his hands.

Diesel gave him space, resuming his knitting. After a few minutes, Michael lifted his head, cast his gaze about frantically for something to look at besides Diesel, and settled on his laptop screen.

"What's that?"

"Oh." It was Diesel's turn to hesitate. He wasn't ashamed of his hacking, but he was loath to drag Michael into his business. The kid was pretty good at keeping secrets—he'd kept the one about Scott King killing his stepfather for more than a week, after all—but that didn't mean Diesel wanted to burden him with having to keep a secret of this weight. What Ritz was doing was . . . illegal. And Diesel had designed the program himself, so he couldn't blame anyone else.

Michael's lips twitched. "I know what you do. Greg told me last night."

Diesel put the sock down, brows furrowed in an involuntary frown. "He did?"

Michael's smile broadened. "He didn't mean to. I guessed and he didn't tell me I was wrong. He tried to tell me I was wrong, actually, but he's a really bad liar."

Diesel laughed. "Good to know. How did you guess?"

"We were talking about video games. He was telling me that he was learning game design, that he wanted to go to school for it. He showed me the game he was working on. Just simple, you know. But cool. He said that Meredith's grandfather was helping him. They Skype."

Diesel smiled fondly at the thought of the old man. "Clarke Fallon is a legend in game design." He'd also become the kind of grandfather that Diesel had never had before. He hadn't realized Clarke was helping Greg, but it didn't surprise him.

Michael's eyes grew round with excitement. "I know! I looked him up and couldn't believe Greg knows him. I've played some of the games Mr. Fallon designed. Then Greg said that you were also friends with Mr. Fallon, that you helped him beta test games." He tilted his head, his eyes going cagey. "Greg said that you were good with all kinds of computer stuff and then he kind of . . ." He exaggerated snapping his mouth shut. "I watched you on your computer on Saturday, when I was reading and Dr. Dani was cooking. You weren't playing games then. And you said you investigated for your lawyer friend, Mr. Clausing." He shrugged his bony shoulders. "I asked Greg if you were a hacker."

"That's kind of a leap," Diesel said dryly.

"Well, Greg already told me that he'd done some hacking. I asked how he learned and he said he had a mentor."

"I think Greg and I need to have a talk about discretion."

Michael laughed quietly. "Don't tell him I told. I like him. He's a nice guy."

"He is nice. Has a really big mouth, unfortunately."

Michael shrugged again. "I'm not stupid. I would have figured it out." He pointed to the laptop screen. "You're hash cracking."

Diesel's mouth fell open. He tried to ask a question, but nothing came out. He was indeed cracking the hashed values—the combinations of letters and numbers into which the passwords had been encrypted.

Michael looked delighted. "I'm right! Aren't I?"

"You're dangerous," Diesel managed, but he was impressed. "How do you know about hash cracking?"

"I read. A lot. Not always books. I sometimes go to the library on campus at UC. You can always tell the programmers. I . . . shoulder surf."

"You really are dangerous," Diesel muttered, then remembered to sign when Michael frowned his confusion. "Sorry."

Michael regarded him very seriously. "You're a white hat."

A good guy who didn't use his hacking for personal profit. "You sound sure."

"I am sure. You said you were going to keep us safe. Find the bald man who killed Brewer. Is that what you're doing? What you were doing last night when you left Dani's house?"

Super, super dangerous kid, Diesel marveled. *So damn smart.* "Yeah. So . . . what are you going to do with this information?"

Michael blinked. "I'm not going to tell. I keep secrets better than Greg does."

Diesel laughed. "I should hope so."

Michael smiled a little, then grew serious again. "I'm going to say thank you for keeping me safe. For keeping Joshua safe. Then later I'm going to ask you to teach me how to do that." He pointed to the screen, then stilled. "It found something."

Diesel's attention veered from Michael's face to

his laptop screen. He no longer had his phone, which would have alarmed to let him know Ritz had finished. He'd had to give his phone to Adam when they'd been brought to the safe house, just in case it was being used to track them, although there was no way anyone could break into his phone to track them. Nevertheless, he'd wiped it first, resetting it to factory settings. He had the backup stored in safe places, so he'd be able to restore it later.

Michael was correct. Ritz had finished, finding Scott King's password to the super-secret database, to which only he and casino owner Richard Fischer had access. *KingOfTheWorld666*.

Well, at least King was consistent. His e-mail password was *GoodToBeKing666*. The guy liked 666, for sure. Diesel wondered what his real name was. It wasn't King. The guy had too much fun with the name. Plus, there was the real Scott King. The nursing home guard who'd disappeared from Indianapolis a year ago.

Stone had been planning to drive to Indy today to check the guy out. In all the excitement last night, Diesel had forgotten.

Michael had been staring at the screen, but now turned to Diesel. "It's Scott King's password, isn't it?"

Diesel wasn't going to insult the boy's intelligence. "Yes. But I'm going to ask that you go play a video game. I . . . I don't know what I'm going to find," he said when Michael's eyes flashed in anger, the boy's hands rising, poised to sign angrily.

"It's going to be no good," Michael snapped, twin flags of color staining his pale cheeks. "I'm not stupid. Brewer knocked Joshua out. With a drug." He mimed a syringe in his arm. "He was taking him out of the house." His eyes narrowed. "I know what he did to me. I know what he was planning to do to Joshua."

Diesel opened his mouth, lifted his hands. Then lowered his hands, closing his mouth, because he didn't know how to respond. "You're right," he finally signed. "It's going to be no good. And I know what you've been through. *I know.*" He let the kid see his own hurt. His own torment. And he knew the moment that Michael understood because he reared back in stunned disbelief.

"No." Michael's eyes filled with tears once again. "You?"

Diesel nodded. "Me. So I know what you see in your mind, and I don't want you to have to see it on my computer screen. I care about you too much already. I don't want more pictures in your head."

Michael blinked, sending the tears down his cheeks. "But . . . you put them in yours," he signed, his movements small.

"And when you're older, you may choose to do the same. For now, do you trust me?" Diesel held his breath, waiting for Michael's answer.

"Yes." The sign was immediate and firm. Adamant. Certain.

The crack in Diesel's heart widened painfully. "Then let me do this. For you and for Joshua. And for the other kids who don't get a choice. Who can't ignore the pictures in their minds. Please. Go play a game. For me."

Michael swallowed hard. "Okay." He stood, unsteady on his feet. "Thank you."

"You're welcome." Diesel watched as the boy slowly walked to the room he'd been assigned and shut the door. Then he picked up his laptop from the coffee table and headed for the office with its lockable door. It was time somebody besides Scott King and Richard Fischer saw what was in their super-secret database.

Cincinnati, Ohio
Monday, March 18, 4:05 p.m.

Goddammit. Cade peeled the bandages from his leg with a grimace. He'd hoped a few hours' sleep would help his leg heal, but the wounds looked worse.

Neither was a big bullet hole. Both through-and-through. Little more than grazes. He'd had worse. Hell, his own father had done a lot worse with a sharpened belt buckle. In those days his mother had made him a poultice, crushing herbs with her mortar and pestle and boiling them, mixing them with flour and covering them with cheesecloth.

He didn't have any of those things here in the old pedo's house. All he had was a bottle of antibiotics that turned out to be expired and a tube of over-the-counter antibiotic cream he'd bought when he'd ventured into a drugstore after ditching Evelyn's mobile grooming salon and stealing another minivan.

Into which he'd stowed Evelyn and Junior and brought them here. He hadn't let them go. He'd never intended to let them go.

But he hadn't eliminated Michael Rowland as he'd intended. Instead, he'd created an even bigger mess. He was going to need to make a break for the border. A hostage might be the difference between safe passage and prison.

Or another firefight, because he wasn't being taken away without one. If they were hauling his ass to prison, he'd take out as many of them as he could.

He briefly wondered if Evelyn knew how to make a poultice, then rejected the idea. She'd made her opinions very clear when he'd dumped her and Junior in the basement cell with Andrew McNab, the still-unconscious interpreter. She wished Cade would die. *I'll take my chances with WebMD.*

He powered up his tablet, needing to know if he should cover the wounds or leave them open to the air to dry out, because they were red and oozing. And they fucking *hurt*.

Goddamn Feds. Cade wished he'd killed them when he had the ch—

He froze. *Motherfucking bitch.* His browser had opened to the last page he'd been watching—the local news. Which now featured Millicent, the nursing home receptionist who'd tried to lure him with the offer of free hockey tickets.

When was that? Saturday?

He clicked on the video, scowling at the woman, who was reveling in her fifteen minutes of fame. Less, actually. It was only a ninety-second clip.

"He seemed so nice." Millicent shuddered, wrapping her arms around herself. She was wearing a dress that was cut low in the front and high at the thigh. Her crossed arms plumped up her already outstanding cleavage, and the cameraman could not get enough. The lens nearly took her head off, trying to zoom in on her boobs.

Bitch.

"His name isn't Scott King, though," she went on, and Cade's blood ran cold. "He's Cade Kaiser. His father is a retired lawyer, a patient at the nursing home where I work."

"Where you *used* to work, bitch," Cade corrected with a snarl. The woman had broken so many HIPAA laws, revealing information about patients.

Focus, he snapped at himself. It didn't matter what laws the receptionist had broken. She'd outed him. Revealed his real name to the entire Internet.

His heart was racing so hard that his head hurt. He drew a breath, trying to calm himself. He was safe here in the old pedo's house. Nobody knew he was here. Nobody knew that he was connected to the old man whose body had long been claimed by the river.

I'm safe here. And I have hostages.

He could still get away. He *would* get away. Then he'd find a way to kill that receptionist bitch from wherever he ended up. He'd make it hurt, too.

"I can't believe I was almost alone with him." Millicent was crying into the camera and the picture abruptly shifted to a picture of the nursing home's exterior.

A photo of his father flashed on the screen, taken before Konrad Kaiser had had his "stroke." When he was still a healthy man. When he could still beat the shit out of anyone who crossed him.

Including his mother. Her photo appeared next to her husband's as the news reporter shared the fact that Konrad Kaiser had been accused of killing his wife, but had been cleared of all suspicion.

Because he'd *lied*. His old man had used his influence to lie. He'd called in favors with colleagues and old clients and even a few cops to establish an alibi. He couldn't have killed his wife, he'd claimed.

Even though I saw him do it.

"Now we have to wonder who did kill Myra Kaiser nine years ago," the reporter mused. "It seems more likely that her son had a hand in it—"

"No!" Cade thundered. He had not killed her. He was not taking the rap for what his piece-of-shit father had done. There was no fucking way.

"—now that we know he's suspected of killing at least ten people," the reporter was saying. "There are the seven bodies that the police have pulled from the river, the pediatrician who originally discovered the bodies, a CSU technician, and the wife of victim John Brewer."

They'd found Stella, then. Cade had zero regrets about killing her.

"If you see this man, please call the following number." A new photo flashed on the screen and he could only stare dully. *A photo of me.* It was a real photo, not the sketch the cops had been circulating everywhere since Michael Rowland had described him on Saturday.

He had to get away. Had to find someone to change his face.

I should have run before now. Because now he

couldn't run. His wounds were dark red and oozing. If he hit the road now, they could turn gangrenous, and that was a very bad way to go.

He'd stay here in the house. At least for now he was safe.

Chapter Twenty-Three

Cincinnati, Ohio
Monday, March 18, 5:30 p.m.

"Diesel? Baby, are you okay?"

Dani's soft voice—even calling him "baby"—was actually the last thing he wanted to hear as he hugged the toilet in the condo's gleamingly clean bathroom. He rested his cheek on the cold rim, wishing he could tell her to go away, but unable to speak the words. *Not to her. Not ever to her.*

He heard the running of water in the sink, then felt the cool wetness of the washcloth she pressed to the back of his neck. The palm she ran over his stubbled head was gentle. Soothing.

"What do you need?" she asked.

He couldn't answer. He couldn't even shake his head. He didn't have the energy. And his body wasn't getting any of the messages his brain was frantically firing. *Go. Make sure nobody sees . . .*

He hadn't closed his laptop before running for the bathroom. *Go. Close it. Nobody else should have to see that . . .*

Oh God. That.

He heard a whimpering sound and realized it was coming from him.

"Shh." Dani knelt beside him, her arms wrapping around his shoulders, her head a welcome weight against his back. He heard sniffling and knew she was crying. *For me.* "I've got you," she murmured. "You're not alone. I've got you."

A sob sat hard in his throat. He couldn't let it go, so it stayed there, growing harder and bigger until he couldn't breathe. He gasped, and she took the wet cloth from the back of his neck and wiped his face.

Then she held him. Saying nothing. Not demanding answers.

She just held him until he could feel the wetness of her tears seeping through his shirt to his back. Eventually her quiet crying stopped and she shuddered out a breath. Still she said nothing.

Rising to her feet, she pressed a kiss to his temple, then filled a glass with water. "Drink," she said softly. "Please." She cupped his chin, holding his head up, and pressed the glass to his lips. "Please."

He drank because he could deny her nothing when she said "please" like that.

She leaned in to rest her forehead against his. "Go lie down. I closed your laptop. Should I shut it off, too?"

His eyes opened, his gaze flying up to meet hers in panic. She'd seen. *Oh God.* She'd seen . . . *that.*

"I'm sorry," he croaked, his voice sounding like a rusty crank.

"Oh, baby. Me, too. So sorry." Her hand caressed his head again and he leaned into her touch. "Come with me. Let me help you. Please."

She stood, holding out her hand, her beautiful eyes full of sorrow, and somehow Diesel knew that she knew about him.

How? How did she know? Marcus hadn't said a word. Of that, Diesel was certain. He trusted Marcus O'Bannion with his life. *So how does she know?*

But he was too tired to figure it out now. Somehow he managed to get his body moving, bracing one hand on the marble tub to shove himself to his feet.

He looked at her hand, still outstretched. Waiting.

He didn't want to touch her. Didn't want to . . . dirty her.

Her eyes narrowed and she grabbed his hand, squeezing it hard. "I don't know what you just thought, but I don't ever want you to think it again. Okay? Just . . . don't." Her gaze softened. "Please, don't. You don't have to tell me, Diesel. You never have to tell anyone. But . . ." She pressed her lips together like she was trying not to cry anymore. Then blinked and sent new tears falling. "You waited for me for a long time. Don't push me away now." She brought his hand to her lips and kissed his fingers, one at a time.

Relief was a tidal wave, sweeping him under. He tugged his hand free to wrap his arms around her, his stupid body still trembling. Her capable hands flattened on his back, hugging him so hard he almost coughed.

It felt better than words could say. So he said nothing, just held her back until his trembling ebbed. "You saw my computer screen?" he asked gruffly.

"One thing, yes." He heard her swallow.

"Did . . . Who else saw? I should have closed it before I came in here."

"Nobody. I was in our room when I heard the door to the office slam open. I went to check and saw you running for the bathroom and Michael coming out of his room. He gave me this look, Diesel. Like he knew. But he didn't see your laptop."

Thank God. "And Joshua?"

"With Agent Troy in the kitchen." He felt her smile against his chest. "They're making cookies."

More relief swamped him. "I'm sorry. I should have made sure—"

She cut him off, pulling far enough away to press her fingers to his lips. "Stop. No harm done."

"Yes, there was. You saw it."

She sighed. "I've seen things like that before. Doesn't get easier, but I saw child victims of sexual assault come through the ER. I sometimes see them in the clinic."

His cheeks went hot now, shame replacing the relief. "You never threw up."

She gave him another look, this one full of challenge. "Yes, I did. And I still do. Almost every time I see a patient who's been sexually assaulted. Adults and kids. I wanted to on Saturday, after I saw that Michael was bleeding on my exam table. I knew what had been done to him. And I wanted to kill his stepfather then, too. I wanted to run from the exam room to my office and cry and vomit and scream."

"But you didn't." She was a strong woman. *Stronger than me.*

"No, I didn't." She cupped his cheek in her palm. "Because when I came out of my office, there you were. And you let me lean on you."

She had, he remembered. Just her forehead against his chest, but she'd leaned on him and it had been one of the sweetest moments of his life.

She was smiling gently. "Lean on me. Let me help you like you helped me."

So he did. There in the condo's bathroom, he took the comfort she offered. The strength. It was just enough for him to tell her what he'd seen on the casino's network. It wasn't enough for him to tell her what had happened to him personally, at least not today. Maybe not ever.

But to tell her what Scott King and Richard Fischer had done? Yeah, he could do that. He leaned in to whisper in her ear, just in case anyone was listening at the door. "I don't think Richard Fischer—the casino owner—knows that Scott King had access to the database. If he did know, I don't think King would still be alive. I don't think Richard's clients know, or *Richard* wouldn't still be alive."

She frowned up at him. "What was Richard doing?"

"You mean, what *is* he doing. The most recent entry

was this past Friday. I think it's a poker game. Very exclusive. Very expensive."

"High rollers?"

"High stakes, at least. It doesn't look like money changes hands. Participants bet things. Black-market things."

She swallowed hard. "And people? Children?"

"Yes. And yes. At least five women, one man. And at least two kids." The photo she'd seen had been of a teenage girl. Luckily he'd already closed out of the photos Brewer had taken of Joshua, so she hadn't seen those.

But Diesel had. He closed his eyes, resting his head on Dani's shoulder. He'd been transported back in time. *Back there.* He'd been five years old. Six years old. Seven . . . Twelve . . .

"Hey." Dani's hands were alternating between rubbing his back and patting to get his attention. "Diesel. Come back to me."

He looked up, realized his mind had . . . strayed. "Sorry."

"No sorries. Focus on Richard Fischer. Focus on making the bastard pay."

He tightened his jaw. She was right. Affection filled him, surprising him with its sweetness. Of course she was right.

"Okay. Other than people, participants staked real estate, exotic animals. Jewelry. Art. Organs—and not the musical kind."

Her eyes popped wide. "Like . . . kidneys?"

"Mostly. One heart was on offer as well." Diesel imagined the FBI would be very interested in that.

"Oh my God," she breathed. "It's like an exclusive, black-market swap meet."

"Pretty much, yeah."

"And the casino owner's role?"

"He's like a matchmaker. He has a 'wants' column and an 'offers' column. Those people end up playing in games together. Only on Friday nights. That's when the riverboat sets sail. Other nights it's docked."

She still looked stunned. "And nobody suspected anything? None of the participants talked?"

Her horror was kind of refreshing. Diesel was afraid he'd become desensitized to what humans were capable of doing to one another after all of his investigations for the *Ledger*. "I imagine it's a mutual-deniability thing. If one tells, he's telling on himself, too. If one tells, the others retaliate. So nobody tells."

"Jesus," she whispered. "Brewer was a participant?"

"Yeah. The guy who wanted a five-year-old boy was named Blake Emerson."

"And now Brewer's dead. I wonder if Emerson is, too." She looked away for a moment, her brow furrowed in thought. Then her confused gaze shot back to Diesel's. "Scott King was the security manager. He killed Brewer. And then came back to check on Joshua. Was he . . . *protecting* Joshua?"

Diesel nodded. "That was my take. King was working every Friday night. I think he was the game's security guard."

"And he saw what was happening. Or heard it. I wonder why he didn't kill Richard Fischer."

"Maybe he did. Nobody can find Fischer, according to the news. I called Adam to find out if they'd questioned him and he confirmed that they were looking for the guy. They were about to search his house."

"House," Dani murmured, as if to herself. "What about the boys' house? Why did LJM Industries buy it? How does that fit?"

God, she was smart. Diesel loved her brain as much as the rest of her. "Good question. Richard didn't pair the same people in more than one game very often, but he put Blake Emerson and John Brewer together twice. The first time was two Fridays ago. John's stake was his house. Emerson's was a kilo of heroin."

"Oh. John wanted the heroin for Stella."

"More likely to resell," Diesel said flatly. "He'd already gone through the boys' trust funds and he was broke."

"Goddammit," she whispered. "What's the street value of a kilo?"

"Six hundred grand plus change, which is the estimated value of the house."

She bit at her lip. "Does Richard keep photos of his clients in that database?"

"Yeah." He dug his phone from the pocket of his jeans. "I didn't download anything from the casino's server. I went old-school and snapped a picture." He held out his phone, open to the photo he'd taken. "Meet Blake Emerson."

Her mouth fell open in stunned surprise. "That's Wesley Masterson, Laurel's cop brother. Marcus found his photo online last night. You're saying that Wesley Masterson was buying *children*?"

Her reaction was the same as his had been. "I'm saying that's what Richard Fischer entered into his database. He also has Blake Emerson owning a company called Liberation Junction Mining Industries, located in Michigan's Upper Peninsula."

"LJM," Dani whispered.

"Exactly," he said grimly. "I ran a background check on Blake Emerson. On the surface, he looks legit, but if you dig deeper, it's suspicious. Liberation Junction Mining is a real company, incorporated in Michigan. Blake Emerson's listed as the president of the company, which does have a website and a phone number, but calls go to voice mail with a generic 'Please leave a message' greeting. The company has an address in Houghton, Michigan, which is where many of the copper mines are located, but the address is that of an abandoned mine site."

She shook her head, still dazed by the revelation that Wesley Masterson had tried to buy Joshua. "So the mining company doesn't really exist?"

"It doesn't appear to have a physical location. It does, however, have cash assets. You remember the bank statement that John Brewer received before his disappearance?"

"Yes. It showed LJM's account balance with a handwritten message basically saying that the company had the funds and that Brewer should turn over the title to his house, which he then did, right?"

Diesel nodded. "Right. Richard had the bank statement attached to Blake Emerson's name. Emerson—or Wesley Masterson—offered up Liberation Junction Mining as his source of income, but gave Richard a bank statement for LJM, an entirely different entity, incorporated here in Ohio."

"If Richard had dissected LJM like we did, he would have seen the same clues. He would have known someone was trying to avenge Laurel Masterson."

Diesel shrugged. "I think all he looked at was LJM's bank balance, because Blake Emerson has a checkmark in the 'approved' column next to his name. If he had dug even a little deeper, he would have been suspicious of Emerson."

"But why would Wesley Masterson fake an identity like that?" Dani asked, then blinked. "Wait. Was Laurel one of the women Richard sold?"

He nodded. "I found her listed under 'offers,' with a date of September of a year and a half ago. It fits with when she abruptly withdrew from med school."

Dani was frowning thoughtfully. "Wesley Masterson is a narcotics detective. He spent two years undercover, even got a commendation for his work. He'd know how to fake an identity."

Diesel blinked, surprised. He'd forgotten that Masterson was Narcotics. "Either he'd know or he'd have resources that could do it. Are you thinking that he infiltrated Richard's secret poker game because he was investigating his sister's disappearance?"

Her eyes had brightened. "It's possible, isn't it?"

"Yes," he acknowledged. "But . . . if it's true, he'll need to explain a few things." He hesitated because Dani looked so hopeful that Wesley Masterson had infiltrated the poker game with good intentions, and Diesel wasn't so sure.

Her brows lifted. "Like?"

"Like how the men who actually bought and sold Laurel both ended up dead, shot during home invasions." Although if Masterson had learned their identities and killed them, Diesel could understand the cop's rage.

She drew a breath. "Well, I can't truthfully say that I'm sorry they're dead. Who were they?"

"Richard lists the seller as Anatoly Markov and the buyer as Clinton Stern. I didn't get a chance to look at the crime reports for the details, but both dying the same way seems too coincidental to me."

Her shoulders sagged. "To me, too. That seems like revenge."

Diesel shrugged. "Raguel, the vengeance dude."

She sighed. "I guess I'd understand Wesley's reasons if he did find and kill them, but that doesn't give him the right to be judge, jury, and executioner."

Diesel opened his mouth, then shut it again, suddenly unwilling to remind her that his hacking was much the same thing.

She narrowed her eyes. "I can tell that you're thinking something I probably won't like."

He forced himself to say the words, hoping she'd respond the way he wanted her to. "I do the same thing. So do Marcus and Stone and the rest of the team at the *Ledger*. We take matters into our hands. We're judge and jury, too."

"But not executioner." She stared at him, her gaze intense. "You don't kill people, do you?"

Relief was like a smack to his chest. That was exactly what he'd hoped she'd say. "No." He could answer with complete honesty. "Not anymore. I did in Iraq."

"But that was war. That's different. What you do at the *Ledger* saves lives, Diesel. Every time you force an abusive asshole away from his family, that's one less beat-up wife I have to tend in the ER. One less child with a broken arm." She swallowed hard. "One less rape kit I have to do on a child."

He'd known that doctors did rape kits on child victims of sexual assault, but the thought of Dani having to do one made him physically ill. "Thank you."

She smiled tremulously. "Same to you. Now, was that all Wesley will have to explain or is there more?"

There was more. "Blake Emerson put up a kilo of heroin to deal into Richard's poker game. Richard attaches documentation of each player's stake when they agree to play. He had the title to Brewer's house, photos of Joshua, and a photo of Emerson holding a brick of heroin."

"Wesley Masterson got his hands on a brick of heroin," she murmured. "And he was a narcotics detective. I wonder if Cleveland PD realizes they have six hundred grand worth of heroin missing."

"Or if it ever made it to the evidence locker in the first place," Diesel added. "That's a lot of temptation for detectives, handling all those drugs. Sometimes they take a little for themselves. Wesley Masterson took a helluva lot more than a little."

"Maybe he's operating under Cleveland PD's direction," Dani suggested. "I mean, he allowed Richard to have photographic evidence of his theft. That doesn't sound like he's worried about getting caught."

"Maybe," Diesel murmured, but he was more inclined to believe that Wesley Masterson simply didn't think anyone would be looking at his involvement, and he wondered why. A seasoned detective would know how to cover his tracks, but Masterson hadn't covered his very well. He was about to say as much when he realized that Dani had gone very still and was studying him with an intensity that made him more than a little nervous.

"What?" he asked quietly.

"How many photos did you see in Richard's secret database?"

Not nearly all of them, but still too many. The photos of the human beings flashed through his mind, a torturous slide show. He lifted one shoulder. "Enough."

"Are there more?"

He nodded stiffly. "A lot more." He dreaded sorting through them, dreaded seeing more photos like the ones of Joshua and the teenage girl who'd been "offered" a few nights before.

"I don't want you to look at any more. I can check them for you."

He wanted to say that it was okay, that he would do it, but he found himself nodding his thanks. "I'm . . . not good with the photos."

She caressed his face. "I know."

He couldn't meet her eyes, afraid of the pity he'd see there. "We need to get this information to Deacon and Adam. Without telling them where I got it."

"I think they've figured it out by now," Dani said dryly. "Adam said they were about to search Fischer's house. At a minimum they might find evidence of the game. They might find Richard himself."

He finally met her eyes and saw no pity. Just respect. And something more. He wasn't going to jinx it by giving it a name too soon. But it loosened his chest enough that he could smile at her. "Thank you."

She didn't pretend to misunderstand. "You're welcome. Now, we should get out of this bathroom or someone might get the wrong idea."

"What? That we're discussing my illegal hacking and Richard Fischer's even more illegal black-market swap meet?"

Her lips quirked up. "I was going to say that we were having sex, but yeah, let's go with that."

He made a face. "I think my retching was loud enough that Troy heard it. And I don't think sex afterward sounds very romantic."

She shrugged. "Don't judge. It might be some-body's kink."

He gaped at her. "What?"

"I saw a lot of shit in the ER, Diesel. Even you would be shocked. I'll wait for you outside." She saun-tered out of the room, leaving him to stare after her.

Kicking himself into motion, he rinsed his mouth with the mouthwash stocked in the medicine cabinet, then followed her out the door.

Where Agent Troy stood, looking grim. For a split second Diesel worried that the Fed had heard every-thing, but Troy was holding out his phone. "I've got some things you need to see."

Cincinnati, Ohio
Monday, March 18, 6:00 p.m.

Grant drew a deep breath as he exited the hospital's elevator on the ICU floor. *I'm going straight to hell. Impersonating a damn priest.* He prayed this would work.

He also prayed that he wouldn't asphyxiate before he got to Stone O'Bannion's room, because the cleri-cal collar seemed more like a noose. Grant couldn't imagine his brother wearing the priest's cassock, as his neck was thicker, far more muscular. Wes would have choked to death.

Grant stumbled a little at the thought. Wes might acutally have been choked to death. Grant had to stop walking, leaning against the wall for support as his knees buckled. He hoped Wes had been choked or shot or something. Before he was dismembered and thrown into the river.

You don't know that that's what happened. But he knew. Somehow he just knew.

"You okay there, Father?" a nurse asked in con-cern.

"Yes," Grant managed, realizing she was talk-ing to him. *Get a grip. Stand up straight. You're not helping Wes by holding up the wall.* "I'm fine. Thank you."

The nurse smiled uncertainly. "Can I help you, then?"

"Yes. I'm here to see Stone O'Bannion."

"He's got a restricted guest list." The nurse pointed through a window in the unit's double doors, to one of the ICU rooms where a uniformed cop stood. "But they might let you in. Heads up, they'll frisk you. We get searched every time we leave the floor and come back in to make sure we haven't smuggled a gun into the ICU. Mr. O'Bannion is a recent victim of a crime."

"I know. I read about it. I'm an admirer of Mr. O'Bannion's work, and the *Ledger* has sponsored my parish's Little League team." The *Ledger* had sponsored the intramural boys' team of one of the inner-city churches, as well as a girls' team. St. Ambrose's Father Trace was the coordinator. That tidbit—and the fact that Father Trace was the uncle of Stone O'Bannion's sister-in-law Scarlett Bishop—had been part of Grant's research. He hoped he hadn't gone too far by dropping the reference. "I was hoping to ask if the family needed anything."

He gripped the large Bible he held, relieved that he'd left Wes's guns at his brother's apartment. It would have looked too suspicious to turn back now, and there was nowhere he could have hidden a gun under this cassock. He did, however, have Wesley's detective shield and his phone. Just in case.

In case of what, he had no idea.

"Well, that's lovely, Father Emerson," the nurse said, peering at the ID badge that Grant wore, the one he'd found in the cassock's pocket. Wesley had been very thorough as he'd built his Blake Emerson alias. "Come with me."

Using her badge, she opened the ICU's inner doors and walked Grant through the unit, smiling at the cop on duty. "This is Father Emerson. He'd like to see Mr. O'Bannion."

The cop noted Grant's ID and wrote his name on a clipboard. Then he stuck his head in the doorway. "I got a Father Emerson to see Mr. O'Bannion?"

Grant stuck his own head in, next to the cop's. "I won't stay long, Mr. O'Bannion. I promise."

Stone lay in the hospital bed, his skin pale. At his side were two people—an older man wearing black gloves and a young, petite blonde. The older man stood. "I'm sorry, but Stone isn't taking visitors."

But Stone's eyes widened in sudden recognition and Grant knew he was thinking of their brief encounter outside the casino the night before.

"It's okay, Dad. I'll see him. Can you ask Marcus to join us? And maybe you can take Delores to get something to eat." Stone brought the woman's hand to his lips. "Go and eat, honey. You're gonna need your strength to put up with me when I get out of here. Remember how cranky I was the last time I got shot."

"And you promised you wouldn't let it happen again," Delores said, but leaned in to kiss Stone's mouth gently. "I'll be back soon." She linked her arm through the older man's. "Come on, Dad. Let's get some of that yummy hospital cafeteria food."

The man looked doubtful. "We're going to be eating candy out of the machine again, aren't we?"

"Probably," the blonde said, then paused. "Don't upset him," she whispered to Grant, loudly enough for Stone to hear from the bed. "Or you'll be hearing *my* confession, and there aren't enough Hail Marys to forgive what I'll do to you."

Grant smiled at her. She reminded him of Cora. "So noted. I promise." Then he held his arms out, allowing the cop to frisk him.

"He's clean," the cop told the pair. "Go and eat. You've been here for hours."

"I'll send Marcus in," the blonde said. "He's in the waiting room."

So Grant had only about a minute alone with Stone before his brother arrived.

"You're a little late, Padre," Stone said with a weak smile as Grant approached the bed. "I coded a couple times last night. I should have said my last confession then." Then he sobered. "Are you a *gambling* man, Father?"

"No. And my name isn't Emerson. It's Masterson."

The spark of recognition in Stone's eyes surprised him. "Wesley?"

"No. He's my brother. I'm Grant."

"The accountant."

Grant frowned. "How do you know about us?"

"Ask my brother. He has all the details. Why were you at the casino?"

"I'm looking for *my* brother. He's been missing for more than a week. I think he got involved in something dangerous there."

Stone said nothing for a few excruciating seconds. "Why are you here?"

"To give you this." Grant held out the Bible, tilting it so that Stone could see as he opened the cover quickly before closing it again. The man flicked his gaze upward to Grant, indicating that he'd spotted the book that Grant had hidden inside the Bible's pages. It had taken him nearly an hour to carve out the necessary space. "You seem like a man of integrity, Stone. I'm not from this city and I don't know which cops to trust. My sister was abducted and a Cincinnati detective failed to report it." Detective Bert Stuart had to have been on the take. It was the only explanation.

"Your sister was Laurel," Stone murmured. "LJM Industries."

Grant frowned. Laurel's initials. "Laurel is my sister, but what is LJM Industries?"

Stone drew a breath and let it out slowly, not for dramatic effect, but because he was clearly exhausted by the effort of speaking. "Talk to Marcus. Or Diesel. Especially Diesel."

"That's Mr. Kennedy?"

"Yes. He has the whole picture. Him and his girl-friend, Dani."

"Dr. Novak."

"You know a lot, Father Emerson," Stone said, looking over Grant's shoulder. "I'd like you to meet my brother, Marcus, and my sister-in-law, Detective Scarlett Bishop. Guys, this is Father Emerson."

Marcus looked at Grant through narrowed eyes. "Like hell he is. He's—"

Stone gave him a sharp look. "Take him to the *Ledger*. Let him talk to Diesel."

Marcus started to answer, but Detective Bishop sucked in a breath. *"You."*

Grant met her gaze, his heart beginning to pound. "Me?" Had she seen Wes? The two of them looked enough like each other that it would be an understandable mistake.

"Scarlett," Stone warned. "Please."

"Yes, you," she whispered to Grant, the lowering of her voice her only concession to the man in the hospital bed. "You were at Richard Fischer's house yesterday. We saw you on his security video."

"I was. I went to see him, but he didn't appear to be home. If you saw the security video, you know I didn't enter the house."

She stared at him, as though trying to read his mind. "I know. I think we need to talk, *Father*."

Grant nodded. "I agree. Can I ask why you were at Richard Fischer's house?"

Marcus and his wife shared a long look with Stone, then each other. "Because Fischer is dead," Detective Bishop said.

Grant shuddered out a breath. "Oh." *One more dead.* He looked at Stone. "What about the Word of God?" he asked, tapping the Bible.

"Give it to them," Stone said, his words beginning

to slur. He closed his eyes, a goofy smile curving his lips, a painkiller obviously kicking in. "Scar's a good one. But don't tell her I said that. She'll get a big head."

Detective Bishop sighed, but leaned over the hospital rail to kiss Stone's cheek. "You're an idiot and I love you. Stop getting shot."

"I will. I promise. I gotta teach my nephew how to cheat at poker."

"You'd better," she scolded, then straightened and aimed a glare at Grant. "Let's go, *Father*."

Cincinnati, Ohio
Monday, March 18, 6:00 p.m.

Dani left the condo's bathroom, still shaken but hoping she'd hidden it. Seeing Diesel so broken . . . It had nearly broken her. She didn't know his story, what had led him to have such a visceral reaction to seeing the photo of a young woman being trafficked. She suspected, of course, but knowing the details . . . She almost hoped he wouldn't tell her. She wasn't sure she could take it.

But she would. If Diesel ever did want her to know, she'd listen. *And I'll take it. I'll be strong for him.* So that he could be strong in the times when she needed him.

She forced herself to focus on Agent Troy, who'd handed Diesel his cell phone. She was surprised to see they had a visitor. Agent Quincy Taylor stood just inside the condo's front foyer.

"Quincy," she said, trying to shake her mood and sound welcoming. "Please come in."

He did so, checking the bottoms of his boots first. "I've been at your property, Diesel, processing last night's crime scene."

Diesel was frowning at Troy's phone, but looked up to greet Quincy. "Hey, Quincy. Did you find anything?"

"Tire treads," Quincy said. "They match treads found near the river where George Garrett was . . ." He cut himself off midsentence, smiling down at Joshua, who'd wandered in from the kitchen. "Hello."

"Joshua," Dani said, "this is Agent Taylor, but you can call him Mr. Quincy. He works with my brother and my cousin."

Joshua blinked up at Quincy, wide-eyed. "Are you an FBI guy, too?"

Quincy bit his lip, trying not to smile, Dani thought. "I am," he said seriously. "I hear you like superheroes."

Joshua nodded suspiciously. "How did you know?"

"Miss Kate is my friend."

Joshua smiled at that. "Her dog is Cap. After Captain America. And she has fingernails with shields on them."

"Exactly. She told me that you like Spider-Man."

"He's on my jammies." Joshua pinched the fabric of his pj's, which he'd begged to wear all day. "See? I got to stay in them because we're still camping."

Quincy nodded sagely. "I do see. I brought you something. If it's okay with Dr. Dani." From his backpack he pulled a wrapped box and Joshua whipped around to meet Dani's eyes.

"Can I have it?" he asked.

Dani smiled. "Of course. But remember to thank Mr. Quincy."

Joshua beamed. "Thank you! I'm gonna show Michael!" He took the package and ran for the kitchen.

"It's just a Spider-Man action figure," Quincy said. "I saw that he had a few action figures in his bedroom at his mother's house." He sighed. "I was at that crime scene, too. I stopped by Walmart and found a figure that he didn't have at home. That way, in case he wants those toys at some point, he won't have doubles."

"You've been busy," Dani said. "If you saw Kate, you've been to the hospital, too."

"Wanted to check on Decker," Quincy kind of mumbled. "He said to say hi."

Dani squeezed the shy man's arm. "Thank you, Quincy. That was thoughtful."

Quincy shrugged. "He's just a kid. He shouldn't have to go through this."

"No, he shouldn't." She hesitated, then leaned up and kissed his cheek. "It was still thoughtful."

Quincy blushed. "I got something for Michael, too. Kate said he and Greg talked video games non-stop. It's the newest *Kingdom Hearts* game. Kate said you've got Xbox, so that's the one I picked."

Dani felt hot tears stinging her eyes and wondered that she still had any left to shed. "That was so sweet," she whispered. "He'll love it."

"You had to tell him that his mom was gone. I thought . . ." Quincy shrugged again, then grunted when Dani hugged him. "It's not violent," he managed through the hug. "Just cartoon-type monster killing. I figured you'd be okay with it."

"She's okay with it," Troy said mildly. "Chill, Quince."

Dani remembered the unspoken conversation the two had had the night before and wondered what was going on between them. She hoped it was something wonderful, because Troy and Quincy both seemed like nice guys.

"I didn't come just to give the gifts, though," Quincy said. "Well, not just for the kids anyway. I've got something for you, too."

Diesel passed Troy's phone to Dani. "Nursing home receptionist ID'd Scott King as Cade Kaiser. His father is a patient at the home."

"Yeah," Troy said sourly. "She went to the news first, not the cops."

"And dressed to the nines for her interview," Dani noted. She gave Troy his phone. "I hope she enjoys her fifteen minutes of fame."

Diesel rolled his eyes. "I hope she realizes that

King or Kaiser, or whoever the hell he is, is a serial killer and will probably go after her for outing him."

"If she'd come to us first, we might have given her protection," Troy said, then shrugged. "There's more you need to know, though. Do you know an Evelyn Keys?"

Dani went still. "Yeah. She's my dog groomer. I help her with her baby when he's sick." A new ball of dread formed in her belly. "Why?"

"She's missing," Troy said gently. "She didn't show up for her first appointment and never dropped her son off at day care. Her grooming van was found abandoned near Mount Airy Forest."

"Oh my God," Dani whispered, physically swaying from the horror of the realization, grateful when Diesel wrapped his arm around her shoulders to hold her up. "He got away, didn't he? Scott King or Cade Kaiser or whatever the hell his name is? He got away and he used Evelyn and Jimmy to do it."

"That's the way it looks," Troy agreed. "We didn't find any sign of violence. No blood. He may have taken them hostage, and if so, he won't hurt them. He'll need them as negotiating leverage."

Diesel kissed her temple. "Breathe, honey. We're going to find him."

Dani nodded. He was right. So was Troy. But at the same time, they weren't. "I've been a hostage before. He doesn't have to physically hurt her to do harm."

Diesel pulled her even tighter against him. "I know. But we *will* find him. We're getting closer. Just focus on that."

She closed her eyes. "I'll try. I will. It's just . . . Evelyn is so sweet. She wouldn't hurt a fly. And she and Jimmy don't have anyone."

"They have you in their corner," Diesel told her. "And they have the FBI. Which is almost as good as having you."

She forced her lips to curve. "You're right."

Straightening her spine, she gave Troy her full attention. "Anything else?"

Troy still looked upset from having had to tell her about Evelyn, but he nodded. "The casino owner is dead."

Diesel sighed at that. "Yeah, I kind of thought so. Who found him?"

"His housekeeper," Quincy answered. "She didn't get far enough into the house to disturb anything, luckily. She smelled his body, backed out, and called the cops. Security video supports her story."

"How did he die?" Dani asked, clenching her teeth. "I hope it hurt. A lot."

Quincy's brows winged up at the venom in her voice. "ME hasn't determined yet, but first responders found a syringe on his nightstand. He was an insulin-dependent type 1 diabetic. We're testing the remnants of the syringe to see if it was his insulin."

"When?" Diesel asked grimly.

Quincy shrugged. "Hard to say. Rigor had passed, so at least twenty-four to thirty-six hours. He was seen at the casino on Friday night, so sometime between then and yesterday noon. I don't believe either of you are suspects, of course."

"Of course," Dani murmured. "Deacon and Adam are aware?"

"Yep," Troy said. "They called to tell me themselves."

Diesel gave Quincy a questioning look. "You said you had a gift for us. Sorry, dude, but none of this news seems like much of a gift."

Quincy's lips twitched. "No, *dude*, it's not. This might be, though." He handed Diesel a piece of paper.

Diesel opened it, Dani leaning on his arm to read along with him. She met Diesel's gaze, then looked at Quincy, her eyes wide. "You ran financials on Laurel Masterson's med school roommate."

"I don't know what you mean," Quincy said. "I found that on a printer."

Troy rolled his eyes. "I asked him to run it."

"I found it on a printer," Quincy insisted, glaring at Troy.

"Like *they're* gonna tell," Troy said with another eye-roll. "It's *fine*, Quince."

Diesel snickered. "Blaming it on the printer was never going to work, Quincy. But thanks, and I won't tell a soul. Why did you ask him to run it, Troy?"

"Because I didn't like how she answered Jeremy's questions last night when we asked her about Laurel's disappearance. And she drives a brand-new Miata."

"Not that expensive," Dani said, taking the printout and scanning the numbers, "unless you're a third-year med student."

"With no visible means of support," Troy added. "Her student loans are being paid monthly by someone else and she's got a nice balance in her bank account."

"With a big fat deposit the month after Laurel Masterson dropped out of med school," Diesel said. "I'll look into who's paying her loans."

Troy smiled. "I kind of thought you might."

"But why didn't the cops find this when Laurel's brother insisted she hadn't just run away with this guy?" Diesel demanded.

"I don't know," Troy said honestly. "And we can't ask Detective Stuart, who investigated the case. He's dead, killed in a home invasion."

Dani jerked her head up from the printout, her gaze colliding with Diesel's. "Home invasion," she repeated quietly. Like the two men involved in Laurel being sold into slavery.

"Why do I get the idea that you two know more than we do?" Troy asked.

Diesel ran both hands over his stubbled skull, winced, then rubbed his palms on his T-shirt like they stung. "Fuck," he muttered, then looked over his shoulder to make sure that Joshua hadn't overheard him swear. "You need to check the casino's server. Now."

Quincy tilted his head. "I take it you have. What led you there?"

"John Brewer's financials," Dani answered. "Brewer transferred the title to the family home, but no money changed hands."

"LJM Industries bought it," Quincy murmured. "Troy told me last night, on our way to the casino after it was raided. We were looking for Scott King. Or Cade Kaiser. We didn't dig deeper, but now that the casino owner is dead, we will. Obviously. Thank you, Diesel."

Diesel pointed to the paper Dani held. "And we thank your printer. It's more of the puzzle. Are you going to pick up the roommate for questioning?"

"You bet we are," Troy said with a scowl.

Diesel rubbed his head again. "Did the roommate mention a man named Anatoly Markov?"

Troy blinked. "Yes, that was the name of Laurel's boyfriend. The one she supposedly ran away with."

Dani smoothed her hand up Diesel's back, standing on her toes to massage his neck, noting his stress. He so wanted to tell them everything, but she knew why he didn't. It was less a fear of arrest and more a need to provide information in a way that they could legally use.

"I'm betting he's paying the roommate's student loan," Dani offered.

"Will we find his name on the casino's server?" Quincy asked quietly, saving Diesel from having to decide what to say.

Diesel nodded. "Among others. Like John Brewer."

"And a guy named Blake Emerson," Dani said. "Who looks enough like Wesley Masterson, Laurel's cop brother, to *be* him."

Quincy rubbed his temples. "I haven't gotten enough sleep for this tangle."

"We need to tell Adam and Deacon," Dani said. "Now."

"I'll call . . ." Troy glanced at his phone. "Speak of the devils. Adam just texted. He's on his way to pick you up. Command performance for both of you."

"With whom?" Diesel asked warily.

"Marcus, Scarlett, Deacon, Adam." Troy pursed his lips. "And Grant Masterson."

"Now we know where Grant went on his 'vacation,'" Dani said to Diesel, air-quoting. "I'll tell the boys that we're leaving for a bit. You'll stay with them, Troy?"

Troy nodded. "I will. Adam's dropping Meredith off, too, along with an interpreter. She thought the kids might need to talk to someone after she heard about their mother's murder."

"Joshua might be ready," Diesel said. "Michael probably isn't. Not yet."

Quincy held out a wrapped package. "Michael's video game. Will you give it to him for me?"

Dani smiled at him. "Of course. Thank you, Quincy."

Diesel reached for her hand. "We'll tell them together that we're leaving *and* coming back. They need to hear that we're coming back, Dani."

She gave his hand a squeeze, her heart squeezing even harder. This giant of a man was so very gentle. So very sensitive to the feelings of children. *And my feelings, too. Why did I make him wait so long?* "You're right."

He kissed her hand. "And before we leave, I want you to put your processor on. I want you to be able to hear everything around you. So that we keep our promise to these kids and come back."

She took her processor from her pocket and snapped it on. "Right again."

Chapter Twenty-Four

Cincinnati, Ohio
Monday, March 18, 7:15 p.m.

Diesel almost laughed when he saw the group gathered in the *Ledger* office. "Just like Stone to get shot to avoid talking to all these cops," he said.

Marcus chuckled. "Ain't that the truth."

"Sit down," Scarlett complained. "I'm getting a crick in my neck looking at you."

Diesel pulled out a chair for Dani, then sat next to her. Marcus and Adam flanked Scarlett, and Deacon took the seat on Dani's other side. The only stranger at the table was dressed in a starched white shirt and dark pants—with a clerical cassock neatly folded in front of him.

Diesel recognized him right away. "You're the guy Stone and I saw last night when we were leaving the casino."

"Yes," the man said. "I'm Grant Masterson."

He didn't look like the photo on the website of his accounting firm. He looked a lot older. Wearier. He looked a lot like his brother.

"I'm Diesel Kennedy and this is Dr. Dani Novak."

Grant nodded once. "My wife told me you called, Dr. Novak. My apologies, but I haven't gotten around to calling you back. I've been busy."

"I guess you have," Dani said quietly. "You're not a priest."

"He used the disguise to get into Stone's room," Scarlett said frostily.

"Why?" Dani asked him.

Grant's cheeks reddened. "I didn't think they'd just let a stranger into his room in ICU. They nearly didn't let a priest in, but Stone recognized me, too."

Dani shook her head. "No, I mean why did you want to get into Stone's room in the first place?"

"To give him this," Grant said, moving the folded cassock aside to reveal a big Bible, the kind that churches set on stands or that families used for their genealogy. He lifted the cover to show that the Bible had a hole carved into the pages. In it was nestled a book bound in green leather cover with purple flowers.

"Mountain laurel," Dani said.

"Texas mountain laurel, to be exact," Grant said. "It was our sister's favorite flower. She drew it on everything." He pulled a pair of latex gloves from his pocket and lifted the book from its hiding place. "I wanted Stone to have this. I didn't know who else to trust."

"Why did you think you could trust him?" Diesel asked. "He told you he was a cop."

Scarlett made a small sound of surprise. "He did what?"

"He was kidding," Diesel said. "Being a goofball to cheer me up."

Dani's gaze swung from the book to Diesel's face. "Sorry."

He covered her thigh with his hand. "Shh. We're done with that, right?"

"Right." She turned back to Grant. "Why did you trust Stone?"

"I read some of his articles, both in the *Ledger* and when he was embedded with the troops. I read that he went to jail once because he wouldn't give up a source. And I read that some of his *Ledger* investigations put some very bad people away. When I saw that he was also a victim of Scott King and all this . . . mess, I wasn't sure what to do. But I figured he'd make sure the information got to the right people."

"I still don't understand why you didn't go to the police," Scarlett said.

"Because of Detective Bert Stuart," Diesel said.

Grant stared at him in shock. "How do you know that?"

Diesel sighed. "I think we all know different pieces of this puzzle."

"Who is Bert Stuart?" Deacon asked.

"Detective Stuart was assigned to investigate Laurel Masterson's disappearance," Dani said. "But he didn't. We couldn't even find a filed missing person report. He also didn't investigate the roommate who conveniently said that Laurel had run away with her boyfriend. The roommate who now drives a new car and has a very nice apartment that she shares with no one."

"She was bribed," Scarlett said flatly. "You think Detective Stuart was, too?"

"We can't ask him," Diesel said, watching Grant closely. "He's dead. Killed in a home invasion."

Grant flinched, confirming Diesel's suspicion that he knew a lot more of the puzzle than they did.

"And the boyfriend?" Scarlett asked.

Diesel hesitated, and Deacon rolled his eyes. "Speak freely, Diesel. We know what you do."

"And we trust you not to abuse our trust," Adam added.

Diesel relaxed. "The boyfriend was really a . . . supplier. Of women."

Grant paled. "A supplier?" he whispered hoarsely.

Diesel winced, reminding himself sternly that Laurel Masterson was Grant's sister. "Yes," he said, gentling his normally gravelly tone as much as he could. "We don't know all the details, but it appears that Laurel was . . . trafficked."

Grant's throat worked as he tried to swallow. "Oh God." The words were half moan, half whimper. "Oh my God."

Dani slid her hand over Grant's, her expression concerned. "Do you need to take a break?"

Grant shook his head. "No," he rasped. "Tell me. Please."

Diesel sighed. "His name was Anatoly Markov. He's also dead. Killed in a home invasion, just like Detective Stuart."

Grant closed his eyes. "Wesley," he whispered.

"Okay," Scarlett said, her frost thawing. "Now I get why you didn't go to the police. Let's start at the beginning."

Diesel nodded, still watching Grant with concern. "Okay. Michael Rowland witnessed his stepfather's murder on March ninth, at the hand of a bald guy."

"Scott King, a.k.a. Cade Kaiser," Deacon said. "Whose birth name is Cadeyrn, by the way, which means 'king.' His father is Konrad, which also means 'king.'"

"Wow," Dani murmured. "Hubris much?"

"Much," Deacon said with a nod. "So, Diesel, you investigated Cade Kaiser."

"Not at the beginning. I started out by following the money, all the way through, because I knew Michael hadn't killed his stepfather. We were worried that the big bald guy would come after Michael because he'd seen his face, so I tried to find who else would have wanted to kill the stepfather. I checked John Brewer's finances. He was broke, had cleaned out the boys' trust funds, and had transferred the title of the house to LJM Industries."

Grant stiffened. "LJM are Laurel's initials, but I've never heard of that company."

"We're pretty sure your brother created it," Diesel said cautiously, because Grant's head had begun to wag side to side in denial.

"That's impossible," Grant said. "I do his taxes. I'd

have seen it." Then he closed his eyes again. "Unless he hid it from me, like he hid everything else."

Oh. It suddenly made sense, why Wesley Masterson had named the businesses the way he had. Leaving the clues in plain sight had been a message to his brother, in case he wasn't able to tell Grant himself.

Because Wesley wasn't sure he'd survive whatever it was that he was trying to do.

Beside him, Dani sucked in a quiet breath, glancing up at him from the corner of her eye. She'd gotten it, too. He gave her a slight nod, silently telling her to continue.

"We've been wondering why the businesses were set up the way they were, because it didn't make sense." Dani also kept her tone gentle, because Grant's skin had grayed and he was taking short, shallow breaths. "Your brother created a maze of shell companies. It starts at LJM and crisscrosses with at least eighty different companies before ending at Raguel Management Services."

"Raguel?" Grant whispered. "I don't know him, either."

Dani patted his hand. "Raguel was an angel of vengeance."

"Oh." Grant mouthed the word, his voice failing him.

"The company names describe Laurel," Dani went on. "Her time on the lacrosse team at LaGrange High, the dance club, her figure skating, the boy bands that she loved, the fact that she went to the University of Cincinnati's medical school and completed her first year. That she got an A-minus in Human Gross Anatomy."

Grant's eyes grew glassy with tears. "She was so proud of that A-minus."

Dani smiled at him sadly. "She should have been. It's a hard course. There were business names that made us believe she graduated from UC and lived at

Scioto Hall. That narrowed down her graduating class."

"Because Scioto Hall just opened recently after renovations," Scarlett said. "I got my degree from UC, too. Very nice work, Dani."

Dani gave her a quick smile of thanks before returning her attention to Grant. "There were companies called Laurels Awards & Trophies, LaGrange Lacrosse Laurels, and Laurels Lilies, Rosemary & Poppies. That gave us her first name. At first we thought they were referring to a plant or an award, but then we realized that they pointed to Laurel's name."

Grant cleared his throat. "Why lilies, rosemary, and poppies? Those weren't her favorites."

He doesn't know that she's dead. Grant may have suspected it, maybe even feared it, but he didn't know. "Rosemary and poppies are for remembrance," Diesel said quietly. "Plus there's a company called Seaheaven 42N x 82W. Those coordinates are over Lake Erie." He hesitated. "We figured that's where her ashes were scattered."

Grant recoiled as if Diesel had struck him. "She's dead? She's really dead? I thought she was still missing, but Wesley *knew*. He *knew*," he repeated furiously, then blinked, sending tears streaming down his cheeks. Closing his eyes, he drew in big gulps of air as he tried to regain his composure. Marcus passed him a box of tissues, and everyone around the table waited in patient silence as he began to process his grief and rage. Finally he opened his eyes, emotionally drained. "When did Wes establish these companies?"

"The first was in January last year," Diesel answered.

"When he discovered she was missing," Grant said bitterly. "I was so busy with my own life then that I didn't even realize something was wrong. My wife was pregnant with twins and had just been put on bed rest when I got the e-mail from Laurel saying she was spending the holidays with her new boyfriend. I didn't think anything about it. I e-mailed her back and told her to have a good time. When Wesley came out from undercover and realized she was really missing, he was so . . . angry with me. And he had a right to be. If I'd bugged them to investigate sooner . . ." He sighed wearily. "But I didn't, and I have to live with that." He rubbed his temples. "What about the other companies? When were they established?"

"All but Raguel, Rosemary & Poppies, Seaheaven 42N x 82W, and Brothers Grim were established eleven months ago," Diesel said, watching Grant for a sign that the date meant something to him.

Grant shook his head, frowning. "Eleven months ago? I don't know . . ." He cut himself off, shoulders sagging. "That's when Wes took time off for rehab. He'd had a problem for years, but when we found out that Laurel was missing, he went off the deep end. He showed up at my office last April completely wasted. Crying." He briefly clenched his eyes shut, looking like he was in pain. "I yelled at him. Told him to pull himself together. It was the fourth or fifth time he'd shown up at my office drunk, but this time was two weeks before April fifteenth and I'd been up all night with one of the twins because my wife was sick. I was so tired . . ." He shuddered. "I lost my temper. I wish I'd listened to him."

"You shouldn't blame yourself for that," Dani said softly. "I know you will, but you shouldn't. Your brother could have come back when he'd sobered up to tell you what had happened."

"Instead, he went off and . . ." He shook his head. "And the others? The poppies and Seaheaven companies?"

"They were established two months later, in June," Dani said. "We think that's when Wesley knew she was dead."

New tears streamed down his cheeks. "Oh my God. All this time. He knew and he didn't tell me. Why didn't he *tell* me?"

"Maybe because he was going for vengeance," Dani said gently. "He was protecting you. You have a family. Your wife sounds nice. You have babies. Maybe he didn't want to drag you into it. And he did tell you, just not up front."

Grant met her gaze through his tears. "The companies. I would have found out when I did his taxes."

Dani put her hand on his forearm. "We wondered why whoever set up the companies would lay it out so plainly. Anyone who took the time to unwind them would know that Laurel was gone and that someone was going for revenge. But now I can see that this was all for you, Grant. It was a code, so that you'd know what he'd done. So that you'd know where Laurel rested."

"Because he didn't think he'd come back to tell me himself." Grant was openly weeping now, his head in his hands. "Oh my God. God*damn* you, Wesley."

Diesel waited until Grant's weeping ceased and the man had dried his eyes. "I'm glad that we know why he set up the companies the way he did, but we still have questions."

"Lots of questions," Deacon added quietly. "But we can take another few minutes if you need a break."

Grant straightened his spine. "No, I'm okay. Go ahead."

Grant was not okay, Diesel thought, but he nodded anyway. "Wesley may have set all this up as bread crumbs for you to follow, but he had the company financed very well. I thought at the beginning that John Brewer had a gambling problem, and that's been confirmed. He needed a stake to continue gambling and put up his house. I figured that whoever established LJM was using the business to prove they were financially solvent enough to gamble for Brewer's house. That they had a sufficient stake to get into the game. But LJM was worth a million dollars. That was real money. Where did Wesley get it?"

Grant sighed. "I got worried on Saturday. His partner said that he'd taken vacation days, but hadn't come back. Wesley had a drinking problem before Laurel disappeared. Afterward . . . Well, he had to go to rehab. At least that's where he said he was. I don't know anything for sure now." He mopped his face and blew his nose. "Anyway, when I heard he'd gone AWOL, I went to his apartment. And opened his safe. The combination was Laurel's birthday." He glanced at Dani. "That the companies were a message to me is consistent with all the other clues he left, leading me to this." He patted the green leather book.

"What was in the safe?" Adam asked.

"Money. A lot of money. Five hundred thousand dollars."

"Holy shit," Scarlett muttered.

"That's what I said," Grant said numbly. "And . . . a brick of heroin."

More heroin, Diesel thought grimly, stealing a glance at Dani only to find she was glancing at him. He gave a minute shake of his head, hoping she understood not to mention the photo from Richard's secret database of Wesley holding the heroin. Her slight eye-roll was his answer. Of course she wouldn't tell.

Adam whistled quietly. "That'd fund LJM nicely. Where'd he get it?"

Grant shrugged. "He's Narcotics. Maybe he took it from a criminal. *Another* criminal," he corrected himself bitterly. "There were also papers—bills he'd paid to maintain an apartment here, downtown. They were in the name of Blake Emerson."

Dani sighed. "We've seen that name, but we'll get to that."

"The apartment is expensive," Grant said. "He'd had the place for six months. Right around the time he established those final three companies. He was creating a persona. A high roller."

"So you came to Cincinnati to look for him," Dani prodded.

"Yes." A wry smile lifted Grant's lips. "He left me

a key to the apartment in his home safe. I let myself right in." He touched the cassock. "I found this in the closet, along with other uniforms. And I found another safe."

"Same combo as the safe in his home in Cleveland?" Adam asked.

"Yes. This one held his detective shield, his service weapon, and his phone."

"Same combo for the phone?" Adam asked again.

"I don't know. I never had to put in a code. It recognized my face."

"You look alike," Dani commented.

"People used to think we were twins," Grant said sadly. "I checked his calendar and found two entries, both on Friday night. The first said 'LOTR Richard.' The second said 'LOTR Poker.' So I knew that the casino was important." He hesitated, then shrugged. "I also found an unregistered gun. The clip was missing four bullets. One was in the chamber. He'd used three."

Diesel looked at Dani, who was holding herself too rigidly. *Never play poker, baby,* he thought. *You'll lose every time.*

"Wesley shot Detective Stuart and the supplier— Anatoly Markov—with those bullets, didn't he?" Scarlett asked. "Who got the third bullet?"

"A guy named Clinton Stern. He was the . . . buyer. And yes, I'll tell you how I know," Diesel promised. "Let Grant finish first."

Grant exhaled heavily. "I searched the pocket of Wesley's suit and found a matchbook for the *Lady of the River*. It was a special matchbook, not like the ones they give out at the bar. It had a joker card embossed in gold on the inside cover. And the date, March eighth."

"Friday night," Diesel murmured. "It all fits. So you went to the casino yesterday to find him?"

"No. Well, I'd hoped to find him. I went to the casino on Saturday night, looking for Richard Fischer.

One of his managers told me he was the owner. I found his address and went to see him yesterday at his house." Grant looked over at Scarlett. "That's when you saw me on the surveillance video."

"Who was the woman banging on his front door?" Scarlett asked. "The security tapes were just video. No audio."

"She told me her name was Dawn Daley. D-a-l-e-y. She works at the casino, waiting tables. She went home with Richard on Friday night and they had sex. The next morning, he tossed her out and she was pissed off."

"I could see that," Scarlett said dryly. "Why was she banging on the door?"

"Oh." Grant snapped his fingers. "I forgot. She left her earrings in his bedroom. I had Wes's badge with me and . . . I might have told her I was a cop. She asked if I'd report the earrings missing and I said I would. She said they're not valuable, but they were her mother's."

Scarlett smiled. "I'll make sure she gets them back at some point."

"Thank you. She told me that she hadn't seen my sister. I didn't ask if she'd seen Wes."

"Because you *might* have used his badge and said you were a cop," Scarlett said dryly. "And then?"

"She suggested I talk to Scott King. I went back last night to see him." Grant frowned. "Hard to believe it was just last night. I was on my way in when you and Stone came out," he said to Diesel. "After the cops came, I went back to Wesley's apartment and went to sleep. This morning I saw that your house had been attacked, Dr. Novak. And that Stone had been shot and that Scott King was believed responsible. But that didn't tell me what had happened to Wes, so I kept looking."

He bit at his lip. "When we were kids, we had an old globe that had been handed down from our grandfather. Worthless, really, but it opened. Well, we opened it. At the time we were disappointed because we were sure we'd find treasure in it. I figured that if Wes really wanted me to find all this stuff, he'd hide the other important things where I could find them. The study in his apartment has a globe, so I sliced it open."

He was caressing the book, his hand no longer gloved. He realized it and yanked his hand back. "I found this book in the globe. It's got a column for names and a column for . . . things, all in Wes's handwriting. One of the names is John Brewer. His name is in here twice. The first time the thing is an address. That must be the house you mentioned."

"And the second?" Diesel asked, although he already knew.

"It says 'Joshua.' Wes made a note that he'd be wired."

Dani turned to Diesel. "Wesley *was* going in undercover."

Diesel nodded. "You were right."

Scarlett tapped the table impatiently. "How did you know? Diesel, what did you find?"

"I found calendar entries on John Brewer's computer for several of the area casinos. The most recent was *Lady of the River*, so I went there last night. Stone joined me. After I was mistaken for Scott King, I called Adam to let him know and we left. I went home and started searching for King. I couldn't find him."

"Because he's really Cade Kaiser," Scarlett said.

"Yes, but as Stone pointed out, he'd need to pass a background check to get a job in a casino. I found a security guard named Scott King in Indianapolis. He'd disappeared."

"One of Cade Kaiser's old addresses was Indianapolis," Adam said. "He lists his current address as a house in northern Kentucky, but that house is in his father's name. The earnings on the father's investments are being used to pay for his nursing care. Neighbors say they haven't seen Cade in years."

"Where's he living, then?" Diesel asked sharply. Because until they caught King, Michael wasn't safe, nor was anyone around him.

"We don't know," Deacon answered. "We were hoping you knew."

Diesel shook his head. He took Dani's hand, because she'd gone pale. "Michael is safe, Dani. He and Joshua are being guarded. They're *safe*."

"I know, but . . . Kaiser's out there somewhere." She glanced at Grant. "I'm sorry. I don't mean to be insensitive to your brother, because I know he's still missing, but Michael is a child."

"He's the boy who was accused of his stepfather's murder?" Grant asked.

"Originally," Dani said. "But he didn't do it."

"Cade Kaiser is looking for him," Grant said. "Why?"

"Because Michael can identify him." Dani swallowed. "He's my foster son."

Grant's smile was small, but sincere. "Then I understand. I have three kids of my own. I'd protect them with my life." He abruptly stilled. "My wife and kids. They're alone right now."

"I contacted Cleveland PD on the way over here," Scarlett said. "They've got someone watching your house."

Grant sagged in his chair. "Thank you."

"I didn't do it to keep them safe," Scarlett admitted. "I didn't want your wife running, since we had no idea how you were connected to all this. But I'm glad that keeping her and your kids safe is a side benefit." She speared Diesel with a hard look. "Continue, please. My baby will be in college by the time you finish."

Diesel found he could still smile. "Okay. I wanted Scott King's home address, so I . . . gained entrée to the casino's network last night, hoping the administrator would have it.'"

"'Gained entrée.'" Scarlett shook her head. "And when you found it?"

"I was going to give it to you guys. Seriously," Diesel insisted when Scarlett rolled her eyes.

"You would have given it to us while you were driving there yourself," Scarlett said.

Diesel shrugged. "That's fair. But Kaiser's address is just a PO box. However, I found that there was a database on the casino's server only Richard Fischer and Scott King had access to. It had columns for people and their stake." He pulled out his cell phone and tapped some buttons. "Just texted you, Deacon, and Adam the photos I took of my screen. I didn't download anything. I have screenshots on my laptop, so I can send you clearer copies later. You'll see that on Friday, March first, John Brewer's stake was his house. The following Friday, a few hours before Michael saw him murdered, his stake was 'five-year-old boy.'"

Three phones dinged with the receipt of his text. Scarlett, Deacon, and Adam put their heads together, studying the contents. Marcus leaned in to Scarlett to see her screen. They looked at each other, then back at Diesel.

"Joshua," Scarlett murmured, her jaw tight. "He put Joshua up as his stake."

"Probably to get the house back," Diesel said flatly. Even knowing that Brewer was dead, he still felt the slow burn of rage at what might have happened.

"Brewer drugged Joshua that night," Dani said. "Michael saw him carrying Joshua from the house and he and Brewer fought. Michael hit him with the fireplace shovel, grabbed Joshua, and ran. He hid in some trees and that's when he saw Cade Kaiser pull into the driveway. Kaiser got out, grabbed Brewer from his car. Brewer tried to pull a gun and Kaiser killed him. Kaiser drove away with Brewer in the back of his SUV, but came back later to check on Joshua."

Grant held up his hands. "Wait. You're saying that Cade Kaiser killed John Brewer to *protect* Joshua?"

"Best we can figure," Diesel said.

Grant closed his eyes. "Did you find my brother's body in the river?"

Diesel watched Deacon and Adam share a glance. "Did he have a tattoo or any markings?" Adam asked.

"A tattoo on his right shoulder." Grant opened his eyes and pointed at the purple flowers that decorated the green leather book. "Like this—a Texas mountain laurel." His shoulders sagged, defeated. "You found him?"

Adam nodded. "Yes."

"I'm sorry," Deacon added.

Grant swallowed hard, then laughed almost hysterically. "It's ironic. My brother wanted to expose a pedophile, so he posed as one. Cade Kaiser believed he was one so he killed him."

It *was* damn ironic, Diesel thought sadly.

"Ironic," Deacon agreed, "but also what happens when people take the law into their own hands." He shot a sharp look of warning at Diesel before turning back to Grant. "If your brother had gone through channels, we would have protected him."

Adam and Scarlett were nodding earnestly. Marcus stared up at the ceiling, but Diesel still caught the roll of his eyes. They both knew that law enforcement's hands were often tied by the very law they enforced. Sometimes channels were too dirty to navigate.

"Except Wesley tried that," Diesel reminded them mildly, "but Detective Stuart was corrupt and, for reasons we might not ever know, didn't do his duty."

Deacon shook his head. "That might be true, but we won't know Stuart's reasons, because he's dead. So is Wesley Masterson. It's a risk of vigilantism."

Dani cleared her throat, her gaze moving pointedly to Grant's stricken expression. "I think we can all agree that Wesley paid a high price for taking the law into his own hands. Maybe you can have this conversation another time?"

Deacon looked at Grant and winced at the pain on the man's face. "I'm sorry, Grant. That was insensitive of me."

But Diesel knew that Deacon's comments had really been aimed at Marcus and himself, because he cared about their safety. "Point taken," Diesel murmured. He gestured to their phones. "Does the list I sent you help?"

"Absolutely," Deacon said with a wry smile. "We know where to start looking."

"And," Adam added, "it matches up. We've identified two more of the . . . recent bodies. They're both on this list. One offered his underage niece. The other had admitted liking underage girls."

"Why did Cade Kaiser kill Richard Fischer *when* he did?" Dani asked. "This poker game has been going on for a while."

"Maybe Joshua was the first time Cade knew that people were being trafficked," Diesel suggested.

"Is . . ." Grant faltered, then cleared his throat. "Is Laurel on that list?"

"She is," Diesel said gently. "But Kaiser didn't start working at the casino until a few months after Laurel went missing. He had nothing to do with her disappearance."

"You mentioned a Clinton Stern as the . . ." Grant swallowed. "The buyer. He's on the list?"

"He is," Diesel confirmed. "He's also dead, killed in a home invasion."

"Wesley," Grant murmured. "I can't say I'm sorry he did it."

"Neither can I," Dani told him in a whisper.

Scarlett tapped the table to get their attention. "I agree that Kaiser didn't kill Laurel. But you do assume that he killed Richard?"

"Well, yeah," Dani said. "Don't you?"

"Yeah," Scarlett admitted. "Unfortunately, we don't have Kaiser on the security vids from Richard's house. The alarm system was turned off from eight twenty a.m. on Saturday through one p.m." She glanced at Grant. "You're not a suspect. We traced your credit cards, and you were getting gas in Cleveland when the alarm system was reactivated."

"If Kaiser was Richard's security manager at the riverboat, he may have had access to his home security as well," Diesel said. "He'd probably know how to deactivate Richard's alarm." He rubbed his forehead. He was so tired. "That's all I know except that I'm starving and my head is pounding like hell."

"I'll take you back to the safe house," Adam said.

"We'd like to search your brother's apartment," Deacon told Grant. "We'll also need to take your prints so we can eliminate them." He pulled on a pair of gloves and slipped the green leather book into an evidence bag. "Thank you. I'm so sorry about your sister and your brother. But we appreciate the light you've shed. Will you be returning to Cleveland?"

"Soon," Grant murmured. "When will you release my brother's body?"

"As soon as the ME is finished with her exam," Deacon promised. "I'll ask her to conduct Wesley's autopsy next."

Diesel stood, feeling shaky from hunger and stress. He put his arm around Dani's waist, relieved when she leaned into him.

"There is one more thing," Marcus said as he helped Scarlett to her feet. "How did Wesley find out that Laurel was dead or even where to start looking?"

Everyone went still and looked at Grant.

Grant shrugged. "I don't know. I was hoping you did."

Diesel studied the man's face. Grant knew something more that he wasn't saying, but he'd shut down. The man was done. At least for the moment. But then he'd just learned that his brother and sister were dead. A man was allowed to shut down for a little while after getting news like that.

Grant dug a single key from his pants pocket. "This is the key to Wes's apartment. I'll sign whatever I need to so that you have permission to search. But if I don't have to be there, I don't want to be."

"You don't have to be," Deacon said. "But we would like the opportunity to talk to you again before you go back to Cleveland—just in case we have more questions after searching your brother's things."

Grant's lips curved bitterly. "So in other words, don't leave town. I won't."

Cincinnati, Ohio
Monday, March 18, 10:40 p.m.

"Here." Cade shoved a thermos full of warm water through the bars of the old pedo's basement cell. "You can mix it with the formula."

He'd gone to the store and paid a loitering teenager a few bucks to buy him some more antibiotic cream, some rubbing alcohol, more painkillers, Epsom salts, a few cans of baby formula, and a bag of diapers. The teenager had been so happy to get a twenty for his troubles—in advance—that he hadn't given Cade a second look.

But he'd lingered in the store just a little too long, and when he'd come out, Cade had already second-guessed his own decision to keep the kid alive. He hadn't been thorough with Stone O'Bannion—who according to the news hadn't been a detective after all, the bastard—and look where it had gotten him.

Here, a virtual prisoner in the old pedo's house, with an infected leg and a fever that had climbed over a hundred and one. Cade wasn't a doctor, but he sure as hell knew that a fever was bad. And that the greenish pus oozing out of the wounds on his leg was likely to blame.

So he'd dragged the kid to the back of the store

and put a bullet in the back of his head, listening with his stethoscope to make sure he was actually dead.

"Thank you," Evelyn said quietly, taking the thermos. "Jimmy's hungry."

Cade scowled. "I know. I could hear him screaming all the way upstairs. Lucky for me, my nearest neighbor is a mile away."

She looked down at the thermos. "What are you going to do with us?"

It was a valid question and asked respectfully, so he answered it. "I'm going to use you to get out of here once my leg is healed. You're going to tell the press that I'm not a bad person. That I was good to you and Junior and performed a vital service to the community." He looked around the basement. "This house? It belonged to an old pedo who'd drugged a kid and had him tied up in the back of his Toyota Sequoia."

"The same SUV that you blew up with a hand grenade?" Evelyn asked, but it still wasn't a disrespectful question, so he shrugged.

"Seemed like a good idea at the time, but like all my plans for yesterday, it bombed abominably." He chuckled at his pun, but Evelyn wasn't smiling. "That wasn't supposed to happen. I wasn't supposed to need your help, but I do. The way I see it, you can cooperate and you and Junior live, or you can play the judgmental hero and watch your kid die of starvation, because nobody knows you're here."

She nodded once. "I have been cooperating."

"Yes, you have. Which is why I got the damn baby formula. Which you should give to your kid before he bursts a blood vessel crying."

She pulled an empty bottle from her diaper bag—which Cade had thoroughly searched—and scooped formula from the can, adding water from the thermos. "So this house belonged to a pedo?" she asked, shaking it hard.

"Yeah. I left the kid he'd snatched in the park for

the cops to find, fed the pedo to the fishes, then came here. You know what I found?"

She swallowed. "No."

"A body. A teenager. He was dead." Cade pointed to the airtight room next to the cell. "In there. Suffocated. I also left his body where the cops could find him. Gave his parents closure and saved the kids in this city from a pedophile. Does that seem like something a bad guy would do?"

She shook her head. "That was decent of you."

"That's what I'm sayin'. So when it comes time for me to run, I expect you to remember that I'm decent. I don't hurt kids."

Unless they'd been an eyewitness to murder, but that was different. That was self-preservation. It would have allowed him to continue serving the community by eliminating pedos and abusive bastards. But Michael had given the cops his description.

The kid had ruined everything.

And now I'm on the run for real. His face and real name on the news. *Shit.*

"What about him?" she asked, pointing to Andrew McNab, the interpreter.

The guy I shouldn't have let live. The guy Cade had drugged so that he and Evelyn couldn't cook up an escape plan. "Depends. Has he woken up yet?"

"No," she said, casting a worried look at the man who still lay as Cade had left him. "I thought he was once, but he kind of moaned and fell back asleep. He's been beaten badly." Her words were stiff and awkward, as if she feared making Cade angry by accusing him of doing the beating. *Good. She should be afraid.* "He could die."

"Then he does. He's not your concern," Cade said, and meant it. "You worry about you and Junior. If the man dies, I'll drag him out of there." He turned on his heel and grunted loudly when his knee buckled. He grabbed on to the cell bars to hold himself upright. *Dammit, that hurt.*

"I think you're going to need something stronger for your leg," Evelyn said softly. "Maybe an antibiotic injection."

"I know," he snapped, happy when she recoiled. They weren't friends. She was his ticket out. Nothing more. "But unless you're a doctor, you can't help me."

He blinked. No . . . she wasn't a doctor. But Dani Novak was, and she ran a free clinic. Places like that stocked medicines. Antibiotics and maybe even pain-killers. And it wasn't a twenty-four-hour operation. They had to close sometime. When the staff left for the night, he'd slip in, get a few handfuls of meds, and get out.

That was a good plan. If he was still running a fever by tomorrow, he'd clean out Dani Novak's pharmacy.

Chapter Twenty-Five

"That was good!" Joshua exclaimed as the credits for *The Incredibles* rolled up the theater room's TV screen, larger than the entire living room wall in Dani's house. She'd held Joshua on her lap, her head on Diesel's shoulder while they watched the movie, Michael sitting on the floor between their feet. Like a family.

We could be a family. It was still a heady thought and she fought not to get her hopes up. But why not? The boys had no one else. She could keep them. Care for them. Make them happy. *We could make them happy.*

She and the man at her side, who'd been lightly snoring for the last half hour.

"I'm glad you liked it," Dani said, laughing when Joshua bounced on her lap. The little boy had been stuck to either her or Diesel like glue ever since they'd returned from the meeting at the *Ledger* office.

Michael had been quieter, reading a book while they watched the movie. He'd joined them physically in the theater room, but it was clear his mind was elsewhere. The only one he paid attention to was

Hawkeye, who had only left his side when he'd been taken for walks outside by one of the agents on duty.

Michael's fingers had raked through Hawkeye's soft fur almost constantly, stopping only to turn the pages of his book. Which didn't happen often, as Michael stared at the pages unseeingly.

He'd had a therapy session with Meredith while they'd been gone and Dani figured that was the root of his preoccupation. The boy had lost his mother. Had suffered so much before that. She could remember the pain of losing her own mom. The grief that had clutched her insides, clawing until she'd wanted to die, too.

Michael's mother had been abusive to him, but kids still loved their parents, even through abuse. It didn't make sense, but it was true nonetheless.

For now they'd give him space and let him grieve. But not too much space. She leaned over and ran her hand over his hair, smiling when he looked up at her in question. "It's late," she signed. "I'm going to put Joshua to bed. You should be going to bed, too."

Eventually she'd get these children on a proper schedule. But these were not normal days, so she cut them all a little slack.

Michael shook his head. "I'm not tired," he signed back with one hand, choosing to put the book down rather than give up his hold on Hawkeye.

"You can read in bed. Meredith brought your lamp from your room at home and put it on your nightstand." So he'd have a night-light, but she didn't add that part. It was enough that Michael knew what she meant.

His eyes flashed gratitude and a little shame before he gathered his book and stood up. He put the book under one arm. "When this is over, *I'll* walk Hawkeye at night." His chin lifted a little with the declaration, as if daring her to disagree.

"I'd appreciate it," Dani said evenly. "He needs more walking than I have time to do. More groom-

ing, too. He loves to be brushed. I'll have to ask
Merry or one of the others to bring a dog brush the
next time they visit."

"And bathed?" Michael asked. "I can bathe
him, too."

Dani had to force herself to smile, because Evelyn
Keys was still missing. *Not your fault.* And she knew
that was true. But it was still hard not to feel responsible. The woman might be dead simply because she
lived in Dani's neighborhood.

And Michael might have been dead had Kaiser
been successful, simply because he'd been protecting
Joshua and was in the wrong place at the wrong time
and had witnessed Brewer's murder.

She hoped Kaiser wasn't hurting Evelyn and Jimmy.
Part of her brain had been shouting all through the
movie that she should be *doing* something, trying to
find them. But she *had* been doing something. She'd
been doing her job, taking care of two scared boys
who'd just lost everything they'd ever known.

"Hawk doesn't like baths that much, but he's good
in the tub," she told Michael. "He just looks so sad
when he's all wet, like you stole his best bone."

Michael laughed out loud, and Diesel made a disgruntled sound, abruptly sitting up straighter. "I think
I fell asleep during the last part of the movie."

"You snored," Joshua informed him. "But it's okay.
Dani put the captions on."

"You can read the captions?" Diesel asked him,
covering a yawn with his hand.

Joshua nodded seriously. "Some of the words."

Michael ruffled his hair. "He's smart," he said,
making the little boy beam proudly. "He can read a
lot of words."

Diesel stood up, all broad chest and hard muscles,
and Dani felt a shiver of anticipation. They'd put off
gratification earlier that day, saving it for when the
boys were asleep.

She hoped that the boys fell asleep quickly. "Time for bed, Joshua," she said.

Joshua slid off her lap and turned to Diesel. "I picked a different story for tonight. It's a chapter book about a little boy who's really a mouse."

"*Stuart Little*," Diesel said knowingly. "I saw it next to your bed earlier. But just one chapter, okay?" He lifted Joshua into his arms, parking him on his hip, then threw a wink at Dani. "They're really short chapters," he mouthed.

Dani bit back a grin. "'Night, Joshua." She turned to Michael, who was watching Diesel with an unreadable expression. She touched his arm. "Michael?"

He jerked, then relaxed. "Sorry. I was thinking."

"About?"

Michael bit his lip. "Nothing."

Dani tilted her head, studying him. "You don't have to tell me, but know that you can, okay?"

He nodded, continuing to bite his lip and then his hands were moving fast and intensely. "Coach said that you started the paperwork to keep us."

Dani nodded. "He's right. Is that okay?"

Michael let out a shaky breath. "Yeah. I know I wasn't supposed to get Joshua's hopes up, but he started crying when you and Coach left. I told him that you were trying to make it so we could live with you permanently. I'm sorry, but I didn't know what else to say to make him stop crying. He was afraid we'd get separated."

Dani understood Michael's need to soothe his brother, but if it didn't work out, the little boy would be crushed. Then her spine straightened. *If it doesn't work out, I'll be crushed. So I'm going to make it work out.* She gave Michael an encouraging smile. "It was okay to tell him. I don't want him to be afraid, ever."

"But what if the state says no? What if they make us leave?"

There was something more to Michael's fear,

something she was missing. "Why are you afraid it won't work out?"

His eyes darted around, looking everywhere but at her. "I saw the medication in the bathroom. Your medication. I'm sorry. I wasn't snooping, honest."

Ah. "You saw my antiretroviral drugs." She was impressed that he'd known what they were for. Michael was going to keep her on her toes. "I'm HIV positive, but my viral loads are undetectable. Do you know what that means?"

"It means you can't give it to anyone. I wasn't afraid of that." He swallowed hard. "I . . . I asked Greg about it. On Skype. Agent Troy said it was okay. He let me use his laptop and I didn't touch anything on it, I swear."

"It's okay, Michael. I'm not upset and I'm sure Agent Troy knew you'd be respectful with his computer. I'm glad you asked Greg."

"Greg said you'd say that. He told me about transmission and stuff. I was freaked out," he admitted. "A little."

"Understandable. I was freaked out, too, at the beginning."

"He said your boyfriend gave it to you."

Dani nodded again. "That's true."

He frowned, his cheeks growing red. "Coach knows? Greg said he did."

Dani smiled. "He knows. He's okay with it." More than okay, which still blew her mind.

Michael crossed his arms over his chest, then released the hold he had on himself to sign. "What if the state finds out? They won't let you keep us."

"Oh," she breathed. "Oh, honey, they already know. I had to submit my health records to be approved for emergency foster care. They're not allowed to discriminate against me for my positive status any more than they can discriminate against you and Greg because you're deaf. That's the law."

His shoulders relaxed. "That's what Greg said."

Her lips twitched. "Greg's pretty smart."

"He thinks you're a hero," Michael signed shyly.

Dani's eyes stung. "He said that?"

"Yeah. He said that Joshua and I are lucky to be living with you." He looked at his feet, his next signs kind of a mush. "I agreed."

Dani cupped his face, happy when he leaned into her. This boy was seriously touch-deprived. *Just like Diesel.* "I think we're all lucky we found one another. Was that the only thing bothering you?"

He swallowed hard. "Mostly. A few other things."

"Tell me if you want to, but you don't have to. I'm glad you talked to Meredith, though. That will help you."

"She's nice. She brought an interpreter and I didn't even have to ask."

Thankfully, the interpreter had agreed to be blind-folded on the drive over, the only way Deacon would approve her admittance to the safe house. "Meredith knows the law. I know the law, too. From here on out, you have an advocate in your corner, Michael. I won't let anyone deprive you of your rights."

His lips trembled and he firmed them. "Thank you. That other agent—Agent Taylor—he brought us presents. Why?"

"He's a nice man. My friends are all nice people. You'll see that."

Hope flickered in his eyes. "I wrote a thank-you note. With a pen."

Dani chuckled. "Going old-school?"

He rolled his eyes. "Agent Troy said he'd give it to Agent Taylor."

"Then he will." She patted his face sweetly. "Go to bed, Michael. We'll talk more in the morning. I have to get my sleep. It helps keep my levels undetectable."

Michael nodded hard, mention of her health spurring him into motion. "I will. Thanks, Dani." But he stopped, hesitating once more.

"Go ahead and ask," she said with a smile. "What's on your mind?"

"Joshua asked if you'd let him call you 'Mom' someday. I didn't know what to tell him. So I told him I'd ask you."

Dani's breath left her in a whoosh. *Oh wow.* She hadn't expected this. Hadn't dared to.

"It's okay," Michael said, misunderstanding her lack of response. "I'll tell him that he should call you by your name."

She held up her hands. "No, it's good. It's just . . . it makes me really happy to think about that. About him wanting to call me that. Tell him . . . yes. When he's ready. No rush."

Michael's smile was shy. "Thanks. Good night."

She watched him go into his room and shut the door, too overwhelmed to move, even when Diesel left Joshua's room and approached her.

"Hey," he said softly, stroking her hair. "What's wrong?"

"Nothing." She smiled up at him. "Well, other than the fact that Michael will probably move to the floor next to Joshua's bed as soon as we go to sleep." She sighed. "And that Cade Kaiser is still out there, trying to hurt our boys."

He wrapped his arms around her, and for that moment she felt so safe. So . . . wanted. *Happy,* she realized. *I'm happy.*

He kissed her forehead. "It won't hurt Michael to sleep on the floor for a while. He'll return to his bed when he's ready. And if it goes on too long, we'll ask Meredith what to do. As for Kaiser, we'll worry about him in the morning. Come on. Let's go to bed." He nuzzled the side of her neck, making her shiver. "I've been waiting all day to get you alone."

"Me, too." She turned her head, her lips finding his. It started out sweet, but he took control, growling against her mouth. "I love that sound," she confessed.

"Come with me, and I'll make it again."

She laughed. "I hope to." She lifted a brow. "To come with you."

"You're very bad, Dr. Novak. I love it." He tugged on her hand, threading their fingers together as he led her to the bedroom. It was sweet. Chaste, even.

Which was really nice, she thought, but not what she wanted at the moment. She waited until they were in their room before opening her mouth to say exactly that, but all she could do was moan, because Diesel had her back against the bedroom door and his hand down her pants before she could blink.

He took her mouth in a bruising kiss that was everything she'd wanted and his fingers . . . "Oh my God," she moaned, but it was muffled because he wouldn't stop kissing her. Her hips bucked, trying to get his fingertips where she needed them.

He lifted his head, breathing hard, his dark eyes nearly black and glittering with undisguised hunger. Dani let her head fall back against the door, closed her eyes, and let herself feel.

"More," she whispered. "God, Diesel." She worked her hands between their bodies and jerked at the snap on her pants, kicking off her shoes as she lowered her zipper. Then her pants and panties were gone, the cool air of the bedroom feeling so good against her heated skin.

Her sweater was yanked over her head and she had a second of clarity to act before her bra met the same fate as the one she'd been wearing the night before. She brushed his hands away when he grabbed at the front clasp, and released it herself. "I don't have another one with me," she murmured on a hushed chuckle, "so you can't rip this one."

His laugh was breathless. "Fair enough. There's something else I want." Then he dropped to his knees, not giving her even a moment to prepare before his face was between her legs and his tongue . . .

She'd thought his fingers were talented, but his tongue . . .

She covered her mouth with her hand to quiet the whimpers that she couldn't seem to control. She'd thought she'd be embarrassed, but she couldn't take her eyes off him. She couldn't stop looking at what he was doing to her.

He looked up, his eyes wicked, his lips shiny and wet. "Do you like that?" he asked hoarsely.

She opened her mouth to speak, but no words came out. Just another whimper. That seemed to be good enough for him because he draped her legs over his shoulders and stabbed his tongue in deeper.

"Diesel," she choked out, more loudly than she'd intended. She clamped her lips together, suddenly conscious of the guards standing on both sides of the front door. And Joshua across the hall. Michael wouldn't hear them, but the others might.

Diesel pulled back far enough to frown. "What?" he demanded. "You went quiet. I want to hear every sound I pull out of you. They're mine, all the sounds."

She shivered again, her hips grinding against his face of their own accord. "People. Outside."

He looked like he was going to tell her to ignore them, but he gently pushed her legs off his shoulders and stood up, surprising her.

"I didn't mean for you to stop," she hissed.

He laughed. "Just a small break," he promised, then picked her up, his hands on her ass. She wrapped her arms around his neck and her legs around his waist.

Then she froze. "Diesel, wait." He'd been licking into her. Unprotected. "Dental dam. We need one. I don't have any with me."

He shook his head, carrying her into the bathroom. "No." Not letting her go, he supported her weight with one hand, turning on the water in the shower with the other. He then gently removed her processor from behind her ear and laid it on the sink, all while he held her so steadily that she could have performed surgery. His strength was hotter than hell, but she wasn't going to be distracted.

"We can't do oral without protection."

He met her gaze, his piercing. "I'll do condoms,

even though those aren't really necessary, either, but no dental dams. I don't want anything between my mouth and your—"

"Diesel," she hissed.

He merely raised a brow, unbothered. "Are you undetectable?"

"Yes, but—"

"Is the CDC a reputable organization?" he interrupted.

The Centers for Disease Control? "Yes, of course, but—"

He kissed her quiet, and she tasted herself on his mouth. It was all she could do not to moan. "The CDC says 'Undetectable equals Untransmittable,'" he said. "They have it on their website. 'U equals U.' There are posters for the doctors' offices. You have one on the wall in your very own clinic."

"I know, but—"

He kissed her again. "Are you a good doctor?"

"Yes, but—"

Another kiss. "Would you post medical advice in your clinic that wasn't true?"

"No."

He grinned. "No buts?"

"No. You'll just kiss me again. Which, y'know, is fine, but—"

He kissed her again, but he smiled through it. "Dani, I'm taking Truvada. You're taking your antiretroviral meds. You get your levels tested how often?"

"Every month."

"How often is the recommended frequency?"

She let out a breath, knowing he already knew the answer. "For positive patients with undetectable viral loads who are taking their medications, every three to four months. I go more often because I'm a medical professional."

He smiled down at her. "So you're covered. *We're* covered. We can use condoms because you don't want to get pregnant and I'm okay with that, but I do not want to use dental dams. I will if your viral loads become detectable, but if that never happens, why should we?"

She stared at him desperately. "If I made you sick, I'd never forgive myself."

"If *we* made me *positive*, *we'd* share the responsibility equally. But we're not going to make me positive. Honey, listen to yourself. You're boxing with shadows. A lot of energy for no payout. I don't know about you, but I'd prefer to expend my energy on more . . . pleasurable pursuits."

She closed her eyes. He was right. She knew he was right. If she were her own patient, she'd be telling herself the exact same thing. She wasn't sure why she was fighting so hard. "You deserve so many pleasurable pursuits." Far more than she could give him.

He kissed her closed eyelids so gently. "Dani? Honey, look at me."

She forced herself to open her eyes. And her breath caught in her throat at the sheer adoration she saw there.

He leaned his forehead against hers, his hands cradling her ass like she didn't weigh anything. "*You* deserve to have pleasurable sex, too," he whispered. "And if that voice in your head is telling you otherwise, you should tell it to fuck off."

She laughed, but it sounded like a sob. Because he was right. That was why she was fighting herself so hard. She could hear the voice now and it sounded so much like her uncle. *If you'd kept your legs together, you wouldn't be diseased. You're trash. A slut. What kind of example are you? What kind of doctor are you?*

A damn good doctor, she answered the voice, and she *knew* that to be true. *I am a damn good doctor.*

Diesel was right, and that voice in her head was wrong.

"I'm so glad you didn't give up on me," she said quietly.

"I couldn't." He kissed her mouth, then trailed his lips along her jaw to whisper in her good ear. "I tried, but I couldn't. Now, I'm planning to get into the shower with you. I'm going to go down on you and I want to hear every little sound, okay? I want to hear you scream my name. And with the water going, nobody else will hear you. Just me. Can I do that?"

She nodded, a new shiver rippling over her skin. "Yes. Except . . ."

He lifted his head to look at her, his exasperation beginning to show. "Except?"

"You're still wearing all your clothes."

He chuckled. "Then take them off me."

So she did, wiggling out of his hold and unwrapping his body like it was a Christmas present. "You are a sight, Mr. Kennedy," she murmured when she had him naked, raking her gaze over each inch of exposed skin, over every curve of his ink. "I could look at you all night long."

"Maybe another night," he said and took her into the shower. And made her scream his name. And then he took her to bed and did it again.

When he finally came, his expression was the most beautiful thing she'd ever seen in her life.

And when he fell asleep, holding her tight in his arms, she knew there wasn't anywhere else on the planet that she'd rather be.

Cincinnati, Ohio
Monday, March 18, 11:55 p.m.

Grant trudged into the hotel room and sank onto the edge of the bed, lowering his head to his hands. He was so damn tired.

And empty. And angry. *So damn angry.*

Angry with Wesley for taking all of this onto his own shoulders. Angry with him for stealing heroin and selling it for money to finance this . . . cover of his. Angry with him for getting himself killed.

Angry with Cade Kaiser for being judge, jury, and executioner.

Angry with the Cincinnati detective who'd covered up Laurel's disappearance because he'd been on the take. And with her roommate for the same.

He was just so damn angry.

He sighed, exhausted by the weight of it all. Before he knew it, he had his cell in his hand and was dialing his wife. "Hey," he said.

Cora shuddered out a relieved breath and he realized he hadn't spoken with her since she'd called that afternoon to tell him that Dani Novak had made contact. "Hey, yourself," she said, her voice rough, the way it got when she was crying and didn't want anyone to know.

"I worried you," he said. "I'm so sorry."

"It's okay. I'm fine. Are you?"

Was he fine? "No," he whispered. "I don't think I am. I'm safe," he added before she could freak. "But I'm not fine."

"Where are you?" she asked gently.

"In a hotel. The cops closed off Wes's apartment. Looking for evidence."

"Of . . . ?" Cora asked warily.

Grant huffed bitterly. "Well, Wes is dead. And so is Laurel." He told her everything, and when he was finished, he was even more tired than before.

"Oh, baby," Cora murmured. "I'm so sorry. I'm sorry that Wes is dead, but he left you to deal with all of this and that wasn't fair. When are you coming home?"

She didn't ask it in a nagging kind of way, but more like the "Come home and I'll hug you" kind of way that always made him feel warm. He missed her. Missed the kids. Missed the normalcy of it all. He hated Wes's crazy life.

"Not yet. I'm at the Westin in Cincinnati. I have to make arrangements for . . ." He exhaled. "For Wes's body. The detectives gave me the name of a local

mortuary service." A sob was building and he tried
to shove it down. "The detectives were all nice."

Nicer than they should have been, considering he'd
withheld evidence from them. Hadn't immediately
reported the brick of heroin in Wes's safe or the piles
of cash. "I met Dr. Novak," he said. "She was lovely."

"What did she have that connected to Laurel?"

Grant shook his head in disbelief. "A house. But it
isn't really Laurel's. Wes won it in a very illegal poker
game."

"Who *does* the house belong to, then?"

"Legally? I don't know. Maybe me. But we don't
need a house. We have one."

"We have a lovely house that'll just get lovelier
when you're back in it."

The tightness in Grant's chest eased a fraction.
"The house really belongs to two boys, Michael and
Joshua Rowland, sons of a couple who were murdered
by the same man who killed Wes. If it is legally mine,
I'll sell it and put the money in trust for them. If it's
not, Dani will figure it out. She's their foster parent."

"I think that sounds like a very good plan. Those
kids are going to need all the support they can get."

"Thank you," he whispered.

"For what?"

"For being so honest and generous. Some wives
might have wanted to keep the house or the money
from its sale. I'm so glad I married you."

She sniffled. "Come home, honey. We love you
and miss you."

"I will, as soon as I can. Love you, too. Kiss the
kids."

He ended the call and toed off his shoes.

The detectives really had been nice. He wondered
if they would be tomorrow, once they realized what
he *hadn't* given them.

Wearily, he dug into his pocket for Wes's cell phone
and placed it on the nightstand. He wasn't sure why
he'd kept it, other than it was the one thing he had left

that was truly his brother's. Wes had made Laurel's graduation photo his wallpaper, and the only other photos he'd kept were of Grant's kids.

He'd loved them. Wes had truly loved them.

Dani Novak was right. Wes had wanted to spare them the pain—and possible incarceration—associated with his mission of vengeance.

Raguel, the angel of vengeance. Wesley had assumed the role knowing he might not survive it, so he'd left the trail of bread crumbs.

Numbly, Grant held up the phone, breathing a small sigh of relief when it recognized his face. He hadn't been sure if it would work again. Grant had looked in the mirror and thought that he'd aged twenty years since yesterday, so surely the phone would detect it.

But it hadn't. He was now staring at Wesley's wallpaper again, Wesley and Laurel smiling for the camera.

How *had* Wesley known that Laurel was dead? How *had* he known where to start looking? How had he found Richard Fischer and the *Lady of the River*?

The answers were somewhere, of that Grant was certain. Wes had left him a trail to follow, every step of the way. And as he blinked away tears, bringing the photo of Wes and Laurel back into focus, he knew where to find the answers.

He swiped the phone's screen, bypassing the normal apps. Wes never bothered with Facebook or Twitter or any other social media. He didn't play games.

He had, however, kept safes with the information he wanted Grant to find. And there, on the last page of his phone screen, was a vault app, meant to hide important, personal things from prying eyes.

Grant tapped the app's icon and a second later, a password screen popped up. He put in Laurel's birthday, just like he had for the other safes. And it opened—to a journaling app. Heart heavy, he tapped it.

The first entry read: *Nita Rubio.* There was a phone number with an area code that Grant didn't recognize. He swiped to the next page, finding it blank. As were the next and the next. The name and phone number were the only entry.

Hands trembling, Grant searched the area code and found it served Seattle. It was still early there, just after nine. So, using his own phone, he dialed the number.

"Hello," a soft female voice answered. It wasn't a question, like one would normally answer the phone. It was a statement. Almost as if his call had been expected.

"My name is Grant Masterson."

"I know. I've been waiting for you to call. Is . . . is Wesley all right?"

The sob he'd been holding back barreled out. "No. He's dead."

The woman sighed. "I was afraid of that. My name is Nita Rubio. Or it was. Your brother helped me get a new identity, a new life."

Through his tears, Grant managed to speak. "You knew my sister?"

A long, long moment of silence. "I was with Laurel when she died. We were taken at different times, but sold to the same man, Clinton Stern. I was able to steal one of his burner phones one day and made the call to Wesley. Laurel said he'd help us. But we didn't know where we were. Wesley tried to find us, but he couldn't. A few weeks passed and Laurel saw an opportunity to take a letter addressed to Stern, but he caught her and . . ." Her swallow was audible. "Beat her. Badly."

"No," Grant whispered.

"I'm so sorry," she said mournfully. "Stern was so angry that he nearly killed me, too. He had to leave the house, and he was so upset that, for the first time, he didn't lock the door. I got Laurel out. Half carried, half dragged her to one of his cars and I drove her to a clinic. I didn't give our names. I didn't want Stern to find us. I did call Wesley and he came right away. But he was too late for Laurel."

Grant swiped at his eyes, trying to see through his tears. "But not for you."

"I'm sorry," she said again, this time very timidly, like she feared his anger.

"I'm not sorry that he saved you," Grant said quickly. "You're okay now?"

"Yes. I have a good job and a good life. But Stern had powerful friends, so I'm no longer Nita Rubio."

"And you're not going to tell me your new name. I get it." Grant truly did. He'd do the same in her position. "Stern is dead."

"I know. Wesley told me that he'd killed him."

"So is the man who took Laurel, Anatoly Markov." He spat the name out.

"I know. And so is the man who took me. Wesley told me that, too."

Grant sucked in a breath, remembering the third bullet. "Bert Stuart, the detective?"

"Yes. He didn't go by that name, though. He had a street persona, kinda like Blake Emerson was for Wesley. I think I was the only one he took and sold. He said he needed the money. It always comes down to money."

"It does. How did Wes find out about Richard Fischer and his riverboat?"

"The *Lady of the River*?" she asked bitterly. "I told him. Laurel was never taken aboard the riverboat, but I was. I remembered everything I could, but it wasn't enough."

Ultimately, it *had* been enough, because Fischer's operation had been stopped. But not in time for Nita or Laurel or any of Richard Fischer's other victims. "This phone number. Is it yours?"

"Not after this call. I'm throwing the phone away." She sighed quietly. "Go back to your wife and kids,

Grant. Have a good life. That's what Wesley wanted for you."

The call ended and Grant stared at the phone for a long, long time. Then he put it on the nightstand and fell into bed, still wearing his clothes.

He went to sleep with the light on.

Chapter Twenty-Six

Diesel came awake with a jerk, his eyes flying open. He'd heard a noise. A mewling sound.

No, a sobbing sound. Someone was crying. He glanced at the woman in his arms, relieved to find she was still asleep. She needed her rest. All the literature he'd read said that rest and nutrition would keep her healthy. Would help her keep her levels undetectable, which was Diesel's highest priority.

Keep her healthy. Keep her happy. Keep her screaming his name when he made her come. Like he'd done twice tonight. And yes, he was damn proud of himself, thank you.

He slipped out from under her body, covering her with the blanket when she curled up into the warm spot he'd left behind. He pulled on a pair of sweats and a T-shirt, then crept from the bedroom, closing the door as quietly as he could.

And stopped short, because Agent Troy was standing on the other side of his door, his fist raised to knock.

"Sorry," Troy said softly. "It's Michael. He's crying."

Diesel wasn't surprised. The kid had put on a brave face—a hardened face—most of yesterday. "I heard. I'll take care of it. Thanks, man."

"I'll make sure you guys aren't disturbed. You should have privacy." Troy looked over his shoulder, his eyes sad. "The kid's breaking my heart, Diesel."

"I know. Mine, too."

Troy returned to the chair he'd placed by the front door and Diesel went in search of Michael. He wasn't in his room, so Diesel went to Joshua's room. Where, of course, Michael lay on the floor, face buried in a pillow.

Diesel stepped hard onto the floor, to warn the boy that he was coming. Michael stilled, then seemed to sag, but he wouldn't show his face.

Diesel crouched and put his hand on Michael's shoulder, giving it a squeeze, then a light tap. Michael shook his head, so Diesel repeated the squeeze-tap. Michael turned enough that one eye was revealed. One very red and swollen eye.

"You're going to wake Joshua," Diesel signed without voicing. "If he sees you crying, he's going to worry. Come on. I'll make us some tea. We can sit in the kitchen."

Michael rolled to his feet, expression sullen. "I don't want to talk," he signed.

"That's okay. You don't have to talk. You don't even have to drink the tea." Diesel left the room, aware that Michael was following. He pointed to a chair in the kitchen, and Michael flopped into it. Hawkeye crawled under the table and flopped to his belly in a similar motion.

Diesel busied himself making the tea, then placed two cups on the table and poured. "This is Dani's tea. It's chocolate mint. I like it."

They sipped in silence for a few minutes, then Michael glanced at the kitchen doorway. "Troy's still here?"

"At the front door," Diesel signed, still not voicing.

Michael raised miserable eyes to Diesel. "He knows about me. What happened to me. Everyone's going to know. Everyone's going to know that I couldn't fight him off." Two tears rolled down his cheeks. "That I'm weak. Brewer always said that to me. That I'm weak. Skinny." He swallowed hard. "That I'll never be a real man."

Diesel flattened his hands on the table, unable to breathe through the tightness in his chest. Once again he wished that he could snap Brewer's neck himself. Killing the bastard might have been the only good thing Cade Kaiser had done.

And then he made a decision. Because Brewer's words took him back. Made him hear almost the same words, but in an older voice. A smoother voice.

A rapist's voice.

He needed to get this off his chest for Michael's sake. *Because there's no fucking way on God's green earth that I'll let Michael believe he's weak.*

He forced his hands to relax and he began to sign. "Troy doesn't know what happened to you. Not what Brewer did, anyway. Kate and Decker don't know, either. They only know that you witnessed Brewer's murder. Only Officer Cullen, Deacon, and Adam know, because they were with you on Saturday."

He paused when he heard a soft footstep on the other side of the open doorway. And smelled chocolate shampoo.

Dani was there, making sure that Michael was okay. *That I'm okay. Well, Michael's not okay. And neither am I.*

Diesel steeled his spine, hoping that Dani had put her processor back on. He didn't want to have to say any of this again. Ever. "But," he said to Michael, this time voicing quietly, "Agent Decker knows about *me.* What happened to me."

He watched Michael's eyes pop wide. And he heard Dani's indrawn breath. *Good. She can hear me.*

"You told Agent Decker?" Michael asked, stunned, and Diesel nodded.

"Not the details," he added. "Nobody knows the details."

"You never told?" Michael asked.

"No," Diesel signed, still voicing quietly. "But I'm going to tell you." *And Dani. Please, God, let me get through this. Just once.*

"Why?" Michael asked.

Diesel met the boy's gaze. "Am I weak?"

"No," Michael replied quickly. "Never. You're strong. Nobody can hurt you."

Oh, no. You're wrong there. "Am I a man?"

Michael frowned. "Yes."

"But I wasn't always a man. I was a little boy, just like Joshua. Then I was a teenager, just like you. I didn't hit a growth spurt until I was sixteen. Before then, I was skinny. Bony. Not strong."

"You were a kid."

"So are you."

Michael's mouth opened. Then closed. He folded his hands on the table and sat silently for several seconds. Then he nodded. "Okay. I'm a kid."

Diesel drew a deep breath, pursed his lips. "I'm thirty-five years old and thinking about the man who hurt me when I was six still makes me throw up."

Michael grew so sad that Diesel didn't think he could stand it. "I'm sorry."

Diesel's eyes stung. His nose burned. Finally he blinked and swiped at the tears that fell. Then he pointed to his wet face. "Am I weak now?"

Michael shook his head. "No." He didn't use his hands, just mouthed the word.

"My dad took off before I was born. I never knew him. My mother was only seventeen when she had me. And her very Catholic family threw her out, so she raised me alone."

"Was . . ." Michael hesitated. "Was she good?"

"Yes." And that was true. "She was a good person,

kind and gentle. And she tried really hard to be a good mother. For a long time it was just the two of us. She got a scholarship to college—she loved computers—but she had to give it up because she had me. She worked at night and went to community college during the day. She took me with her to her job sometimes. She cleaned office buildings, and when I was really little, I'd help. I don't think I was actually much help, but my mom always made me feel like I was indispensable."

"She sounds nice."

"She was."

Michael bit at his lip. "Is she dead?"

Diesel nodded sadly. "Yes. She died when I was fourteen. Car accident."

"Did you go to foster care?"

"For a few months. Then her father took me in. We . . . didn't get along."

"He threw her out when she was pregnant," Michael said. "I hate him and I don't even know him."

That made Diesel smile a little, but he couldn't hold on to it and his shoulders drooped. "My mother hated him, too. So much so that she converted to another religion because her father had used his as an excuse to shame her. She wanted no part of the Catholic church. Anyway, she got her associate's degree in office management when I was six years old, and went to work as a receptionist in a doctor's office. She was making pretty decent money and we moved to a nicer apartment. I got a bicycle and a few toys. I went to a better school than the one I would have gone to before we moved. My mother was so grateful to the doctor for giving her a job."

Michael had grown still, his dread a palpable thing. "It was the doctor."

Diesel nodded. "It was the doctor," he echoed, still signing and voicing so that Dani could hear. "He let my mom bring me to work when I didn't have school. There was a playroom in the back of the office. It had toys, a worktable. And a door that locked."

Michael's throat worked as he tried to swallow. "You were Joshua's age."

"A year older, yeah. The first time."

"It hurt," Michael signed, his hand movements so small that Diesel would have missed them had Michael not chosen to also speak the words.

Diesel wasn't going to lie to the boy. "I was six. I was small. So yeah. It hurt a lot and I cried and begged him to stop. So he spanked me. Hard. Then he told me not to tell my mother. That it would be our secret. That she wouldn't like knowing that I'd been bad and he'd had to spank me."

Diesel could hear Dani's gasp and her shuddered exhale. It sounded wet. Like she was crying. He'd expected as much. Which was why this was an easier way to tell her. He didn't think he could stand to see the sorrow in her eyes.

Michael's sorrow was different. It was more . . . a sorrow of understanding. Not pity or even sympathy.

"He was wrong," Michael said aloud, his voice breaking.

"Yes, he was. But I didn't know that then. I was six." Diesel drew in a breath. "And then seven and then eight. I started to act out in school when I was nine. Got a reputation as a bad kid. Figured I'd earn the rep and I beat up a lot of the other students. I was skinny, but I wasn't gonna be weak. Even if that meant beating up on kids smaller than me."

"You were angry," Michael signed and Diesel knew he was talking about himself as well.

"You're right. I was very angry," he said for Dani's benefit. Her sniffling was audible now. She had to know that he knew she was there.

She had to know this was the only way he was going to be able to tell her.

"I got older. The abuse went on. My mother didn't know what to do with me."

"Did she keep working for the doctor?"

"Yes." Diesel needed a second so he poured himself some more tea. "She married him when I was ten." It had been the single worst day of his life. He'd had to be dragged into the church by one of his mother's friends, who scolded him for being so selfish. He'd left the reception to throw up. Much as he'd done when he'd seen the photos in Richard Fischer's super-secret database.

"Oh God," Michael signed, his face growing pale.

"Oh God," Dani whispered on the other side of the doorway. He could hear the slide of her body against the wall as she sank to the floor.

"She admired him," Diesel went on. "All her friends said how lucky she was to marry a doctor. We moved to a nicer house. His house. And he didn't need a playroom any longer."

"He came to your room," Michael signed numbly.

"Yes, he came to my room. Not every night, and that almost made it worse. I was never sure if he was coming or not. I never slept. I still have trouble sleeping."

Michael looked at his hands, then back up, ashamed. "I sleep with the light on."

"I did, too, until I was in the army." Diesel's lips quirked up. "They wouldn't let me."

"Dani got me a lamp with a night-light."

"She's good that way. She helps other people. Sometimes she forgets to help herself, so we're going to have to remind her, okay?"

Michael nodded. "When did he stop?"

"He stopped the day he ran a red light and hit a car that had the green light. He and my mom were killed instantly. He'd been drinking. The family of the people in the other car sued his estate for damages, so there was nothing left for me."

"Then your grandfather took you in?"

"Yeah. My grandfather was strict. He'd heard about the trouble I got into at school, all the fights. The poor grades. He was going to fix me or die trying."

"Did he? Die trying?"

Diesel chuckled ruefully. "No, but he gave it his best effort. He sent me to an all-boy Catholic school. But it wasn't what you think," he added when Michael blanched. "There may have been bad priests at the school and the parish, but I never knew any. After the doctor, the priests were like a vacation. I got decent grades. As and Bs without cracking a book. They'd tell me that I could be so successful if I'd just apply myself."

"I get that, too," Michael said glumly.

"Well, they were right about me, even though I hate to admit it. I didn't get serious about school until I'd almost graduated. I was a high school senior."

"What changed?"

Diesel smiled. "My chemistry teacher changed everything. His name was Father Walter Dyson. At the beginning of the school year, he thought I was a thug. I'd hit my growth spurt the year before and was huge. My grandfather would complain about me going through shoes like sticks of gum, which was fair."

"Just because you were big didn't mean you were a thug," Michael protested.

"It was because I acted up in his class. I wasn't nice. I didn't even know why. I *was* a thug, outside of school. When I got some size, I stomped on some of the kids who'd bullied me when I first moved to my grandfather's. I'm still not sorry for that. They deserved to be stomped. But I got carried away and made some unfortunate friends. I have no doubt that I would have ended up in jail, because every single one of those guys did—a few of them for murder. Father Dyson saved my life."

Michael was leaning forward, into the story now. "What did he do?"

"He sat me down one day and asked me why I hated him so much. I didn't know what to say. He said he'd talked to my other teachers and they said that I didn't make trouble in their classes. And then he asked for my forgiveness. He didn't know what he'd done, but he was sorry for it. No one had ever asked for my forgiveness before. He said that he didn't want my future to be messed up because I got a bad grade in his class or I got expelled for 'thuggery.'" Diesel finger-spelled the word. "I'd never heard the word before or since." He smiled at the memory. "I didn't know how to react, but I was . . . hyper inside. I was always hyper inside when I was in his class. Nobody else's. But Father Dyson was pretty smart. He could read chemical formulas and people. He stood up and took off his white lab coat, balled it up, and put it in a drawer, out of sight. Immediately, I calmed down."

"The white coat?" Michael asked. "Why?"

"The doctor wore a white coat when he'd . . ." Diesel filled his lungs and held the breath for a few seconds, hoping to quiet his racing heart. He wished he could knit and sign at the same time. His hands were itching for his knitting needles. "When he raped me."

Michael flinched. "Oh."

"Oh," Dani echoed from her hiding place. "I get it now."

He'd figured she would. He sighed loudly. "So after that, Father Dyson never wore a lab coat when he was teaching class. He asked the sister school for their girls to make us smocks for when we did labs. The girls made it a class project. Dyson made it a party and we all gathered together to help. The girls made similar smocks for their own chemistry class, so no one knew that he'd done it for me."

"Wow," Michael voiced softly. "That was nice."

"It was. And I got an A in chemistry."

"Did you go to college?"

Diesel nodded. "I went to college after the army, yes."

"Why did you join the army?"

"Because I'd waited too long to get serious about school and my grades weren't awful, but not good enough for scholarships. I joined the army to get money to go to college. Ended up meeting Marcus O'Bannion on my very first day in boot camp."

"And you became friends."

"We did. And then I met Stone, and when Marcus came home after his tours, I came to work for him at the *Ledger*. My grandfather had died by then, and my mother was an only child, so I didn't have a family. The O'Bannions sucked me into theirs. And I love them."

Michael smiled. "I'm glad." He looked away, his cheeks pinking up at his show of emotion. Or maybe at Diesel's. It didn't matter. Diesel was going to make sure this boy had a family, no matter what happened between himself and Dani. He was going to make sure this boy knew that somebody loved him. "What did you go to college for?" Michael asked, changing the subject.

"Majored in computer science and physics. Minored in religious studies, because Father Dyson had. And I worked construction to keep my body strong, because I never wanted to be weak again."

Michael looked thoughtful. "Can you teach me? To have muscles?"

"We can work out. You might not be as tall as me, or as big, but we can make your body its strongest, whatever that is. Don't measure yourself against other people, Michael. Just be the best *you* that you can be. Be kind and take care of the people around you. That's what being a real man is."

Michael gave a quick nod, but the flicker in his eyes said that he'd understood the words. "What happened to Father Dyson?"

"He retired. My grandfather had died while I was in Iraq, so I came home for his funeral and found out that he'd left the house to me. I sold it to Father Dyson for a song." He paused. "You know that idiom— 'for a song'?" Because he'd learned from Greg that English idioms didn't always translate when signed.

"It means for cheap."

"Close enough. Anyway, Father Dyson lives there now, and he has the most amazing vegetable garden in the summer. I've always wanted a garden like that."

Michael's gaze became intense. "Did Father Dyson coach little kids in soccer?"

Diesel's mouth curved. God, the kid was quick. "He coached the Pee Wee leagues. Still does."

"You're trying to be like him. Mentoring kids like Greg. And me. And Joshua."

Diesel nodded. "All but the priest thing. I like Dani too much to take a vow of chastity."

Michael laughed, a real laugh. Then he sobered. "Did you ever tell Father Dyson why the white coats bothered you?"

"Nope. And he never asked. He may have guessed, but we've never talked about it. He just made sure no one wore white coats when I was around. He's a good man."

Michael's eyes grew shiny. "I'm glad you had him," he signed.

"I'm glad I had him, too," Diesel said.

"Me, too," Dani murmured from the other side of the doorway.

Diesel stood up and gathered the tea things. When his back was to Michael, he said, "We're wrapping up, Dani. If you don't want him to know you were sitting there, you should go now."

"I will. I'll wait for you in our room."

Our room. Hearing the words was more of a relief than he'd expected. He'd known Dani wouldn't blame him for what happened to him as a child, but he must have been afraid that she'd back away from him.

But she hadn't. *Our room.*

He turned back to Michael. "I'm going back to bed. Should I text Meredith and ask her to come for a session tomorrow? I mean today. After we've all slept."

"Yes, please. And Coach?"

"Yes, Michael?"

The boy's swallow was audible. "Thank you. For telling me. I know you didn't have to."

He met Michael's gaze head-on. "Do you think worse of me, knowing that my mother's husband raped me?"

"No."

"Good. Your story is nobody's business but yours, Michael. If you never want anyone to know, that's your decision. But the people who love you—the ones who really matter—won't think worse of you. I never told Marcus, but he guessed. And he's still my best friend."

Michael's nod was shaky. "I still hate my mother."

"For what it's worth? I hate her, too, and I'm not sorry for it."

Another shaky nod. "Good night, Coach."

Diesel pulled the boy in for a hard hug, then let him go. "Good night, Michael. Oh, I ordered an inflatable mattress for you. You can use it for as long as you need to sleep next to Joshua's bed. That way you're not on the hard floor. It'll be delivered sometime after noon, and whoever's guarding the front door will open the box."

And when he returned to the bedroom, Dani waited, her face tearstained. Slowly he approached, lowering himself to sit next to her on the bed.

"You're an amazing man, Elvis Kennedy," she said, resting her head on his shoulder. "I am so very proud of you right now."

"Ditto, Dr. Novak," he replied lightly, when he really wanted to say three other little words. Maybe on a different night when they weren't so emotionally raw.

"I'm serious. What you did for Michael . . . I know it wasn't easy, but for you to trust him with that was . . . Well, I'm proud of you."

Diesel craved her praise, but wasn't exactly sure what to do with it. "I couldn't let him think that he was weak. Or that he was alone."

She drew a deep breath, then wiped her eyes. "I swore I wasn't going to cry any more."

"Don't. Don't cry for me."

"I'm not—not right now anyway. And I will if I want to. But these . . ." She swiped under her eyes again. "These are because you have a beautiful heart. I want to meet Father Dyson even more now. He sounds a lot like my stepfather, Bruce."

"We'll invite him out when this is over."

She sighed, her shoulders sagging. "What are we going to do, Diesel? We can't hide here forever. We have lives. The boys need a home."

"I know, and you're right. But first we're going to sleep. Tomorrow we're going to gather everything we know about Cade Kaiser and find him. And make sure he never sees the light of day as a free man ever again."

Cincinnati, Ohio
Tuesday, March 19, 2:20 p.m.

"I'm sorry, Dani," Deacon said soberly. "Still no word on Evelyn Keys."

Dani gripped the phone a little tighter. She'd put off calling Deacon for a few hours after she'd woken, hoping he'd call her and tell her that Kaiser had been taken into custody while they slept. But she'd finally given in and dialed his number.

"No demands from Kaiser?" she asked, trying not to let her desperation leak into her voice, because though Joshua was far enough away not to hear her words, the child was adept at listening for tone. Which probably had come from years of living with an abusive mother. "He's not asking for safe passage out of the country or money or anything?"

"No. Nothing." Deacon's voice grew muffled. "Be there in a minute."

Dani could hear the slamming of a car door in the background. "Where are you?"

He hesitated, then sighed. "You'll read about it

online soon enough. A young man was killed last night outside a convenience store in Miamitown."

Dani closed her eyes. "How old?"

"Eighteen. He'd bought some baby formula, diapers, a bottle of Advil, rubbing alcohol, Epsom salts, and antibiotic cream. He was found this morning when the shift changed."

She felt a frisson of relief, followed by immediate guilt. "Evelyn and Jimmy are still alive, then." But a young man was dead.

"I think we can assume that," Deacon said. "And we're hoping that the antibiotic cream is because our bullets did some damage to Kaiser's leg."

"I hope it goes gangrenous and falls off," Dani said viciously, then reined her anger in when Joshua looked up from the picture he was coloring at the kitchen table. His little face had grown abruptly tense, and she made herself smile. "It's okay, Joshua. I'm not mad at you or Michael. Just the bad guy who started the fire at our house."

Joshua nodded warily, then pushed the coloring book aside. "I wanna go outside and play. This is boring."

Dani knew the feeling. "I need to go, Deacon. Will you update me later, please? Even if it's to tell me there's no change. We're going a little stir-crazy here."

"I'll try," Deacon said and she could hear the exhaustion in his voice. "We've been a little busy, though."

Guilt reared its head again because Deacon had been burning the candle from both ends between this case and the hours he'd spent at the hospital. "I'm sorry. Go, do what you need to do. We're fine."

"Thanks, Dani. Talk to you later."

She ended the call and sat at the table with Joshua. "I want to go outside, too. But we can't. Not until the bad guy is caught."

Joshua's lower lip trembled. "I wanna go home."

Me, too, baby. Me, too. But Joshua wasn't going home, not ever again. "Sweetie," she started, then sighed. "Your mom's not coming back, Joshua. She's dead. So you can't go home."

He blinked up at her, his expression very serious. "I meant our house, Dani. With Hawkeye and Coach and Michael."

"Oh." She pulled him onto her lap and hugged him hard. "That we can do. Just not today. Wanna see a movie?"

"No." His lip came out and his voice grew cross. "Tired of movies. I wanna *play*."

Dani was spared a response by the appearance of Meredith and Maria, the interpreter who'd helped during Michael's exam that first day in the clinic. Meredith appeared serene. Maria looked shaken.

Dani was well aware that the interpreter's expression was a more honest representation of her true feelings. The serene face was Meredith's way of dealing with the harsh realities of her job.

Michael's session must have been brutal, and no wonder, after the conversation he and Diesel had had the night before. Dani was still raw from hearing it. She'd lain awake for hours, her good ear on the steady thumping of Diesel's heart. Diesel, on the other hand, had slept like a baby, waking up bright-eyed and refreshed. Maybe sharing his story the night before had brought him some peace. Or maybe it was that they were finally together as he'd hoped for so long. Either way, she was glad one of them had slept.

"Is Michael okay?" Joshua asked in a tremulous voice, reminding them once again how intuitive—and adult—this child had been forced to become.

Meredith ruffled his hair. "He will be. Give him a little space for now. I, for one, could use a cup of tea. Maria, can I get you something?"

Maria looked up from her phone, distracted. "What? Oh. No, thank you. I need . . ." She faltered, frowning at her phone again. "Dani, can I talk to you for a moment? Privately?"

Dani shared a quick look with Meredith, noting that her friend looked bewildered. "I'll be right back," she told Joshua, kissing him on the cheek, then settling him back in his own chair.

She led Maria to the entertainment room, which sat empty. Michael was still in the condo's office, where they'd had his session, and Diesel was working in the bedroom they shared.

"It's Andrew McNab," Maria said as soon as Dani had closed the door.

The dread that had been sitting heavy in Dani's gut immediately grew to fill her chest, making it hard to breathe. "The interpreter who helped when Michael went to the police station. What about him?"

"He didn't show up for work this morning and would never miss work without calling in for a substitute. He interprets in an elementary school. He'd never leave the child without support. The agency switchboard said he'd been called to the police station on Sunday to interpret for a deaf man who'd been arrested. Our office manager called the police. They haven't made any arrests in the deaf community for weeks."

Dani hit Deacon's speed dial. "This is important," she said before her brother could say a word. She handed the phone to Maria. "My brother, Agent Novak. Tell him what you told me."

A light knock on the door startled her. She'd put on her processor that morning without Diesel having to remind her and small sounds from behind her had been driving her crazy all day. The door opened and Diesel stuck his head in.

"You okay?" he mouthed.

Dani motioned him in so that he could hear what Maria was telling Deacon. Diesel's shoulders sagged. "Kaiser?" he murmured.

Dani shrugged. "I don't know." But she did. And so did Diesel.

He rubbed his hand over his head, a gesture that was becoming increasingly familiar. "He needed to confirm that Michael was an eyewitness. Needed to know if he'd given the cops that sketch."

"We can't tell Michael," Dani whispered. "Not yet. He feels guilty enough about Stone and Decker getting hurt."

Diesel nodded. "He's fragile right now. I heard Meredith come out of the office. She's wearing her face." He grimaced. "You know what I mean."

Dani knew what he meant. She'd seen it, too. The mask of serenity.

"Oh," Maria said, sinking into one of the soft chairs in front of the huge TV. "I never even thought about that. Th-thank you. I will. Good-bye." She handed the phone to Dani. "He's sending a team to investigate," she said quietly. "I'm not supposed to leave by myself. He's assigning me an escort. He says I may be in danger because I've been interpreting Michael's therapy sessions." She looked up, her eyes full of fear. "I have kids. What about my kids?"

"Where are they?" Dani asked, then texted the children's school information to Deacon. "He'll take care of it."

The three of them left the TV room, only to be met by the sound of Joshua's sobs. Dani ran for the kitchen and stopped short. Joshua sat at the table, his head on his crossed arms, crying like his heart was broken.

Something *had* actually broken, though. Remnants of a colorful plate lay on the kitchen floor in pieces. Meredith sat with Joshua, rubbing his back. "Michael came out of the office," she said quietly. "Started to make himself a sandwich. Joshua got up to hug him, but Michael pushed him away. The two of them signed something I didn't understand. Then Michael threw the plate on the floor. He's out there." She pointed to the sliding glass doors.

Michael stood on the terrace, his back to them, but his shoulders were shaking. He was crying, too.

Dani let out a breath, trying to stay calm when she also wanted to cry. "Joshua, honey, what happened?"

"He pushed me down. Michael pushed me."

Dani crouched beside his chair, ignoring the broken plate. They all were wearing shoes and the mess could wait. "Are you hurt?"

Joshua shook his head, then lifted it, the picture of misery. "But he never pushes me. Never. He's never mad at me. But he is now."

Dani brushed the tears from his cheeks, biting back the urge to make excuses for Michael. Not until she understood the facts. "That wasn't okay of him to push you. That's not ever okay. What did you say to him?" she asked gently.

"I asked if he'd play with me." More tears fell. "That's when he pushed me. Said he didn't have time to play with a baby."

Dani glanced to the terrace, then at Meredith. "What happened then?"

"He looked shocked," Meredith said, still rubbing Joshua's back. "Then he ran."

Diesel squeezed Dani's shoulder. "I'll talk to him."

"Tell him I'm sorry," Joshua cried. "I'm sorry."

"Oh, baby," Dani crooned. "You didn't do anything wrong. Michael's just had a hard few days, okay? We all have." She wiped at his tears, somehow managing to keep her own at bay. Diesel was out on the terrace, his big arms around Michael, rocking them both where they stood.

Dani made a decision. She stood up and squared her shoulders. "We need to get out of here, even if it's just for a little while."

Meredith nodded once. "I think that's a very good idea."

Chapter Twenty-Seven

Loveland, Ohio
Tuesday, March 19, 5:05 p.m.

"Thank you for bringing us here," Michael signed to Coach, who hadn't even frowned at him after he'd lost it with Joshua. Coach should have. So should Dani. *Everyone* should have. *Because I'm like them.* In a minute of temper and self-pity, he'd become the mother and stepfather he'd despised.

"You're welcome. Don't you want to play with the puppies?" Coach signed back.

Dani and Coach had somehow managed to get them out of that condo, which couldn't have been easy. They had four FBI agents as bodyguards, and the men all seemed super-tense, always looking around for danger. Dani told him that her brother Deacon hadn't wanted them to go, but that she'd convinced him that their mental health—Michael's mental health—was important, so Deacon had sent them the extra two bodyguards.

Michael considered telling Dani that it was all right, that they could just stay, but he'd needed to escape the condo more than he'd needed to breathe.

He shivered just thinking the word. *Condo.* It was more like a prison. It was a nice place. Nicer than any place that Michael had ever seen. Still a prison.

It wasn't Dani's house. It wasn't home.

Delores's shelter wasn't Dani's house, either, but it was nicer than the condo. Plus, there were animals. Dogs and cats and rabbits and even a ferret. Plus three pygmy goats and a llama in the field behind the house that connected to the shelter. They all had names and Delores knew every one of them.

She'd been nice enough to meet them out here, taking time away from sitting with Stone in the hospital. She'd waved off Michael's thanks, telling him that she needed to shower anyway. She knew a few signs because Greg came out here to volunteer sometimes, cleaning cages and grooming animals.

Michael thought that was something he'd also like to do.

Drawing in a breath of fresh air, he looked at the litter of four puppies playing in a pen. Delores claimed they were a giant schnauzer–Doberman mix. Michael only cared that Joshua was in the middle of them, laughing nonstop. He wished he could hear, just so he could hear his brother laugh.

"No, I don't need to pet the puppies. I'm good watching Joshua."

Coach just nodded and the two of them stood there together. Michael felt quiet inside his mind for the first time he could remember. And in the quiet, his brain was screaming that he'd fucked up.

"Joshua won't trust me anymore," Michael signed.

Coach touched his shoulder, then tipped his chin up, forcing Michael to meet his gentle gaze. "You didn't break anything between you and Joshua that can't be fixed," he signed back. "Tell him you're sorry, then let him decide when he's ready to trust you again. He worships you. You can fix this."

"I pushed him." Michael couldn't believe he'd done that. "I always promised myself that I'd never hurt him, that I'd never be like *them*."

"Your mom and stepfather?" Coach asked and Michael nodded. Coach bent down until they were eye to eye. "You are nothing like them. Were they ever sorry when they hit you?"

"No. My mom would apologize sometimes, but only when the social workers came and threatened to take me away. But I *am* sorry. God, how could I do that?"

"Because you're human. I told you that I bullied kids when I was in school. I'm not proud of that. I've contacted a lot of them to apologize, to make amends." He finger-spelled the word. "You can, too. But now you know what you're capable of doing. You have to work to control your anger so that it doesn't push you to use your strength against someone else. That's what a real man does."

Coach would know, Michael thought. "I told Meredith what happened to me," he blurted out, signing it fast before he could change his mind.

"I'm glad," Coach said simply. "You can always come to me, too, whenever you need to talk." Then he pointed at Joshua, who held a squirming puppy on his lap, giggling every time the little dog licked his face. "What do you want to bet that we take that puppy to Dani's once it's safe for you to go home with her?"

Michael smiled, relieved that he still could. "That's a sucker bet, Coach."

Coach grinned. "I agree." He gave Michael a tiny nudge toward his brother. "Go. Talk to him. You'll feel better and so will he."

I hope so. His stomach hurting with nerves and shame, Michael approached Joshua, kneeling outside the pen. "He's cute."

Joshua nodded, his joy changing to a careful study of the puppy's giant paws.

Michael sighed and tried again, voicing this time. "What's his name?"

Joshua looked up, eyes wary when they'd never been before, and right there and then Michael vowed he'd never hurt his brother again. He'd learn to control his anger. He didn't care how many times he had to spill his guts to Meredith.

"She's a girl," Joshua signed, letting go of the dog as he did so, but the puppy remained exactly where she was—cuddled safely in his lap. "I'm gonna call her Storm. From *X-Men*."

"That's a good name. She's going to get really big."

Joshua's chin lifted, like he was preparing for an argument. "She'll keep me safe."

Ouch. The *because you won't* didn't have to be said. Michael ran a hand over his head before slowly signing his reply so that Joshua would know he was serious.

"I'm sorry, Joshua. It was wrong, what I did. I wasn't mad at you. I was mad at myself." And life. And the nightmare he couldn't seem to escape. "I lost my temper and didn't take care of you. It won't happen again. I promise. Please forgive me."

Joshua stared up at him for a long, long moment. Then he smiled and, putting the puppy down, lifted his arms to Michael.

Michael picked him up, breathing again when Joshua's arms and legs came around him like a spider monkey. Joshua squeezed him hard and Michael squeezed hard right back. They stood like that for a long time, Joshua burying his face in Michael's neck.

At last the little boy squirmed to get down and Michael had to let him go. Joshua tugged his hand, urging him to get into the pen with him and the puppies. Michael obeyed, sitting on the ground with Joshua and the new puppy in his lap.

He saw Dani watching him soberly from outside the pen. "You don't have to take care of him anymore," she signed without speaking. "Not alone, anyway. We'll help you. And we'll take care of you, too. It's your turn to be a kid now."

New tears burned his eyes and it was like he could suddenly breathe. "Thanks," he mouthed.

Dani just smiled.

Yeah, Joshua was totally getting his own dog.

Cincinnati, Ohio
Tuesday, March 19, 6:10 p.m.

Cade backed the minivan he'd stolen into the alley behind the free clinic. He needed to get in and out quickly. The clinic probably had an alarm, and he was moving too slowly to get away before it sounded.

His leg hurt. And he felt sick. And hot. And so damned tired. His fever had spiked sometime before dawn—over a hundred and four. He'd downed some Advil and taken cold shower after cold shower to bring it down. It was hovering around a hundred and two now. Not great, but at least he was able to move without falling down.

He got out of the minivan and clutched the frame when new dizziness slammed him hard. *Fuck, fuck, fuck.*

He'd been saying that all day, cursing when he'd woken that morning to find it was after ten a.m. The clinic had already opened, and he wasn't going to attempt a B&E when there were people there. So he'd waited, taking more cold showers and using all the antibiotic cream on the fucking wounds, which continued to be swollen and oozing. Red streaks traveled from them in all directions, a sure sign of blood poisoning. Sepsis. *Fucking hell.*

He was going septic, and according to the Internet, he could die. *Fucking hell.* After all this, he could *die* from a fucking *infection.*

"Not going to happen," he muttered through gritted teeth.

Evelyn had been right. He needed antibiotics, and fast. He'd already Googled how to give himself an IV, so that he could do it quickly if he found the supplies. He hoped his hands wouldn't shake too much to get a needle into himself.

He also hoped they wouldn't shake while he was trying to pick the lock on the clinic's rear door. Taking his lockpick set from his pocket, he fought against the chills that continued to rack his whole body.

This is what I get for trying to do the right thing. I never should have checked on that damn kid. Joshua fucking Rowland. I should have gone home to bed. Then Michael Rowland never would have seen him and he wouldn't be in this mess.

But thinking like that wasn't going to help him now. Now he needed antibiotics. As soon as he got inside, he was grabbing every antibiotic he could find, in whatever form he could find it. He could use some painkillers, too, but the clinic's website clearly stated that they did not dispense narcotics of any kind.

He frowned. The website also clearly stated that their hours were eight to five, but the doorknob turned easily, before he'd even tried to pick the lock. Either someone had been stupid and not locked up, or someone was here.

He hesitated, his hand on the cool metal of the handle. If someone was here . . . He shook his head hard, trying to clear his vision. It didn't matter who else was here. *He* was here and he wasn't going to back out now. He was going to get the damn antibiotics, because he was not going to die.

He slipped through the door, closing it quietly, and checked for an alarm panel. There it was, next to the door. The light was green. *Green is good.* Green meant no alarm had been set. He was safe for now.

Creeping through the hallway, he looked for the drugs, pulling on every door until he found one that said SUPPLY CLOSET.

That was simple enough. Except that it had a combination lock, not a keyed lock. He exhaled as quietly as he could. *Fuck.* He couldn't pick that.

He drew the gun from his pocket, tempted to shoot the lock off, but that only worked in the movies. With his luck, the bullet would ricochet and hit him, giving him *another* wound and even *more* infection.

Maybe it was good that someone was here. Especially if they knew the combination to that lock. If they knew, they'd tell him or he'd . . .

He'd figure that out if they refused. Maybe they'd just give him the medication. They were supposed to heal people, right?

He took another shaky step, then froze. A man stood at the other end of the hall, silhouetted by the light behind him. For a moment they simply stared at each other, then the man spoke.

"What do you want?"

Cade blinked hard. The man was holding something in his right hand, lifting it into the air. A gun.

Cade fired twice, the suppressor keeping the sound to a quiet *pop-pop*. The man crumpled to the floor, arm outstretched.

A woman screamed. "Miles! Oh my God, Miles!"

A few things became apparent in the next few seconds. Miles wasn't holding a gun. It was a cordless phone. *Fuck*.

And Miles wasn't wearing a shirt. Neither was the woman who now knelt beside him, frantically taking his pulse, still shouting his name.

The woman, who wore only a bra and a pair of scrub bottoms, looked right at Cade, her eyes wide with shock. "You shot him."

"Get away from him," Cade gritted out, motioning with his gun. "Come here and open the supply closet." Irritated when she didn't respond, he fired another bullet into the man's leg. He didn't have time for this. He also didn't know if the man had managed to get a call in to 911 like George Garrett had. "Kick the phone toward me. *Do it!*"

The woman just stared at him, then back down at the fallen man. "Miles? Miles, open your eyes, baby. Please." She rose on shaky legs, turning for one of the exam rooms.

"Stop," Cade hissed. Dragging his leg behind him, he grabbed her and spun her toward him. He shoved her back against the wall, looming over her. "I said to open the damn supply closet."

Her eyes widened farther as recognition mixed with her terror. "You," she whispered.

"You know who I am, so you know what I'll do to you." He slung her toward the supply closet. "Open that fucking door!"

"I can't." She took a step back, holding one hand out, bloody palm up. As if *that* was going to stop him.

"You're lying. Open the closet. I need antibiotics."

"I'd open it if I could, but I don't know the combination. Only the doctor can dispense medication."

"Then get the damn doctor to open the door."

Her eyes flashed. "You just *shot* the damn doctor."

Fuck, fuck, fuck. "Then call another one. And fast, before your lover boy over there bleeds out."

Her nostrils flared. "Let me get my phone. It's in the pocket of my top. In the exam room."

He motioned with his gun. "Then go. Now." He followed her, picking his way around the bleeding man on the floor, making sure to stay out of his reach. Just in case he was playing possum.

He didn't appear to be, though. The woman gave the doctor an agonized look, a sob rattling in her chest.

"Keep going," Cade ordered. She stumbled forward, going into the first exam room on the left. She headed for her scrubs top, but Cade spied her cell phone on the counter. "Stop," he barked. "Your phone's right there. Behind you."

She stopped. "Thank you," she said stiffly. She walked toward the counter, her face an impassive mask. When she got there, she slowly reached for the phone with her left hand, then yanked at one of the drawers with her right.

She wheeled around, her arm raised high, and Cade saw the glint of a blade just in time. He grabbed her wrist and squeezed hard until she dropped the scalpel with a cry of pain. It clattered to the floor and he twisted her arm behind her, shoving the barrel of his gun at her head.

"Don't fuck with me, lady," he growled. "Open the damn supply closet."

"No," she seethed, breathing hard. "You'll kill me either way, so why should I?"

Then she did a move he was not expecting, twisting her body so that she almost broke free. She kicked at his knee and he swore.

And shot her.

She dropped to the floor and he cursed. Now he'd never get the damn door open. He sank into the patient chair next to the counter and gave himself a second to regroup.

He needed a doctor. That was the most important thing. If he didn't get medical help, he was going to go septic and die, and that was unacceptable. His gaze landed on the woman's cell phone, still on the counter.

If she wouldn't call a doctor for him, he'd call one himself.

He leaned forward and grabbed her phone, then reached for her hand, now limp. The phone was an old-style iPhone with the button at the bottom. Hoping she used fingerprint ID, he pressed her index finger to the button and breathed a sigh of relief when the phone unlocked.

He quickly found *Novak, Dani* in her contacts. But what to say? He'd need to text, of course. Something that would make Dani hurry to the clinic.

Preferably alone, without her bodyguards. Which there was no way she'd do. She wasn't stupid.

Unless . . . He looked at the next name in the woman's contact list.

Novak, Greg. Dani Novak's little brother, the dog walker who was deaf.

I can do something with that number. Brother and

sister would most likely use texting as their primary communication, so neither would think twice about receiving one.

It might work. Then again, it might bring the FBI and the entire Cincinnati PD down on his head. Prison would be a sure thing.

His vision abruptly blurred. He didn't want to know what his body temperature was at the moment. All he knew was that he had to try to get Dani Novak here, or he wasn't going to live long enough to make it to a holding cell, let alone drive to Canada.

Cincinnati, Ohio
Tuesday, March 19, 6:15 p.m.

"And we'll go back, right?" Joshua asked for the tenth time. "We'll go back for Storm, right?"

Dani looked over her shoulder to where Joshua sat in the very back of the windowless FBI van in his booster seat and patiently answered as she had the previous nine times. "Yes, we'll go back. Storm isn't ready to leave her mom yet anyway. Delores said she needs to drink her mama's milk for another week."

Dani hoped like hell that all this would be over by then, and they'd be back home in a week. The outing had been necessary for the boys' mental health, but it had been a bitch to plan and execute. They'd taken two different vans from the Mount Adams condo to Delores's shelter in the northeastern part of the city. Troy drove their van, with Diesel riding shotgun. Literally, she suspected.

He wore a loose-fitting sweatshirt today instead of the tight T-shirts he seemed to prefer. She had a feeling he was wearing a weapon under the sweatshirt, but she wasn't asking. She didn't want to know and she didn't think Troy wanted to know, either.

Besides, Diesel had a concealed-carry permit, so on this he was actually legal. She wasn't going to complain either way, because Michael was sitting beside her, looking more peaceful than he had when they'd left the condo. The firepower in this van and the one that trailed them had enabled that to happen.

The other van was being driven by Agent Parrish Colby, a newer addition to their circle of friends. He was more Meredith's friend than hers, but Meredith trusted him and that was good enough for Dani. Colby was accompanied by one of the other agents who were on guard duty at the condo today. They'd left one man behind to ensure that the apartment remained secure.

Dani didn't want to think about how many strings her brother and cousin had needed to pull to get them this kind of coverage. Although she suspected that Troy was volunteering his time. He hadn't left them since he'd arrived at the condo Monday morning, sleeping in a chair by the front door overnight.

"Troy, are you on vacation this week?" she asked.

He glanced at her in the rearview mirror, his eyes narrowed. And guilty looking. "Why would you ask that?"

"Never mind," she said softly. "You just answered me. I just wanted to say thank you."

His eyes crinkled in the mirror as he smiled. "You're welcome."

Dani leaned back and closed her eyes. She hadn't slept well at all the night before, Diesel's story continuing to break her heart even after he'd fallen asleep.

She'd dozed off when the buzzing of her cell phone woke her. Struggling to sit up, she stared at the message with a frown. "What the . . ."

Diesel turned in the front passenger seat to look at her. "What's wrong?"

"This text. It doesn't make sense. It's from Greg. It says, 'On my way.'"

"Maybe he sent it to you by mistake," Michael signed, but he looked worried.

"Maybe." Dani typed in a reply. *On your way where?*

There was no reply. Dani glared at the screen, willing Greg to answer. *Dammit,* she texted. *Text me!*

Diesel was still watching her from the front seat, his dark brows furrowed in concern. "I'm calling Adam."

"I'll call Deacon," Dani said. "This could be nothing, but let's make sure," she added, because Joshua had the pinched look on his face that said he was scared. "I got Deacon's voice mail," she muttered.

"He's way out in Miamitown," Troy said. "At a crime scene."

The kid who was killed after buying baby formula and diapers. Miamitown was on the far west side, at least thirty minutes away this time of day. So she texted everyone in their circle in a group message, asking if anyone had seen Greg.

Faith replied first. *He's at home. Why?*

Alone? Dani asked.

Her phone rang. "Yes, alone," Faith said. "Why?"

Dani told her about the single-line text she'd received.

"Shit," Faith muttered. "Give me a second. I'm still at the office, but I can track his phone."

"You can?" Dani was surprised. "Does he know you can?"

"It was a condition of him driving alone," Faith said. "He wanted to drive my car, so he said yes. It looks like he's driving, and he's not allowed to touch his phone while he's driving." A slight pause. "It looks like he's headed to the clinic."

Dani was suddenly very cold. "I didn't tell him to meet me at the clinic."

Troy swerved abruptly, crossing several lanes of traffic to take the next exit. Car horns blared at them, but he ignored them as he called for backup.

"No," Diesel said firmly. "We're not going to the

clinic, Troy. Kaiser could be trying to lure Michael there."

Michael tapped Dani's shoulder frantically, because no one was signing. Dani reluctantly interpreted, not wanting to scare Michael, but knowing that, had he been hearing, he'd already know what was happening.

Troy gave Diesel a look of reproof. "I know that. But doesn't Dani want to try to catch him before he goes in? Deacon's thirty minutes out and I don't know where Adam is. Someone who signs needs to catch Greg before he enters the clinic."

Troy was right, Dani thought, but Diesel was shaking his head.

"No. I won't let Dani put herself in danger. I'll go."

Dani ground her teeth. "Troy, can you stop the van and let Diesel and me get into the other van? You should continue to the condo with the boys and we'll go to the clinic. I need to make sure that Greg is okay."

Troy glanced at Diesel, then nodded warily. "I can do that."

Diesel turned fully in his seat to glare at her, but he must have seen something in her expression, because he muttered a particularly salty curse.

"That's a bad word!" Joshua said loudly.

Diesel briefly closed his eyes. "Sorry, Joshua, you're right. Michael, we need you to stay down, okay? Do whatever Agent Troy says."

Michael was pale, but he nodded. "Okay. You're coming back."

He'd signed it as a statement, but Dani knew that it was really a question.

"We are coming back," she assured him. "This could be nothing at all. Either way, we will be back."

Troy was on the phone with the other van, and both vehicles pulled into a nearby parking lot. Diesel got out, but looked back at Troy.

"With my life," Troy said mildly before Diesel could say anything at all.

Diesel nodded once, then helped Dani out of the

van. "See you later, guys," he said. "Pick a movie for tonight. We'll make popcorn."

But neither boy smiled, and Joshua was crying.

Before Dani could question her choice, Troy was driving away, taking the kids to safety, and Agent Parrish Colby had opened the van's sliding door for them to get in.

Dani buckled up and called Faith. "Where is Greg?"

"Three minutes from the clinic," Faith said tightly. "I texted him, too, in case by some chance he is looking at his phone. I told him not to go to the clinic and to call either me or you, but he's still not answering. Dammit. He fights the rules every day. Why does he pick *now* to obey? Where are you?"

Dani's heart was beating in her throat. *Let me be paranoid. Let this be nothing. Let Greg be on his way somewhere else.* "We just got off at Taft."

"Five minutes," Parrish said. Putting the emergency lights on, he took off with a squeal of tires. "Hang on."

Chapter Twenty-Eight

Cincinnati, Ohio
Tuesday, March 19, 6:25 p.m.

Agent Parrish Colby got them to the clinic in four minutes, slowing down when Diesel spied Greg walking from where he'd parked on the street. Greg was walking with his head down, texting on his phone.

Parrish leaned on the horn, but Greg didn't stop.

Dani wanted to throttle her brother. "If he's not wearing his hearing aids, he can't hear anything." And even if he was, it wasn't enough just to hear a car horn. "We're going to have to catch him, because he's not watching for us. Stop the van. *Stop the van!*" she shouted when they still hadn't rolled to a stop.

Parrish stopped with a jerk, opening the doors for Dani to get out. But Diesel was first and he sprinted toward Greg, catching up to him just as Greg was pulling at the clinic's front door.

Diesel grabbed Greg around the waist, spinning him around.

Greg shrank back, his face gone white. "What the fuck?" he voiced.

Diesel didn't answer, dragging Greg between two parked cars on the street and hunkering down. Dani caught up to them, breathing hard as she dropped into a crouch beside them. "It's a trap, Greg," she signed, her hands shaking. "I didn't ask you to meet me here."

Greg's face went even paler. "Oh my God. It's him? Kaiser?"

Dani nodded, trying to catch her breath. "I think so."

"But . . . how?" Greg was trembling, head to toe. "How did he get my number? How did he know yours? The text came from you."

"He must have spoofed it," Diesel said, but he was looking up and down the street. "Let's go. Parrish Colby's going to get us out of here. Now."

Dani didn't move. "How *did* he get our numbers, Diesel? Did you get any other texts, Greg?"

Greg nodded. "One from Jenny, right as I got out of the car. That's what I was looking at when Diesel grabbed me. She said to hurry."

Dani sucked in a breath that hurt. One text had been sent from her own account and the next from the nurse at the clinic? This wasn't good.

"Jenny was on duty today," she explained to Diesel. "If Kaiser's using her phone . . ."

Diesel pressed his lips together. "Okay, this is what's going to happen. Greg, you're going to get into Parrish's van and stay down. Dani . . ." He trailed off and just shook his head. "You're going to do what you're going to do."

Damn straight, she thought. "Just wait," she told him, then took Greg's arm and ran with him to the FBI van. "Parrish, we need you. Greg, get in the van. Stay with Agent . . . I don't know your name."

"Agent Rocha, ma'am," the other man said as he slid over the middle console and into the driver's seat.

"Thank you. Greg, stick to Agent Rocha like glue. And stay down." Without waiting for agreement, she ran back to Diesel.

If Cade Kaiser had her nurse's phone, it meant Jenny was hurt. "Where's Adam?" she asked Parrish.

"I don't know," Parrish said from behind her and Dani was grateful that she'd remembered to wear her processor. She wouldn't have been able to hear him otherwise.

"Can you try Meredith? She might know where he is."

"I did," he replied. "Neither of them is answering."

"What about your backup?"

"On the way," Parrish said, then blew out a breath. "Shit. What the fuck's he doing?"

Dani's heart skittered as she realized that Diesel was no longer hiding between the parked cars.

He'd just entered the clinic.

She burst in behind him. And skidded to a stop, staring at all the blood on the floor. "Oh my God. *Miles.*" The other clinic doctor was on the floor, unmoving.

Diesel was checking for a pulse. "It's so faint, I can barely feel it."

Dani started toward them, but Parrish Colby grabbed her arm. "Wait. Let me clear the area," he said.

So Dani waited impatiently while he searched, clearing each room. She heard him call out from one of the exam rooms and rushed in after him. "Jenny!"

Her nurse was down, a wide swath of blood behind her, like she'd dragged herself across the floor. Dani grabbed a pair of gloves from the box on the counter and dropped to her knees to take her pulse.

"She's alive," Dani said, relieved.

"I called for an ambulance already," Parrish said. "The interior is clear. I'm going to check outside and direct our backup."

"Thanks," Dani murmured, already focused on Jenny. The nurse wore only a bra, which had once been white but was now crimson except for a few inches of the straps. She'd been shot in the upper abdomen. Her arm was outstretched, reaching for her scrubs top, which lay on the floor.

Still on her knees, Dani crawled to the cabinet and threw open the lower doors, grabbing all the gauze she could find. If she couldn't stem the bleeding, Jenny wasn't going to make it.

She was packing the wound when Jenny's eyes opened and her mouth moved. Dani lowered her ear so that she could hear whatever Jenny was trying to say.

"Pocket," Jenny barely breathed. "Please."

Dani reached for Jenny's top and felt something heavy in the pocket. It was the switchblade that the woman always carried because she feared the neighborhood, especially at night. It wasn't going to help her now.

Dani had dropped the scrubs and was returning her attention to Jenny's gunshot wound when she heard it.

A small pop. Like a champagne cork, but softer. Fear had her grabbing for Jenny's blade, sliding it up the sleeve of her sweater seconds before she heard the footsteps behind her.

She pivoted on her knees, only to look up into the face of Cade Kaiser.

"You look like shit," she said, because it was the first thing that came to mind.

His skin was an unhealthy gray, and he swayed unsteadily. Even from a few feet away she could smell the putrid odor of infection.

His wounds were going septic. But that wasn't what held her attention.

That would be the gun in his hand. With a silencer on the end of the barrel.

Oh no. Suddenly her mind processed the pop she'd heard. *Oh God.*

"Diesel!" she yelled and tried to rush past Kaiser, aiming for the exam room door, but he grabbed her wrist, yanking her to her feet. A moment later the barrel of the gun was pressed to her head.

"He's dead," Kaiser said flatly, "and you will be,

too, if you don't open the damn supply closet and get me some medicine."

Cincinnati, Ohio
Tuesday, March 19, 6:29 p.m.

Cade blinked hard, fighting to keep his body upright. He leaned into Dani Novak, pushing her toward the exam room door.

"Go. And don't try anything heroic. I've got literally nothing to lose."

The doctor stumbled, and he jerked her wrist behind her back to keep her from falling. Her hiss of pain was welcome and he latched on to it, using it to fuel each step forward. This woman was responsible for this. For all of this. Her and her goddamn bodyguards.

Her "platoon." Her friends and family.

He wanted to gut them all, but he'd content himself with her. He'd already taken care of the behemoth who'd charged into the clinic like a rabid bull, shocking him. He'd been expecting the doctor's younger brother, not a man who looked so much like himself. For a moment he'd stared, thinking the fever was making him delusional.

Then the man had dropped to the male doctor's side and Cade had managed to clear the back door, evading notice.

He'd been forced back inside the clinic, though, when a man in a suit ran around the back, weapon drawn, shouting "FBI." The Fed had dropped like a rock when Cade shot him in the leg, the same place the redheaded female Fed had shot Cade.

He'd pulled a stack of flattened boxes over the downed Fed and fled back into the clinic, desperately trying to figure out his next step. And then he'd heard her. The doctor. Dr. Dani Novak, a.k.a. his ticket to freedom.

Now he shoved Novak through the exam room door, jamming the barrel of his gun into her temple with more force than he needed to. Except that he *did* need to. He needed to hear her gasp, her whimper when she saw the carnage in the hall outside the exam room.

"Supply closet," he snapped when she faltered at the sight of the behemoth's body lying facedown beside the shirtless male doctor. A dark stain was spreading on the back of the brute's sweatshirt.

Diesel. She'd called him Diesel. What the fuck kind of name was that? This was the man he'd heard with Dani Novak the night he'd shot Not-a-Detective Stone. According to the news article on the shooting, the property he'd thought was a safe house belonged to Elvis Kennedy, a.k.a. Diesel.

Well, *Diesel* was one problem Cade no longer had to worry about.

Cade gave the doctor another shove. "Move it, Dr. Novak. I don't have all day."

She stopped abruptly, her breaths coming in jagged pants. "No."

He tightened his hold on her arm. "No? Did you just tell me *no*?"

"I did." She stood ramrod straight now, her body trembling. "I was agreeing with you. You *don't* have all day. This place will be surrounded by cops and FBI, if it's not already."

"They'll let me go," he said. But his hand shook, which made him angrier. "You're my ticket out of here."

"No," she said again. "They won't let you go."

He stilled for a moment, then snarled. "Of course they will. Your brother and your cousin will let me go because they want you to live."

"No, they won't. They will not let you go to save me." She drew a shuddering breath. "Not because they won't want to save me, because they will. And when they catch you, they're going to make you pay for forcing them to make that choice."

He shook her, glad to hear a whimper, because she'd made him doubt what he knew to be true. Of course they'd choose her. Of course they'd let him go. They'd do anything to keep her alive. *She's messing with my mind.* "Stop arguing and get to the supply closet. I want antibiotics."

She bowed her head, her free hand clenching at her side. "No."

It sounded like a sob.

He shoved her hard, and she went to her knees. He jerked her arm, twisting it higher behind her back. "Get up," he snarled, dragging her to her feet. Feeding on her cry of pain, letting it center him. "Get up, or you'll be dead on the floor with your bodyguard."

And then the bodyguard moved. In a flash, the big man was lurching from the floor, lunging toward them.

Huge hands closed around Cade's throat, squeezing, lifting him off his feet, making him gasp for air. The doctor twisted from his hold and he dimly heard something clatter to the ground. His gun? No, he still had that.

I still have my gun. Shoot him. Now.

Cade worked the weapon between their bodies, shoving the barrel into the man's chest, but his vision was going black, his fingers numb. *Pull the trigger, dammit,* he told himself. *Pull it.*

Then he froze as the tip of a knife jabbed into the back of his neck.

"Drop the gun," Dani hissed. "Or I will kill you where you stand. Don't you dare think I won't, you sonofabitch."

The behemoth wrenched the gun from Cade's hand, then stepped back, his hand visibly shaking as he pointed the weapon at Cade. "On the floor," he commanded. "Hands out where I can see them."

No. No, no, no. It wasn't supposed to end like this. He'd come so far . . .

Too far to stop fighting.

He spun around, going for the doctor's wrist, but a sharp pain ripped through his gut just as he was knocked to the floor by the bodyguard. He had only enough time to register Dr Novak's bloody knife and satisfied expression before a beefy fist connected with his jaw, then another fist. And another.

Through blurry eyes, Cade looked up to see the bodyguard looming over him, snarling like a beast. Then the fist smashed into his eye and he couldn't see anything.

"Diesel." The doctor's voice cut through the fog. "Diesel!"

More hits, to his face, to his stomach, as the doctor continued to yell the bodyguard's name. "Diesel, baby." She panted the words. "You need to stop."

The attack stopped abruptly and the only sound was heavy breathing. Hers. The bodyguard's. His own.

The pain was excruciating and he had to strain to catch her words.

"He's down," she said softly. "He's not getting up again."

"He hurt you," the big man growled. "He put his hands on you."

"He won't do that again, baby. He won't hurt anyone again."

And then the doors burst open and, through the pain, there was chaos.

Cincinnati, Ohio
Tuesday, March 19, 6:35 p.m.

Motherfucking hell. Diesel had never been so glad to see cops in all his life. They poured in, surrounding Kaiser, guns drawn, Adam leading the charge.

"You're late," Diesel griped at them.

"Shh," Dani whispered. She'd had her arms around his shoulders, having dragged him off the bastard who lay bleeding at his feet. Now she lowered Diesel to the floor, raising his sweatshirt, her mismatched eyes full of worry. She scanned his chest. "Where are you hit?"

"Back," Diesel rasped. The asshole had snuck up behind him while he was checking on the clinic's other doctor. "But it's not bad."

Adam dropped to his knees beside him. "What happened? Why the fuck did you run in before we got here? Greg was safe."

"Heard a crash." Diesel pointed to a toppled display of pamphlets. "And a groan. Thought it was the nurse. Saw the doc on the floor. He's still alive, but barely."

"Same with Jenny," Dani said, her head whipping to the exam room.

"EMS is here." Adam pointed to the team of paramedics who were pushing a stretcher through the doors, followed closely by a second team with another stretcher. One of the teams rushed to where Miles lay, the doctor's chest barely moving up and down as he took shallow breaths. But he was still alive.

When the second team of medics approached Diesel, he waved them off. "Jenny needs you more." Once they'd pushed the stretcher into the exam room, Diesel lifted his head to take in the room. "Is Kaiser dead?"

Dani turned on her knees to look. "Actively bleeding from a knife wound to his lower abdomen. But still alive."

"Shit." Diesel closed his eyes. "Let the fucker die."

"I can't."

Diesel opened his eyes to see Dani staring at Kaiser, her eyes tormented and uncertain. "Why?"

"Because he knows where Evelyn and her baby are."

Shit. He'd forgotten about them. "Do what you need to do. I'm okay."

"No, you're not, but you're more okay than he is." She pressed a hard kiss to his mouth. "I'll be back. Adam, see that the next medics take Diesel. I think he's worse than he's admitting."

Diesel closed his eyes, swallowing a groan so she wouldn't know exactly how right she was. "What the fuck took you so long, Kimble?"

Adam shrugged out of his suit coat and rolled up his sleeves. "We didn't know you'd gone into the clinic, dipshit," he snapped. He waved his hand and Diesel heard the clatter of a third stretcher. "Help me over here," he called out. "He's been shot in the back." Then he added in a mutter, "Fucking idiot."

"Love you, too," Diesel grunted as the paramedics turned him onto his side. Seconds later he felt cool air on his back as his sweatshirt was cut away.

Adam crouched beside him, letting the paramedics do their job. "I swear to God, Diesel Kennedy, if you die, you will break my wife's heart, and that is not okay."

Diesel found himself smiling. It was Adam's way of saying that he cared, too. "Got it." Then he frowned. "Where's Greg? And Parrish Colby? Parrish followed us in, then went out back." He'd cleared the interior, Diesel remembered.

"Kaiser shot him," Adam said grimly. "He's being transported to the ER as we speak. It took us a minute or two to find him. Greg had to tell us that Parrish's partner had *left him alone* in the van to go search for you guys because Parrish wasn't answering his phone." He shook his head. "Gonna have that idiot's badge."

Diesel agreed. Leaving Greg alone? What had the agent been thinking? "Where is Greg?" he asked again.

"Safe," Adam assured him. "He's with Parrish's partner and two uniforms." He raised a pointed brow. "Greg was the only person who did what he was supposed to. He stayed put and stayed down. Parrish didn't wait for backup because you and Dani rushed in here all save-the-day."

Diesel understood that Adam's rant was more a release of pent-up fear than any real anger. "Kaiser had hidden Parrish under some boxes," Adam went on. "We thought you two were with him, but then realized you weren't. We were about to come in when we looked through the window and saw Kaiser with his gun to Dani's head."

Diesel growled again, the image too clear in his mind, then yelped when the paramedic began putting pressure on his wound.

"Diesel?" Dani called from where she sat tending Kaiser, her tone worried.

"Tell her I'm okay," Diesel muttered to Adam.

Adam snuck a peek at Diesel's back and grimaced. "You're not okay."

"Then *lie*. If that guy dies, we'll never find the dog groomer and Dani won't forgive herself, even if that's stupid."

Adam blew out a sigh. "He's okay," he called to his cousin. "Just being a baby."

Diesel scowled. "You are *so* going to pay for that."

"You can't be that hurt if you're threatening me," Adam said lightly.

"The boys are with Troy." Diesel clenched his teeth because it hurt, dammit. "Tell them that we're okay and we'll be home soon."

Adam grabbed his hand and held it tight, absorbing the pain when Diesel crushed his fingers. "I will. Don't worry."

Diesel wasn't worried. Not about his little family. But they weren't done yet. Kaiser still had hostages. "How's Dani doing over there?"

Adam looked grim. "She's saving the bastard's life."

Diesel knew it was necessary. Still . . . "Fuck."

"Yeah," Adam agreed. "That about sums it up."

Cincinnati, Ohio
Tuesday, March 19, 7:55 p.m.

"Thank you," Grant said, accepting the mortician's card. "I appreciate you staying open late to help me with my brother's . . . arrangements."

Wesley's cremation.

"We're happy to be of service," the mortician said. "And we are very sorry for your family's loss."

Grant jerked a nod. He'd heard that phrase several times today. Everyone from the Cincinnati PD to the medical examiner to Wesley's boss in Cleveland. Of course, the Cleveland commander over the narcotics division had a lot more to say than that.

There were lots of questions about Wesley's possession of a brick of heroin and five hundred grand in cash. So many questions that Grant's head ached. He supposed he was lucky that he wasn't being arrested for conspiracy or aiding and abetting a felony.

"We'll call you when his remains are prepared for pickup," the mortician was saying, and Grant realized he'd been standing there staring into space.

"I'm sorry. My mind wandered."

The mortician smiled kindly. "Perfectly normal. Please take care."

Nodding numbly, Grant left the mortician's office and made his way to the front of the funeral home. Then paused when a lively conversation between two employees stopped the moment he saw them.

He frowned. "What?" he asked, because the two men were staring at him.

"Um . . . nothing," one of them said.

The other shot his coworker a disapproving look. "We just saw that Cade Kaiser has been apprehended. We thought that seeing as he was responsible for your loss, maybe you'd like to know."

Grant grabbed onto a support column, feeling lightheaded. "They caught him? When? Where?"

"An hour ago. He'd taken some hostages in the free clinic in Over-the-Rhine."

Grant's blood went cold. "The free clinic?" That was Dani Novak's clinic. He'd read up on her when he'd woken this morning, wanting to know about the woman who'd been so kind when she hadn't had to be.

He'd read up on Diesel, too. They were good people. "Was anyone hurt?"

Both men hesitated. "There are reports of several injuries," the second man said. "They're keeping pretty quiet on the details."

"Thank you," Grant said and hurried out, dialing Dani Novak's cell phone number as he ran to his car.

"Hello?" Dani answered. "Grant?"

"Oh my God." His breath rushed out of him. "I heard there was a shooting at your clinic. But you're okay."

"I'm fine," she said, reassuring him. "Diesel was shot, but he'll recover. An FBI agent, one of the clinic's doctors, and my nurse are in stable condition."

"And Kaiser?" Grant pressed. "Is he dead?"

"No. Kaiser survived." She drew a breath and exhaled loudly. "I saved his life."

"What?" Grant shouted, then apologized. "I'm sorry, I'm so sorry. But . . . why?"

"He has other hostages. And he should face justice. He should pay for what he did, all the people he hurt."

Grant unlocked his car and slid behind the wheel, so damn tired. "You're right." He still wanted Kaiser dead, but she was right. "Is he talking?"

"Not yet. He's in ICU. He's alive, but . . . well, it doesn't look good. If he were a religious man, I'd say he should be asking for a priest right now." The last was uttered with a dark humor that Grant suspected was helping her to cope. "How are you, Grant?"

"I'm . . ." He started the engine. "I'm leaving the funeral home."

A beat of silence. "I'm sorry." And she was. He could hear it in her voice.

"Thanks. You take care of Diesel, okay?"

"I will. You take care of yourself."

Grant ended the call, then sat staring through his windshield. He switched on the wipers when the glass became blurry, then realized that it wasn't raining. He wiped his eyes and pulled out of the parking lot. He still had one more thing to do before he left this city and never came back.

Chapter Twenty-Nine

Cincinnati, Ohio
Wednesday, March 20, 1:30 a.m.

"Mr. Kennedy, we do not advise this," the doctor said firmly.

Dani would have said the same thing to a patient with Diesel's injury. But Diesel wasn't just any patient. He was in pain, but refusing painkillers.

Not here, he'd whispered to her when she'd tried to get him to take the damn pill while he lay in the ER. *I can't. Not here. I will at home. With you. But not here.*

And then she'd understood. Ten years ago he'd woken in a military hospital surrounded by white coats and, in a post-sedated state, had lashed out with such vehemence that they'd had to restrain him. Which had, of course, made it worse.

Now, hours after being shot, he was pale and trembling and hanging on to his composure by a thread. He'd conquered most of his fear of white coats for Dani, but some of that fear remained, especially when he was the one in the hospital bed.

Diesel held out his hand for the clipboard the nurse held. "I'll sign the form."

The nurse hesitated and the doctor sighed. "Dr. Novak, please explain to Mr. Kennedy the risks of leaving the hospital with an injury as serious as his."

"Mr. Kennedy is lucid and understands the risks," she said. "You need to respect that." But Diesel also needed to understand that he *was* injured, he *should* be under the care of a medical professional, and he *would* be. *Me.*

The doctor, who was so young that he had to be a first-year attending, gave the nurse a curt nod, and she handed Diesel the clipboard. The doctor then turned an evil eye on Dani while Diesel signed the Against Medical Advice form.

"The only reason I'm not having him evaluated for mental competency is because you're taking him home," the doctor said, and Dani could feel the rumble of Diesel's low growl.

His hand tightened on the pen and it snapped. "Sorry." He gave the leaking pen and the clipboard back to the nurse. "I signed. Can I go now?"

The doctor waved in a flourish. "You're free to go. You have the scripts for the antibiotics and painkillers. Dr. Novak, please call me with his status tomorrow."

She gave the young man a smile. "That I can do." When the doctor was gone, she kissed Diesel's temple. "Just a little longer, okay? We have to wait for someone to bring a wheelchair so that you can leave." She covered his mouth with hers when he started to argue. "That's not negotiable," she murmured against his lips. "Hospital rule. If you want out of here, you have to comply. Okay?"

He nodded silently. Grumpily.

She chuckled. "I don't think you're going to be a good patient. But that's okay. I can handle you."

He looked up, his dark eyes suddenly intense. "I love you. I'm sorry if it's too soon, but tonight when he had a gun to your head, I didn't think I'd get to say it."

Oh. Tears stung her eyes. It sounded so much nicer than she'd imagined, and she'd imagined it quite a bit. Resting her forehead against his, she cupped his cheek, the terror of seeing his body motionless and bleeding still way too fresh. "I didn't think I'd live to hear you say it. Or to say it back." Her throat closed and she had to clear it. "But I do," she whispered. "I love you, too. I think I have ever since you saved my life."

He closed his eyes, shuddering out a breath. "I was so scared that night. Tonight, too. We have to be done with this dangerous stuff. We've got kids now."

He said it with such seriousness that she had to smile. "We do. And I think they'll be happiest once you've healed up. So obey your doctor, okay?"

That made him smile. "As long as that doctor is you."

"Aww, look at you guys. Aren't they cute, Scarlett?"

Dani and Diesel backed away from each other at Marcus's teasing voice.

Scarlett was grinning. "So damn cute."

"Fuck off, assholes," Diesel said, but he was trying not to smile.

"That's no way to talk to your chauffeurs," Marcus said lightly.

Scarlett nodded. "Are you ready to go home, tough guy?"

Diesel looked at Dani. "You called them?"

Dani nodded. "I was pretty sure you'd be asking for the AMA form, and I don't have a car here." She did, however, have their phones. Troy had given them back when they'd left for Delores's shelter and Dani had spent most of the first hour texting everyone to let them know that she and Diesel were okay.

She'd asked Marcus to help because she needed someone with enough muscle to get Diesel in and out of a vehicle, and anyone else who was strong enough was either on duty or in the hospital themselves.

They would have had their pick of chauffeurs had Kaiser attacked them on the west side of town, closer to Diesel's house, because that was where Stone was hospitalized. Dani's free clinic was practically next door to the hospital downtown, so their friends and family had been driving back and forth all evening.

The proximity to the downtown hospital had, however, saved Jenny's life. She was out of surgery with a hopeful prognosis. Her sister was with her now. Jenny had only woken once, asking after Miles, but fell back into unconsciousness before anyone could tell her that Dr. Miles Kristoff was alive, but still in surgery.

Neither Jenny's sister nor Dani had realized that Jenny and Miles were even seeing each other. Thankfully both Jenny and Miles had family in the area, because for now she had to focus on Diesel, making sure he got the care he needed once they were home.

"We were going to start a pool on how many hours you'd stay in the hospital," Scarlett said, "but nobody would take the bet." She leaned in to kiss Diesel's cheek. "Tell me that you're okay," she whispered, all levity gone.

"I'm okay. Been better, been a lot worse."

"And he'll be even better soon," Dani said firmly. "They did a chest X-ray while they were checking for tonight's damage." Which, thankfully, hadn't been nearly as bad as it could have been, the bullet missing all his major organs. "The cardiothoracic surgeon said he could remove that other bullet as soon as Diesel is recovered from tonight. That he could have removed the sucker ten years ago."

Marcus's face broke into a bright smile. "How did you manage to get a surgeon to evaluate him? You've only been here a few hours."

"Your dad helped," she told him. Jeremy and Keith had been the first of Diesel's family to burst into the ER. They'd been on the way from their home to the west side, where Stone was still hospitalized, but veered off the highway in much the same way Agent Troy had, detouring to make sure that Diesel was all right. "Jeremy saw one of his former colleagues walking through the ER and flagged him down. I asked him about removing bullets and he asked to see Diesel's X-ray." She arched a brow at Diesel. "And then Mr. Kennedy here admitted to the surgeon that Jeremy said the same thing years ago. Diesel's just been too . . . 'busy' to have it done."

Marcus's smile turned to a scowl. "If you weren't hurt, I'd hurt you myself. Why didn't Dad insist?"

"Because Diesel is a 'grown-up.'" Dani used air quotes. "His wishes had to be respected and your dad also respected his confidentiality. But I'm not that nice, so I'm making him do it." She glared at Diesel. "Because we've got kids now."

Diesel's cheeks heated. "I hate it when you're right," he mumbled, then brightened at the sight of a wheelchair being pushed toward them. "Hey, look, the chair is here."

Dani snorted, but kissed the top of his head, which was now covered in chocolate brown fuzz, still a little prickly against her lips. His hair would be so pretty if he grew it out. But that would be his call. The only thing she wasn't budging on was that damn bullet next to his heart.

Because that heart belonged to her now. He'd made it so the moment he'd told her he loved her. She wanted to shout it to whoever would listen, but remained content to be quietly happy as she walked alongside Diesel's wheelchair.

When they got outside, he drew a deep breath, immediately and visibly calmer.

Dani nodded to the nurse who'd pushed the chair. "We'll take it from here."

"I'll go get the car," Marcus said. "Sit tight."

"Wait," Diesel said and Marcus turned to him, concerned.

"Are you okay?" he demanded. "Do you need to go back in there?"

"Yeah," Diesel said. "But not like you think." He looked up at Dani. "I want to see him."

Scarlett frowned. "Why?"

But Dani understood. "Nothing against law enforcement, Scar. But I think we need to see him with our own eyes. I went in the ambulance with Jenny and Adam went with Diesel. We didn't see Kaiser delivered to the hospital. We need to see him *here*." She squeezed Diesel's shoulder. "Because we're going to pick up Joshua and Michael from the condo and take them home. I want to look them in the eye and say, 'Yes, Kaiser is handcuffed to a hospital bed and he can't ever hurt you again.'"

Diesel nodded, gratitude in his eyes. "What she said."

"Then let's go," Scarlett said. "I can flash my badge if they give us any trouble."

Cincinnati, Ohio
Wednesday, March 20, 2:00 a.m.

"Good evening, Father," the nurse said in greeting. "How can I help you?"

Grant nodded once, acknowledging her. "I'm Father Emerson. I've come to see Mr. Kaiser."

The nurse's smile fell away. "He's not allowed visitors."

"I'm not here on a social call, ma'am. I'm here to see if Mr. Kaiser would like to offer a last confession."

The nurse looked uncertain. "He's conscious and aware. Mostly. I suppose he can say no."

"And if he does, I'll leave. I promise." But he hoped that Kaiser would want to talk, though he wasn't entirely certain what he wanted the man to say.

Perhaps give an apology, he thought, then had yet another moment of self-doubt. This was stupid. Maybe even illegal. But not dangerous. The man was no threat to anyone now. He'd paced outside the hospital for hours before forcing himself to come in. Now he was here and he was going to talk to the bastard. He at least needed to know *why.*

Although he knew why. At least he knew what Diesel, Dani, and the cops believed to be true. That Kaiser had thought Wesley was a pedophile and had eliminated him along with John Brewer.

But deep down, Grant could admit that he wished Wesley's death had been an accident. That maybe, just maybe, he'd been killed because he'd tried to protect one of Kaiser's other victims. That he'd died heroically.

Not because Wes had been blinded by his need for revenge and gone into a sting completely vulnerable, without backup. Without caring if he survived or not.

That would be a waste of a life, and Wesley deserved better than that. Laurel deserved better than that. *Hell, I deserve better, too.*

"This way, Father," the nurse said, leading him to the ICU room that housed the man who'd killed his brother. A police officer stood outside the door, feet planted firmly. "This is Father Emerson," she said to the cop, and he gave Grant a nod.

Damn, that was easy. If he'd wanted to kill the guy, he could have. Nobody had frisked him. Nobody had even double-checked his ID.

He paused inside Kaiser's room, his own thought penetrating the numbness in his mind. *If I wanted to kill the guy, I could.*

Do I want to?

Yes. But there were hostages. Innocent people. A woman and her baby. Grant had read the articles online. Kaiser had used the woman to escape, then killed another young man after hiring him to buy baby supplies. He was keeping the woman and baby alive to buy his escape.

Except now, he couldn't escape. Cade Kaiser lay in the hospital bed, cuffed to the side rails. Machines beeped quietly as the man's chest rose and fell.

He was still alive. But barely, according to Dani Novak.

"Hello," Grant said softly.

Kaiser's eyes opened, but they weren't sharp. He was probably on some heavy painkillers. *Too bad.* Grant wanted him to suffer. This man had been responsible for hurting so many people. Though he *had* tried to protect John Brewer's stepson, Joshua.

Then tried to kill the other stepson, Michael. Kaiser was insane.

"Go to hell, Father," Kaiser rasped.

Well, then, Grant thought. *Gloves are off.* The man wasn't going to simply confess. "Maybe I will," he said, abandoning his priest persona. "If I do, I'm sure to see you there."

Kaiser blinked slowly. Then laughed, a broken, rusty sound. "We can get a beer. Maybe a few hookers."

Grant pulled up the chair beside Kaiser's bed and leaned in close. "Maybe the beer. I'm married."

"Then you're a . . ." Kaiser drew a labored breath. "Shitty priest." But then something flickered in his eyes and he blanched, pressing his head into the thin pillow. "Fucking hell," he whispered.

Grant studied the man, who looked like he'd seen a ghost. And maybe he had. *Because he killed my brother.* "Something wrong, Mr. Kaiser?"

Kaiser squinted, then shook his head. "Thought you looked . . . familiar."

"I have that kind of face. Just one of the crowd."

Kaiser swallowed hard. "Why . . . are you here?"

I'm not sure. "I wanted to meet you." True enough. "I wanted to find out *why*." Truer still. "Maybe I wanted to get your autograph," he added.

Kaiser looked at him, clearly uncertain. "You're crazy."

"Probably." He made a split-second decision, one of so many since Wesley's partner had visited his office. "I'm a writer. I've interviewed a lot of killers. I like to know why. But you're different. You killed to protect people."

"You're a cop," Kaiser said flatly. "You're trying to . . . trick me."

"No, I'm not a cop. I promise you that." Grant leaned a little closer. "You're going to die, Mr. Kaiser. It's just a matter of time. It might be here. Or it might be in prison. If you do survive, you're standing trial for a lot of murders."

Kaiser's lip curled. "Fuck off, *Father*."

"You will stand trial," Grant continued as if Kaiser hadn't spoken. "Wouldn't you like the jury to know *why* you killed all those people? And if you do die, don't you want to be remembered for the good you did?"

Kaiser's eyes narrowed. "What do you mean?"

"I mean that you'll be tried in a courtroom, but if the public knows the real you, you might even get a humanitarian award. John Brewer was trash. Killing him was a public service."

"Him and all the others," Kaiser mumbled.

"So you'll tell me?" Grant asked.

"What's in it for you?"

"I write a book and make money. And my curiosity is satisfied."

"I can . . . understand that. You think . . . it'll help? With a jury?"

Grant made himself shrug nonchalantly. "Can't hurt. If you die, you're a hero. If you live, the jury might see the truth. Who was the first person you killed?"

Kaiser's smile was eerily beatific. "The first was an old pedo. Name was Leigh Gladwin."

"When was that?"

"Four years ago."

"And the next?"

"Henry Lindquist. A guy who'd beaten his wife to death in front of his kid."

Grant reached into the pocket of the black suit coat for the small Bible he'd taken from the hotel's nightstand drawer. He'd had to give Wesley's cassock to the cops, but he'd managed to find a black suit and a detachable collar in a Brooks Brothers store at the mall. He looked like every priest he'd ever known.

The Bible had been a last-minute addition, intended to be part of the costume, but now he was happy he'd brought it. He found a blank page, pulled out a pen from the hotel, and wrote down the first two names.

Then he looked up at Kaiser, who wore a wistful expression, like he was enjoying this walk down memory lane. "And then, Mr. Kaiser? Who was next?"

Cincinnati, Ohio
Wednesday, March 20, 2:05 a.m.

There was a different dynamic entering the hospital as a visitor, Diesel thought. Even in a hospital wheelchair.

Marcus skillfully navigated the hallways, getting them to the ICU. Diesel didn't even mind the curious looks they got in the elevator, or the smug smirks on Marcus's and Scarlett's faces.

Because Dani had finally said it. *She loves me, too.* His chest felt tight, like his happiness was too big to fit.

Until they rolled out of the elevator into the ICU and the reason for his being there crashed through his mind. *Cade Kaiser.*

Who was still alive.

They stopped at the desk and asked to see Kaiser. The nurse directed them to the waiting room, telling them that "Mr. Kaiser" had another visitor at the moment, but that they should be done soon.

They sat in silence, Dani holding Diesel's hand tightly, but after a few minutes, her cell phone buzzed with an incoming call.

"It's a Cleveland area code," she murmured, then hit ACCEPT. "Hello?" She blinked in surprise. "Mrs. Masterson, hello. How can I help you?" She listened for a moment, then turned to Scarlett. "Do you know where Grant is? His wife is here in Cincinnati and he's not at his hotel."

"Put her on speaker," Scarlett said, then greeted Grant's wife. "I haven't talked to your husband since yesterday evening. I have tried calling him several times, though. I think he forgot to give us something last night."

"What was that?" Mrs. Masterson asked warily.

"His brother's cell phone. He mentioned that it was in the safe in Wesley's apartment here in town, but it wasn't there when we inventoried the evidence."

"I don't know anything about that," the woman said. "But I'm worried. I drove down this afternoon so that I could be with him while he made the funeral arrangements. I got to the hotel after eight, and fell asleep. When I woke up, he still wasn't back."

"I talked to him around eight," Dani said. "He was leaving the funeral home." She opened her mouth, then closed it again. "Can I call you right back?" she asked.

"Of course. Please hurry, though. I'm worried sick."

"I will," Dani assured her and ended the call.

"What's going on?" Diesel asked her.

"I don't know. Hold on." She walked quickly to the nurses' station and spoke for less than a minute before returning to them, her face abruptly drawn. "Kaiser's visitor is Father Emerson. He's giving him last rites."

"Holy shit," Scarlett muttered. She drew her badge from her pocket and motioned them to follow her. She spoke with the same nurse, who led them through the double doors into the unit.

Quietly they crossed to Kaiser's room, Marcus pushing Diesel's chair. Sure enough, there was Grant Masterson standing by Kaiser's bed. Holding a folded blanket in his hands, looking down at the killer with absolutely no expression at all.

"Get me in there," Diesel said to Marcus.

Scarlett flashed her badge to the cop on guard

duty, who frowned at her but let Marcus push Diesel into the room. Diesel caught the last part of what Grant was saying.

"—my *brother*, you sonofabitch. An undercover *cop*. You killed him."

Kaiser's eyes were wide. And scared. "You're . . ." He gasped. "Lying."

"No, but you're right about one thing," Grant said, so very quietly that Diesel had to strain to hear. "We *will* meet each other in hell."

"Father Emerson," Diesel said softly. "Grant," he snapped when the man didn't move.

Grant turned, his eyes flickering with something like horror. And maybe relief? His gaze focused on Diesel, swung to take in the group at the door, then back. "Mr. Kennedy. We meet again."

"And not in hell." Diesel made himself smile, even though part of him wanted to tell Grant to *do it*, to smother the bastard. But that would make Grant a murderer, and they might never find Evelyn Keys and her baby. "Cora is here. Waiting for you."

Grant faltered. "What?"

"She's here," Diesel repeated. "Waiting for you at your hotel. She loves you, Grant, and you've worried her today."

Grant's eyes filled with tears and he looked at the blanket he held. "Oh God," he whispered, and put the blanket down. "Oh my God." Picking up a Bible from the chair at Kaiser's bedside, he walked toward Diesel, his gait stiff, like he'd woken from a long sleep. He glanced at Marcus, then at Scarlett, who stood in the doorway. "I thought I could listen to him and I'd be okay. But I couldn't. I just got so mad." He blinked and the tears fell. "I'm just so damned angry."

"I know," Diesel murmured. "So am I. Come on, Grant. Let's get out of here. The bastard's not worth any more of your energy. Save it for your wife and kids."

That was what Diesel was doing—channeling his anger into the focus he needed to get through the pain so that he could get somewhere safe. With Dani.

She was his safe place.

He heard her, always thoughtful, telling the nurse that "Father Emerson" needed just a moment to collect himself. She too understood the rage that came with loss. Understood how it could drag you under if you allowed it.

Diesel held his breath as Marcus pulled the wheelchair from the room and Grant followed. The officer on duty resumed his post, seemingly unaware of what had nearly transpired.

When they were clear of the room, Scarlett took Grant's arm and led him from the ICU into the hall by the elevator. Then, thankfully, let him go.

Diesel hadn't been sure that she would. He thought he'd have to intervene on behalf of the man who'd learned in one day that he had lost both his siblings. But Diesel saw nothing but compassion in Scarlett's eyes. And Dani's. He couldn't see Marcus, but he assumed the same.

"What did you mean?" Diesel asked. "You thought you could listen to him?"

Grant's shoulders sagged. "I wanted to know *why*. He told himself he was protecting people. He might have even believed it. But he fed on their pain. He . . ." He swallowed. "He cut them up while they were still alive. He did that to Wesley. He told me how my brother suffered. He . . . got off on it. I think I just lost it."

Dani rubbed Grant's back comfortingly. "That had to be hard to hear."

"Yeah." Grant shuddered, then looked Scarlett in the eye. "Here." He dug in his pocket and Scarlett stiffened, going for the gun holstered at her hip, then relaxed when Grant handed her Wesley's cell phone.

"You 'forgot' to give it to me last night?" Scarlett said wryly.

"That's right," Grant said with a nod. "Password is Laurel's birthday." Then he handed Diesel the Bible he'd picked up from Kaiser's room. "For you, with my thanks. I hope you mend quickly. Give my best to Stone. I'm going to find my wife."

Cincinnati, Ohio
Wednesday, March 20, 3:00 a.m.

"Where to?" Marcus asked when they were all in his Subaru.

Dani grabbed Diesel's hand. She'd just finished a quick call to Grant's wife, telling her he was on his way. "The condo for a few hours so Diesel can sleep. Deacon and Faith are there with the boys, and they're asleep, too. We can go back to my house when everyone's woken up."

Scarlett twisted around from the front passenger seat to look at them. "The kids must have been so scared. But Troy said they were so good in the van. They did everything he told them while he was getting them back to the condo for safety."

"We called them as soon as we got to the hospital," Dani told her. "FaceTimed them so we could talk to Michael, too." The relief on their faces still made her eyes sting. "We promised them that I'd at least be there when they woke up in the morning."

"Actually," Diesel said, his head leaned back, his eyes closed, his jaw clenched tight against what had to be incredible pain, "I'd like to go to my house. Just to grab a few things," he added when Dani jolted in surprise.

"You need to rest," she said. "Take your pain meds and rest."

"I can pack you a bag and bring it to you," Scarlett said warily. "If you're okay with me going through your things."

Diesel's mouth quirked up, even though his eyes remained closed. "I do trust you, Scar, if that's what you're asking. I don't trust all the cops who swarmed my place when Stone got shot. I promise I'll obey doctor's orders when we get to the condo, but I'd sleep better knowing that nobody touched my stuff."

His "stuff," Dani thought, was all the computers in his office. He'd brought only one laptop with him when they'd raced from his house to the condo. "Can we load some of his hardware into the back?" she asked, thumbing at the cargo hold.

"Of course." Marcus set a course, and for a while, nobody spoke. Diesel's breathing had softened, slowing, and Dani hoped he would be able to sleep for the twenty minutes it would take to get there.

A thump got her attention and Dani realized she'd dozed as well. The thump was the Bible that Grant had given Diesel falling from his finally relaxed hand to the floorboard at his feet. Taking care not to jostle him, she leaned over to pick it up, then gave it a hard look.

Grant had hidden his brother's journal in the last Bible. She wondered if he'd hidden anything in this one. She opened it, a little disappointed to see that no hole had been carved inside. Idly she turned the first few pages.

And then stared. *Names.* She counted them quickly. Nearly a dozen names. Scott King was one of them. And near the bottom of the list?

John Brewer, Blake Emerson, and Richard Fischer. *Oh. My. God.*

"What's wrong?" Diesel asked, rolling his head sideways, a frown on his face. "You just said, 'Oh my God.' What is it?"

A little laugh bubbled up Dani's throat, sounding hysterical when it burst free. "Grant actually got him to confess. Kaiser, I mean. I was kidding when I told him that Kaiser would need a priest, but Grant did it. This is a list of Kaiser's victims."

Scarlett twisted in her seat, stunned. "What the hell? Gimme."

Diesel took the book from Dani's hands, suddenly alert. "He gave *you* the phone, Scarlett. He gave *me* the book."

Scarlett's eyes narrowed. "Diesel," she warned.

"Chill, Scar," Marcus said soothingly. "He'll hand it over. Let him look first."

Diesel was doing more than looking. He had his phone out, searching the names. Dani held the Bible open, tilting it so that the lights from the interstate's lamps illuminated the page, allowing Diesel to type with one hand while holding his phone with the other.

"Missing," he muttered, then searched for another name. "Missing. Suicide. Missing." Fifteen minutes had passed and they were nearing the exit for Diesel's house when he lifted his head. "They're all reported missing or dead, either accidental causes or suicide. All except one. Leigh Gladwin. Don't get off here," he ordered when Marcus moved to the exit lane. "We're getting off at New Haven. Hurry."

"Why?" Scarlett asked, clearly impatient.

Marcus said nothing, merely moving over a lane and flooring it.

Diesel leaned back, deep lines etched in his cheeks. "Henry Lindquist fell down his basement stairs three and a half years ago, breaking his neck."

"Like Charlie Akers," Dani said. "Quincy's CSU tech."

"Yes." Diesel spoke heavily, his teeth still clenched. Still in pain. "But Leigh Gladwin, the first name on the list, hasn't been reported dead or missing or anything. He's still paying property taxes on his house. In Harrison."

Dani understood. "That's not far from where the guy was killed after buying Pampers and baby formula."

Diesel handed his phone to Scarlett, then fell back against the seat. "There's the address."

Scarlett plugged it into her GPS. "Step on it, Marcus."

Harrison, Ohio
Wednesday, March 20, 3:40 a.m.

"Getting shot sucks," Diesel grumbled. He'd watched
Scarlett kick in the front door of the house supposedly owned by Leigh Gladwin, a seventy-year-old
veteran of the Vietnam War. Dani had followed her
in, against everyone's wishes, especially Diesel's. But
she'd argued that if Evelyn and her baby were there,
they might need her help, and Scarlett had reluctantly
agreed.

But they'd been in the house for a long time. Actually it had been less than a minute, but it *felt* like a
fucking long time.

Marcus chuckled. He was standing outside the
Subaru, talking to Diesel through a lowered window.
Diesel knew his friend really wanted to be at his
wife's side, but had stayed behind to keep Diesel safe.
"That's what you said the last time you got shot."

Diesel pressed the heel of his hand to his chest,
over the bullet that he'd carried for ten years. He'd
gotten used to it, he realized. "It's gonna be weird,
not having it anymore," he said, knowing Marcus
would understand what he meant.

"I can't believe you wouldn't let Dad help you.
You're a real asshole, Diesel."

"Yeah," Diesel agreed. "It's . . . I don't know. It's
almost like I needed to keep it."

Marcus looked at him sharply. "Why? So that I'd
feel guilty all these years, knowing you were walking
around with my bullet in your heart?"

Diesel blinked at him. "What? Why would you . . ."
Oh. It had honestly never occurred to him, not in *all
these years*, that Marcus would feel guilty that Diesel
had taken a bullet meant for him. *But it should have.*

And maybe he had wanted Marcus to feel guilty.
Or at least responsible. A little. *No, not really.* "I
didn't want you to feel guilty. But I did like being . . .
part of you guys. Part of the family." And the bullet

had been his entrée. He'd earned his place at the O'Bannion family's table.

Marcus was scowling at him. "You fucking asshole. Did you really think we only love you because you almost *died* for me? My God, Diesel. I can't—" He yanked open Diesel's door and leaned in so that they were nose to nose. "We love you for *you*, you idiot." He hooked his hand around Diesel's neck, then stilled, his touch gentling. "Sorry, man. You got me so mad that I forgot you were hurt." He let him go, bracing his hands on the vehicle's frame. "But tell me that you believe me that we don't care about the damn bullet. We care about *you*."

They love me for me. "I know." He'd always known it, down deep.

"Do you?" Marcus shook his head. "Do you really? Goddammit, when you're better, I'm going to kick your ass."

"Nothing says love like an ass-kicking," Diesel said dryly, but he was smiling. "I knew, Marcus. I did. But maybe I . . . I don't know. Maybe I didn't feel like I deserved it for only being me."

And maybe he and Dani Novak had even more in common than he'd thought.

Marcus's expression softened. "But you feel different now?"

Diesel thought about the woman who'd dedicated her life to caring for others so that she'd be more deserving. When everyone who mattered already loved her for herself. "Yeah. I think I get it now."

He hoped Dani did. If she didn't, he'd spend the rest of his life convincing her.

Marcus smiled slyly. "So? You and Dani? Finally?"

Diesel realized that he and Marcus hadn't talked since the night Stone was shot. "Yeah. It's all good. Finally."

Marcus swallowed hard. "Good. I want my child's godfather to be happy."

Diesel's mouth fell open. "But . . ."

Marcus grinned. "Still not naming him Elvis."

"Thank God," Diesel muttered. "What about Stone, though? Won't he want to be the godfather?"

"He can be godfather for the next one. He's happy to be an uncle. And Diesel, I can't think of a better role model for my kid."

Diesel wiped his eyes with his sleeve. "Shit. Not fair, man."

Marcus ran a hand over Diesel's head, but Diesel could feel his hand tremble. "I can't get used to you with hair. It's been forever."

Subject changed. *Thank God.* Too much emotion for one night.

The front door of Gladwin's house opened and Marcus straightened abruptly. "It's Scar and she's got the woman and her baby. Be right back."

"Where's Dani?" Diesel yelled after him. He heaved his body, managing to turn himself in the seat, but had to stop with only his feet out of the door, because the world started to spin.

And it *hurt.* Mother*fuck*, it hurt. It had been bad when he'd remained still. But moving? "Shit."

The passenger door opened on the other side of the Subaru. "Diesel, get your ass back in the car," Marcus snapped, then his voice gentled. "Sorry, Evelyn. My friend just left the hospital against medical advice. Diesel, Evelyn. Evelyn, Diesel. Sit tight, Evelyn. The ambulance will be here soon."

Diesel edged himself back into the seat. The woman was in her late twenties but looked a lot older due to the circles under her eyes. "Hi, Evelyn. Where is Dani?"

The woman's lips curved slightly as she climbed into the car, her arms reaching for the baby that Marcus held. Once her child was safely in her arms, she turned to Diesel. "Dani says for you to stay the hell put and that she is fine." She sighed wearily. "There's a guy down there and she's taking care of him. He's been in and out of consciousness since Kaiser stuck me in there. I don't even know how long ago that was."

It took Diesel a moment. "It's Wednesday morning and he escaped with you on Monday morning, so two days. Do you know who the guy is?"

"Andrew McNab. He came to enough to tell me that."

"Oh, good," Diesel breathed out. The interpreter wasn't dead. "And how are you?"

"Unhurt. Just . . . tired. I'm so tired."

"Join the club," Diesel said and she laughed wearily.

"Dani said that you found me. That you found this place. Thank you." Her voice broke. "Thank you so much."

Diesel gave her a nod, then they both lapsed into silence until several police cruisers and two ambulances arrived. The first ambulance took Evelyn and her baby. Paramedics raced from the second, carrying a stretcher into the basement.

Minutes later they reappeared, a man strapped to the stretcher, followed by Dani. She stopped at the ambulance to talk to the paramedics, then stepped back when they drove away, siren screeching.

She dropped into the seat Evelyn had just vacated. "Andrew the interpreter."

"Will he be okay?" Diesel asked.

"I think so. He came out of it for a few minutes and the first thing he asked was if Michael was okay." She settled in the seat so that she was looking at him. "I don't know how much longer he would have lasted. He's got some internal bleeding and he's terribly dehydrated. So thank you, Diesel Kennedy."

He took her hand and kissed it. "Love you."

She smiled. "Love you, too."

"I think I'm going to let Scarlett and Marcus pack up my computers." He lifted a brow. "Can I stay with you for a while until I'm all healed up?"

She blinked. "You have to ask? Silly man. Of course you can. Besides, you have to read Joshua's bedtime stories. He likes how you do the voices."

Marcus got behind the wheel. "Scar's going to get a ride back with one of the uniforms. She told me to find you somewhere that you can rest."

Diesel closed his eyes. "Then let's go get the boys and go home."

Epilogue

Hands closed over Dani's shoulders, giving her a tiny shake. "Go outside," Deacon said. "Everything is perfect. Go enjoy your party."

Dani dried her hands on a towel, then turned and pressed a kiss to her brother's cheek. "I'm going to. Just had to get the cake ready."

"It's perfect," Deacon said again, and it was. Decorated with Hawkeye and Storm action figures plus cartoon images of the dogs that were their namesakes, it was big enough to feed thirty people—or ten people and two teenagers. And in bold letters in the middle of the cake were the words HAPPY BIRTHDAY TO OUR FAMILY.

Deacon picked up the cake platter. "Hold the door open. I'll carry it outside."

Dani did and took a deep breath of crisp fall air. It had been hot in the kitchen, as she'd had her oven going since the night before. But it was worth it. *So worth it.*

The weather had cooperated, giving them a beautiful day for their celebration. Most of their guests wore jeans and heavy sweaters, but a few still wore the suits and dresses they'd worn to court, she and Deacon among them.

It had been an easy adoption, all things considered. Joshua and Michael had no living relatives, so there'd been no need to terminate parental rights.

Freeing the boys of their unstable mother and abusive stepfather was probably the only really good thing Cade Kaiser had done. Dani had found herself ethically torn on the other murders. Except for Wesley Masterson, Charlie Akers, George Garrett, and the innocent kid who'd bought Kaiser diapers and antibiotic cream, his victims had been the scum of the earth and deserved to die. But it was difficult to condone Kaiser's vigilantism. Yes, Diesel was also a vigilante, but he didn't kill anyone. He saved women and children all over the city from abusers. But Kaiser had *enjoyed* torturing his victims—and he'd tried to kill Michael, several times. That fact alone erased any other good he might have claimed credit for.

But they never had to worry about Cade Kaiser again. The man had held on for another day in the ICU, but had died, alone and in pain. *Not enough pain,* Dani thought, but brushed the anger aside. She wasn't sorry she'd stabbed him. She only had to look at her two sons to know she'd done exactly the right thing.

Michael and Joshua were happy kids. Happy, healthy kids who knew that they were loved. That was the most important thing.

She found Joshua easily. He was "introducing" Storm—who was already gigantic—to Scarlett's daughter, now a month old. Scarlett and Marcus had named her Michelle, after Marcus and Stone's younger brother, Mikhail, who'd been killed five years before.

Jeremy and Keith were the proudest grandparents Dani had ever seen—although they'd made it clear to Joshua and Michael that little Michelle was their third grandchild. Michael and Joshua were the first two, because Diesel was their adopted son.

Michael had grinned for days. So had Diesel. And

if Dani hadn't already loved the two men who'd taken them all under their collective fatherly wings, she certainly would now.

"Dani?" Deacon said in her good ear. "Stop grinning like a lunatic and tell me where to put this cake. I'm not getting any younger, y'know."

Laughing, Dani pointed to the space she'd cleared at the end of the long table filled with food. "There. Thanks, Deacon."

"You're welcome." He gave her a little nudge with his foot. "Go. Mingle."

She did as he suggested, chatting with the guests, making sure all the pregnant women had what they needed. Scarlett's announcement had triggered a rash of baby making, with Faith and Meredith due within weeks of each other. Delores wasn't far behind.

Apparently Stone had healed *very* quickly, but he had just muttered something like "I'm rubber and you're glue" when Diesel had teased him about it, because they truly were ten years old. And because Diesel had healed quickly, too.

Thank God for that, Dani thought with an inner smirk. There would be no babies for them, but that didn't stop them from "perfecting the technique," as Diesel termed it.

Parrish had also recovered, as had Jenny and Miles. Mostly. Miles was still on leave from the clinic, and the nerve damage Jenny had sustained might mean the end of her nursing career.

Thankfully, Andrew McNab was back to work—and he and Evelyn had become cozy during his convalescence. They stood together off to the side of the yard, Evelyn's baby on Andrew's hip. Dani thought she'd seen a ring on Evelyn's finger earlier, but hadn't had time to ask for details. She would before the afternoon was over.

Her own ring had already been oohed and aahed over. Diesel had proposed two months after he'd been shot, the night before he'd gone in for surgery to remove the bullet poised next to his heart. Which had, of course, been successful, just as Jeremy had been telling him for years.

They'd be married on Christmas Eve, with Scarlett's uncle Trace conducting the ceremony. The invitations had gone out, both of them stunned at how many people they knew. Life was very good.

Neighbors milled around, smiling and chatting. It had been a little dicey directly after Kaiser had blown up the neighborhood, and Dani and Diesel had campaigned hard to regain the favor of their neighbors, working with the insurance company to fix the damage. But all it had really taken was one look at Joshua's winsome smile and the neighbors had been putty in their hands.

"Mama." Joshua tugged on her jacket. "When can we eat the cake?"

She smiled down at him. "Good question. Let's go find your dad and brother so we can cut it all together." Joshua had slid into calling them Mama and Dad pretty quickly. It had taken Michael longer, and he still called them Dani and Coach more often than not, but that was okay. Even if he never called them Mom and Dad, he still knew they loved him.

She held out her hand for Joshua and he took it, chattering about how much the new baby liked Storm. The overgrown puppy was exactly what the little boy had needed, giving him a sense of permanence and safety. Storm never left his side, just like Hawkeye never strayed from Michael's.

She saw Hawkeye before she found Diesel and Michael, the dog's wagging tail visible beyond the far corner of the house. Diesel and Michael stood shoulder to shoulder, each holding one edge of a large piece of paper. Greg stood next to Michael, signing animatedly. The older man on Diesel's left had been a surprise arrival—his old teacher, Walt Dyson, who'd been delighted to see Diesel so happy. Marcus completed the group. He was pointing to the paper with one hand and pointing up at the house with the other.

"Um, guys?" Dani said. "What's going on?"

Diesel and Michael both spun, each trying to hide the paper behind their backs, then laughing when they both dropped it. "We wanted to show Father Dyson," Michael signed, beaming. "It's a surprise. For you."

She narrowed her eyes in mock suspicion. "What kind of surprise?"

"You'll like it," Joshua said with a giggle.

"You knew, too?" She smiled at him. His giggles were bright spots in every day. "Am I the only one who isn't in on it?"

Diesel picked up the paper and held it for her to see. "Take a look."

"It's a blueprint," she said cautiously, stepping closer to study it. "For what?"

Diesel nervously rubbed one hand over his bald-again head. He did indeed have a gorgeous head of hair, but he'd shaved it after a few months, saying it was "too damn much trouble." Either way, he was the sexiest man she'd ever seen, especially in the suit he was wearing, which fit him perfectly. He'd tugged the tie loose, revealing a glimpse of the ink she loved so much.

"For the house," he said, then met her eyes. "We're filled up now, and I know you've had to turn away two deaf foster kids who needed you."

It was true, and it had broken her heart to turn them away, but Michael and Joshua were her sons now. They came first. She and Diesel were trying to figure out how to fit a small bedroom into the available space in the basement, but there wasn't enough room.

Then his words sank in and she realized what she was looking at. She jerked her gaze up to stare at him, shocked. "Is this an extension to the house?"

He nodded once. Nervously. "Yes. Marcus and I are going to build it."

She blinked rapidly. "But how are we going to pay for it?"

"I have some money put aside," Diesel said. "And Marcus, Stone, and Jeremy are putting up the rest."

"It'll be our wedding present to you," Marcus explained.

"Do you like it?" Greg asked, his signs as nervous as Diesel seemed.

But Dani was speechless, and could only stare.

"We got zoning approval to add three bedrooms, two bathrooms, and a second playroom," Diesel explained. "Walt's got three pinball machines he's going to give us. Plus the game systems and some board games and puzzles and maybe—"

She leaped, throwing herself at him, her arms wrapping around his neck. He caught her as he always did, supporting her like she weighed nothing as he held her inches off the ground. "It's perfect," she said into his neck. "*You're* perfect. Thank you, thank you."

"I think she likes it," Joshua said, making them laugh. He tugged on her jacket again. "Can we *please* have cake now?"

Dani gave Diesel's neck one last hard squeeze and he lowered her to the ground. "Yes, Joshua," she said. "Let's go have cake." To Diesel, she whispered, "You are *so* getting lucky later."

Chuckling, Diesel signed, "I'm lucky every day." He waggled his brows. "I get to wake up to you."

Michael groaned. "Please. You promised no gross . . . stuff." But his smile was as bright as Joshua's. "Come on. Let's get cake."

My dear readers,

I hope you enjoyed Into the Dark! *This is a story of my heart in so many ways. The characters have become like friends, and I hope it will be the same for you.*

Dani Novak and her brothers, Deacon and Greg, have Waardenburg syndrome, just as I do. I didn't realize that I was subconsciously writing the syndrome into Deacon's character until it was time to write his book, and then his white hair and unusual eyes suddenly made all the sense in the world!

FYI, Waardenburg syndrome is a genetic condition that primarily impacts hearing and pigmentation (in hair, eyes, and skin). It is hereditary, with a worldwide incidence of about one in forty thousand. It is carried by the women in my family, although in some families, it's carried by the men.

Dani Novak has dark hair with white streaks and she's deaf in one ear, just like me. She has a blue and a brown eye, just like my aunt and uncle do. (My cousin's eyes are bicolored, similar to Deacon's.) Dani's brother Greg is completely deaf, like my own daughter.

The use of sign language in Into the Dark *is based upon my own experiences over the years. My husband and I began to study sign language when our younger daughter was only a few weeks old. We had so much to learn!*

Many authors will differentiate signed dialog and spoken/"hearing" dialog with italics or special *punctuation, like <<Hello>>. I chose to present the signed dialog in the same way as spoken dialog. The characters are communicating, whether their words come off their hands or from their mouths.*

This is perhaps the biggest personal "aha!" moment I had while learning to sign. Language and speech are not the same. *Language is the communication of concepts and ideas. Speech is merely one method of communication.*

Here are some other things I learned that you'll find useful now that you have read Into the Dark:

- *Sign language is not universal. American Sign Language (ASL) evolved from French Sign Language. British Sign Language is so different from ASL that an American deaf person and a British deaf person would need an interpreter to communicate with each other.*
- *ASL is its own language, with its own syntax and grammatical structure.*
- *There are many methods of visual communication. In our family, we relied on three: ASL, Signed Exact English (SEE), and Pidgin Signed English (PSE). SEE is useful when signing and speaking at the same time, as it associates a sign with each of the English words. (It's very useful when teaching someone to read English.) However, SEE is a bit cumbersome, so we usually used Pidgin Signed English. PSE is a bit of ASL, a bit of SEE, and a bit of family/ local sign. When Dani and Diesel sign to Michael and Greg in* Into the Dark, *they're usually using PSE.*
- *Not all parents of deaf children learn to sign. Studies show that over ninety percent of deaf children are born to hearing parents. Less than twenty percent of those parents learn to sign, less than ten percent with any fluency. Many people are shocked by this. I certainly was. There are a number of reasons for this statistic, however.*

- *First and foremost, many doctors tell parents of a deaf child that if they use sign language at home, their child will never speak and will never be "normal."*
- *Doctors often urge the use of a cochlear implant, a device that converts sound to digital pulses the brain can interpret. Importantly, CI is not a "cure" for deafness. It is an aid, much like a wheelchair or a cane. When a CI user takes off their processor, they are still deaf.*
- *Some parents don't have the means or opportunity to take ASL classes.*
- *Some, like Michael's mother in* Into the Dark, *simply don't care to learn, or they only learn the "discipline" signs—no, bad, stop, go, come, bed.*

- *Not all deaf people speech read or "read lips." It's a learned skill, and some are better at it than others. Don't assume a deaf person can speech read.*

There are so many topics I didn't even touch on in this book, the biggest of which is Deaf culture. That's a book all in itself! If you'd like to learn more about these topics and others, I recommend the book For Hearing People Only: Answers to Some of the Most Commonly Asked Questions about the Deaf Community, Its Culture, and "Deaf Reality," *by Matthew Moore and Linda Levitan.*

> *All the best, and thank you for reading* Into the Dark,
> *Karen*

If you missed the first book in Karen Rose's
Cincinnati series, keep reading for an excerpt of . . .

CLOSER THAN YOU THINK

Available now!

"It's only a house." Dr. Faith Corcoran gripped her steering wheel, willing herself to look at the house in question as she slowed her Jeep to a crawl. "Just four walls and some floors."

She drove past, eyes stubbornly pointed forward. She didn't need to see. She knew exactly what it looked like. She knew that it was three stories of gray brick and hewn stone. That it had fifty-two windows and a square central tower that pointed straight to heaven. She knew that the foyer floor was Italian marble, that the wide staircase had an elegantly curved banister made out of mahogany, and that the chandelier in the dining room could sparkle like a million diamonds. She knew the house top to bottom.

And she also knew that it wasn't the four walls and floors that she really feared, but what lay beneath them. *Twelve steps and a basement.*

She did a U-turn and stopped the Jeep in front of the house. Her heart was beating faster, she thought clinically. "That's a normal physiological response. It's just stress. It will pass."

As the words slipped out, she wondered who she

was trying to convince. The dread had been steadily building with every mile she'd driven the past two days. By the time she crossed the river into Cincinnati, it had become a physical pain in her chest. Thirty minutes later, she was close to hyperventilating, which was both ridiculous and unacceptable.

"For God's sake, grow the hell up," she snapped, killing the engine and yanking her keys from the ignition. She leapt from the Jeep, angry when her knees wobbled. Angry that, after all this time, the thought of the house could make her feel like she was nine years old.

You are not *nine. You are a thirty-two-year-old adult who has survived multiple attempts on your life. You are* not *afraid of an old house.*

Drawing strength from her anger, Faith lifted her eyes, looking at the place directly for the first time in twenty-three years. It looked . . . *Not that different,* she thought, drawing an easier breath. *It's old and massive. Oppressive.* It was more than a little run-down, yet still imposing.

It looked old because it *was* old. The house had stood on O'Bannion land for more than a hundred and fifty years, a testament to a way of life long gone. The three stories of brick and stone loomed large and dark, the tower demanding that all visitors look up.

Faith obeyed, of course. As a child, she'd never been able to resist the tower. That hadn't changed. Nor had the tower. It maintained its solitary dignity, even with its windows boarded up.

All fifty-two windows were boarded up, in fact, because the O'Bannion house had been abandoned twenty-three years ago. And it showed.

The brick stood, weathered but intact, but the gingerbread woodwork she'd once loved was faded and cracked. The porch sagged, the glass of the front door covered with decades of grime.

Gingerly, she picked her way across the patchy grass to the front gate. The fence was wrought iron.

Old-fashioned. Built to last, like the house itself. The hinges were rusty, but the gate swung open. The sidewalk was cracked, allowing weeds to flourish.

Faith took a moment to calm her racing heart before testing the first step up to the porch.

No, not the porch. The veranda. Her grandmother had always called it "the veranda" because it wrapped around the entire house. They used to sit out there and sip lemonade, she and Gran. *And Mama, too.* Before, of course. Afterward . . . there was no lemonade.

There was no anything. For a long time, there was absolutely nothing.

Faith swallowed hard against the acrid taste that filled her mouth, but the memory of her mother remained. *Don't think about her. Think about Gran and how she loved this old place. She'd be so sad to see it like this.*

But, of course, Gran never would see it again, because she was dead. *Which is why I'm here.* The house and all it contained now belonged to Faith. Whether she wanted it or not.

"You don't have to live here," she told herself. "Just sell the property and go . . ."

Go where? Not back to Miami, that was for damn sure. *You're just running away.*

Well, yeah. Duh. Of course she'd run away. Any sensible person would run if she'd been stalked for the past year by a homicidal ex-con who'd nearly killed her once before.

Some had said that she shouldn't be surprised she'd been stalked, that by doing therapy with scum-of-the-earth sex offenders, she'd put herself in harm's way. Some even had said she cared more about the criminals than the victims.

Those people were wrong. None of them knew what she'd done to keep the offenders from hurting anyone else. What she'd risked.

Peter Combs had attacked her four years ago because he'd believed that her "snitching" to his probation officer about missed therapy sessions had sent his reoffending ass to prison. Faith shuddered to think of what he would have done had he known the truth back then, that her role in his reincarceration had been far more than marking him absent. But given the cat-and-mouse game he'd played with her in the year following his release, the fact that his stalking had escalated to attempted murder four times now . . . Maybe he did know. Maybe he'd figured it out.

Slipping her hand into the pocket of her jacket, Faith's fingers brushed the cold barrel of the Walther PK380 she hadn't left her Miami apartment without in almost four years. Miami PD hadn't been any help at all, so she'd taken her safety into her own hands.

She was sensible. Prepared. But still scared. *I'm so tired of being afraid.*

Suddenly aware that she'd dropped her gaze to her feet, she defiantly lifted her chin to look up at the house. Yeah, she'd run, all right. She'd run to the one place she feared almost as much as the place she'd left behind. Which sounded about as crazy now as it had when she'd fled Miami two days ago. But it had been her only choice. *No one else will die because of me.*

She'd packed the Jeep with as many of her possessions as she could make fit and left everything else behind, including her career as a mental-health therapist and the name under which she'd built it. A legal name change, sealed by the court for confidentiality, had ensured that Faith Frye was no more.

Faith Corcoran was a clean slate. She was starting fresh. No one she'd left behind in Miami—friend or foe—knew about this house. No one knew her grandmother had died, so no one could tell Peter Combs. He would never think to look for her here.

She even had a new job—a sensible job in the HR department of a bank in downtown Cincinnati. She would have coworkers who wore conservative suits and stared at spreadsheets. She would make an actual living wage and receive benefits for the very first time. But the most valuable benefit would be the bank's security, just in case her efforts to lose Faith Frye hadn't been quite good enough.

Lightly, she touched her throat. Although the wound had healed long ago, the scar remained, a permanent illustration of what the man who hunted her was capable of doing. But at least she'd lived. Gordon hadn't been so fortunate.

Guilt and grief welled up in equal measures, choking her. *I'm so sorry, Gordon.* Her former boss had had the bad luck to be standing next to her when the bullets started to fly—bullets meant for her. Now his wife was a widow, his children fatherless.

She couldn't bring Gordon back. But she could do everything in her power to make sure it never happened again. If Combs couldn't find her, he couldn't hurt her or anyone else. Her grandmother's passing had presented her with a place to run to when she'd needed it most.

The house was a gift. That it was also her oldest nightmare couldn't stop her from accepting it. Forcing her feet to move, she marched up the remaining two steps to the front door, dug the key from her pocket, and went to open the door.

But the key wouldn't open the lock. After the third try, it finally sank in that the key didn't fit. Her grandmother's attorney had given her the wrong key.

She couldn't have gone inside if she'd wanted to. Not today, anyway. The relief that geysered up inside her made her a little ashamed. *You're a coward, Faith.*

It was just a delay of one day, she reasoned. Tomorrow she would get the right key, but for the moment her inability to enter bolstered her courage.

Peeking through the dirty glass on the front door, she saw a room full of furniture, draped in sheets. Her grandmother had taken only a few favorite pieces when she'd left the house for a townhouse in the city twenty-three years ago. The rest she'd left to Faith.

The thought of unveiling the furnishings elicited the first spark of excitement Faith had felt in a long time. Many of the items were museum-quality, or so her mother had told her on many occasions. *This will all be mine someday, Faith, and when I die it'll be yours, so pay attention. This is your legacy and it's high time you learned to appreciate it.*

The memory of her mother's voice doused her excitement. She could recall the fear that had filled her at her mother's words as if it were yesterday. *But I don't want my legacy,* she'd replied. *Not if it makes you die, Mama.*

An affectionate tug on her pigtail. *Silly girl, I'm not going anywhere for years and years. You'll be Gran's age before this place is yours.*

And in her eight-year-old eyes, Gran was already ancient. *Then I have lots of time to learn about my legacy, don't I?* She'd hidden her relief with a roll of her eyes, she remembered. She'd also remembered being far more interested in the golden retriever that belonged to the cook's son than in the silver teapot in her mother's hands. *Can I go outside and play? Pleeeease?*

An exasperated sigh had escaped her mother's lips. *Fine. Just don't get dirty. Your father will be back soon with the car and we'll head home. But next time we're here, young lady . . .* Her mother had shaken her finger at her with a smile. *We do teapots, 101.*

But the next time Faith had come to this house there had been no talk of teapots or anything else that was happy. Her mother was gone, leaving her life irrevocably changed.

Faith ruthlessly shoved the memory from her mind. Dwelling on the past would make her crazy. She had enough problems in the present without dredging up old hurts.

Except . . . this was a hurt that needed dredging. And then purging. She hadn't been back to this place since that last horrible day. Never told her mother how angry she was. She'd never told anyone. She'd covered up her rage and hurt and fear and moved forward. Or so she'd told herself, but here she was, twenty-three years later. Still hurting. Still angry. And still afraid.

Time to deal, Faith. Do it now. Resolute, she walked around the house before she could change her mind, not realizing that she was holding her breath until it came rushing out.

There it was, off in the corner of the backyard. *A respectable distance from the house,* as Gran had always said. Someone had kept it tidy all these years, pulling the weeds, cutting the grass around the wrought-iron fence, fashioned in the same style as the one bordering the front. The historical society, Faith remembered. Gran's attorney had told her that the local historical society paid for the upkeep because the O'Bannion cemetery was a historic landmark.

Her family was buried here, all the way back to Zeke O'Bannion, who'd died at the Battle of Shiloh in 1862. She knew who rested here, remembered all of their stories, because, unlike silver teapots, she'd found their stories riveting. They'd been real people, lived real lives. Like a faithful dog, she'd followed her mother whenever she visited the graves, helping her pull weeds, hanging on her every word as she talked about their ancestors.

Faith pushed at the gate, frowning when it refused to budge. A glance down revealed the issue—a padlock. Her grandmother's attorney hadn't given her any other keys, so she walked around the fence until she came to the most recent headstone, carved in black marble.

It was a double stone, the inscription on the left weathered over twenty-three years. *Tobias William O'Bannion.* Faith remembered her grandfather as a stern, severe man who'd attended Mass every single day of his life. *Probably to confess losing his temper,* she thought wryly. He'd had a wicked one.

The inscription on the other side of the black marble was crisp and new. *Barbara Agnes Corcoran O'Bannion. Beloved wife, mother, grandmother. Philanthropist.*

Most of that was true. Gran had been a strong supporter of a number of charities. And Tobias had loved her in his own way. *I loved her.* Enough, in fact, to have taken her name.

Most of her children had loved her. Faith's mother's younger brother Jordan had taken care of Gran uncomplainingly until she'd drawn her last breath. Faith's mother had been devoted to Gran, although Faith wasn't sure how much of her devotion had been love. And the jury was out on Jeremy, her grandmother's only other living child. He was . . . estranged.

Faith's grandmother had been quietly laid to rest next to her grandfather in a very private service with only her priest and Faith's uncle Jordan in attendance, in accordance with her grandmother's wishes. Faith thought it was likely due to the fact that Tobias's funeral had become a bitter battleground that had shattered the O'Bannion family.

And her own little family as well, she thought as she moved past the next five headstones, all children of Barbara and Tobias who had not survived into adulthood. She stopped at the sixth headstone. Its design was identical to that of her grandparents', the inscription as weathered as Tobias's. Not surprising since they'd been bought and carved at the same time.

One side, her father's, was mercifully blank. The other bore a terrible lie.

MARGARET O'BANNION SULLIVAN
BELOVED WIFE AND MOTHER

"Hello, Mother," Faith murmured. "It's been a while."

A high-pitched scream floated across the air as if

in response. Startled, Faith did a three-sixty, looking for the source, but saw nothing. No one had followed her, of that she'd made certain. There was nothing like being stalked to teach a woman to be careful.

No one was here. It was just Faith, the house, and the fifty acres of fallow farmland that was all that remained of the O'Bannion family holdings. She patted the pocket of her jacket, calmed by the presence of her gun. "It was a dog howling," she said firmly. "That's all."

Or it could simply have been her mind playing tricks, echoing the scream from her nightmares. *Twelve steps and a basement.* Sometimes she woke from the nightmare to find herself screaming for real—which had scared the hell out of her ex-husband, a fact that gave Faith a level of satisfaction that was admittedly immature. Officer Charlie Frye deserved a hell of a lot more than a start in the night for what he'd done.

Her mother had done so much worse to her dad. "Dad deserved a hell of a lot better than what you did to him. So did I. I still do." She hesitated, then spat the words out. "I have hated you for twenty-three years. I *lied* for you. I lied to Dad so that he'd never know what you did. So if you meant to hurt him, you failed. If you meant to hurt me, then congratulations. You hit the bull's-eye."

It suddenly occurred to her that her best revenge might be to live as her mother had always expected to—as mistress of the manor. It was almost enough to make Faith smile, but the memory of her father's devastation made her angry all over again.

The thought of her father brought to mind the promise she'd made. Reluctantly, she snapped a photo of Margaret's headstone with her phone and texted it to her dad. He'd made a pilgrimage to her grave every few years, but a recent stroke had him housebound. Faith had promised him the photo so he'd know for sure that her grave was okay.

Got here safely, she typed. *All is well. Mama's grave is—*

Her finger paused as she searched for the right words, rejecting all the wrong ones that would be sure to hurt her father, who still believed the inscription to be true. "Well cared for" was honest, she decided, so she typed it. *Will call from the hotel.*

She didn't dare call now. Standing here, looking at her mother's headstone . . . She wouldn't be able to keep the bitterness from her voice. Swallowing hard, she hit SEND, then she turned back to her Jeep with a sigh. If she couldn't get into the house, there was nothing more to be accomplished here today. She'd hit the Walmart near her hotel to buy some cleaning supplies and turn in early. She had a busy day tomorrow.

Mt. Carmel, Ohio
Sunday, November 2, 6:05 p.m.

His hand froze, midstrike, as the light in the ceiling began to flash. *What the hell?*

The alarm. Someone was outside.

"Fuck," he bit out. It couldn't be the caretaker. He'd mown the grass a few days before. It was a trespasser. Rage bubbled up, threatening to break free. Someone had the nerve to trespass here? To interrupt him *now*?

He glanced down at the young woman on his table. Her mouth was open, her breath sawing in and out of her lungs, her expression one of desperation. It had taken him two fucking days to get her to this point. After fighting him tooth and nail, she'd finally begun to scream.

She had the most remarkable threshold for pain. He'd be able to play with her for a long, long time. But not right now. Someone had trespassed and needed to be dealt with.

If he was lucky, it was someone who was lost, looking for directions. When they realized the house was abandoned, they'd leave. If not . . .

He smiled. He'd have another playmate.

He put the knife aside, several feet away. Just in case. The woman on his table had proven to be smart and strong. A little too smart and strong for his liking, but he'd soon fix that. The moment his captives' wills broke, the moment they realized that no one would come to save them, that he was their master for as long as he chose . . . He smiled. *That* was satisfaction.

Closing the door behind him, he left the torture room and went to his office. Powering up his laptop, he brought up the cameras, expecting to see a salesman or someone stranded—

He stared at the monitor, shock rendering him motionless for several long seconds.

It can't be. It simply can't be. But it was. It was *her.* She was *here.* Standing at the cemetery fence. Staring at the grave markers, her face as cold as ice.

How can she be here? He'd seen the news reports, the pictures of her little blue Prius, twisted and smashed. She could not have walked away from that. *I know I killed her.*

"Fuck," he whispered. Obviously, he had not. The girl had more lives than a damn cat.

Go, finish the job. But first he had to make sure she was alone. He switched to the camera out front and got another jolt. A Jeep Cherokee, bright red. Filled with boxes.

She'd already bought a new car, but at least there were no other passengers. *Good.* He'd take care of her once and for all. He'd have to catch her unaware because the bitch carried a gun. He couldn't allow her the opportunity to use it. *She's all alone out there. Kill her now.*

He switched back to the cemetery camera, then cursed again. She had a cell phone out, taking a picture. He ran to the stairs, taking them two at a time.

Skidded to a stop at the back door and peered through the gap between the boards that covered its window.

His heart sank. She was typing into the phone, giving it a final tap.

She'd sent a text. She'd texted a damn photo.

Somebody would know she'd been here. He couldn't kill her now. Not here. *Never here.* Disappointment mixed with his panic. He couldn't risk it. Couldn't risk the law coming around, poking into his business. Or even worse, the press.

Find her and kill her, but not here. He edged his way to the front room, peered out the window. His pulse pounding in his head, he watched her get in the Jeep and drive away.

Part of him wanted to jump in his van and follow her. To kill her now.

But he made himself slow down and think. He liked to plan. To know exactly what he'd do at every phase of a hunt. At the moment he was too rattled— and anyone would be, seeing her at the cemetery like that. He'd been so sure he'd killed her. But she was obviously quite alive.

That would soon be remedied.

He drew a deep breath. He was calming down now. More in control. This was better. A rattled man made mistakes. Mistakes drew attention, requiring even more drastic cleanup. This he had learned the hard way.

He'd find her easily enough. He'd followed her long enough to know her preference in hotels—and Faith was even more of a creature of habit than he was. Although she'd surprised him with the Jeep. A red one, even. That didn't seem to be her style, but perhaps she'd been forced to be less choosy when her old car had become a pile of twisted metal.

How she'd walked away from the wreck was a detail that she would divulge before he killed her. Because he *would* kill her. He'd find her and lure her

someplace else and *end* her, once and for all. Nobody
could come looking for her here, to this place. *My
place.* Nobody could know. They'd spoil everything.
Everything he'd built. Everything he treasured.

They'll take my things. My things. That would not
happen. *Think carefully. Plan.*

Flinching at a sudden pain in his hand, he looked
down to realize he was holding his keys in a white-
knuckled fist. He was more rattled than he'd thought.

Which was . . . normal, he supposed. But ultimately unnecessary. *She's just a woman, just like all
the others.* Easily overpowered. When he found her,
she'd be sorry she'd threatened him.

Except . . . Faith wasn't easily overpowered. He'd
tried to kill her too many times. She'd become careful, aloof. Now she never allowed herself to be unprotected. So he'd just have to work a little harder to lure
her to a place of his choosing. *And if you don't manage to lure her far enough away? If she comes back
here? If she tries to come in?*

Then he'd have to kill her here, which might bring
the cops. *They'll take my things.*

He drew a deep breath, let it out. Refused to allow
the panic to overwhelm him. He would not lose his
things. If he had to, he'd move them. All of them.

*Nobody will ever take my things again. Not now.
Not ever.*

Mt. Carmel, Ohio
Sunday, November 2, 6:20 p.m.

Once Faith had reached the paved road, she began
dictating a new to-do list into her phone. Her lists had
helped her stay sane, enabling her to accomplish everything she'd needed to do to leave Miami as Faith
Corcoran, leaving Faith Frye behind, in an insanely
short period of time.

She'd learned the magic of lists after her mother
died and her father began turning to the bottle for

comfort. She'd had to run their little household back then, and she'd been only nine years old. Lists were her salvation.

Tomorrow, she'd contact her grandmother's attorney to get the correct house key and then call the utilities to have the power and water turned on. She'd need a landline, too, because cell service was spotty out—

Oh no. Her heart sank as she realized what she'd forgotten. *Cell service. Dammit.* She stared at the phone she held clutched in her hand. She'd changed her name, her address, her driver's license and credit cards, but she hadn't changed her cell phone number.

Irritation swept through her. How the hell had she forgotten about her phone? Not only was it still in her old name, it was a damn homing signal.

She stopped the Jeep in the middle of the road and pulled the chip from the phone. She'd get a new one tomorrow. An untraceable one, just like some of her former ex-con clients carried.

Then, once she got all her ducks in a row, she'd return to the house to begin what was sure to be a massive cleanup job. *Correction. It's not "the" house. It's "your" house. Get used to saying it and going inside next time will be a lot easier.*

Relax. You left Peter Combs in Miami. No one is stalking you. No one is trying to kill you. There's nothing to be afraid of here.

NEW YORK TIMES BESTSELLING AUTHOR

KAREN ROSE

"Few writers succeed at [romantic suspense]
as well as Karen Rose."
—*The New York Times*

For a complete list of titles,
please visit prh.com/karenrose